Almudena Grandes is one of Spain's top-selling authors. Her first book, *The Ages of Lulu*, sold over a million copies worldwide and was translated into 21 languages. She has won several prizes including the Crisol Readers Prize which is awarded directly by customers' votes. Two of her books have been made into films.

The
Wind from
the East

Almudena Grandes

*Translated from the Spanish
by Sonia Soto*

PHOENIX

A PHOENIX PAPERBACK

First published in Great Britain in 2006
by Weidenfeld & Nicolson
This paperback edition published in 2007
by Phoenix,
an imprint of Orion Books Ltd,
Orion House, 5 Upper St Martin's Lane,
London WC2H 9EA

First published in Spain in 2002
as *Los Aires Difíciles*
by Tusquets Editores, SA

The publication of this work has been made
possible through a subsidy received from the
Directorate General for Books, Archives and
Libraries of the Spanish Ministry of Culture.

1 3 5 7 9 10 8 6 4 2

A CIP catalogue record for this book
is available from the British Library.

ISBN 978-0-7538-2159-6

Typeset at The Spartan Press Ltd,
Lymington, Hants

Printed and bound in Great Britain by
Clays Ltd, St Ives plc

The Orion Publishing Group's policy is to use papers
that are natural, renewable and recyclable products and
made from wood grown in sustainable forests. The logging
and manufacturing processes are expected to conform to
the environmental regulations of the country of origin.

www.orionbooks.co.uk

To Luis,
For the light of every summer

I would have preferred
to be an orphan in death,
to be without you there, in the mystery
than here, in what I know.

To have died before,
to feel your absence
in the treacherous wind.

Manuel Altoloaguirre, *Soledades Juntas*

Two Beginnings

꧁꧂

The east wind was blowing when the Olmedo family arrived at their new home. It lifted the canvas awnings from their aluminium frames, swelling them out then dropping them suddenly before inflating them again, producing a continuous, dull, heavy noise like a flock of monstrously large birds flapping their wings. All around, neighbours were hurriedly taking down their awnings, all of them green, all identical. From time to time, the rhythmic, high-pitched squeal of rusty metal could be heard beneath the sound of the wind, a piercing noise that Juan Olmedo immediately recognised as the scraping of the metal bars in their rings. He reflected that he'd been unlucky. There was something sinister about the contrast between the bright blue sky and the brilliant sun reflecting off the facades of the houses – all of them white, all identical – and this hostile, savage wind. A couple of times, on the journey from Jerez, he had promised Tamara that he would take her for a swim in the sea before lunch; but the perfect sunny morning that had seemed so tempting through the car windows had suddenly been transformed into this nightmarish storm. Now the girl was one step behind him, looking around warily, seeing it all for the first time but saying nothing. Alfonso had remained behind but Juan didn't notice until he unlocked the front door of number thirty-seven. The unmistakable smell of decorating sprang at him like a cat covered in paint and varnish, and an old yellowed newspaper, stiff with droplets of paint, trembled slightly before flying out of the door and scattering in the wind. Juan watched as the loose pages danced in the gusts of air, swirling suddenly upwards or being dragged along the ground. Then caught sight of his brother standing like a post at the intersection of two streets paved identically in red, his legs planted firmly apart, his arms hanging limply down, his head swaying slowly from side to side. Alfonso's face was raised up to the wind, and he was frowning, his mouth open. Juan glanced down at Alfonso's flies – a check he made so often now it had become almost instinctive – and saw with relief that they were closed. His poor brother, sniffing the air like a clumsy, disorientated animal, was conspicuous enough without exposing his clumsy disorientated penis. Juan went over to him and hugged him gently, smiling, then kissed him on the cheek before leading him away, an arm around his shoulders. Alfonso nodded several times, vigorously, as if trying to detach his head from his neck. As the two brothers made their way along the narrow pavement, the wind showered them in a flurry of pink, red and purple bougainvillea petals. At last Alfonso Olmedo smiled. Tamara was waiting for them, leaning against a wall, clutching a brightly coloured jewellery box, a couple of books and a Barbie doll. She burst out laughing when she saw her two uncles 'in bloom'. Alfonso's bald head, Juan's hair and their trousers, shirts and arms were all covered in petals, making them look like a comical cross between a pair of badly camouflaged soldiers and two mimes dressed up as flowering shrubs. Juan joined in the laughter as he brushed the petals off himself and Alfonso and gently ushered his family into the hall. As he shut the door, he wondered whether this wasn't all a big mistake – the new house, new job, new town hundreds of miles from their old home. But then it was still much too soon to tell.

Sara Gómez had watched the entire scene from her bedroom window, which was firmly shut to keep out the wind. She had been checking that the shutters were secure when she'd noticed a tall, dark man in the distance, followed closely by a little girl who was also dark, with hair cut in a bob, and the disproportionately long legs of a child in the middle of a growth spurt. She had watched them with interest because that day, 13 August, was a Sunday, the shops were closed and the wind was blowing furiously – a combination that forced her to rest, reluctantly. She'd been very busy for the past few weeks. Setting up a new home, with all the myriad little tasks that she considered essential, was turning out to be more time-consuming than she'd expected. When she had finally found a cheese grater she liked, she realised she needed a garlic crusher, but when she found that, she realised that the toilet mirror was too small, or that she couldn't let one more day pass without ordering mosquito screens for all the bedrooms. Time slipped by quickly in the car parks of shopping centres, taking the summer along with it, and with summer, all those hot sunny days at the beach that had lured her to this town, this landscape so very different from the big city where she was born and grew up, where she had lived for her not especially outstanding fifty-three years. That was why she had resolved not to let a single sunny morning pass without swimming in the sea, no good afternoon with a low tide go by without strolling along the wet sand leaving every last bather behind. The imminent arrival of September worried her. Although she could not recall ever having made as satisfying a decision as the purchase of this house, she still wasn't sure how people lived in autumn in a small town where the taxis didn't have meters and where you could go almost anywhere on foot.

The other new arrivals felt a similar anxiety, although Sara couldn't yet know that. She wasn't even sure they were here to stay. House number thirty-seven was still under construction when she decided to buy number thirty-one, which was already complete except for the finishing touches. That was why she had chosen it, and she hadn't enquired about the neighbours. Instead of the distasteful railings that she'd pictured before she visited the development, she found that the garden of each house was surrounded by solid, whitewashed walls over four feet high providing total privacy. With the awnings up, there wasn't the slightest gap for a curious passer-by to see what was happening on the porch of the house opposite, and if she hadn't been looking out of an upstairs window at the time of the Olmedos' arrival, she would have been quite unaware of their presence. She had been so pleased with the privacy the walls provided that she hadn't paid much attention to the estate agent when he explained to her in a monotonous voice – a speech he had clearly made many times before – that the walls were designed to shelter the garden from the constant winds. Alternately dry and loaded with sand, or else damp and surprisingly cold, these winds could be a blessing at certain times of year but even so, they were almost always destructive, although the estate agent preferred to describe them as merely 'inconvenient'.

On 13 August 2000, Sara Gómez was only beginning to learn about the nature of the local winds. Peering from her bedroom window, she watched as the shutters of number thirty-seven were opened one by one – all of them green, newly painted and identical. The wind caught hold of them, crashing them violently against the walls of the house, banging them repeatedly over and over again, until a member of the rather odd family returned in alarm and fastened them to the wall. Sara watched the Olmedos, not only because she was worried at the thought of living opposite a house that was rented out for weeks at a time, or because the weather was unsuitable for going to the beach, or because the shops were shut. She watched them because she couldn't fathom who they were, how they were linked, or why they lived together. Like many children who spent a great deal of time alone, Sara Gómez had enjoyed playing a game in which she invented lives for the strangers she encountered. Now she began to imagine a story in which this tall, dark, forty-something man was the father of the little girl walking a few paces behind him, trying to shelter from the wind. From afar, they looked very much alike. Dark and tall like him, slender and long-boned, the child must have been about ten or eleven. Sara, who could not know that the only thing she had guessed right was their ages, wondered what the girl's mother must look like. She must have stayed behind in the car, searching for something, or perhaps she had gone for a quick walk around the development; surely she was the person the husband went to find among the swirl of newspaper pages, floating in the air like big yellow parentheses in a cloud of bougainvillea petals. Up to this point, the scene was so predictable it was boring. But then the child stopped and waited by the open front door, not even attempting to enter the house. Leaning against the wall, hugging some books and a blonde doll tightly to her chest, she stood frozen, motionless, her eyes large and alert as if she really didn't want to be there and distrusted everything around her. The stranger observing her wondered what kind of child could resist the urge to rush into a new house, and she began to suspect that no mother was going to appear. In fact she was now fairly sure that the father must be separated, on holiday here with or without his new partner, accompanied by his child, who no doubt had a lengthy list of daughterly resentments, some of them justified. But then Sara caught sight of the tall dark man again, walking very slowly, with his arm around a second man; this was a possibility she hadn't considered. The other man was walking like a badly coordinated puppet, tilting his head to look at the sky with his mouth hanging open, meekly leaning against the companion who was guiding him confidently, obviously used to taking care of someone who couldn't take care of himself. Although he was fat rather than stocky, and almost completely bald,

Sara guessed correctly when she estimated that the man must be about thirty. She quickly realised that she had been wrong about everything else, however, when she saw the smile that lit up the child's face as soon as they approached. The tall dark man put his left arm around her and hugged her to him, his right arm still encircling the other man, and he kissed them both several times on the head and face, before gently pushing them inside the house. He closed the door, and it occurred to his new neighbour that he seemed rather sad.

Very soon all the windows of house number thirty-seven were open, all the shutters secured, and Sara Gómez moved away from her bedroom window feeling vaguely guilty, as if she'd committed a sin by witnessing the new arrivals' grief, their paltry joy. Sitting on the sofa in her vacant living room, a series of empty spaces crying out for the furniture that had already been ordered in half a dozen shops, Sara listened to the shrieking of the wind. Without the flap of the loose awnings, its howling seemed even more ferocious, like the soundtrack of a reality unfolding ceaselessly beyond her garden. With nothing to keep her company save the deafening roar of the wind and a packet of cigarettes, she began to doubt her own anxiety, to question whether the furtive, almost clandestine air she'd detected in every one of her new neighbours' movements had really existed. She was, after all, learning what the wind had to teach. She already suspected that on a quiet day, a peaceful, sunny day good for the beach, her new neighbours would not have seemed so strange.

A spectacular band of deep orange lay on the horizon between the sea and the sky. The sun was about to set, but even before he got to the beach, Juan Olmedo could see the silhouettes of some of the strange encampments that had so surprised him that morning. The cars of the Sunday day-trippers, most of them from Seville, had filled both sides of the road right from the entrance to the estate to the first sand dune, like a corridor of fans applauding anyone shrewd enough to have chosen a house so close to the sea. Juan had congratulated himself and remarked out loud, to mollify Tamara, that today, 14 August, a Monday as splendid and sunny as a postcard, was the day before a public holiday and therefore a holiday too, indeed the most popular holiday of the season. But the little girl seemed so pleased that the wind had finally died down that she wasn't even listening. Nothing could spoil her mood. Even Alfonso, who was walking between them holding their hands, looked happy.

The beach had been as crowded as they expected it to be. What Juan had not anticipated, however, were the peculiar habits of these weekend nomads. Entire families, including decrepit pensioners and tiny babies, would occupy an area of beach from first thing in the morning, before it was even hot, investing hours laboriously setting up a new version of home with tents, canvas windbreaks and portable furniture, until the beach looked like an extraordinary makeshift shanty town. As they looked for a place closer to the water's edge where they could lay their humble mats, Juan saw an elderly woman having her breakfast of coffee and *churros* using a plastic plate and cup and a patterned fabric napkin. It made him smile. The spectacle of other people's strange habits took his mind off his own litany of misfortune. In addition, he realised that the crowds at the water's edge were having the same useful effect as they did in big cities – the bathers were so busy searching for a place to enter or exit the water, or chasing their little white ball amongst the dozens of other identical balls bouncing up and down the damp sand, or keeping an eye on their children's buckets and spades, or anointing each other with suntan lotion, that they had neither the time nor the inclination to stare at Alfonso, who looked more conspicuous and helpless than ever in the stripy Bermuda shorts that Tamara had chosen for him. Juan couldn't remember a time when he hadn't been anxious about his younger brother and by now he was completely immune to the curiosity of others, but Tamara had inherited her mother's steely intransigence, and could not bear the sympathy of strangers. That morning, however, all three were able to swim and play in the waves without Tamara having to shout – 'Hey, what are you staring at, idiot?' – at unwelcome spectators. In the afternoon, they had eaten grilled sardines at the only bar nearby, and had another swim before going home, exhausted from all the sun and sea. Everything had gone so well that a couple of hours later, when Alfonso fell asleep on the sofa, Juan was able to go out for another walk. He felt like being on his own for a while, so he headed back to the beach.

He had thought that the setting sun would induce everyone to go home, but he was only partly right. There was no longer anybody in the water, but semi-naked bodies still lay beneath parasols and sunshades, and there were children playing football, groups of adults on plastic sunloungers chatting, while others slowly, despondently, gathered all the chairs, mats and tents that they had set out so energetically that morning. Juan Olmedo gave them a wide berth on his way to the water's edge. He wasn't sure whether they really were all staring at him, or whether the uncomfortable sensation of being watched was an inevitable consequence of feeling that he looked ridiculous. He walked faster. He had lived on the coast for a few years before, but in a city like Cadiz it had been very different. There, he wouldn't have stood out in his immaculate white trousers, long-sleeved navy-blue T-shirt and lightweight moccasins, but here, over a mile from the town's seafront, everyone walking along the beach was wearing shorts and trainers. Juan realised he'd have to dress the same if he didn't want to become known as 'the pretentious poser from Madrid', and set off towards a section of the beach that was studded with fishing rods.

He felt as if the east wind had dissipated only on the

surface, but was still battering him mercilessly inside. He felt anxious, but more than that, confused, uncertain, weighed down by responsibility. He had never had to make so many decisions in such a short space of time, never had such a narrow margin in which to ponder the wisdom of each choice he made. When he realised that Madrid was no longer a good place for them to live, he chose what had, at the time, seemed the best option. Making the most of the general confusion that prevailed at the start of the holidays, they had slipped away discreetly. After all, no one would notice their absence with all the summer migrations. The plan was simple. During his time in Cadiz, Juan had become very good friends with Miguel Barroso, who was now head of the orthopaedic department at Jerez Hospital, and Juan had felt sure that Miguel would support his application for a job. It was the main reason he'd moved to this region rather than any other part of Spain, although he already knew he'd like many things about the area – the climate, the light, the people – the same factors that had influenced his choice the first time he moved away. His parents came from a village in the wilderness of Extremadura, but he had only ever visited the area a couple of times, before Alfonso was born, and he had no links there other than a few old songs, odd words slipping quietly from his memory. Juan Olmedo was from Madrid and he knew he would miss it, but his own nostalgia, which had already destroyed his life once, was less of a concern to him than the thought that Tamara might not get used to living so far from home, or the even more worrying possibility that his brother's mental state might suffer as a result of the inevitable isolation of the first few months and of having to deal with unfamiliar teachers and pupils at a new daycare centre. Now that there was no going back, Juan felt that perhaps his choices had been too hasty. Perhaps they needn't have left Madrid. Perhaps it would have been enough simply to change minor details – a new house, new part of town, new hospital, new school. Perhaps there was no real reason to be so afraid.

The fishing rods weren't as far away, or as close together as they'd seemed. As he walked past them one by one, he also realised that the rocks he'd had to walk around for some time now were not a natural formation, especially on this beach where the sand was so fine. Moulded into smooth, grey, slippery blocks by the imperceptible tenacity of the waves, they formed a perpendicular line into the sea where they met another line of rocks that ran more or less parallel to the beach, interrupting the path of the waves and forming a barrier in the water. Juan recalled that someone had mentioned there was a trap-net site in the area near the housing development, and he now understood why fishermen brought their tackle all this way, so far from the centre of town. He watched some children armed with nets and plastic buckets as they jumped from rock to rock and, in the dim light of the dying sun, searched unsuccessfully for crabs and crayfish trapped in the pools closest to the shore. They were ignoring the insistent calls of a woman, assuring them, unconvincingly, that this was the last time they'd be allowed on the beach if they didn't come out of the water right now, this minute. Juan stopped for a moment and saw that the children hadn't the least intention of leaving. He walked on, comforted by the familiar elements of this little holiday scene.

The small town the Olmedo family had just moved to was the only aspect of their new life that Juan was certain he had got right. He had decided from the start not to live in Jerez, not only because it was quite a distance from the coast, but because there was no point in leaving one big city to move to a smaller version, an embryo of the same thing. This was why he had also decided against El Puerto de Santa Maria; still too big, too urban, too formal for what he wanted. He'd tried to convince Tamara that the move was an inevitable consequence of his job, a decision taken for him by faceless strangers, a risk that all doctors working in the national health service ran, but he had a feeling she knew this wasn't true, even though she was only ten. The child's happiness was so important to him that he had done everything he could to ensure it, providing her with a completely different life from the one she had known so far – a house by the beach, on a private development with swimming pools, gardens, tennis courts and lots of other children, a school that she could cycle to when the weather was good, and a small, pretty town that was quiet in winter, busy in summer, its population of some thirty thousand inhabitants swelling to over a hundred thousand during the months of July and August; a place small enough that she wouldn't keep comparing it to Madrid, but big enough that she wouldn't feel stifled by the size of the streets.

He could have found a cheaper house, but he didn't even consider it. He could have looked at other towns around the bay, but he didn't have the time, or the inclination. His new boss had recommended this development, and it fulfilled everything he had envisaged for Tamara when he first began thinking about moving. He'd put his top-floor flat in the Calle Martin de los Heros up for sale in mid-April, a few months after having made the last payment on a mortgage he'd taken twelve years to pay off, and by the end of June he'd found a buyer who didn't need the flat until September. He hoped that the price difference between a square foot of land in the centre of Madrid and a housing development on the outskirts of a provincial town would mean he could easily afford a large and attractive house. He was right, and it took him even less time to buy the house than it had to sell the flat. On his first day off in July, he took an early-morning flight to Jerez, where he met Miguel at the hospital, visited the centre where he planned to send Alfonso in September and, that afternoon, selected house number thirty-seven from the plans for the development. He'd only viewed the show home, but that was enough. The estate agent was astonished when Juan handed him a cheque and left quickly, saying he couldn't afford to miss his plane back to Madrid. In the few minutes it took for Juan to get out his cheque book, note down the amount he was paying as a deposit and fill in the rest of the cheque, he told the estate agent he wanted plain tiles in the bathrooms, that he'd rather have all the kitchen units along a single wall, and that he'd be very grateful if, before the decorators set to work, the electricians could be informed that he didn't want spotlights in the ceilings, just a single light fitting. He assumed, of course, that the house would be finished by the beginning of August. The estate agent, who'd never met anyone who could think of so many things simultaneously, nodded. A little later, when he stopped off at a bar for a glass of *anis*, as he did every evening on his way home for supper, he recounted the story to all his cronies and none of them had ever heard anything like it.

Though he wasn't prepared to admit it – even to himself – as he strolled along the deserted beach, Juan Olmedo had fled Madrid. He'd done so mainly for Tamara's sake, but, that night, their second in the new house, he suspected that he would probably enjoy the benefits of the place before she did. He stopped worrying about the thirty-mile commute to and from work he would have every day after sending Alfonso off on the bus to the daycare centre. This sudden acceptance of the small routine inconveniences the move entailed reduced his anxiety over the more serious problems he faced. It was as if the pleasure of taking a solitary evening stroll along the beach were a balm, a promise of future harmony. By the time he turned round to return to the house, Juan was in a much better mood.

On the way back he encountered only a couple of dog walkers and then, as he turned down the path that led from the beach, a woman. The light was so dim that at first all he could see was a cream shape with dark stripes on its upper half. As they walked towards each other, as if their meeting were planned, he could see that she was wearing the type of outfit that people from inland considered nautical: wide-legged trousers and a navy-blue striped top – unmistakable clues to the woman's origin. Juan Olmedo immediately recognised another recent arrival from Madrid. She was one of those well-preserved women who maintained an appearance of youthful maturity despite her forty-odd years and would probably continue to do so until the first ravages of old age. She had a pleasant, even attractive face, but although she had beautiful eyes you couldn't exactly say that she was pretty. This was all Juan had time to notice, but it was enough for him to be sure that they had definitely never met. As she passed him, however, she greeted him in a friendly manner. He greeted her back casually, purely out of politeness, as if the instinct to wish each other a good evening were part of a ritual of recognition amongst equals, fellow exiles from Madrid with a confused notion of seaside elegance. His niece was much more observant and, had she witnessed the scene, she would have been able to tell him that the woman, while still a stranger, lived in the house opposite.

I

Weariness and Need

In the kitchen of number thirty-one, the units ran along two walls. In the middle of the room was an aluminium table and two folding aluminium chairs, which added a functional, almost industrial touch to the decor. The occupant was clearly at home with adapting the suggestions of the glossy magazines to suit her own style. Sara Gómez had always had very good taste, but little time and even less money. Now, the abundant crop of zeros flourishing in her bank statements was producing magnificent results.

Sara had also made her mark at the estate agents' offices, but for very different reasons than Juan Olmedo. She had arrived after visiting other parts of the coast of Andalusia, evaluating all the houses for sale so conscientiously that by now she could tell at a glance whether a place was worth viewing. Her expedition had begun in mid-March, and as she had no intention of returning to Madrid, the search was open-ended. As she crossed from Malaga into the province of Cadiz, her intention had been to explore the Atlantic coast all the way to the Portuguese border before choosing a place to spend the rest of her life; but soon she was so fed up with travelling, and so discouraged with the results so far, that she settled on a place before she planned to, taking on the challenge of the only house that, in two otherwise fruitless months, had managed to surprise her.

She could easily have afforded one of the more expensive, more luxurious houses she'd been offered on the Costa del Sol but although she'd liked some of them very much, in the end she found them all too ostentatious. And she didn't want to live surrounded by foreigners, an anomaly in a crowd of pale-skinned neighbours. If she'd wanted to attract attention, she could have stayed in Madrid and bought herself a house in El Viso. No, what she was looking for was the exact opposite, and she'd found it at last on a secluded development, discreetly luxurious, and inhabited by upper-middle-class professionals; a place where she would easily merge into the background. Located on the outskirts of a popular tourist resort, it lacked the dubious elegance that might attract hordes of Arab sheikhs or showy *nouveaux riches* like the Lopez Ruiz family, bogus cousins she never wanted to set eyes on again. Sheltered from the wind and from prying eyes by walls so high that, from the road, you could only just glimpse the roofs of the houses, nothing betrayed the privileged nature of this secluded enclave; a place that turned in on itself like the leaves of a plant at nightfall, always seeking the centre. As she walked around the development for the first time, having visited dozens of similar projects over the last few weeks, Sara was impressed by the intelligence of the layout. It all seemed simple as she walked through it, but secretly labyrinthine when she looked back, and it was impossible to tell from their rather uniform back walls that the houses looked out onto attractive gardens. From outside the complex, there was no hint of how big the swimming pools, the children's play areas or the sports facilities were, and to Sara it seemed that they grew larger with every step. The mysteriously elastic quality of the space became even more noticeable when she went inside the show home, a square house on two floors with a large roof terrace. It was so well designed that she had to ask the estate agent for a tape measure in order to measure the rooms one by one before she could concede that their generous size wasn't an optical illusion. But even this wasn't enough to convince Sara Gómez.

Having shown her around the house twice, in a viewing so thorough that he noticed things he'd never even seen before although he'd been showing clients around daily for the past six months, the estate agent dared to sit down on the doorstep, just to take a break from this well-heeled client who must be a quantity surveyor at the very least. But Sara seemed quite unmoved by his weariness and continued asking questions, firing the inexhaustible machine gun of her curiosity at his limited knowledge until she'd pinned him against every wall in the house. He'd had to say 'I don't know' so many times that he ended up simply shrugging to save himself the embarrassment. Nobody had ever asked him why one of the light fittings in the sitting room was not close to the obvious place for a side table, why there weren't taps for hoses on every terrace, why it had been assumed, judging by the distance between light switches, that all double beds were a metre and a half wide, why all the fitted cupboards had only two drawers, why the unit containing the plate rack had been placed to the left of the double sink, as if all housewives were left-handed, and why such and such a choice had been made in another hundred matters of similarly negligible importance. He was convinced that the woman would vanish into thin air like a bad dream when, having pointed out all the defects of a house whose quality he would have vouched for earlier that morning, she smiled and announced that she had almost decided to buy it. Inwardly awarding himself a medal for being the most long-suffering estate agent in the area, her opponent smiled back, feeling as if he'd overcome the most testing ordeal of his professional life. But she disabused him of this notion immediately and, after informing him that she assumed that he must agree with her that it was vital to examine which way a house faced before making a final choice, she asked him what time would suit him the following day to show her all the available houses on the development. Then, with a compassionate intelligence that he appreciated, she added that she had plenty of free time.

Sara Gómez, buyer, and Ramón Martínez, estate agent, almost became friends in the following weeks. She had rented a furnished flat in the town so as to keep a close eye on completion of the finishing touches, and she became the person he spent most of his time with from Monday to Friday apart from his wife. Every day she came to the office with some new idea, and he had to admit that they were nearly all good, though they invariably involved him hanging on the phone for an age, finding out names and addresses that he kept so that he could suggest Sara's improvements to subsequent clients as if they were his own ideas. She was rather amused by this little ruse and although she realised his actions were beneficial to them both, she would reward him every evening by buying him a drink in a nearby bar. He insisted on paying for the drinks every other day, however, and he chased the electricians and decorators so that number thirty-one would be finished even earlier than the agreed date, 1 July 2000. The only thing he couldn't do for the future occupant of the house was recommend a trustworthy cleaner, but he did well when he suggested she speak to Jerónimo, the gardener, who thought immediately of his cousin, Maribel.

Sara's cleaner was thirty, with a son of eleven, a broken marriage behind her, and a substantial amount of excess weight, pleasingly distributed over an old-fashioned figure. She made the best of her solid, curvaceous body by wearing tight, low-cut dresses, the mere sight of which would have caused anyone who really had been well-heeled all her life to reject her without even asking how much she charged. But Sara wasn't quite what she seemed, and she found the showy gold rings Maribel wore on every finger – tarnished by bleach and ruining the effect that the woman was aiming for – so touching that she hired her on the spot. She didn't regret it. Maribel was hardworking and spirited, as capable of using her own initiative as she was of accepting all kinds of instructions without a word. Even the two apparent drawbacks that had caused Sara to have some doubts about her at first turned out to be advantages. Andrés, Maribel's son, who was forced to waste his holidays accompanying his mother to work every morning, was a lonely, withdrawn child, older than his years. He would sit quietly on a chair, reading a comic, with a toy car or robot clasped in his fist, until Sara, who soon grew fond of him, encouraged him to go out and play in the garden or suggested they go to the beach. In contrast, and refuting the laws of heredity at one stroke, his mother was incapable of keeping quiet. A steady stream of words poured from her mouth as she went about her tasks, and each time she drew breath, it was as if she was winding herself up for another torrent. She was the best source of information that her employer had at her disposal, once her ephemeral friendship with the estate agent had waned. From Maribel, Sara could find out about life in the town, what went on, and what kind of people lived there. And it was also Maribel who, on the first working day after the August bank holiday, told Sara that the new arrivals were called Olmedo.

'I'm so sorry, I know I'm late!' she declared in greeting, clicking into the kitchen on her high heels. She found the mistress of the house sitting on one of those peculiar metal chairs that she still hadn't become used to. 'I've just come from Dr Olmedo's, you know who I mean, don't you?'

'No, I don't,' Sara replied, turning her attention to the elusive figure of the boy standing by the door, peering in shyly. 'Come on in, Andrés. Come and sit here with me. That's right. Have you had breakfast?' He nodded. 'Sure? You don't feel like eating something?' He shook his head this time, still saying nothing. Sara took his hand, squeezed it, and readied herself to hear all about their visit to the doctor. 'The boy isn't ill, is he?'

'What boy?'

'Your son, Maribel; who else would I mean?'

Maribel frowned as if Sara's words had completely confused her, and asked: 'Why would he be ill?'

'Well,' Sara sighed, as if she couldn't struggle on with so much air in her body – a feeling she experienced every time her cleaner, an uneducated but intelligent woman, became stuck in a deep pool of incomprehension – 'because you said you'd just been to the doctor's.'

'Oh, right! You had me worried. No, no, that's not it,' she went on, struggling out of the teetering sandals whose fine straps had left pink marks on her feet and ankles, and donning a pair of tatty old espadrilles with frayed rope soles. 'Dr Olmedo owns number thirty-seven, he's just moved in. Jeró called me last night and said that Dr Olmedo had asked him if he knew someone who could come in and clean for him, and I . . . well, I was thrilled, after having found you, getting another job, right next door, and so near to where I live. I'm going to get changed.'

Maribel was wearing her best and newest dress that day, a tight red Lycra number – the kind sold on market stalls that lose their shape with every wash – but she would have taken just as much care had she been wearing any of her other dresses: her long black dress with a tiny flower print that buttoned down the front, for instance, or the short piqué dress, always gleaming white if a little worn. Before even turning on a tap, Maribel would shut herself in the bathroom, reappearing a moment later in an old pink housecoat spattered with bleach, and carrying what she called her 'good clothes', now neatly folded. She did the same this morning, but was so excited by all her news that she went on talking from the bathroom, speaking more loudly so that she could be heard through the door.

'So, we got up early this morning, and I went straight there to see them. It's really good, you know, because I was worried the job will only be for the summer, but no, they're going to live here all year round. They're from Madrid too. He's a doctor, he works at the hospital in Jerez, maybe you know them, their name's Olmedo . . .'

'No, I don't know them.'

'Sure?' Now squeezed into her pink housecoat, Maribel put her new dress in a canvas bag before giving her employer a second chance. 'But they're from Madrid.'

'No, Maribel,' said Sara, smiling at the obstinate scepticism of her cleaner, who couldn't quite believe that everyone from Madrid didn't know one another. 'I've told you before, Madrid must be over a hundred times bigger than this little town. I couldn't possibly know everyone who lives there. And it's no coincidence that we bump into one another all over the place, we're like flies – there are swarms of us.'

'Right . . .' Maribel, leaning over the dishwasher, seemed to accept this. 'Well, anyway, they're from Madrid, and they're here because of his work—'

'What about her?' interrupted Sara. 'Does she work too?'

'What "her"?' asked Maribel, straightening up and staring at Sara.

'Well, the doctor's wife. He is married, isn't he?'

'No. That's the strange thing, you see. I mean he doesn't look like a poof and he's quite good-looking. Well, maybe not good-looking, you know, handsome, blond and all that, but he's definitely very attractive . . .' She stopped stacking the dishwasher for a moment and started listing Dr Olmedo's attributes, counting them off on the fingers of one hand. 'He's tall, slim but not puny, dark not balding, well dressed. A pretty good catch, if you ask me. And being a doctor he must earn a packet. But he definitely doesn't have a wife. Maybe he's divorced. And the child isn't his, that's for sure, because she calls him "Uncle Juan".'

'He has a little girl living with him?' remarked Sara

neutrally, trying to divert the torrent of words in the direction that most interested her.

'Yes, she's about this one's age, and really pretty, gorgeous, even though she isn't blonde and doesn't have blue eyes or anything. Her name's Tamara. Sounds lovely, doesn't it?' Maribel had her back to her employer so she didn't see Sara give a start when she heard the child's name, instead taking her silence as a sign of agreement. 'I think so too. If I ever have a daughter, maybe I'll call her Tamara. Well, anyway, the niece looks just like her uncle. Her face is softer, more delicate, and rounder like all kids, but apart from that, she's the spitting image. Same eyes, same mouth, same nose, same everything. Apparently she's his brother's daughter. He and his brother must have looked identical, if you ask me, though who knows, because I didn't find out much else – he's like you, doesn't go around telling you his life story. He said the child's an orphan, that's all, and only because I asked. I think it's because of the retarded one. They live with a man who's not all there, if you know what I mean, and the less you talk about that kind of thing and the less people you tell, the better. That's what I think. He's the doctor's brother too, like the little girl's father was. When you see him around, you'll know it's him straight away, because he's bald and you can see how retarded he is, the way he moves and talks and all that. Shame, isn't it? It was because of a difficult birth, apparently. Imagine, he's been like that all his life, thirty-two years! Of course, I won't ever be left alone with him, thank God, because those people – I know you're supposed to pity them and all that – but they give me the creeps, they really do. What if he had a fit or something, with only me in the house? People like that have seizures and they get violent, you wouldn't believe it, a neighbour of mine, she's got a daughter like that and she really whacks her mother sometimes. But this one seems quiet and he'll be going to a school for people like him, in El Puerto. He'll be having lunch there and everything. The girl too, except she'll be at the school near here of course. Anyway, the arrangement suits me down to the ground, because I'll leave here at one, do four hours over there so the house is all clean and tidy when they get back around five, and then off I go to put my feet up, because I'll be knackered after all that. But I won't have any more money worries, at long last. I've been thinking that, if I keep cleaning the stairwell I've got in the village, what with your house and the doctor's, I'll be earning as much as a builder! The problem will be Christmas, and then next summer, because the retard's school – his name's Alfonso – has holidays the same way normal schools do. The doctor's already warned me, and he doesn't dare leave him alone all day with his niece, so I'll have to be there for longer, but anyway, we'll manage somehow, won't we, Andrés?'

Maribel turned to the boy and gave him a long, solid look, like a bridge between them, forcing a smile that seemed strangely independent of her face. Sara, who had witnessed such scenes before, was struck once more by the mysterious, secret intensity of the relationship that bound Maribel to Andrés. Beneath the cleaner's overt preoccupation with painting her toenails and other trivia, beneath the apparent indifference and even contempt with which she sometimes treated her son, ran a violent undercurrent that occasionally forced itself to the surface. At times like this, Sara came to doubt her incipient theories about Maribel's moral weaknesses and came close to understanding the truth of her brutal history, symbolised perhaps by Maribel's childish addiction to the shiny things, cheap cosmetics and fripperies that made life worth living, that made her feel human. The little boy was so serious, with such a strong sense of responsibility towards his mother, that he was capable of playing for weeks at a time with one of those small toys you get inside a chocolate egg. Sara was sure he had never felt neglected, but that didn't stop her feeling protective when she saw him every morning, a skinny little kid with neatly combed hair, looking uncomfortable in his hand-me-downs, a ridiculous pair of flowery trunks that were too long for him and a green T-shirt so tight you could count his ribs through it. Now she took advantage of the first gap in Maribel's monologue to include him in the conversation.

'So, that little girl will probably be in your class, won't she?' she said, smiling at the boy.

'Maybe,' he answered. 'She'll be in my year, but they might put her in a different class.'

'Does she seem nice?'

'Well . . .' Andrés thought a moment. 'Yes, but she sounds very posh.'

'Like me.'

'Yes, but with you it doesn't make me laugh.'

'What is he talking about?' his mother interrupted harshly. 'He didn't laugh at her, he didn't even open his mouth. This son of mine's an idiot. Can you believe he didn't go anywhere near Tamara? I was so cross with him. The little girl kept on showing him things and he wouldn't say a word, acted as if he was deaf and dumb. God, this kid's such a pain!'

'Well, she didn't want to play either,' complained Andrés, sitting up in his chair. 'Her uncle made her, otherwise she wouldn't have got out a single toy. And it's not true, I did go and look at them.'

'Rubbish! You didn't show an interest in anything!'

'But kids are like that, Maribel,' Sara intervened. 'Children can be very shy, it takes them a while to make friends. You shouldn't be angry with him for that.'

'That's right, go on, defend him! You always side with him! It's quite incredible, because, no offence, but you spoil him more than his own grandmother, all day long doting on him, so he's always "Sara says this", "Sara says that", arguing with me from the minute he gets up till he goes to bed at night. You're going to spoil him if you keep giving him so much attention.'

'Don't be ridiculous, Maribel!' Sara burst out laughing. She stroked Andrés's hair, ruffling it and then smoothing it down again.

She had her own secret feelings about the boy, but she couldn't tell anyone about them, not even Maribel because she wouldn't understand. Nobody would understand what Sara Gómez felt the first time she realised that, when she thought of Andrés, she could remember him only in black and white.

Arcadio Gómez Gómez was a dark man. In those days, almost all men were, but young Sara had learnt to distinguish between limited shades of grey. At one end of the scale were all the gentlemen who came to call at the flat in the Calle Velázquez: Don Julio, doctor to her godmother's husband Don Antonio, and Don Fernando, the solicitor, and Don César and Don Rafael, who had been friends of Don Antonio's since attending the same Jesuit college as children, long before he became ill and before they won the war with the army in which they all three enlisted the same morning. They were all very much alike, from their heads – all three usually wore stiff hats with a band round the crown – to their feet clad in pointed shoes of punched leather. Each had a little moustache so fine and straight that it looked as if it had been painted on with a brush, dividing the space between the bottom of the nose and the upper lip into two precisely equal halves. They always wore grey suits, sometimes made from a light cloth that had a metallic sheen, sometimes in a heavier, dark flannel that was soft to the touch. And they always wore a badge in the buttonhole of their jacket, except Don Julio, who was a widower and wore a button covered in black fabric to show that he was in mourning. Doña Sara, the younger Sara's godmother, enjoyed teaching the little girl about different fabrics, and the cut and style of her own clothes, but she never told her much about the uniform elegance of Spanish gentlemen in the 1950s, except that all those suits – so intrinsically grey they appeared grey even when they were navy blue – had been made in England, while the ties, with discreetly bold polka dots or little stars on plain backgrounds that sometimes even dared to be deep red, were always Italian and made of silk.

These men in grey made up for the dry monotony of their appearance with the sophisticated elegance of all their gestures, from the studied nonchalance with which they handed their hats to the maid at the door, to the skilful way they tapped – always three times and with just the right force – the end of the cigarettes they were about to light on a silver cigarette case pulled with a magician's dexterity from the inside pocket of their jackets. Secretly watching them through the crack of a half-open door, Sara enjoyed everything about these visits, especially when it was Don César and Don Rafael, who always seemed so youthful and full of jokes that their mere appearance lit up the gloomy drawing room with the sparkle of a party. But the little girl, who was only allowed in to greet the adults and then leave, had fun witnessing these adult gatherings from afar, even when the visitor was just Brother José, the Father confessor, an imposing Dominican friar, tall, fat, bearded, who sweated profusely even in winter and had mad eyes that Sara found frightening. The Father, as they called him, had only one subject of conversation: El Pardo, the official residence of General Franco. Every time he uttered these two words, it was with the kind of reverence reserved for a person's name, but he spoke so elliptically that it was impossible to make out what he was really trying to say. 'It's always the same, Antonio,' Doña Sara would conclude after seeing the monk out, 'all that boasting and trying to make himself sound important, but he really doesn't have a clue.' Although Sara didn't understand this criticism any more than the gibberish spouted by the coarse monk himself, she took a dislike to him and although she continued to watch him from afar, she never lurked behind any more, hoping to be invited to stay, when he was the one seated on the guest sofa. But not even Brother José, in his food-stained habit, a rough cord tied round his waist and wooden rosary bumping against his thigh, was as dark a man as Arcadio Gómez Gómez, her father, a solitary figure at the other end of the spectrum from the pearly sheen of the gentlemen, a denizen of the margin where grey merged dangerously into black.

Every Sunday at midday, her father would be waiting by the front door. He never missed their appointment and he was never late. Winter or summer, rain or shine, he was always there, leaning against the same tree, when she returned with her godmother from eleven o'clock Mass. As they turned the corner, they could see his grey, opaque form, a grotesque mistake in these elegant surroundings, an image cut from an old photograph, flat and dull, and set down at random in front of the majestic front door. Arcadio Gómez Gómez was a shadow at the centre of a world that ignored him. When Sara and her godmother first caught sight of his figure, they became nervous. He quickly removed his hat and squeezed it without realising what he was doing, shuffling sideways, measuring the width of the pavement with his feet, three or four steps in one direction, three or four in the other, still looking at them both but not daring to come any closer. Instead, Doña Sara would stop dead and search her bag for a cigarette with her right hand, still gripping the little girl's hand firmly with her left. It was as if she couldn't face this defenceless man without the comfort of a cigarette. Young Sara was divided between her own anxiety, which made her glance around to make sure none of her schoolmates was nearby, and the fear emanating from both adults, the mysterious tremor she detected in her godmother and the uneasiness of her father as he tugged repeatedly at his shirt collar. In those days, when she was eight or nine, she never wondered exactly what it was that she felt every Sunday morning. She was an unusual child, she always had been, she couldn't know how much she had gained and how much she had lost when she was allotted a destiny that didn't belong to her.

'There he is again . . .' Having consumed half her cigarette in three or four greedy drags, Doña Sara barely disguised her displeasure. 'I've told your mother, let her come to fetch you, not him, I really can't bear that terrible man. She pays absolutely no attention to me. Every week, I have to put up with the sight of him standing there, damn him. Really! The things one has to endure.'

Sara didn't like her godmother talking like this, breaking her own rules with a vehemence that was disconcerting. At the house in Calle Velázquez, nobody ever mentioned Sara's parents, whether to speak ill or well of them. When the lady of the house referred to the child's mother she used her Christian name, as if she were merely an acquaintance – 'Years ago Sebastiana washed a pair of curtains like these and she ruined them; Sebastiana used to cook a delicious roast chicken; Sebastiana used to clean windows with water and bleach and despite the smell, they were marvellous', and so on. When her god-daughter came back on Sunday afternoons, Doña Sara never asked the girl if she'd had a good time, or if they'd gone for a walk or had a nice lunch – the smiling interrogation she always subjected the child to when she got back from a birthday party or a school outing. Those hours remained outside time, suspended inside a parenthesis of silence, detached from a reality that paused at midday on Sunday and recommenced eight hours later with a bath, supper and prayers, just like every other night. These were the rules that governed young Sara's life, strict and immutable except on the days when she returned from eleven o'clock Mass, in the hundred metres of pavement that seemed to give way beneath her feet, registering the crack that her godmother's uncharacteristically harsh words opened up in her comfortable existence. She didn't like it when Doña Sara spoke like that, as if every syllable was an invisible knife peeling away the good, kind woman Sara had always known, to reveal a harder, drier, hidden skin, like a vague threat that made her ask questions of herself that she didn't want to answer. And she was even more disconcerted by her godmother's sudden return to courtesy and correctness, for she couldn't imagine which button Doña Sara pressed when she wanted to switch back to the charming, polite lady they were all accustomed to.

'Hello, Arcadio.' At the decisive moment, nobody seeing the genuine freshness of her smile would have doubted her sincerity. 'How are you? How is Sebastiana? And the children?'

'Well, they're all fine, thank you,' he would mumble, holding out his rough, dry hand in the direction of the light, tapering glove that extended from the sleeve of her coat.

Arcadio Gómez Gómez never wore a coat. In winter, when it was very cold, he wore a thick, dark green, woollen jumper, hand-knitted and expertly darned in several places, under a strange cape with a vaguely military look despite its plain, black buttons. It was made from a thin, cardboard-like fabric and when it rained, Arcadio turned up his lapels, exposing the underside which was made from a less unusual type of cloth. Once, his daughter dared to ask him where he'd got his odd coat from, but he was reluctant to answer at first.

'It's not that odd,' he said eventually, when she'd given up hope of an answer. 'The thing is, your mother took it apart and turned it inside out. This used to be the lining.'

'Ah!' accepted the child. 'Why did she do that?'

'Just because.'

Arcadio didn't talk much, but he expressed himself in other ways. On Sundays, once Doña Sara had left him alone with his daughter, he always lifted her up and looked into her eyes, before hugging her fiercely but also with just the right amount of gentleness. He would put his arms right round her until he was touching his own sides with his fingertips, and hold her tight as if he wanted to absorb her, carry her inside him, merge with her so that they were a single body, but he was always very careful not to hurt her. Then, when the child crossed her legs firmly around his waist, he'd rest his face against hers and say very softly, 'Sari', using the pet name that infuriated her godmother and which Sara hated until she heard his hoarse warm voice whisper it in her ear – Sari – two syllables that later, when she was a grown woman, would always bring a lump to her throat. But not when she was a child. Then she just looked into his watery eyes, which changed colour depending on the light, sometimes grey-brown, sometimes chestnut, but always vaguely green, and saw a tremor in their depths. Those eyes would have been a perfect replica of her own had it not been for the dusty lines, as deep as scars, that ran from their corners, joining those on his cheeks. In that ashen face, that barely differed in colour from the curly hair – two white hairs for every black – that framed his face, only the mouth, with its thick, fleshy lips (which she was lucky enough not to inherit) showed his true age. Arcadio Gómez Gómez was not yet forty when, in 1947, his youngest daughter, his fifth child, was born. He had wanted to name her Adela, after his mother, but the little girl was named Sara after her godmother. She always believed that the person she went to meet every Sunday morning was an old man.

He would take Sara firmly by the hand and squeeze it in his rough palm when they crossed the road on the way to the metro. There, until she was at least nine years old, he would pick her up and carry her down the steps. The woman at the ticket office was used to seeing them every week, but occasionally a curious onlooker stopped and watched the strange pair, unable to guess the connection between the dark man and the luminous child at his side. But the sparks of surprise in strangers' eyes became fewer with every stop, just as the glow of the platform lights faded from the carriage as the train moved off again. By the time they arrived at Sol, the carriage was so crowded with people all jostling to get out, that nobody looked beyond the end of their own feet. This was Arcadio's territory; he manoeuvred skilfully, carrying her through the air and depositing her safely on the platform, so that she had no idea how they had avoided all the pushing and shoving that made the other passengers stagger. But this floating sense of immunity seemed as natural to her as these mysterious Sunday outings. Before she could even walk, she'd already learnt to fly above the ragged outline of reality, holding the edges of her immaculate clothes with the tips of her fingers.

Reality awaited her at the exit of the metro station at the Puerta del Sol but, as long as she could elude its grasp, she never recognised it. She walked along holding her father's hand not really understanding what the word reality meant. She accepted his tenderness like a sad, lukewarm prize she didn't feel she deserved, and everything else seemed hazy like the words to a song, or the faces of children in very old photographs, or the rules of a playground game. She moved through the chaos of winding dirty streets as if she had just entered a film, looking around with the mild and transient curiosity of a casual spectator. The district was bursting with movement and colour, as busy as a beehive, but instinctively Sara merged all the different tones into an oppressive, uniform sepia, like the dust that gathered everywhere: on the wooden blinds resting over the railings of balconies; in the windows of the tiny shops displaying only a couple of empty milk bottles and a basket of eggs on a cracked counter; on the red and white tiled floors glimpsed through the doorways of bars; and on the clothes of the amputees begging on the pavement. Sometimes, when they saw that she was afraid of them, these men would try to frighten her just for fun, thrusting their crutches out at her, or suddenly raising an arm that ended in a stump and pointing it at her. Her father greeted the people he knew by their Christian names, and smiled at everyone else, but he was careful to avoid the heavily made-up women who gathered in groups of two or three at different street corners.

'Well, here we are.' With these words Arcadio hailed the facade of the Santa Cruz palace, whose ancient, austere beauty jarred with the polished modernity of his daughter's world. She preferred to wait for him outside on the pavement, staring up at the dark mansion with its pointed towers, like those of a witch's castle, while he went into a bar to collect his demijohn of red wine. 'Right, come on, let's go home . . .'

Arcadio Gómez Gómez and his wife, Sebastiana Morales Pereira, lived in the Calle Concepción Jerónima next to the Ministry of Foreign Affairs, in a building that was falling apart. The edifice was the indefinable colour of dirt and neglect, displaying its wounds with the serene acquiescence of a leper. In some places the stucco had fallen away and deeper gashes revealed patches of a grey amalgam or exposed the building's brick skeleton. By one of the balconies on the first floor bullet holes were still clearly visible. Beneath it was the entrance, with its wooden door painted brown and a lock so ancient it required a large, rusty, iron key, with one end shaped like a clover leaf. Arcadio, who always carried it in his pocket, had to struggle with the lock for a moment before they could enter a dark, dank hallway. He felt along the wall until he found the switch, and turned on the dim, yellowish light. The staircase, with its steps worn down in the middle and wrought-iron banisters that barely served as a reminder of better times, was at the end of the hallway. On the left-hand side of the third floor, it always smelled of cooking, and shouting could be heard from behind the door. This was Arcadio's home. But not Sara's.

'Oh, darling!' cried Sebastiana. She'd come running down the passage as soon as she heard the key in the lock, embracing Sara with hands that always felt damp however much she wiped them on her apron. 'Let me look at you. You look lovely! I think you might even have grown! Come here, let me give you a kiss.'

Her mother would kneel down and hug her. A few months younger than her husband, Sebastiana's sparse, brown hair was badly dyed and scraped back into a bun, exposing a round face with fat cheeks that seemed to squash her small, dark, button-like eyes. Her body had a soft, compact quality to it, making her black skirt and blouse look as if they were stuffed with pillows. But unlike Fray José, Sebastiana Morales always smelled clean, of soap and water, and her plumpness exuded warmth, constancy, an indefinable promise of protection. Perhaps this was why Sara was more affected by her kisses – loud, quick, interspersed with words – than by Arcadio's solid embraces. When her mother's eyes softened, as she succumbed to an emotion that she could no longer express in words, Sara felt her own eyes begin to fill with tears. At that moment, just before everything became blurred, her father intervened and drew them apart.

'That's enough, Sebas. Don't start.'

Her mother would immediately spring up with an agility surprising in one so heavy, and rub her eyes on her cardigan sleeve, nodding in agreement with her husband. Meanwhile, their daughter stood stock-still in the middle of the tiny hall, never knowing what to say or do, or where to go once she'd quickly fought back her tears. She was never really sure what they expected of her so she preferred to remain where she was, waiting for someone else to take the lead so that she could respond in kind, being careful and polite, just as her godmother told her to be whenever they went to visit anyone. Her Sunday lunches were nothing like those afternoon teas with ladies who ate their cake using dainty knives and forks. She'd learnt from the stories her godmother told her – which never featured wicked stepmothers – that poor, very, very poor parents cried a lot when they said goodbye to their children, and that if they sent them out into the world to earn their living when they were small, it wasn't because they didn't love them but because there wasn't enough food to go around. That was why she didn't like the tale of Hansel and Gretel, or any of the adventures about defenceless children who found their way into the castle of a hungry ogre and stole his treasure. In the end, all those children returned home laden with gold, and the parents wept all over again, with joy this time, at their return. But Sara would never have known which home to return to, especially since she had noticed that in the flat on the Calle Concepción Jerónima, they only seemed to eat twice a day.

Although she almost always felt sure she didn't want to be like them, she sometimes wondered why her four older brothers and sisters lived with their parents while she was so far away, in a different house, in a different part of town, with a different family. But she never dared demand a definite answer, because she realised that Arcadio and Sebastiana were suffering, each in their own way – he, proud, terse but tender at the same time; she, much more humble and tearful. Her brothers and sisters, on the other hand, treated her with an indifference that varied from the distrust of the older ones, whom Sara would always regard as hostile adults, to the curiosity of Socorrito, the youngest girl. Socorrito had been born seven years before Sara, and she was the only one who went near Sara of her own free will, always kissing her before taking her coat and giving her an old smock to put on over her dress, following instructions from Sebastiana that made Arcadio furious. Socorrito made no effort to hide her interest and she liked touching her sister's things – the hats that always matched her coats, the gloves, the patent shoes, the purse, and a white leather missal with gilded edges and a pair of angels on the title page that Sara almost always forgot to hand to her godmother when they got back from church. Doña Sara made sure to send her god-daughter to the Calle Concepción Jerónima in the plainest outfit possible, and would make her wear a dress from the previous year even though the skirt was too short or the armholes a little tight. This was why Sari, as they called her at her parents' house, had no choice but to disappoint her sister Socorro, week after week.

'Have you brought your Mariquita Pérez doll?' she'd whisper in Sara's ear as she led her to the kitchen. When Sara shook her head Socorro stamped and frowned and glared at her, screwing her eyes up into two furious slits. 'You really are horrible!'

'But they won't let me,' Sara would mumble defensively.

'You're mean, and nasty and . . . God! It's not as if I'm going to eat your silly doll, or break her. I was looking forward to seeing her. I bet she's got a coat just like yours, hasn't she, with the same kind of fur collar, and a hat.'

Sara managed to smuggle her possessions out of the house on the Calle Velázquez only three or four times during her childhood, the most popular being the famous doll with straight dark hair and big round eyes that was dressed like a real little girl. But though her sister Socorro's joy – the sincere hugs and kisses with which she rewarded Sara – was much greater than she'd expected, she couldn't help feeling a pang of guilt at the thought of her godmother, who was in bed with a temperature, missing her, not suspecting how her god-daughter had made the most of her illness or how quick she'd been to betray her. This was why, after a while and although she'd always had too many toys to grow fond of any one in particular, she ended up snatching the doll from Socorrito and carrying it around all day. She didn't feel happy until she'd placed it back on the little chair beside the trunk where she kept all her clothes, near the head of her bed, which is where it stayed for the next two or three weeks, until one afternoon she thought of playing with it again.

The emotional chaos churning inside Sara squashed her spirit as if it were a ball of bread, something soft and breakable that could come apart in your fingers, or else harden, becoming dry and unyielding. She almost never knew what she wanted, and she felt guilty about being so indecisive, but she kept going, always kept going, and so on Saturday nights she always slept badly, then on Sundays she felt the warmth of her father's embrace, and tears trembled in her mother's eyes as they did in her own, but she was disgusted by the chicken and rice that her mother always served for lunch, though she ate it and said how delicious it was, and she liked it when Sebastiana made her come and sit on her lap after lunch, and she found it revolting seeing a loaf of bread just sitting directly on the table, but she broke off a piece just like everyone else, and she thought her two brothers, Arcadio and Pablo, were oafs, a pair of dirty rude idiots, but she tried very hard to be nice to them, and her sister Sebastiana was ugly and already as fat as her mother, but Sara was pleased when she let her come into the bathroom and watch her apply her turquoise eye shadow, and she knew that she was going to be bored when they all set out for a walk dressed in their Sunday best, but she'd lay her head on her father's arm and fall asleep on the sofa, and she got tired walking around the Plaza Mayor, but she liked holding a different person by the hand on each side, and she couldn't wait for it to be seven o'clock, but she was dreading it, and she breathed a sigh of relief when it was time to head for Sol metro station, but she didn't want to arrive at the station, and she hugged her mother with all her might and with tears in her eyes when she said goodbye to her at the foot of the stairs, but she was relieved at not having to see her again until the following Sunday, and she felt regret with every passing station, but she counted the remaining stations with excitement, and her father looked darker than ever when she saw him again on the pavement in the Calle Velázquez, but she never felt so sure that she loved him as she did then, and she couldn't have wanted to get home more, but she couldn't have wanted to get home less, and as she glimpsed the bars of the entrance to the house she realised with blinding clarity that the Gómez Morales family were strangers to her, but the bars at the entrance insisted on shouting with deafening clarity that she was a Gómez Morales just like them, and she was upset when Arcadio left, but she was pleased when Arcadio left, and the marble lions at the front steps in the Calle Velázquez looked at her like old friends, but she didn't recognise the marble lions, and she kept going, she kept going, letting go of her father's hand to take the hand of the maid waiting for her, not looking back, always looking ahead, because she would never have known which home to return to.

'Children always live in the moment,' her godmother would say when Sara got back, seeing traces of sadness and confusion on her face, the fissure dividing her self.

And for a time, Sara managed to convince herself that her godmother was right, because for the rest of the week she barely thought of Arcadio, or Sebastiana, or her brothers and sisters. Doña Sara would take her to the bathroom and undress her in silence beside the bath, as if she knew that the companionable warmth of the water and foam would warm up her heart until it was the same temperature as her skin, and this was indeed what happened. By the time her god-mother came back to help her into her nightdress and comb her hair and cover her in too much eau de cologne, which she always loved, they could talk and joke about any old thing, back in the comforting intimacy they had always shared. Later, on the kitchen table, she always found a plate of freshly cooked croquettes, or a large slice of potato omelette, or a bowl of *cocido* soup with noodles and *picadillo*, her favourite dishes. On Sunday evenings she never had to eat green beans in tomato sauce, or vegetable stew, or garlic soup, things she hated.

But not even the supper on Sunday nights could entirely erase the effects of that single moment of shock that paralysed her on the doorstep of the only place she could consider as home, when the door opened to reveal the figure of Doña Sara, slim, smartly dressed, with a double string of pearls at the neck of a pale angora sweater, her hair done up in a bun and backcombed so that it resembled a cloud of candyfloss, looking as she always did, yet suddenly unfamiliar. Her shock lasted only a second but had as its source the stranger at the door and the form of her husband, whom Sara could make out through the living-room door, sitting in his wheelchair, impeccably dressed in a suit and tie, a permanent sneer of contempt on his lips and a glass of brandy warming in his hand. Then, just for a moment, she wondered who they were, and felt a bitter, impossible pang of regret for another family, another house, another life, one that she had never lived.

It was something she could never forget, either on school days or holidays, when she was happy or when she was sad, alone in her bedroom or surrounded by dozens of guests. However hard she tried, she never quite managed to escape the fleeting shadow of melancholy, and yet, when her godmother, who acted as if Sunday were a day like any other, put her to bed and told her a story in which there was never a wicked stepmother, and turned off the lamp on her bedside table, and kissed her goodnight, images of the day filled the horizon as she closed her eyes, and, just before she fell asleep,

Sara realised that she could remember nothing more than odd images in black and white, like figures cut from old photographs, people and objects the colour of things that only half-exist.

Sara Gómez would never have declared out loud that she loved children, but she was always emphatically on their side. She hadn't had any children of her own, and she had never spent much time with any of her nephews or nieces, so she had never experienced even the basics – what they weighed, how they felt, their unique smell – but when she saw a baby in the park as she sat enjoying the sun, she liked to observe the way it became fascinated by its own hands or by the leaves on a tree fluttering in the wind. With babies of friends or family, she was more circumspect; it terrified her that a confident mother might try to please her by depositing the surprisingly warm, light bundle in her arms, a creature with a fragile head and soft skin that scratched the air with its ten delicate little nails and waggled its tiny podgy legs. She preferred older children, who didn't disconcert her by asking to be helped onto the toilet, but who still faced the world with the wide-eyed puzzlement that optimistic parents took for innocence. Pre-adolescents, with their sudden mood swings and ability to go from hysterical laughter, violent anger to torrential tears all within the space of a minute, scared her as much as babies, but she almost always found a way of understanding the sharp edges of their sadness. Then, when they turned eighteen, she lost interest in them, as she did with most adults.

Although she could almost never do anything for them and might only ever get a weak smile in return for her efforts, Sara stood up for children, defended them, supported them, silently encouraging them as they passed by the periphery of her life. She observed them from a distance, tight-lipped and alert, never intervening but always trying to anticipate their

41

reactions, to guess what sort of questions they were trying not to ask themselves, and what sort of answers they were avoiding, for Sara was searching for herself in their embraces and their quarrels, in their joy and their boredom, in their identity and in all the people they pretended to be. In all the children she encountered, she tried to find the little girl she had once been and to understand what had happened, what it was she had felt when she had so carefully avoided her own feelings, what had become twisted and broken. She was convinced that in the chaotic recesses of her mind there slumbered an answer that she might never entirely decode, a simple formula for hating or for loving her own memories.

Sara was used to other adults interpreting her interest in children as unfulfilled maternal instincts, and she realised immediately that her new cleaner would be no different. Nor was she surprised when Maribel's initial joy at her son feeling so much at home in a stranger's house changed into dark mutterings about how all this fuss would ruin the boy for ever. Sara never took Maribel's fears seriously as she felt that her own experiences protected her from any excess, Andrés from any lack, and Maribel from her own jealousy. And she knew that spoiling a child wasn't the same as paying attention to it, offering to have a long, open-ended conversation about anything under the sun.

This was the connection between Sara and Andrés, a relationship without expensive presents, empty kisses, or showy displays of affection. While Maribel cleaned the kitchen, Sara and Andrés went out into the garden and chatted. She asked him about the winds, how many types there were, the significance of each one, what effect they had on fishing, on plants, on people's moods. The locals seemed to plan their entire lives around the east wind, the west wind, the south wind, the hot, cold, damp or dry wind, making it advisable, or not, to do the washing, go out or stay in, open the windows or shut them to keep out the sand which got into

food, ruined kitchen appliances, collected in the gaps between tiles and could never be entirely eliminated, however
much one swept. Andrés smiled, as if he couldn't understand
how such a simple thing managed to cause confusion in the
mind of such a clever and grown-up woman. He explained it
all to her patiently and clearly, savouring the rare feeling of
being important.

'Imagine you're on the beach.' And he stretched out his
arms, as if he were holding Sara by the waist at the water's
edge. 'Right? If it's blowing from the left, it's the east wind,
if it's blowing from the right, it's the west wind, if it's
blowing in your face, it's the south wind.'

'And what if I'm not on the beach?'

'It's still easy. When the east wind's blowing it's hot, really
hot in summer, and it's very dry, you can feel it in your
mouth and your throat. It knocks all the flies out, but it
brings in lots of weird insects, caterpillars, bumblebees, but
mainly "diablillos", which are like big mosquitoes, with two
long thin wings on either side. They look horrible but they
don't bite. If I see one, I'll show it to you. That way, when
you see one, you'll know the east wind's coming. The west
wind is cool, but it can be quite sticky. You can feel it on
your clothes, because you sweat more.'

'So it's damp,' she dared conclude for him, wondering
how long it would take for her to get lost this time.

'If it's towards the south, yes. If not, it depends. But it
always makes you leave the beach in the afternoons, because
it suddenly gets cold. Of course, the south wind's worse,
even colder, and you can feel it on your sheets at night –
suddenly they're freezing.'

'Right.' Sara hesitated, faced with the first difficulty.
'And how can you tell if it's the south wind blowing or the
east?'

'Well . . .' Andrés stopped, as if she were being stupid.
'Because you can just tell. Because it blows from a different

direction. And the west wind is drier, but not as dry as the east wind.'

'The worst one.'

'In summer, yes. Especially when it's calm, I mean, when you know it's going to start blowing, but it hasn't started yet, and sometimes it goes away without blowing at all, like last week, do you remember?' Sara shook her head, but this didn't discourage him. 'Well, it doesn't matter. The thing is, it's really horrible, because it gets really hot, like a furnace, so you get all sweaty and it just pours off you. Bleuh! You can't go out, or play football, or anything. You open the front door and it's like you've been smacked in the face, and you just want to go and lie down in the dark, and not do anything. But in winter, the east wind's good, because it clears the air, and dries the washing hanging out on the line, and it's nice getting dressed for school in the morning without having to dry the edges of your jumper with the hairdryer.'

'And when it's calm?'

'In winter?' For a moment, it was the boy's turn to be confused. 'No, in winter, you never notice it. It's never calm. It's like the west wind, it can blow or not blow, but there's never any warning that it's going to start, not in winter or in summer. With the south wind, it's the same. Of course, in winter, the south wind's worse than the west wind, because it's a lot colder, but in spring, the west wind . . .'

At this stage Sara surrendered, holding up her hand as if she were waving a white flag.

'Don't worry, Andrés, it doesn't matter. However much you explain, I'll never understand.'

'What?' And he burst out laughing, feeling more important than ever. 'But it's so easy!'

Sometimes it was the boy who started the conversation. Crossing the living room en route to the garden, he'd point at one of the large illustrated books that occupied the lowest bookshelf. Sara would carry it outside and show it to him, at last finding a use for all the heavy tomes she had begun to accumulate over the past few years – *The Prado Museum*, *Spanish Fauna*, *The Hermitage*, *Nature Reserves of Europe*, *The Masterpieces of Michelangelo*, *Australia*, *Picasso* – since her god-mother had tired of giving perfume or scarves to an old spinster like herself. It made Sara feel useful, reading out the names of the paintings or statues or monuments or places in the photos, although she sometimes felt overwhelmed by Andrés's omnivorous curiosity.

'And the duck-billed platypus?' he'd ask suddenly, as if she knew what he was talking about.

'What?'

'The duck-billed platypus. It's a disgusting animal that's got boobs but it lays eggs, and it's got a duck's beak, I think. It lives in Australia, but it isn't in this book.'

'Oh, yes?' Sara cast her eyes over the list of illustrations several times, but in vain. 'Well, I don't know. Maybe it never lets anyone take photos of it. Or maybe it's extinct.'

'No,' he'd answer, suddenly as sure of this piece of information as he was of the direction of the wind. 'I'd know about it. But it must almost be extinct, which is a shame, because I'd really like to see one. In my science book last year there was only a drawing of it.'

'Well, I'll try to find a photo of it in another book. The thing is, it isn't easy here, but remind me about it the next time I go to Cadiz.'

'Or Madrid,' suggested Andrés, his eyes suddenly shining, because he liked to imagine that, one day, she'd take him with her and show him the city she came from. 'It'd be easier in Madrid.'

'Yes, but the thing is I don't think I'll be going back to Madrid.' Sara tried to let him down gently. 'At least not for the time being.'

'Ah!' Andrés acquiesced, never daring to ask her why, and

then he was off again, saying he'd love to see the photo of the strange mountain that was so flat it looked as if the top had been lopped off with a knife.

Andrés was a quick learner, and he'd repeat the names over to himself so that he wouldn't forget them. Sara would watch him, recalling how much energy it took to deal with all that information, all those names and titles, dismantling concepts with the tools of the mind and then nailing them into memory through sheer will, and every time the boy managed to link one concept with another, or dared to voice a correct supposition, it pleased Sara even more than it did him. She felt that Andrés was a special boy, that his seriousness, his focus and his melancholy nature were symptoms of an unease that bordered on anguish. Perhaps it was simply that she was too old to kneel down on the floor and play toy cars with him, but the wound seemed to go deeper than that. Difficult lives produce difficult children – she knew that herself – and Maribel's lot was not an easy one.

'Well, what can I tell you?' When Sara finally got Maribel to confide in her, almost unintentionally, about the boy's father, it took only a few sentences to clear up the mystery. It was a banal story, like so many others. 'What a disaster. I left school at fourteen. My teachers said I was bright but my family wasn't well off, so I went to work in a supermarket, as a messenger at first and then in the fruit and veg department. That's where I met Andrés's father – he's called Andrés too, he's the son of a haulier and he drove a small lorry. I saw him every day, because he delivered the bread and rolls. They called him "Tasty Bread" because he was so good-looking. You should have seen him, gorgeous, not very tall, but so handsome it wasn't true. He had a really good body, and he was cocky, that's for sure. He always went on about having a good time, saying he'd only had three hours' sleep, how he'd been to a bullfight in El Puerto, he'd gone for a big night out in Jerez, that he'd burned himself out at the Trebujena fair, he was friends with flamenco singers – Paula, Camarón, all of them. Anyway, I was just crazy about him. I loved to listen to him and the way he could convince anyone he was important. He seemed to live life to the full. I even liked the way he pulled so many girls, always bragging about this one or that one, and showing off about how many tourists he'd scored. God, I was stupid. I thought I could change him, that with me it would be different. He knew I had plenty of blokes after me too. It's true, I really did, I had to push them out of the way just to get into my house. And with all the men I had running after me, I had to go and pick the worst one. When I think about it now I could kill myself! Anyway, I started going out with him, and we got engaged. He gave me some coral earrings, and took me round the festival on his horse. It was the most amazing thing that had ever happened to me, that's for sure, but the minute we got off that horse, I got pregnant. Until then, it had all been very nice, but then . . . He didn't want to marry me, and my dad was livid. You should have heard him, and Andrés's father was the same, so in the end we got married. He never spent three nights in a row at home, even in the first week we were married, and when the boy was eighteen months old, he cleared off for good. He moved in with another woman, two streets away, and when she got fed up with him and threw him out, he took up with another one, who runs a bar and puts up with everything. She must be at least ten years older than him. So anyway, there he is, living on the Chipiona road.'

Maribel had told the whole story in one go, folding and re-folding the yellow cloth that she used to wipe the work-tops, and not taking her eyes off her son, who was reading a comic in the garden. Sara understood everything except the woman's apparent calm, the neutral, flat, almost casual tone with which she had told the simple tale of her small wretched life, the brief smile that appeared on her face as she recalled

47

the glory of a morning at the festival. Then, in the silence that followed, she tried to smile again, but her lips just drooped, and she kept passing the cloth from one hand to the other as if it were on fire. Then suddenly she turned round and threw herself into wiping the same marble surface she'd just cleaned with an energy that shook her entire body.

'On the Chipiona road,' she said again, thickly. 'Cocky bastard, that's exactly what he is.'

And with that the conversation ended. Sara never dared to bring the subject up again, but she gleaned other facts from the anger in the eyes of Jerónimo, the obliging gardener who found jobs for people, as his cousin Maribel clicked around the kitchen on her high heels; in Andrés's scowl of displeasure as his mother put on a dress that was too tight when she changed out of her pink housecoat; in the hard look in the eyes of the cashier at the supermarket as she ignored Maribel when she and Sara went shopping together; and in the smile with which her cleaner greeted the wolf whistles of the traders at the Wednesday street market. Maribel was very young, Sara thought, and she wasn't doing anything that any other thirty-year-old woman wasn't doing: going out in the evenings, going to clubs, flirting, having drinks, wearing make-up, not wearing a bra with a low-cut dress, sleeping with lots of different men, maybe ones she didn't want to see again but keeping her sights set on a different, better kind of man, one she could stay with for ever. None of this had anything to do with her son, or with those cheap rings tarnished by bleach, but Sara was sure that Andrés's interest in Madrid, the way he begged her again and again to tell him what the streets, the houses, the football pitches were like, sprang from a desire to escape, to blend his tracks with thousands of others, though perhaps his mother's social life pained him less than the absence of his father, who rushed into the nearest bar to avoid him if he saw him in the street. Sara could do nothing for the difficult boy other than to love him cautiously and pay attention to him, encouraging him to keep going, always keep going.

It was through Andrés that Sara finally got to know the Olmedo family. As the dying days of August stole light from the evenings, and the car parks began to empty, the boy, who had continued to go to the beach with Sara every morning, even after his mother started working for the new neighbours, suddenly announced that he was fed up with salt, sand and having to walk back at lunchtime, and anyway his lilo had a puncture, so he'd much rather stay by the pool. 'You can carry on going to the beach, if you like,' he added, and Sara found his equivocal remark so amusing – both possessive and tolerant – that she decided to go with him to the pool, although now it was she who trailed him, and not the other way round. So the two of them got used to seeing Tamara, who usually arrived at the pool around mid-morning, almost always on her own, with her towel, her bikini-clad Barbie, and a fabulous water pistol the size of a machine gun, with two water tanks and three cannons on different levels that Andrés coveted from the moment he saw it. Sara told him he should ask the girl if he could have a go, and after they'd had their first water battle, Tamara began laying her towel next to Andrés's every morning. But the little girl, who was almost unbearably pretty, didn't much like talking about herself, or her home, or her family, and she hardly ever asked Sara to explain when she didn't understand something Andrés, her future schoolmate, said, as he spoke very fast and with a strong Andalusian accent. Her Uncle Juan, who sometimes came to fetch her and have a quick swim before lunch, confirmed the different impressions that Sara and Maribel had formed on seeing him for the first time. An attractive but serious man, extremely polite but distant, calm but with an anxious expression, mysterious yet ordinary at the same time, deliberately restrained yet seductive almost despite himself, tall, dark and slim, looking much younger than his forty years, there really was no reason why he should stand out, but for some reason he did.

And yet, as September wore on, Sara began to see the Olmedos in a different light, possibly suspecting that they all – both she and her neighbours – were destined to live side by side like the only survivors of a shipwreck, tossed onto the beach of a desert island by a capricious sea. The development, which only a few weeks earlier had been full of children, pregnant women, tanned pensioners, and fathers in shorts, suddenly turned into a model of itself, like a giant film set with fake houses, their shutters firmly closed, their gardens deserted, this picture of abandonment seemingly confirmed by the few disorientated people remaining, their presence compounding the worrying thickness of the air instead of dispelling it. The startling arrival of the west wind, bringing autumn to what should have been a peaceful summer afternoon, crashed against the dozen or so remaining parasols like a sudden full stop.

Juan Olmedo enjoyed his work, and although he was always affected by the general mood of despondency that hung over the last few days of the holidays, he usually got back into his daily routine of white coat and broken bones without too much trouble. That year, however, the first of September felt ominous, like the tremulous first tile in a spiral of dominoes that could send everything else tumbling down. Starting at a new hospital didn't worry him too much, because all hospitals were alike. He knew it was possible that news of his friendship with the head of department might have preceded him and provoked some envy or suspicion, but he was confident that his abilities and lack of bureaucratic ambition would soon dispel any enmity. He was also aware that the opposite could happen: that once word spread that there was a new doctor in Orthopaedics – unmarried, apparently single, who didn't appear to be gay – the atmosphere could become stifling.

But he'd spent many years in the same situation, and he was sure it wouldn't be much of a problem compared with everything else that might befall him.

He was much more concerned about leaving Tamara alone in the house for so long, however much Maribel, who seemed very efficient, assured him that she'd drop in to check on her first thing every morning, on her way to number thirty-one, and that she'd have the little girl's lunch ready by the time she and her son got back from the swimming pool. Ostensibly Tamara would only be on her own for about two weeks, until term began, but Juan knew that, deep down, her loneliness would last much longer; in fact he couldn't see an end to it. The blows his niece had had to endure – the death of her mother, then her father soon afterwards – had turned her relationship with him into an almost unhealthy dependency, a form of permanent emotional blackmail, more like that of a baby than a child her age. Juan realised that she was afraid of losing him as well, because he was all she had left, but he felt uncomfortable as a hostage to her love, not so much because it limited the freedom he'd become so accustomed to, having lived alone for so many years. No, it was because the anxiety that made the child's eyes grow wide every time she saw him start up the car was only a glimpse of the monstrous solitude that stalked her like a shadow.

And yet Juan was convinced that life was beginning to improve for the child, whilst he couldn't be so sure about Alfonso. It was his brother who worried him most, who was constantly on his mind. When, on the first of September, at seven in the morning, he went into Alfonso's room and found him sleeping on his back, with the bedclothes thrown off and his pyjama top all twisted around his body, he regretted not having a god of any kind to pray to. He sat down beside his brother, called his name and shook him, gently at first, then a little more energetically. Alfonso kicked him a few times before he finally sat up and the first thing he said, in his strained, nasal voice, was that he didn't want to go. But he gave in to his older brother's authority as Juan made him get out of bed, straightened his pyjamas, and led him downstairs to the kitchen. There, Juan listened to Alfonso complaining while he prepared breakfast.

'I don't want to go,' Alfonso said over and over, waving a finger for emphasis. 'No, no, no. I'm staying here. Home sweet home, home sweet home.'

Spreading a slice of toast with butter, Juan said nothing,

concentrating on somehow filling the hole that had opened up where his stomach used to be, stunned by the mixture of pity, fear, anger, love and sadness he felt every time he had to force his brother to do something he didn't want to do.

'Look, Juanito, look at my tears. They're running down here, and here. I don't want to go, don't want to, don't want to . . . don't, and that's that.'

'Why not, Alfonso?' Juan said at last, putting a cup of hot chocolate before him and sitting down. 'What do you want to do? Stay in the house all day on your own? You'd be bored.'

'I wouldn't. I'd watch TV. I know how to change channels.' And he held out his right hand, tapping with his index finger as if he were pressing on a remote control. 'Zap zap, zap! See? I can change channels myself. Like that.'

'And who's going to get your lunch, eh?'

'You.' He smiled, pleased at having found a solution. 'You could get it.'

'But I won't be here. I'll be going to work each morning and I won't get back until late afternoon.'

'You!' Alfonso exclaimed, meekly at first but growing more and more angry. 'You get my lunch, you, you!'

'Don't shout, you'll wake Tamara up. I can't, Alfonso, I've got to go to—'

'You!' Alfonso shouted again and then threw himself on the floor.

Half an hour later, Juan had finally managed to get him dressed, although he hadn't brushed his teeth. This wasn't Alfonso's only reprisal. He refused to accompany Juan upstairs to say goodbye to Tamara, and while Juan was out of the room he threw his cup of hot chocolate into the sink. As it was boiling hot, he managed to burn his hand and the whole drama started again.

'Do you want me to get cross, Alfonso? Do you?'

As usual, the threat triggered a new phase in Alfonso's

onslaught. Even though he'd been up for only an hour, Juan was already exhausted and drove in silence to El Puerto de Santa Maria, while his brother, strapped into the back seat, complained and insulted Juan in equal measure.

'You're bad, very bad,' Alfonso said one last time, as they parked outside the centre.

The day couldn't have got off to a worse start, thought Juan, as he pushed open the door to the clean, new building, with large windows and spacious, square classrooms that had so impressed him at the beginning of July, when he was arranging his brother's enrolment. Surprisingly, Alfonso also seemed to like the place, because as soon as he entered the foyer he stopped crying and started looking around with interest. Suddenly the day changed direction, like a ball rising in the air after striking the ground.

Juan gave his name to the receptionist who told him to wait there. She went over to Alfonso and asked him, in the firm but soothing tone teachers use to negotiate with small children, if he'd like her to show him his classroom. They had just headed off down the corridor when a woman in a white coat came across the foyer towards Juan.

'Hello, I'm Isabel Gutiérrez.' She looked about thirty-five, had discreetly dyed hair, wore no make-up, and had a wedding ring on her right hand. She projected a promising air of efficiency. 'I'm a psychiatrist and the Assistant Director of the centre. You must be Mr Olmedo. Would you like to come with me? I need to ask you a few questions about your brother, so that we can focus our plan of action.'

As he followed her down a bright corridor, punctuated at intervals with enormous dark green aspidistras, Juan reflected on the woman's choice of phrase, and appreciated the nuance that separated it from other terms she could easily have used, such as 'treatment' or 'programme'. This re-assured him about the tone of the conversation he was about to have.

'I believe you're a doctor yourself,' she said, offering him the chair on the other side of her desk and opening Alfonso's file.

'Yes, but my speciality is broken bones,' he said, and she smiled. 'I'm an orthopaedic surgeon.'

'We'll make sure we give you a call if we ever break anything! Now, let's see. Your brother's condition is the result of oxygen deprivation during childbirth, is that right?'

'Yes, they didn't realise that the umbilical cord was twisted around his neck. At some point his brain was starved of oxygen. We don't know exactly why or for how long.'

'The usual incompetence.'

'Well, yes, that's true, it was a complete mess. The labour was very quick, it was my mother's fifth. She became fully dilated in the car on the way to hospital, so when she arrived the doctors sent her directly to the delivery room, but they wouldn't wait and opted to use forceps straight away. They must have been in a hurry that morning.'

Dr Gutiérrez consulted her notes, underlining things from time to time, avoiding his eyes as she asked questions.

'He was her last child?'

'Yes. All the other births were fine, quite normal. After Alfonso was born, she didn't realise there was anything wrong. She wasn't an educated woman so she didn't fully understand what had happened to him. She didn't make any sort of formal complaint either – she just put it all down to the will of God.'

'And she brought him up exactly like her other children?'

'Exactly the same.'

'So Alfonso has always lived with the family?'

'Always.'

The doctor smiled appreciatively at his response.

'First he lived with my parents,' Juan continued, 'then, when my father died, he stayed on with my mother. She was always fit and active, and very strong physically, until she had a brain haemorrhage seven years ago. So then Alfonso went to live with my brother Damián, as he was better off than my two sisters. He had a large house with a garden, in the Estrecho district, near to where we all grew up. Everybody in the area already knew Alfonso and he could manage quite well on his own. Damián was married to a girl who'd lived next door to us for years, and she was very fond of Alfonso. Her name was Charo, and he adored her. Their house was very well organised, with a live-in maid and another girl who came in the afternoons to look after their daughter, my niece Tamara, who was only a baby at the time. So Alfonso's arrival didn't alter their way of life too much. I'm the eldest, but I live on my own. Well, not now; I mean that I lived alone back then, and that's why it seemed the best solution.'

'So what happened?' the doctor asked. As he remained silent, she decided to press him further. 'I'm only asking because Alfonso now lives with you.'

'Yes.' Juan took a breath and answered in one go. 'My sister-in-law died in a car accident eighteen months ago. My brother was the driver. He suffered very serious injuries, including brain damage, which was what eventually killed him seven months later. My sisters' situations were both still very difficult – they each have three children, and the younger of the two is divorced. I've always been closer to Alfonso than they have and I've always spent a great deal of time with him. I'd take him out at weekends, for lunch, or to the cinema, and he'd sometimes stay at my place on Saturday nights. We'd go away on short trips in the summer. I tried to help my brother and sister-in-law, to give them some breathing space. As you can imagine, Alfonso can be quite exhausting. Damián and I were always very close too. I was only eleven months older than him and I knew his wife very well – we were all part of the same group of friends when we were kids. I went to visit them a lot, I often had lunch there on Sundays, and I'd stay with Alfonso and Tamara if they couldn't find a babysitter. My niece only saw my sisters at Christmas, on her birthday or her cousins' birthdays, so when her parents died, I decided to take care of both her and Alfonso.'

'That was very brave of you.'

'No.' This time it was Juan who looked away. 'I simply accepted my responsibility.'

'And the change of location? I expect you realised that this could have an adverse effect on your brother.'

'Yes, but I was more worried about my niece.' Juan had foreseen this question. 'She was deeply affected by the loss of her mother, and when in the end her father died too, she became very withdrawn, she wouldn't speak to anyone, and she began to do badly at school. I thought it would be a good idea to have a change, to leave a house that would always remind her of her parents.'

'Of course, of course, I understand,' the psychiatrist said quickly, apologetically, as if Juan's words had called her expertise into question. 'I'm sorry. I'd forgotten about the child. She must be about ten, is that right? I fully understand your decision. Now, tell me more about Alfonso. He must have been very upset over his brother's death as well.'

'Yes, but he was much more affected by my sister-in-law's death. I'm just telling you because he still talks to her a lot, as if she were some kind of invisible friend. He tells her what's going on, talks to her at the table and asks her if she likes the food, asks us to tell her to come upstairs and give him a kiss at bedtime, that kind of thing. He was extremely fond of her because she was like a second mother to him. He had a different relationship with Damián. Damián had a very forceful personality, and well . . . he could be a little abrupt and impatient. It's not that he didn't love Alfonso, it was just that he insisted on treating him like a normal person. He expected him to do things he couldn't possibly do, and imposed rules he couldn't follow. He insisted on trying to get him to eat properly, stand up straight, keep his shirt tucked into his trousers. He was furious if Alfonso spilt soup down his chin.'

Juan stopped and, looking up, saw that the doctor was now staring at him. He'd known that the question would come up and he'd decided to be open for Alfonso's sake, not minimising the ugly facts for which he somehow felt responsible, and without exaggerating them so as to comfort himself for obscure reasons that this woman would never know.

'I would rather not ask you this, but I hope you agree that I really don't have a choice. Did your brother hit Alfonso?'

'Yes.' Juan met her gaze. 'I'm very ashamed to admit it, but he did. Never when I was there, of course, or his wife – she'd always stop him – but . . . It was never systematic violence, it didn't happen every day, or even every week, it was just sudden bursts of anger. Sometimes, Damián simply felt he couldn't take it any more, and he hit Alfonso. He didn't actually beat him, he'd just strike him once or twice until he'd calmed down. But he frequently threatened to hit him, and when Alfonso did something wrong, Damián would ask him, "Do you want me to get cross?" He acted as if there wasn't a problem, but a couple of times I managed to get him to talk about it, and I even suggested that we put Alfonso in a residential home, but he'd never agree to it. He wanted to have his brother living at home, but he also wanted him to be different, so they were at an impasse. Damián was a complex character. I don't think he could stand being the second child, he would have given anything to be me as I was the eldest. He had an obsession with being the head of the family, the patriarch, maybe because he started earning a lot of money when he was very young – he was the typical, successful young businessman. He liked to take care of my parents, buy them expensive, showy presents, give my sisters money at Christmas, and he always had to be the one who gave the most expensive toys to all the kids on their birthdays. Anyway, he wanted to be a father figure to all of us and he wasn't used to people not doing as he said. Poor Alfonso wouldn't, and this was the result.'

'Alfonso was scared of him,' concluded the doctor.

'Terrified. He couldn't stand being alone with him. It was all right if there were other people around, but when they were on their own, Alfonso would suddenly start crying, or wet his pants, which only made things worse.'

'I see,' she said simply, before scribbling a long paragraph on one of the forms from her folder. 'This kind of thing can have serious consequences, but you mustn't blame yourself. It's very common, unfortunately, even among educated people, who you would expect to know better. Let's talk some more about Alfonso. You've signed him up for the bus service, so I take it that he's obedient and fairly independent.'

'Yes, I'm sure he'll be perfectly OK making the journey here and back. I'll bring him myself next week, on my way to work, and I'll collect him on the way home, but after that I'd like him to take the bus. I've told the hospital where I work about the situation, and they've let me off night shifts for three months, until Alfonso gets used to the routine here, but it's only a special concession until after Christmas. Anyway, I have a lot more expenses than before, so the night shifts will come in handy. I thought I'd hire someone to stay overnight when I'm not at home, and I think it's best that Alfonso gets used to being fairly independent as soon as possible. That's why I decided he should start today, even though it's a Friday. Anyway, I don't think he'll give you too much trouble. He hates change, that's true, he doesn't feel secure in new surroundings, but he's quite docile and sweet-tempered – he doesn't often get angry or violent. He's never harmed himself, or attacked anyone. He gets on well with people and he's very affectionate. He can control his bladder and bowels, get himself dressed in the mornings, feed himself, brush his teeth, and do small errands. He has the mental age of a child of six or seven.'

'Which is quite a lot.' The doctor nodded. 'Is there anything special I should know?'

'Yes. He loves tomato ketchup. We put it on everything for him – meat, fried fish. It's a way of guaranteeing he'll eat it. And he also likes to masturbate. This was what infuriated my brother Damián the most. The thing is, he'll do it wherever and whenever he can, and it doesn't bother him if someone else is looking. I've managed to convince him to go to the bathroom when my niece is at home, but that's about as far as I've got.' He smiled, and the doctor smiled back.

'Does he reach orgasm?'

'Not necessarily. Sometimes he does, but sometimes he just stops halfway through. For him, it's just a way of passing the time.'

'Right. Well, don't worry, nobody here will be shocked. We've got enough recreational masturbators to make a couple of football teams. It's fairly common. Anything else?'

'Yes, I . . .' Juan paused for a moment, searching for the right words. 'You might find that he's a little spoilt. I can't really explain it properly but, after everything that's happened, I find it hard to be strict with either him or my niece. We've all been through so much in the last couple of years, that I'm probably spoiling them both. The thing is, I love my brother very much.'

'I'm glad to hear it.' Dr Gutiérrez stood up, bringing the meeting to an end. 'We'll do our best for him. Well, I don't think there's anything else. Ah yes, I always forget. There's something I should tell you, but we can do that en route. I'll walk you back to the entrance.'

They left the office and headed back along the corridor with the aspidistras.

'What I wanted to tell you about is the wind,' said Dr Gutiérrez. 'We should have mentioned it to you back in

July, when you came to enrol your brother, but I was on holiday at the time and my secretary only told me this morning that she had forgotten to say anything. The thing is, she was born here, and I get the feeling she doesn't really take it seriously – she thinks I'm making too much of it. But it can be a real issue. You should be careful of the east wind because it's still dangerous in September. Later on, in autumn and winter, it's not so much of a problem, because, it's very strange, the characteristics of the wind change with the temperature. Don't ask me why. I'm from Salamanca and though I've lived here for over ten years and I'm married to a native, I still don't quite understand it. The east wind can be very pleasant when the weather's cold, because then it's a warm, dry wind, but in spring it can have a very bad effect on people, and even more so in summer with the hot weather. People with learning difficulties often feel it much more intensely than we do, because they have less self-control. So, when the east wind is blowing, you'll need all the patience you can muster. It's very likely you'll find that your brother is more irritable, more impatient, more depressed, and he may even be more violent than usual. It might seem like a lot of nonsense, but that's how it is. For instance, what kind of mood was Alfonso in when he woke up this morning?'

'Terrible,' admitted Juan. 'He said he didn't want to come here, he was complaining and crying and calling me names; he even spilt a cup of chocolate over himself.'

'Because the east wind has been blowing since yesterday evening.' The doctor nodded emphatically.

'But, I don't know, it all seems a little far-fetched. I don't think it can . . .' Juan made no attempt to hide his scepticism, but neither could he complete his sentence when he looked the doctor in the eye. 'Or can it?'

'Well, the courts here allow the east wind to be cited as an extenuating circumstance in cases of assault and battery, physical abuse, even murder. And there is a higher number of mentally disabled patients on the coast around Cadiz – particularly near the Straits, where the winds blow even stronger than here – than anywhere else in the country, with the exception of the Costa Brava, where there's the *tramontane*, which is more or less the same thing. This is why you need to be on your guard. You might not feel the wind change, but Alfonso will. Remember that.'

Her warning still echoed in Juan's ears when he emerged into a hot, sunny morning and it accompanied him as he drove to the hospital, along a road lined with peaceful fields, a reminder that even the most serene of landscapes can conceal malevolent forces. Later, as he met his new colleagues and found his way round a new building and a new system, Juan Olmedo's mood improved. He was sure he was going to like it here in Jerez. His old friend and new boss, Miguel Barroso, had thought of everything. He introduced him to all the staff, took him round every last corner of the department, and had even filled in all the documents Juan needed for his transfer, so that all Juan had to do was sign on the dotted line. 'And I've collected your post,' he said, handing over an envelope bearing the letterhead of the Puerta de Hierro clinic and a postmark dated 22 August. Inside there was another smaller envelope, long, cream and with his name and old address written in purple ink, in a pointed elegant hand that Juan recognised immediately as that of the fragile and bewildered figure of Señora Ruiz.

On Saturday, 24 April 1999, Dr Olmedo went on duty at the Orthopaedics Department of the Puerta de Hierro Clinic in Madrid at eight in the evening. Just before nine o'clock, the first car-accident victim was brought in, a boy of nineteen who'd decided to jump a red light in the Plaza de España just as a jeep was heading down the Gran Vía at eighty kilometres an hour. It struck him from the side and he ended up with a broken arm, two broken ribs and a broken collarbone. In contrast, the motorcyclist who came in at eleven thirty hadn't been wearing a helmet and there was nothing anyone could do for him. Juan Olmedo didn't even see him, because he was dealing with an old lady who'd recently had a hip replacement and had fallen over in her bathroom. At two in the morning, a car came off the road on one of the slopes of Dehesa de la Villa and crashed into a tree. The driver, who was drunk, had confused the pedals and pressed the accelerator instead of the brake. Both he and his girlfriend arrived at A & E completely bathed in blood, but neither was seriously wounded. Dr Olmedo treated the girlfriend's injuries. At four thirty in the morning, as a porter was wheeling his patient to her room, Juan checked to see if anyone else was waiting to be treated, then sat down and smoked a cigarette, staring morosely at the bed ready for the next patient. He hated weekend shifts so much that from time to time he even considered changing to another branch of medicine, leaving the distressing discipline of shattered bodies for a more pleasant field; but then he'd spent too many years working in a hospital to believe that other jobs were as stress-free as they appeared. Anyway, he didn't have time to think much during these Saturday shifts, and the night of the twenty-fourth was no exception. At twenty to five, he was informed that a young girl had been run over by a car outside a nightclub. It sounded horrific, but her injuries were only superficial. At six, he decided to lie down for a moment, and fell asleep as soon as his head hit the pillow. Fifteen minutes later, a nurse woke him.

'Yes?' he said, at once fully awake. 'What is it now?'

'No, no, it isn't that . . . It's just that your brother's here, asking for you. It seems a member of your family has had an accident, but he wouldn't tell me any more. He looks very upset.'

'Thanks.' Juan leapt to his feet. 'Where is he?'

'At the nurses' desk.'

Damián was circling the spot where the nurse had left him. He was quite alone in the soulless corridor with its greenish walls, hung at regular intervals with lists of instructions about what do in the event of an accident, and pictures of muscles and bones shown in full colour that, in Juan's opinion, always made them look more sinister than they did in real life. Perhaps this was why, when he saw his brother pacing round and round, trapped in that sad place, he realised that he was still capable of feeling compassion for him, as he did when they were children. This unexpected rush of empathy made him greet his brother with a kiss on the cheek instead of a simple pat on the back. He realised that he hadn't kissed Damián since the day of their mother's funeral, seven years earlier.

'What's the matter?' he asked. 'Is it Alfonso?'

He was sure that the emergency must involve Alfonso. It was the first thing that had occurred to him when the nurse told him his brother was there to see him, and he'd repeated the thought to himself as he crossed the tiled floor that led to the corridor. Alfonso was capable of all sorts of mischief. Maybe he'd burned himself, or hurt himself jumping off a piece of furniture, or maybe he'd had a fall or even escaped from the house – it could be anything. This certainty both calmed and worried him at the same time. 'It must be Alfonso,' he repeated one last time as he waited for Damián to answer. But before his brother had uttered a single word, the look in his eyes told Juan that he was mistaken.

'No.' His wary, furious expression was not that of a man who was simply alarmed. 'Charo.'

'Charo?' Juan dug the nails of his right hand into the palm of his left hand, but he couldn't control his breathing, and he could hear himself gasping as he broke out into a cold sweat. 'But how?'

'That's what I'd like to know!' The nurse who'd come to

64

fetch Juan and was now back at her desk motioned at Damián to be quiet, a finger to her lips.

'Don't shout, Damián,' said Juan. Suddenly he felt a furious wave of resentment towards his brother. 'This is a hospital.'

'I'm sorry.' He glanced at the nurse and then went on in a whisper, gritting his teeth with the effort, 'The police called a short time ago to ask if a María Rosario Fernández was related to me. They confirmed the address and so on, and then they told me that she'd just been involved in a car crash on the old Galapagar road. I told them it was impossible, that my wife had left for Navalmoral de la Mata yesterday, to see her mother. The officer said he couldn't tell me any more for the time being. I've called Nicanor and asked him to go over there, to talk to them. He said he would come and pick me up, but I wanted to go with you, in case it really is her . . . if she has to go to hospital, you'll be able to tell me what's wrong. Shit! I don't know . . . I'm in a real state. I don't know what to think.'

Juan relaxed his hands and stared at the white marks his nails had left on his palm, wishing he had other, longer nails to jab into his brain. He shook his head and forced himself to think, automatically falling back on the discipline he'd acquired through many years of dealing with emergencies.

'How are things here, Pilar?'

'Pretty quiet,' answered the nurse, who had listened in silence to Damián's story. She glanced at her watch. 'I think the worst is probably over, it's nearly six thirty. I can have a word with Dr Villamil, if you like.'

'No, thanks, that's OK, I'll go myself.' Juan took hold of his brother's arms and spoke slowly, making sure he was understood. 'Did you come here by car?'

'No.'

'Good. We can go in mine. I'll drive. Go down to the cafeteria and order two large espressos. You have one of

65

them and wait for me there. If you think it'll do you any good, order a brandy and drink that, but do it quickly. I'm supposed to be on duty for another hour and a half, so I'll have to go and tell my boss that I'm leaving. I'll get changed and I need a coffee too, because I haven't slept. I'll see you in about five minutes. We'd better get there as quickly as possible, because there's always a lot of confusion at an accident, and if more than one car's involved, they can get mixed up about the ambulances and which hospital the injured have been sent to. Do you understand me?'

'Yes.' Damián looked even more frightened now than when he first arrived, and he nodded with a meekness Juan hadn't seen since their school days. But all Juan's compassion was reserved for himself.

While he was telling his colleagues what had happened, while he was changing as quickly as he could, while he drank a coffee before it had even cooled or the sugar dissolved, while he pressed down on the accelerator as his car headed up the ramp of the underground car park, Juan Olmedo tried to replace the images of all the corpses he had ever witnessed with the memory of all the victims who had managed to survive before his very eyes. He tried to remember every hospital bed, every recovery exercise, every furtive tear, every conscious smile, every vase of flowers, as the only things capable of dislodging all the other images of bodies without legs, arms, eyes, a head, without any real body at all, all the deaths he'd seen pronounced or had to pronounce himself. He'd never experienced this kind of pressure before, or felt so detached from himself. Nor could he remember ever having been as afraid as he was then. He wanted to scream, pound his fists on the dashboard and tear at his face; but he could do nothing except drive as fast, and prudently, as he could, and with all the hope he could muster.

'You don't think she's dead, do you?' asked Damián, as if he could read Juan's mind, as they turned onto the La

Coruña road. 'They would have told me, wouldn't they, if she was dead?'

Juan kept staring straight ahead as he answered. 'I don't know.'

But he did know. He was fully familiar with the system that handled every car accident – he'd spent the last fifteen years being part of it. He knew that until a doctor had certified the death of a victim, the court wasn't contacted, and until the judge on duty turned up and authorised the removal of the bodies, the relatives of the victims couldn't be informed. He knew that nobody said their official farewell to life until several strangers had confirmed that he or she was definitely dead, and that the first stretch of the Galapagar road came under the jurisdiction of the courts of Plaza de Castilla. He knew that in the municipal district of Madrid, Friday and Saturday nights were lethal, and that at weekends the courts were as overworked as the emergency departments. He knew that the judge often arrived late, and that the relatives almost always got there before he did. He knew all this, but he said nothing because he remembered how many times he himself had wished Charo dead, gone, vanished, transported to the other side of the universe. He remembered all the sleepless nights he'd spent imagining her death, all the glasses he'd raised to toast her imaginary funeral, all the times the phone had rung, torturing him over the years, all the restaurant tables set for two where he'd ended up eating alone, all the lives he'd given up, all the girlfriends he'd left, all the opportunities he'd turned down just so that he could go on experiencing the glorious torment of waiting for the phone to ring, of sitting alone at restaurant tables, of sleepless nights, and of the tanned body of the love of his life. You can't resign from hell, Juan Olmedo told himself while there was still time, because hell never stops. Hell has legs, two long legs that leave their taut, sinuous, luxuriant imprint on the retinas of the condemned, and they can always outrun even the fastest unwary wretch. You can't say no, because hell has no ears for the word no; Juan knew this better than anyone because he'd spent half his life uttering it in vain. 'Surely I wouldn't free myself of you so easily,' Juan Olmedo said to himself. It would be too simple, too casual, too appalling. 'It can't be true, it can't be,' he repeated to himself, because there was still time. And somehow an image slipped behind his eyes, like a transparency: a hospital room, with a single bed near the window, the sun shining in, and against the dazzling white sheets a Charo who was slimmer, very tired and pale, with untidy hair and burning eyes, her head to one side, lightly resting her cheek against the hand of a man dressed in green standing beside the bed, and it was him, Dr Olmedo, and he'd arranged for his sister-in-law to be transferred to his floor so that he could personally supervise her recovery, and at last he'd managed to get her all to himself, from the time he took her breakfast in the morning until he said good night. 'I'll heal you,' he thought, 'I'll take care of you, I'll look after you,' and he savoured every syllable of those three lines because there was still time. 'I'll repair every bone in your body, I'll make sure you get to sleep each night, I'll see to it that you don't feel even a hint of pain, and we'll talk,' he added, still to himself, feeling more and more euphoric, 'we'll talk about the things we always talk about, but you'll have experienced death close up and life will be more dear to you, and I'll take care of Damián, I'll explain everything to him, we'll leave together, we'll go far away.' He managed to lose himself so abruptly, so suddenly, so desperately in this searing fantasy, that he almost took the wrong turning. As he rounded the next bend, Juan saw the lights of the ambulance in the background, parked in the middle of the road. Before he got out of the car, he searched for Charo but he couldn't see her.

'Damián! Damián!'

Juan Olmedo heard someone shout his brother's name,

and recognised the voice of Nicanor Martos, an inspector in the National Police force, and his brother's best friend. He looked for him, but couldn't see him amongst the dozen or so men and women, some in uniform, clustered around the ambulance, the crane and the van carrying officials – two police cars with their lights flashing and several other cars parked haphazardly completed the scene. As he made his way through the crowd, Juan saw a man's shoe lying on the ground on its side, a very clean and almost new shoe, the leather sole barely marked. In that instant, Juan knew that Charo was dead. He felt overwhelmed by a sudden tide of nausea, as if all the fluid in his healthy, living body was smashing against the walls of his skull, pounding his eyes, ears, temples and nose in increasingly violent, painful waves. His legs felt hollow, his arms numb, his chest empty, while his head seemed to swell like a sponge, useless, saturated. Images swam before his eyes as if through a blurred, liquid veil, and his ears were unable to process the sounds because of the monstrous waves crashing together repeatedly in the centre of his forehead. Through this blurred tableau, he finally caught sight of Nicanor, coming towards him with one arm raised, frozen in warning. He turned his head out of some vague instinct, and saw two shapes covered in thick brownish-grey blankets, lying beside the white line at the edge of the road.

'Damián!'

Juan thought Nicanor was shouting to him, but Nicanor repeated the name one more time and Juan realised that his brother was still beside him and that his own legs were trembling, close to collapse.

'Don't come any closer, Damián. She's dead.'

The policeman, as accustomed as any doctor to breaking bad news, was a cold-blooded creature. Juan knew this, for he knew him well. Nicanor Martos, who had chosen the same career as his father and grandfather, did not have a good reputation in Estrecho when the Olmedos moved there in the mid-seventies. For the first few days, as Juan was wandering about trying to get his bearings in the new district, he saw Nicanor a few times, always on his own, walking up and down the streets in a green loden coat and expensive shoes that seemed incongruous with his greasy, acne-covered face. In those days, he was already tall and rather fat, and on his lapel he always wore the right-wing Falangist Party badge. He made it clear that he wasn't simply looking at people, he was watching them. But then he met Damián and the rest of the world receded. He became the younger Olmedo's shadow: he grew his hair, began wearing black boots with a flamenco heel, and bought a tight denim jacket to match his jeans, as was the fashion in Villaverde at that time. From then on they were inseparable. Damián was the only friend Nicanor had ever had, and was still the only person who really mattered to him. Perhaps twenty years had not been long enough to repay in full the debt of gratitude and admiration that Nicanor felt he owed Damián. Although he had viewed the dead bodies of the victims with indifference, his eyes were clouded as he hugged Damián.

'It's her. She's dead,' he said again, to make sure that Damián understood. 'There's nothing we can do.'

Juan closed his eyes but then he felt something strike his shoulder – it was his brother staggering, swaying from side to side. Nicanor grabbed hold of him and helped him over to one of the police cars, so that he could lean against it. Juan, who had grown used to holding himself upright, to controlling every syllable, every silence, in a decade of furtive love, stood motionless. His mouth was dry, his throat suddenly raw, and he realised he felt dizzy too. He made his way over to Damián and Nicanor.

'What happened?' Damián was slurring his words as if he were drunk, his features frozen and his eyes unfocused, until he turned to look at his friend, who couldn't begin to find a way to answer him.

'Tell me what happened,' Damián insisted. 'I want to know.'

'It must have taken place about five thirty this morning.' Nicanor glanced at his notebook, where he'd entered the cold, cruel data. 'It seems the driver must have been blind drunk, at the very least. The doctor who examined him told the police he'd probably taken something else too, maybe coke or ecstasy, who knows. He was heading away from Madrid at over 180 kilometres an hour. He came off the road, crashed through the barrier and slammed the Audi into the cliff face. Neither of them was wearing a seat belt. The police had to use a special crane to prise the car away from the rock – it was wedged so tightly into a fissure that they weren't able to pull it out using the normal hooks and chains. Both of the passengers were killed instantly. Charo's airbag inflated but a piece of the car's bodywork, or maybe it was the barrier, sliced through her femoral artery. His airbag didn't even inflate, the collision must have been too violent. The emergency services had a difficult job getting the bodies out and they're in a pretty bad state, so I think it's best if you don't see her.' Nicanor stopped, lit a cigarette, and placed his left hand round his friend's neck, as if this were the greatest show of tenderness he could allow himself. 'I'm so sorry, Damián,' he murmured, 'I'm sorry about everything, that Charo's dead, that she died like this . . .'

'Who was he?'

'It doesn't matter, Damián, don't think about that now.'

'But it *does* matter.' He looked at his friend in disbelief. 'It matters to me. Who was he?'

Nicanor flicked through his notebook again, clenching his jaws so tightly it looked almost painful.

'José Ignacio Ruiz Perelló,' he said at last, after clearing his throat a couple of times. 'Age forty-one, born in Valencia, living in Madrid, in the Parque del Conde de Orgaz. He was married to a woman from a very good family, with lots of money, and he was a civil engineer, with a post high up in the Ministry of Public Works and Town Planning. The people in the bar over there knew him. His wife's got a swanky house a couple of kilometres away, one of those old holiday homes with a huge garden. Charo and he must have been on their way there when they had the accident. The wife had no idea, of course, she was stunned – Perelló had told her he was going to Lisbon for the opening of a joint Spanish–Portuguese dam on the river Tagus, or something like that. She got here before you did – she's the woman in the mink coat over there, the one with the dyed blonde hair.'

There was a long deep silence, thick, loaded with bitter memories, which was interrupted only when Damián slammed his clenched fist on the roof of the car.

'Whore!' he muttered, his fist raised. 'Whore, whore!' he repeated, crashing his fist down again and again and shouting more loudly with every blow, before at last breaking down in tears. 'Whore, whore, the fucking whore!'

Juan flinched with every word. His brother's raging pierced his mind like so many long sharp needles, until he felt he couldn't bear another moment.

'I'm going to see her,' he whispered to Nicanor, who nodded, smoking silently and not taking his eyes off Damián, ready to catch him when he fell.

Juan walked away as quickly as he could. As he reached the place where the bodies were lying, a traffic policeman stepped in front of him.

'Can I help you, sir?' Inside the uniform was a very young man, no more than twenty-three or twenty-four, with the look of a recently qualified cadet, still trying to follow the rules to the letter, but without much experience of imposing them on others.

'I'd like to see the woman.'

'Are you a relative?'

'Yes, I'm her brother-in-law. My brother can't see her. He's completely devastated. He's the one over there, the one pounding the car.'

The policeman raised his eyebrows with a look that seemed almost comical.

'I know she's been identified, but I'd like to see her anyway.'

'Right. But I have to warn you, the body is in a very bad state.'

'I can imagine.'

'Yes, but the thing is we couldn't get her out . . . with her legs.'

'I don't care. I'm a doctor, I work in a hospital. I can assure you I've seen worse things than this.'

'Well, if you say so.' The policeman seemed more shocked than Juan as he leant over Charo's body and lifted the blanket, turning his head away.

Juan crouched down and tried to examine the body as a forensic pathologist would, noticing out of the corner of his eye that the young policeman had decided to avoid a second viewing of the corpse. The woman, aged about thirty-five, about five foot seven inches tall, weighing about sixty-five kilos, with dark hair and eyes, Caucasian, had indeed died as a result of a severed femoral artery. The right leg had been cut clean through. And that was all. Part of her left leg, to just above the knee, remained attached to the rest of her body. Her right thigh. Her left thigh. Her legs the colour of caramel. Shards of shattered bone, bloody pulped flesh, shreds of skin. Her thighs. Her knees that were no longer there. Juan instinctively tried to loosen his shirt collar, but could find nothing to loosen – the top two buttons of his shirt were already undone, but still he felt he couldn't breathe. Her head and torso were in good condition – she had simply bled to death and her deep crimson lipstick stood out obscenely against her pale, white face, tinged with mauve. Juan Olmedo opened his own mouth, gasping for air, as he stared into the dead woman's eyes. Her black eyeliner had run, creating dark shadows under her eyes, and some of her mascara had come off her lashes, sprinkling her cheeks with tiny black specks. Charo had carefully re-applied her lipstick, ignoring the rest of her make-up, before leaving Madrid, as she had always done the minute she was dressed when she left her brother-in-law's house to return to her own. Juan recognised the colour: it was very different from the pale pink, almost beige, lipstick she wore at family meals. He understood its meaning, and for the last time felt Charo's legs, legs that were no longer there, around his neck. Then, without moving his shoulders or leaning towards the corpse, so that no one behind him would notice what he was doing, he put out his hand and quickly undid two of the buttons on her maroon blouse, revealing the edge of a lace bra of the same colour. Juan couldn't bear to look at it. He closed his eyes and bent his head forward, resting his forehead for a moment on the lifeless chest, the unbearably cold skin.

'Hey!' A second later he heard a gruff voice – not that of the young policeman who had left him alone with her – and footsteps approaching. 'What d'you think you're doing? Who are you? You can't touch the bodies. The judge hasn't arrived yet.'

'I'm sorry,' said Juan in a loud voice, hurriedly doing up the buttons of her blouse. 'I didn't realise.'

He stood up quickly and didn't stop to see the furious expression of the older policeman, who was still berating him as he covered Charo's body with the blanket again. He had already decided what he was going to do next. Nicanor had left Damián by the car for a moment and seemed to be heading in Juan's direction, perhaps because he had seen everything, or perhaps because he had seen nothing and wanted to find out what had happened, but this didn't seem reason enough for Juan to change his plans. He walked up to the ambulance team, talked to one of the paramedics, identifying himself, and requested a sedative for his brother. He then returned to the car. Nicanor was back with Damián, who was staring blankly into space, his arms hanging loose at his sides. He looked pitiful and useless, like a dirty, shrivelled balloon.

'Here.' He handed Nicanor a foil packet containing two pills. 'They're sedatives. If he shows signs of needing them again, give him one of them, but only one. It'll do him good. Take him home and stay with him. I'll get there as soon as I can. I've got to stop off at the hospital to check they're OK and pick up a few things. I was on duty when—'

'All right,' Nicanor interrupted, nodding. 'That's fine.'

Juan looked at them both for a moment, and was once again amazed at how alike they looked. Damián was shorter than Nicanor, wider and more heavily built, with curly hair and a very thick neck. He'd always looked a lot like their mother. Juan had no idea who Nicanor looked like, but he was sure that if any of the strangers around them were asked to guess which of the three were brothers, they would point out Nicanor and Damián rather than himself. And Juan, who had always resembled his father, thought that in some ways they would be right. He didn't much like Nicanor, or Damián for that matter. Even now, he didn't feel guilty for having slept with Damián's wife for ten years. His brother's wife. His wife. The ephemeral mistress of a stranger. But still, he took a step forward and embraced Charo's only official widower.

'I'm so sorry, Damián.'

'I'm not.'

Later, recalling the scene, he wondered how he had managed to control himself, restrain every impulse, simply move back a few feet and watch as the red car drove away; then turn on his heels and go into the small quiet bar that had had to open its doors with an urgency that was unusual along such a deserted road. But, instead of killing his brother, this was exactly what he did. He usually drank whisky, but this time he ordered a double brandy and carried it out back to a rather unwelcoming terrace with a plain cement surface, three metal chairs – two painted blue, one green – where it was as cold as the barman had predicted. He thought the cold would do him good. He sat down on the green chair and drank half the brandy in one gulp. It didn't make him feel any better. The deafening noise of a car horn sounding repeatedly on the other side of the building cracked his defences, and he let himself go. The tears fell gently at first, sliding slowly down his dry face, but this miserable, concise, controlled weeping was choking him. He hadn't wanted to collapse entirely, not in public, but now the sobs broke out involuntarily, allowing his lungs to take in air again, and the unbearable pressure inside his head gave way at last as a warm salty tide flowed down his tight, distorted face, his mouth open in a soundless cry.

When it was all over, Juan felt empty, but at least this made him feel he was back inside his own body. He looked up and only then did he notice the woman with the dyed blonde hair and mink coat – the woman Nicanor had pointed out to him earlier. She and the young policeman were standing at the door to the terrace. Juan stared at them in surprise, unable to believe that the noise inside him had been so deafening that it had prevented him from hearing the arrival of two strangers who should never have seen him weeping. They stared back at him, both equally astonished, as if they couldn't relate this explosion of grief with the sober, calm, severe figure of the doctor who had taken charge of the situation when his brother had completely collapsed.

'Hello,' Juan Olmedo greeted the blonde with a feeble remnant of his usual voice, before lighting a cigarette.

Looking pale and exhausted (in a way that Charo never would again), the woman had deep shadows under her eyes and her lips trembled. On the outside, she looked the very picture of a traditional, middle-aged woman, the kind who would stifle even the most searing inner pain in order to behave like a 'proper lady'. But thanks to years spent working in hospitals Juan was a shrewd observer of the suffering of others, and he realised that she was drawing on the last of her strength. He felt no surprise when she came towards him, very slowly.

'Could I have one?' she asked, jerking her chin towards the smoke from his cigarette. 'I've run out.'

She lit the cigarette with her own lighter, took a long deep drag, and glanced round the small, bare space, looking very lost. Then she chose one of the blue chairs and moved it next to his.

'Do you mind if I sit here with you?'

'Of course not.'

The policeman muttered that he had to go, and left them. The two sat in silence, smoking their cigarettes right down to the filter, stubbing them out on the ground almost at the same time. She turned towards Juan.

'I'm the wife of—' The muscles in her neck tensed and her lips trembled. She was obviously about to cry but managed to squeeze a few more words out: 'Well, I'm sure you . . .'

It was still only eight o'clock in the morning and although the sun was shining brightly by now, it provided no warmth. But Juan Olmedo was grateful for the light, the immaculate reflections in the dirty windows of the bar, the rows of empty bottles huddling in a corner of the terrace, the metal buckles of the woman's leather handbag sitting on the cement floor. He witnessed her grief, comforting her automatically with an arm around her shoulders, as he did on weekend shifts every time he had to face another mother of a young boy killed on a motorbike.

'We were very happy, you know,' she whispered several times. 'I thought we were happy.'

Juan didn't say a word, but he stayed with her until another woman, who looked very much like her – also with dyed blonde hair, also wrapped in furs – came to fetch her. He paid for his drink, got into his car, and drove to his brother's house. That day was no worse than the next, which in turn was no worse than the one after that, and yet the woman stayed in his thoughts, during the silent family reunions dominated by Damián's rage, with Alfonso, confused and desperate, wandering up and down the stairs, while Juan spent hours holding Tamara in his arms, the television playing pointlessly in the background, as the child cried, very quietly, still too weak to ask any questions. Even at the worst point during the funeral – the wooden box being lowered into its trench in the earth, tearing Charo away from him for ever – he couldn't stop thinking of that lonely woman, doubly abandoned. So he wasn't surprised to find her one morning in the hospital corridor, when his own thoughts were still dominated by the shapeless grey form of a body covered with a blanket.

'Hello, do you remember me?'

It was less than three weeks since they had met, but in that time she had lost a lot of weight, too much, even considering her situation – seven, maybe eight kilos, Juan estimated. She looked as if she hadn't had a proper meal since that day, and from the dark rings beneath her eyes and puffy red eyelids, she probably hadn't slept for more than six hours in a row. More than grief-stricken or even devastated by her loss, the widow of Charo's last lover actually looked ill, with a face gaunt from total exhaustion and a body that could barely support its own weight.

'Of course,' answered Juan. Though it was painful even to look at her, he asked the standard question with which he greeted all his patients: 'How are you?'

'Bad.' She smiled gloomily, making no attempt to soften the bluntness of her response. 'Very bad, to tell you the truth. That's why I'm here. I'd like to have a quick word with you, if that's OK.'

'Of course. Would you mind waiting for a quarter of an hour, then we can go and have a coffee.'

In the end, she would only accept a small bottle of mineral water, playing with the plastic seal for some time before she could bring herself to speak.

'I'm in a very bad way, as I said, though I know it's not your concern. Perhaps you're thinking who am I to come bothering you like this, and you'd be right, but the thing is, there are things I would like to know, questions I have to ask, so that I can believe what's happened. I was very much in love with my husband. At least, I'd never stopped to ask myself whether I was still in love with him or not, which is a way of still being in love after living together for eighteen years, I suppose. I knew nothing about his affair. That's the truth, and I don't care if that makes me seem pathetic, or ridiculous. My sister told me not to come and speak to you, and my friends said the same, because Ignacio's dead, so what difference does it make now? They keep saying "remember the good times, don't torture yourself", but I can't remember anything, good or bad, until I know what happened, who that woman was, how long . . . Even my mother says I'm being morbid, mad, rash. I understand what they mean, you know, I'm not stupid. I know that when something like this happens, the more you know, the worse it is in the end, but I can't go on like this, suspecting that everybody knows more than I do, that they're all hiding part of the truth from me, all lying to me – my mother, my brothers, his parents, his brothers and sisters, my friends. I think I have a right to

79

know what was going on . . .' She paused for some time, fiddling with the seal from the water bottle, twisting it around her fingers then straightening it out, over and over again. 'It didn't even occur to me that my husband might not be faithful to me. Naive, perhaps, but it's true, Ignacio was very good-natured, he was amusing and affectionate. He spent a lot of time with the children, and he was very good to me. He never forgot my birthday or anything like that, and he was always buying me pretty things – flowers and plants and books, even jewellery sometimes – for no reason. My friends were very envious. Now I keep thinking that perhaps all the presents were his way of making up for his infidelity. But the fact remains that we were very happy, at least I was. And then suddenly this. Not just that he's dead, which is the worst thing of all, but suddenly finding out that he had another life, that he was lying to me, cheating on me, making fun of me. I need to get him back somehow – I want to understand him, maybe even forgive him, or hate him, you know, tear up all his photos and dance on his grave. Even that would do. What I can't do is go on like this, not knowing what to think, what to do, what to feel. I don't know whether to grieve for him or not, whether this is an end or a beginning.' She stopped again, and looked Juan in the eyes. 'Do you understand?'

'Of course I do,' he said. 'I understand perfectly, but I don't think I can help you. I didn't know your husband.'

'But you knew her – Rosario – didn't you? You knew her.'

Juan nodded and the widow lowered her voice, adding what could only be a suspicion: 'You knew her well.' Juan nodded again. 'I don't dare talk to your brother, and it wouldn't make sense. I saw him on the day of the accident and he looked as if he was in an even worse state than me. I was almost afraid of him, to tell you the truth. But you . . . I don't know, you seem different, and after we met in that bar,

I thought maybe you wouldn't mind talking to me, and that you might know if . . .'

She didn't dare finish her sentence, but Juan knew what she meant. He realised that the widow had guessed the nature of his relationship with the woman whose name she could barely bring herself to say; but it didn't make him feel uncomfortable or offended, as if the stroke of fate that had brought them together on the terrace of a roadside bar at one of the worst moments of their lives was, in itself, a guarantee of intimacy. Juan Olmedo looked into the mirror of this stranger's eyes, and when he recognised himself, he understood that both of them had no choice but to learn how to survive the effects of this disaster.

'If you're worried about whether your husband and my sister-in-law had been having an affair for a long time, whether they had a long-term relationship, you can rest assured – that wasn't the case.' He spoke slowly, intending to sound sympathetic and to inspire trust, using the same tone he used when trying to minimise the severity of his diagnosis to a terrified patient. She nodded at almost every syllable, taking in everything he said, not suspecting perhaps that the words were also for Juan himself; that he was saying something he too needed to hear. 'I'm absolutely sure about that. I don't know when or how they met, but I'm convinced their weekend together had no great significance for either of them. Charo was a very attractive woman, extremely beautiful, and more than that . . .' Juan Olmedo thought for a moment, struggling for words to define exactly what he felt. 'I don't know, I can't explain it. She was irresistible, dazzling, seductive . . . I know those are clichés and I must sound like an advert or something, but that's exactly what she was like. I've never known anybody like her; she had so many good qualities and so many bad ones too. Ever since she was fourteen, which is when I met her, she's always had men – or boys in those days – buzzing around her. And yet she was never satisfied with what she had. It was like a curse or an incurable illness. She didn't know how to enjoy life, she couldn't appreciate her own worth, or derive any pleasure from the things she had. When she got something, she just dropped it and ran off after something that was harder to get, and it wasn't because she thought she deserved better, quite the opposite. She was her own worst enemy, a very self-destructive person. I'm telling you all of this so that you can understand what might have driven Charo to have a relationship with your husband. I'm absolutely certain she would never have tried to take him from you – it was just another way of making her life even more complicated, another reason to keep running away. And if they hadn't had the accident, your husband would probably have escaped from her the first chance he got. Being with Charo was very difficult. Extremely difficult. I knew her very well, much better than my brother did, but even I never managed to fully understand her. The truth is that, in reality, I never knew who she was. So what you should do is forget all about her.'

A year and a half later, Señora Ruiz was finding it easier to dance on her husband's grave than to forget about Charo, but Juan Olmedo was still happy for her. He never saw her again, but she wrote to him occasionally to tell him of the bitter progress of her investigations, the pace at which she was piecing together her husband's long and prolific career of adultery. She went back to using her maiden name when she decided that the best option was hatred, and although he never answered any of her letters, Juan understood her decision, because it's easier to hate. This was why, in her last letter that reached him in Jerez, she was saying goodbye for she was on the threshold of a new life. She had met a man, in his fifties, divorced, with grown-up children and a desire to complicate his life, and she suddenly felt so strong again that they were all spending the summer together at her house in Galapagar, the house she'd sworn she'd never set foot in again.

As he drove from Jerez to El Puerto, Juan was glad he'd resisted the urge to tear up the letter. For this stranger whom fate had made his double seemed to be assuring him between the lines that the future could hold a place for him. Alfonso was waiting for him at the entrance of the centre, looking calm, hair neatly combed, with three other classmates, two of them younger, one not much more than a child. Juan observed his brother for a moment before going in. He didn't like to presume too much, but his brother seemed to be in a good mood: he came running up and threw his arms around Juan jubilantly. His teacher said that Alfonso had been extremely wary and shy at first, which was quite understandable given that both the routine and environment were new to him, but this hadn't prevented him from showing an interest in the others' activities and demonstrating an ability to participate and interact with his classmates. Juan was sufficiently familiar with this kind of language to realise that he needn't worry about Alfonso having any violent outbursts, which was what he had feared most while his brother was adapting to a new situation, and he breathed a sigh of relief, gratefully accepting the small respite that fate seemed to be offering him.

'Did you have fun?' he asked his brother as they walked to the car.

'Yes,' Alfonso admitted. 'But I'm not coming back tomorrow. Today's OK, but not tomorrow, because I already came here today, so I don't need to come back.'

'All right.' Juan smiled, because he had already reckoned on such complicated calculations. 'Tomorrow's Saturday, and the day after's Sunday, so you definitely won't have to come back then. We'll see on Monday.'

'OK,' his brother answered, so incapable of seeing things in the long term that he was happy with this response.

During the journey Alfonso told Juan about his day – he'd seen a film, he'd liked the food but not the pudding, because it was quince jelly with cheese and he'd only eaten the cheese, he'd done a painting, his teacher was pretty, they'd gone out into the garden twice, once in the morning and once after lunch. Juan chatted with him, answered his questions, and tried to be encouraging, while studying the bushes that grew here and there along the roadside out of the corner of his eye. They were completely still now, every branch, every leaf motionless, as if they had sprung from the bucolic whim of a decorator rather than from roots deep in the earth; the east wind had vanished without a trace. Juan was still reluctant to believe that such a simple, physical phenomenon could really be the diabolical spirit the assistant director had depicted that morning, but he was surprised to find his own nightmares had receded with the wind. By the time he got home to find Tamara sitting quietly on the porch, her face washed, hair tied back, wearing a T-shirt and matching shorts, between two piles of old comics – those she'd read on the right, those she hadn't on the left – he'd forgotten his fears, the terrifying visions of all the disasters that might be caused by a bored little girl, alone at home, which his morbid imagination had been concocting all day while he tried to concentrate on his work.

'They're cool, aren't they?' The little girl kissed her uncle and showed him her trove, pointing to the piles of comics and grinning proudly. 'Andrés lent them to me. He has a huge collection, because they come with the newspaper at the weekend, and Sara saves them for him. I think I'm going to collect them now, from the day after tomorrow. It's a great idea, isn't it?'

'Yes, of course. But tell me how you got on. What did you do all day?'

'Well, I had a good time. Maribel got me up, at nine, I think. I had breakfast and watched TV and then I went to fetch Andrés at Sara's house. Then the three of us went to the swimming pool, then Maribel came to get us and we ate macaroni with *chorizo*, which was really nice, and then we watched TV for a bit after lunch because we didn't feel like swimming. Then Andrés went back to his house and he brought me his comics, and I swapped them for my water gun, and he left again when his mother left, a while ago, and I stayed here reading. Sara said that, if you let me, she'll take me and Andrés out for pizza one day during the week. I can go, can't I?'

Juan nodded absently and went inside the house, pleased that he'd remembered just in time that the woman Tamara called by her first name, with a casualness he found slightly unnerving, was in fact the neighbour who lived in the house opposite. As he searched for the cleaner's phone number, he realised wearily that Sara's invitation had given him something more to think about, just when he had decided to disconnect all his anxiety. Maribel confirmed that there had been no problems during the day, though she didn't hide her surprise at all his questions ('What on earth could have happened?' she even asked a couple of times), and her tone reminded him that he was now living a different life, subject to different rules. The woman at number thirty-one lived alone and she was probably bored. Perhaps she was one of those women who adore children, or perhaps she was missing her own children, or grandchildren. In a small town like this, where everybody knew everybody, the line between concern and nosiness was blurred, gossip didn't extend beyond healthy curiosity, and watching over children was, like the gardener's wages, an obligation shared by the whole community. So, having conscientiously reined in his fears, he decided to pop over to Sara's house, to thank her for keeping an eye on Tamara and for the pizza invitation, but she wasn't at home. The following day he looked out for her on the beach, which was almost entirely empty even though the weather was beautiful, but either she was one of those who renounced summer rituals as soon as August had been torn from the calendar, or else she had better things to do. Then on Sunday evening he came across her again by the fishing nets, looking as elegant as she had the first time.

'Hello.' As Juan spoke he compared his blue espadrilles and worn jeans to the full, long, white canvas skirt and white T-shirt his neighbour was wearing, and he had doubts about his decision to dress more casually. 'I'm glad I bumped into you! I went over to your house on Friday afternoon but you weren't in. I wanted to thank you for inviting Tamara out for pizza, and for going with her to the pool and so on.'

'Oh!' Sara was barefoot and carrying her sandals which she shook in feeble protest. 'But it's nothing! I like spending time with the children and I was going to the pool anyway. They don't bother me at all, and I know it means that Maribel doesn't have to worry about them if I'm with them.'

'Nor do I. I don't really like the idea of leaving Tamara in the house on her own, but she wouldn't hear of me hiring a babysitter to look after her during the day. She said she was old enough to take care of herself, she didn't need anyone to look after her, and as Maribel offered to keep an eye on her and give her lunch . . .'

'Of course. It's a wonderful arrangement. Maribel is completely trustworthy, and when she's not at your house, she's just opposite, at mine. Anyway, your niece seems quite capable of taking care of herself, I don't know if you've noticed, but as soon as I got here, I realised that the children have much more freedom than they do in somewhere like Madrid. It's good, because that way they learn to be responsible at a younger age. Anyway, I told Tamara that she can come and get me if she ever needs anything. I tend to stay at home in the mornings. I'm quite tanned enough as it is.' She smiled. 'I prefer to come to the beach at this time of day.'

'Me too.' Juan smiled back. 'When I lived in Madrid, I couldn't imagine that these walks would be what I enjoy most about living here.'

'Yes,' Sara turned away from the sea, 'it's the same for me.'

They headed back together. They were walking slowly, speaking about little things like the wind and the climate here on the coast, life in big cities and in beach resorts that emptied at the end of summer, when Sara suddenly stopped and, grabbing his arm, gave a little cry.

'Look!' she said, pointing down at the sand. But Juan couldn't make anything out in the dim light of the setting sun, which had now slipped down behind the cliffs. 'At last! Look! I've been waiting by the fishing nets just to see them and not a single one appeared.'

'Really?' he said, trying to be polite. 'But, what is it? I can't see anything.'

'A crab.' Sara knelt down on the sand and signalled for him to do likewise. 'Here, look.'

Juan had to peer very closely at the ground before he could make out a tiny crab, whose sepia-coloured shell with darker spots camouflaged it admirably in the sand. The little creature, which had frozen when it had sensed the proximity of the two strangers, now fled sideways, tracing a wide parabola with its symmetrical, almost transparent, legs, as fine and delicate as wires.

'Do you see?' asked Sara, tracking it with her gaze. 'People always say that crabs walk backwards, but they don't! They walk sideways!'

Juan saw that this was true.

'That's right,' he said, as delighted as a little child. 'It's incredible!'

'Isn't it?' she went on. 'The first time I saw it I was amazed. All this time hearing the same thing, and now it turns out not to be true. That's why I like them. Because they don't move backwards when they find an obstacle, they simply go round it. The poor little things are crafty, not cowards.'

'Yes,' Juan agreed. 'Such a bad reputation, and so undeserved.'

Crabs walk sideways. Juan Olmedo reflected on this as he fell asleep that night, and remembered it the following morning, when Alfonso offered only token resistance to getting up early for the drive to El Puerto. Sideways, he said to himself again, on his way to work, not backwards, but sideways, and he promised himself not to forget this when the bad times inevitably came. Every trivial domestic setback, every minor battle he managed to win – as utter inexperience gave way to such absolute control of the daily routine that he was amazed – opened the way to a life that he would never have chosen but which drew closer every day. Before him stretched a dry monotonous horizon of weariness and need – the weariness of always being needed, the need never to admit to his weariness. He hadn't allowed for this when they left Madrid, or during the exhausting whirl of days following the move, when everything was difficult, new, unknown, and time flew by so quickly he couldn't even start half of the things he intended to do. First came fear, then haste, and the everyday trivia of fitting lampshades, hanging pictures, buying pots and pans, finding their way round the market, finding a cleaner, negotiating with the gardener, arranging his hours at the hospital around Tamara's and Alfonso's schedules, learning that three people could dine on a packet of spaghetti and a tin of tomatoes without even having to open the empty fridge. The domestic appliances were all working, the larder was full, there was a blanket for every bed in every wardrobe, all the enrolment fees were paid, the furniture was all in place, the Serrano ham was placed on a new ham stand, Maribel was given a set of front door keys, and there was even an unemployed nurse waiting by the phone, ready to come and babysit when Juan was on night duty. Now there was nothing left to do but wait for the real beginning of the life he had wanted to live with Charo, to start living that life without her, and like the best poker player, to soberly accept the heavy irony of his destiny without letting his feelings show. Sometimes, Juan almost found it funny, even if he couldn't find any reason to smile at his fate. He was an excellent doctor, one of the best of his generation in his field. This meant that over the years he had grown used to receiving spectacular job offers from private sports clinics, the kind that flourished thanks to footballers' broken knees and shins, tennis players' wrists and motor-cyclists' spines. The possibility of becoming nursemaid to a dozen spoilt young multimillionaires had always seemed the epitome of hell, but he would willingly have accepted such a fate in exchange for a footballer's salary and the simple opportunity to be with her, however remote that might have been. But now, he – who had always been prepared to risk everything for Charo, had told her a million times that he was willing to take on all her responsibilities, all her expenses, all her sins – had found himself with all her responsibilities and expenses, and all her sins as well as his own, at the ridiculous cost of losing her for ever. What was going to be everything with Charo had turned out to be everything without Charo, and he couldn't even blame fate, because the only one responsible for the situation was himself.

From the moment he accepted that the decision was out of his hands, Juan Olmedo had never stopped to think about the future of his private life. What had seemed like the obligatory renunciation of any sense of control over his love life had given him many years of dissatisfaction and a few moments of intense suffering, but he realised now that it had been an easy way to live. The uncontrollable, supreme, desperate desire to possess his sister-in-law completely and for ever had allowed him a superficial freedom, time to himself, which had vanished the moment he had to divide himself up between the demands of an orphan and the tyranny of a mentally disabled man. Juan, who missed Charo infinitely, missed the sporadic splendour of moments snatched with her, was reluctant to accept that he also felt a certain nostalgia for the rest of his past – for neutral, weightless days, for sleeping all morning, arranging to meet a friend for lunch, spending the afternoon lazing in front of the TV, reading, going to the cinema alone, inviting a junior doctor out to dinner, flirting with a rather ordinary girl in a bar. He was unwilling to accept that he missed all of this as well, but he did. And now that it was all behind him, and the exhausting daily routine could function on autopilot, now that Alfonso and Tamara depended on him as they had never depended on anyone before, vulgar nostalgia for his private leisure, his laziness, his boredom, was what scared him the most.

To avoid the risk of weariness and need, all he had to draw on was will power and self-discipline, but the crab's strategy kept him company, and he tried to remind himself regularly that they didn't walk backwards but sideways, going round obstacles rather than giving up. He was still thinking of this as the mornings hardened with a whitish chill, while the evenings sadly shed the last flecks of summer and the nights grew longer. He thought of it as he celebrated small victories, when the school took charge of Tamara from nine till five thirty, and Alfonso resigned himself to taking the bus without complaining. Juan suddenly found himself with empty hours in the middle of the afternoon, while his brother meekly watched television and his niece was in her room doing her homework, and discovered he didn't really know what to do with them. He thought of the crab's strategy as he embarked on a new social life, accepting Miguel Barroso's invitations to go out for lunch on a Sunday, or occasionally having a drink with a colleague after work, forcing himself gradually to master his fear of the possible catastrophes his absence might allow in such a precarious and hard-won domestic order. And he thought of it one cold, wet and windy Friday evening in October, when he should really have stayed at home and tried out the fireplace rather than phoning the nurse to see if she could babysit. She assured him it was no problem and she was happy to stay the night, but couldn't resist making a remark about what a night the doctor had chosen for his first evening out. 'It's the stag night of one of the junior doctors in my department,' he explained, 'and he's invited me even though I've only known him for a few weeks, so I feel I have to go.' 'That's fine,' she said quickly, 'I was just saying.' As he hung up, he realised that he hadn't sounded convincing even to himself. But still, at precisely nine o'clock, he got into his car and set off for Jerez, driving with great care. He found the restaurant without getting lost, he greeted everyone pleasantly, everyone greeted him back, and, as if he were quite used to this kind of thing, he slotted easily and naturally into a lively dinner with excellent fish and jaded dirty jokes. He wasn't expecting a girl to jump naked out of a cake, and there wasn't one. He was, on the other hand, expecting someone to suggest they continue the evening elsewhere, and the suggestion came between the first and second drink. 'I'm off home, Miguel, I'm a bit worried about the kid,' he whispered to his new boss. 'You must be joking, Juanito, you're coming to San-lúcar,' came the reply. 'We'll have another drink and then head off. The girls there don't bite, so don't give me that bullshit.' Juan wasn't sure what kind of a dive they were off to, but it was clear there were prostitutes involved, and he'd never felt comfortable in that kind of place. The name 'Lady's' spelt out in neon seemed to confirm his worst fears, but the bar turned out to be a spacious place with smart new furniture and comfortable low lighting. Maybe this was why the sudden appearance of a girl dressed in red made such an impression on him. She kept at a reassuringly safe distance, as a swarm of avid smiles fluttered around this promising group of late customers. Juan tried to analyse her with the eyes of a pathologist – five foot seven, sixty-five kilos, dark hair and eyes, Caucasian, and worryingly similar to María Rosario Fernández, deceased. Her hair was longer than Charo's, her eyes were smaller, and her arms thinner, but he still felt a shiver as she headed towards him. 'Come with me,' she said simply, 'you won't be sorry.' Juan Olmedo shook his head, and didn't change his mind, but just then he remembered again that crabs walk sideways. Not backwards, but sideways.

It was the first day of the 2000/2001 school year, and the entrance hall of the school smelled of overcooked green beans. The new girl, Tamara Olmedo Fernández, discreetly wrinkled her nose at the horrible, depressing smell, and a parallel crease appeared in her damaged spirit. 'Beans at nine in the morning,' she thought, 'how disgusting!' Glancing at her new watch, which had a second hand, the date, a light and could also be used as a stopwatch, she saw that she still had ten minutes before the bell rang, and decided to spend them outside, sitting on the top step by the main entrance to the building. She chose a protected spot, a corner, with the wall behind her. She soon realised, however, that almost all the children climbing the steps – taking them three at a time, shouting and pushing and jostling one another, the usual soundtrack to the first day of term – stopped for a moment when they reached her, their attention drawn to her new shoes, new rucksack, new uniform: a new girl sitting on her own. Having had the whole summer to prepare herself for this, Tamara gazed back at them calmly, steadily. In previous Septembers she had been one of the ones staring, with the same intent curiosity, at the new kids like Ferrán, who was from Gerona and had a very strong accent that made them all laugh at first; or Laura who, though her surname was López García, was born in Kansas City and couldn't speak Spanish too well; or Felipe, or Silvia, or blonde Carmen, or Tall Nacho, as he'd been called when he arrived in the third year, to distinguish him from another, shorter Nacho, who'd been at nursery school with Tamara. Today, Ferrán, and Laura, and Tall Nacho, seasoned veterans by now, would be thinking of her, wondering aloud what her new house, new school and new friends would be like. Or maybe they wouldn't, she thought, pressing her lips together, and feeling a lump in her throat. She wondered why the memory of her old school made her feel so sad, when she'd always found it such a boring place. Now it was as if she had never been bored there, as if all the tastes, opinions and feelings she'd had at the time counted for nothing, because today she was missing it so terribly.

Tears welled up in her eyes, but she forced them back, counting backwards, first three by three from a hundred down to fifty, then from fifty down to zero using only the odd numbers. By the time she reached twenty-three the urge to cry had gone. Since she'd been living in the house by the beach, she'd cried only three times – once because she thought of her mother, and the other two times because she felt sad without knowing why. She always cried at night, when nobody could see or hear her. Sadness lived inside her all the time like a drowsy beast crouching in a hollow in her belly, its neck tense and paws trembling greedily, always ready to pounce, but Tamara kept it in check during the day thanks to numbers, a block of precisely one hundred numbers that allowed themselves to be manipulated without complaint, unlike memories. She wished it were the other way round, that she could summon, rearrange or dispel certain images and voices she remembered at will, like the numbers she manipulated in sets of two, three or four, according to her whim. But she'd learnt that some memories cannot be altered, however much a person might wish to tell themselves a different story. This was why she only ever allowed herself to cry on the hazy edge of sleep, when the lines between the different story she desired and the reality she knew to be true became blurred.

Tamara Olmedo Fernández, new girl, didn't like it that her new home, her permanent home, the house she would be living in all year round, was really a summer home, with stone floors and green awnings, and a porch with teak furniture opening onto a garden full of bougainvillea and hibiscus that were in bloom even in winter. A real home had wooden floors and small windows and balconies instead of all those huge French windows. Outside, it had old trees that were so tall you couldn't take them in with a single glance, and a constant, tireless rumble of traffic. 'Real houses should be far away from the sea,' thought Tamara. Yet she acted as if every day held the promise of endless fun, and she forced herself to smile as, each morning, the punctual violence of autumn stole another sliver of summer light, taking with it the last of the fictional normality she'd inhabited during the good weather. Her smile later that afternoon would be equally radiant, and she'd never complain to Juan that her new school smelled horrible. Although they hadn't mentioned the subject since leaving Madrid, Tamara realised that her uncle was absolutely determined that things would work out here, and in his determination, which she had never fully understood, there was something more than the need to change jobs, more than the opportunity to live by the sea all year round, much more than the promise of the distraction and solace that his family needed. Tamara had never figured out the real reasons behind their hurried and arbitrary move, but in Juan's insistence, his optimism and his displays of endless enthusiasm that never fully disguised his uncertainty, she found sufficient reason to hope that her uncle would be right. And when she lost heart, when she was in a shop and couldn't understand the assistant's accent, when the wind howled at night as if it were trying to tear her from her bed, when the sea no longer smelled of brine but reeked instead of rotten seaweed, a gentle, luminous memory came to her, an image that was painful but which she never wanted to lose, the memory of an afternoon long ago, in the warm, obliging light of a better, fairer autumn.

Her mother never let her go to bed without brushing her teeth, always made her have a bath before supper and, even if she was going out for the evening, she always looked over Tamara's homework before dragging her off to the bath. But she also had wonderful ideas, the kind of thing that never occurred to Tamara's father, like coming to collect her from school as a surprise on the second day of term when she was five years old and didn't yet have lessons in the afternoon because she was too young. 'Papa called to say he wouldn't be home for lunch,' her mother explained as she carried her to the car, 'so I thought we could go into town and have a hamburger, and then maybe go to the cinema to see that film you've been talking about. How does that sound?' Tamara hugged her tightly and kissed her face repeatedly, because she couldn't find words to express her joy. But although they went to the Gran Vía, their favourite area, for lunch and Mama let her have two chocolate ice creams, and they had the best seats because the cinema was empty, Tamara ended up in tears that afternoon, because the film told the story of a little girl whose uncle and aunt sent her to a boarding school after her parents were killed in a car crash. It was a lovely story but also very sad. Tamara came out of the cinema with puffy eyes, and though her mother hugged her and comforted her and tried to cheer her up on the way back, reminding her that the film had a happy ending because the little girl found a new family in the teachers and girls at her school, Tamara was still tearful when they arrived home. This was why, when her mother sat on one of the chairs in the garden – the garden with its bare earth, simple trained vine and a few, huge trees, just like real gardens should be – Tamara climbed into her lap, looked her in the eye and asked what would happen if she died one day. 'I'm not going to die, silly,' her mother said, smiling, but she must have taken the question seriously because she cradled Tamara as if she were a baby and gave her lots of kisses, the kind of special kisses that only she knew how to give, kisses that weren't like any others, her lips imprinting themselves on Tamara's forehead, cheeks and hair; kisses that took an age to fade, kisses like tunnels, like bridges, like double bows – Mama's kisses. 'I'm not going to die,' she said over and over again, 'I'm not going to die.' She was smiling, but Tamara cried anyway. 'What'll happen to me if you die? It could happen, couldn't it? What'll happen if you die?' Her mother suddenly became serious, put her hands on Tamara's cheeks, looked into her eyes, and spoke very quietly. 'If I die, Juan will take care of you,' she said. That was all. 'Nothing bad will ever happen to you because Juan will take care of you.' She didn't mention Tamara's father, or her grandparents, or any school for orphans. Just that. 'Juan will take care of you,' she said again, and kept on kissing her until, eventually, Tamara stopped crying.

Now, five years later, whenever she felt she was on the verge of the kind of tantrum she used to have in the old days, Tamara remembered that she had lost everything, that her mother had died despite her reassuring smiles, that her father had died too, but that Juan was taking care of her and that was enough. The generosity with which her uncle had kept her mother's promise deserved blind, solid loyalty in return, whatever happened. Tamara was reminding herself of this as she wondered whether she'd be able to think of anything to tell Juan later that day, other than that the school smelled of overcooked vegetables. Suddenly she heard a familiar voice.

'What are you doing here?'

Andrés was peering at her with the slightly perplexed but serene look with which he viewed almost everything. Tamara was more pleased to see him than she'd expected, and immediately forgot the cautionary speech her uncle had made that morning at breakfast, advising her not to pester Andrés, not to stick to him like a limpet all day, to understand that he must have his own gang of friends, and that he'd be keen to spend time with them after the holidays. 'Andrés is the only friend you've got here,' Juan said again as he left her at the school gates, 'so be careful and don't pester him.'

'I was waiting for you,' said Tamara as she stood up, telling herself that waiting for someone wasn't the same thing as pestering them.

'Oh!' Andrés didn't seem bothered. 'Have you been inside to see what class they've put us in?'

'No, not yet.'

'Well, come with me. I think I know which one it's going to be.'

Andrés stepped inside decisively, without turning to see if she was following, and Tamara noticed his rucksack: it was very clean but had been washed so many times that the lettering on the flap, what must once have been four large capital letters in red, was no longer legible. One of the straps had been sewn back on with thick black thread, and both straps were frayed. The rucksack was so tiny its owner had to carry a lot of his books in his arms. Tamara thought Andrés might do better with her old rucksack, which was a bit dirty but much bigger and newer than his, but the moment she opened her mouth to suggest this she shut it again, unsure of how her offer would be received.

'This is it,' he said, stopping before a door that was identical to all the others in a corridor decorated with large colourful pictures and collages. 'Come on.'

He entered the classroom without glancing at anyone in particular, although he acknowledged a couple of other children with a nod and even responded with a laconic 'hello' to some of his classmates' more effusive greetings. Tamara clearly heard giggling from the back of the classroom. His hair neatly combed down with eau de cologne, Andrés tried to see where it was coming from, turning his head with a violent expression Tamara had never seen before. Two boys and a girl were whispering together, and pretended not to notice. Without a word, Andrés chose a desk on one of the central aisles and began taking his things out of his rucksack. Tamara sat beside him and did likewise.

'I'll sit here with you,' she said, not looking at him. 'Is that OK?'

'It's OK.'

The teacher's name was Doña Maria. Tamara thought she must be about Sara's age, and she was short, slight and chatty, and very smartly dressed. She seemed to know almost all the children, including Andrés, by name, and addressed a few pleasant words to each of them: 'Don't you look nice? Haven't you grown? You look as if you've done a lot of swimming this summer. Long hair suits you.' Once she'd finished, she told them they all had to give a special welcome to two new classmates, and she asked Tamara and a fair-haired boy called Ivan to stand up. Tamara had been expecting something like this, but it didn't make it any easier and she tried to hide her blushing by looking down, as if she were suddenly fascinated by her shoes. When the teacher got on to all the usual boring stuff – the plan for the year, the syllabus for each subject, the things they had to bring in the following week, the dates of exams and the best way to plan their homework – she felt better, because she'd heard spiels like this so many times before that it was almost comforting, even if it was delivered with an unfamiliar Andalusian accent.

The bell rang at eleven o'clock. Andrés reacted slowly, which surprised Tamara, for she had expected to find herself alone at break time. She was already almost out of the classroom door when she realised he was still sitting at his desk.

'To get to the playground you have to turn left, the way

we came in,' he said when at last he made up his mind to join her, taking small weary steps, like an old man.

'Aren't you coming?'

'No, I . . . I have to do something.'

'Are you going to the toilet?'

He shook his head and set off slowly, turning right. He couldn't have gone more than five steps when he turned round and saw that she was still standing in the corridor, by the classroom door.

'Where are you going?' she asked, taking his backward glance as an invitation.

'Somewhere.'

'Where?' He didn't answer, so Tamara followed him. 'I'll come with you.'

'No.'

'Oh, go on, let me come with you. I don't know anyone here and . . .'

'I said no.' Andrés shook his head firmly. 'You can't come with me, I mean it.'

'Why not?' she asked, stamping her foot. 'And why won't you tell me where you're going?'

'I'm going to see my grandmother,' Andrés said at last, almost angrily. 'She works here. Happy now?'

Tamara blushed for the second time that morning and didn't even try to think of an answer, as if the fact that Andrés had a grandmother who worked at the school was reason enough for him to exclude her from his plans. Andrés disappeared through a door at the end of the corridor and she went out to the playground. She sat on a bench and watched the other children playing. A quarter of an hour later she caught sight of Andrés, heading towards her holding a large mortadella sandwich and looking apologetic.

'D'you want some?' he asked, sitting down beside her. 'It's very big.'

'Did your grandmother give it to you?' she asked,

accepting some, even though she'd already eaten a doughnut.

'Yes. She's the cook.'

'Do you have to go and see her every day?'

'Yes. But only to get my sandwich. She gets cross with me if I bring one in. Today was different, because she and my mum don't talk to each other, so I haven't seen her for at least a month, and that's why I had to stay longer.' For a while Andrés ate his sandwich in silence and then offered Tamara the last piece. 'Do you want it? I'm full. Anyway,' he added, as she finished it off, 'you wouldn't like her. She's grumpy. She spends all day moaning and pretending to cry.'

Tamara didn't ask anything else, but she could see that Andrés was now not only friendlier, he looked happier too, as if he was relieved his visit to the kitchens was over. And even he would have had to admit that his grandmother was a very good cook, because the rice with tomato sauce, roast chicken and crème caramel at lunch were all much better than the food Tamara had had at her school in Madrid. She even gave up trying to identify where the depressing smell of beans came from and scarcely noticed it now. After lunch, she and Andrés went out to the playground and joined in a game of tag, although it was called something else here and had slightly different rules. She didn't run as much as Andrés, but she had a lot of fun, and when the bell went, sentencing them to an afternoon of classes, it sounded familiar, ordinary. The first lesson seemed to go unbearably slowly, as it always did, but the second hour simply flew by. Andrés said good-bye to her at the classroom door, because he had to go and meet two kids who lived next door to him. They were in the same year but another class. 'We always go to school to-gether,' he said, 'they're the two I was talking to in the playground, after lunch, remember?' She didn't, but she said she did, and as she made her way out, she thought she'd been lucky that Andrés hadn't left her to be with his friends until then, by which time her new school had started to seem less new, and more just like school.

She thought she'd walk home but as she ambled alongside the fence enclosing the school, a grey BMW with a Madrid number plate drew up beside her and honked its horn. Tamara recognised it immediately and already had her hand on the door handle by the time the tinted window rolled down and Sara offered her a lift home.

'How did it go?' she asked, after a kiss from Tamara, who was delighted to see her. 'Today was your first day, wasn't it?'

'Yes, it wasn't too bad, actually. My teacher's nice. Andrés says she's really prissy, but she gives high marks, and that's the important thing.'

'And what about Andrés? Did he introduce you to lots of kids?'

'Yes, well, after lunch we played tag, and that was fun. But a lot of the time I don't understand what they're saying to me, because they use weird words and everything they say sounds funny. They don't say their "s" on the end of words, and they always sound as if they're singing.'

'You'll get used to that.'

'That's what my uncle says, and he thinks I'll end up speaking like them, but I don't know. Anyway, when I don't understand something, Andrés explains it, so that's lucky, isn't it? Juan told me this morning that I should leave Andrés alone and not pester him, he's got his own friends, but we spent most of the day together. Andrés's best friends aren't in our class, they're in a different one, and he didn't go and find them until the last bell went, just now.'

Sara smiled to herself remembering the advice she and Maribel had swamped poor Andrés with over the last few days, the exact opposite of the speech she could imagine Juan making: 'Remember Tamara doesn't know anyone apart from you,' they'd told him, 'look after her, don't leave her on her own, introduce her to the other kids.' She was relieved that he'd accepted the task, because the last time they'd talked about it she felt she'd pressed him too hard. She was thinking about this when her passenger asked her if she knew that Andrés's grandmother was the school cook.

'Yes, of course,' she answered, searching in her handbag for the remote control to the gates of the development.

'Right,' said Tamara, and said no more, as if she needed to ponder Sara's answer.

Sara wondered if a ten-year-old child was capable of drawing conclusions from such information and decided that she wasn't. She had been surprised when she learnt that Maribel sent Andrés to a private school, however close it was to their home, particularly in view of the fact that there were several state schools near by. She didn't dare ask Maribel why, but eventually the cleaner told her: it didn't cost her a penny, because her mother worked there and her contract gave Andrés a free place. Maribel detested being in debt to her mother, but when Andrés started school she had very little money and was doing several jobs, cleaning a couple of offices and houses. She lived from hand to mouth, working different hours every day of the week, which didn't fit in with Andrés's schedule, so she had no choice but to accept the offer. Her mother would pick Andrés up at eight on the dot, an hour before school started, take him with her to work and give him breakfast there, then look after him in the afternoon until Maribel could collect him. 'Anyway,' Maribel added, 'it's a brilliant school, it has playing fields, a swimming pool, a lab, it gives them two hours of English a day and loads of other activities, so I'm not sorry – especially now that Andrés is older and he doesn't need anyone to take care of him, so I don't have to put up with my mother. I never see her,' she added. 'I know she tells everyone that I'm ungrateful, and foul-mouthed, and . . . worse things than that, but I don't care. Things were bad enough when my husband left me, I didn't want to go back home and spend the rest of my life there. That was all I needed, at twenty; to have to listen to my mother all day long. The first thing she asked me when she found out that he'd gone was what had *I* done to make him leave! I think she fancies him, you know. She's after my husband! I know it sounds weird, but that must be it because otherwise I can't understand the things she said to me, the things she still says – you can imagine.' Sara didn't try to imagine anything, although she understood precisely what Maribel was saying. This didn't prevent her from being disconcerted by the direction that Tamara's intuition was now taking:

'I asked you because . . . well, I don't know how to explain it, but I think Andrés is really embarrassed about his grandmother, you know? I don't understand, because there's nothing wrong with it, is there? But when we went into class this morning, some kids were laughing at him and then, during break, he wouldn't let me go with him to see her, and it made me think, well, maybe it annoys him that he never sees his father. Well, of course it annoys him, but what I mean is, he's got an odd family. It's like he doesn't have a father, but then he does, so that makes it even worse. But he shouldn't care because odd families are normal now. That's what Juan says, anyway – years ago if your mum wasn't married it was awful, and if your parents split up that was bad too, but now there's loads of kids with families like that. Like me, I'm an orphan, I live with my uncles instead of going to boarding school, but it's OK, nobody says they feel sorry for me, and they don't call me names or anything like that.' She held her head rigid as she spoke, staring straight ahead at the wall of the car park, but she was gesticulating a lot, as if this helped her find the words she needed. When she finished she turned to look at Sara. 'What do you think?'

'I don't know, Tam. I think that what's difficult about having an odd family is how you feel inside, not what other people think.' The little girl shook her head a couple of times, hesitating, before nodding reluctantly. 'And I suppose having an odd family is still complicated, though it used to be much worse, that's for sure, your uncle's right about that.'

The last act began in 1963, on the first Saturday in February, at her best friend Maruchi's sixteenth birthday party. Maruchi dragged her off into a corner of the living room, and whispered that Juan Mari fancied her. At the time, Sara had never wondered why her real mother, Sebastiana, had had four children in just over six years and there was a seven-year gap between her and her older sister Socorrito. But she had begun to notice that Juan Mari was gazing at her with love-struck eyes, a novelty so pleasant that it caused an unsuspected weakness in her own eyes. As she walked into the space that served as a dance floor with Juan Mari, a pleasant boy from Vitoria who was studying to be an industrial engineer, Sara knew nothing of the terms of the agreement that Doña Sara had made with Sebastiana just before holding her in her arms for the first time, when she was only eight months old. Fifteen years later, other arms now encircled her, dancing to a sentimental, hypnotic song – *sapore di sale, sapore di mare* – and she decided she wanted a party like this on her own birthday, to give Juan Mari – *sapore di te* – the opportunity to declare his love. Then, at a quarter to ten, as she was saying goodbye to Maruchi amidst nervous giggles, he appeared at her side. Although he didn't have a car, he said quite clearly, 'I'll take you home,' and the young Sara realised he didn't need any other opportunity. She walked along the street beside him, her hands in her coat pockets, yearning to put her arm through his, wondering what her life would be like if they were married some day, where they would live, how many children they would have, what they would call them, and she didn't realise that this was the first time she had ever allowed herself to wonder what kind of life lay ahead of her. At the entrance to her house, he looked into her eyes, blew away the lank fringe that kept flopping over his eye, and told her to wait a moment, because he had something very important to ask her. Sara, who knew the story of Doña Sara's engagement to Don Antonio by heart, was unaware that her own parents had become engaged at that very door, twenty-one years before she was born. Juan Mari asked her to be his girlfriend, and Sara said yes. He took her hands and she squeezed his back, he kissed her on the lips and she closed her eyes because it was her first kiss. Then they said goodbye, agreeing to meet the following day. He was very happy, and so was she.

Arcadio Gómez Gómez was taken to the prison on the Calle General Díaz Porlier on 16 July 1939. On the morning of the seventeenth, he was tried by a military court. As the following day was a public holiday, he was condemned to be executed at dawn the day after that, 19 July. The execution did not take place on the appointed date, however, because that same afternoon the prison authorities received a phone call. The wife of a glorious ex-soldier, heiress to the fortune of one of the city's great families, had taken an interest in the prisoner's fate; so the officer in charge of executions decided to relegate Gómez Gómez's file to the bottom of a large pile of matters pending – indefinitely – showing an instinctive prudence that would ensure he rose to the rank of general in a very few years. A few weeks earlier, the *abc* newspaper had published, amongst many other similar items, an article describing how certain residents of the building at number ten on the Corredera Alta de San Pablo had collected five hundred pesetas and given it to the concierge of their building, as a way of recognising the immeasurable debt of gratitude they owed her for her help during the worst moments of the Bolshevik terror. It was this same old lady (who had effectively risked her life when she stood up to gangs of wild militiamen when they tried to search the building) who saw Sebastiana Morales Pereira in the Plaza de San Ildefonso one morning. Sebastiana lived in one of the attic flats in the concierge's building and was the wife of a plumber in the UGT, the General Union of Workers. This plumber had become a soldier, then a corporal, then an NCO and even a captain in the Republican army, and had completely disappeared, been swallowed up by the earth. The concierge was struck by the sight of her neighbour stopping dead in the middle of the pavement and, after glancing suspiciously to left and right, bending down to pick up an object that she quickly stuffed into her pocket. The concierge hurried to catch up with her. At first she'd thought that Sebastiana must have found a purse, but now she could see that it was a packet of cigarettes. She put two and two together, and guessed where the missing man was hiding. It was not recorded whether she received any reward for reporting Arcadio Gómez Gómez to the authorities.

Sara didn't have a front door key. When she rang the bell, at twelve minutes past ten, Doña Sara greeted her, tapping her with her index finger. Her god-daughter responded by hugging her and kissing her loudly on each cheek before apologising: 'I'm so sorry, Mami, but I was enjoying myself so much that I lost track of time. It's the truth.' This outburst of affection, an unexpected reminder of the loving child Sara had always been before the sour sullenness of adolescence suddenly infected her, mollified Doña Sara more than the flushed look on the young girl's face. But she shushed her because she knew that her husband, who was already at the table, drumming his fingers on the tablecloth so as to leave no one in any doubt about how much it annoyed him to delay dinner because of this extravagant show of weakness on his wife's part, would never show any understanding with regard to her god-daughter's misdemeanours. In his opinion, Sara should still have been eating her meals in the kitchen, however well she had learnt to handle a knife and fork. The girl's stay under his roof was subject to one condition: Doña Sara was Sara's godmother, but this didn't mean that Don Antonio was her godfather. Sara rarely spoke to him, and always used the more formal *usted* when addressing him. She tried to go unnoticed in his presence, because she knew that the grumpy invalid held his wife responsible for anything Sara did wrong, and she feared his reprisals. As the two women had supper with Don Antonio Ochoa that evening, they knew that the best, most prudent tactic would be to say nothing, engulfing the meal in silence. But Sara was so excited, amazed and delighted by the events that had sud- denly expanded her life, that she forgot the rules and, break- ing one of the long silences that invariably occurred between courses, asked her godmother if she could have a party for her birthday. The air turned thick, as dense as fog, pierced by Don Antonio's sudden, furious glance, at which Doña Sara flinched and looked down at the tablecloth. 'I don't know, darling, we'll see.' Sara knew that Don Antonio didn't like having parties at the house, and she couldn't fail to notice the glance, but she wasn't sure just how much anger and disbelief it contained.

Sebastiana Morales Pereira began working as a servant in the Villamarín household in the spring of 1920. For the first week, she cried every night because she felt lonely and frightened, and because she was only twelve years old. Her mother, Socorro, did ironing at a dressmaker's workshop opposite their home, not stopping even for meals. When her mother had told her she'd found her a position with a very good family, one of the dressmaker's best clients, Sebastiana had not protested, or even been surprised at the news. Her two older sisters had gone into service at a similar age, and there were still two younger children at home. The eldest son had re-enlisted in the Spanish Legion after doing his military service in Morocco, but there were still too many mouths to feed and not enough pesetas coming into the flat on the Calle Espíritu Santo, where Sebastiana had lived all her life. Though she had left school at eight, Sebastiana had learnt to read and write and do simple arithmetic. She took care of the shopping and cooking and looked after her younger siblings until their mother got back from the workshop, almost always late at night, and exhausted after spending twelve hours on her feet. Their father was out all day, supposedly looking for work, though all he ever seemed to find were bars selling cheap wine. Perhaps this was why Sebastiana noticed Arcadio Gómez, a good-looking but shy boy, serious and quiet, who worked as a plumber and whom she saw occasionally in his workplace on the Corredera Alta, a dark little room where he and his father kept their tools and collected their messages. By then, Sebastiana had grown up somewhat, and didn't dislike her position. She was a bright, responsible girl and her mistress trusted her, sending her out on errands almost every day, often asking her to take along her daughter Sara, who was seven years younger than Sebastiana. Sebastiana went to the Calle Espíritu Santo a couple of days a week, to deliver and collect laundry, because she'd managed to persuade Señora Villamarín and some of her friends to send their ironing to her mother, who now worked from home, which allowed her to spend less time on her feet and earn twice as much as before. On all these errands, even when the little girl was with her, she always passed by the Corredera Alta, both on the way there and on the way back, looking out for Arcadio and making sure he looked out for her, until they became formally engaged. The engagement lasted seven years, which was the time it took Arcadio to save the money he needed to move out of his parents' house, while she collected her trousseau and made her own wedding dress. In 1932, Sebastiana was married at last, wearing a short black dress, with no bouquet but with a gardenia pinned to her breast, just as all the women in her family had done.

Some nights, when she couldn't sleep, Sara thought about what would happen if she and Juan Mari were girlfriend and boyfriend for years and years, until it was time to make serious plans for marriage. She knew she was still very young to worry about such things, but sleeplessness painted black shapes on the iridescent gloom of her childish bedroom, twisting the outlines of the white furniture that was built for a child, a defiant challenge to the passing of time. This was what worried her. She was starting to like Juan Mari very much, so much that she could now admit to herself that really she'd said yes to him simply because he was the first acceptable boy who'd declared his love to her. He was about to finish the first year of his industrial engineering course. Sara wanted to go to university as well. Although her favourite subject was maths, she'd more or less decided to study French, like Maruchi, because any form of science didn't seem appropriate for a girl. But she'd always been a good student, and time passes quickly, so quickly that she soon found, to her surprise, that her legs no longer fitted under her desk when she sat there to do her homework. And if it wasn't Juan Mari, it would be someone else, another boy from a good family in the Salamanca district who would have vaguely heard that Sara Gómez Morales had been orphaned when she was little more than a baby, and had been adopted by close friends of her parents, who had wanted her to keep her original surname. This was the story that Doña Sara always told, the story all Sara's school friends knew, but it wasn't the truth. The truth emerged of its own accord at a restaurant on the Calle Mayor one spring afternoon in the terrible year of 1963, at the wedding banquet of her sister Socorro. Sara was given a prominent place at the bride and groom's table, sitting between her father, Arcadio Gómez Gómez, and her mother, Sebastiana Morales Pereira. Neither of them sensed the distraction of their youngest daughter as she remained transfixed by the expression of astonishment, shock and horror that would have graced her boyfriend's face if some evil spirit had allowed him to witness the scene. Unless time stood still, unless the years stopped passing, Sara would one day have to tell a wealthy, elegant, polite future husband the truth. The mere thought of it made her legs freeze with fear. 'You can't lie to your husband,' she repeated to herself; a friend, an acquaintance, a schoolmate, yes, but not a husband. This was the nightmare tormenting Sara Gómez Morales just when she thought her future was secure, and when she thought there could be no greater obstacle to her happiness than the prospect of this confession.

Antonio Ochoa Gorostiza was the tallest and strongest of his mother's children, and she was sure he would be saved. She had had many conversations with God and with the Virgin of El Carmen, before embarking for the third time on the bitter adventure for which she had been so painfully prepared. Her eldest son, Francisco, had fallen ill at the age of three, when he didn't yet have the words to describe what was happening to him, the strange, painless tingling that preceded the loss of control in the muscles of his right leg, then the muscles in his neck, then his hands, perfect and as useless as those of a doll. Her daughter Carmencita's illness took a quite different course. When she was born she was as healthy as her older brother had been, and it wasn't until she had just turned twelve, and was already taller than her mother, that her body broke down; her arms, legs, neck, hands and feet suddenly slackening like a large, beautiful balloon being punctured by a branch just as it begins to rise. Three years later, her mother had to arrange her eldest son's funeral on the date she had hoped would be the coming-out of her only daughter, who attended the funeral in a wheelchair. The doctors had no idea why the illness had struck both her children so cruelly, but they strongly advised her against another pregnancy. Señora Ochoa asked if they were sure that the disease, which seemed to have attacked Carmencita less savagely than it had Francisco, would also affect a third child. The doctors couldn't say for sure, so she decided to talk to God, and when she held her new baby in her arms, she believed that God had listened. Weighing over five kilos and looking like he was already three months old, Antonio was the chubbiest newborn baby the family had ever produced, and he grew to adulthood big, strong and healthy. He was a full-grown man, with qualifications and even a fiancée when, just before his twenty-fourth birthday, his mother noticed something odd about his back. His right shoulder blade looked sunken and it had nothing to do with the movements of his arm. That night, Señora Ochoa wept as she had not wept in many years, but she said nothing to her son. It wasn't long before he realised what was happening himself, only a few weeks before his wedding to Sara Villamarín. He discussed the issue with his mother and she advised him not to mention it to anyone. 'I had many conversations with God and with the Virgin of El Carmen when I was expecting you,' she said, 'and They heard me, I'm sure of it. The shoulder blade is a useless part of the body, and it probably has nothing to do with your brother's and sister's illness. It always affected their arms or their legs first. Don't even think of saying anything to Sara. What would be the point? You'd upset her for no reason, over something trivial.'

Though she had not dared raise the subject again since Don Antonio thought he had settled the matter with his one, furious glance, Sara was convinced that on the last Saturday in May she would be having a party to celebrate her sixteenth birthday. That certainty was born of habit – she had always, always got her own way, especially on special occasions like Christmas and birthdays. Spoilt and indulged beyond measure by a woman bound for life to an embittered husband, Sara was used to having more, newer, prettier, more fashionable and more expensive things than all her friends, and she never wondered why. Questions were superfluous when tears took care of the dirty work so effectively. Doña Sara took her god-daughter's weeping as a sign of personal failure, and she would resort to any means within reach of her bank account to put things right. It was true that, in the last two years, since the disparity between the size of the furniture and the size of herself had begun to make her feel like she was in an illustration in *Alice in Wonderland*, Sara had found that her relationship with her godmother was changing. She didn't attach too much importance to the matter because none of her friends got on well with their mothers either. All the mothers tried desperately to prolong their daughters' childhoods – they all forbade them to wear make-up, or high heels, or go out with boys, and demanded they get home by nine o'clock, then nine thirty, then ten. All the daughters put up a fight, screaming, raging, bursting into tears, getting home late, secretly meeting boyfriends and locking themselves in their bedrooms. There was no reason why Sara should be any different, except that she, in the end, always got her own way. Sara believed this constant struggle to be the cause of the weariness that appeared on her godmother's withered face every time they began to argue, and it never occurred to her to read anything else into Doña Sara's reluctant resignation. And, in her god-daughter's presence, Doña Sara herself never touched upon the hidden keys to their conflict – gratitude, ingratitude, childhood, middle age, compromise, intransigence – words she held back, although they were always on the tip of her tongue, rebuttals she never allowed herself to utter out of a strange combination of pride and modesty. So, in early April, taking advantage of a visit from

Doña Sara's other god-daughter, Amparito, the daughter of a cousin who lived in Oviedo and of whom her godmother was not very fond, Sara decided to begin her campaign, sighing for no reason, falling silent suddenly, staring into space with a sour expression. She was slightly too old for tears now, but she was confident that her sudden bout of melancholy over the Easter holidays would do the trick, particularly in contrast to Amparito's insipid, provincial prissiness.

The birth of Doña Sara, who came into the world as Sara Villamarín Ruiz, was a surprise. Her mother had grown tired of repeating that God was mad – all those impecunious wretches without two pennies to rub together who kept sprouting children like there was no tomorrow, like her only sister, married to a pen-pusher from Asturias, having babies every other year – and there she was, her dream of holding a baby in her arms unfulfilled and a dozen cot sheets yellowing in a drawer. Señor Villamarín, who would do anything rather than leave a penny to his wife's nieces and nephews, had even begun to consider recognising some of his illegitimate children, when his wife, at the age of forty-five and more astounded than delighted, announced that she wasn't menopausal but pregnant. More than good news, this was a miracle, and in the autumn of 1915, the aged mother gave birth to a healthy, rosy baby girl. Her father, who had thought he would rather have a son until the moment he saw the little girl, swore that he would spare no expense and that no one and nothing would stand in the way of that baby growing up to be a happy woman. But not even the strongest love can slow the march of time and, as the daughter grew, so did her boredom; she was condemned to wandering alone through the rooms of a vast, gloomy apartment as an army of ailing servants persisted in the domestic rituals developed during a quarter of a century of life without children, indifferent to the needs of the little nuisance they

respectfully addressed as 'Señorita'. To alleviate her loneliness, Señora Villamarín would invite a niece to stay from
time to time; but the girl, called Amparo, though the youngest of her family, was still quite a lot older than Sara
Villamarín and, although they were fond of each other, they
didn't have much fun together. For many years, with
Amparo or without her, in the enormous apartment on the
Calle Velázquez, Sara's saviour was Sebastiana. Sara would
follow her everywhere, with the tenacious admiration ordin-
arily reserved for older brothers or sisters, appreciating her
spirit and energy as a rare treasure. But she did not miss her
when Sebastiana left to get married; by then Sara had been
welcomed into the select social circles in which her parents
moved. Shortly afterwards, she announced her own engagement to Antonio Ochoa Gorostiza, a handsome young
man from a very good family and heir to a considerable if
indisputably lesser fortune than the one she would soon
inherit. Her parents were delighted by the news, certain that
they had done everything in their power for their daughter.
Afraid that they would not live long enough to see their
grandchildren, they agreed with the mother of the groom
that it would not be advisable to delay the wedding. They
admired and welcomed the woman's fortitude when she
proceeded with the wedding despite the regrettable accident
that had cost her daughter, Carmencita, her life. They were
never told the precise details but they gathered that the
unfortunate girl had managed to swallow, with nothing but
her own saliva, almost an entire bottle of sleeping pills that
she could only hold by pressing it against the palm of her
other hand with her only functioning finger. When they
found her, she was dead, her mouth full of a white paste
speckled with pink and the remains of the last few pills that
she had chewed with rage at not being able to swallow any
more. Her funeral, a secret rather than private affair, did
nothing to dim the brilliance of her brother Antonio's

wedding, which took place a week later, in the spring of 1935. The guests stopped remarking that the groom was better looking than the bride when Sara appeared in a magnificent white satin dress with an extraordinarily long veil of Belgian lace held in place by a spectacular pearl and diamond tiara. They also approved of the solemnity of the ceremony and opulence of the wedding reception, which turned the banqueting rooms of the Ritz into an oasis of comfort and tradition, balm to the spirit in a Madrid that was becoming increasingly hostile, strange and dangerous every day, full of workers who had ideas above their station and risible revolutionaries. They all wept, but the mother of the groom wept more than anyone, alternating her tears with a radiant smile. And with good reason. She had just lumbered one of the richest heiresses in the capital with an invalid. Antonio Ochoa Gorostiza had begun to complain of a strange, painless tingling that occasionally took over the right side of his back, but by then he was already married to Sara Villamarín Ruiz. For better, for worse, in sickness and in health, for ever and ever, amen.

Monday was laundry and cleaning day. Mid-morning on Tuesdays, a woman came to iron and starch all the freshly laundered clothes. The young Sara hardly saw her because the woman spent all her time in the laundry room. On the other hand, she very much enjoyed the company of Pura, the woman who came on Wednesdays to do the sewing. Pura was sociable and liked to sit mending the clothes in a corner of the kitchen, chatting to the cook. She also dealt with all the basic sewing, making dishcloths, dusters, aprons, dustcovers for the furniture and other items that required no more skill than sound stitching. A couple of times a year, Doña Alicia, the dressmaker who made Sara's clothes, came to the house and very occasionally she was also commissioned to make a dress for the mistress of the house. The dressmaker was delighted by these isolated signs of

Doña Sara's faith in her, because she knew that Señora Ochoa bought her own clothes from a prestigious fashion house near the Puerta de Alcalá. This was why the dressmaker took such care over her god-daughter's clothes, making Sara have four or five fittings for every dress, with the result that Sara loathed her. Mid-morning on a Thursday, Encarna, the mistress's hairdresser, would arrive. Doña Sara couldn't bring herself to go to a salon, preferring to have her hair styled at home, as her mother had always done. The cycle came to an end on Friday afternoons with the visit of the manicurist, Encarnita, Encarna's daughter. At the age of fifteen, Sara began attending these appointments with her godmother, though they became a source of weekly conflict as she always wanted her nails painted red and Doña Sara would forbid anything other than a coat of clear varnish. Apart from these ritual arguments, the life of Sara Gómez Morales was as well organised as the house she lived in. She rose every morning at eight o'clock on the dot, ate the breakfast set out for her on a tray, walked to school, came home for lunch, went back for her afternoon classes, dawdled on the journey home chatting to her friends, had tea, did her homework, went out for a walk or went shopping with her godmother, found her bath ready for her at eight fifteen, took her bath, donned her nightdress, had supper and, a little later, went to bed. The only change to this schedule was the introduction of Juan Mari, who phoned her every evening and sometimes came to fetch her in the afternoon, to take her out for a coffee or go for a walk. Sara loved his visits, but one afternoon in April, she had to cancel their meeting only moments after arranging it. Doña Sara had just told her that she wouldn't be free that afternoon as she was taking her to the dressmaker's. 'What's the matter with Doña Alicia?' she asked, surprised. 'Is she ill?' 'No,' Doña Sara smiled, 'we're not going to see Doña Alicia, we're going to another dressmaker, my dressmaker. If you're going to have a birthday party, you'll need a new dress, something special.'

Arcadio Gómez Gómez thought he wasn't interested in politics, but the first time he heard talk of class-consciousness, he realised there was a name for his anger. The discovery changed his life. His father, who believed in God and in the eternal division between rich and poor, told him not to talk nonsense. His fiancée, who seemed resigned to a poverty he could never accept, asked him not to get into trouble now they were so close to the wedding. But Arcadio didn't lose heart. He loved his father, who had worked like a beast of burden to provide his family with its modest standard of living, and he was very much in love with Sebastiana, but he felt that there was plenty of room in his heart for others, and the more he thought about it, the more clearly he understood that he had a duty towards them too, towards this vast universal family of those who had nothing. So he joined the union and attended all its meetings. Eventually, he realised how he could make himself more useful, and he signed up for the literacy course organised by Don Mario, a young schoolmaster who, after a whole day spent struggling with children, taught workers to read and write in his own home for free. Sebastiana burst into tears the first time her husband was able to read the sign in a shop window. For that alone, and also because her future husband looked so handsome when he was trying to convince others he was right, she began to have sympathy for the cause. In just a few years, this man, who had been working since the age of seven and had never had time to go to school, was more eloquent than a priest, using strange words that his wife, stuck at home all day washing nappies, could not understand. Arcadio explained them to her slowly, just as Don Mario explained them to him when they went for a glass of wine together after class. There was only one term he avoided, the obstacle upon which Arcadio had stumbled time and time again, the weak point in this essential theory that Sebastiana was assimilating so quickly and so vehemently. When Arcadio asked Don Mario what exactly was meant by the term 'proletarian internationalism', the schoolmaster looked at him with surprise. Arcadio explained quickly that he understood the word 'internationalism' but not the other bit. Don Mario smiled and said that the word 'proletarian' came from 'proletariat', and talked of the position of the workers, whose only valuable possessions were their children. Arcadio raised his eyebrows. He and Sebastiana had been married for just over three years and already had two kids, and so far they were poorer than they had ever been. 'I don't understand, Don Mario,' he said after a moment, 'children are extra mouths to feed, they need new clothes all the time because they're always growing, and medicines because they fall ill every five minutes.' 'No, no, Arcadio,' insisted Don Mario, 'think about it. Children are the only wealth the poor have.' 'If you say so,' conceded Arcadio, but he didn't change his mind. In secret he thought, 'What rubbish.'

Doña Sara was thinking of a white dress, in a short modern style, the same colour as the evening dress she had worn at her own coming-out ball. She'd always known that her goddaughter would never have such a ball, but when all was said and done, the birthday party that she so desperately wanted was the first social event of any importance arranged in her honour. Had Sara been aware of her godmother's musings, she would have burst out laughing. It had never occurred to her or any of her friends that they might have any kind of 'coming out' ceremony. In 1963 there was nothing more ridiculous, old-fashioned or tacky as the idea of a 'debut' in society. So when the mellifluous manageress of the large, luxurious shop began showing her dresses, Sara chose an Italian design with a loud, multicoloured and radically modern print. At a strategic moment when the saleswoman and her assistants had left them alone in one of the little rooms reserved for their best clients, Doña Sara made one plea for the white dress, while Sara defended her first choice. For once, their disagreement didn't lead to a real argument; instead they hurriedly compromised on a yellow raw silk dress which was as far from the dull, home-grown standard of elegance as it was from the suspect, imported extravagance. Sara was very moved by her godmother's generosity. Doña Sara had had to embark upon a complicated operation to keep her husband in the dark about her plans. His friend, Don César, had volunteered to join in the scheme, but moving Don Antonio anywhere was complicated, even though the estate in Toledo where he got together with his cronies was less than an hour and a half away by car. Doña Sara, for her part, had decided that she would do everything she could to make sure that Sara enjoyed this special birthday. She didn't waver from this decision, even when the manageress of the shop took it for granted that they would be ordering shoes made of the same fabric as the dress, even though she knew that Sara would get much more wear out of a good pair of black leather dress shoes and pointed this out. But before the corners of Sara's mouth drooped with disappointment, she added quickly: 'Well, if you want shoes in the same fabric, you shall have them, darling, and that's that.'

On 19 July 1939, Sebastiana Morales Pereira paused for a moment between the pair of marble lions at the front door to the Ochoa household. She took from her bag a dark scarf with which she covered her head, knotting it firmly beneath her chin. She normally never wore scarves, but she wanted to look as similar as possible to the way Señora Ochoa had looked when she rang at the door of the attic room on the Corredera Alta, three years and four days ago, on 15 July 1936. In those days, the rich would never have dared to wander about the working-class neighbourhoods of Madrid without disguising their wealth, so at first Sebastiana didn't recognise the woman dressed in a worn grey coat, her face half-hidden beneath a black scarf. 'We're leaving for San Sebastián this afternoon,' Doña Sara told her as she accepted the coffee that Sebastiana offered her, her head now held high. 'My parents have been there for the last six weeks, since the beginning of June. They go there every year, but Antonio insisted on staying here until the situation is resolved. He didn't want to just drop everything and go. Everything we own is here, our house, our possessions, everything, but now, after the business with Calvo Sotelo . . . I don't know, to tell you the truth I'm scared. I don't think things are going to get any better, they're just going to get worse. Anyway, we're leaving Madrid today, so I wanted you to know, and I also wanted to ask you a favour . . .' There was a different concierge now. Sebastiana didn't know the strange man who rushed up to ask what floor she was going to and sent her to the tradesmen's entrance. She obeyed meekly. As she went up the steps she wondered what had happened to the previous concierge, a friendly man from Asturias who always chatted to her when she went to check on her employer's apartment, to make sure that the document that she herself had nailed to the front door was having the desired effect – keeping the apartment safe. This piece of paper had caused a tremendous row with her husband. She could still remember Arcadio's every word: 'You'll never learn, will you, Sebastiana? No, you're still at their beck and call, you don't know how to live without a master.' And the contempt with which he threw into her lap a typed sheet bearing the words *These premises have been seized by the Metalworkers' Union of Madrid, General Union of Workers* – two lines with no signature followed by a stamp in red ink, large and clear, with the three powerful capital letters symbolising the General Union of Workers beneath it: UGT. But that humble piece of paper had now become the life insurance of Arcadio Gómez Gómez, sentenced by a military court to be executed at dawn. At least, this was what his wife hoped as she rang the bell on the fourth floor, though it didn't prevent her from feeling a thick, anarchic rage that made her want to tear down the door with her bare hands. When a maid answered, however, she simply said that her name was Sebastiana Morales and that she needed to see the lady of the house. Doña Sara received her and listened in silence right to the end. 'Help me, Sara. You can help me now. He's a good man, he hasn't done anything wrong. He doesn't deserve to die. Remember, when our side was winning, you asked for my help and I helped you. Now you can help me, Sara. Please save him. He's a trade unionist and a revolutionary, but he's not a murderer. He never went about waving a gun at people, he was only interested in politics. He doesn't deserve to die, he's never killed anyone, he hasn't done anything.' 'Now, now,' said Señora Ochoa, after a while. 'He did do something – he fought.' Then Sebastiana Morales Pereira stood up and raised her voice. 'It was the same war your husband fought in, Sara,' she said, with her fists clenched. 'In war, people kill and people die. Arcadio didn't do anything your husband didn't do.' Señora Ochoa looked at the woman and stubbed out her cigarette with a sharp tinkling of gold bracelets. There was a silence. Her soul on tenterhooks, Sebastiana counted five, ten, fifteen, twenty seconds, until the bracelets tinkled again as Señora Ochoa picked up the phone. Nine days later, a guard fetched Arcadio Gómez Gómez from his cell and took him to an officer. The officer didn't ask him to sit down. 'A notification has arrived for you,' he said simply. 'I'm going to read it to you.' This was how Arcadio found out that his death sentence had been commuted to thirty years in prison, with a possible reduction in the sentence if he undertook hard labour. He was so scared that he didn't dare tell the lieutenant that he could have read the document himself.

The problem with Maruchi was that she had always been

an envious bitch. When she started to make excuses about the record player, young Sara Gómez Morales could think of a long list of similar offences, going right back to the very beginning of their friendship when they were children. Maruchi couldn't stand it if anyone was better off than herself. Sara was well aware of this and she was sure that, however much Maruchi promised she'd lend her the record player for the party, she never actually would. Fortunately, a friend of Juan Mari's had one that was even better, newer, and he was happy to lend it to her in return for an invitation to the party. Sara agreed, delighted. If Maruchi wanted war, then she'd get it. Already the battle of the guest list had been won. Sara would be having at least twenty more people at her party than her friend had had; the Ochoas' apartment, with its three interconnecting living rooms, the dining room, her godmother's little sitting room and Don Antonio's study, was twice as big as Maruchi's parents' flat. And then there was the dress, of course. True, Maruchi had worn a lovely outfit at her party, but it wasn't new. Sara knew this because she'd been invited to Maruchi's older brother's wedding, and she'd seen her wear it then. She, on the other hand, was increasingly pleased with her new dress; the colour really suited her and the cut flattered her figure. Of course, Sara had a very good figure anyway, while poor Maruchi, although she had a pretty face, had a bottom as big as two footballs. As for the food and drinks, there wasn't much she could do, because Maruchi's party had been magnificent, but Doña Sara tipped the scales once and for all in her god-daughter's favour when she ordered a dozen centrepieces of yellow roses and lily of the valley, thus decorating the house with flowers that matched the hostess's dress and the pearls Doña Sara would be lending her for the occasion. Sara was deeply grateful to her and, for once, she forced herself to admit, aloud, that her godmother definitely had style.

When General Franco led the uprising that began the

Civil War, Arcadio Gómez Gómez was a very strong man. Before he became ill, Antonio Ochoa Gorostiza had been too. On more than one occasion, Arcadio's strength and skill had proved invaluable to the artillery brigade to which he was assigned when he enlisted with the Spanish Republican Army. Antonio's toughness also became legendary amongst the rebel ranks, though he never had to demonstrate it assembling and dismantling a cannon weighing several tons at top speed. When he enlisted with the rebel forces, only a few days after the early fall of San Sebastián, an uncle, who was a general, immediately made him an officer. Second Lieutenant Ochoa never had to wield a pick or a spade, or drag sandbags, or carry the wounded, but he wasn't a coward and before long had accumulated as many ribbons on his uniform as Captain Gómez would earn on the other side of the Ebro. Nor did he ever seek to obtain a safer post in the rearguard, and he quickly realised that his daily flirtation with death made him horny. From then on, he made the most of any leave, breaking his own records for sexual exploits, which had already made him famous with the most exclusive whores in Madrid before the war. 'Bloody hell, Antoñito, who can keep up with you?' his colonel would say when they bumped into each other leaving one of the improvised bordellos that followed the soldiers from place to place, despite the denunciations of the army chaplains. He always answered with the same thing, 'I'm just a Spanish gentleman,' and the sentence became famous. Captain Ochoa took the teasing about his sexual prowess with good humour, not guessing how bitter a memory it would later become. The former Captain Gómez, on the other hand, soon came to regret his own excesses. When the soldiers came for him, Sebastiana was pregnant again, two months gone. The baby was their fourth and Arcadio wondered if he would ever see the child. By the time it was born, Arcadio was in a prison work battalion rebuilding the access roads to Madrid. This was where he ceased to be a strong man. The person in charge of the battalion was not at all happy with his lot. A card-carrying member of the Falangist Party, with several honourable mentions for his conduct in the field and even a medal, he considered this shitty posting (to which his wife had refused to follow him) a humiliation. He was therefore intent on delivering outstanding results at any price, so he saved all he could on the prisoners' rations and extended their working day, until, after three years in exile, his brilliant management at last earned him a decent office in Madrid. His successor was a good man who took several measures to improve the prisoners' lot, re-establishing the right of the convicts to send letters to their families even though stamps cost money. Arcadio wrote two identical letters to his wife. He sent one to their old address on the Corredera Alta, even though he thought Sebastiana probably hadn't been able to go on living there, and the other to the house on the Calle Velázquez where his wife had been employed when he first met her, hoping that someone there would know where she was. She answered by return of post, telling him that in February 1940 she had given birth to another girl, whom she'd called Socorro after her mother, that the older children were well and all going to school, that they'd moved to an attic flat on the Calle Concepción Jerónima, very near the Plaza Mayor, that she'd gone back to work for Doña Sara, spending about nine or ten hours there every day except Sunday, that Doña Sara treated her very well and let her bring her youngest to work, that the poor woman had had very bad luck because her husband had a very strange illness that made his right leg useless, that Arcadio shouldn't worry about anything, some old friends were helping her as much as they could, that she didn't need to see him to go on loving him, and that she loved him.

The party was a huge success, from start to finish. Not only did everybody who was invited turn up, but at the last minute some college friends of Juan Mari's arrived, making the number of girls and boys almost even. Sara received many presents, but her favourite came from her boyfriend, who gave her a pair of round black sunglasses with very dark lenses, like the ones the Beatles wore on tour. She was also given several records, so the dancing started straight away, though Juan Mari's friends, victims of the culinary torture at their halls of residence, were still wolfing down the food. At first, the owner of the record player, a boy from Alicante called Ramón who seemed particularly hungry, looked after the music; but once he'd found a dancing partner, he put a shy, sad-looking boy in charge, telling him which records to play. At first they all danced together in large groups but around eight thirty, as the maids finished clearing away the cake plates and Doña Sara ran out of excuses for being there, the owner of the record player returned to his original station and put on some slow records. Juan Mari took Sara by the hand and led her to the middle of the room without a word. They had been going out for almost four months by then, so he didn't need to ask her to dance. She put her arms round his neck and clung to him, resting her head on his shoulder. They danced like this for one song, then another, then another, but then some prankster turned out too many lights at once, giving the mistress of the house a reason to return. Juan Mari got nervous and he suddenly let go. But the sound of Doña Sara's heels, as she advanced in a zigzag switching on lights as she went, was so familiar to her god-daughter that Sara was the only one who remained calm. Moving a step away from Juan Mari, she made him put his arms back round her waist and went on dancing, albeit in a slightly less intimate fashion. When her godmother approached, Sara gave her a kiss and said, 'Mami, I'd like to introduce you to my friend.'

Arcadio Gómez Gómez wrote to his wife every week, and every week he received a letter back. He didn't have much to say, but he told her everything that was happening to him until, in mid-1945, he began to cough up blood. This he kept silent from Sebastiana. The other news that did not reach Sebastiana was that around the same time as lung disease was sapping the last vestiges of her husband's strength, the legendary fortitude of a Spanish gentleman was collapsing in spectacular fashion. The process was slow, painfully slow. It began with a few failures in his much lauded sexual potency, but as his condition deteriorated, Don Antonio Ochoa – who could still walk with a single crutch – gradually reduced the frequency of his extramarital adventures until he had eliminated them completely, not because he wanted to, but because he was afraid of looking ridiculous. He didn't know what was happening to him. His doctor understood as little about the cause of the illness as he did about its progress. 'All I know is that it attacks the muscles,' the doctor said many times, 'weakening them until you lose the use of the body part they control. But it's like Russian roulette – you never know what will be next – a finger, a thigh, maybe even your face.' Nobody ever dared mention the penis, but when the tingling spread to the lower abdomen, Antonio Ochoa realised his days as a 'Spanish gentleman' were numbered. At the age of thirty-four, Doña Sara's husband had to make the most of the rare opportunities his treacherous body presented him with, and in the end he would have been satisfied simply with getting his wife pregnant. But he didn't succeed. By early 1945, he was permanently in a wheelchair, and the couple's attempts at lovemaking became more and more infrequent, ceasing entirely just after the summer. Antonio Ochoa Gorostiza suffered deeply, and somehow his own shame made Doña Sara's company unbearable, with the result that he agreed to anything she asked as long as she left him alone. Sebastiana grew used to seeing her mistress crying, spending the afternoons staring out of the window, a crumpled handkerchief clutched in her hand. As for the master, he never left his study. She didn't understand what was going on, but then, in January 1946, she stopped caring when she received a letter from Arcadio saying that he had been ill for over a year. Don Esteban, the battalion commander, was aware of new measures to give special pardons to prisoners of war who had served half their sentences in hard labour, and he was prepared to request one for Arcadio. At a rate of three days of prison for every day of labour, in the seven years Arcadio had been there, he had redeemed almost two-thirds, but his original death sentence required additional guarantees. Don Esteban had signed one guarantee. If Doña Sara's husband would sign the other, he could be free by the beginning of April. That afternoon, Sebastiana wept even more than her mistress. Doña Sara read the letter, went into Don Antonio's study without knocking, and returned a minute later with the document signed.

Sara had not dared tell her godmother that she had a boyfriend, but she assumed that Doña Sara must have guessed from all the comings and goings and phone calls of the last few months. When her godmother decided to make a final appearance at the party just before ten o'clock, just as the tumult of guests thronged into the hall in search of their coats, she was sure that Doña Sara knew everything. Her godmother took advantage of the general confusion to sidle over to Juan Mari, who had stayed behind in the sitting room, obviously intending to leave last. Sara glimpsed this dangerous encounter out of the corner of her eye and hurriedly abandoned her duties as hostess. By the time she reached them, her godmother had discovered that Juan Mari's second surname was Ibargüengoitia, the same as her husband's fourth surname, and she was about to establish that they were related, unquestionably if remotely, via a village in Alava and a shipping company in Bilbao. 'Imagine,' she said to Sara. 'What a coincidence! This boy's mother must be Antonio's second cousin, there's no doubt about it.' Juan Mari was nodding, embarrassed. 'Amazing,' said Sara, for the sake of saying something. Then, thankfully, Ramón returned to ask Juan Mari to help him carry the records, and the uncomfortable trio dissolved amid polite goodbyes. The look of relief on Juan Mari's face was unmistakable. Sara told herself that her godmother hadn't done anything any other mother wouldn't do, and she decided she would have to talk to her that very evening. But Doña Sara got in first, as soon as the last guest left. 'Are you happy?' she asked her. 'Very,' Sara answered as she took off the pearl earrings and necklace, 'it went fantastically well.' 'You must be exhausted,' her godmother replied, putting her arm around Sara's waist and walking her along the corridor. 'Look, I tell you what, put on something comfortable and come to my sitting room. I need to talk to you.'

When Arcadio Gómez Gómez got out of prison, he was ill and weak, but he still had his pride. The city he found on 6 April 1946 was quite unlike the city he remembered and he soon realised his fears about his wife's ambiguous allusion to 'old friends' contained in her first letter were correct. Many of his comrades in the union were dead, quite a few others were still in prison, but some had been lucky enough to disappear just in time in the colossal confusion of defeat. Of these, most would have sworn that they never knew him if they happened to bump into him in the street, and the new Arcadio, a man sick of feeling alone, of being scared, hungry and exhausted, would not have dared reproach them for it. But a few were true to their memories, and had helped his wife and children as much as they could. Now they helped him in the only way they knew how – Arcadio had been free barely a month before he found a job. 'We're through the worst,' he told Sebastiana then, 'everything's going to be fine now, you'll see.' They would both have liked to sever all links with their unfortunate past, but it seemed advisable that Sebastiana should continue working for Doña Sara, on the same terms, for at least a few more months. Former convicts didn't tend to find jobs so easily, and the friends who had called upon every distant acquaintance to find work for an excellent, experienced plumber, who'd just arrived from a village in La Mancha looking for a better life, didn't deserve to run any more risks. And with two wage packets, they were finally able to move down from the attic room to a third-floor flat with four rooms, where the boys could have a separate bedroom from the girls for the first time. Life was still difficult, but it seemed to have stabilised at a tolerable level of difficulty when, in mid-September, Sebastiana found that she was pregnant again. The news was a complete disaster. Speechless, stunned, unable to react, Arcadio simply felt guilty as his eyes followed his wife round the room. Sebastiana, on the other hand, couldn't keep still, pacing around the flat with the desperation of a caged beast, whimpering and cursing under her breath, 'This was all we needed, just what we needed.' The pregnancy progressed despite the expectant mother's dismay. She was inconsolable. She did her sums over and over again, but she could see only two possible options: either go through the same hell as she did when Socorrito was a baby, taking her to work, leaving her in her basket in a corner of the kitchen, unable to go to her when she cried; or take her daughter Sebas, now aged eleven, out of school and have her look after the newborn baby, turning her into a poor wretch like her mother instead of the hairdresser she wanted to be. There was no point in sending her eldest son out to work, because his wage as an apprentice would not make up for the loss of her own; nor could they move back to the attic flat, as there would now be seven of them. There was another solution, but it was Doña Sara, not Sebastiana, who thought of it. 'Look,' she said one autumn morning as they were having coffee at the kitchen table, 'I've had an idea, but above all I want you to remember that it's just that – an idea. I know you're indebted to me,

131

but I want you to listen and think about it, and I don't want any decision you make to be influenced by your husband's situation, or your own, or anything I might have done for you both in the past. I'm mentioning this first of all because I don't want to have anything weighing on my conscience.'

Sara took off her clothes, had a quick shower and put on a white piqué dressing gown, going over in her head all the calm assurances she intended to give her godmother – that Juan Mari was a wonderful boy, that he treated her with all the respect and dignity a respectable girl could wish for. But when she reached the door to the little sitting room, she could see that her godmother was behaving oddly, and she knew that Doña Sara would be the first to speak. Sara feared the worst, although at this point she had no real idea of what that word could mean. 'Now, darling, I have something to tell you. I probably should have told you before but . . . I don't know . . . it's difficult.' Her godmother sounded hesitant and couldn't look Sara in the eye, her gaze fixed on a napkin that she slowly twisted in her hands. 'Now, darling,' she continued after a moment, sighing, 'when you were born, Spain was a very different place than it is today. We'd had a war. Afterwards, the situation was very bad – the harvests had been lost, cities had been destroyed, people were hungry and would do anything to survive. In those days, your mother used to work here – well, you already know that. When she became pregnant, it wasn't that she didn't love you, Sara, of course she loved you, and so did your father, but things were difficult for them. They already had four children, they didn't know how they were going to give you what you needed, feed you, educate you, help you to get on in life. Anyway, we've talked about this before. By that stage I knew that I wouldn't be able to have children, but I did have this big house, and the means to look after you, and to pay for your education – you know this too. What you don't know is that – well, my husband and I never legally adopted you. Your father wouldn't have agreed to it and it wasn't exactly what we intended. We . . . we came to a kind of agreement that best suited all of us. I undertook to make a lady of you, and what I'm trying to tell you is . . . well, I've fulfilled my part of the agreement. In two weeks' time, you'll be finishing school. There's no point in you continuing with your studies because . . . That's why when I saw you with that boy – Juan Mari, isn't it? – well, I started thinking. I'm sure it's not serious yet, at your age these things are never serious but . . . It's probably my fault. I should have told you all this a lot sooner. The fact is that you have to prepare yourself, Sara, because this evening's party was a kind of farewell. When term ends and we leave for Cercedilla, you'll go home.' As she said this, she raised her head and looked at her god-daughter. Sara, for her part, seemed to be staring at something far away, a point in the distance, a vague shadow on the horizon. 'Home?' she asked after a while. 'Yes,' said Doña Sara, 'to your parents' home. Your home, darling.'

That afternoon in the autumn of 1946, Sebastiana Morales Pereira left her employer's house with dry eyes. Her veins felt as cold and heavy as lead, and her mouth was filled with a metallic taste that was familiar: Sebastiana had listened and learnt, and would never forget the taste of fear. She recognised it again as she walked along the street, taking small steps, mired in loss, defenceless against the sadness that made her ears ring, the roots of her nails ache, the soles of her feet seem frozen. There was always some new sadness to encounter, and only a dirty old rag to fight it with. Doña Sara had said that she was going to be absolutely honest with her – her husband, Don Antonio, would not hear of her legally adopting the child, so her intention wasn't to keep it for ever, only to bring it up, give it a good education, equip it with the means to do well in life, and return the child to them having turned it into a gentleman, if it was a boy, or a lady, if it was a girl. Her words were convincing, which was why Sebastiana repeated them to herself so many times, walking round and round the Puerta del Sol like an idiot, not daring to go home. The words were convincing, but she still hadn't found a way of swallowing them by the time it grew late and she simply had to return home. When she got there, Arcadio was waiting at the front door, worried, Socorrito in his arms. Seeing him there, as serious as ever, still very thin, his hair now grey and with the cough that he couldn't shake off, Sebastiana realised that she loved this man more than the child she didn't yet know growing within her. But still, remembering the smell of a newborn baby, its softness, the strange peace that filled her when she withdrew to suckle it alone in the gloom of her bedroom, she felt as if she was suffocating, and decided not to say anything to her husband until after supper, once the children had gone to bed. Only then did she sit facing him: she took his hands, looked him straight in the eye, and started talking. The words sounded good, but Arcadio didn't wait to hear them. 'Out of the question!' he said straight away, banging his fist on the table. 'It's absolutely out of the question, do you hear me? I don't care that they haven't got children of their own! I don't know how you could even consider something like this.' She wanted to cry, but she'd resolved not to burden her husband with her tears. So, because of this, and because she couldn't tell him the whole truth, forcing him to share her worst anxiety – Doña Sara's words that hung like a sword above her head – she looked into his eyes with an intensity that made him fall silent and then, for the first and last time in her life, she spoke disrespectfully to him. 'How can I consider something like this?' Sebastiana Morales Pereira hissed in a whisper, her lips tight, emphasising every word with her eyebrows, punching the air with her white clenched fists, but not daring to raise her voice in case the neighbours heard. 'What's the matter with you, have you gone mad? Where have you been all these years, Arcadio, in prison or on the moon? In case you haven't noticed, you don't give the orders any more, do you hear me? You're not the one in charge, that all ended years ago. You take orders now, like me, like all of us – get it through your head. We're like pigs at the slaughterhouse, tied up with a knife to our throat – that's how life is for us now, for you, and me, and there's nothing we can do about it, Arcadio. We have no choice.' As Arcadio looked at her, she saw his infinite helplessness, the uncertainty of a child lost in a crowd, the foreboding of a final, decisive defeat, and she covered her face with her apron, turned, and ran away to the kitchen to escape the appalling humiliation in his eyes. Children are the only wealth the poor have. When he was alone, Arcadio Gómez Gómez remembered Don Mario as he'd last seen him, at the front at Teruel, as sickly as ever, so thin he was lost inside his uniform, with his glasses that were always dirty and carrying a rifle that weighed more than he did. Arcadio remembered Don Mario's joy, his enthusiasm, the fervour with which he believed in the offensive that would cost him his life the very next day. Children are the only wealth the poor have. Arcadio Gómez Gómez swallowed his pride and a void opened up inside him. He closed his eyes, leant his forehead on his knees, interlaced his fingers behind his head, and wished that he too had been killed at Teruel, like Don Mario.

On 21 June 1963, a taxi took over a dozen suitcases and boxes containing most of Sara Gómez Morales's belongings from the Calle Velázquez to the Calle Concepción Jerónima. She followed, with the rest of her things, in a second taxi. When she arrived at her home, her parents embraced her with an intensity that did nothing to mask their uncertainty, even fear. Their daughter responded to every movement, every embrace, every kiss, mechanically, meekly, and with the same coldness that had frozen Doña Sara's blood half an hour earlier, as she took leave of her god-daughter at the front door with the two marble lions. 'Come with me,' Sebastiana said to her now, 'we thought you'd prefer the boys' room, it's bigger than your sisters' room. I didn't mention it to you last Sunday because I wanted it to be a surprise, but your father's repainted it, and he's laid a new carpet – blue, it's your favourite colour, isn't it? I hope you like it.' Sara had never realised that the floor of the room sloped, but that morning it was the first thing she noticed as she stood on the new carpet. She said nothing. Her mother supposed aloud that she must want to unpack and Sara nodded, but when she was alone she sat on the bed and did nothing, didn't even move, until they called her for lunch. She was exhausted. She had no tears left, or fear, or rage, or pity, or bitterness, or hatred, or nostalgia. She felt dried up, shrivelled, as if she'd been boiled vigorously in her own confusion until all that was left was a mannequin of skin and bone. Three days passed in this way. Mid-morning on the fourth day, her father knocked on the door and entered determinedly. He sat beside her on the bed and told her an old story. It was murky, cruel, absurd, barbarous and true. It was the story of a girl called Sara Gómez Morales. Her story.

This west wind is really getting into my bones . . . The first time she muttered these words under her breath, Sara Gómez smiled to herself; yet this sign that she had at last begun to decode the mystery of the winds did nothing to lessen the crushing sadness of an autumn afternoon. In summer, with the shutters half closed to stop the sun reaching into the living room, the sound of children laughing as they splashed around in the pool, and the friendly heat – making rain seem welcome and silence miraculous – it would have been different. In summer she would have been delighted by this modest progress, but now she was worried about a more pressing lesson she needed to learn – the way to govern time.

Neither the calendar, nor the barometer, nor the capricious tyranny of the hour change that suddenly brought darkness, were of any use. It was the ticking lethargy of the clock that she needed to master; the sickly, ailing motion of the minute hand as it measured each and every passive moment. Over the last few decades, as she devoted herself to planning her future in minute, obsessive detail, making sure every element was under her control in order to secure the life that should always have been hers, it had never occurred to her that the success of her scheme might also carry this risk. She had not reckoned on the fact that, if her plan worked – and it had – time would become her enemy, and that clocks would administer her punishment with frugal, aimless cruelty.

Since that spring so long ago when she had quarrelled for the last time with Maruchi over a record player, Sara had not had any friends. The universal distrust with which she had armed herself during that long taxi journey from the Calle Velázquez to the Calle Concepción Jerónima, had prevented her from ever running such a risk again. But this lack of friends didn't worry her, because she always had so much to do, and there were plenty of agreeable, even likeable people around with whom she could exchange a pleasant word. Before she disappeared without a trace, Sara Gómez had had many acquaintances, neighbours, colleagues, and distant relatives with whom she occasionally went shopping or to the cinema, although she invariably would have been just as happy to go alone. She didn't miss the capacity for surprise, faith or joy that she had suppressed, because she knew that the distrust that had hardened inside her was also the key to her strength; the thick, solid, indestructible beam that kept her upright when she most wanted to collapse. The only constant in the torturous path of Sara Gómez's life had been her resolute intention to keep going, always keep going; yet now, the certainty that spring would unfailingly follow winter was no longer enough. This sudden, unforeseen helplessness was a challenge to the choices she had made, a question mark over the route she had taken. But when she tired of laughing at destiny's joke, when she resigned herself to accepting loneliness and the slow hostility of clocks as one more requirement of the difficult peace she had made with herself, when she understood that she had always kept going because she was looking for a place to stop, only then did she begin to let go of her old ways of thinking. Until that moment Sara had lived for revenge; now she had to learn to survive the consequences of vengeance. Her goals had changed, and with that, her life, and the rhythm of her days, her pleasures and her needs. She had sensed something of this towards the end of the summer: as Andrés and Tamara counted down the remaining days of their holiday, she was surprised to find that she was missing them already. And although she hadn't been aware of any change in herself, the old, hard, leathery scales on which she had depended for survival were gradually peeling away and floating silently, light as feathers, to the ground.

The discovery that distrust no longer served her did not make the clock hands move any faster, but it restored to her – even though it was too little, too late – a way of seeing, of relating to others without calculating beforehand all the possible consequences of every word she said, every gesture or movement she made. At fifty-three, she was too old to recover her innocence, but she could still joyfully regain her curiosity.

It was Maribel who began to help her see things in a different way. When she took her on, Sara had not factored in that she would be spending so much time with Maribel, Monday to Friday, chatting, and she felt a little uncomfortable, even ridiculous, when she realised that Maribel thought her new employer rather odd. After all, here was a middle-aged woman living alone in a large, though not huge, house with no dogs, no invalids to care for, and no children, yet she employed Maribel to clean it for four hours a day. The truth was that, from the outset, Sara tried to make as much mess as she could and, more than once, after clearing up and taking her glass or plate to the kitchen, she would go and put it back again. She found it more difficult to get used to leaving towels on the floor when she got out of the bath, but even then she didn't consider renouncing the sentimental need that compelled her to adopt such luxuriously lazy ways. This inner evolution led to other changes, to small pockets of trust that allowed other people in – first Andrés, then Tamara, and finally Maribel herself.

The west wind got into their bones, and the gloomy sky bore down on the coast, the fields, the houses, daubing everything with a dirty shade of grey-brown. Sara could feel the clouds – although it never actually rained – spread a fine film of water over every surface, on eyelids, in mouths and throats. She had no desire to do anything, and even essential tasks seemed laborious. The palm trees and swimming pools, the whitewashed walls and the bougainvillea, the refreshment stalls on the beach with their palm roofs and the forgotten bicycles all seemed to share the general air of despondency, the discord of the south awakening to a day that seems more fitting to the north. And yet, the day it really did start to rain, Maribel arrived humming a rumba and wearing a smile so broad it barely fitted on her face. She placed a strange package on the table, a large round object that she had covered with a plastic bag to protect it from the rain.

'This is for you.'

'For me?'

'Yes. It's a present.'

'A present?' Sara carefully removed the plastic bag and uncovered a wicker basket containing African violets of several different colours – purple, pink, fuchsia, white, blue. 'They're lovely, Maribel! Thank you so much. But I don't know why—'

'Wait a second,' Maribel interrupted, holding up her hand. Without even taking off her raincoat or putting down her bag, Maribel sat opposite Sara and continued, 'You're not going to believe this! I couldn't believe it either but something *very* good has happened and I want to celebrate. You see . . .' She paused, took a deep breath and slowly let it out before she went on: 'My grandfather, my father's father, had some land on the outskirts of town. You know the old road to Chipiona, near the Playa de la Ballena. It's a big piece of land with good soil, but it's quite far away, so that's why nobody's wanted to farm it since he died. Before, when I was little, it was lovely. My grandfather went there by donkey every day, and he grew potatoes, pumpkins, melons, tomatoes, peppers and carnations – he always grew carnations, and he sold them at a good price. He gave us the ones with snapped stems, so we always had loads of flowers in the house. Well, the thing is, when he died nobody wanted to go on with it. Farming doesn't pay much, you know, and his children had jobs, and my cousins, well, they didn't want to farm it either. Anyway, the land just lay there, going to waste. Then at the beginning of the summer a builder from Sanlúcar turned up and said he'd like to take a look at it. He went there a lot, and took people to measure it, and dug some holes to see what was underneath, and then he said he wanted to buy it. He offered fifty million pesetas, can you believe it, for that little piece of land we thought wasn't worth anything – fifty million! Of course he wants to build on it because it's near the beach – a little inland, but pretty near, about ten minutes' walk at the most. And you know how much they're building round there, they've built a whole town in a couple of years. Anyway, I didn't want to get my hopes up because my dad, God rest his soul, he would have got twelve million, and I thought my mother would keep it and that she wouldn't give me a penny. Well, yesterday my sister told me that's not what's going to happen. We're going to split my dad's share between the three of us, because it turns out my grandfather had made a will. I had no idea, but he had, because he got married twice, and when he met my grandmother he was a widower and already had a young son, José, who's always been like my uncle, like my father's brother, and a brother to the other two, even though he had a different mother. We've never talked about it in my family because he called my grandmother "Mama", and my grandmother always said he was her eldest son, and everybody was happy. But my grandfather made a will just in case, and it's all quite clear. He didn't leave the land at La Ballena, which wasn't worth much then, to his children but his grandchildren – and not in equal shares, because the will said it had to be divided into four parts, one for each son, and these parts were then divided up amongst their children in equal shares. Just think,' she looked at Sara with wide eyes and a smile that showed all her teeth, 'nobody even remembered.'

'So you'll be getting four million,' Sara said.

'Well, yes. And because my grandfather died years ago, we don't have to pay any tax or anything. So, what do you think? I'd have given anything to see the look on my mum's face when the notary told her that no, the papers for the sale couldn't be signed because the land didn't belong to her. Anyway, in two weeks' time we have to sign and they'll pay us part of the money. We'll get some more in January next year, and then the last part in March. Isn't it incredible?'

'No, not incredible, Maribel.' Sara burst out laughing. 'It's wonderful. I'm so happy for you, and for Andrés, of course. What do you think you'll do with the money?'

'I don't know, I haven't thought about it yet. But I'm taking Andrés to Disneyland Paris, that's for sure, or to the other one in Florida, it's bigger. Then maybe I'll get myself a car. I'd have to learn to drive, of course, but that's no big deal, is it? And, I don't know, I haven't had time to think what else.'

Maribel couldn't have known that Sara had too much time on her hands and too little to think about, but she would soon find out. There were many things she didn't know about her employer's past, including the way apparently trivial things, such as plants bought in shops or the rough reddened skin of Maribel's gesticulating hands, had an effect on her. Then there were more substantial things, such as the glow that surrounded Maribel as she sat in the kitchen that morning, wondering aloud what to do with the money, bewildered by this sudden stroke of luck, facing a woman who had spent her whole life waiting for an opportunity. She would never know this, and yet this woman, whom she barely knew, would change the course of her life in a way her grandfather's will alone would never have done.

That day, Sara thought a lot about Maribel. She went on thinking about her the following day, and the one after that, and the one after that. She realised that the money, which her cleaner had not yet received, was starting to oppress Maribel, to obsess her, prompting her to devise ways of spending it as quickly as possible. Sara knew the feeling – the banknotes burning a hole in your pocket, the churning of your insides when you've never had anything before, when luck suddenly fills your hands with a perverse generosity – because with the gift bestowed by good fortune comes the impulse to squander it and nostalgia for the time when your pockets were empty. She was used to taking an interest in others, waiting to see how they reacted, taking care of them, but she had always kept her opinions to herself. She had never been close enough to anyone to try to influence their life. Yet Maribel's bewilderment and anxiety, as she listed ever more foolish choices, totally lost in the deluge of adverts on TV, moved Sara so deeply that one morning, as she listened to Maribel wondering whether to have electrolysis or buy her son a jet ski, Sara decided to intervene. She reminded herself that she had always thought her cleaner a bright woman, and she wanted Maribel to prove her right.

'Look, Maribel.' She didn't give Maribel a chance to speak first, as she usually did, or to answer. 'Sit down here. Come on, I want to ask you something. Now, let's see. How much do you save?'

'Me?' said Maribel, confused. 'How much do I what?'

'How much do you save? How much of what you earn do you have left over each month?'

'Me?' she repeated, pointing at herself even though there was nobody else there. 'Well, nothing. I don't have a penny left over.'

But Sara had never been one to give up easily, and she'd been expecting this answer.

'But before this summer,' she insisted, 'you lived on less money. And you still managed to pay your rent, and do your shopping, and you bought Andrés whatever he needed, didn't you?' Maribel nodded, still looking a little puzzled. 'So why do you still spend every last peseta now?'

'Because I bought a TV.'

'Yes, I know. With your July wages. And a deep-fat fryer with your August wages. And a games console, or whatever they're called, with your September wages. And you're paying for it all in instalments, aren't you?'

'Not the fryer,' said Maribel, her eyes wide. She was bemused by this interrogation, and her tone was cautious, defensive, as if she wanted to protect herself from Sara. 'I bought that in one go because it didn't cost much.'

'It doesn't matter. The thing is, you bought it, didn't you?' Maribel nodded. 'But that's not the point. Buying fewer things, using the ones you've already got while they're still working, not spending money foolishly, keeping the money from the inheritance and adding the money you've got left over – that's saving.'

'What do I want to save for?'

'To buy yourself a flat.'

Maribel was so surprised that her eyebrows practically flew off her face. She stared, open-mouthed, her lips forming a perfect parabola framing her even, white teeth.

'A flat!' she said, almost shouted, at last. 'Me? A flat?'

'Yes,' insisted Sara, 'you, a flat.'

'You don't know what you're saying.' Maribel suddenly seemed to relax and burst out laughing, as if she'd just been told a joke. 'With four million pesetas? Do you know how much flats cost around here, with all the holidaymakers who'll pay anything? I don't even have enough for a deposit. It's ridiculous. I'll go and get changed – I'd better start work.'

'Absolutely not,' said Sara, her firm tone stopping Maribel in her tracks. 'You're going to put on the coffee and get out the coffee cups, then you're going to sit down here and you're going to listen to me. Look, Maribel, there are lots of things I don't understand, but I do know about this. Money's cheap at the moment. It means that paying a mortgage is easier than ever, because of the interest rate. Do you understand? Interest rates are low right now. Things might change in the future, but you can get fixed-rate mortgages that . . . Anyway, that's something we'd have to look into. You've got four million, and that's almost half the amount you need, because you wouldn't need to buy a very big place. Thanks to those four million, you'll be able to move to a new flat and pay it off every month for not much more than the rent you're paying now. Think about it. Andrés might say that going to Disneyland is the thing he wants most in the whole world, and he might have got it into his head that he wants a jet ski. Last week he said he wanted a little boat to go out fishing, even though he doesn't know anything about fishing and doesn't have the time. Think about him. What would be best for him – to inherit a flat or a couple of photos of Mickey Mouse? And what about you? What would be best for you? You've been waxing your legs for fifteen years. Do you really want to spend a fortune on electrolysis? Think, Maribel. You might never get another inheritance, and houses don't lose their value, quite the opposite, they go up over time. They're a safer investment than a savings account, and they last for ever. And if you don't have any money left over to buy furniture, well, you can make do with what you have now. And when you finish paying this mortgage, you can get another one. It's all much easier than it seems, and after all, you're only thirty, you've got your whole life ahead of you. You've been lucky for once, very lucky. Make the most of it. Listen to me – save the money and buy a flat. Think about it, Maribel. Think carefully.'

Maribel sat down again. For a few seconds, she didn't move, staring down at her skirt. Then she looked up very slowly. Since she'd known her, Sara had been sure that despite her appearance, her lack of education, her loud voice and laugh, and her unpredictable logic, Maribel was intelligent, and she didn't disappoint her that morning.

'But I don't have a regular wage,' she said simply. 'Banks won't give you a mortgage if you don't have a regular wage.'

'Yes, they will, because you've got four million pesetas, and that's a guarantee. If you stopped paying the mortgage, the bank would get your money, you see. It makes you worthwhile as a customer. Anyway, I can write you a certificate of earnings, and we could have a word with Juan Olmedo. I'll be seeing him on Saturday at Tamara's birthday party. She's invited Andrés, hasn't she? I'm sure Dr Olmedo would be happy to write you one too.'

'No, no way!' Maribel sat back suddenly, stirring her coffee so violently that she spilt some of it on the tablecloth. 'Believe me, you can't trust that man.'

'Why not? He seems like a good person, he's responsible and very generous. I don't think there are too many men out there who'd be prepared to take on—'

'Yes, I know what you're going to say,' interrupted Maribel. 'I know, and it's probably true, I'm not saying it isn't, but there are other things too.'

'Like what?'

'Like some things I know.'

'OK,' Sara snorted. 'What things do you know?'

'Look, I don't like to bad-mouth people because I don't like it when people say bad things about me and I've never hurt anyone. But the other day, that bastard Andrés, my ex, you know? Well, he was making fun of me. I don't know how he does it, I hardly ever see him but when I do, he always finds some way of needling me. The other day he told me he saw "that doctor you work for", as he calls him, in Sanlúcar, in a prostitutes' bar. What do you say to that? That's how Dr Olmedo spends his money, all generous and responsible that he is! I mean, really, men are all the same. What are you laughing at? I don't think it's funny.'

Sara wasn't really laughing, but she couldn't help smiling. She had just realised that Maribel had been thinking, or was still thinking, of seducing Juan Olmedo. It was the only explanation for both her ex-husband's taunts and Maribel's acute indignation, an explanation that, above all, provided her with yet more proof that her neighbour was the type of man you could trust. But she resorted to other arguments to justify her reaction.

'Why shouldn't I laugh, Maribel? Well, really! What did you expect? He's a young man and he has a difficult life, looking after a mentally disabled person and a little girl all the time, and working too. Besides, he's new to the area, he doesn't know anyone, and I imagine he can scarcely find the time to have a beer in peace, let alone to go and meet women. It doesn't seem all that bad to me.'

'Oh, doesn't it?' Maribel was unable to formulate a more complex answer, so she expressed her disapproval by going to the sink and attacking the washing-up as if the fate of the universe depended on it.

'Well, no, it doesn't. I don't mean that I'm in favour of men going to prostitutes, but life is complicated, you know that.'

Maribel didn't answer. In the silence that followed, Sara Gómez, who had thought many times that it was very odd that a doctor should give up a permanent post in a Madrid hospital and move to one in Jerez, now began to wonder what had made Juan Olmedo take this step, as if Maribel's revelation might somehow be the key to the mystery. The fact was, she did find it difficult to imagine her neighbour in a bar with prostitutes, but she didn't judge him too harshly for it. As she was absorbed in these thoughts, Maribel turned round from the sink and looked at her for a moment before exclaiming:

'It's a shame you never got married. You would have made your husband so happy! I mean, you know everything. It's amazing – everything! You can tell you've been lucky in life, you can really tell.'

'W hat's your name?'
'You know it's Elia.'

'No, I mean your real name.'

'Ah!' She burst out laughing, showing ugly teeth like a cat's, a cluster of narrow yellow incisors between two pointed eye teeth. 'Well, it's nearly the same: Aurelia.'

'Good.' Juan Olmedo nodded, thinking to himself that it would be better if this pretty girl didn't smile during her working hours. 'That makes it easier to call you Elia.'

She closed her mouth, but a mischievous smile still played on her lips. While he dressed slowly, sitting on the edge of the bed, Juan looked at her closely, as if he'd never seen her before. Close up, and with the lights on, she didn't look much like Charo, but her face had a similar disturbing beauty – full, dark and stormy – a strange perfection in features that might have seemed ugly in another woman. The angle of her jaw, the shape of her chin, her cheekbones, the line of her nose, had all the harmony of a Renaissance painting, the balanced geometry of a marble sculpture, punctuated by deep black eyes that burned dangerously. She would never have been cast as the ingénue in a film; she would, on the other hand, have made a perfect villain, a *femme fatale*, for any man too inexperienced to fully under-stand the complex depths such a role entailed. For Juan knew that, despite everything, in spite of the fatal aura that surrounded everything she did, Charo had always been a good person. Elia probably was too, though her face lacked the strategic fleshiness – full lips and a slight plumpness of the cheeks – that had given his sister-in-law her mysterious combination of perversity and sweetness. But Elia's body was like a copy of the one he had lost, an earlier, younger version, showing the same lack of proportion that had characterised Charo's body before she had a child: her breasts and hips had seemed too big for her slim arms and narrow waist, the sharp edges of her shoulders and collar-bones jutting out beneath taut, smooth, glossy skin. Elia, who couldn't have been more than twenty-two or twenty-three, was observing him now as she lay stretched out on the bed. Juan tried to imagine her in ten or fifteen years' time, when her body had undergone the changes that had balanced out Charo's body, making it rounder and more solid, thickening her waist, her arms, and her thighs, but pleasing him no less. He found Charo attractive whatever she looked like. Sometimes, while she was still alive, when she still had a future, Juan liked to imagine her at fifty – well preserved, carefully made up, her hair always immaculate, wearing tight, fitted dresses that showed her body still had curves, a kind of rebellious and disconcerted Liz Taylor, because that's how it would have been, and he would still have found her attractive.

He had almost finished buttoning his shirt when he felt a sudden, surprisingly intense desire to take off his clothes, lie down and pull Elia on top of him again. He turned slightly and placed a hand on her belly. She seemed to straighten suddenly and look at him differently, half-closing her eyes to soften her shrewd expression, a kind of pleased, pleasing alertness that convinced Juan Olmedo that she had guessed what was going through his mind. 'What is it?' she asked him. 'No, nothing,' he answered, and though this moment-ary show of insight had truly moved him, he managed to get up a fraction of a second before she came towards him to make him change his mind. Elia withdrew instantly and began to play with her hair, showing him that she was not bothered by his decision. Juan smiled to himself, because this unspoken struggle, this quiet power play, had restored Charo to him much more vividly than his forensic deconstruction of her body. He knew this kind of combat well, except that Charo would have won, she always did, ever since she'd learnt to control him by pulling the elusive strings of his desire. Now he was pleased he had resisted. He had never intended to dance on anyone's grave, and he wasn't prepared to hate her; he didn't need or want to, and he certainly wouldn't allow himself to. He suspected that the memory of his lost love would inevitably fade one day; Charo's features, her voice, her words slowly receding until everything was buried beneath the fine, cold sand of the passing hours and days, the weeks and months. He was determined to experience this moment; to become this serene figure, untroubled by emotion, watching the last of the man he'd been slip away with the last memory of the woman he'd loved. The image made him feel dizzy, a vague combination of anxiety and expectation, although he knew that the sands of time would eventually bury him as well. He had always been the most intelligent of the three. Though Charo had discovered it too late, and Damián had never realised it, Juan had always been the most intelligent of the three; and that was why, that night, in that comfortably anonymous room, with its red plush wallpaper and simple double bed, he hurriedly finished dressing.

'Will you be back?'

The question rekindled the desire still throbbing in his head.

'Of course,' he replied, and he meant it. 'Some day soon.'

She got up from the bed and came towards him, conscious of her nakedness with every step. She put her arms around him, and kissed him on the mouth as if she hadn't been paid for it. Juan responded enthusiastically, because he liked her very much and because he was in a good mood. Later, as he made his way outside, the first breath of the damp morning air released the knot inside him, and he was able to breathe freely for the first time in hours. As he closed the car door and turned the key in the ignition, he realised that the woman, Elia, or Aurelia, had probably misinterpreted his departure. He'd left because he liked her and he wanted to preserve the desire that now coursed within him as much as his new smiling exterior, the good mood that surprised him more than anything else that had happened that night.

Over the three weeks that had passed since he first caught sight of her in the dimly lit interior of the bar, he'd thought often of the girl in red who looked like Charo from a distance. He hadn't obsessed about her, of course – he had too much experience of obsession already – but her image had remained with him without tormenting him, and he was forced to calculate how long it had been since he last slept with a woman. Seven months of celibacy is a long time but, at the age of forty, he was too old to face a sexual debut casually, or without the sneaking fear that he might be making a fool of himself. He would have remained in this state of paralysis had Miguel Barroso not suggested going for a drink that afternoon, because his wife had gone to Seville with the kids, to spend the weekend with their grandmother, and it was a Friday, and he couldn't think of anything better to do. Juan agreed, but it wasn't until they got to the bar and found a very attractive young anaesthetist waiting for them that Juan realised what was really going on. He'd seen this woman with his friend several times over the last few days, in the cafeteria, or in the corridor. Juan said hello to her, ordered the mandatory drink, and prepared himself for the thankless role of third fiddle in a song made for two. Miguel and the anaesthetist gazed at each other, smiling, brushing against each other, completely oblivious to Juan even as a spectator. He spent the next three-quarters of an hour reading the labels on all the bottles lining the shelves on the back wall of the bar, but when he tried to leave, the woman grabbed his arm, insisting that he stay with them for dinner. When she went to the toilet, Miguel pleaded with him not to leave them alone too soon: 'Shit, don't do this to me, Juanito. What's it to you?' So Juan phoned home and Tamara sounded delighted by the prospect of a takeaway pizza for supper. He also called the babysitter who promised she'd be right there and would take care of everything. These assurances didn't make the evening ahead seem any more enticing: he was going to have dinner with two consenting adults who were married, almost middle-aged, whose previous experience of adultery had not diminished their enthusiasm for the courtship ritual. And this was exactly what happened. By the time the first course arrived, the prospective lovers had fired an entire arsenal of signals at each other across the table – eyelash fluttering, sighing, daring gestures, stroking the air as if it were skin – and everything they said began to sound like an endearment, until the conversation slid gradually onto even more awkward and embarrassing terrain. Then, as their desire spread across the tablecloth like spilt wine, as it strengthened with every passing minute, threatening to eclipse him completely, Juan Olmedo suddenly felt implicated in every sentence he heard, in the nervous tension that distorted his companions' voices and made their hands shake, in the furtive activity of their legs and feet that hinted at plans beyond this table cluttered with dirty plates and empty glasses, this reassuring, cheap restaurant.

Excitement – ordinary, happy sexual excitement – running through his body with the crazy discipline of a colony of ants, was the first feeling he became aware of, though not the most intense. Then, nested within its shiny, luxurious wrapper, came envy, nostalgia, loneliness, the temptation to feel sorry for himself and the arrogance that overcame it. He felt a sudden burst of vitality, an imaginary torrent of clean red blood cells activating a sophisticated system of tiny valves and ducts as fine as threads, the organic, chemical labyrinth that fired both his excitement and his awareness of it. Desire made him selfish and it made him strong. He found himself thinking that the girl in red was a woman like any other, and that his money was his own and he could spend it on whatever he chose. He no longer needed arguments, excuses or moral considerations of any kind. After coffee, he got up and quickly said goodbye; by then Miguel was quite happy for Juan to leave. Juan felt anxious, but he didn't let it show as he left the restaurant and got into his car, only just keeping within the speed limit as he drove past the turning he took every day to get home. He was anxious and he couldn't do anything about it, but she didn't seem to notice as she got up from her stool and headed straight towards him when he entered the bar. 'I've been waiting for you,' she said. Juan's eyes swept her earlobe, her jaw, the curve of her neck, the glossy skin of her cleavage, and the sight calmed him.

He would have preferred to follow her immediately, wherever it was that women like her took men like him, but he didn't dare say a word. He didn't want the girl in red to know it was his first time with a prostitute, and he would rather forget his one previous experience, his spectacular failure, aged twenty, when faced with a pair of magnificent legs and a lacy, black body stocking. He could still remember Damián's taunts, the ridiculous refrain that ran through Juan's mind for months – 'What's dignity got to do with your prick?' – every time he looked at himself in the bathroom mirror, every time he and Damián bumped into each other on the stairs or in the hallway, every time he passed Mingo's bar and saw them there, Nicanor and Damián, laughing like idiots, sitting at a table strewn with bottle tops, chanting that stupid, annoying little question, 'What's the answer to this: dignity and your prick – what do they have in common?' But in those days, Juan's dignity and his prick were so closely linked that they sometimes ended up being one and the same. He would have liked to forget this, not because he feared being unworthy of a Juan Olmedo who now seemed more authentic, purer, better than the one produced by the past twenty years, but because the claustrophobic memory took him back to a youthful insecurity that he wasn't quite sure he'd ever overcome. He was no longer intimidated by naked women, but he was wary of this girl even before she undressed. He followed her to the bar and asked her what she'd like to drink before ordering one for himself, using the same tone, movements and words he would have used with any other girl in any other bar. Secretly, he wanted to tell her not to behave like a prostitute; he wanted to fuck her and he didn't mind paying for it, but he didn't think he could endure any purring, moaning, endearments or pouting. He didn't dare say so, but he didn't need to – she was very well trained. She must have learnt to guess exactly what her clients wanted, because she gave him exactly what he needed, which was the reason for his good mood.

He got up late on Saturday and as he had breakfast, he noticed that his mood hadn't deteriorated during the night; on the contrary. Alfonso in the meantime was playing with the TV remote control – a source of enduring fascination ever since he'd learnt to use it – altering the volume and changing channels, switching endlessly from one lot of cartoons to another, or turning the sound off and on. Tamara was upstairs in her room with Andrés, trying unsuccessfully to get to the end of a difficult computer game that exasperated her so much that Juan could hear her screaming and stamping on the floor just above his head. But despite the noise, the chaos surrounding him like a storm, he was able to enjoy his breakfast in peace, savouring

154

memories of the night before: the delicate skin at the edge of her armpits, the smooth channel between her breasts, the almost invisible line of pale down on her flat, taut stomach, her toenails painted silver, the small red spiral tattooed on her right buttock. These images accompanied him during the day, as he did the shopping, prepared lunch, chose a film for them all to watch, sweetening his exhausting weekend as father, mother, housekeeper, tutor and occasional therapist. On the Monday, he resisted the tug of desire that made the memories sharpen and plague him more frequently, replacing the details of her body with moving pictures, the reactions of his own body instead of her touch, smell, weight. He was expecting to feel bad about it at some stage, to discover that he'd made a mistake, to hear the harsh voice of his betrayed youth; he thought he might regret what he'd done, realise that it made no sense to fantasise about a whore, however much he liked her, however good she was. He expected all of this, yet nothing happened, and on the Tuesday as he left work, his prick and dignity by now quite dissociated, he decided to put up with the confusion and headed for Sanlúcar.

'I was expecting you yesterday,' she said. This time she didn't even have to walk across the bar to get him.

'Well, I'm here today,' he said, hearing a new confidence in his voice.

He enjoyed it as much as the first time, and as much as he would the third, the fourth, the fifth, and all the other times he would go to her during the autumn and winter that followed. The physical euphoria – beneficial, real, solid – lasted throughout, but his good mood turned out to be less enduring. A couple of months after he'd met her, Elia had become an essential part of his daily life, as essential as the washing machine or the boiler. By then, Juan Olmedo had discovered that she wasn't dangerous at all – not that bright, a bit of a gossip, sweet, sentimental and very jealous, she was just a good girl who'd appeared by chance in his troubled life. She was uncomplicated and could absorb Juan's inner turmoil without offering even a pale reflection of it; he didn't know whether to be pleased or sorry about this, but one thing he was sure of was that Elia closed a circle. Alfonso, Tamara, the hospital in Jerez, his friend Miguel, a house in a small town, a beach on which to discover that crabs walk sideways, and her; points on the map of a moderate life, which could have been worse and was the best he could have chosen at that point in time. Not a great comfort on a winter's night, but then winters in the south are just as warm as spring in the north.

When he realised that he'd followed them to the entrance of the most famous, most elegant banqueting suite in all Estrecho, he was furious with himself for having been deceived yet again. Damián announced loudly that they'd arrived, but then walked straight past the large glass doors, the crystal chandelier and regal staircase with its ornate banisters that were the envy of every bride from Cuatro Caminos to Tetuán, and headed down a different staircase, this one narrow and foul-smelling, that led straight off the street under a neon sign, GAMES ARCADE, with half the letters missing. The clicking of snooker balls, and the sharp metallic crash of the table football, guided them towards a huge basement. The air was thick with smoke and aggression, at odds with the sweet tinkling that came from a row of slot machines. This was home to a throng of cocky teenagers, flick-knives bulging in their back pockets, a louche, contemptuous smirk on their lips and a girl, almost always much younger and heavily made up, hanging around them to light fags, watch over beers and hold snooker cues when the boys went for a piss. At the back of the room, above a black door, a pink neon sign indicated the entrance to the bar.

Damián and Nicanor walked through the middle of the room, ignoring the admiring glances of the players who seemed to part down the central aisle like a guard of honour. On that evening in late May, as he followed Damián and Nicanor, Juan had had the uncomfortable but familiar feeling of being out of place, a third-year medical student who felt nervous in front of this gang of louts even though they probably hadn't even finished school yet – that is, if they hadn't been expelled. These hardened habitués were, nevertheless, banned from going through the black door, where a badly spelt handwritten sign stated that there was no entry to anyone under eighteen. Aware of thirty pairs of eyes following his every move, Damián, who had just turned nineteen, pushed the door open with the arrogance bestowed by his great age, while somewhere upstairs a wedding march began. It was eight thirty and Juan, here for the first time and having therefore never yearned for the forbidden black door, felt a sudden stab of melancholy, a shameful remnant of childish vulnerability, as he heard the familiar, saccharine chords. Meanwhile, a wizened old vixen with dyed-black hair scraped back into a bun and huge hoop earrings, smiled, welcoming him to this most miserable circle of hell.

'Conchi's place', as they called it, was as long and narrow as a railway carriage, a dank tunnel with curving walls. Despite the pretentious decor – a confused mix of nautical motifs and hunting prints in gilded frames that you could tell were plastic even from a distance – it was a dive. Parts of the domed ceiling were covered with egg cartons painted gold, a legacy from the previous manager of the premises, who had tried unsuccessfully to turn the snooker hall into a nightclub, also installing a small dance floor at one end. His successor, Conchi, had shown more imagination and better judgement by making it a kind of improvised illegal brothel, under the inoffensive guise of a games arcade. She ran this thriving business with her husband while the landlords of the building turned a blind eye. Nicanor told Juan all of this in a hoarse whisper while Damián pretended to dance with the skinny old bird. Forced to hear the murky secrets of the place, Juan could easily imagine what a wonderful source of customers the snooker hall was, packed with frustrated teenagers who spent years fantasising about what went on behind the forbidden door. This was the recent past that his brother was trying to distance himself from, affecting a casual familiarity, a calculated combination of indifference and interest. The smirking Nicanor was attempting to do the same, but with less success. He hadn't yet donned a policeman's uniform, but he followed his friend Damián around like a faithful dog.

'Juanito,' said Damián, coming up to him with his arm around the woman's waist, 'I'd like to introduce you to a friend of mine. Conchi, this moron is my elder brother.'

Nicanor sniggered, and even Juan smiled.

'Yes,' said Conchi, tugging at Juan's shirt as if she wanted to straighten his collar. Her long crimson talons turned this gesture, which his mother made when seeing him off at the door every morning, into something worrying, alien. 'You can say what you like, Damián, but he's a lot better-looking than you, you know.' She turned suddenly as if wanting to trap Damián, who was grinning. 'Now I know why you haven't brought him here before.'

'Who, him?' Damián pointed at Juan, then waved a hand dismissively. 'He's always got his nose buried in a book, the idiot. He'd drown in a glass of water.'

'Fine.' She stroked Juan's throat with the edges of her nails. 'Whatever you say. But he's going to have another drink. My treat. You know I have a weakness for nice young men.'

It was the second time that day that a woman had called him 'nice' and Juan Olmedo felt tempted to answer that he must have a weakness for bad women. He watched Conchi as she headed back behind the bar: she was too old, too like some gargoyle on a Gothic cathedral, to remind him of Charo, yet it was Charo who had spoken these words on the phone, ruining his dessert that day, and the following day, and the day after that, and many more to come. Their conversation still stung his ears, and he couldn't get rid of the suddenly bitter taste of the strawberries that had frozen in his mouth as he held the phone to his ear for seconds that felt like years. 'Too nice' – a couple of syllables to chew on, but ones he'd never fully managed to digest. Too nice. Nothing and nobody in this world was too nice, nothing and nobody, he repeated to himself, nothing was too good, too nice, nobody except him.

Even his second whisky didn't clear away the bitter taste, but it did promise to dull the endless looping of those two words inside his head. Now accustomed to the gloom, Juan examined his surroundings and saw in greater detail the faces and bodies, the hunters and dogs, the knots and anchors on the walls. The bar was small, and fairly empty. To his left, Nicanor was shaking his head rhythmically, as if he couldn't decide between a skinny girl with long dirty-blonde hair and eyes furiously ringed with black who looked like a junkie, and an older woman of about thirty, with short hair, who looked healthy and experienced, and who was leaning against the wall smoking. Juan would have chosen the second girl, but he didn't intend to compete for her with Nicanor, because he didn't like her enough to prove to himself that Charo was wrong. Nor did he much like the look of the two girls his brother had chosen to joke around with on the dance floor, or the sad-looking woman with frizzy hair who was chatting to a grey-haired man at a nearby table. Damián was soon fed up with dancing and came back to the bar with his two companions. At the far end of the room, Juan suddenly caught sight of two magnificent, perfect, endless legs, extending between a red patent mini-skirt and a pair of black stilettos. As he continued to stare, the owner of the legs uncrossed and stretched them briefly before standing up, as if she wanted to display the full range of their possibilities to her admirer. She headed towards him, walking around the raised dance floor, taking her time. Juan ran his eyes over the rest of her body and concluded that, on the whole, it was up to the standard of her amazing legs. She wasn't exactly young, but she wasn't middle-aged either. She had a slender waist, full hips, a slim torso with narrow shoulders, and round breasts squeezed into a tight, black body stocking, that made them look like ripe fruit, tempting, almost edible.

When she was halfway across the room, the woman with the frizzy hair put out a hand to stop her, as if she wanted to say something; the owner of the amazing legs leant in to listen. From that angle, her cleavage would have driven any man crazy, but by then Juan had been able to see her face – it was angular, tired and beautiful in a difficult, unconventional way. Her hair was dyed mahogany, and there were dark circles beneath her eyes; she had a large nose, and something else, something he couldn't quite capture, a familiar air that toyed with him, masking its origin. He couldn't possibly know her, yet Juan had the feeling that he did, or that he knew somebody very like her.

'Hey!' he said to Nicanor, who was still shaking his head to left and right. 'Who's that girl?'

'Oh, yeah, Gogo – her real name's Carmen, but they call her Gogo because she used to dance in a club. She's hot.'

'Yes.' It was true, she really was.

'And she's bloody good. I'd recommend her, seriously.'

But just then, Juan realised without a shadow of a doubt who she was.

'She's the wife of that locksmith in the Calle Avila, the one who cuts keys, isn't she?'

'Correct,' answered Nicanor, nodding. 'The very same.'

Juan had seen her many times before – the same tired face, the same dark circles – enveloped in baggy, green overalls covered with metal shavings, her right hand on the lever that kept the keys in place, her eyes on the saw cutting the outline of the copy. He'd often spoken to her, an ordinary woman, with a scrubbed face and hair tied back in a ponytail, almost always alone in the shop because the locksmith was out opening locks or fitting them in people's homes.

'But she works with her husband! I see her all the time, we always take our keys there. What's she doing here?'

Nicanor stared at him as if he didn't understand the question, and took a few seconds to answer:

'What do you think she's doing? Earning cash, like the rest of them.'

'Cash.'

'Yes. Things are pretty rough and ready here, they're not professionals. Conchi—' He broke off suddenly as Juan took out a thousand-peseta note and placed it on the bar. 'What are you doing?'

'I'm leaving.'

'What?' Nicanor curled his lip in a mocking smile. 'Come on, Juan, get back here. You don't want to prove your brother right, do you?'

But Juan left anyway, although he wasn't fast enough to avoid hearing the woman's voice as she called out to him.

'Hey!' she shouted. 'Hey, boy!' ('Right, this is ready,' Juan heard.) 'Where are you going?' ('If it doesn't fit the lock, you tell your mother to send it back and I'll file it down.') 'Come back!' ('No need to pay for it now, your mother can pay me when she sees me.')

Outside, he realised that his cheeks were burning. He didn't need a mirror to know that he was blushing, but he couldn't tell whether it was because he was ashamed of himself, of his nervousness, of running away, or of the locksmith's wife who worked as a prostitute in her spare time. Perhaps he was simply ashamed that places like this existed, one metro stop away from his home. In that moment, he knew only that he felt uncomfortable in his own body, that his arms and legs seemed heavy, as if they didn't belong to him, that his cheeks were still bright red despite the cool evening air, and that he never, ever should have let Damián talk him into going.

He headed down Bravo Murillo, no particular destination in mind. He would have carried on walking to the ends of the earth, but he knew himself, and he knew that sooner or later he would head home, walk past Charo's front door, open his own, go straight to his room, take out his books and start studying with the same ferocious determination as ever. He knew it, this was his personality, his nature, the best of him, the worst, the punishment he rewarded himself with when he was alone, the prize for which others tormented him; the hard shiny rock of a difficult but burning ambition that the verdict of a local princess had crushed to a pile of dust.

'Look, Juan,' she'd said, and he knew that something bad was coming. 'The thing is, I . . . I think it'd be best if we left it, you know? Because, it's not that I don't like you – you're good-looking, you're sweet and all that – but you spend all day sitting at home studying. I hardly ever see you, and then when I do . . . You don't like parties, or discos, or any of that stuff. The thing is I need something else, something more lively. I like going to the cinema, and I like sitting around chatting, but really what I like most is going out with a gang of people, dancing, having a good time. But you don't like my friends. You're always saying they're arrogant and childish, and well, maybe they are, but they're my friends, you know? And, OK, we're going out together, so it's normal for us to kiss and cuddle, but I don't want to spend the whole afternoon in a bar doing that . . . It's not that I'm

bored, I like kissing you, but I can't explain it, I just want
something else. I think you're too nice for me, Juan, that's
what it is. It's not that I'm bad, but I like guys who think
about more than just passing their exams. Guys who know
how to have fun. I don't mean that you don't know how to,
it's just that you're not even interested in having fun, Juan,
that's the truth.'

This was what she'd said, and if Damián had been listening, he would have agreed. He might even have applauded.
This was what Charo had said and Juan hadn't even defended
himself, because all he could think of saying was what he
always said: 'But if I don't get good marks in June I might
lose my grant.' Charo knew this, she'd heard it a thousand
times, but she didn't care, it didn't matter to her, the way it
didn't matter to his father, who still made him work shifts at
the bakery at weekends even when he was in the middle of
exams; the way it didn't matter to his brother, who came
home and put his music on full blast and said that if Juan
didn't like it he could go and do his homework elsewhere;
the way it didn't even seem to matter, deep down, to his
mother, who was always telling everyone how proud she was
but then did nothing to make his life easier. And that evening, when he reached Cuatro Caminos, saw from his watch
that it was nine thirty, and kept on walking, he started to
think that maybe they were right, because that's how things
had always been, right from the beginning.

The beginning was in Villaverde Alto in a tiny flat next to
a park, over an hour away, first by van and then by metro,
from the bakery in Calle Hermosilla. The bakery was what
had brought his parents to Madrid only a few months before
Juan was born. Juan's only memory of Aunt Remedios, a fat,
clumsy and sour-faced old lady, was of her shaking a finger at
him and saying she'd cut off his hand if she saw him take so
much as one piece of bubble gum without paying for it. Yet
it was Aunt Remedios who had asked Juan's father, her

youngest nephew, to help her with the shop when she became a widow. He was newly married, and as the only alternative open to him was labouring on a farm, he didn't hesitate. So Juan's parents ended up in Villaverde Alto and with the prospect of inheriting the business in a few years, not even the exhausting routine of early mornings, endless journeys there and back, and even working on Sundays made them lose heart. By the time Damián was a year old, their father was staying at home on Mondays, and it was their mother who did all the work at the shop while Aunt Remedios barked orders from her chair behind the counter. But Juan had no memory of this, although he clearly remembered his great-aunt's funeral, because it was pouring with rain, and the cemetery was awash with mud. His mother, in the early months of pregnancy, was very pale and had to put her hand in front of her mouth every so often. Damián, holding their father's hand, wouldn't stop crying, and their father was carrying their little sister Paquita, who had just learnt to walk and couldn't keep still. The gravediggers were cursing under their breath because their boots kept slipping on the slick mud. Eventually Mama moved away a few paces and vomited, holding onto a tree. Everything was sad and dirty and wet. But Juan was happy, because the bakery now belonged to Papa, and before setting out that morning his parents had explained that he could be happy but he mustn't let it show.

The rainy morning of the funeral, Juan was five and Damián was almost four. A few months later, when Trini was born, they all had their photograph taken, and their mother placed it on the sideboard in the hall. His mother was in the middle, holding the baby wrapped in a shawl that trailed over her skirt. Damián was sitting on her left, looking very serious, wearing short trousers and resting his hands on his thighs. Their father was standing behind, resting one hand on his son's head and the other on his wife's shoulder.

To their right, beside the bench and also standing, was Juan, grinning at the camera and carrying a very blonde and smiling Paquita in his arms. Alfonso was born three years later, and they had a new photograph taken; this was also placed on the sideboard in the hall. The two photographs were very similar: Damián was again sitting on the bench, between Mama with a baby in her lap and Paquita, more serious this time, and with darker hair. As before, Papa was standing behind them, and this time Juan was next to him, but not smiling, perhaps because he was carrying Trini who was crying. By then, Damián was seven, but he never – either then or later on – appeared in a photograph carrying any of his younger brothers or sisters.

And he never went to the hospital. It was Juan who went with his mother and the baby to the teaching hospital, where a team of specialists monitored Alfonso's development every two weeks so that they could give a definitive diagnosis. He would always recall those trips with horror. They began with tense expectation, punctuated with smiles and erroneous predictions – 'This time, Juanito, you'll see, I'm telling you he's fine. He follows my finger with his eyes, I'm sure he does, haven't you seen? You just haven't noticed, but he is focusing, really he is. I should know, I gave birth to him' – and ended with stunned, angry weeping, his mother clasping the child to her breast and covering his head with kisses. Juan would hurry out after her, holding on to the hem of her coat, suspecting that she wouldn't even have noticed if she left him behind or he became lost in the crowd on the way to the metro. While the doctors were examining Alfonso, Juan waited outside on his own in a room full of photos of chubby healthy babies, and it was here, one afternoon, that he decided he would become a doctor, but that he would never look after sick children. The news that Alfonso's impairment was irrevocable confirmed his decision. By the age of nine, Juan Olmedo felt an imaginary duty, born of guilt, to love his younger brother and to somehow compensate his parents for having a child who would always be defenceless. Since then, he had been both the cleverest and the stupidest member of his family.

'Hey, you, Juanito, come here!' Damián would call from the living room, from the street, from the schoolyard. 'Bet you can't do this!'

And he'd fit the final piece into a complicated structure of little sticks which would fall to pieces shortly after; or he'd write out four numbers that looked like a bearded man when he turned the piece of paper upside down; or he'd launch into a long list of calculations to which he could always guess the answer; or he'd strike a match on the sole of his boot, or imitate the sound of a banjo by doing strange things with his mouth. Juan would shake his head and smile admiringly, before admitting the obvious:

'No, I can't do that.'

'Of course you can't!' his brother would shoot back, laughing his head off. 'You can't do anything!'

Juan had admired Damián sincerely, faithfully, for as long as he had things to learn from him. Everyone admired Damián – their parents, their younger sisters, their school friends, the kids in the street. Dami was as flexible as an acrobat, as surprising as a magician, as fast as an athlete, as shrewd as an adult, a good friend, as unpredictable as his tricks, as hilarious as his jokes, always full of good ideas for making a wet Sunday afternoon fly by. A great brother, thought Juan, who loved him without jealousy or resentment, and without feeling the need to be like him. The two of them were a team, an unbalanced but efficient pair. And, after Alfonso's last hospital visit, when their parents received a typewritten letter bringing with it a dark despair that seeped slowly, gradually into the furniture and the walls, the eyes and the skin, Juan and Damián became the backbone of the family. In good moments, Dami seemed to be a catalyst for joy, reaping loud laughter and kisses that almost seemed to colour the air around them; in bad moments, only he could dispel tension, counteract sadness, crush despondency with a joke or prank that made everyone at the dining table smile. But there wouldn't have been as many good times if Juan hadn't always been ready to anticipate the bad ones, whisking the little ones out of the way a moment before their mother started shouting, rushing downstairs for cold beer when he saw his father standing cursing in front of the open fridge, taking the girls to the park or cinema when Alfonso was ill, spending a whole night going through a school book with Damián when he admitted that he hadn't even glanced at the chapter headings and had a test the following day.

For many years, Juan had unquestionably been the older brother, the only one to whom important tasks could be entrusted, the guardian of the little ones, almost foolishly kind. He was also nearly always the clever one, while Damián was the funny one, the incorrigible one who made you want to hug him even when you were reprimanding him, sharp as a tack and sometimes clever too. Back then everything was as it should be – they loved each other, needed each other, and were on a level when it came to what they did and didn't know. Damián taught Juan to smoke, and to masturbate. He'd borrow money from him and lend him dirty magazines in return. Juan taught Damián to solve polynomial equations and physics problems. He'd cover for him when he got home late and lend him novels with passages underlined that were more exciting than the photos in the magazines. That was until the day they decided they knew it all and their paths diverged; the day the removal van arrived and their parents closed the door of the rented flat in Villaverde Alto for the last time. They were moving to what would, after twenty years of monthly mortgage payments, be the first place they had ever owned – a large sunny third-floor apartment, in an old but not too ancient building with views, on one side, of the Dehesa de la Villa park, and on the other, of the end of Francos Rodriguez, the widest street in the district of Estrecho.

Their father, delighted to be moving as he would now be able to get to work by metro (six stops with a change at Bilbao, virtually a stone's throw away), asked them, at breakfast, if they would be so kind as to not piss him off today. So Juan kept his mouth shut, and worked without a rest all morning, filling and taping up boxes, marking their contents on the outside then carrying them downstairs. For him, the move was a disaster. The beginning of term was barely a week away, and he'd been refused a transfer of his grant because there were no places available in the university entrance subjects he was studying at any school in the district they were moving to. This meant he'd have to travel back to Villaverde every day, and he wouldn't be able to go home for lunch. In this working-class suburb there weren't too many students preparing for university. Many of his friends had left school at sixteen and started vocational training or been apprenticed in some trade, and even among those who had stayed on, fewer than half had signed up for the university entrance exams. Of these, only two shared Juan's ambition to go to the best university in Madrid, the one that rejected the most applicants. This was why they had to study their core science subjects in the morning and return to class mid-afternoon for their optional subjects. It wouldn't have been a big deal had the Olmedos stayed in Villaverde for another year – just one more year – but now Juan would have to spend all day in the school library, with only a sandwich for lunch, and would arrive home after eleven o'clock at night.

He didn't dare complain, or suggest they postpone the move to make his life easier. The rest of the family was too delighted at the prospect of the new flat to pay attention to anything else, and when he explained his problem to them, their lack of understanding plunged him into a resentful stupor with eruptions of injured pride. It was this that was secretly driving his frenetic activity. He worked harder, better and faster than anyone else all morning, and yet he was the only one who felt that there was no reward for all this effort.

'Leave the boxes from the kitchen till last,' said his mother when the removal man asked where they should start. 'Then I can tidy everything up while you load the furniture.'

Juan looked around him and saw a pile of unmarked boxes on the pavement alongside Damián, who was singing, and doing such a convincing impersonation of the kitsch singer Raphael that the removal men were staring at him, amazed.

'Who packed up the kitchen?' asked Juan, although he'd heard the same singing coming from the kitchen all morning. His brother, still holding an imaginary microphone in his right hand, raised his other hand in response.

'Which boxes are they?'

Damián turned round, interrupting his performance and holding out his hands, to find Juan coming towards him with a felt-tip pen.

'Shit!' Damián said.

His mother reprimanded him quietly, 'Mind your language, Dami,' as she wiped Alfonso's nose.

'Well, I was putting them here, but then I went to the girls' room, and Papa handed me boxes from the living room.'

'So that means you've got no bloody idea.'

'Mind your language, Juanito,' muttered their mother, quite oblivious to the rising tension.

'All you had to do was pick up a pen and write K-I-T-C-H-E-N on them.'

'Yes, I know,' Damián said. 'But nobody told me to.'

'You shouldn't have to be told, dickhead.'

Frightened, their mother said nothing this time.

'For Christ's sake, it's obvious. Only a fucking moron like you would do this. It's not rocket science, you idiot.'

'Look, the only idiot here is you.' Damián came towards him, riled by the fact that the removal men had been nodding in agreement with Juan. Their father came between them just as they were about to start fighting.

'Stop that, Dami, your brother's right. He may not have told you what to do with the kitchen stuff, but I did. And you listen to me too, Juan,' he said to his eldest son, not letting go of Damián. 'I'm fed up with that tone of yours, d'you hear me? If you've got something to say, say it without wrinkling up your nose, because none of us smells like shit here. I've done my best for all of you even if I didn't get much of an education, understood?'

'Yeah, well it shows.'

The words came out unbidden, as if a mischievous demon-self had slipped them into his mouth, and the world suddenly shrank. His father turned abruptly and took two huge, furious strides towards him. Juan saw him, he must have seen him, but he would always remember the scene in slow motion – his mother hunched, tilting her head to one side, lips drawn in fear, looking like a frightened child before an approaching storm, and Damián's mouth slowly opening, eyes full of surprise fixed on Juan, and Paquita gaping, frozen. It must all have happened very quickly, in an instant, but that's not how he remembered it. In his memory, a deep, hollow echo would always surround his father's disbelieving question and the utter foolishness of his own reply.

'What did you say?'

'I said it shows, that you didn't get an education.'

The hand made a sound of its own as it flew through the air – ffmmmmmm! – before striking his left cheek. Juan reeled from the slap, staggering as if he were drunk, and

170

while reality suddenly recovered its normal speed and colour, the fingers of his father's hand left a shameful, and as yet pale, imprint on his face. But the worst thing was the pain he felt inside, the first urgent tears that he failed to hold back, and the loneliness that engulfed him, treacherously, suddenly, on that stretch of pavement crowded with people, his own family, a forest of empty eyes all desperately looking at anything but him.

'A good wallop, yes, sir.' Damián was the only one who dared come near him, whispering triumphantly and patting Juan on the back. 'A good old wallop. But you deserved it, Juan, you really did.'

Then he left too. Juan stood there a little longer, motionless, feet together, arms hanging by his sides, with a swollen cheek and a vague burning sensation in his ear, jaw and throat. He was trying to understand, wondering how on earth he could have said such a stupid thing, made such a brutal challenge so calmly, inviting his father's blow and his own shame. It had been silly, unfair, even cruel of him; it certainly wasn't what he really thought, and he didn't know why he had said it. His father shouldn't have picked on him when he was telling Damián off, he shouldn't have, because Juan didn't deserve it – he'd worked solidly all morning, without skiving or complaining. His father's insistence on balance irritated Juan. He always told the two brothers off together, with a peculiar understanding of justice that made him the most capricious and arbitrary of judges. This wasn't the first time it had happened, and Juan knew as well as Damián that joint punishments were more ephemeral for being shared, more bearable than those handed out singly. Their father was quick to anger, but had a bad memory. If you rode out the initial storm, harmony returned within ten minutes as if nothing had ever happened.

The day of the move, something changed, although Juan

Olmedo didn't fully realise it at the time. Four years later, as night fell between Quevedo and Bilbao metro stations, he knew that his uncontrolled burst of arrogance, his furious defence of his own merits, always destined to be overshadowed by a Raphael impersonation or the latest joke about General Franco's funeral, had been the end of his fervent admiration for Damián. He hadn't felt proud of himself at the time, and he was still ashamed when he thought of it now, but although he should never have been rude to his father, although he had made a poor decision and it had turned out badly for him, the events of the day had been a revelation. For the very first time, Juan had a sense of his own will, his ability to make his own way in life, and it freed him of the temptation to bemoan his fate, to blame his troubles on destiny or on being in Damián's shadow. From then on, he learnt to do without the support of others. And ever since then, he'd been alone.

'Don't worry about the old man,' his brother had said that night, as they collapsed, exhausted, onto their new beds, surrounded by piles of unopened boxes. 'He's forgotten it already.'

'I know,' answered Juan. A few hours earlier, he'd helped his father carry the wardrobe up to his bedroom, the last item of furniture leaning, dismantled, against the wall of the apartment building. They got one of the doors safely into the lift, but when they tried to get the other one in, the mirrored panel cracked from top to bottom, although it didn't shatter completely. It was the only serious mishap of the day, but his father's tired and sweaty face suddenly looked so defeated that Juan started apologising: 'I'm so sorry about what I said before, Papa, I'm such an idiot. It's not what I think, really, I don't know what came over me.' 'I'm the one who's sorry, son, I'm sorry,' said his father. They carried the rest of the wardrobe upstairs without mentioning the subject again.

'Now he's pissed off with me,' Damián said just before falling asleep. 'I told him I want to leave school, and he said there was no way, I'd have to do my exams and then we'd talk about it again.'

When at last he reached Bilbao metro station, where he planned to turn round, Juan's legs suddenly felt tired and he searched his pockets without conviction. He didn't find much – a few pesetas, a box of matches from Mingo's Bar and a crumpled cinema ticket. The thousand-peseta note he'd thrown down on the bar at Conchi's with the swagger of a cowboy in a spaghetti western was all the money he'd had.

He sat down to rest on a bench, resigned to the fact that he'd have to go home on foot, and suddenly felt scared by just how much he missed her. Charo hated benches, and long walks, but the only money Juan had was what he earned working in his father's shop on Saturday and Sunday mornings, and it didn't go very far. Even-handed when he told his sons off, their father was obsessively careful when it came to their weekly pay, and he was not distinguished by his generosity as a boss. Things had been different in the beginning, when he and Charo first started dating – he'd still had his small Christmas bonus and the money he received as gifts. Charo had already turned him down twice, always with the same excuse, that she was too young to have a boyfriend, but always with the same inviting smile that compelled him to try again, in early March, when she turned seventeen. This time she said yes, and he felt as if he was walking on air. The first time he kissed her on the mouth, he found an unexpected softness and sweetness, like caramel. He'd never been as happy as he was then, during the early days. She showed him off proudly to her friends and laughed at anything he said, and kissed him at traffic lights, and put her arms around him out of the blue in the middle of the street. But the time came when he had used up all his savings, and his exams were getting closer, and it occurred to her to wonder why he didn't have a car, and why he shut himself up in his room every afternoon with his books, and why, at the weekend, they spent all their time just sitting on park benches or going for walks, and having no more than one drink each. She never complained to him about any of this, but Juan could tell what she felt from the weary look in her eyes, the impatient curl of her lips, her curt, lazy answers, and he felt that the prestige of his age and status was quickly deflating, like a balloon whizzing around the room before it emptied completely. This was why, the previous Saturday, in one last desperate attempt to keep her, he had asked Damián to lend him five thousand pesetas so he could take her to one of the biggest and most expensive clubs in town.

'Get off me! For fuck's sake!' Only a moment before she'd seemed dazzled, delighted by the lights, the mirrors, the dark velvet upholstery, the gilded boxes, and the majestic foyer of the converted old theatre. But now she pushed him away violently, almost as soon as they sat down on one of the sofas. 'It's unbelievable. You're so serious but then you can't keep your hands to yourself. Unbelievable.'

'It's only because I like you so much.' He always gave the same response, and it was terrifying because it was true. He liked her so much that when he wasn't with her, he saw her everywhere – on the library ceiling, in the windows of cake shops, in his coffee at breakfast every morning, in the section of sky that he could see from the balcony of his room. And when he was with her, he couldn't take his eyes, or his hands, or his mouth, off her, he was all over her, he couldn't help it, he just had to touch her, kiss her, hold her in his arms until he could feel the shape of her ribs beneath his fingers. He liked her, more than a lot, more than anything else in the world.

'OK, I like you too, but I don't smother you. I'm not on top of you all the time like a bear,' she said, rearranging her clothes. She moved away slightly and looked at him. 'Just control yourself and don't paw at me, not here.'

Juan moved a little way from her, grabbed his glass, put his feet up on the table in front of them, and with his shoulders hunched, sat in a pained silence befitting his offended dignity. When Charo got up and asked him to dance, he just shook his head, and did so each time she came over and held out her hand to him. At midnight, the lights were dimmed to a cool white like a misty moon, to signal the start of the slow dances. Charo came to him once more, taking him by the hand and dragging him on to the dance floor, where she let him put his arms around her.

'I'm sorry, Charo,' he whispered in her ear, feeling the shape of her body against his. 'It's just that I like you so much, seriously, I don't know, it makes me crazy. I can't help it when I'm with you. Please don't be angry with me, Charo, that's all it is, I just like you so much.' He paused and waited for a word, a movement, a signal from her, but he could feel no change in the body moving against his, and impatience prompted his first mistake: 'I couldn't bear it if this ended, if you left me.' She still didn't react, so he abased himself further: 'You're not going to leave me, are you? Tell me you're not.'

He'd received his answer that afternoon, on the phone, just as the family was eating dessert. Juan Olmedo glanced at his watch – it was almost eleven. He lit his last cigarette, got up and set off home. It was a very long way, too long for him to be able to sustain the fantasy of a possible future – quiet years of transition until he'd finished his degree and begun work in a hospital, swapped his wages as a part-time baker for a doctor's salary, and could buy himself a car, and a house; until his real life began and he was somebody at last, no longer the rough draft of a person that he seemed to have been for years. Then she'd realise she'd made a mistake, and she'd come for him, and everything would go back to the way it was before. This thought cheered him for the first stretch of the journey, but he was still a long way from home, his legs weighed a ton, he didn't even have enough money to take the underground, and Charo had left him. Defeat, like a clean, absolute horizon, crushed all his dreams.

Once, he'd had the world in the palm of his hand. He remembered its weight, its size, its perfect spherical fullness. He remembered the heat of that first June morning, the furious blue of a sky that was a furnace even before the sun had fully risen. He could feel the heat of the pavement, which hadn't had a chance to cool during the long, sultry fly-ridden night, through the rubber soles of his trainers. That morning, the ten o'clock bus was full of tired, sweaty people, who looked more bored than ever at having to go to work when the holidays were only a fortnight away. But Juan didn't pay them any attention. Freshly showered and very much awake, he was so nervous he didn't even notice how stiflingly hot it was inside the packed bus. Holding on to the rail with one hand, a full head taller than most other passengers, he went over the exam questions again and again, wavering between the memory of his euphoria as he handed in his script, and fear of possible disaster, the same deep ambivalence that had been eating him up for weeks.

He wasn't the last to arrive at the school, nor was he one of the first, though the office door was still shut. Their tutor smiled when he saw them all – a dozen teenagers, rigid with nerves, some on the verge of hysteria – and muttered, 'It wasn't too bad, not too bad at all,' before going into the office with three or four other teachers. Handing over the exam results was no more than this, a simple formality, so quick that Juan was almost surprised to find himself standing before his tutor's desk.

'Congratulations, Olmedo,' his teacher said as he handed over a small white piece of paper bearing Juan's name, his registration number and another number – an unbelievably, inconceivably, patently absurd, high mark.

'Is this my grade?' Juan asked in disbelief, pointing to the magical number. The teachers all nodded, laughing at his bewilderment. 'Nine point seven two? I got nine point seven two?'

'Yes, the second-highest mark in the entire province of Madrid.' His tutor looked even more happy and proud than Juan himself. 'That's why you were given the second decimal place, to distinguish you from a girl at the Lope de Vega School who also got a nine point seven. In the end, they gave her the higher mark but hers was in Arts subjects and, whatever they say, well, you know . . . Anyway, we've never had anything like it in Villaverde. You deserve it, Olmedo. Congratulations.'

'Shit!' At last Juan looked up from the piece of paper, glanced round at the other teachers seated at the table and then looked at his mark again. 'Shit! Shit! I knew it had gone well, but not this well! I really wasn't expecting it. Shit! I don't know what to say. I still can't believe it!'

He was even more lost for words when his teachers all stood up and started clapping. Their uncharacteristic behaviour attracted the attention of the students waiting behind him, and the first one to see Juan's results started shouting. Soon everyone knew his mark as his classmates carried him out of the office on their shoulders and around the garden of the school. They took off his T-shirt and trainers, and sprayed him with a hose, and he just let them, delighted, stunned, drunk with joy and pride, his faith in himself finally confirmed. He could never have imagined that life would feel as good as it felt when he held this little piece of white paper, with his name on it and the second-best exam results in all of Madrid.

'Olmedo!' Waving another piece of paper in her hand, his favourite teacher called to him as he was leaving. 'Here. I have a friend on the board of examiners and I asked him if I could have this – you can keep it as a souvenir.'

It was his biology exam script. At the top of the first page, in the middle, somebody had written '10' in red felt tip, surrounded it with exclamation marks, and underlined it three times.

'Thanks!'

'No, thank you.' She leant forward and kissed him on both cheeks. 'It's been a pleasure teaching you, Juan, a privilege. We're going to miss you.'

On the journey home, Juan Olmedo felt a new serenity, a new command over himself and others, an utterly new feeling of control over his present and his future. That perfect ten defined him – perhaps even more than his own name. He'd achieved this all by himself, and he was determined to go even further. This was what he was thinking as he got off the bus, opposite his house, and he smiled as he remembered how anxious he'd felt on the outward journey. As he crossed the road, the ground somehow felt more solid beneath his feet. The entrance to the building, like a cool dark cave, welcomed him. The lift was at the top floor, and any other day he would have walked up to the third floor, but this morning he was in no hurry. So, he pressed the button and waited. And then he heard the music.

The laboured, monotonous rhythm of that summer's hit song seemed to bounce off the walls of the building, its absurdly festive chorus and tinny percussion ringing in Juan's ears. Suddenly curious, Juan Olmedo followed the trail of music along a corridor that he'd been down only a couple of times, until he reached the inner courtyard of the building. Square and not very large, the residents used it only for hanging out clothes and storing useless bits of old furniture. There, amongst the junk, he spotted the cracked mirror from his parents' wardrobe; he'd put it there himself when they'd bought a new one. In front of it, staring at herself in the glass, a dark-haired girl was dancing.

When he saw her, Juan Olmedo moved back a few steps and hid behind the door that opened onto the courtyard. Standing close to the wall so that she wouldn't catch sight of him in the mirror, Juan could see a portable record player on the ground, with a single on the turntable. The girl was fairly tall, lithe and young. She was wearing black high-heeled shoes that were too big for her, despite the woollen socks she was wearing that must have been stiflingly hot in the midsummer heat, a tiny checked skirt and a white shirt that she'd tied in a knot around her middle, leaving half her back exposed.

For the moment, that was all he could see. But then the song ended. The girl crouched down beside the turntable to put the record on again, giving him a glimpse of her perfect profile. She had eyelashes that were so thick they looked false, a small straight nose, and a large mouth with full lips; there was something indefinable about the harmony of her features which meant that Juan couldn't take his eyes off her. She stood up, moving in time to the opening bars of the music, wiped her hands on her skirt and returned to her position in front of the mirror. Before she began to dance again, she pulled something that looked like a ballpoint pen from the untidy knot of her long black hair, and it fell, glossy and straight, down her back. She gathered it up again, twisting it like a freshly washed sheet and pinning it skilfully to the top of her head in a bun, exposing the nape of her neck. This movement sent a first shiver down Juan's spine and he gazed, transfixed, at her shamelessly bared skin, following the trails of sweat running down into her shirt. He was still vaguely conscious of what he was doing, but then, when the girl began to swing her hips from side to side, when her long bare legs quivered, electrified, as she released a sudden furious burst of stamping, when she started to rock her pelvis in time to the movements of her arms, Juan lost all sense of who he was, his own name, even the dirty, crumpled piece of paper in his hand. She brought her hands to her body, caressing it, circling her hips lower and lower to the ground in a suggestive, almost obscene movement. From time to time, like the dancers on TV, she would suddenly turn and dance with her back to the mirror, as if she were dancing for him alone, and he felt a sharp, delicious stab in the chest that left him breathless.

'Chariii!' somebody shouted, loud enough that it could be heard above the music. 'What are you up to? Have you borrowed my black shoes again? Come back upstairs right now!'

The girl didn't answer and went on dancing, tracing with her body the most magnificent sequence of figure eights that Juan had ever seen – this was one maths problem he would never be able to solve.

'Chariii!' the woman shouted again, this time more impatiently. 'Did you hear me?'

'Yes, Mama!' she shouted back.

'Well, come upstairs right now!'

'Comiiiing!'

The girl tried out a few more dance moves, twirling round completely before turning off the record player. She put it in its case, carefully covered the mirror with an old door that was leaning against the wall beside it, took off her shoes and turned to go, carrying them in one hand. As he saw her coming towards him, Juan suddenly recovered his senses and realised that she wouldn't be too pleased to find him there hiding behind the door. He told himself he ought to run away, get out of there, but the urge to see her up close was too strong.

'What the . . . ?' She gave a start when she saw him,

against the wall, his biology exam script crumpled into a ball in his hand. 'What are you doing there?'

'Nothing,' he said, his voice so weak he scarcely recognised it.

'Nothing?' She laughed, as if she found his answer funny. 'That's a good one! Who are you anyway?'

'I'm . . .' Juan began hoarsely. He dug his nails into the ball of paper in his hand until he was sure that his voice wouldn't crack again. 'My name's Juan. Juan Olmedo.'

'Oh, yes! You must be the brother of those little girls who always dress the same, and the guy who hangs around with that idiot Nicanor. What's his name? It's Damián, isn't it?' He nodded. 'So why've I never seen you before?' she asked with surprise.

'I've been studying at the school where we used to live, in Villaverde Alto, and at weekends, well . . .' He tailed off, wondering whether the truth would show him in a good light. He knew it probably wouldn't, but he couldn't think of anything better. 'I help my father at the bakery in the mornings, so I'm hardly ever around.'

'You're at school?'

'Yes, well, I've just finished. Next year I'm going to university. To study medicine.'

'Medicine?' she asked, and Juan nodded, blushing despite himself. 'OK, well, if I ever catch you spying on me again, there'll be trouble.'

She moved past him with an angry look that wasn't very convincing, and after only a few steps, she suddenly turned round, barely suppressing a smile.

'And close your mouth, Juan Olmedo, or you'll swallow a fly!'

He smiled too now, a sort of automatic grin that conquered his lips. He was still smiling as he watched her disappear down the corridor, with her black hair, white shirt and short skirt, her thighs the colour of honey. He stayed there for a long time, alone with his smile and violently beating heart. When he set off along the corridor, his legs seemed to move of their own accord as if he were some wind-up toy, still tied to the girl's golden legs, the rivulets of sweat running down her neck, hypnotised by her bare waist.

'How did it go?' asked his mother as she opened the door.

'How did what go?'

'Well, what do you think? Your university entrance exam. What mark did you get?'

'Oh, that! I did well – really well,' he answered. The vision of white cotton knickers glimpsed fleetingly beneath a pleated skirt that was much too short flashed through his mind, triggering a brutal sudden pressure in the centre of his forehead. 'I got one of the top marks – nine point seven.'

'My dear Juan!' His mother flung her arms around him and covered him in kisses. He had trouble reacting even when she took his face in her hands. 'How wonderful, Juanito, but that's wonderful!'

'Yes, I . . .' he began. He looked at the ball of dirty crumpled paper in his hands and lobbed it quickly, neatly, into the umbrella stand. 'It's brilliant. I'm really pleased, but I'm a bit tired now, you know, Mama? I'm going to my room for a while. Will you call me when lunch is ready?'

'I'm so happy, Juan!' cried his mother, sounding very emotional and following him down the hallway. 'I'm so happy for you, son!'

When he flung himself down on his bed, intending to do nothing but preserve this moment of joyous frustration, he didn't realise that Charo's sudden arrival in his life had undermined his first great triumph in an instant, like a naughty child knocking down a house of cards with a swipe of her hand. Later on he thought about it many times – he'd have twenty years to think about it, to curse that loud music and her body, both calling to him; also to bless it just as fervently. Back then, he didn't understand that just when he'd achieved something, when that emphatic red 'ten' put the world in his hands for the brief interlude of a bus journey, a much more pure, intense desire had snatched the winner's medal from him and placed the goal beyond his reach. That morning, Juan Olmedo experienced desire and loss for the first time, and it made him a man. But he was unaware of it as he lay there on his bed, hugging his pillow with his arms and legs, his insides churning. His skin was tingling, his eyes were strangely moist though he didn't want to cry, and he had a sudden, powerful erection from which he felt strangely detached.

His skin never lost that tingling sensation. In the warm dawn that followed the spring day when everything seemed to have ended, he could feel it still, though he was exhausted from his long walk, his pockets were empty, and Charo's poisonous words on the phone were still ringing in his ears. At the entrance to his building, he screwed up his eyes and ran towards the stairs, as if a powerful, cunning enemy lay in wait in the gloomy courtyard. Upstairs, the flat was dark, but his desk lamp greeted him with a warm glow, like the embrace of an old friend. He opened the book he'd been working on that afternoon and decided to run through the diagram of the human skeleton, each bone labelled with its name and description, its size and function; it almost seemed pleased to see him. He had only reached the spine when he heard the front door open. It was a quarter to one in the morning. Even though Damián had already opened a bakery of his own, he rarely returned home this early. Juan closed his eyes, feeling infinitely weary.

'Well, well,' said Damián, raising his eyebrows in mock surprise, 'if it isn't Marie Curie.'

He closed the door quietly and flung his jacket on the bed with a flourish, like a bullfighter tossing his cape. He sat down in the armchair, stretched out his legs and put his bare feet up on the desk, only a few inches from Juan's anatomy textbook.

'What the hell's wrong with you?' Damián asked irritably as he unbuttoned his shirt. 'You're a disgrace, I can't take you anywhere.'

'Leave me alone,' Juan muttered, still not looking at him.

'Leave you alone? Yeah, I should. All you do is show me up. What's the matter with you?'

Juan's silence propelled Damián out of the armchair, like an invisible spring. He removed his shirt and threw it on top of his jacket, then leant over and gripped Juan's shoulder, hissing in his ear:

'OK, I'll tell you, Juanito. The thing is, Charo's too much for you, that's what. You thought I didn't know? Mama told me after supper and that's why I took you to Conchi's, to cheer you up, but even that didn't work. You should stick to the reliable old bangers and leave the sports cars to the experts. It was so obvious, you should have seen it coming. What did you think you were doing with a girl like that, you sad bastard? She's out of your league.'

Juan hadn't intended to react, to say or do anything, but suddenly he turned and thrust his fist into his brother's face. He missed, because Damián was expecting it.

'Hey!' Damián ducked to avoid the punch and caught Juan off-balance, grabbing both his wrists. 'You want to hit me? Oh, I'm so scared! Come on, tell me: bet you haven't even fucked her, have you?' He laughed, as if he found his own question funny. 'It's so obvious you haven't. And she's begging for it, just begging for it, you can see it a mile away. You're an idiot, Juan, a real idiot! All that studying . . .'

Damián suddenly let go of his wrists and finished undressing as if there was no one else in the room. Juan closed his eyes, and clenched his fists. And as he turned back to the diagram of the spine, he wondered what sound human bones would make as they shattered.

On the day of Tamara's eleventh birthday, Andrés almost
didn't go to her party. The previous afternoon, as the west
wind brought with it billions of tiny, invisible droplets of
water that seeped into everything, he had a rare row with his
mother, in the only hypermarket in town. Andrés hated
shopping at the best of times and normally couldn't have
cared less about his clothes. He was the one who tried to
cheer up Maribel when she bemoaned the fact that her only
child always had to wear second-hand clothes, hand-me-
downs from his cousins, neighbours or acquaintances who
suddenly thought of him just as they were about to throw the
clothes away. This time, though, it was different.

That afternoon, when he got home from school, before
even saying hello or taking off his rucksack, Andrés reminded
his mother that she had to take him shopping. He didn't
want to watch his cartoons and wouldn't even sit down to
eat. He ate his sandwich at the bus stop and when they got to
the shops he didn't ask his mother to buy him a water or a
Coke, even though he was thirsty, because he wanted her to
be in a good mood. Together they looked for the CD that
Tamara really wanted, and then they went to the children's
clothes section, where he spent a long time choosing a long-
sleeved shirt with wide blue and white stripes, and a plain
blue fleece. But he turned round to find that he was on his
own. His mother was heading back towards him carrying a
shirt on a hanger.

'Look at this cute little T-shirt,' she said, holding out a
very light short-sleeved polo shirt with horizontal green and
brown stripes. 'How about this?'

'No,' he said, shaking his head emphatically. 'I want this
one, Mama.'

'Let's see,' said Maribel. Pursing her lips disapprovingly,
she examined the shirt and glanced at the price tag, not even
bothering to look at the fleece her son was holding out to

her. 'No. No way. Why would you want a long-sleeved shirt? You're not going to a wedding or anything. You'd only wear it once, and as for this big, thick thing, it's never cold enough to wear something like that here! Now you could wear this little T-shirt in summer as well. And I'll get you one of those nice, light V-neck jumpers in green or brown to match.'

'I said no!' Andrés thrust out his arms, clenched his fists and shook them, in a gesture that was almost comical. 'I'm not going to wear it. No way! I won't go to the party tomorrow, I'll stay at home, and that's that.'

'What's wrong with you? I don't understand.'

'I'm not going to the party dressed like a hick, Mama, don't you get it? I don't want to. I'd rather not go.'

'Like a hick?' said Maribel, looking warily at her son. 'What do you mean? Who's been putting these ideas into your head? Sara? Tamara? Like a hick! You don't know what you're talking about.'

'Yes, I do,' muttered Andrés, his anger giving way to dismay, his voice now thin, like a thread about to break. 'And I don't need anyone else to tell me. I can see things for myself.'

'I can see everything, Mama,' he thought to himself.

For a moment, they stared at each other, without a word, the mother cross and a little worried, the son ready to stand his ground, anticipating how upset Maribel would be the next day when he really did refuse to go to the party, even though he wanted to go very much.

'Well,' Maribel said at last, in a rather final tone. 'Come on, I'd like to look at . . .'

'No,' said Andrés, sitting down on the floor. He hugged his legs and put his head between his knees. 'I'm not going anywhere and no way am I going to wear that stupid outfit. Don't buy it, I'm sick of . . . of . . .'

He hunched his head even further, feeling the welcoming,

almost velvety softness of his worn jeans against his forehead. He didn't want to cry, and he didn't want to tell his mother the truth, or say a single word he might regret later. And anyway, his mother wouldn't understand. Maribel would never understand what the arrival of Sara and the Olmedo family had meant to her son, to his life of cheap T-shirts and his free place at a school for rich kids. The first time the silver BMW, which was so big it barely fitted down the narrow streets in the centre of town, stopped by the school gates and its door opened just for him, Andrés looked round before getting into the passenger seat and saw instant envy, and shock, in the murky eyes of his schoolmates. It was quite a triumph. There was Alonso, the son of the locksmith who'd made a fortune providing the locks for all the developments in the area, and Medina, whose family now built villas on what had once been farmland, and Solís, who was a real moron and always got bad marks, but whose future was assured thanks to his father's property company, and Auxi, Medina's cousin, who'd been boasting about her mother's expensive new car. There they all were, frozen still, quiet for once. Then Andrés made a bet with himself that things would be different from now on, and they were. So far this term, he hadn't had to get into any fights he knew he'd lose. Nobody had called his mother a servant, nobody had made snide remarks about her going out every night, nobody had asked where his father was, nobody had laughed at his tatty old rucksack or complained about the school food his grandmother cooked.

And his friendship with Tamara had only added to his new status. Andrés suspected that all the boys in his class had a crush on her, and the girls, though they made fun of her accent and her clothes, would have given anything to be like her. Tamara – who sounded so posh, and was good at English, and was so tall and pretty and trendy and clever, and from the big city – was his, because she never left his side. Andrés couldn't understand it, but he accepted this unusual piece of luck and did everything he could not to lose it. Tamara was a strange child; she never said or did anything that any normal girl wouldn't say or do, but there was a solitary air about her even when she was smiling, or playing with the others. He knew her better than anyone else, and he assumed that this was what had made them such good friends, because she was the only person he felt comfortable with. Sometimes, after school, they went into town on their bikes, and they just sat in the harbour and watched the boats; they could stay like that for ages, just the two of them, and they didn't even have to say a word until one of them realised it was time to go home. Andrés felt that his friend had a secret, but he never asked her because he didn't want to share his own secrets, and he always said the same – 'Don't know' – when Sara or Maribel asked him about her.

Maribel had been asking him a lot of questions recently, and it made him feel uncomfortable. Andrés loved his mother, loved her very much, but he didn't like it when she embarrassed him, or forced him to do things that he found embarrassing, like going to the party wearing hideous clothes. Andrés had been eleven for months, and he knew it was silly to attach too much importance to clothes, but he also knew how things were and that it wasn't his fault. Tamara was like a miracle, like hitting the jackpot, and he didn't want to risk anyone laughing at him in front of her, because he was old enough to know that you couldn't always rely on miracles.

'What do you think?'

His mother's voice made him look up; she was determined to sound as if nothing had happened. Squeezed into a tight, low-cut, purple Lycra dress, its long narrow skirt slit up to mid-thigh, Maribel was turning round, smiling and looking pleased with herself. It was just the kind of dress she liked, the kind that made men stare in the street, that made builders wolf-whistle as she walked past, that made shopkeepers come outside when they saw her looking in their shop window, the kind of dress that made Andrés ashamed to be seen with her. So he pursed his lips and watched unhappily as Maribel tried to smooth the wrinkles out across her hips.

'You don't like it,' she said at last.

'No,' said the boy. 'It's too small for you.'

'Small?' said Maribel, opening her eyes so wide that her son couldn't tell if she really did find this hard to believe, or if she was only pretending to be surprised. 'What do you mean, small? This is how it's meant to look – close fitting. It's stretchy, see?'

'OK, well, it doesn't look nice on you. It makes your stomach look fat and it's all creased up at the back.'

And then the thing that Andrés dreaded the most happened. Maribel suddenly went very red and looked up at the ceiling, blinking furiously and muttering to herself, 'Maybe, maybe.' Then she rushed back to the changing room, leaving her son feeling even worse than he had when they'd been arguing. He jumped up off the floor as if it were red-hot and, stuffing his hands into his pockets, tried to think of a way to tell his mother that she was very pretty, but she'd look better if she dressed like other mothers, even if it meant her getting less attention in the streets. He couldn't find her, and when she, looking defenceless and almost childlike, finally found him, she didn't know what to say either.

'You're right, you know,' said Maribel, breaking the silence at last. She put the purple dress down on a table. 'I had a good look at it in the mirror, and it isn't all that pretty. Definitely not worth the money. And I was thinking, if you really want that shirt, we could look for a jumper to go with it, one of the ones with a V-neck I was telling you about, in blue, instead of green. But you've got to promise you'll wear it, OK? I want to start saving up for a flat, so we can't go spending our money on silly things.'

Standing on tiptoes, Andrés stretched up to give his mother a kiss and, as she leant forward, he put his arms around her neck, as if he wanted to hang on. It wasn't the first time he'd had the vague feeling that he was the one looking after this adult woman who in turn looked after him, who tucked him up in bed at night and gave him medicine when he was ill. In some of the old westerns he watched on TV, Indian attacks would force the white farmers to ride out, leaving their wives alone to look after the farm and the children. As the men prepared to leave – with a woman in a long dress and white apron always weeping quietly in the background, cradling a baby in her arms – the man of the house would address the eldest son, a boy of Andrés's age, handing him a rifle and telling him that he would now have to protect his mother. Andrés always saw himself in the brave faces of those children; Andrés's mother wasn't holding a baby in her arms, and she didn't have a husband, but they too lived on the frontier, with one foot in enemy territory, although it wasn't Indians they had to worry about. Andrés was very young, but he felt that his love for his mother somehow kept her safe, like the rifle in the shaky hands of the boy on the remote farm, the last gun before the wilderness. Beyond this conviction, his moods went up and down like a yo-yo as he defended his mother to his grandmother for things that he secretly disapproved of himself, or forced her, as he had that afternoon, without really knowing why, to give up things that would have made her happy. The most prominent feature of this endless inner confusion was something that Maribel would never be able to understand – his friendship with Sara Gómez, the affection that had become a necessity. Sara had shown him that his mother's habits were no more than that, and they weren't important. Every time Sara laughed at his grandmother's criticisms of Maribel, or when she asked Maribel casually where she'd been on Friday night and whether she'd had a good time, whenever she offered to have him stay at her house so that Maribel could go to a party or a wedding, Andrés admired the supremely casual way that Sara made life seem so simple, and he started to think that perhaps the world really was more straightforward than he thought.

Sara was also the first to compliment him the following day, when he arrived at the Olmedos' in his new clothes.

'Wow, Andrés!' she whispered in his ear, after giving him a kiss. 'You look so handsome, and so smart!'

Just as Maribel came through the door, wearing one of the dresses Andrés actually liked, Tamara's uncle said loudly, so that all eyes turned to him:

'Hey, we look as if we're on the same team!' And it was true, they did – they were dressed identically. Andrés glanced at his mother, and she smiled. He told himself it must be because she was also pleased with his new stripy shirt, blue jumper and jeans. Tamara looked lovely in her present from Juan – a red polka-dot flamenco dress, with a matching shawl, bead necklaces, combs, bracelets and shoes with slight heels that made her a whole head taller than Andrés, instead of the usual half. But it didn't matter – he felt good, so good that he dared show off a little in front of the other kids from school who'd been invited to the party, and during tea he ran to the kitchen a couple of times to get glasses and spoons without having to ask anyone where they were. He even switched on Tamara's games console in the absence of its owner to show off his skills. Time passed by in a flash until, around eight thirty, the doorbell began to ring at regular intervals, gradually reclaiming all the other guests. Andrés already knew that he would probably be the last to leave because his mother would insist on helping Juan to do the washing-up, and he was right. But he was the first to find Alfonso, when the adults returned to the living room and were surprised not to find him there with the children.

Alfonso Olmedo was in the garden, standing almost rigid, with his arms hanging by his sides and his head tilted, eyes fixed on a point in the sky. Andrés saw him through the living-room window and went outside, guessing what was happening even before he opened the door. The wind slapped him in the face like an invisible enemy lying in wait, before sweeping into the room and hurling the discarded wrapping paper against the far wall with a violence that seemed deliberate, almost human. In the yellow light of the street lamps, Andrés immediately saw the impossible sight of two seagulls hanging absolutely motionless in the wind. Wings outstretched, heads straight, beaks shut, the birds looked artificial, like an illustration or a doctored photograph, an image held by an invisible hand in front of the insubstantial sky. But they were seagulls, and they were alive. Alfonso Olmedo knew it, and he jerked his chin in their direction, his eyes wide with fear, as Andrés joined him. The boy placed a hand on Alfonso's back, telling him not to worry, trying to comfort him. They were standing like this when Juan found them. At first, the scene baffled him.

'It's the east wind,' explained Andrés, pointing at the sky with one hand, while leaving the other comfortingly on Alfonso's back. 'It's just risen, but it's coming. It makes the gulls go mad. See that? They don't know which way to fly. At first they just go round and round in circles. They go one way, then the other way, then they suddenly drop – it's like they've forgotten how to fly. Sooner or later, they hit the wind head on and they can't go forward. They keep trying for a bit and then they just keep still and wait for the wind to drop. It's creepy, isn't it?'

Andrés looked up and saw in both Juan's and Sara's eyes that they agreed, even though neither of them answered.

'It's sinister,' said Juan at last, as if he had been searching for the right word to describe what he was seeing.

'Yes,' said Sara, frowning. 'Poor things.'

'It's only the wind,' said Andrés, shaking his head. 'But it is scary. I'm scared that one day we'll all end up mad, just like the birds.'

II

❦

The Price of
Rifles

The following day, a Sunday, Sara Gómez got up late with a feeling of well-being so unfamiliar that, at first, she scarcely recognised it. She sat up in bed and looked round the room suspiciously, as if something – the furniture, her belongings – had been rearranged during the night as she slept; but there was nothing within the four walls of her bedroom that could explain this sudden change. Her head felt heavy and she had that pleasant woolly feeling that comes with a good hangover – the kind that numbs the brutal process of awakening, but without the headaches and guilt produced by a serious binge. She lay down again, curling up in the bed with the covers up to her nose, savouring every last drop of this unexpected and mysterious sensation.

After a fickle and tumultuous love affair with alcohol that had lasted almost thirty years, Sara had reached a state of disciplined abstinence that could be summed up with one basic rule: she never drank when she was alone. But she did allow herself one drink, or two, if she was in the company of others, because that didn't frighten her. Since she had moved to her home by the sea, these rules had changed a little, yielding to the will of the landscape and the different nature of her solitude. The previous night had been an exception, she told herself, and she hadn't drunk to excess. This conviction lulled her back to sleep.

Her father had always had a brandy after dinner. Sara couldn't remember the point when she began to feel envi-ous, but by the time she decided to join him, she was already smoking at home and bringing in a wage at the end of every month. When her mother first saw Sara with a glass of brandy in her hand, she covered her face with her apron: the universal gesture she used to express indignation, joy, shock, surprise, sadness. But her husband saw nothing wrong in Sara drinking. Arcadio knew his daughter better than Sebastiana did, for in her face, in the firm set of her mouth and her determined brow, in the particular way she lifted her head as if scenting a threat, he could see himself and the man he had once been. So, every time he refilled his own glass, he poured a little into Sara's and frowned in silent response to his wife's endless, droning complaints that drinking was for men; men, not young girls – even the adverts said so.

But despite what the adverts claimed, brandy did provide warmth and comfort to women. It protected them, within and without, mercifully blanketing them from their memories, covering their eyes with the grey neutral veil of sleep. When she discovered this, Sara threw herself into its warm embrace with the joyful recklessness of a young girl falling in love for the first time, and, in the absence of other loves, she cultivated it impatiently and tenaciously. Until she saw its true face. Then, her own poverty saved her. People with more interests, more worries, more properties, more prospects than her, would have succumbed to the gentle fires of dissipation, but Sara had nothing but herself, and she couldn't afford to lose herself like this, drop by drop, waking each dawn with a dry muddy paste filling every recess of her mouth and a thick, solid thirst gripping her between the last drink and the next one. This was why, one unremarkable evening, she discovered she couldn't meet her father's eye. Dignity was her first reason to stop drinking.

But difficult lives produce difficult adults, and it was difficult to shake off the memory – and the ease – of the amber-coloured liquid. It was comforting, it was cheap, and sometimes it was indispensable. Sara Gómez didn't want to start drinking again, but she went back to it, time and time again, each time her path seemed unclear and she lost her direction, every time she couldn't move forward and found herself rooted to the spot. She was familiar with this variety of panic, the extreme weariness that comes from being stuck in a rut. Alone, she might have found a way out, but she wasn't alone; she was responsible for two exhausted adults who had been ill-treated by life and who deserved, at the very least, a peaceful end. When she faltered, she turned back to brandy to give her the warmth and comfort she needed, until her tongue began to taste muddy once more. Then she would stop, but at the back of her mind she always knew that it wouldn't be for good. The constant premonition of a relapse didn't torment her because she'd learnt to live with ambiguity the way a fish swims in water, out of necessity, instinct. The little girl split down the middle who changed the way she saw things as easily as she changed dresses, who could see in colour and in black and white, had grown into a discreet figure, an ordinary woman, but one who never quite fitted in. She had adapted to the emotional chaos of her life as best she could, but beyond this, she no longer expected or aspired to anything. And then, suddenly, everything changed. The gears of the universe shifted, a star changed trajectory, and all of a sudden, the woman without a future saw the light. When Sara Gómez finally understood that she could grasp her destiny in her own hands, she also realised that sobriety would be essential if her plans were to succeed. From that moment on, she had to be much more canny, to think fast, be alert to the smallest detail, and take scrupulous care of her reputation. She bade farewell to brandy with a melancholy kiss and some regret, like leaving a treacherous lover. Yet she didn't miss it in the frenzy of the fraudulent existence she was about to begin, nor in the explosive events that led to a much better life, a brand-new normality that she would never have dared imagine for herself.

Now, living here by the sea, she discovered that brandy had changed with her. The taste was different – subtler, less harsh – and so was its power. After thirty years of passion and guilt, Sara Gómez had finally learnt to drink for pleasure rather than the meagre reward of forgetfulness and a long and heavy sleep. Once again she drank alone but only a single glass, never quite full, after dinner – and even then, not every night. The silent ritual of warming the drink in her hands, sipping it slowly, gazing at the sky or reading a book, had become the best moment in many of her days.

The night before, she had suddenly renounced this discipline. She wasn't entirely sorry, because her body had been magnanimous enough not to make her pay. During the party and particularly afterwards, when all the children had gone home and Juan Olmedo had asked her to stay for one last drink in the middle of the battlefield to which his living room had been reduced, she had been much more aware of what was going on around her than of how much she was drinking. Except for the moment of terror that had paralysed Alfonso – the sight of a pair of seagulls suspended motionless in the sky – nothing odd had happened. Tamara had seemed happy, calm, and as tired as was to be expected after so many hours of being the centre of attention. But Sara couldn't stop thinking about how anxious Juan had seemed beforehand, and the nervous edge to his voice when he decided to confide in her, in advance of the party – a revelation she had not expected or prompted, but which was delivered with the fluency of a well-rehearsed speech. His dark fears seemed excessive, especially in view of the placid scenes she then witnessed, but Sara knew from her own experience that an excess of caution could be more significant than its absence. Something didn't quite fit, there was some important detail missing in the gaps between his brief, ordered speech.

'My brother Damián, Tamara's father, died exactly a year

ago,' he'd explained as they walked briskly, with the wind against them, down the town's main shopping street. 'On Tamara's birthday. She had waited for him all afternoon before cutting her birthday cake, but he didn't arrive in time. He only got back after midnight and Tamara was already asleep by then, although she'd had a huge tantrum earlier in the evening. Damián had had a lot to drink and his reflexes were slow. I was waiting up for him because I was worried he hadn't phoned to say he'd be late, nobody knew where he was, and I was angry with him for being in such a state – he was always drunk, he wasn't eating or sleeping . . . he just kept overdoing it. Anyway, we had an argument, he became very agitated, and then he lost his balance and fell down the stairs. It was a very long, straight staircase with no landings, and he was unlucky, very unlucky, because he cracked his skull on a step. My sister-in-law, his wife, had died seven months earlier in a car crash. I'm worried about how Tamara is going to react to this birthday. I would have preferred not to celebrate it, but she insists on having a party and I suppose she's right. I think it might be worse, over-emphasising the fact that this is the anniversary of her father's death. That's why I wasn't listening to you. I'm sorry.'

That morning, Juan Olmedo had called her from work. His niece's birthday was only a couple of days away, and though he'd been wondering for weeks about what to get her, he hadn't come up with anything until the previous night, just before he fell asleep. It was a great idea: a flamenco dress. He was sure she'd like it – it was the sort of thing every little girl would like – and it also seemed to be a way of confirming her in her new life, helping her to set down roots in the place where they were now living. A colleague at the hospital had given him the name of a dressmaker who sold the dresses, and he was ringing to ask if Sara would come with him, because he wasn't sure he'd be able to choose properly. 'I could have asked Maribel,' he added, 'but I'm not too confident of her taste.' Sara smiled and replied that she didn't have any plans for that afternoon and would be delighted to go shopping with him. She also thought to herself that it would be an excellent opportunity to discuss her ideas about Maribel's future and Maribel buying a property of her own.

They arranged to meet mid-afternoon in a bar in the centre of town. Sara brought the subject up straight away, before they'd even finished their coffee. Juan agreed that although she seemed slightly frivolous and impulsive, Maribel was actually a very hardworking, responsible woman, and that it did seem like a good idea for her to invest the money she'd inherited. But then his attention seemed to wander as they walked along the street, reduced to a series of mechanical nods and grunts of approval. Sara realised that he wasn't listening.

'Well,' she snorted halfway through the list of possibilities she was weighing up, 'I can tell you find this absolutely fascinating.'

'No, it's not that,' he said, meeting her eye for the first time since they'd left the bar, 'I'm just slightly preoccupied. I'm sorry.'

So then he told her the story of how his brother, Tamara's father, had died. After this, neither of them spoke, until the dress they chose for Tamara gave them a comfortably trivial subject of conversation for the way back.

From then on, Sara Gómez had not stopped analysing Juan's dry account of Damián Olmedo's death. Whatever she was doing – having a shower, cooking, watching television – the image of a man falling down the stairs stayed with her, as if it were permanently imprinted on her memory. She went over his account with methodical thoroughness, searching for any crack, any chink that would allow her to prise it open and see what lay beneath. But all the questions that came to mind had immediate, obvious answers. After all, people died every day in accidents in the home, silly, cruel accidents – choking on a plum stone, falling off a roof, electrocuting themselves – and these deaths were so trivial, so brutally reasonable that they didn't even deserve a mention in the papers. Juan Olmedo had been there when the accident happened, but there was nothing strange in that. Families tended to get together for children's birthdays, and Juan was probably very close to Tamara, to her parents, because otherwise he wouldn't have taken her in when she was left on her own. That he had seen his brother fall and die did add a sinister dimension to his story, but it was still within the bounds of logic. If he was there, at the top of the stairs, he wouldn't have been able to prevent the accident, and if he was at the bottom and saw his brother fall towards him, he wouldn't have had time to react. When Sara first met the family the previous summer, Tamara had told her that her parents had died in an accident, and that was about all she'd said. Sara had assumed that the child was talking about a car accident, and later Tamara had confirmed that this was the case, adding odd pieces of information. Now Sara realised that she was talking only about the accident in which her mother had died, but even that had a simple explanation. For if her father had arrived home late and drunk on her birthday, if he'd had a row about it with his brother and had fallen down the stairs, the memory would seem like a nightmare to the small child. Perhaps she felt it had been partly her fault and, even if this wasn't the case, the version of the story in which both parents died together would always seem simpler than the truth; nobody asked too many questions about a car crash. Perhaps it was Juan himself who had advised his niece to tell this half-truth, and Sara would not only have understood it, but would have approved of the strategy. The story had enough ingredients to make it seem credible, yet something made Sara go back to the beginning, sifting all the information once more, wondering where the error lay.

The worries that Juan had provoked burst like soap bubbles when she saw how easily Tamara played the part of hostess at her party. And yet, while she was chatting to Juan in a corner of the sitting room, Sara felt that perhaps the child's failure to react badly only deepened the mystery – it would have seemed more normal for Tamara to be depressed or withdrawn, for her smiles to seem forced, for her to get upset when blowing out her candles. In Tamara's cheerful demeanour, there seemed to be no space, no corner for the memory of her dead father.

The following morning Sara hadn't entirely forgotten her unease, but when she finally managed to get out of bed, at about eleven, she was much more interested in the unusual feeling of well-being that she couldn't quite place. She opened the bathroom door and an icy draught froze her to the spot for a moment. 'That's what happens when you go to bed drunk,' she thought, realising she'd left the bathroom window open all night. Although she was shivering, she didn't feel like closing it because the cold air cleared her head, and the sky, still arrogantly blue so near to December, boasted a bright round sun, like an assurance of spring. She wrapped herself tightly in her bathrobe and, on feeling the fabric against her skin, she suddenly understood. The bath-robe was dry, perfectly dry, as thick and stiff as if she'd just taken it down from the washing line in the middle of August. It was over a month, maybe two, since she'd felt anything like it. Then she knew what the seagulls knew, and under-stood at last the strange phrase the people of the town used when speaking of the wind which they couldn't live without in winter. 'The east wind blows it all away,' they said, and it was true. Sara returned to the bedroom, opened wide the windows to the balcony, and gave herself up to the wind. It beat against her face, blasted through her hair, danced inside her head and filled her lungs, sweeping away the murky sadness of the shortest days. Everything fled before the formidable force of the wind, like some powerful classical god.

Sara ran downstairs, secured the doors to stop them banging, improvised a series of paperweights from ashtrays and pans, and opened all the windows. She'd forgotten the other face of the east wind, the spiteful devil that made the sky boil, and tempers fray, in the immense cauldron of summer's most hellish days. As things started to fly about the room despite all her precautions, she thought again of the previous night and imagined the mess her neighbours' house must still be in this morning. It was as if the wind had the power to sweep away foolish ideas too, because she was suddenly amazed that she'd devoted so much time to something that was simply a tragic accident. The twists and turns of fate were always mysterious – and she should know that better than anyone. If Juan Olmedo ever heard her own story, he'd wonder how she could possibly have come up with such a strange tale.

Once the east wind had had its fun, she went to the kitchen and made herself some coffee. She didn't want to eat anything because it was already very late. She pictured herself exchanging a few words with the newspaper seller or perhaps with a waiter in a bar if she managed to go for a walk in the afternoon, and as she stirred sugar into her coffee, she pondered the pattern of her Sunday mornings.

'The truth is, I'm bored,' she said quietly, even though her neighbour couldn't hear her or absolve her for all her suspicions. 'That's all it is . . .'

In October 1963, Sara Gómez Morales began to attend classes far removed from the prestigious schooling of her recent past. She remembered the torments of algebra and compared that to learning shorthand, which she viewed as a pastime, a simple technique to be mastered through hours of practice. She felt similarly about typing, although the typewriter seemed alien to someone accustomed to using only a pen and paper. That summer she had learnt many other strange things: working out how much bleach was needed to wash white clothes without damaging the fabric or turning it yellow, for instance. Ironing a jacket through a wet cloth. Knowing exactly when a sauce made from tomatoes was ready, the moment when the flesh had given up its juices but the oil hadn't yet risen to the surface. Cleaning anchovies, removing the head and backbone without damaging the flesh. Beating the doormat with that giant wicker carpet beater. Cleaning the grouting between the old, dull tiles, applying a foul-smelling liquid with a little brush, and later, once it was dry, spreading it over the tiles with a cloth in an attempt to restore some of the shine stolen by the years, rubbing until her arms ached.

Sara learnt how to do all of this with the same determination, the same sharp stubbornness with which she had sweated over maths problems, muttering under her breath that those two bloody trains that left Madrid and Barcelona at the same time and passed through Calatayud thirty-five minutes apart wouldn't get the better of her. This sense of pride, this unconditional self-belief, was the only thing she had, the only aspect of her life that wasn't given to her by other people. It defined her and was both a flaw and a virtue, changing the course of her life one fine morning in July. Sara had returned from the walk she took every day on the pretext of buying bread, to find her room tidied, her clothes hanging in the wardrobe and her bed made.

Until then, she'd lived with her parents like a guest, a visitor, the natural successor to the little girl from another home who came only for Sunday lunch. For a fortnight they had all played their part in this fiction. She emerged from her room only at mealtimes and nobody else went in there. Dirty clothes piled up on the bed with open books, biscuit wrappers and half-eaten bags of crisps. That morning, her mother had broken the unspoken rule by tidying her room, and Sara didn't even have to wonder why she flushed with shame at the thought of it. But the room, with its sloping floor, now seemed bigger, more comfortable and more welcoming than before. At that moment, Sara Gómez Morales finally confronted her destiny. Everyone had treated her gently but she had only managed to survive the confusion of her precarious existence by learning to be hard on herself. When her godmother had said goodbye to her at the door to the house in the Calle Velázquez, there had been no mercy, and there would be none now either. Sara thought of the room in her dolls' house that was a mirror image of the one she used to inhabit, a world created for a little girl whose only sin had been to grow up. And once again she felt the anger she'd felt on a night a lifetime ago, the night she turned sixteen, when she suddenly understood not only why she could no longer fit her legs under her desk, but also why she would never have another desk made for her. Doña Sara had grown tired of playing mother and didn't deserve to see her shed so much as a tear. What Sara could not allow now was that her own mother, who never even had the chance to teach her to play, should treat her like the young lady she no longer was.

Her mother was in the kitchen, chopping onions, garlic and parsley on a wooden chopping board. Sara went and stood beside her, not knowing what to say, where to start. The seconds passed slowly. The garlic was chopped so finely it was almost a paste. The knife reduced the onion to tiny pieces, and Sara silently envied the happy unconcern of the blade. She couldn't bring herself to risk either humiliating her mother by thanking her, or offending her by asking her never to clean her room again. Then, Sebastiana turned and scraped the contents of the chopping board into a frying pan, wiped her hands on her apron, and smiled.

'Hello, dear,' she greeted her daughter in a bright voice. 'How are things going?'

'Fine,' answered Sara. 'What are you making?'

'Beef stew, for lunch.'

'Lovely! Are you adding potatoes?'

'Yes, but not till later,' said her mother, looking away, glancing at the pan, as if confused by this sudden curiosity and her daughter's exaggerated enthusiasm. 'Potatoes are softer than meat, so they cook quickly. If I put them in now, they'll go mushy. So that's why you have to wait until almost the end. Half an hour is plenty.'

'Oh,' murmured Sara, 'I didn't know that.'

Neither of them could find anything more to say. Sebastiana washed her hands, and once she'd dried them thoroughly, she washed the chopping board and dried it with the same excessive care she had applied to her fingers, cuticles and nails. Sara realised how ill at ease her mother was, but her own hands were empty and she wouldn't find a knife in any drawer that could cut through the tough, invisible membrane that separated them, keeping them at a polite, cautious distance from each other. They had never learnt to talk to each other and both could feel the weight of the air above their heads, pressing down on them like a plunger. Then Sebastiana put her hand to her forehead and smiled.

'The washing!' she exclaimed, relieved to have found something to say at last. 'I've got to hang out the washing, I forgot.'

'No, Mama,' Sara said quickly, looking round for the washing basket, which was on a chair. She grabbed it before her mother could get to it. 'I'll do it.'

She opened the window and found a little basket of pegs on the ledge. She struggled with the pulleys until she realised that clothes were only hung beyond the knot. She was determined not to make any more mistakes after that. 'It's easy,' she told herself every time she pegged an item of clothing to the line. 'Easy.' She worked slowly, taking care over every movement, thinking she mustn't let anything drop down into the courtyard. She took a shirt from the washing basket and turned it upside down, then the right way up, then upside down again.

'Mama,' she said at last, 'how do you hang shirts – by the shoulders or by the hem?'

'By the hem. And it's better if you peg it at the seams, because that way the peg marks don't show quite as much and it's easier to iron.'

Sara hung out the shirts correctly but almost everything else was wrong, though she did manage to pair up all the socks and hang out the entire basket without anything falling into the courtyard. When she'd finished she felt quite pleased with herself, not realising that taking twenty-five minutes over this simple task was ridiculous.

'Right,' she said as she closed the window and turned around, holding the washing basket, not really knowing what to do with it. 'That's done.'

And then she fell silent. Her mother was standing very near, looking at Sara with moist eyes, wringing her apron. Sara couldn't bear the tremble in her mother's eyes, the veiled tears dancing in her pupils.

'Don't cry, Mama.' Sara threw down the washing basket and went to her, choking back violent sobs. 'I'm so sorry.'

'Why should you be sorry, dear?'

'I don't know, Mama, I don't know.'

Sebastiana opened her short, thick arms, and Sara, who was much taller, shrank into them. They stayed like that for a long time, belatedly learning to communicate without words. Meanwhile, the stew caught on the bottom of the pan. That day they had to have fried eggs and potatoes for lunch. When Arcadio arrived home at two that afternoon he didn't ask any questions, but realised that something had changed.

If Sara Gómez Morales was ever cruel and merciless, it was then, when she decided to tear off her old skin with her own fingernails. This was the moment when she actively chose –

or thought she was choosing – the only life left to her, and fed her anger until she had suppressed any temptation to look back. Sometimes, at night, she found herself thinking of Juan Mari, Maruchi, and the Beatles, amiable inhabitants of a distant shore, but she quickly tried to forget them, to bury them beneath other memories. Even in her worst moments, when she felt utterly miserable, Sara remained cool-headed enough to understand that anything – hate, bitterness, revenge – would do her less harm than the soft, rosy nostalgia of a string of broken dreams.

And, for a time, she succeeded, especially during the day. Sara threw herself into a frenzied schedule of activities that kept her busier than she'd ever been before. She made sure to keep herself occupied inwardly too, rigorously controlling the flow and nature of her thoughts as she concentrated on the new tasks she tackled each morning. Sometimes she ended up with a headache as she forced herself to be perpetually cheerful. At others, she resorted to the same childish fantasising that she had indulged in only a few months earlier, when she daydreamed about married life with Juan Mari – their honeymoon in Venice, a spacious, elegant home, summers by a quiet beach in the north, a couple of beautiful blond children in due course – but now she planned a very different future, limited to the confines of a poky, old third-floor flat. She imagined doing up the bathroom and kitchen, enlarging the windows, laying wooden floors, knocking down half the walls and erecting others – mad schemes that would have seemed less so if she had ever learnt to plane floorboards or mix cement herself.

Her parents listened to her, their shoulders hunched, exchanging alarmed looks as they watched her going about the house, never stopping, moving furniture and then moving it back again, tying back the curtains and then letting them go, tidying things that were already tidy, battling against dust that wasn't there.

'I don't know, Arcadio, she's behaving very oddly,' whispered Sebastiana occasionally. 'She's like a nun.'

He nodded without a word, playing the part his daughter had assigned him in a belated, painful and unlikely rebirth.

'Well . . .'

Sometimes, after supper, Sara would take out a cardboard box from the chest of drawers where her mother kept the linen. She sat on the sofa beside Arcadio, and made him look at the dog-eared, yellowed old photographs it contained. He would have preferred never to set eyes on them again, but he gathered his patience and answered the questions of this wilful, confused girl whose curiosity seemed never to be satisfied.

'This is you, isn't it?'

Arcadio in his militiaman's uniform, holding a rifle, with a cartridge belt slung across his body, standing beside a large granite rock.

'Where was it taken?'

'In the *sierra*, near Guadarrama.'

'When was that?'

'I'm not sure, dear, I don't remember. It must have been at the start of the war.'

'And who took the photo?'

'A German photographer who was a friend of Don Mario.'

'Who was Don Mario?'

'Somebody I knew.'

But Sara wouldn't accept this, wouldn't accept only scraps of information from a remote past that was beginning to seem desperately important to her. She forced her father to talk, to search his memory for names, dates, details as trivial as breadcrumbs that she ground down with her teeth until she had absorbed them completely.

'And here?'

A group of trade unionists photographed outside the

headquarters of the Workers' Party in Madrid, dressed in their Sunday best and holding their hats, the younger ones smiling. Some had raised their fists – Arcadio among them – and they were gathered round a man dressed in black, who wore a tie and a hat, and had pale eyes and an aquiline nose. He was smiling at the camera confidently, seductively.

'And this gentleman?'

'Largo Caballero.'

'Was he on your side?'

'Yes, of course. He was a leader. One of the most important ones.'

'He looks very elegant.'

'Does he? There were much more elegant men than him, believe me. But he was my leader.'

'And what was he doing there?'

'Well, I don't know. He must have come for a meeting, or a conference. I don't remember, it was a long time ago.'

'And this person here is Don Mario, isn't it?'

'That's right,' said Arcadio, smiling despite himself. 'This is Don Mario.'

Sara knew all the features of the rough, sunburned faces by heart, the names, and the stories hidden behind each picture. But still she went on looking at each photograph over and over again, pointing to it, interpreting its edges and curves, presences and absences, shadows and symbols, as if the images were some new kind of alphabet.

'Mama, could you come here for a moment, please?'

Her parents' wedding photo, large, oblong, the faces foreshortened, the bodies cut off at the chest; she wearing a dark dress with a white flower pinned to the lapel, he with a dazzling white shirt buttoned all the way up but without a tie.

'You made your own dress, didn't you?' asked Sara. Sebastiana nodded. 'Why didn't you wear white?'

'Because it wasn't the fashion then.'

'But Doña Sara got married in white.'

'Doña Sara was a lady. She could afford to have a dress made specially for her and wear it only once.'

'And you, Papa?'

'What about me?'

'You were wearing a new suit.'

'Yes.'

'But you weren't wearing a tie.'

'What would I want with a tie?'

'Largo Caballero wore one.'

'Largo Caballero was a politician. I was just a plumber.'

'I suppose so. And afterwards you all went to have hot chocolate and *churros*.'

'Yes.'

'You didn't have a wedding reception.'

'No.'

They both answered in unison but Sebastiana slipped away, inventing some excuse, before the more difficult photos appeared: And these people? Why are they here? They're not members of our family, are they? They look like a couple of saints in an engraving. The heroes of Jaca? What heroes? A mutiny? In Jaca? I had no idea, I never studied that at school. What were their names? Galán and who? García Hernández, Galán and García Hernández, right. And this, where did you get this? They were handing them out in the street? And when was that? And what rank were they? So what happened? They were shot? Sebastiana had already answered quite enough questions during the day and knew her role. She was the one who went shopping with Sara, did errands together and Sara always made sure she kept Sebastiana close by whenever she began to take on the heavier chores. It was her mother who had to devise answers to Sara's more intimate questions, to explain other kinds of conflict and defeat. Like her husband, Sebastiana answered even though she didn't really want to, and sometimes thought her daughter was wrong to push her. But Sebastiana talked to Sara because it was her duty, because she owed it to her, and she gradually told her the whole story – when she had met Doña Sara, what her life was like in the Calle Velázquez, what it was that made her first notice Arcadio, how long they were engaged, what she felt when the war broke out, when she realised their side was going to lose, when her husband was taken prisoner, when she went to plead for his life, and what she felt when, in the end, after so many years, she had finally to pay the price. She did enjoy the walks Sara took her on every afternoon. Sebastiana went with her daughter to the old district, walked with her around the Calle Espíritu Santo, the Plaza de San Ildefonso, the Corredera Alta and the Corredera Baja, remembering aloud the name of every shop and bar, every neighbour, every friend of her father's, every customer of her mother's, gradually filling in details from her memory – the fairs, the Republic, the war, prison, the post-war years – until she had completed the map of a city that her daughter did not know at all.

Sara's passion for the past lasted all summer. By the time the days started to draw in and the leaves began to fall, Sara was almost sure she'd succeeded: the memory of another life crouched at her feet like a tame animal, a tired old dog, and her small daily achievements stood up well to the loss of novelty's shine. But summer was coming to an end, and reality began to reassert itself, calling her out of the refuge she had built so carefully. One evening in September the phone rang. Her mother went to answer and, when she returned, she announced that Doña Sara was back from Cercedilla.

'She'd like you to go and visit her tomorrow, Sari,' she said, her voice becoming a whisper when she saw her daughter's frown. 'She'd like you to go for lunch.'

'I'm not going,' Sara answered flatly, firmly, clearly, as a thick, dangerous silence invaded the room, an echo of the icy climate of her early days back in her parents' home.

'She won't understand,' countered Sebastiana timidly after a long pause. 'She says she misses you and she's dying to see you. I don't think it would be too much effort for you to go.'

'If she wants to see me, let her come here,' said Sara, cutting her mother off curtly. 'I'm not going there.'

'But . . .'

'Leave the child alone, Sebastiana,' Arcadio intervened suddenly, emerging from the cocoon of his own private grief. 'She's told you twice. Do you want her to have to tell you three times?'

'But I think, well,' continued his wife, as if she hadn't heard him, 'she's been like a mother to you all these years. She's done a lot for you.'

'For me?' Sara screamed, as if her mother's last few words had hurt her ears. More pained than incredulous she repeated: 'For me?'

'What do I know?' said Sebastiana, wiping her face with her apron, her eyes clouded and her hands trembling. 'I might not be the most intelligent person, dear, but if there's one thing I've learnt – it's what my mother taught me, and I've said it to your father many times, although he never takes any notice – it's that pride is something we can't afford, Sari. Pride doesn't put food on the table.'

'But it's all I've got, Mama!' Sara said, shouting over Arcadio, who was telling his wife to be quiet. Sara stood up, head held high. 'It's all I've got,' she repeated, more quietly now, before running to her room and locking herself in. She flung herself on the bed and burst into tears, crying in a way she had forbidden herself to ever again.

Sara Gómez Morales was sixteen years old and had little experience of the world. This was why, that night, she tossed and turned without finding any relief, any way out from the anger that consumed her but she couldn't quite understand.

It would be many years before she realised the irony implicit in her situation: that it was, in fact, Doña Sara who had equipped her with the tools to stand up for herself and to resist her godmother's affection. Toying with a little girl's mind and heart without even being conscious of it, without ever stopping to consider the consequences, Doña Sara had given her god-daughter the inner strength that would keep her firmly rooted, like an enormous oak tree with ancient, twisted, dry roots. When she left the house in the Calle Velázquez, Sara was a scale model of the woman who had brought her up, who had taught her to peel prawns with a fish knife and fork, and to be horrified by the outfits of civil servants' wives, who had forbidden her to swim in public swimming pools or to go out in slippers, who had encouraged her to choose her friends carefully and to be polite to servants, the woman who had sat and chatted to Sara for a little while in French every afternoon. But this realisation, which would change her life as an adult, was way beyond the understanding of a wounded, confused teenager whose only wish was to be left in peace. And it had not yet occurred to her that pride, a dangerous luxury, was the only privilege that her godmother, the source of all her privileges, could not take away.

Sebastiana wasn't as clever or as strong as her youngest daughter, but she'd had much more experience of life and she knew that some things were as certain as the sun rising in the east each day. She knew, for instance, that if the word 'humble' seemed ambiguous it was only because reality almost never was, that if the poor were meek, it was because the meek were almost always poor. But as she and Sara sat having breakfast the following morning, she chose other words to stop her daughter brooding over the scene from the evening before.

'Look, love, don't misunderstand me. I'm not fond of your godmother – quite the opposite – but I don't think she's a bad person. She's . . . she's just the way she thinks she ought to be, just like everyone else in her class, like her parents and her grandparents before them. They're the masters, and that makes them think they're good people, because they go to Mass, and confession, and they sleep peacefully in their beds at night. This doesn't mean I'm defending her, that I'm on her side, because I'm not. I'm on your side, dear, that's the main thing. Your father doesn't see that. He's very clever, that's for sure, but he can also be very blind when he wants to be. I'm not saying he isn't right, because he is, but you don't get anywhere from being right and I can't believe that he doesn't realise that with everything he's been through. The fact is, life is hard, and I think it would be best if you didn't fall out with your godmother, because she has money and we don't, and being right is neither here nor there. You have been in my thoughts all these years, Sari, and you still are – I worry about what's going to happen to you, what you're going to do, how you're going to earn your living. You can't spend the rest of your life like this, shut up at home, learning to cook. It might seem OK for now, because it's new to you, but this is a wretched way to live. You can do so much more, Sari – find a good job, earn money, marry and live well, and not end up like me. You're clever and you've had too good an education to end up like this. You can't. You've got to do something. I wish I didn't have to say any of this to you, I dearly wish I could just tell you to go out and have fun. But I can't lie to you, love, I can't, because that's how things are. That's why I suck up to your godmother. So now you know.'

Sara learnt no new skills that morning. She didn't prepare lunch, she didn't dust, she didn't clean the bathroom, or jot down ideas for making the most of the living room or covering up scratches on the furniture. At first, she couldn't even bring herself to move at all. For a long time, over two hours, she sat in the same Formica chair where she'd had her morning coffee, feeling neither hungry nor thirsty, cold or hot, happy or sad. Her fate was already sealed, it seemed. She tried to think, but didn't get very far. She understood all her mother's arguments but she also understood that agreeing with her meant that all her efforts were in vain, that there was no point in resisting the divided self she had dragged through the tunnels of the metro every Sunday of her life. The only thing on the other side of the scales was her pride – a delicate, unstable, nebulous substance that was a comfort to her but didn't put food on the table.

Sara thought things over for a long time, from every angle, in the hours and days that followed. She thought about her father, the cheerful arrogance of his young, uniformed self, his strength, his faith, the treacherous delusion of the rifle he held as if it were a symbol of truth. For her, there would be no rifles, no lies. 'Things are the way they are,' her mother had said. 'There's nothing you can do about it.' Certainly Sebastiana's other children thought so. Sara considered them too, her equals, her brothers and sisters, vaguely familiar shadows that roamed the house only in her parents' memories and who phoned every Sunday. They were all far away: Arcadio working in Germany, freezing to death but happy and earning plenty of money, according to his letters; the young Sebastiana in Avilés, where she'd gone with her husband, a metalworker from Asturias. The two younger ones were still in Madrid, but because the city was now so big, it didn't seem like it. Pablo lived in San Fernando de Henares, worked for ITT and was married to a woman who was a cleaner for the Mahou beer company. They had two young children and were so exhausted by the weekend that they preferred to go to the trouble of cooking a meal at home rather than to come all the way into town. Socorrito had been married less than a year and was already pregnant. She and her husband lived in Puente de Vallecas with his mother, an ailing, bad-tempered old lady whom Socorrito would never be rid of because her husband, a welder, was an only child. Socorrito visited more often than the others, usually in the evening and always in a hurry, as if she had to steal away from home to visit her own mother. Sara was always pleased to see her because she had fond memories of the precarious intimacy that had united them around the Mariquita Pérez doll, and she made use of the only practical thing the nuns at school had taught her by spending the evenings knitting a white jumper for the baby. For her part, Socorro behaved like an older sister from the start, complicit and protective, and confided in Sara about her husband, her home, her life in Vallecas. Sara grew very fond of her, but she also knew she didn't want to become like her. Or like the maids at Doña Sara's. So she went on thinking, dreaming of rifles, of any solution that would enable her to square her pride with a future that seemed bearable. It seemed as if she would never find a solution and for several days she fell into despair, until one evening her father said something that encouraged her to start thinking again, in a direction that would be unreservedly right.

'We didn't know anything. We believed whatever they told us – the Party, the ones who had an education and were good at giving orders. They knew. They told us we had to resist, so we did, that we had to wait, so we did, that anyone who wanted to would be able to leave Madrid in time. They deceived us, they treated us like idiots, and that's what we were – complete idiots. They made sure they got out in time, of course; Casado first of all, and fast. He handed us over to them on a plate. I can still hear him: "General Franco has given us guarantees," he said over the radio, "anyone who hasn't shed blood need not fear reprisals." Had I shed blood? No. Well, they sentenced me to death two days after capturing me, that's what they did. How was I to know? I didn't learn to read until I was thirty.'

Six days later, in the middle of the afternoon, Sara Gómez Morales rang at the door of the Ochoa household, where everyone recognised her immediately. But she was no longer the same girl – the carefree, capricious teenager they all remembered. She was an impostor, determined never to trust anyone again and never to take a single step, for the rest of her life, without anticipating even the most trivial consequences. This resolve had led her by the hand into her godmother's presence, keeping her pride intact, but secretly squirrelled away in an inner sanctum so deep that it was safe from lies, treacherous promises and hypocritical smiles. Even if it meant shrivelling up inside, daily swallowing the bitter pill of resignation and humiliation, she would not be overcome. When all was said and done, rifles didn't simply appear, you had to earn them, snatch them from the enemy, know how to steal them or save up to buy them, and if this was the price to pay, she'd pay it. But she would not be humble, she would not be meek, she would not be stupid. There was only one possible path if she was going to advance: she had to arm herself. This was the only conclusion Sara reached after thinking and thinking. If her mother was right, so too was her father. She had to end up being one of the ones who had an education, who were good at giving orders, the ones who knew, and that meant, for a start, getting a good job and earning lots of money. 'After that, we'll see,' she promised herself whenever she had any doubts about her plans. 'We'll see.' And she thought of Socorro, of Sebastiana with all those children, their anxiety as the end of each month approached, and she gritted her teeth and repeated it to herself, like an order, a mantra – 'We'll see.'

'I thought I'd do a short course – to become a bilingual secretary, for instance, so that I can use my French. Then, once I've started work, I can learn English, and do other courses. I like studying and I'm good at it, but I wanted to know what you think.'

She was repeating – with small, well-chosen variations – what Doña Sara had told her mother about her plans for Sara's future. Even before she'd reached the end of her speech, Sara saw that she'd got it right.

'Well, that sounds very sensible, darling. I'm so glad to have you back, to have you here again. You can't imagine how much I've missed you.'

While her godmother's eyes showed emotion, Sara no longer cared whether this was genuine or not. There was to be no room for compassion and she kept her lips tightly shut to suppress any sudden outburst. Instead, she opened her own eyes wide to respond in kind, and discovered that this quiet deception did not affect her, or so she thought. She was wrong, but mistakes, like people, mature slowly.

'My friend Loreto – you remember her, don't you?' Doña Sara went on with the gratuitous magnanimity of those who don't need to fight to win their wars, and Sara nodded. 'You'll pay for this, you bitch, you'll pay for it all,' she thought, sitting on the edge of her chair decorously, discreet and attentive as would be expected of a young lady. 'Her sister is married to the owner of a chain of academies across Madrid. They prepare their students for Civil Service exams, and offer shorthand and secretarial courses. The main school is in the Calle Espoz y Mina, very near to where you live. It's a bit late so they might not be taking any new students, but I'm sure Loreto would do me a favour and get you a place. You could do a three-year course, and be fully qualified by the end of it. Then we could look for a good position for you. What do you think?'

Doña Sara looked at her with an expectant smile, her hands folded in her lap. Sara had come to know the meaning of that smile very well, an expression of indulgent generosity, a woman who felt very pleased with herself. The last time she had seen it was when her godmother had agreed to allow her the party shoes in yellow silk, an expression that said she was bestowing a gift and demanded overflowing gratitude in response. Sara faithfully observed the rule. Afterwards, she went to say hello to Don Antonio, who barely answered, and passed by the kitchen to say goodbye to the servants. Then she ran down the stairs, rushing to get outside as soon as possible. When at last she breathed in the warm, soothing breeze that fluttered through the tree tops, her whole body hurt. 'I'll get used to it,' she told herself, 'I'll get used to it eventually, no doubt.' And though her legs felt weak and shaky, she forced them to move and hurried down into the metro.

She thought she'd come through the worst, the period of shipwreck. She had plans now, another refuge to build, a purpose to cling to with the hope and desperation she would need. But reality still lay in wait for her, and it was ugly, even more so than the vulgarity of mentioning money, the price of things, in an intimate family conversation.

The Robles School of Shorthand, Typing and Secretarial Skills occupied the first floor of a building so old it had forgotten every vestige of its past splendour. The huge, labyrinthine apartment, the result of successive chaotic additions to a small, original nucleus, had one central corridor that branched off into other, smaller corridors, some of which ended abruptly in a blank wall. On either side of the corridors, there were countless old doors, all of them uniformly covered in layer after layer of thick white gloss paint, like geological strata. These doors opened onto tiny rooms, grandly designated classrooms. They contained an odd selection of furniture, often including six or seven different styles of chair in a single row, almost all of them with a little attachment on one side that served as a desk. Some were made of wood, others of plywood with a synthetic laminate, or of plastic, a few of them folded, and some had a little rack beneath the seat for books. Señor Robles, whom Sara did not see once in the four years she spent there gaining her qualification as a bilingual secretary, re-used desks thrown out by schools, paying only a little more for them than the rag-and-bone men would. The typewriters were so old that you could only manage, and then not always, to produce letters on the page by viciously pounding the keys. They were always being sent to be repaired, and even so it was a rare one that didn't have a broken key or two. The official explanation was that it was good for the students to learn on difficult keyboards so that they'd do even better when they worked on comfortable modern typewriters, but this argument didn't explain why the ceiling lights always had a blown tube, or why the French teacher, a woman in her fifties with a red nose and an accent slurred with *anis*, spoke the language worse than Sara did.

However most of the students couldn't have cared less about any of this. Apart from the occasional enterprising office worker investing his spare time with a view to a promotion, the Robles School fed mainly on girls of Sara's age, from lower-middle-class families who were trying to provide some training for their daughters, but could not afford to send to them to university (although this wasn't always the case for their brothers). The girls didn't mind that much. Almost every week, one of them dropped out, having started a course just to try it out or to avoid speeches like the one Sara had had from her mother. Many of them would have preferred to be working as trainee hairdressers or make-up artists or in a clothes shop, the three points that delimited the unvarying triangle of their interests. They all knew how to put their hair in curlers, how to iron it, how to pin it up, and they wore a lot of make-up even to class, with thick black lines ringing their eyes, pastel eye shadow on their eyelids, and skilfully applied false lashes like a row of insect legs. Short skirts were in fashion, and theirs were extremely short. Knee-high boots were in fashion, and theirs were extremely high. They subscribed to a singular aesthetic in all aspects of their appearance and behaviour, and Sara stared apprehensively at their nails, long and curved as razor shells, with deep-red polish that chipped as the week wore on, their bouffant hairdos stiff with lacquer, their dozens of necklaces, their cheap, showy plastic earrings. She listened to them talking in loud piercing voices, slapping themselves suddenly on the thighs as they laughed, repeating the same expressions of amazement or amusement, 'Oh, my God, take a look at her, can you believe what she's wearing?' On Mondays, a kind of general conclave was held in the corridors, where they exchanged gossip about dances and boyfriends, the two things that seemed to determine their happiness. Sara felt more like an alien than ever, and she sensed their distrust, the hostility and contempt that rose to the surface in their glances, the whispers as she passed. But she couldn't make friends with the swots either, dull, timid little things who applied themselves to their studies in the hope of one day resembling their idol, Isabelita Sevilla.

Señorita Sevilla had an impressive collection of plastic hairbands placed strategically on her head so that they accentuated the architectural magnificence of her hairdo. At the front, there was a chestnut fringe, furiously backcombed, and behind it a dome of short hair so hollow, so bouffant, that it looked like a meringue straight out of a recipe book. Señorita Sevilla was the typing teacher, and the kind of woman who would rather go out naked than carry a handbag that didn't match her shoes. At the Robles School, this second-rate lady, who was proud of her small waist and never admitted her age, was taken to be the acme of refinement and good taste, even though she occasionally let slip disastrous errors in grammar. This weakness never compromised her prestige because the only student who noticed had no one to talk to, no one she could laugh about it with.

Señorita Sevilla, though she would never know it, was also the very model of the averagely well-off, averagely capable, averagely attractive, averagely educated, averagely elegant, averagely single, averagely contented woman that Doña Sara Villamarín de Ochoa had envisaged her god-daughter might become, an average future of plastic hairbands and six different pairs of shoes as the grand prize in a lottery of the unexceptional.

But Sara Gómez Morales was not, and would never be, an average woman. Reality was ugly, very ugly, and life more wretched than hard. This was the most important thing she learnt at the Robles School of Shorthand, Typing and Secretarial Skills, along with the knowledge that if she didn't watch out, she'd end up like Señorita Sevilla. As for the rest, she passed all her exams and practical assessments with amazing ease. The shorthand teacher – and virtual director of the school, whose proprietor, if the rumours were to be believed, was also her lover – held Sara up as an example to the other students. This status made Sara's relationship with her classmates even more complicated, but she didn't care.

In less than a year, Sara Gómez Morales had gone from a well-to-do adolescence, to being ejected from the social class in which she had grown up, from the rigours of revolutionary frenzy, to a cold and calculating, life-long desire for revenge. She'd pondered each critical step taken, her reasons, the advantages and risks of each choice. She'd even succeeded in controlling her own feelings, and yet one day everything suddenly seemed to pall, and she felt she no longer cared about anything. Time dragged, and the years passed by imperceptibly. She was determined to be successful, and she managed it easily, on the modest scale of successes that were within her reach. By the time she started her third year at the Robles School she was already working in the afternoons, managing the books of several shops in her district. Then she found out how much classes at the school cost, and was shocked at how tiny the outlay that her godmother had portrayed as a privilege actually was. She telephoned Doña Sara to tell her that she no longer needed to make the payments, and was amazed that she did not feel more triumphant at what should have been the first major victory of her life.

Her other victories didn't make her any happier. At the age of twenty she got a job in the offices of a pharmaceutical laboratory, a modern company that didn't pay a great salary but gave her a few hours off in the afternoon so that she could continue her studies. This was when she began to flirt with brandy. She bought a television set for her parents, enrolled for the first year of English at one of the official language schools, changed jobs, did a few odd courses in advanced book-keeping, drew up her own savings schedule, got an advanced qualification in tax law. She spent all her weekends at home, had no friends, either male or female, went to the cinema alone, studied hard, and drank quite a bit. She took a short course in customs regulations, had the kitchen at the flat in Concepción Jerónima redecorated, got a job as an accountant for a shipping agent, started earning more money than Arcadio Gómez Gómez had ever dreamed of, did up the bathroom, turned twenty-five, redid the floors throughout the flat, obtained an official qualification in English, realised that it wasn't sensible to invest a single penny more in a rented flat, and began to admit certain things to herself:

That the necessarily fabricated love that bound her to her parents could not fill all the gaps in her life. That she was fed up with her mother continually asking about her colleagues at work and inventing imaginary boyfriends for her at the slightest opportunity. That she was just as fed up with her father living her life for her, overwhelming her with useless advice and suggestions that only seemed to confirm he would have done it all much better himself. That her father and mother were poor uneducated people who understood nothing, neither what she liked, nor what she wanted to achieve, nor what she hoped to do. That her godmother had been right, that her relationship with Juan Mari had not been serious but that now, when she was old enough to cultivate nostalgia, she missed her adolescent fantasies of life with him, missed the exaggerated elegance of the details. That although she hardly ever went to visit her godmother in the Calle Velázquez – and even then, did so reluctantly – she liked seeing the furniture, using the things, breathing the air of the apartment. However much she berated herself afterwards, she couldn't rid herself of this weakness. This was why she didn't have a boyfriend, or any friends, and went to the cinema alone, studied hard and drank quite a bit. She had no one to talk to. She would always be in limbo, neither a lady nor an office worker, neither her godmother's Sara, nor her parents' Sari, none and all of these things at once, everything and nothing, with an endless burden of dissatisfaction imprinted on her brain.

Sometimes, the ugliness of the world bore down on her, but she still found the strength to fight it. Sometimes her hidden pride, appeased, beaten down by routine, rose in her throat, burning the roof of her mouth and forcing her to see that what she had was not enough. Each of the modest diplomas gained from correspondence courses that her mother insisted on framing and hanging on Sara's bedroom wall, resigned to not being allowed to hang them in the dining room, was a product of these unpredictable rages, of this furious crippled ambition. But nothing was as strong as the fever that took hold of her in the summer of 1974.

Sara was twenty-seven years old and she told herself that enough was enough. She did it in under a month, twenty-two days from first looking at job ads in the paper to moving into her office in the accounts department of a large construction firm. She enrolled for an economics degree at the

Open University and made a down payment on a flat still under construction, on a rather pretentious development by the Plaza de Castilla. Then she joined what had once been her father's trade union. With her cold, meticulous, arithmetical mind she immediately stood out at meetings where temperatures, blood, words and promises were all overheated. Perhaps this was why Vicente noticed her immediately. She noticed him the moment he walked through the door of the warehouse where the meeting was being held that day.

Vicente González – in fact his full surname was González de Sandoval, but he always cut off the more aristocratic-sounding second half – was eight years older than Sara and the only son of one of the largest shareholders in the company. With a PhD in economics, he was a Marxist by conviction, but with plenty of supporting arguments. When he'd finished his degree, he'd tried to sever all links with his family, whose history, politics and business both embarrassed and disgusted him. He managed this successfully thanks to a temporary teaching vacancy at the university where he'd done his degree. He'd grown his hair and a beard, rented an attic flat in Argüelles, shacked up with an aspiring actress from Cordoba who sang in a bar, and for a time had fun and was satisfied with his life. He was also involved in organising the student uprisings of '68. Arrested and tried, he was sentenced to two years in prison, the leniency of the sentence owing something to the true length of his surname. The court, however, did not take into account the allergic asthma he had suffered from since childhood and which seemed to take him, with every attack, to the brink of death. He had a terrible time in prison, so terrible that after three consecutive asthma attacks, he was released on health grounds, and confined to house arrest at the family home for the remainder of his sentence. He no longer felt like doing anything foolish and his mother welcomed him with open arms. She made

228

him shave off his beard and cut his hair, gave him his old room and lovingly fed him hot soup and fish with potatoes. Vicente had almost forgotten the taste of fresh fish. And María Belén, his childhood sweetheart, came to keep him company every afternoon with a self-abnegation that would have moved a dead man. As he was still alive but reluctant to discuss the matter, it was she who told him one day that she knew everything and forgave him and that they'd have to start thinking about a date for the wedding. Vicente doubted she knew everything – in particular the prodigious capabilities with which the actress from Cordoba had seduced him. But he agreed, persuaded partly by the fish dinners, partly by the conviction that he had no choice. They were married in 1971, in church, and three hundred and fifty guests attended the reception at their country club. By then, Vicente was already a senior executive in his father's construction company. In 1972, his first child was born, the umpteenth Vicente González de Sandoval. In 1973, he began to suffer from insomnia, and seriously wondered if he was going mad. By 1974, the year he met Sara, he thought of himself as an amoeba, a germ, a bug, but above all a complete and utter fool. A few months earlier, his wife had told him she was pregnant again and that with luck it would be a girl so she could call her Begoña, after her grandmother. That same day, he'd bumped into a quantity surveyor in the corridor who knew him from his old days of political activism at university. Through this man, he started to forge links with the union leaders at the firm, who welcomed him warmly, aware of the benefits such a contact might provide. Vicente didn't dare ask to join the union because he was afraid he might be refused, but he quietly attended their meetings and, always in private, passed information, made suggestions, and felt that at least he was being useful.

Sara knew from the start why she had noticed him. He was tall and sturdy, but had a slightly pallid look that suited him, softening a heavy brow, large nose and thick neck that hinted deceptively at peasant stock. In fact, this quiet man, who observed everything with curiosity, possessed the same innate elegance, the same silvery, luminous quality as the gentlemen Sara had not seen close up since she was a child; the brilliance that went beyond the labels and the impeccable cut of his clothes, manifesting itself instead in his way of sitting, lighting a cigarette, putting out a hand to refuse something with the wordless courtesy of one who has always had plenty of everything. She asked about him and heard his story, and after that she looked at him with tenderness. He, who already looked at her so insistently, responded by moving ever closer, until one day he was sitting next to her.

'Why do you stare at me so much?' she whispered, without turning her head, her eyes fixed on the speaker.

'Because I like staring at you,' Vicente answered with a certainty to which Sara could find no response.

Later, after the meeting, Vicente followed her to the door of her office without saying a word. Sometimes, Sara laughed at his mutely stubborn courtship, and then he laughed too, like a little boy, because he had the audacious, jubilant feeling that the good times had returned at last.

'Well,' she said when they reached the end of the corridor. 'Here we are.'

'Who are you, comrade?' he asked jokingly, for the first time using the word that would become an ironic, though sincere, code between them. 'Where did you spring from?'

Sara breathed out, leant against the door and looked deep into his eyes. She had an answer to his question; she had spent weeks thinking about it.

'I am your opposite,' she said. 'Your equal and your opposite. Like your reflection in a mirror.'

The first time, they went to a very smart, very expensive, very discreet hotel, near the airport. As they were leaving,

Sara noticed a little cardboard box sitting unopened on a shelf in the bathroom, containing two plastic bottles of shower gel, two of shampoo and two of cologne, two tiny soap dishes, a small sponge, and a miniature sewing kit. 'My mother would just love this,' she thought and put out her hand to take it. But, just in time, she remembered that ladies never took anything from hotel rooms. As she walked down the corridor, she longed for the box of toiletries, and felt sure that Sebastiana would have been delighted with the gift, opening all the little bottles, smelling them, closing them again, placing them in a prominent place in the bathroom, dusting, touching, smelling them every day; but Sara also felt darker, more complex emotions, a deep indefinable nostalgia for a time that had not quite passed. Sara had been out with several men, she had even slept with a few, but she hadn't really liked any of them, not the way she liked this man, an impossible choice. The intensity of those hours stung her skin and her eyes, softened every one of her muscles, every drop of blood, every bruised fold of her memory. Perhaps the small things her mother so loved would make sense one day. But perhaps there wouldn't be another chance.

When she reached the lift, she pretended to search for something in her bag, then asked Vicente for the room key, making the first excuse that came to mind: 'I've got to go back, I think I've left my earrings in the room.' She rushed back, and it didn't occur to her that he might have noticed she hadn't been wearing earrings that afternoon. She'd just taken apart the little box so that she could fit it and its contents into her bag, when she saw his reflection in the mirror. He was standing in the corridor, next to the bathroom door, watching her in silence. She blushed, not knowing what to say. A second went by, then another, and another, and neither of them spoke. Then Vicente went to her, put his arms around her and kissed her on the mouth for a long time.

Years afterwards, when it was too late to change anything, Sara Gómez Morales, with her prodigious talent for calculation, realised that it was that moment, precisely that moment, that had been the origin of the principal, most serious, and only truly important error she had ever made in her life.

The east wind blew for eight days and eight nights – too much and too long for anyone to preserve even the vestige of a happy memory of its arrival. When it went, it left a clean, peaceful world, days of sun and calm, and air that was kinder than the daytime dew that permeated everything when the west wind blew.

'Looks like we're going to have a good winter,' said Maribel one afternoon. She'd let Sara drag her out to take a look at some of the new apartment blocks being built in the area. 'Mild and dry. That's the thing about the east wind: it's quite unbearable, but you couldn't live without it.'

Sara, who felt slightly married to the wind herself, was amused by Maribel's conjugal resignation, but she didn't say anything. She would soon discover that Maribel was right, however. For Sara too, that winter would be better than the autumn.

After all, life, like an old, disloyal friend, had made her an expert at change. Her ability to adapt had been honed throughout her youth, her middle age and beyond, in a long succession of settings, real and fictitious, public and private, in which she had never been able to settle for long. This time the process was different. Now she had arrived, alone, objectively and irretrievably alone, in this ghost station on a disused track; abandoned to its fate except, perhaps, as a home for the poppies that might one day flourish amongst its dusty sleepers. This was why, admitting that she was bored, and without disavowing the bitter taste of disappointment, Sara accepted the small destiny of wild flowers and, that winter, learnt to live again. Once she had managed to assimilate the stillness, to become reconciled to the slowness of clocks, everything began to seem easier.

She grew used to doing everything slowly, without counting the minutes, and her days began to acquire a modest stability, an almost ritual serenity that eventually affected her peace of mind too. Reading without keeping count of the books she had got through in the week, getting hooked on the most frivolous TV programmes, becoming a regular customer of the video shops in town, making the most of the mild climate by going for walks on the beach, setting herself the goal of reaching a specific rock, and turning round once she'd got there without even pausing to enjoy the silent company of the crabs, shutting herself in the kitchen occasionally with a book of complicated recipes and spending much more time than was reasonable making an irresistible cake and then eating it all on her own for tea, and enjoying it. All these milestones were significant in themselves, like rooms used for the first time that had not yet been fully explored, in a life that only then began to feel different from all the others she had known. Sara Gómez finally began to relax. When she accomplished the feat of letting a whole Sunday go by without speaking to anyone and not feeling bad about it, Sara understood that this move had been as complete as the final one would be. Death would find her by the sea, caught between love and hatred of the winds.

In the midst of her new indolent lifestyle, Sara did allow herself one exception – a task that had nothing to do with her own needs. She was determined to turn Maribel into a property owner because, regardless of any altruistic impulses, it was a more entertaining project than any book, TV programme or film. Poring over specifications from developers and then picking them apart word by word, suggesting endless improvements to the plans, and covering reams of paper in calculations had always been one of her favourite pastimes. Everything else was put on hold. But then, on 14

December, at ten to five in the afternoon, the front doorbell rang insistently, proving that she still couldn't rely on every day being identical to the one before.

'Hello,' said Andrés. He was wearing his school tracksuit and trainers, and was twisting the sleeves of his anorak apologetically.

'Hello,' said Tamara, who was dressed the same as Andrés and looked just as nervous.

'What are you two doing here?' asked Sara, glancing at her watch, surprised and even a little alarmed, though the children's anxious faces didn't seem to show any signs of a disaster.

'We're off school in the afternoons now.'

'Today, and tomorrow, and all next week.'

'We've already done our homework.'

'Yes, so we thought . . .'

'Because my uncle won't get back from work till six thirty . . .'

'And you've got a car . . .'

'We wondered if you'd like to go for a drive.'

'To Jerez.'

'Or to the port.'

'Or to Sanlúcar.'

'For ice cream.'

'Or to go shopping.'

'Or to the cinema.'

'We've got money.'

'Not much.'

'But we've got some.'

'Yes.'

'If you don't feel like it, it doesn't matter.'

'I hope you don't think we're being cheeky.'

'But it's too cold to play outside.'

'And we're a bit fed up with going into town.'

'And there's nothing good on TV.'

'And we can't think of anything to do.'

'And we're bored.'

They stood staring at her, while Sara gathered her thoughts. But she soon rewarded their patience with a smile, and invited them inside. As she followed them into the sitting room, she cast a rueful glance at a folder lying on the table, containing the details of a new development that was so expensive Maribel couldn't understand why Sara even wanted her to look at it. But then she remembered how much she'd missed the children when they'd gone back to school, and although she was reluctant to go out again at this time, now the winter nights drew in so quickly, she sat down opposite them and smiled again, because she had learnt from her father that loyalty could overcome lethargy.

'Now, let's see. Where do you want to go?'

'Well, loads of places really.' This time it was Tamara who spoke first.

'I'd like to go and look at the new computer games so that I can decide which one I'm going to ask for, for Christmas,' said Andrés.

'Me too. And I'd like to buy a Christmas tree, and decorations. We haven't got one here.'

'I think they've set up one of those Nativity scenes at the Corte Inglés store, with those figures that move and speak.'

'Maybe they've got things at the other shopping centres too.'

'I bet they have. Last year, at one in El Puerto, they had a big tank of balls with slides and nets to climb up. It was great. I couldn't go, because mum doesn't have a car, but maybe they'll have it again this year.'

'And someone told us there's a Christmas street market near here.'

'And there's a really good film, about space, that's just come out.'

'And one about twins who get lost.'

'That one's rubbish.'

'Well, I want to see it.'

'Well, I don't.'

'OK!' shouted Sara, holding up her hands to get them to be quiet. 'We can go and see the one about space one day, and the one with the twins another day.'

They would have time to see two more films as well – a big American blockbuster supposedly retelling a medieval legend, and a Japanese animated film – before the holidays ended. For almost an entire month, Sara regained the feeling of not having enough time to do all the things she'd set out to do in a day. On the days the children had to go to school in the mornings, they arrived at her house just after lunch, doing their homework there to save time. Later on, the main novelty was no longer the new timetable, but the fact that there were three of them instead of two.

'We've got to bring Alfonso with us, Sara,' Tamara informed her contritely, when Sara opened the door to her one day and found her holding her disabled uncle's hand. 'We've got no choice,' she went on, still using the plural as if Sara were the one who had been dreaming about going to El Puerto to see if they'd set up the tank of balls. 'His centre is closed for the holidays and Juan said I've got to keep him company, because Maribel doesn't want to be left on her own with him. She's scared he'll go all strange on her. But he won't, he's very good, aren't you?' Alfonso nodded vigorously, three times. 'OK, Alfonso, stay here a minute. I'm going to get Andrés.'

Tamara kissed him before letting go of his hand and ran into the house. Sara shrugged slightly, not daring to look directly at this unexpected guest. She'd been around Alfonso Olmedo a few times before, but always when his older brother was there, and she'd noticed the way Juan handled him with a careful combination of strictness and leniency; he was firm when asking Alfonso to do things he knew he was capable of, but forgave him mistakes quickly and easily whenever he tried something new. However Sara wasn't sure where the line between naughtiness and clumsiness fell, so she was thinking that the best course would probably be to treat him like an ordinary adult, when she noticed that he was staring at her. She held his gaze, and then Alfonso proffered his hand, like a little child who wants to be taken for a walk. Sara took the man's soft, large, hairy hand and squeezed it, feeling its size and shape and how readily he entrusted it to her. The situation seemed so ridiculous that she let out a nervous giggle.

'It's fun, eh?' said Alfonso. He spoke with difficulty in a guttural voice that betrayed his disability, no matter how correctly he pronounced every syllable.

'Yes,' said Sara, not knowing what else to say.

'What is?' Alfonso asked then.

'Well, I don't know. That we're going for a walk, and having lunch out, and . . .'

She was saved by the arrival of the children, but although she breathed a sigh of relief that she wouldn't have to answer any more of Alfonso's questions, Sara suddenly felt that this had to stop, things had gone too far. She wasn't the mother of these children, and she couldn't be expected to take them here, there and everywhere all day like an unpaid chauffeur or nanny. She hadn't thought of it like this until now. She'd found the films amusing, and she'd enjoyed their walks through the winter streets full of lights, and the colour and bustle of the street markets, where she'd been so carried away by the atmosphere that she'd bought a wreath of dried flowers to hang on her front door (the only clue that it was Christmas, rather than October, or April). She sometimes felt a trifle bored by the children's endless comparisons of various computer games, but on the whole she'd enjoyed watching them have fun, and took pleasure in having a packed schedule, filled with things to do. So far, all of this, and the pleasure of putting her feet up when she got home, exhausted, had seemed fine, and she would even have said that it had been worth it. It wasn't as if taking the children out had eaten up valuable time – she had nothing to do that couldn't wait a couple of weeks, or months, or even whole years if need be. But while it bothered her to discover that she shared some of Maribel's irrational fear, the addition of Alfonso to the group was simply too much. 'After today, that's it,' she told herself as she got out of the car, oblivious to Andrés's and Tamara's delight when they saw the complex edifice of brightly coloured plastic. She steeled herself for an odd, disjointed conversation with Alfonso while the two children exhausted themselves, jumping off the seemingly endless number of ramps and spirals, but this wasn't what happened. Tamara went up to the attendant and gave him a long, pathetic speech about her uncle, and the man let Alfonso in, much to Sara's surprise. Then she was amazed to see him climb and jump with considerable agility. She realised then that physical exercise must have been part of his therapy since childhood. On the immense and fairly empty apparatus, Alfonso Olmedo stood out only because of his size, and he was having as much fun as everyone else.

By the time their sixty minutes were up, Sara Gómez had calmed down enough to search within herself for the cause of the uneasiness that had almost ruined the day. Her investigation began and ended in the same familiar place: Christmas always put her in a bad mood. Having resorted to a wide variety of tactics for sweetening this troublesome time over the years, she'd eventually opted for simply ignoring the whole business. But this hadn't worked much better than trying to celebrate it on her own, or eschewing solitude to stay at her sister Socorro's, or being consumed with sadness at a smart hotel in a village in Castile, where she'd had to eat in a dining room full of single diners, all the other fools from Madrid who'd had the same stupid idea as herself. This was the main reason that she'd submitted so meekly to all of Andrés's and Tamara's whims. Self-interest lurked beneath her generous self-denial whenever Juan or Maribel asked her not to pay the children so much attention, when she insisted that she loved taking them to the cinema and driving them around. She hoped that the children's company, their energy and enthusiasm, their endless capacity to want things, would protect her from her feelings of desolation, the thick sense of failure that flooded her being when the sound of the first Christmas carol forced open the floodgates of her memory. She didn't hate Christmas, she didn't have a reason to hate it, or anyone to hate it with – it just put her in a bad mood. A really, really bad mood. Such a bad mood that it took her a whole morning to realise that it wasn't Alfonso Olmedo's fault that in more than fifty years she hadn't found security, a home to return to, with her hands empty or full of gold, when Christmas came around once more.

Apart from anything else, Alfonso was perfectly behaved. He did as he was told and didn't wander off even once. And Tamara kept a close eye on him the whole time, as if, despite Sara's attempts to hide her feelings, she knew what was at stake for them all that morning. But later, when Sara rushed to take the only free table in the burger bar, Alfonso immediately sat beside her, with the innocent passivity of one who is used to having everything done for him, and Tamara said she and Andrés would go and get the food. In the few minutes she was away, the only mishap of the day occurred. It made Sara very nervous, but later on she felt pleased that she had been there, because only then did she begin to think of Alfonso Olmedo as a complete being, a person separate from his brother and his niece, a pair of eyes and a voice that had their own story to tell.

The scene seemed perfectly normal, when suddenly Alfonso pushed back his chair and tried to hide behind it. Sara scrambled to grasp what had happened, what had changed, what new element had been introduced into the monotonous landscape of plastic tables and brightly coloured signs. But however much she tried, she wouldn't have been able to pinpoint anything had Alfonso not grasped her arm and whispered a strange word into her ear, a name that sounded quaint, almost funny, like the name of a character in an old-fashioned comedy.

'Nicanorrr,' he said, extending the last syllable out like chewing gum, in a way that would have been comical if he hadn't looked so afraid. 'Nicanor, Nicanor.'

'Who?' asked Sara. She didn't dare raise her voice and the question emerged as a nervous whisper. She looked around, bewildered. She didn't understand what was happening; all she knew was that Alfonso was becoming very agitated. 'What is it? What do you mean?'

'Nicanor,' Alfonso repeated, as if he thought Sara should understand, and grew increasingly frustrated when he saw that she didn't. 'Nicanor, Nicanor,' he said again, and then suddenly, more precisely: 'That uniform – see that? It's Nicanor.'

She looked towards the front of the restaurant and suddenly began to understand. A pair of policemen, one young, fair-haired and solid, the other older, almost completely bald and fatter, had been queuing for food for quite a while. Apart from the waiters, they were the only people in uniform in the place, so she guessed Alfonso must mean one of them. Sara turned back round to look at Alfonso and was alarmed to see how pale he was, beads of sweat running down his forehead. Instinctively, she put out a hand to stroke his face.

'The policeman?' she said quietly, still stroking Alfonso's cheek. 'You mean one of those policemen, don't you? You know him and his name is Nicanor. Is that right?' He nodded, not looking at her, his eyes fixed on the two men in their blue uniforms. 'Which one is it? The fair-haired one?' Alfonso shook his head, and Sara corrected herself. 'No, the other one, the taller one – he's Nicanor.'

'Yes. I don't like him. Juanito doesn't either. He's bad, Nicanor, he's bad, he does tests on me, he hits me, he does tests on me. I hate tests, I hate them.'

'He hits you?'

'Bam, bam.' Alfonso started waving his hand from side to side, insisting on sound effects. 'Bam, bam, this is what he does, bam, bam.'

'What's happening?' asked Tamara, rushing up with a tray. She dropped it down on the table and put her arms around her uncle. 'What's the matter, Alfonso?' She turned to Sara, looking more frightened than Sara or Andrés had ever seen her. 'What's happened to him?'

'I'm not altogether sure. It started when those policemen came in. He seemed very anxious, even frightened, and started saying that one of them was called Nicanor, and that he knows him. I don't know, maybe he's seen him at the daycare centre, or maybe he looks like one of the security guards there.'

'No, it's not that,' Tamara said, shaking her head vigorously. She didn't stop to explain, but turned back to her uncle. 'Look, Alfonso, listen to me. That's not Nicanor, do you understand? Nicanor isn't here, Nicanor lives in Madrid, and we're not in Madrid. We live here now and we're very far away, very, very far away. Don't you remember?' But Alfonso, clinging to his niece, didn't seem ready to understand. 'What d'you bet it isn't him? Look, he's coming this way. You see, it isn't Nicanor, is it?'

Alfonso looked up now. He stared at the policeman, who was searching for an empty table, and then he flushed.

'No, it isn't.'

Tamara gave him three kisses – one on the forehead and one on each cheek – and squeezed his hand. Then she sat down beside him and proceeded to eat two hamburgers in a row, as if nothing had happened. Alfonso took a little longer to recover, but did so eventually. Meanwhile Sara decided to follow Andrés's example. He had watched the entire scene wide-eyed, not daring to intervene or ask any questions. After some ice cream, they decided to return to the tank of balls before going home. Tamara let Alfonso go on ahead with Andrés and walked beside Sara, taking her hand.

'Nicanor isn't someone at the daycare centre,' she said. 'He was a friend of my father's and he's a policeman. We never see him now. Alfonso was very scared of him, because he always had a gun and a truncheon, and he's really horrible. Alfonso must have got confused.'

'Of course,' answered Sara, sensing behind Tamara's poorly concealed anxiety the weight of a lie she repeated, not for the sake of it, but because it was best for everyone. Sara didn't mention the incident again, but from that moment on, she watched Alfonso Olmedo with greater interest.

At the end of the holidays, Alfonso went back to his daycare centre, Tamara and Andrés went back to school, and Sara missed them even more than she had in September. This time, though, she didn't feel as lonely. And not just because the children, now almost always accompanied by Alfonso, seemed to have decided that Sara's timid invitation to tea on the first Sunday in January was extended indefinitely, or because that first afternoon they each arrived with a present – a cup, vase and ashtray, all decorated by hand – making up for Father Christmas's amnesia towards her over the previous decades. That Christmas ended with something more than the certainty that long, silent Sundays were a thing of the past. From now on, whenever she grew tired of her plans for Maribel's flat, Sara could amuse herself by imagining myriad different stories about Juan Olmedo, and she no longer felt guilty about it, or blamed it on her boredom. The stories and silences of the house opposite bound her to its occupants by an invisible thread, keeping her awake, and keeping her company.

The year began with a stroke of luck for Dr Olmedo. Although he'd never played the lottery regularly, he'd sometimes joined in at the hospital in Madrid, where there was always some older and astonishingly efficient nurse who took charge of buying the tickets. His winnings had been minimal so far and at first it seemed that this would also be the case in Jerez. But then, in the New Year draw, the Rehab Department won one of the big prizes. The money was divided up amongst all the patients and staff, as well as some of the nurses and doctors in other departments. Juan Olmedo was one of them, and received two million pesetas.

He was delighted, although it occurred to him that the sum he'd won was a little awkward. He didn't say so, of course, and outwardly he seemed as happy as was to be expected, paying for the meal the next time he went out to dinner with Miguel Barroso and a few other colleagues, and buying two large trays — one of cakes, another of canapés and savoury tarts — as a treat for the rest of the staff. This last ritual, an essential precaution to ward off the misfortune that might be hitching a ride on the tail of luck, was a kind of tribute to his mother. Though never wealthy, she had always carried loose change in her purse out of superstition, to give to anyone she saw begging in the street. When Damián began to do well in business, she often told him that if he didn't share some of what he earned, he'd end up with nothing sooner or later. Her prediction had come true, although not in the way she'd expected. When he died, Damián was richer than ever, having discovered that his true vocation was earning money.

Juan didn't really know what to do with the two million pesetas. Had he won a tenth of the amount, he would have spent it on something trivial; had it been ten times greater he would have had no choice but to invest it. But two million – too much money to fritter away on expensive dinners – was a derisory sum to invest, particularly when the single beneficiary of this modest amount, and any interest it might yield, would one day be a very wealthy woman anyway. Tamara's parents had died without leaving a will, but circumstances had turned Juan into his niece's guardian and, in that capacity, he had had a meeting before leaving Madrid with Damián's lawyer and tax adviser in order to make plans for Tamara's inheritance. After looking carefully at the state of his brother's businesses, he decided not to sell Tamara's interest in any of them. He didn't know whether the other partners were trustworthy or not, but he certainly trusted Antonio, an old friend from the area where they grew up whom Damián had gradually made into a kind of general representative on his behalf, thanks to an initial recommendation from Juan. Many years earlier, when all three of them were still in their twenties, Juan had helped Antonio to come off heroin, and then asked Damián to give him a job. Juan knew that in his radical transformation into a respectable man, Antonio had not forgotten his past. Following Damián's death, Antonio advised that it would not be a good idea to dispose of the chain of bakeries, and another of cafés, as they'd been more or less running themselves for years and were as dependably profitable as slot machines. And he promised Juan he'd watch over Tamara's interests as if they were his own. Juan knew the value of Antonio's word, so he accepted, even before Damián's legal advisers supported the decision. He sold only a few properties –

Damián's cars and two plots of land that hadn't yet been built on in a development in El Escorial.

Juan did, however, keep the two houses in which Tamara had lived with her parents, and where it was conceivable she might some day live with her own children. The house in Estepona, with a small garden and its own tiny swimming pool, was only a bungalow, but it was worth a lot of money because it was on a luxurious estate, a sort of private club for millionaires with services provided so that it had all the advantages of a hotel. The company that ran the estate also operated as a rental agent, letting out the properties for weeks, months or years at a time, when they were not being used by their owners. Juan handed them the keys to his brother's house and soon saw from the bank statements that it had become one more source of income.

The house in the Colonia Bellas Vistas in Madrid, on the other hand, remained closed. Antonio took charge of paying a gardener and getting a cleaning company to go in every six months to keep the house in good condition. It was the kind of house that Juan, and all the other teenagers in the Estrecho district, had sworn they would one day live in. The street of houses, all with gardens, was separated from the rest of the world by railings that constituted much more than a boundary. Initially these houses were planned as holiday homes in the days when Madrid stretched only as far as Cuatro Caminos. But by the middle of the twentieth century, the unrestrained advance of the cranes had turned what had once been an outlying district into an area as central as any that could be reached by metro. Since then, the street, with its leafy gardens, ancient acacias, plane trees, and vine-clad pergolas that absorbed the coolness from the earth beneath, had been like an island, an oasis immune to the noisy eruption of blocks of flats that soon surrounded it on all sides.

Within the wrought-iron railings, not all the houses were

the same. Some had been knocked down many years earlier and the plots of land on which they stood divided into two or three, with smaller houses that bore little relation to the ambitious proportions of the originals. At first Damián had bought one of the smaller houses, waiting patiently for almost ten years until he could afford to buy something bigger: a magnificent place built over three floors with a Swiss chalet-style exterior that had been the whim of the banker who built it in the twenties, together with many other unusual decorative features, such as the fabulous mahogany staircase – one long, straight flight of stairs – that would eventually claim Damián's life.

After Damián's dramatic fall, Juan moved into one of the guest bedrooms until he came to a decision about Alfonso's and Tamara's futures, accepting from the start that their fate would determine his. In the months after Tamara's tenth birthday until the summer of the following year, he had plenty of opportunity to appreciate the privileged life that the occupants of such a house enjoyed, but he never felt comfortable there. When he gathered the rest of the family to tell them that he was thinking of closing it up, selling his own flat, and moving to a small town on the coast, his two sisters couldn't understand. Paca, the sister who was most like him, felt his forehead as if checking for a fever, and asked him if he was delirious. Leaving such a beautiful, pleasant home, taking Tamara out of school and Alfonso away from his daycare centre, and embarking on a totally new life in a remote town, would have seemed like madness even if Juan had some experience of running a home. 'I know you, and this is ridiculous,' she warned him, 'absolutely crazy.' Their other sister, Trini, was as ambitious and mercenary as Damián, but had had a very different life from him. She weakly agreed with Paca for the time it took her to analyse the situation and assess how she could use it to her benefit, then suddenly changed sides and backed Juan, suggesting that she and her three children could move into the house in Bellas Vistas to keep it in good condition until Tamara was old enough to decide what to do with it. 'Closing up a house like that is as good as abandoning it,' she added, 'that's obvious.' Juan knew just what Trini was capable of – her divorce had been a long, sordid legal battle with a man who was even more crafty, selfish and, if possible, more money-grubbing than her. So Juan refused to let her move into the house from the start, and his younger sister called him all the names under the sun, swearing that she'd never speak to him again. Paca burst out laughing when she heard this and, after Trini had left, slamming the door behind her, warned Juan that the main risk of his plan was that, if he really was going to live by a beach, Trini would sooner or later come to stay and spend the whole summer scrounging off him.

This proved to be an accurate prediction: on Christmas Day in 2000, Trini phoned Juan, after only four months of not speaking to him. 'We really miss you,' she said in a theatrically emotional tone that didn't actually sound entirely false. 'Are you thinking of coming to visit us? No? Well, let's see if we can come to you, when the children are on holiday.' Juan assured her they were welcome to stay, and tried to sound as if he meant it. He was happy to have his sister and her children enjoying his home as long as they didn't take advantage of what was still, in a way, Damián's hospitality.

He had been so rigidly scrupulous about not using any of his brother's money, that there came a time when he realised it might actually be detrimental. But if, outwardly, he seemed to relax his standards, it was mainly to avoid questions he didn't want to answer.

'I'm sorry, Juanito, but I don't understand,' said Antonio one day, reflecting the views of Damián's other financial advisers. 'I can see why you do it for Alfonso – he's your younger brother, so he's your direct responsibility, you might say – but Tamara? She's not your daughter, she's Damián's, and she has plenty of money, even though she's only ten. So why should you pay all her expenses? It doesn't make sense.'

'But I don't mind.'

'What does that have to do with it? We're not talking about your feelings, we're talking about money.'

'About money I don't need.'

'At the moment – you don't need it at the moment, because you're single and you don't have any expensive vices. But you might want to get married some day.'

'No.'

'You might want to get married,' Antonio went on as if he hadn't heard, 'and have a couple of children of your own.'

'I'm not going to have any children.'

'You don't know that, Juan. You can't know, nobody does. And your circumstances might change for the worse. You might become ill, have an accident, fall into a depression, I don't know. Then you'll need money, and you'll be sorry you spent it all unnecessarily. Please listen to me. Pay for Tamara's school fees out of her own money, at least. Aren't the mortgages on the Madrid house and the house by the beach still being paid out of her inheritance? Well, this is the same: a direct investment in her future. If you're worried that people will think you're taking advantage of the child's money, you're wrong. I'd like to remind you that her income is considerably greater than yours.'

'That's not it, Antonio, that's not it at all,' said Juan, shaking his head stubbornly.

'Isn't it?' Antonio looked sceptical, unwilling to believe otherwise. 'So what is it, then?'

Juan didn't want to answer Antonio's question, so he ended up agreeing to award himself a kind of allowance, a modest amount equivalent to Tamara's school fees augmented by ten per cent. The first day of every month, he received a transfer to a bank account opened specially for the purpose and from which he never withdrew a single peseta. Month after month, term after term, all the money he didn't want to spend would accumulate, until Tamara finished school. He considered paying his lottery winnings into this account instead of spending them, but in the end he decided that this would be no better than buying a new car, a state-of-the-art music system or a huge flat-screen TV. He preferred not to mix his own money with Damián's, not even in the clean anonymity of nameless numbers.

But his brother was with him, wherever he went, asleep or awake, even when there was nothing around to prompt the memory. He had never walked along a beach in winter with Damián, but the sea brought him back, and so did the wind flattening the tops of the palm trees that you wouldn't find in Madrid, and the stealthy doodle of a lizard scurrying across a white wall, shaded by bougainvilleas, in the garden of a house that his brother had never seen. Any movement, any landscape, any gesture could summon the presence of a strong, agile boy, swift and good with his hands, smiling; Dami, as they called him in those days, aged ten or eleven, sitting on the kerb outside the house in Villaverde Alto, legs crossed, holding something in his lap, head tilted to one side and the sun glinting reddish-gold in his curly, chestnut hair. This was how Juan pictured him wherever he went: always sitting on the kerb, oblivious to the wheels of the cars and the feet of the passers-by, in shorts and one of the stripy T-shirts he and Juan jointly owned before either of them thought he had the right to anything of his own. Dami the magnificent, the best, repairing his mother's coffee grinder, or trying out a card trick, or holding some piece of junk that he'd found in the street. In his memory, Juan went up to him slowly and stood beside him. His brother looked up and, recognising him, smiled with his whole face, his eyebrows, his eyes, his chapped lips, his dazzlingly white teeth. And across the years, the oblique, perverse laws of love and resentment, Juan still took delight in that smile. Damián was dead but his smile would break as rhythmically as the tides as long as Juan was alive to nourish it with his memory and his guilt.

Juan didn't want to picture Damián, didn't want to remember him as he was when he loved him more than anyone else, but he never managed to shut his eyes in time, as Dami stood up and showed him the gadget he'd just made. The world would have been a better place without him, Juan thought as he heard the distant, innocent echo of his own childish voice, admiring Damián's inventiveness with fervent devotion. The world just had to be a better place without Damián, Juan repeated to himself as he watched him wipe his hands on his trousers and fell into step beside him, his own arm around his brother's neck. The world would be a better place without Damián. Meanwhile, the two Olmedo boys returned home, the clever one and the foolish one, the good one and the bad one, arm in arm, letting go only at the foot of the stairs, Dami always getting to the front door first. The world wasn't a better place without Damián. As he turned to look at Juan, and smiled again, and waited for him before ringing the bell, Juan tried desperately to manipulate the image, to superimpose a frown on Damián's smooth brow, trouble in the clear, bright, hazel eyes, a thin, disgusted mouth on the cool, parted lips, elements that should have slipped easily over his brother's features as they expressed him more truly than the lively, naive boy's smile that tormented Juan but that he could never quite erase. He could clearly remember the face that Damián had created for himself over the years, the face he deserved in the end: the double chin, the veins in his neck that bulged when he raised his voice, the permanent dark rings from all those late nights, the bloated cheeks on mornings when he had a hangover, the way he breathed in quickly through his nose when he was nervous, and the slack lips, the lower one always drooping, folded over itself like an old man's, even when he looked pleased. Juan clearly remembered all these details, summoning them easily to his memory, but he could never quite banish the image of the little boy sitting on the kerb, who looked back through the eyes of the man he became.

When Damián slipped and fell down the stairs, Juan composed a sentence that he would never get to say out loud, but that would have a decisive effect on the rest of his life. It was not, however, an answer to the question Damián had asked the moment before he lost his balance and found only air instead of the top step: 'D'you think I care?' he'd shouted at Juan, the veins in his neck rigid, his face red, his lips curling with contempt. 'I've always known, I've always . . .' Juan Olmedo never answered Damián's question, nor did he ever manage to complete his brother's unfinished sentence. None of this worried him at the time, as he was absorbed by a single, obsessive thought: the world would have been a much better place if his brother Damián had never lived. This was what Juan was thinking the moment his brother died. And when it was all over, when everything around him seemed to start again, he sometimes repeated a variation of that sentence – 'The world would have been a much better place without you.' He didn't say it to himself, but to the image of a child in shorts and a striped T-shirt, sitting on the kerb.

Dr Juan Olmedo knew the theory behind this phenomenon, the reason his mind clung only to the good memories, the perverse mechanism of nostalgia that made him forget what he knew and brought to the surface things he barely remembered, when everything was as it should be and Dami was the best brother in the world, his other half. He couldn't behave as if he felt guilty, because allowing himself to do so would be to forsake Alfonso, and his niece, the child whose happiness was so important to him. But he knew guilt was there, lying in wait for him, and that the only intelligent thing to do was learn to live with it. At first, he thought this would all pass, that the removal lorries would complete the work accomplished by time and distance. But this didn't happen. In the almost absolute calm of that dry, mild winter by the sea, Dami was still with him, endlessly winning the race. Juan had a feeling he would become accustomed to his mute, smiling vigil, just as he had grown used to so many other things in his life.

Charo finished applying her lipstick and examined her face in the little compact she was holding. Looking pleased with the result, she turned round in her chair to face him.

'Well?' she said. Juan had never seen her with her war paint on. Before he had time to ask her what she meant, she continued: 'Are you going to take me to the cinema or not?'

His sister-in-law's lips, perfectly outlined with a very dark pencil and filled in with a colour more dangerous than red, deeper than crimson, glossy yet almost brown, caught his gaze like the inner petals of a carnivorous flower.

'Well, I don't know,' he stammered. 'If you'd like to go.'

'I would, very much,' she said with a smile he found confusing, because on any other woman's face its meaning would have been unambiguous. 'I'd really like to,' she said, pronouncing the words a little more deliberately than necessary.

'Yes, go on, Juanito, take her to the cinema,' said his mother who was gathering up the tablecloth, wearing her Sunday best. 'You can drop me off at Aunt Carmen's on the way. She's asked me to go over for coffee with Alfonso.'

Juan looked at his mother, trying to appear calm, and then looked at Charo suspiciously, like an adult trying to surprise a small child who has been too quiet for too long. She had just put her cigarettes in her bag and was taking out her sunglasses, looking so casual it seemed impossible that she could have planned this in advance. He was getting used to never knowing how to behave around her. The most sensible thing would be to go straight home, alone, but as he was trying to summon his strength, she called out:

'Well? Are we going?'

'Do you know which film you want to see?'

'Of course I do,' she answered with another equivocal smile. She gave a tiny laugh. Just then, Alfonso came into the sitting room, smelling of cologne, his face freshly washed, and wearing a pristine grey flannel suit.

'Don't I look handsome?' he asked.

'Very handsome,' said Charo. She went to put her arms around him and kissed him lightly, delicately, as she would later kiss her daughter when she was born.

All four of them squeezed into the lift, and it seemed to Juan that Charo was pressing against him a little more than was necessary, although she kept her back to him. He listened as she chatted to Alfonso in the high-pitched, bright voice that she used to get his younger brother's attention, and felt, or thought he felt, his sister-in-law pressing her bottom directly against his right thigh. Scenes like this had occurred regularly since Juan had returned to Madrid, almost a year before. Over the months, certain words, smiles, glances from Damián's wife had completely thrown him, from one Sunday to the next. Sometimes, he felt like the still centre around which Charo turned and turned, her eyes bright with the eager greed of a little girl gazing at a prized toy in a shop window every morning on the way to school. He enjoyed it, but the price of these fleeting stabs of pleasure was much too high. Because a moment after each auspicious gesture from his sister-in-law, often a movement so insignificant that nobody except him seemed to notice, Charo would leave with Damián, going back to the house where they lived, sleeping and waking together in the same bed, while the only thing Juan went back to was the certainty that he was a gullible fool, and the insidious memory of his past humiliation, a hideous wound that had never healed.

On their way to the car, they passed Mingo's Bar. Looking as weary as ever, the proprietor was wiping a table with a dirty cloth. He called out a perfunctory greeting and they answered. Juan glanced to his right and saw the rare threat of Charo's dark-red lips, the outline of her breasts beneath a tight, black, low-cut T-shirt. Juan looked down at the pavement and was taken back to another time, another hot afternoon, not in April this time but towards the end of September, on the verge of a languidly warm autumn. He remembered the heat. Over the past few weeks, café tables had been put away and then set out on the pavement again according to the whim of the thermometer, as if the cruel summer Juan had spent without her was determined to last for ever. It was then that he saw them together for the first time: Damián and Charo sitting next to each other, part of a group in which Juan recognised several of her friends, members of the gang she couldn't do without but whose friendship he had never sought, and some of Damián's friends, including Nicanor. And it was Nicanor who looked round and stared at him, smiling in vicarious but unmistakable triumph, snarling like a guard dog, as if he was the one most pleased by Juan's defeat. Juan shouldn't have stopped, he should have just kept on walking, have passed by without looking round and gone home, but Charo was wearing a low-cut, white T-shirt, and she was very pretty, and very tanned, and Juan couldn't help himself. He stopped in the middle of the pavement, slowly took a pack of cigarettes from his pocket, then a cigarette from the pack, and finally a lighter from another pocket, just so that he could keep watching them and make sure it was really true. Charo with Damián. He couldn't take it in. But he was to feel even worse when Damián, catching sight of him at last, hugged

Charo's body tightly and slid a hand down over her breast, squeezing it from below, pushing it up inside her T-shirt, all the while staring straight at Juan, with a black eye and an even more crooked smile than usual. She let Damián fondle her then realised that he was staring at something. Following the direction of his gaze, she saw Juan, standing there on the pavement. She wriggled out of Damián's embrace as quickly as she could, sat up straight and pretended to be listening to the conversation to her right. She was blushing, but far from this making Juan feel any better, it only increased his fury. He had always treated her with as much respect as his painfully intense desire for her allowed, only to discover, now, that she seemed to enjoy having his brother touch her breasts in public, proving to himself once more that he was an absolute and utter fool.

By the time he got home, he felt worse than he ever remembered having felt in his life. Juan knew that Damián's cocky display of triumph – so typical of him – was a way of getting back at him, a response to the punch that had thrown him to the ground a couple of days earlier. But knowing this didn't do Juan any good. Quite the opposite. At this point in his life, knowledge seemed to have turned against him like an enemy.

'Well, what do you think?' his brother had asked, tossing a newspaper on top of Juan's book. 'And this is just the start.'

That was how it had all begun. What Damián had dropped on Juan's desk was a sort of free newspaper, four sheets of cheap paper folded in two, that the shopkeepers of Estrecho left on their counters for customers to pick up. He'd occasionally leafed through the pages full of adverts interspersed with the odd article or report and a couple of items on aspects of local life. On the front page of the Autumn issue 1980, printed on a surface so porous that all the colours had bled into each other making the print almost illegible, was a photo of Damián in a suit and tie and leaning on an office desk, smiling at the camera. Beneath it was a caption that declared: 'You're never too young to succeed'.

'To be honest, you don't look too good,' said Juan, suppressing a laugh. He couldn't resist the temptation of pointing out Damián's eyes in the photo, smudged with blue, yellow and red. 'You look like you're wearing make-up.'

'Very funny,' said his brother, snatching the paper from him and folding it carefully, as if it were something fragile and precious. Juan said nothing more, because it was obvious that, to Damián, the ridiculous article was exactly that – something precious.

Since finishing school – which he'd done grudgingly, with great difficulty, and only to comply with his father's plans – Damián had started three businesses in just over two years, and all of them were doing very well. There had been nothing to suggest he would have such success when, in return for unexpectedly passing his exams, he got a loan from his father to buy a small sweet shop. The shop, which had been closed for years, was just next door to one of the biggest schools in Madrid, and very close to their home. Damián reopened it, saved up to buy a hot-dog machine, installed another for popcorn, and started selling comics, magazines, cigarettes, ice cream and sandwiches. When he had enough money to pay back the loan, he asked his father if he could delay repayment and got an additional loan from the bank – taken out in Juan's name at first, because Damián was still a few months underage at the time. He then took on a shop that had never, in all its previous incarnations, been successful. There were already quite a few bread shops in the area, but the one Damián started up had a distinctive name, The Bread Boutique, and sold all sorts of exotic bread: bread with raisins, with nuts, with seeds, bagels, rolls of all shapes and sizes, white bread, wholemeal bread, rustic bread, baguettes, breadsticks and savoury snacks. To his family's surprise it was a huge success. He opened the sweet shop at key times, at the beginning and end of the school day, because schoolchildren seemed to have more disposable income than anyone could have imagined and, for a few months, he employed his mother part-time in the bread shop, from eight to nine thirty in the morning and from one till two in the afternoon. His sister Paquita looked after the sweet shop from five till eight in the evening, until he was doing well enough to take on a full-time assistant. Damián's bakery had been open over a year when the shop next door to it became vacant. His parents begged him not to take on too much too soon, not to burden himself with another loan, but the bank manager, who'd appreciated Damián's business acumen from their very first meeting, said he'd lend him as much as he needed. Damián gave it a lot of thought, did his sums, and decided to take the risk. Again the business was a huge success. By the time his business career attracted the attention of the local paper, he owned, in addition to the sweet shop and the bread shop, a café where he served the bread and rolls he sold in the shop next door (with fillings and at greatly inflated prices), thus guaranteeing, as he put it in all his promotional material, the quality and freshness of his products. Juan had followed his brother's progress with the same combination of awe and admiration that half the district felt, and he was amazed that nobody else had ever thought of trying the ideas that were now making Damián rich.

'It's simply a question of perspective,' Damián said to him one evening when an excess of alcohol combined with the intoxication of success made him more talkative than usual. 'Who lives in this area? People like Papa and Mama, who aren't too badly off any more, who started at the bottom and worked hard and have done well in the end. Then, there are people who earn more but who live here because they can't afford a flat in the Calle Serrano yet. So what does that mean? Well, it's no longer a working-class area. Even the worst parts of it are all more or less middle-class now, because it's so central. And opposite the Dehesa park they've just built some blocks of flats for people who've got much more cash than the families in the old blocks, and that's not counting the Bellas Vistas estate. This is a middle-class area now, even if the residents don't know it. And why don't they know it? Because of the shops. Because even if they can't afford a flat in the Calle Serrano, they don't mind paying twenty-five pesetas more for a special loaf of bread, or the extra two hundred pesetas it costs to have a croissant filled with crab and a cinnamon-flavoured coffee in a place like mine, which is smart and has modern furniture, instead of a plain white coffee and a piece of tortilla in Mingo's Bar, where the floor's covered with screwed-up napkins and the tables have all got initials carved into them. They feel flattered into spending their money, because it seems like the kind of thing people from somewhere elegant like Salamanca would spend their money on. It's not always about cutting prices. Sometimes, you earn more by putting prices up. That's the secret.'

But despite the clear, astute, shrewd way Damián presented all of these calculations, Juan knew his brother's weakness, the ambition hidden beneath the self-possessed exterior and the arrogance of his words. On the top shelf of the bookcase they shared, stored in order of date and protected, or hidden, by a plastic folder, was a stack of articles – almost always from magazines or Sunday supplements – featuring young entrepreneurs who were millionaires by the age of twenty, owning chains of clothes shops, software companies or huge nightclubs in Ibiza or the Costa del Sol. Damián might have devoted his energies to convincing his neighbours they lived in a middle-class area but he couldn't resign himself to being like them, to belonging to the same dull, mediocre class. As the young, almost childish, faces in the magazines became celebrities, there grew inside him an unqualified desire to emulate them, and a dark resentment as his merits remained unrecognised.

'Look at this one!' he'd say, pacing around the table that took up most of the space in the small dining room of his flat. 'Inherited a jeweller's from his parents! Can you believe it? And this one! What about this one? I mean, she's thirty! A model agency? Ha! I bet she's the only one on her books. Call that being an entrepreneur? Give me a break!'

When they witnessed these outbursts of indignation, his parents and sisters were supportive, breaking out into all sorts of sympathetic lamentations – 'I know, it's unfair! You've worked so hard, son, and you started from scratch. These articles are always about the same people! All this talk about democracy, but if you don't have a famous name, there's nothing you can do. It's a disgrace, it really is an absolute disgrace' – and Damián would finally shut up. Juan's voice was the only one missing from the shrill, bitter chorus, the noisy exercise in catharsis that the family offered as consolation to Damián, their unsung hero. Damián's insistence on seeking social recognition, the only reward to elude him so far, inspired in Juan a strange mixture of compassion and embarrassment. For him, it was the most disconcerting aspect of his brother's sudden acquisition of wealth. He was as sure as any sane person could be that no writer from a big newspaper would ever pick up the phone to find out about the owner of the smartest bread shop in Estrecho, however thriving it was. In the world to which Damián unrealistically aspired, his business talents didn't elevate him above the status of a pygmy, and even if he did ever manage to turn himself into the 'Bread King' of northern Madrid, it would make no difference, because the glamour shots in these magazines had little to do with the size of a person's bank balance. That Damián didn't realise this, and was so vain with so little pride, was a mystery that Juan couldn't fathom. He couldn't help acknowledging Damián's talent and his great ability, but for the first time in his life, he thought his brother appeared rather foolish, a pathetic caricature, a clown prepared to sell his soul to the devil for three lines and a photo in a newspaper. This was why he said nothing about what would be Damián's first and only media success, a blurry photo with smudged colours that you couldn't even recognise as Damián without squinting. But Damián knew him too well to accept that his silence was neutral, and after filing the interview of which he was so proud in the same folder as the ones that fuelled his ambition, he pulled from his sleeve the only ace that could leave Juan naked, ruined.

'Oh, yes, and another thing – that girl Charo who lives on the second floor, the one you were going out with?' Juan swivelled in his chair and looked at him. 'Well, now she's going out with me.'

This time Juan didn't miss. Damián found himself on the floor before he'd even had time to lose the self-satisfied smirk with which he'd made his announcement. Juan knocked him down with a single blow, a punch directed at his right cheek that reached its target with force and precision. Charo's new boyfriend now had a cut under his eye which, within a few hours, would develop into a magnificent bruise, making Damián look rather more like his photo in the local paper. Though it was many years since Juan had won a fight with Damián, though his victim wasn't even sure how it had happened, Juan knew that his victory had no more value than the miserable little interview that had prompted the fight.

'You bastard,' he said anyway, looking down at him before walking out of the room.

'Ha!' said Damián from the floor, and then again before getting up: 'Ha, ha!'

Forty-eight hours later, that odious little laugh was echoing in Juan Olmedo's head while the image of Charo and Damián naked, caressing each other on a bed, pounded inside him with the merciless, mechanical throb of a pneumatic drill. He recalled the words with which his brother had concluded his hateful speech about Charo being out of Juan's league – 'Bet you haven't fucked her yet, have you? Bet you haven't even fucked her.' He told himself that Damián was an idiot – Juan knew that already, but he couldn't lose to his brother in such a pitiful way. Before he could summon even the appearance of calm, he had to pass through the full gamut of foolishness, alone in his room, pacing up and down in the tiny space, making plans. He'd kidnap Charo – without hurting her – knock her out with chloroform and take her somewhere safe, the boiler room at his old school in Villa-verde Alto, for instance; a huge basement that nobody checked from April to November because the heating wasn't turned on. The padlock on the door was easy to open and he and his friends had forced it many times, going there to smoke joints or make out with girls. He'd take Charo there, tie her to a chair and wait patiently for her to regain consciousness. 'Don't be scared,' he'd say to her, 'I'm not going to hurt you, I just want you to listen. You've got it all wrong, Charito, you've made a big mistake, and I'll prove it to you.' Then he'd tell her the truth, that Damián, with all his businesses, all his money, driving about in his new car acting like a big-shot, was pathetic, a deluded fool who'd sell his own mother for half a page in the Sunday supplement of El Pais, and who couldn't love her. Damián would never love her the way he did, because he was better, more intelligent, more sensitive, more self-aware than his brother, and he was so in love with her that he couldn't find the words to express anything close to how he felt. 'How can you be so blind, Charo?' he'd ask her. 'How could you do this to me? Is it because he takes you to expensive places? Gives big tips to the doormen at nightclubs? What a load of shit that is, Charito. I loved you so much my eyes hurt just from looking at you, and my fingers ached every time I touched you. I would have done anything for you, anything.'

At this point, terrified by his own weakness, Juan fell onto the bed. Reality was very different from his fantasy, and it was also very simple. Charo wasn't tied to a chair, her hair clammy with sweat and sticking to her face, her eyes wide with fear and surprise, showing that she understood at last. He wasn't walking towards her, then slowly circling the chair, he wasn't standing behind her, letting her feel his prick on the back of her neck, or covering her breasts with his hands, or pinching her nipples, or whispering in her ear: 'If this is what you like, I can do this too.' Instead he was alone in his room, lying on his bed, rejected, humiliated by the only girl he'd ever been in love with, and she was out there somewhere, fucking his brother. It was too dreadful, he simply couldn't accept it, even if it was true. So he masturbated slowly, delicately, trying to prolong this break from all the pain. He had a very strong orgasm but felt cold at the same time, and the sticky feel of his semen covering his hand made him feel a combination of pity and disgust. Afterwards, he sat on the edge of the bed, opened his eyes, closed them again, fell back and started to cry like a child.

The following morning the sky was grey, as it would be for many months to come. He didn't see Damián until lunch and then, although he didn't say a single word to him, and nothing happened to distinguish that meal from any other, everything seemed to collapse inside him. Looking at his brother, happily joking with his sisters and complimenting his mother on how delicious her lentils were, he had a precise image of his future life – the constant, unremitting fear of seeing her again, and of seeing her with Damián, fear of bumping into her in the building, at birthday parties, fear of the telephone ringing and having to answer it without knowing whether it would be her on the other end of the line. 'I'm fucked,' he thought as he left the table, 'well and truly fucked.' This feeling never quite went away in the following months, but he grew used to his new situation sooner than he would have thought possible. He became accustomed to seeing Charo every day, hearing her voice in the corridor, finding her sitting at the lunch table on a Sunday, seeing her laugh, and talk, and kiss Damián; accustomed to having her close but not being able to touch her or kiss her, not even wanting to look at her.

Almost eight years later, as he got out of the car in the Calle Altamirano at the entrance to his Aunt Carmen's building, Juan Olmedo barely recognised himself in that boy who had suffered so much, that gauche, withdrawn child who had a strong sense of duty but was too proud, helpful and unsociable at the same time, quiet and a little distracted, excelling only at his studies, sitting glued to his books for hours on end. And yet he retained a memory of the passion too, the violence and desire that had never ceased to torment him over the years. He had never desired Charo more than he did now, when he could imagine with absolute precision the echo of the voice in her ear, the feel and size of the body pressing against hers, the familiar amalgam of words and stock phrases, of movements and gestures, habits and quirks. He knew his brother well, he'd known him all his life, so he could see him even when he didn't want to, his profile against a pillow, his hand on the small waist that Juan could still feel in his own fingers, or sinking into the sex of a satisfied girl who would happily return his every caress. And he was stuck in the middle, caught between them, tied to their bed, unable to shake off the daily torture of their company. Occasionally, he tried to object, to tear himself away from this mysteriously indispensable pain that enslaved him. He tried, but he didn't succeed, and every morning he felt he desired Charo a little more than the day before, and that the hatred he had begun to feel for his brother grew by the same amount. And yet, life continued. Much later, Juan Olmedo would understand that this was the most important lesson of those years – learning to live at any cost and despite everything. He would never forget the taste of fury, nor the mute screams with which he rebuked God during all those agonising years of sleepless nights: 'Give her back to me, God, give her back.' While Damián slept in the next bed, Juan writhed, facing the wall, making no sound: 'Give her back to me and I'll do whatever you want, I'll be whatever you want, I'll give you whatever you ask if you give her back to me.' He hadn't spoken to God since then, but when Charo sat beside him in the passenger seat, and the split in her skirt parted, and she did nothing to rearrange it, he wondered whether the Devil wasn't a little hard of hearing.

'Wait, don't drive off yet,' she said, lowering the sun visor and examining herself in the mirror. 'I need to touch up my make-up.'

'No, you don't,' he said, abandoning himself to his fascination as she re-applied her lipstick with less resistance than he would have liked. 'You look beautiful.'

'Really?'

'Damn you, you bitch,' he thought, but didn't say so. He just turned the key in the ignition and stared straight ahead, as if he hadn't noticed the poisonous sweetness of her last question. It was four in the afternoon on a Sunday and the Gran Vía was almost deserted, but the red lights gave him an opportunity to think. 'Nothing's going to happen,' he told himself. What could happen? She's just teasing me. It's too late – for me, for her, for everything. And yet he was nervous, as if hordes of ants were swarming under his skin. It wasn't the first time his sister-in-law had played this game, but she'd never gone beyond playful teasing and he, too aware of his own scars, hadn't even gone that far. But that afternoon, there was something new and it worried him. It was the first time that he and Charo had been alone since that spring evening, long ago, when he'd persuaded Damián to lend him money so he could take her to the most expensive disco in Madrid. And all of it had happened purely by chance. He'd rung the bell at his mother's house at two on the dot and found Charo there. She'd looked to his left, then his right, checking that no one was with him, before leaning calmly against the door, blocking his path.

'Where's Elena?' she asked.

'She can't make it, she's on duty.'

'That's a shame, isn't it?' she said, and smiled, as if nothing could have made her happier. 'Poor thing, working on a Sunday and missing your mother's paella. It's always so delicious.'

Only then did she let him in, and he followed her down the corridor to the dining room, where Damián was bragging to his in-laws that his friend Nicanor had managed to get two tickets for the royal box at the Calderón Stadium.

'Apparently, you get a drink beforehand,' he was explaining in his booming voice as Juan came in, 'and a cocktail after the match, so I hope we'll be having lunch soon – I've got to shoot off early.'

After he left, without waiting for dessert, Charo moved stealthily to her husband's chair so that she was sitting next to Juan.

'They've left us on our own, Juanito,' she whispered in his ear.

'So it seems.'

'We could go to the cinema,' she said and looked round. The television was on but nobody was near by. 'Like the old days.'

Those words caressed the bruised spine of the desperate boy that Juan had once been, but the man he had become still felt them as keenly as the edge of a knife. He kept his composure so admirably that he felt she must have been offended, and he forced himself to believe that nothing was going to happen, that nothing could happen, nothing at all. On reaching Callao, Charo's skirt revealing a tantalising glimpse of her glossy left thigh and her mouth curved in a private smile that didn't change as he parked the car, he still couldn't accept the possibility that something might happen, that he had been kidding himself, trying to hide from his own irresistible predisposition towards flinging himself into the abyss.

'OK, so where are we going?' he asked, looking at her, and she reacted somewhat strangely. 'You said the cinema you wanted to go to was in Callao, didn't you?'

'Yes, of course,' she said and leant forward so that her skirt slid open even further. 'Let's see. This one will do,' she said pointing at the building to their right. 'Yes, this one's fine.'

'What do you mean, it's fine?' he asked, laughing openly to hide the effects of the spasm that had just gripped his entrails. 'Do you want to see this film or not?'

'Of course I do! What are you talking about?'

Then they both laughed. She stopped and tried to behave casually as if there really was nothing going on as they walked to the entrance of the cinema. When they reached the ticket office, Juan Olmedo finally understood what was at stake. He suddenly felt weak, as vulnerable as when he saw her for the first time, dancing in front of the mirror.

'Get seats upstairs,' she said quickly, as if she could read his mind.

'Upstairs?'

'Of course. I like to watch films from high up,' she said, lying coolly.

'Since when?'

'Since always,' she said with an impatient pout. 'You've got such a bad memory, Juan.'

'The auditorium's almost empty,' said the woman at the ticket office. 'There are good seats downstairs.'

Juan turned to look at his sister-in-law, and she moved closer until she was pressing her body against his.

'Do as I say,' she whispered. 'Don't be silly.'

'OK, two seats upstairs then.'

A few minutes later, when the lights went down, they were the only people sitting in the gallery. The adverts were playing, just as they used to when he flung himself towards her, feeling for her with his mouth, his hands, blindly, and she would angrily protest. This was why he couldn't help leaning towards Charo and closing his eyes, brushing his face against her hair and smelling the air around her. But then he sat up straight in his seat once more and looked ahead at the screen, where a quick sequence of shots introduced the characters in an inane romantic comedy.

'The film's terrible, isn't it?' whispered Charo after a while.

He nodded, and waited.

'It's so boring,' she insisted a moment later. 'And I think I've seen it before. Yes, I saw it about a week ago. I'm such an idiot, aren't I? Unbelievable!'

'Do you want to leave?' he asked, stifling a nervous laugh.

'No, it's all right. Let's stay.'

For a few minutes the only action was limited to the screen. Then Charo moved, turning towards him, and very smoothly and very calmly she undid the top button of his jeans.

'What are you doing, Charo?'

'Well, I'm opening your flies.'

'Right, I got that.' He looked at his sister-in-law and saw her, mouth open, eyes focused on what her hand was doing. 'Why?'

'Because I want to get your prick out. See?'

Juan Olmedo, who had never been less and never more himself than at that moment, did as she suggested and saw his prick, erect in his sister-in-law's hand.

'Stop it, Charo,' he said with little conviction, his voice choking on the last syllable.

'I don't think so,' she answered. 'I've treated you badly, Juanito. It's time I started being nice to you. And I was dying of curiosity. I mean, I've never seen your prick before, or touched it – you were such a good boy back then. And anyway, it seems to like it.'

'But I don't.'

'I don't believe you.'

She began moving her hand slowly, up and down, the scattered first caresses acquiring a precise, unequivocal rhythm. He began to feel good, and his eyes went from his sister-in-law's face – tense, focused like a little girl determined to complete a difficult task – to the response of his pampered, privileged prick. It almost seemed to be smiling at him.

'We're a bit old for this, aren't we?' he protested feebly, trying to make his voice sound firm, even a little contemptuous.

'Oh, don't worry about that,' she said. Her voice was muffled, as if her tongue was swollen, the voice of a woman who was aroused and didn't mind showing it. 'I'll make it better in a minute. But first I'd like you to kiss me. Come on, kiss me, you haven't kissed me in almost eight years.'

As he leant in towards her, he kept his eyes open. His heart clenched at such a callous blow – the exact time they'd been apart, the duration of his pain. Charo parted her lips and welcomed him, but didn't allow her hand to pause even slightly. Her mouth still tasted of caramel but they were on the threshold of a new, savage hunger so different from the gentle delicacy of the first time they kissed, and Juan realised how much he'd changed and just how much he'd lost. Between the hesitant, slow waves of a pleasure that he could still control, he felt the memory of his anger grow, the old dark despair, and, surrendering to Charo's open mouth, he put his arm around her and took hold of her breast, the object of that distant, coarse display, and kneaded and pressed, squeezed and pinched it. In his head, meanwhile, the voice of a gauche, luckless boy who talked to God and said 'I love you' without moving his lips to his brother's girlfriend, struggled with the mature, self-satisfied sarcasm of a man who no longer needed anything from anyone and gritted his teeth as he yelled, 'Screw you now, bitch, screw you.' She didn't complain, didn't say anything, but maybe his pincer-like grip on her nipple prompted her next move, and Juan anticipated it, easily interpreting her intentions when Charo decided to change objective, pulling her head away from him and lunging at his belly. The lips that had looked so smug earlier in the day now ran up and down his prick, causing a familiar, increasing pleasure, and it was good, he could still control it, but at a certain point, near the end, he remembered to open his eyes. In the deceptive gloom of the darkened cinema, he saw her glossy black hair, smooth as a freshly ironed sheet, spilling over his jeans, and then he knew with certainty who he was, who she was, and he spoke to God again without even realising it.

'Now you owe me,' she whispered afterwards, leaning her head on his shoulder and pressing her forehead against his neck with a sudden, helpless urgency.

'Yes,' he admitted, shuddering to his bones. He held her tightly and kissed her on the lips, carefully, as he used to.

Neither of them moved again, or said anything, until the end of the film. Then, it was she who stood up first. She descended the stairs without looking back and she didn't look at him again until they were outside. When she smiled, after glancing at her watch, he realised that he had been waiting for that smile.

'It's only six thirty,' she announced, her voice gentle, neutral. 'We could go for a drink?'

'Of course,' he said, and his heart leapt in his chest with amazing, inappropriate glee. 'Do you still like Vips cafés?'

'Yes, I love them.' She smiled again, and took his arm. 'So you remember that, do you?'

'I remember everything, Charo. Everything.'

To prove it to her, when they sat opposite each other at a small orange table, in the kind of place she'd longed for when all he could afford was one and a half rum and Cokes, he anticipated her desires even before she'd looked at the menu.

'Would you like some pancakes, a hamburger, a triple-decker sandwich?'

'I wasn't referring to that kind of debt . . .'

'Nor was I. I just want you to know that I can afford it all now,' he said, looking into her eyes, and he saw how they suddenly grew dark and she drew away from him, her expression instantly changing from a mischievous grin to a vague grey shadow. 'That was it, wasn't it? That was what was wrong.'

'No,' she answered after a pause. 'Or yes. I don't know. I've never been very clever, as you know. Anyway, I'd like to have a piece of cake. Chocolate cake. And a rum and Coke.'

'And to change the subject,' he added, still looking at her, her eyes drawing him in, reminding him that he could spend his whole life looking at her.

'Well, yes. I'm a bit of a coward too,' she said, laughing, and he laughed too. 'But I've got other things going for me.'

'That's for sure.'

When the waiter brought her cake, she ate it slowly, following a strict system. She would lift a piece of chocolate icing with her fork and put it in her mouth, dissolving it on her tongue, then she cut the section of sponge directly beneath the icing and ate that, chewing delicately, savouring every last morsel. She didn't speak during this operation, only pausing to take long, frequent gulps of the rum and Coke, as if it were water. She seemed to be enjoying the cake so much he was sorry when the plate was empty.

'Would you like another one?'

'Not more cake.'

She smiled sadly, with almost painful intensity, before

looking at her watch and saying it was time to go. When they got outside, the air was warm, but although it was still quite light, Juan felt as if he had just entered a long, dark tunnel, defenceless, confused, and more alone than ever. Charo walked by his side, looking down at her feet, placing them in a straight line so that she stepped only on the cracks in the pavement, playing one of those silly games children enjoy. Then she changed tack suddenly and ran ahead, stopping a few metres away. She turned and watched him as he caught up with her. He didn't hurry, and saw her lips part and close again, uttering a word that was lost in the noise of all the traffic and the people hurrying past, sometimes turning to look – such a young woman standing there in the middle of the pavement, her glorious body tense with fear, or sorrow, her eyes fragile with sorrow, or fear, and uncertainty.

'Kiss me, Juan,' he heard at last as he reached her.

He looked at her lips. They'd lost their earlier bloody perfection – her lips, always promisingly fleshy, were now their own natural colour, and even more powerful, more dangerous than before. The pencil line that had traced their outline a few hours earlier was still there, but smudged. Juan followed it with his eyes, reconstructing it, and his whole life seemed to flash through his mind with the same, fleeting insistence of a condemned man's memories just before his death. As he stared at the blurred dark line, he saw himself, drowning in his own jealousy, working doggedly for his houseman exams, and he saw his brilliant results, and the look of amazement on his classmates' faces when he announced he was going to do his residence outside Madrid, as far away as possible from a city that was her, simply, only her. He had searched the map for the most remote places he could find, and chose Cadiz so that he could gaze at the ocean, the challenge of an unknown, endless expanse with America on the far side rather than the reassuring, familiar company of the Mediterranean. He remembered Cadiz, the year 1983, the light and happiness of the first few months, his obsession with finding her in other women, and seeing Charo herself at Christmas, in the summer, on a few long weekends. She seemed stranger, more alien, more different every time from the woman he carried with him, sewn to his skin, who repelled all intruders, every woman who dared invade her territory. Those poor women of flesh and bone could never compete with the essential perfection of her dazzling incorporeal form. It was this, the shimmering idea of her, that enabled him to see Charo in white and not suffer, to be a witness at her wedding and not believe it, to raise his glass in a toast to the happy couple and feel it was not the beginning of something.

Charo took a step forward. Juan could hear his mother weeping, her voice faltering on the other end of the line, then the words of his sister Paca, who was more composed: 'Papa's dead.' It was one morning in March 1986. 'He seemed fine, hadn't been complaining of anything when he went off to work. At the door to the shop, just as he was unlocking it, he collapsed and fell to the ground. A vein burst, or something, that's what they said, the aorta, I think, you know about that sort of thing. And he died, Juanito, by the time the ambulance got there he was dead.' He did indeed know. 'An aneurysm,' he said to himself as his eyes caressed the soft, smooth skin of Charo's lips, now parted, in a pause that would never last long enough. He knew now something he hadn't wanted to know then, the worm that gnawed at the corners of his anxiety and the guilt that condemned him for not having lived with his father during the last years of his life. He had loved the man, loved him deeply. He'd felt annihilated by the grief he felt as he sat staring out through the train window at the fields; later, embracing his mother as if he wanted to enclose her completely, crying and growing weary of crying, surrendering to the void that opened up inside him when he ran out of tears, all the time torn between the temptation to return and the certainty that it would be better for him to stay away. At the beginning and end there was Charo, and she came before the fears of his mother when she confessed that she didn't feel she could look after Alfonso on her own, she came before the old feeling of responsibility that he'd given up as his brother and sisters learnt to make their own breakfast and get themselves to school. It was Charo who was behind the exemplary speech of the model son offering to request a transfer, to find somewhere to live close to Estrecho and wear a pager so they could always get hold of him. Charo was everywhere, whether she was far away or near, Charo, who had looked at him again during the long nights that followed his father's death, Charo, who was looking at him now, standing on the pavement on the Gran Vía, with dim, blurred eyes that were not the eyes of a happy woman.

'Kiss me,' she said again and grabbed him by the lapels. But she didn't draw him towards her, didn't pull, and Juan looked at her and was frightened by what he saw – the haughty princess, the prettiest, the strongest was about to shatter into pieces in the middle of the street.

He had never stopped to wonder whether she was happy; he had never thought it was any of his business. And yet, as Charo's lips began to tremble, he realised that her happiness did matter to him, and that he would never be able to stand seeing her cry, not ever. She was looking at him as if she was hanging from a bridge clinging to an old, threadbare rope, and he could almost hear the sound of it snapping. Suddenly, a car hooted, and an unexpected image rose unbidden before his eyes. Elena was a paediatrician, she had red hair and the finest backside in the hospital. Juan hadn't thought of her at any time that afternoon, but now he could see her – Elena, who spoke German, and played the cello, and practised naked on Sunday mornings sitting on the edge of the bed, and wanted to marry him and live in the country, and have two kids, one with red hair, the other dark, like Juan. He felt a sudden stab of longing for this life, a placid future that would now never be, and the voice of his girlfriend – a happy, reasonable woman, efficiency personified – made its way from some hidden corner of his mind to suggest an alternative reading of the situation, making a last, desperate attempt to save him. 'She's your brother's wife, isn't she? She left you and then got involved with him, and now they're married. OK, the lady felt capricious and tricked you into going to the cinema so that she could give you a blow job. Great, that's what you got out of it, but what's going to happen now? Well, nothing. I'll forgive you when you tell me about it, you know I will. These things happen. I mean, this isn't going to change your life, or did you think it would? What were you thinking, Juan? For God's sake, you're almost thirty.'

Charo gripped his lapels hard for a moment before suddenly letting go, dropping her arms by her sides, fists clenched, and closing her eyes. Then it was Juan who took a step forward and put his arms around her, almost fearfully, and kissed her. He knew he was risking his life with that kiss, betting everything on a single card – and not the best one, maybe not even a good one at all – but it was the only one he'd ever had.

They walked back to the car park with their arms around each other and neither of them spoke. As he was waiting for his exit ticket, Juan glimpsed his reflection in a mirror and noticed the same metallic pallor that he could see on his sister-in-law's face, the same reddish shadows around the eyes. He suddenly felt very tired. He drove slowly, sorry that the Sunday traffic was so light, looking at Charo each time they stopped at the lights. She was brushing the glow of normality back onto her cheeks by the light of the street lamps.

'Shall I drop you off here?' he asked, trying out his brand-new adulterer's caution for the first time as they reached the entrance to the estate.

'No,' she answered, smiling. 'You can take me right in. Your brother isn't the least bit jealous. He's so sure he's the ideal man, the dream husband, it wouldn't even occur to him that I might look at anyone else. If someone told him I was cheating on him, his first thought would be that I'm an idiot. Then he'd get angry, of course. But at the moment it wouldn't even enter his head. Seriously. And I bet he doesn't know that his prick is smaller than yours. The day he finds that out, he'll slit his wrists.'

The car stopped without Juan being aware of having taken his feet off the pedals.

'It's stalled on you,' said Charo, and laughed.

'And it'll stall on me again if you say that sort of rubbish.'

'It's not rubbish, Juan, it's the truth. I told you before, I'm not that bright. I spend my life making mistakes and I always realise it too late. When I met you, I thought you were too nice, too studious, too serious. Do you remember? I found it too much the way you were always on top of me, pawing at me.' She smiled and turned her head to look straight ahead so that her gaze was lost in the growing darkness of the street. 'In those days I thought tough guys were right for me. And I thought your brother was one, but I was wrong about that too. Damián isn't hard, or soft, he's something else entirely. He simply isn't interested in anything, or anyone. That's why things go so well for him, because he doesn't care about anything. And sometimes . . . Now, when I see you with Elena at your mother's house, all serious like you used to be, so concerned for others, such a good son and a good brother . . . well, I don't think you're too good any more. And I wonder how you are with her, when you're alone, when nobody sees you, and I imagine that you treat her the way you used to treat me. The truth is I'm jealous. I'd love to have a husband who couldn't keep his hands off right now, but I've made such a mess of everything. So that business about the size of your prick isn't important. You don't have to worry, I'm not going to lie to you about that. I'm not all that clever, but I'm not stupid.'

She turned in her seat and looked at him, and Juan looked at her without seeing her, watching two fat tears sliding down her cheeks, her face different, yet the same, the exhausted, dusty face of a girl tied to a chair, her sweat-soaked hair sticking to her face, her eyes wide with fear and surprise, showing that at last she understood, that after all this time, she understood everything.

'Aren't you going to say anything?' Charo asked, shifting in her seat as if she were uncomfortable.

For a moment, Juan Olmedo considered starting up the engine and driving quickly past his brother's house, leaving the estate through the opposite entrance to the one they'd entered by, heading out of town on the first road he found, just driving, not stopping until he found a hotel three or four hundred miles from Madrid. But only for a moment.

'Tell me at least if you were in love with me.'

'You know I was, Charo.' Then it was she who didn't want to say any more, so he went on speaking, because he wasn't ashamed to tell her. 'Of course I was in love with you. Like a fool. Like an animal. Desperately in love.'

Then he started up the car. A couple of hundred yards further on, he saw Damián, standing outside his house chatting to Nicanor. He double-parked, in front of a gap just big enough for Charo to get out, but she didn't move.

'Look at him, so pleased with himself,' she said simply. 'I bet Atletico won. Flash your lights, go on, he hasn't seen us.'

Juan flashed the lights several times and Damián spotted them at last. He raised both hands, the left with three fingers up, the right with only one, before heading towards them.

'Three—one, no?' said Charo, smiling at the approaching

277

figure. 'What a dickhead.' Still looking in Damián's direction and smiling, she said to Juan: 'When's your next night shift?'

'Wednesday.'

'I'll come and see you on Thursday, at five.' Her husband was now beside Juan's car, putting his hand out to open the door. She went on: 'So you can get some sleep.'

'Well!' As he looked inside the car, Damián's face was still jubilant. 'What are you two doing here?'

'We've just been to the cinema,' Charo explained innocently. 'We both wanted to see the same film and as you and Elena both left us on our own . . .'

'That's good. The match was shit hot. Three–one against Bilbao, and it could have been more, because we played bloody brilliantly, really, bloody brilliantly. You'd have enjoyed it, Juanito. How was the film?'

'Well, you know, a silly romantic comedy. Nice, but I think Juan enjoyed it more than me.'

'I told you, he's always been soppy.'

Charo gave Juan a kiss on the cheek before getting out of the car and he drove home, stunned, euphoric, but above all confused, shaken by a current of wild happiness that was dangerous, but also strangely pure. In the following days, he lived at the centre of a storm, a fast, rosy whirlwind that, after all those years, still induced a painless pressure that burned like a fever. This passion receded from time to time and in isolated moments of clarity, when he could see himself objectively, he again heard Elena's voice, a rigorous analysis, both compassionate and cruel, that made him compare what was best for him with what he longed for. He knew he would always follow his desire. The sound of the doorbell made him jump out of his skin, and the telephone's ring made his stomach leap up into his throat, and during his shift on Wednesday night he was so concerned that a little girl who'd broken her arm falling out of a bunk bed should be comfortable and was so nervous when resetting the bone before putting it in plaster, that the nurse who was working with him stared and asked him if he'd had a vision of the Virgin Mary or something. 'No, but I think I've got an appointment with her tomorrow afternoon,' he said, and the nurse laughed and said maybe he shouldn't put any more limbs in plaster for the time being. 'You're likely to cripple someone today,' she added before she left.

On Thursday, at five to five, he prepared himself for disappointment, but she arrived on time. When the doorbell rang, he had to count to ten before standing up, and his legs were still trembling when he opened the door and found Charo standing there, with her impeccable red lips, and her body dressed all in white.

'Aren't you going to offer me a coffee?' she asked as she came in and dropped her handbag on the floor.

'No,' he said, pressing her against the door, a hunger in his hands that was over ten years old.

'That's good.'

That night, when he was alone again, Juan Olmedo had reached certain conclusions. The first and most painful, the one he would rather not have had to accept, was the crushing superiority of the real, flesh-and-bone woman, over the manageable, idealised version that he had created so meticulously over the years. While the universe shrank to fit the narrow confines of his bed, and Charo screamed with pleasure, Juan Olmedo would have given her everything, down to the last drop of his blood. Hours later, he still shivered as he remembered it. 'I'm done for,' he thought to himself, smiling. Completely done for, in love with her to the tips of his fingers, as he had always been and with a woman he didn't trust, who he would never trust. In those moments he thought that this last conclusion was more important than the one before, but time would prove that it was not so. Because from that night on, the only rule, the only aim in his life, would be defined by the colour of a lipstick.

The return of the west wind during the last days of February, ruining the promise of an early spring, was unwelcome to everyone except Juan Olmedo. While his niece complained loudly that her anorak felt heavy, more annoying and cumbersome than ever after almost three weeks of sun and light jackets, he looked up at the cloudy sky with pleasure and welcomed the gusts of wind that left their damp imprint on every window. The return of weather more appropriate to the season seemed to pacify Alfonso. Over the past few weeks he'd shown the kind of demanding, capricious, violent mood swings that Dr Gutiérrez at the daycare centre had warned Juan about when she predicted the effects of a combination of the east wind and good weather. The cold wind calmed Alfonso, but also made him a little depressed and gloomy. Juan wasn't worried because he was used to Alfonso's abruptly changing moods. What he hadn't been prepared for was how emotionally fragile he felt himself while the east wind blew, abandoning the seagulls to their bewildered fate.

Returning to night shifts did him good. He'd had a feeling it would, which was why he'd never thought of using his lottery winnings as a way of getting out of working nights for a year. And however much the extra money would come in handy now that he had so many expenses, it wasn't just a question of money. The thought of being awake and working while all around him the world was unplugging itself with drowsy fingers didn't appeal in itself, but the pleasure of an inverted routine – leaving the hospital at eight in the morning, going to bed when everyone else was getting up, sleeping three or four hours then still having almost the whole day left – more than made up for it. In the early days, he'd greeted the unaccustomed pleasure of having free time in the middle of a Tuesday or a Friday almost as if it were a prize. Later, that feeling became stronger when every night shift was followed by a morning in bed with Charo. Now he didn't have anything like that to look forward to, but he was still sure that working some night shifts would do him good. He had everything planned, although things didn't turn out exactly as he'd expected. Because Dr Olmedo, always conscious of his new domestic responsibilities, swapped better-paid night shifts at the weekends for shifts during the week, and this meant that when he got home, he was never alone.

What began to happen on those mornings and afternoons that had promised to be so tranquil, so indulgently peaceful, was so disconcerting that he ended up blaming the east wind, blowing savagely outside as if it were trying to unstitch the sky. He had been sure, or thought that he was sure, that he wasn't attracted to Maribel. This was what he'd thought when he saw her for the first time – that she was an attractive woman he didn't feel attracted to. He appreciated a certain level of strategic padding in women, and over the years he had gradually increased what he allowed himself to consider an excess, but Maribel was a step beyond this. Her face was too round, her cheeks too chubby and too rosy, like a bouncing baby bursting with health, which was emphasised by her clear eyes and her innocent, even guileless expression. Her body followed the same pattern: her tight clothes revealed the firmness of her flesh, and the healthy flush that coloured her cheeks also gave her arms, her legs, and her cleavage, a fresh, almost appetising look, like a newly washed apple. One day, to his surprise, Juan Olmedo found himself thinking that she must have great breasts, and admitted without surprise that she had a fantastic backside, although her calves were as thick and muscly as a cyclist's; but his interest went no further than these basic observations. Maribel didn't interest him because there was nothing interesting about her, neither her appearance, nor her story, nor her aspirations. This was why he hadn't even let himself be bothered by the discovery – even though it was logical, given the situation they were in – that his cleaner seemed to be entertaining the mad idea of seducing him. He even felt a little sorry for her when he saw her arrive all done up, looking plumper than ever in her new clothes. He felt sorry for her, and for Andrés, but he never thought about his own reaction, because he was sure he didn't find Maribel attractive. Or at least he thought he was sure.

'Good grief, what are you doing here?' Maribel had a bit of a shock the first time she saw him coming down the stairs in pyjamas in the middle of the day. 'Are you ill?'

'No, no,' he assured her. It was only then that he realised she would always be there on his days off, but he wasn't bothered by it, and apologised for not having told her in advance. 'I've just finished a night shift. I'm sorry, Maribel, I should have warned you, but I didn't think. When I get back from work you're usually already gone. I've been working all night so I don't have to go back until tomorrow.'

'Oh, yes, I remember you said something at the beginning, when I started working here. So is it always going to be like this?'

'Well, yes, more or less. I'll be doing one night shift a week, occasionally two, because I want to try to have Saturdays and Sundays off, so that Tamara isn't left on her own with Alfonso.'

'Right,' she said. She thought a moment and then smiled. 'Well, just let me know in advance.' And before he'd had time to wonder why she was smiling, she went on to explain: 'I'll need to know whether to cook lunch for you or not. Because you'll be eating here, won't you? The thing is, when the children aren't here I don't cook anything. I just have a sandwich and that's it.'

'Well, don't put yourself out for me. I'll try to bother you as little as possible.'

She said nothing, only smiled again, and again he didn't wonder why she was smiling. He went to the kitchen, made himself a coffee, got dressed, walked into town along the beach, bought a paper, had a beer, got back home at three, had lunch on a tray in front of the TV – 'It's only steak and chips and salad, I'm sorry I didn't have time to make any-thing else,' she apologised – and lay on the sofa, reading, until his niece got back from school.

A week later, he was already up when Maribel let herself in with her key, at around twenty to one.

'I've brought some stew I made at home,' she announced, taking a Pyrex dish from her plastic bag. 'Stews are always much tastier if they're made the day before. I hope you like it. I can cook some rice later to go with it.'

A couple of hours later, the aroma coming from the kitchen smelled so good that he felt embarrassed about eating the food alone, so he asked Maribel in a tone that was respectful, almost formal, in order to dispel any possible misunderstandings, if she wouldn't like to set the table for the two of them in the living room instead of eating on her own in the kitchen. She nodded, and as she went to and fro, first carrying a tablecloth, then plates, glasses and cutlery, Juan Olmedo noticed that, instead of her usual espadrilles, she was wearing high-heeled shoes that considerably improved the look of her thick calves. He smiled to himself, observing the contrast between the smart shoes and her pink, bleach-spattered housecoat, which was so tight that the row of buttons strained across her front, offering tiny glimpses of flesh. What he was never able to identify later was the exact moment when the tightness of the uncomfortably stretched fabric ceased to be a threat and began to seem more like an enticement. Nor did he ever manage to pinpoint precisely the origin of the pressure that seemed to weigh down on them as they sat down to lunch, making the air they shared seem dense, solid, unbreathable. Although he always switched on the television, forcing himself to watch the screen and eat in silence, although he made sure he complimented her admirable cooking – 'This is delicious, Maribel, wonderful, really, I've never had such a delicious stew' – without turning to look at her, there came a time when his stubborn silence began to deafen him, and his head started to feel as if it were lined with cork. He realised that the strict, excessively cool stance he had adopted as a sign of respect towards her was having the opposite effect, making him seem haughty and almost contemptuous. So he decided to ignore the possible consequences of these lunches with her and enjoy the benefits, looking at Maribel, joking with her, laughing at her jokes, and watching her eat, as she raised her fork to her mouth, parted her lips, took a mouthful and chewed with her mouth closed, then swallowed, while his desire, as yet unacknowledged, twisted these innocent actions into something more obscene. As they chatted, the tension in the air didn't diminish but it changed character, becoming warmer, friendlier, and Juan Olmedo had to admit that, despite all his prejudices, he was enjoying her company.

One month ended and another began, with the east wind still reigning supreme. The sky was so unchangingly blue that it looked like a painted vault, and the sun shone constantly although the wind still threw the occasional tantrum, as if it needed to remind them of its existence. The weeks passed and Juan Olmedo was enjoying chatting to Maribel, seeing her arrive, watching her from a distance, not wanting to admit that this might one day become more than a game. Although he was still convinced he wasn't attracted to her, he had begun to notice certain things. The new confidence, for instance, that had gradually replaced Maribel's previous, desperate efforts to attract him, an assurance that grew with the passing weeks. While he acted like a haughty fly, moving every so often to avoid the fine, glossy threads being spun into an increasingly thick web around him, Maribel, like a fat, cunning spider, stuck doggedly to her task. She was in no hurry. From time to time, Juan needed to prove to himself –

and to her – that he was fully in control now that he was playing at home, on his own turf. He had the feeling once more of being a motionless object around which a woman circled, but this time it caused him no anxiety, no pain, no dark premonitions. He didn't find it alarming, quite the opposite. Being desired felt good, he reflected, intrinsically good, and this was the best he could expect from the situation with Maribel – a clear expression of her desire and a pure, innocent, harmless bit of fun. She would probably be the first to tire of it, he thought.

But there were other mysteries he couldn't unravel, details he couldn't quite understand. He wasn't attracted to this woman, but whenever she got down on all fours right by his feet, searching for the remote or picking up a toy – any excuse really – not only did he start ogling her rear, but more than once he actually raised a hand, as if he were about to slap it. He forced himself to lower his hand immediately, because he wasn't attracted to her. But when, at the end of January, he began to notice that she was losing weight, he was sorry to see that the gaps between the buttons on her housecoat were getting smaller, threatening to deprive him of the sight of the bare flesh beneath. He wasn't attracted to Maribel, but at lunchtime on the last Tuesday in February, when the east wind blew up an unbearable storm before finally taking its leave, he was distracted from his plate of stuffed squid – which was delicious, like everything else she'd cooked for him – by the strong acid fragrance of a peeled orange. And when he looked to his right, he saw that she was sucking a segment between her lips and a trail of sweet, sticky juice was sliding slowly down her neck, losing itself in the furrow between her tight breasts. This image, the obliging slowness with which the pale, fragrant juice slid into her cleavage, made his tongue hurt, his poor, tortured tongue, and all he wanted to do was sink his teeth into her flesh, to taste it, lick it until every last trace of the orange was gone.

This seemed excessive, especially in view of the fact that he certainly wasn't attracted to her, so he was tempted to blame it on the east wind. But although he greeted the arrival of the west wind with joy, hoping that with its return everything would go back to normal, the west wind did not return the compliment.

'What a morning!' said Maribel, shaking her umbrella as he opened the door for her. He wasn't attracted to her, but for weeks now, even though he hadn't got any sleep during his night shift, he always woke up a little before one o'clock.

'And I'd brought you some *arranque* for lunch! I mean, it's March already, and it's been so warm lately that I thought . . . But no way, winter's going to stay with us for a while.'

'It doesn't matter, Maribel,' said Juan, smiling, savouring this new proof of her solicitude. 'I love *arranque* and I haven't had any since at least September. I'll enjoy it just the same, even if the weather is cold.'

'Yes, I know you like it,' she said, her lips forming a mischievous, doting smile, like an adult enjoying the prospect of giving a present to a child. 'That's why I made it. I kept the tomatoes in the sun for about five days, so they were really ripe.'

The *arranque*, a solid, local version of *gazpacho*, was so delicious that Juan wasn't at all bothered by the absence of the hot weather as he ate it. Beside him, Maribel contemplated her omelette unenthused, although she cheered up at the sight of him eating.

'Aren't you going to have any?' asked Juan, surprised. 'It's delicious.'

'All right,' she said, directing her spoon at the bowl to her left. 'Yes, it's good,' she added, as she tasted it. 'Perhaps a bit too much salt?'

'No, I don't think so.'

'OK. The thing is that I'm on this diet and I can't tell what things taste like any more. I put on so much weight last summer, I had to do something about it. Of course, my problem is,' she stopped gesticulating and looked him straight in the eye as she confessed, 'I love eating.'

'Yes, so do I.'

'Yeah, but on you it doesn't show.'

It seemed like a trivial, altogether reasonable comment. She probably hadn't intended it to be anything else, but something he couldn't pinpoint – the sound of her voice, maybe, a little more husky than usual, or a hint of reproach in her words – made Juan look at her closely. Then she burst out laughing, a sudden, nervous laugh.

'You're not trying to provoke me, are you, Maribel?' he asked, intimately. She laughed again, and he joined in. 'Because I've been behaving myself for so long now.'

'And you don't like it?'

'Well, no, I prefer behaving badly.'

'Right.' Then, just when Juan thought she was about to throw herself at him, she leant back in her chair, and behaved as if nothing had happened. 'What I meant is that you don't put on weight.'

'Ah,' he said, and they both laughed again.

The moment seemed to be over, although it was here that everything really began. Maribel, who sometimes seemed so gauche, so stupid, so ignorant of how to do things properly, had the intelligence to ease the pressure, not to force the consequences of the conversation, or try to take advantage of the weakness he'd shown. That afternoon, surprisingly, she found no excuse to bend over, or stand on a chair, or lean across the table to reach something in front of Juan. He, in the meantime, was laboriously chewing over his surprise, going over their slight misunderstanding born of his own wish to misunderstand. After that, until the morning of the following Friday, Juan Olmedo no longer thought about how he wasn't attracted to Maribel, or anything else for that matter. He knew it was mad, crazy, nuts, a ridiculous complication to add to his life, but he refused to acknowledge it; he was too busy keeping good sense at bay. He didn't find this too difficult, because his desire was a mechanism capable of disconnecting all the wires of his conscience, subjecting him entirely to the tyranny of his will. After all, ten years of uninterrupted adultery with his brother's wife had made him an expert in the art of letting himself off the hook when it came to moral probity.

When she let herself in with her key on Friday, Juan was still in bed, wearing his pyjamas. Listening to the sound of Maribel's heels clicking around as she moved about downstairs, he got up, took off his pyjamas and raised the blinds a little. For a couple of seconds there was silence. Then he heard her heels again, in short, hesitant bursts. Juan decided she must be looking for him. He went to the bathroom, turned on the taps, counted to three and turned them off again. He got back into bed, folded the pillow so he could lie back on it, covered himself to the waist with the sheet, crossed his arms and waited.

She had obviously followed his clues because he soon heard her coming up the stairs. He'd left the door to the bedroom ajar, but she knocked before entering.

'Come in,' he said, keeping absolutely still.

'Ah. Oh!' Maribel took a few steps forward and stopped dead. 'But you're still in bed! Did I wake you?'

'No.'

'What's the matter? Are you feeling ill?'

'No,' he said again and smiled. 'I'm fine. I feel great.'

'Oh,' said Maribel, and gave a short, nervous laugh. Scratching her hands as if she suddenly had a rash, she came forward a few steps. 'Would you like me to bring you a coffee?'

'No.'

'Shall I pull up the blinds?'

'No.'

'Would you like me to bring you your pyjamas?'

'No.'

She stood there, a few feet from the bed, smiling at him, not daring to say anything more.

'Come here,' said Juan, patting the bedcovers. 'I'll show you what I want.'

Maribel went towards him slowly, quietly, eyes wide, a look of serious concentration on her face. She sat on the edge of the bed and looked straight at him. Juan turned towards her and began unbuttoning her housecoat, slowly, using both hands. At the first button she closed her eyes. At the third, she opened them again. At the last button, she shrugged off the housecoat and took off the rest of her clothes, surprisingly swiftly and with skilful ease. Possibly to make up for this, she lay down on the bed in one indolent, majestic movement, like a classical muse. Her eyes fixed on Juan's, she made no other movement, as if she was confident that he would appreciate what he was seeing. She still didn't move as he began to slide his hand over her body, downwards from her collarbone, then upwards from her knees, becoming more aroused with every inch of skin he covered, skin that was like a freshly washed apple. He recognised its firmness, the tense elasticity of the hard flesh that yielded to the pressure of his fingers, a deep, velvety tremor at the base of her breasts, in her round hips, in the softly padded small of her back, her round, compact backside, so unbearably perfect that he could feel it on the edge of his teeth as he ran his fingertips over it. There was something to grab hold of everywhere, and he hadn't yet decided what to choose when he put his tongue in her mouth and found a hot, sour taste, the taste of cherries soaked in brandy, the taste of naked women who know exactly what they want. Then he opened his mouth and said something he hadn't been aware of choosing.

'You're amazing, Maribel.'

These simple words were like a switch, a secret, hidden spring. She heard them, interpreted them, and threw herself at him with all that she was, all that she had, growing more assured with every passing minute, until, overcome by her eagerness, the voracity now impelling her, Juan stopped and took command. 'Slow down,' he whispered in her ear, 'we're going to do things my way.' She agreed with a smile, 'OK, anything you say.' And he thought, 'Maribel, don't be so polite to me.' He thought it but didn't say it, because he liked hearing her say it, and then he started to regret what he was doing, which made him like it even more. He liked seeing her tremble, and the liquid shine that filled her eyes when she opened them, and the violence that sharpened her chin when she threw her head back, the almost animal clumsiness of her fingers, the almost childish babbling issuing from her lips, and as they reached climax, the almost painful tension twisting her feet, the slender thread of saliva that trickled from a corner of her mouth and left a damp patch on the sheet. When they'd finished, he felt so satisfied that he even went so far as to acknowledge that he liked Maribel less on the outside than on the inside; her intimate capacity for absolute self-annihilation. As he caressed Maribel, he tried to find a way of telling her this, of thanking her for the generous greed of her flesh, so selfish and so sincere, and so obliging, but she spoke first.

'I can't believe it. I'd never have imagined you'd be like that in bed. I mean, you're normally so serious, so . . . so polite,' she said, smiling. She put out a hand and stroked Juan's face slowly with the tips of her fingers, as if she were afraid of saying something wrong. 'I'd never have guessed that you'd be so, so . . . !'

'Enthusiastic?' he suggested.

'No, not that,' she said, shaking her head. 'Or maybe, but

not quite. What I meant was . . .' At this point she blushed. 'Oh, it doesn't matter.'

'Yes, it does.'

'No, really.'

'Maribel, tell me,' said Juan, taking her face in his hands and forcing her to look at him. 'I want to know.'

'But you might be offended. I mean it in a good way, OK? Remember that. And I'm a bit like that too, I like it. It's just the kind of man I like . . . Anyway, promise you won't be offended?'

'I promise.'

'I would never have thought you'd be so . . . so depraved.'

Juan Olmedo burst out laughing when he heard this, and almost felt like hugging her, kissing her gently on the lips instead, as if she were an innocent, teenage bride.

'Don't worry, Maribel,' he said reassuringly. 'It doesn't bother me at all. In fact, I'm used to it. The fact is, sooner or later, every woman ends up telling me that.'

She hadn't liked him mentioning the existence of other women. At least, this was what Juan feared when he saw her sit up, glance at the clock and jump out of bed. 'It's already half past two! Goodness knows what time I'll get lunch on the table.' Juan didn't feel like eating. He'd have preferred to stay in bed until they both felt like getting up, but he didn't dare ask her to stay because at that moment it suddenly became clear again that she was, after all, his cleaner, and she might take his request as an order. When he was alone, he realised he'd forgotten to tell her she didn't need to be so polite towards him, and hadn't given a moment's thought to all the arguments that had been going round in his head all week. He'd just done something crazy, and half of him was condemning it, making him feel guilty and bad. But the other half of him knew that he was pleased. Part of him was screaming and bombarding his conscience with moral

291

judgements; the other part was quiet, calm, as if it were no concern of his. And it was this latter part that knew that if Maribel had been mad or sensible enough to open the door to his room just then he'd have fucked her again. It had always been like this – a choice he regretted, a regret he chose – and in the midst of it all, something so good he'd never been able to get it from respectable women, the kind he ought to go out with, the kind he could kiss in public without worrying, the kind he could take out to dinner at the weekend with his friends and their wives, remove their clothes with a steady pulse, a level gaze and the fresh, neutral taste of water in his mouth. The kind of women who could speak German, and wore white dressing gowns, and didn't drool when they came. It had always been like this, he didn't know why, but he no longer cared, and he wasn't going to waste time finding out why. But he also couldn't control his thoughts, couldn't mend the crack that split him down the middle each time he struck lucky. After all, he'd never wanted to stop being a good boy. He knew that if he went and found Maribel, and looked into her eyes, and gave her the speech he was composing for her, he'd feel terrible, ridiculous, hypocritical, despicable. But if he didn't do it, he might end up feeling even worse. This certainty didn't manage to drown out a faint, cheerful, sarcastic voice that, by three o'clock, when he went downstairs, still hadn't fallen silent. He now felt ashamed that he'd taken advantage of the situation, of his cleaner's weakness, of his own unforgivable weakness. But he could still hear the voice – 'You idiot, you know you're going to do it again. You know that as soon as she drops her guard, you'll do it again.'

Maribel, on the other hand, was perfectly happy. 'I've made you a tripe stew,' she said, beaming at him like an incestuous mother, not noticing the difference between the smiling naked man she'd left in bed only a little while ago, and the man now heading towards her.

'Delicious!' He hadn't meant to say it, but he couldn't help himself, as if saying this were now an instinctive response at mealtimes.

'I didn't add any chickpeas, because I know you prefer it without.'

Then Juan Olmedo told himself the most sensible thing to do would be to accept this card that destiny had dealt him, sit at the table, eat, drink, joke around for a while, smoke a cigarette and take her to bed again, letting himself be guided by a hunger and thirst that wouldn't be satisfied until he was with her between the sheets once more. But then he remembered her bra. It must have been white long ago but now it was grey after countless washes. The straps were frayed and there was a tear in the lace – he'd noticed. And he'd noticed her flesh-coloured knickers with their worn elastic and dull, threadbare fabric. She'd taken them off quickly so he wouldn't see them, but he had, and he'd compared the tatty underwear with the emphatic splendour of her skin, her hard, taut flesh, and as he remembered it, he pictured himself coming out of a shop with a large box, six sets of satin underwear in different colours, and he realised he couldn't bear the image so he started talking, sure that he was going to say exactly what he needed to say.

'Yes, I do prefer it without chickpeas,' he said, now sounding more curt, serious. 'Maribel, leave that and come and sit down. We have to talk.'

But she remained standing, holding the ladle, her arm frozen on its way to the casserole dish. She was frowning, and rather than seeming upset, or suspicious, or anxious, she simply looked scared.

'You didn't enjoy it,' she murmured, more to herself than to him.

'Of course I did!' said Juan. He leant his elbows on the table, placed his hands over his face and rubbed it vigorously before going on, making the most of a rare opportunity to be equally sincere with both halves of himself. 'I enjoyed it very much. That's the problem.'

She looked at him as if she were unsure whether to believe him, as she served the food with a slightly trembling hand.

'If I hadn't enjoyed it, there'd be nothing to say, Maribel, don't you understand? If it had gone badly, we'd both know there was no chance it would happen again, and that would be that.'

'But it was good,' she said, sitting down at last, very slowly.

'Very good,' he agreed, nodding to underline his words. 'In fact, it was bloody brilliant. And that's the problem. Because it can't happen again, Maribel. We've got to forget about it right now, behave as if we've already forgotten it. I know that sounds ridiculous – like when judges in films ask the jury to discount what they've just heard, even though they've heard it and are bound to remember it. I know you won't forget it, and neither will I, of course I won't. But it's what we've got to do. We've got to sort this out somehow, because we've made a mistake, or rather I've made a mistake. I'm sorry, it's all my fault.'

'Why?' she asked. 'I don't understand.'

'Well, because it is, Maribel, because this is stupid, it's not right, it makes no sense, don't you understand?' He could see from her eyes that she didn't, so he went on: 'Because you work for me, because your son and my niece go to the same school, because they're always together, always hanging around here, and because you're my cleaner and I pay you a wage every month for cleaning the house. This really should never happen again.'

She said nothing for a moment and the expression on her face was calm and focused. It didn't change when she spoke again, quietly.

'But you don't mind paying for it.'

He turned towards her. 'So you know,' he whispered, so surprised and disconcerted he smiled despite himself.

'Of course I know,' said Maribel, and indicated his plate with a jerk of her chin. 'Come on, eat your stew or it'll go stone cold. In small towns like this everybody knows everything.'

'But you . . .' He stopped and took a mouthful of food. He chewed it slowly to gain time, and although it bothered him hugely to admit it at this particular moment, he thought to himself that it was the best tripe stew he'd eaten since moving from Madrid. 'How did you find out?'

'My ex spends his life in that bar and he knows you by sight. He knows who you are. And she shows off a lot. She's very proud of it, apparently.'

'Yes. But that's different, Maribel.'

'Why?'

'Because she's a prostitute,' he said, pausing and looking at her. 'And you're not.'

'Well then!' she said triumphantly, slamming both fists on the table. 'That's what I mean! What's the problem? You pay me to clean your house, I clean it for you, amen. The other has nothing to do with it, it's as if we were somewhere else. It's our private life, you could say.'

'Yes,' he said, smiling at her words. 'But the thing is we're not somewhere else. We're here, in this house. My house.'

'That has nothing to do with anything.'

'Yes, it does, Maribel,' he said. And then he wondered why the fuck he was being so insistent, especially when it went against his own interests. He didn't feel sorry for her, and she didn't seem to be confused, or easily deceived. In fact, she seemed like a woman who knew her own mind, and was expecting a similar resolve from him. 'Of course it does.'

'Look, I . . .' she said and stopped. She sighed, shut her eyes tight a moment, as if she were forcing herself to continue. When she went on, she used a different tone from the one she normally used with him. 'On the twenty-sixth of March I'm going to be thirty-one. I'm quite old enough. I know what I want, and what I don't want, and I know what life has in store for me, even though I might not want it. I know that my life is shit, I know that too, and that I'm not going to get a boyfriend who's any good as long as I live in this town, which is where I'm going to have to live until I die. I have a twelve-year-old son and I've somehow got to help him do well, and that's the most important thing. I know all this. And I know I'm not going to get you, you don't have to worry about that, the idea didn't even occur to me, I know full well you'd never marry me – men like you don't marry girls like me, they never do. Look at all the things I know, loads of things. But if I had to live with everything I know, I'd die. That's my problem.' At this, he thought he saw a tremble in her eyes and sensed she was about to break down, but she shook her head a couple of times and seemed to recover. Her voice, when she went on, was hard. 'Because just as I know you sleep with prostitutes, you must know I've got a bad reputation. I'm sure you know. Well, I don't deserve it, and do you know why? Because I'm not a tart, no matter what they say. So don't give me your spiel. I know exactly what I am. And you're not going to ruin my reputation at this stage. So you can stop worrying about that too. I really didn't expect you to be such a chauvinist.'

'A chauvinist?' Juan Olmedo flung himself back in his chair, placing his hand on his chest, as if a hole had opened up just under his collarbone, and burst out laughing. 'I'm a chauvinist?' he said again, reflecting how ironic it was that she'd picked this to reproach him with, he who couldn't even tell his friends about it each time he screwed a woman. 'No, Maribel, I . . .' Of course he was a chauvinist, he had no choice, he'd been born one, but he tried to hide it. He was sure it was the last word the women he worked with would have chosen to describe him. As for the others, that was different, a tacit agreement, a private pact, an alliance that was beneficial to both parties. Even so, nobody had ever accused him out loud of being a chauvinist. 'I'm not a chauvinist, Maribel. On the contrary. All I'm trying to do is make sure you don't get hurt. I want to protect you – from me.'

'Right. But I know what hurts me and what doesn't. And I don't need you to protect me. I don't need anyone to protect me. I just want you to sleep with me. And when it's over, it's over and that's that.'

Juan Olmedo couldn't quite believe what he was hearing. He felt all his blood rush to his head and, realising he couldn't sit still a moment longer, he suddenly got up and started pacing the room.

'Fine, Maribel, fine,' he repeated several times like an automaton, as if he could find nothing better to say. 'Well, OK, great. If that's what you want. Fine, yes, that's fine.'

He turned and looked at her, and saw that she was staring at him, smiling. But it wasn't his face that had caught her attention – Juan Olmedo suddenly realised that he had an erection, and that it was clearly visible beneath his pyjamas. He smiled too, and sat down.

'Fine, Maribel, fine,' he said for the last time, feeling suddenly euphoric, and resigned to this new twist of fate. 'If that's what you want, then I'll sleep with you. I'd be delighted to. It'd be a pleasure. And I'll do it to the best of my ability, because I can't think of anything I'd rather do, you can be sure of that. But let's agree on one thing. So that I don't feel bad, so that I don't feel like I'm being a patronising male chauvinist, you take the lead, OK? At least for now, until I get used to . . . all this. When you feel like going to bed with me, tell me, or just jump me. I'll try to keep up.'

'What is this, some kind of deal?' she asked, looking amused.

'Yes, something like that.'

'And what if you don't feel like it?'

The thought entered his head for the last time that he wasn't attracted to the woman, then he heard her cry out, and saw the trail of saliva stretching from her mouth, down her chin, onto the sheet, and he was on the verge of screwing her there and then, on the table in the middle of the plates and glasses and the dish of tripe stew without chickpeas.

'Trust me, I'll feel like it, Maribel.'

'Always?'

'If you don't take advantage of me too often.'

'Now, for instance?'

'Yes, now.'

The following morning, as he left for work, Juan Olmedo felt a familiar pressure on his chest, the well-known, almost comforting presence of a secret.

꧁

Sara Gómez didn't usually shop at such a cheap super-market. It stocked strange, unfamiliar brands and the cashiers didn't have plastic bags, even for customers who were willing to pay, but it was the only shop in the town that sold the chocolates the children liked. That was the only thing she was intending to buy that Saturday afternoon, when a man suddenly spoke to her. He was a rather healthy-looking older man, with close-cropped grey hair, and a face with irregular features that might have been interesting had not a rather foolish, placid smile ruined the overall effect.

'I think the coffee ones are the best,' he said in perfectly correct Spanish, but with a strong American accent.

'Yes, I've tried them,' she answered out of politeness, as she chose two boxes of orange-flavoured chocolates and two of the mint ones. 'They're very nice, but the children don't like them.'

She had no wish to prolong the conversation, but as she was heading to the checkout, he said something that made her stop dead in the aisle.

'Yes, I've seen you with the children. In the car, and around town a few times.' Then he managed to frown while still smiling, which left Sara even more confused. 'Are they yours?'

'No,' she said and smiled, falling, without realising it, for the implied compliment.

'They can't be your grandchildren,' he went on,

continuing his flattery unashamedly. 'You're much too young to have grandchildren that age.'

'No, they're not my grandchildren either. They're . . . friends' children, and I'm expecting them for tea, so I'd really better get home.'

He must have noticed the change of tone, her curt, hurried attempt to bring things to an end, but he showed no sign of discouragement.

'Well, see you around,' he said. He took a step forward to shake her hand energetically, and she had no choice but to accept. 'My name's William, but everyone calls me Bill. I live in the pink houses, the development next to yours.'

'Oh, yes, of course! Well, then, see you soon,' she said, but as she was walking away she realised she'd forgotten something: 'My name's Sara.'

Back in the car, she thought briefly about the man – his appearance, his manner, his casual omission, on introducing himself, of any mention of his nationality, as if he'd assumed she'd realise immediately that he was American. By the time she got home she had forgotten all about him. The following Tuesday afternoon, she didn't notice him in the line of people queuing in the fish shop, but he soon came to say hello.

'Are you in a hurry?' he asked, in a solicitous, chivalrous tone. 'You can take my place in the queue, if you like. I don't mind waiting.'

'No, no,' said Sara, glancing discreetly at the fish and realising they would probably have run out of sole by the time it was her turn. But she didn't feel like being in this man's debt. 'I don't have anything urgent to do either.'

He began a trivial conversation about the fish available in the area, making sure to pronounce the names of local varieties as fluently as an expert – *urta, corvina, almendritas, huevos de choco*.

'That's one of the things I like most about living here – the fish. Where I come from, we never eat fish at all.'

'Where are you from?' asked Sara, out of politeness rather than curiosity. His smile grew even wider, pleased by what he must have interpreted as the first sign of interest from this woman, whom he'd met by chance and more or less forced into conversation.

'From the south. A small town in the state of Virginia, not too far from Richmond. Have you ever been to the United States?'

'To New York,' she said, and an old, happy, painful memory returned: Vicente looking frozen, his nose bright red, twice his usual size with all the warm clothes he was wearing, the gloves, scarf and hat Sara had made him put on. He was fooling around, standing on one leg in the middle of Brooklyn Bridge, a thick, white, muffling layer of snow lying all around. 'Only New York.'

'Right, like most people. New York is great, but you should visit the south. It's different, you know? It's . . .' He punched the air enthusiastically, reminding Sara of the gung-ho cheeriness of Coca-Cola ads, so that she had to stop herself from laughing. 'It's authentic.'

'The real thing,' said Sara in English.

'That's right. So you speak English.'

'Yes, but not as well as you speak Spanish.'

It was his turn to be served, then he waited for her when her turn came. Carrying their respective plastic bags, they were about to go their separate ways when Bill suggested they have a beer. Sara said she couldn't, all that waiting in the fish shop had made her late. But on the following Saturday, she couldn't refuse when he asked again. This man, who seemed to have nothing better to do than patrol the town in the vague hope of bumping into her, called out to her in the busy pedestrian precinct where she often went for a walk. She was on her way to the ironmonger's, in a square that offered the temptation of a café terrace, surprising yet welcoming on a warm, sunny morning in February with the east wind blowing. When she sat down, the back of the chair felt icy, however, and Sara was berating herself for succumbing so easily to the illusion created by the sun, when Bill took off his jumper. Underneath, he was wearing a tight black T-shirt that contrasted with the blond hairs on his arms, the firm, tanned skin revealing every line, every shadow, every muscle of a spectacular, younger man's body, a body that had been worked and trained. Sara Gómez had to admit to herself that she was impressed. As she assessed his splendid physique, his pectorals almost offensively obvious beneath the tight T-shirt, she reflected that twenty years ago she would have felt contempt for his macho exhibitionism. But now she was twenty years older and her head was slightly less full of nonsense. She smiled. Aware of exactly what was happening, he smiled back.

'How old are you?' she asked, in a warmer tone than before.

'Fifty-nine.'

'You'd never know it. You're in very good shape.'

'Yes,' he said, and let out exactly the kind of silly laugh that a thirty-three-year-old Sara Gómez would have expected from the owner of such a body. 'Well, in my line of work, you don't have much choice.'

Right, she thought, though she simply nodded, because deep down she knew it, she'd known it from the start if she'd stopped to think about it. What else could an American his age be doing in a town like this? A member of the armed forces, of course. An officer in the United States Navy. Terrific. Still, it was a pleasure to look at him.

From then on, as if the gift of a body glimpsed beneath a simple black T-shirt had inspired a kind of loyalty, Sara stopped resisting the courtship of that southern gentleman, such a gentleman and such a southerner that his naive, inoffensive, almost indolent manner came to be more troubling than reassuring. He continued to bump into her all over town that winter, apparently without any other aim than to walk beside her. He kept her company, told her about himself, insisted on paying when she, who tried to alternate between rejecting and conceding to his proposals, let him convince her to go for a drink. While he talked about his ranch, his happy childhood as the son of a well-to-do farmer, his dogs and his horses, his three failed marriages, he awoke in Sara's spirit a forest of dark shapes, uncomfortable memories that had nothing to do with him. She didn't feel attracted to the man. She wouldn't even have noticed him if he hadn't insisted on striking up a conversation, though sometimes, with a glass of brandy in her hand, she thought it would be nice to find a man like him in her bed in the mornings. A man like him, but not him. But it was William Jefferson Baker – his full name always in her mind since she'd seen him one afternoon in his dazzling, white, annoyingly flattering uniform – who was walking around this town, and there might be no one else. He might be the last one.

It was quite a while since Sara had felt so aware of her age, quite a while since she'd disliked the fact of it so much. She was used to living alone, and hadn't had many opportunities to change this. In fact, she'd had only one, and she had destroyed that herself. She didn't need company, a man in her life, warmth in winter, the shelter of another body on stormy nights, twisted illusions, drunken fantasies, cheap glitter, the worn, threadbare velvet of a theatre set made up of emotional props. She wasn't like that, she wasn't one of those women, she'd never have allowed herself to be. She'd given up everything so that she wouldn't need anyone; that was her goal, her project, the dream of a rifle, the life she'd yearned for. But the innocuous proximity of the man, his calm, quiet strategy, his excessively relaxed approach, more suited to a nineteenth-century courtship between youngsters than to the reasonable aspirations of adults with little time left – she liked it, yet she didn't like it, she felt flattered rather than desired and, in an obscure, unpleasant way, she felt rejected in advance. From time to time, she surrendered to this strange mix of emotions, like a little girl who's just been given a toy she doesn't like but then realises another child is coveting it, a little girl who doesn't even know why she suddenly feels an insuperable need to cling to the gift as if it were something she'd always yearned for. On these occasions, Sara Gómez Morales realised that nothing and no one was competing with her for this man, nothing but the passage of time and her own memory. But she also felt tired and upset by this surprising complication that was interrupting the smooth flow of her uneventful life. By mid-March, after two months of casual encounters, cafés and walks, Bill dared to make a proposal – ingeniously discreet, cautious, restrained, but still a proposal – and Sara realised she didn't know what to do.

This was a situation she wasn't used to. She usually reasoned everything out meticulously, patiently, because she had faith in her ability to reach precise solutions, round numbers that fitted into the column to which she'd assigned them. If, this time, the numbers balked, defied her with impossible decimals, it wasn't because of the way the problem was set out – it was an easy calculation – but a result of the persistent shadow of the difficulties that had overcome her in the past. Or perhaps it was simply that life had gone by, her life, all the years she'd spent learning how to move the pieces on a board instead of others moving them for her, and now she'd drawn a line in the sand and begun a new game. This was what she'd wanted to do.

'It's not him, you know. He's not bad. But, according to him, he's been seeing me around for months whereas I wouldn't even have noticed him if he hadn't insisted on talking to me. I mean, I like him physically, he's a very

304

attractive man, but when he smiles he sometimes looks rather foolish – don't laugh, it's true. But he really does have a very good body, very athletic. He seems much younger, more handsome if you only look at his arms and not his face. Don't look at me like that, you're twenty years younger than me, you still have plenty of time to start working out.'

Walking along the beach beside her, looking amused rather than shocked, Juan Olmedo burst out laughing.

'I wasn't thinking about myself, Sara, I was thinking of you. I don't really understand what's the matter. Go out with him. If you like him, carry on. If you don't, stop.'

'Yes, I know, I've thought that myself. But the thing is, I don't really understand what's wrong. I suppose I'm scared, scared before anything has even happened, which is the silliest way of being scared. I'm afraid of liking him, because deep down I don't want to like him, and I'm afraid of not liking him, because then I'll leave him, and maybe there'll never be anybody else. It's not that I need a man, or that I've been looking for one. Quite the contrary. It was the last thing on my mind when I came to live here, but – I don't know. You know what I'd really like to do? Erase him. Press a key and make him disappear. Or better still, have never had him appear in the first place. The truth is, this sort of thing has never gone well for me. My . . .' She stopped and thought for a moment, searching for the right word, and pursed her lips before going on: 'My love life, let's call it that, has always been a disaster.'

'I'll swap you,' he said, smiling.

'Don't be so sure.'

'I am sure.'

They'd reached Punta Candor, and she was surprised by how short the walk had seemed. She'd left the house around five to get some fresh air, hoping that the breeze and the sunlight, the slanting rays reluctantly leaving the sky in the late afternoon, would dispel her doubts, or perhaps suggest a solution. Then she saw Juan Olmedo on his porch, snoozing on a lounger, covered with a blanket, and she felt the urge to call out to him, to ask if he'd like to come for a walk, and tell him everything. He was so near, it seemed so easy, that she didn't even realise it had been many years since she'd allowed herself the luxury of giving in to an urge. Juan was dozing, but he woke up immediately and accepted her offer, as if he somehow knew that he was the only person at that time, in that place, to whom Sara could turn. He hadn't said much so far, but he was listening carefully and she realised it was doing her good to talk. Now he took the initiative, leading her by the arm up the steps to the bar. It was a small place with large windows, almost always deserted out of season, and without all the noise and semi-naked tourists, there was something melancholy about it, yet welcoming, like beaches in winter.

All the brandies on offer were fairly awful. Juan encouraged her to try the whisky, which was a little better, but she stayed faithful to brandy, although it was sourer and rougher than she was used to, rather like the harsh, anonymous stuff that filled her father's bottles.

'And do you know what the worst thing is? He hasn't even tried to seduce me yet. Here I am, going over and over the same thing all the time, and maybe he's not even thinking like that – I don't know. Maybe he thinks that it's not even worth bothering at our age, although he has asked me to go to Seville with him for the weekend. He's said that we could go and see the coronation of some Virgin or other. In Los Remedios, I think.' She stopped to emphasise her disbelief, eyes wide, eyebrows raised, mouth agape. 'Can you believe it?'

He laughed first, but she soon joined in with a boisterous, childlike complicity, as if they were schoolchildren exchanging dirty words in the playground. Then Sara realised that everything would have been much easier if the long, sedate conversations she'd had with the American had ended in a burst of that same simple, silly laughter, whose only purpose was to bring two people closer together. Afterwards, Juan Olmedo yawned.

'Would you like another drink?' he asked, rubbing his eyes vigorously.

'No, we've got to leave,' said Sara, placing both hands on the table as if she were about to stand up. 'You're going to fall asleep on me, I've been going on for so long.'

'No, no, it's not that,' said Juan, looking round for the waiter and signalling to him for another round of drinks. 'Let's have another drink. I am tired, but it's not because of you. I was on duty last night and I couldn't sleep this morning for some reason. It happens sometimes, but I feel fine, honestly. I was just thinking that if you go to Seville, you'll miss Maribel's birthday treat, the rice with *galeras*.'

Sara nodded as she remembered how disappointed Maribel had been, the pout with which she greeted the news, the vehemence with which she explained that '*galeras*', strange creatures that seemed like the prehistoric ancestors of Dublin Bay prawns, could only be found along a couple of miles of the coast and only at this specific time of year, for six weeks at most, and were hugely expensive. At the restaurant where she'd planned to have her birthday lunch, they couldn't guarantee they would have any, so that was why she'd had to convince her brother, who was a fisherman, to keep her a couple of dozen. 'Well, well,' she'd said to Sara, 'imagine yourself getting an American boyfriend now, when we were all getting along so well.' Sara had quickly denied everything, as if she had something to be ashamed of. 'He's not my boyfriend, Maribel,' she'd said, 'and it's not definite that I'm going to Seville with him. I'm not even sure I feel like going.' Maribel looked sceptical. Her face had changed, becoming more angular, more delicate, more interesting, as she lost weight. It was now, above all, a face that was lit up from inside with a gentle glow, a new softness that erased all memory of the bitterness that sometimes used to twist her lips. 'Well then,' Maribel went on at last, 'like I said, if he was the love of your life or something, I mean if you'd been after him for months, then I'd be happy for you, I swear. But if that's not the case . . . I mean, there are plenty of men in the world! There are loads of them, that's the truth, and they're all the same, they all want the same thing.' Then it was Sara who stared with interest at Maribel. And she reflected that what was mutely expressed by her rosy colour, her eyes, her mouth, was a metamorphosis that could only have been caused by a man, just a man but different from the others. Maribel was sending signals that were as clear as day: she sometimes curled her hair now, and sometimes she wore tights to work instead of the thick socks she used to wear, she checked her nails and she arrived with a clean face, and applied make-up before leaving. 'So what are you saying?' Sara asked while she tried to think of a more delicate phrase than the one in her head. She couldn't find one, so she smiled to soften it: 'If you want a fuck, any man will do? Is that it?' 'That's right!' said Maribel, thumping her fist into the palm of her hand and nodding. Sara smiled again. 'But that's not true, Maribel,' she said, 'just look at you, recently.' Maribel blushed but she still had something to say: 'Well, OK, but bad fucks are useful too, because they put you off it for a while.'

'Yes, I know,' Sara said to Juan once the waiter had brought their drinks. 'We were talking about it yesterday morning, and I think she might even be a little bit cross with me. Although I shouldn't think she really cares that much, because she's got herself a new boyfriend.'

'She's got herself a boyfriend?' Juan asked, eyes wide, neck tense, all signs of tiredness now entirely gone. 'Maribel?'

'Well,' Sara went on cautiously, 'I'm assuming she has, at least. She hasn't told me anything, but she certainly looks as if she's met someone, because she pays more attention to herself, she's on a diet, and she looks reasonably happy. Anyway, I don't think she's about to give up work, you don't have to worry about that. The only thing is, I don't know, I was quite touched that she should be so bothered, so keen for me to be there on her birthday. I didn't expect it.'

'Right.' He smiled, seeming much more relaxed. 'Well, the children are even worse – they're both green with envy. Maribel's told them that if you get involved with the American, you'll probably end up marrying him, and if you do, sooner or later you'll go and live in America.'

'That's ridiculous!' said Sara, shaking her head, while Juan laughed. But she wondered whether this wasn't exactly what she had wanted to hear, whether she hadn't come here to hear those very words.

Juan Olmedo didn't know her story, the toll taken by a childhood of fairy tales without wicked stepmothers, Hansel and Gretel loaded with gold, plastic tiaras and shoes covered in yellow silk as far as the eye could see, Christmas Eve an annual torment and no home to return to. Sara didn't want to tell him any of this but on the walk back she sketched her past for him including the few key elements that outlined why she was different from Maribel, who could blaze, burn, be consumed in a single flame; Sara had never been like that, she had never been able to be. Sara Gómez Morales, mistress of very little, was born with her passions contained, and she couldn't remember how long it had been since someone last said to her that they loved her, loved her for herself, because she was easy to love. 'We'll really miss you if you don't come to the lunch!' said Maribel. 'Andrés really loves you, he looks up to you more than anyone else, and I've become very fond of you, almost without noticing it! That's the good thing about you, you're easy to love.' Juan Olmedo would never understand what those words had meant to her, he'd never guess her real motives; someone who'd always known his way home, always had a place where he belonged, would never understand.

Sara Gómez Morales walked along the beach, and said nothing, she had nothing to say, but she took her neighbour's arm to thank him, and looked straight ahead. The beach seemed to stretch on endlessly, long, white, inexhaustible, as if it were the edge of a world that never ended, but that could be contained in a few gestures – Maribel's warmth as she spoke, the way Alfonso squeezed Sara's hand, Andrés's worried face when he saw her with Bill on the promenade, Tamara nervously touching the handlebars of the bicycle next door without daring to look at it. It didn't seem like much – an employee, a mentally disabled man, a little girl of eleven, a boy of twelve – it wasn't much, yet it was more than she was used to having. In fact it was everything she'd wanted since moving there, a world apart from the risks and rewards that had marked out her earlier life. She'd chosen a discreet house, on a gated development, on the outskirts of a remote town that was neither too big nor too small, to embark on the elegant life of a wealthy outsider, and she believed she had expected nothing more. She'd tried to take refuge in her own strength and found that it wasn't enough, so she'd drawn a line in the sand and faced the unknown, not wanting to recognise a familiar face to her dreams.

Many times in her life, she'd tried to find a place to fit in, to replace the memories of a divided little girl with the certainty of a new future, but it had never worked. Her whole life amounted to a list of attempts and failures. So she'd thrown herself into what had seemed like the definitive opportunity, a project that redressed the balance of her divided self and the brutal severity of her life of distrust. And she'd succeeded at last, she'd achieved it. Yet, as she walked home arm in arm with Juan Olmedo, she realised she'd done nothing different now from what she'd always done. Her conversations with Andrés, with Tamara, the cheerful, instinctive ease with which she let them both exploit her, the casual way she'd accepted Alfonso as part of duties no one had forced her to take on, the stubbornness with which she had convinced Maribel that she had to buy a flat, and even her aim of discovering the key to Juan's past and why he'd come to live there, probably had less to do with boredom, the unbearable slowness of clocks, and more to do with an automatic reflex, so ancient and intimate that she couldn't distinguish it from all the other components of her being – the instinct to be part of something, anything, to feel she had a home that was more than just the building in which she lived.

In the early hours of Saturday morning, the sky was clear and quiet, with no trace of a west wind and no sign of an east wind. The air was still, the sea like a mirror. Sara Gómez got up late, feeling well rested, and found that the world echoed her mood exactly, as far as the eye could see. Three days after its official start, spring seemed confident of its own strength. And she was too. She had a leisurely breakfast, got ready with more care than usual, chose comfortable, light clothes, and at one o'clock went across the road. Andrés and Tamara spotted her. Juan, with his back turned, and Maribel, who was combing Alfonso's hair, heard her cheerful greeting:

'Did you think you'd get to eat all the *galeras* without me then?'

They all looked at her and smiled. As they were all about to set off, Andrés and Tamara both raised their hands. It was their way of claiming the passenger seat next to Sara.

Sara Gómez Morales passed four subjects in her first year of economics, but never registered for the second year. At the time, giving up her plans didn't bother her much, and she never really regretted a decision that more or less took itself, born of weariness – weariness of going to the cinema alone, studying all the time, drinking too much. In exchange,

Vicente González de Sandoval restored brilliance and intensity to her life just at the point when she was about to turn thirty.

'Don't lie to me, Vicente.'

They'd gone out for a coffee mid-morning. They'd had to walk for quite a while before finding a café that neither of them had been to with colleagues. It was eleven thirty in the morning and the coffee machine was noisy, but there was no one in the room. Vicente picked a table with a view of both sides of the street, took her by the hand and began to give her confused explanations. She then asked him not to lie to her, thinking she'd never ask him anything else.

'It's the only thing I ask of you: don't lie to me. I've been told quite enough lies in my life – I don't need any more.'

'Not lie to you . . .' he said, rubbing his eyes, as if to gain time. He turned his head to look out of the window at the street, then turned back to her. 'So what can I tell you? I'm one of your bosses, I'm married, I have two children. The youngest, a little girl named after my wife, María Belén, was born only a few months ago. I didn't want to have a second child, but her mother didn't consult me. We make a good couple. We started going out together when we were at school. When I left home, I left her. When I came back, I went back to her too. My mother adores her. I don't. I like you. I like you a lot. That's it. It's the classic story, isn't it?'

'Yes,' said Sara, smiling. 'It is.'

'And sordid. Ugly . . . sickening.'

'Of course,' said Sara. 'Like all true stories.'

'Almost all true stories,' he said, lifting a finger.

'All right,' she accepted his qualification with a nod. 'Almost all.'

Vicente had been playing with a sugar cube as he spoke, turning it over and over, passing it from one hand to the other, putting it down on the table, flicking it with his index finger, picking it up and starting all over again. Now he unwrapped it slowly and dropped it into his cup. As he stirred his coffee, Sara wondered whether he was genuinely flustered, whether his nervousness was spontaneous or premeditated. Suddenly, he smiled.

'And if I tell you you're the first woman I've been involved with since I got married, you wouldn't believe that either, I suppose?' She laughed, shaking her head, and he laughed too, but as his laughter faded, his face took on a peaceful, almost melancholy look. 'But it's true, in a way.'

'Let's not bother with "ways", Vicente.'

Talking was hard. Everything else, what had happened the Friday before, had been much easier. Sara had been surprised when the quantity surveyor who was also a union member and whom she knew only by sight, had invited her to the dinner, and she accepted only because she couldn't think of an excuse quickly enough. When Vicente, who'd spent the last month walking down corridors with her and paying her numerous little visits, appeared a moment later to say how pleased he was that she'd be going to Miguel Angel's stag party and offered to give her a lift to the restaurant – 'It's quite far out of town, beyond Arturo Soria, even taxi drivers get lost' – Sara recalled having seen him chatting to the surveyor. They had been joking around, elbowing each other when some secretary in a miniskirt went past. So she assumed they were good enough friends for the surveyor to have invited her to the dinner as a favour. It didn't bother her, in fact she quite liked it, because she liked Vicente, and she was starting to experience the same agitation she could see in his eyes, on his lips, in his nervous movements, the sudden tension, an instant reaction like an alarm that made his head jerk up whenever she came into the room. But the certainty that their desire was ripe didn't stop her assessing her situation precisely, just as an apple might calculate the extent and pain of its fall just as it felt the last fibre attaching it to the tree break.

As she dressed, trying to bear in mind that she would probably be getting undressed twice that evening, she real-ised that after all that effort, all those years, all those fierce resolutions, she was going to end up just like Señorita Sevilla, in the arms of her boss's boss, although Vicente González de Sandoval was younger, richer and more elegant than the owner of the secretarial school. She had sworn to herself a thousand times that she would never play a part like the one she was rehearsing that afternoon. He was a Republican of course, and she was a free, independent woman. It was also true, however, that her godmother and her friends would split their sides laughing if they heard her set out the problem in those terms. As the rejected dresses, skirts, blouses and bras piled up on the bed, the feeling that her fate was already sealed, that someone else had written the script of her life, seemed stronger than ever. She wondered how many of the women she saw each morning – secretaries, telephonists, receptionists – had got ready for a night out with Vicente before her. 'This isn't his first time,' she warned herself, 'it can't be.' Yet she still felt happy, and nervous, and hoped that something would happen.

Until that day, men had played only a secondary role in her life. She'd gone out with a few – almost always col-leagues, or acquaintances – and in her last year at the Robles School she'd almost become engaged to an office worker from a village near Ávila who'd pursued her for a whole year without being discouraged by his lack of success. Eventually his perseverance, the tenacity with which he asked her out one Saturday after another, endeared him to her. He wasn't much to look at. He had glasses, was balding, skinny, and always wore one of two jackets, both of which were too big for him. Sara gave him the benefit of the doubt for a couple of months, because she was twenty by then, and she hadn't been out with anyone since Juan Mari. But she found him boring, and despaired because he never seemed to understand the endings of the films they went to see. So she was taken completely by surprise when he attacked her the night she finally agreed to accompany him up to his room, 'Just so you can see where I live,' he said. She could have screamed, she could have shouted for help, waking up the other lodgers, hit him, kicked and bit him; she would probably have been a match for him he was so puny, but she felt sorry for him. His skin was cold, covered in goosebumps, he had a few sparse black hairs on his puny chest, and very narrow shoulders, and he wanted to marry her. He was very nervous, he finished almost immediately, and it was all a disaster. Afterwards, as he gathered his clothes and started dressing, he said sorry, and Sara felt like crying, for him and for herself, for how squalid it all was and how incredibly ugly a man's naked body could be. On Monday, after class, he began to plan a more formal engagement and even started to talk of a wedding. Sara said she didn't want to see him again and refused to answer his questions.

It had been different only once. She was twenty-two. He was a neighbour of her brother Pablo, who worked for ITT. He was thirty-four, had been married for ten years and was alone in Madrid, working in August when most people were away on holiday. She met him by chance one day, when she went to Pablo's to water her sister-in-law's plants. His name was Manuel, he lived in the flat opposite, and she had liked him very much, although she was never really sure why. She had glimpsed him across the courtyard. He was naked from the waist up, with broad shoulders and thick arms, and was holding a bottle of beer. 'Hot, isn't it?' he said, and she replied, 'Well, yes, it is hot,' and went on watering the plants, glancing from time to time at the line of hair that went down his belly, past his perfect navel and disappeared into the top of his trousers. 'Would you like a beer?' he asked after a while, raising the bottle in the air, and she said yes. They chatted and drank beer on the landing until it grew dark. He was funny, telling endless jokes, but then he began to appear nervous, as if he didn't know what to do next, how to behave in such a situation. Sara found his gaucheness touching. At last he said, 'Well, you probably have to go, don't you?' assuming she had plans for the evening because it was a Friday. She said no, she was alone in Madrid too, her parents were in Asturias visiting her sister and she had nothing planned. 'I've just started a new job and I've only got a week's holiday,' she told him, 'it's this week, so I don't have to go to work tomorrow.' 'Nor do I,' he said, brightening up. 'I did a shift for a friend last week, so we could go for a drink if you like.' They had dinner in a Chinese restaurant. They had a great deal to drink in two different bars. He kissed her in the street, with his arms around her, holding her tight against his body, and she liked it. They slept together in a bed that matched the wardrobe and chest of drawers and bedside tables adorned with matching little crochet mats. On the table on Sara's side there was a framed photograph of three children with a fat woman who looked older than her husband. It was only her second time, but he was a gentle, affectionate lover and didn't seem to notice her lack of experience. Nor did he say anything when Sara suggested they sleep at her brother's flat, 'Because here,' she added, 'with all this', and she gestured vaguely at the photo by the bed, 'I don't know.' They spent all of Saturday together and most of Sunday, and he helped her tidy the flat before they left. As they parted, on the landing where they'd met, he looked at her very steadily, and couldn't find anything to say. She kissed him on the cheek and rushed downstairs, but as she got to the entrance, Manuel called: 'Hey, wait!' He ran after her and kissed her on the mouth. 'Next Saturday I've got to go and collect my wife, but maybe . . . Do you have a phone?' 'No,' she lied, 'I haven't.'

As she came out of the metro at the Puerta del Sol, it wasn't quite dark, but Sara felt like she was emerging into a different world, the real world, the only world that was hers. It was as if the time in San Fernando de Henares – her brother's flat, Manuel's body, his face, his hands, the way he moved – was all part of a fiction that had just burst like a soap bubble. She wasn't sure what had just happened or why she'd behaved the way she had, who had taken all the decisions for her. She felt neither ashamed nor pleased, just strange. In time she would come to understand that this episode had sprung from herself, from her own confusion, and was unlike any conscious step she had ever taken before. The favour for her sister-in-law, which had seemed such a hassle, a tiresome journey on a stifling afternoon, had provided her with a rare and precious opportunity to slip into another possible life, the life she might have had if things had been different. Pablo's neighbour, with his curly black hair, pale eyes, and square jaw that balanced the thickness of his lips, was much more than some random good-looking man who'd caught her eye through a window. From across the courtyard, the stranger looked more like Arcadio Gómez Gómez than his own sons did; not the grey, tired, prematurely aged man who had hugged a lonely, confused little girl every Sunday morning, but the young, strong Arcadio of the photographs, the armed, fierce Arcadio, with a strong body and tanned arms. And her brother's flat, its terrazzo floors, hollow doors, aluminium windows, narrow corridor and hideous china figurines, might have been her home had she chosen an employee of ITT, had she been able to live the life she should have led from the very start.

This was what she had loved, this was the dream she had given herself up to in the brown arms of a man who was never simply himself to her, and who never quite made her his in the strange forty-eight hours they spent together. Neither of them thought to switch off Pablo's alarm clock when they got into his bed, but when it went off, at six twenty-five on the Saturday morning, Sara was already

317

awake. It was the first time she'd spent the night with someone and the proximity of a man's body, the heat it gave off and the sound of his breathing, weighed down on her. When the alarm erupted, bouncing off the walls of the room, he sat up immediately and shot out of bed, a reflex. Amazed at how beautiful the body of a naked man could be, Sara watched him look around, bewildered, as if he didn't know where he was. He then turned to her and smiled.

'Oh!' he said, his voice still thick with sleep. 'You're here. Good! I'd forgotten.'

He got back into bed, covering himself with the sheet, put his arms around her and kissed her face, her hair, her neck, and Sara felt his warmth, so pleasant after her sleepless night. She could sense a new greed, a desire growing in her finger-tips, in the space between her parted lips, in the hard penis pressing against her belly, and she felt jealous and strangely grateful. She put her arms around him, placed her hands flat on his back and drew him to her, and he took possession of her slowly, wordlessly, with his eyes open, pulling out just in time. Then they kissed for a long while, still looking at each other, as if they both knew how strange and good it was. 'We've got to buy some condoms,' he said, then added, 'Let's get some more sleep, shall we?' She moved close to him, clung to him. Manuel took her arm and placed it across his chest, as if he were used to sleeping like this. Sara kissed him on the shoulder, once, twice, three times, and as she fell at last into a deep, heavy sleep, she surrendered to the fantasy that this man was her man, this house was her house, and she realised that, however pathetic it might seem, this was the sweetest moment of her life.

Yet never, not even once, did she think of trying to find this man, who asked for bread in a Chinese restaurant, who rested his left arm on his leg as he ate, and who spoke with a thick Madrid accent, again. She didn't even want to go back to her brother's house to take the sheets off the clothes line.

She'd washed them and hung them out to dry, and was planning to iron them and remake the bed. But by the following Monday, when she left work, she couldn't believe that it had really happened, because she was scared of seeing him again and didn't want to prolong the pleasant deception of a life that would never be hers. It hadn't occurred to her that her sister-in-law would be suspicious; but when Sara came across her sitting at the table at her parents' house one Sunday in September, it was obvious she was still annoyed.

'I spilt water on the bed,' Sara said, giving the first excuse she could think of, and not daring to meet Pili's eye. 'That's why I changed your sheets.'

'And that's why you washed them?'

'Well, yes, so they wouldn't smell of damp.'

'Of course,' her sister-in-law spat out with obvious contempt. 'Right little slut you are!'

Pablo got on very badly with his wife, and he didn't dare intervene directly, but he started telling off the children for no reason so as to interrupt the conversation. Sara realised that he too was looking at her differently, conspiratorially, almost admiringly, as if he'd never known her before. Sara reflected that this must be the first time her brother had ever really noticed her, but she was grateful to him for providing the distraction.

'Manuel sends you his regards,' he said to her later, in the kitchen, as she was doing the washing-up and waiting for the coffee to brew. 'He's a mate of mine, we work together on the same floor. He's a good man, so don't worry, he didn't want to tell me any of the details. But I got it out of him – it was obvious that something had happened and not just because of the business with the sheets. Apparently, you put all the pots and pans back in the wrong places. You were the only one who had a key to the flat. You could have brought anyone here, of course, with this place to yourself, so why would you bother going all the way over to ours? And

Gracia, Manuel's wife, told Pili that when she got back she found him very odd, in a bad mood all the time and not wanting to do anything, so, what with one thing and another, it didn't take me long to work it out. The problem is, my wife is good friends with his. They go to the market together, they listen to that serial on the radio every afternoon, they go shopping for clothes, things like that. But I think although they're suspicious, they don't know anything for sure.'

'Oh!' Sara said, raising her eyes from the washing-up and looking at her brother. But she couldn't focus because her eyes were filling with tears.

They heard the clicking of heels approaching down the corridor and her brother, who was eleven years older than her – and was probably already involved with the hairdresser for whom he left his wife a couple of years later, to general consternation but the bitter satisfaction of Sara, who detested her sister-in-law from that day on – comforted her immediately.

'Come on, it's all right,' he whispered quickly, hugging her and kissing her on the temple as if she were a little girl, before turning to intercept his wife. 'The coffee's not ready yet. Will you ask my father if he wants any? I'll bring it in a minute.'

'You?' said Pili in mock amazement, sharp and shrill as a hen. 'You'll bring the coffee in?'

'Yes, I will,' he replied calmly. Sara went on with the washing-up, not even stopping to wipe away the tears; she couldn't understand why she was crying, yet the tears kept flowing. Her brother was getting stroppy with his wife now: 'What's the matter?' he said to her.

'What's the matter?' she bristled. 'Shit! First little miss goody-two-shoes here, and now you, taking the coffee to the table. I can't cope with all the surprises!'

'Oh, go to hell!' Pablo shouted after Pili had left the

kitchen, the sound of her heels receding down the corridor. 'You might be getting another surprise some day soon!'

'Oh, yes?' called his wife, stopping to shout back. 'You watch out, you might get a surprise yourself!'

Sara heard her mother, asking them to calm down, as usual.

'No problem! Where do I sign?' Pablo went on yelling, despite his mother's pleading, also as usual. 'No such luck! No such bloody luck!'

The sound of Pili's heels faded, and Sara could now hear the children's voices. The coffee was ready. Pablo, surprisingly calm after the row, took a tray, and placed the coffee cups and sugar bowl on it.

'Is there anything you want me to tell him?' he asked his sister, almost in her ear.

'No,' she said, shaking her head. 'What would be the point?'

He shrugged, as if conceding she was right, but as he was about to take the tray to the dining room, she whispered, 'Well, remember me to him. Because I do remember him.'

She'd remember him for a long time, never forgetting the feel of his wide, rough-skinned fingers, their instant, analgesic heat when he touched her face, her clothes, her body, fingers that were stronger, more powerful than the confusion of a little girl; she never forgot their warm intimacy between unfamiliar sheets. For years she reproached herself for not having returned to San Fernando, to Manuel's body, on the Monday that convinced her that nothing had happened, or in the days that followed, prolonging the dream of a fragile love, irrevocably condemned to die.

But she was never truly sorry that she hadn't gone back to see him again. Whenever she felt tempted to respond to the understanding look that she got from Pablo across the table several Sundays in a row, she tried to picture her brother's small, cheap flat in the suburbs, to hear his outbursts of barely contained rage, to imagine the rows that were becoming more serious, louder, more ferocious. She imagined the mute presence of the plants her sister-in-law didn't buy in any shop, spider plants and geraniums and money plants that multiplied through shoots and cuttings, changing hands on the stairs, at the market, in the changing rooms at the beer factory where she worked as a cleaner, spontaneous gestures of basic courtesy in a world that was barely decent, a landscape of tired figures, young men who no longer looked young, young women who looked old, and endless children, shrieking, running, crying, constantly demanding. Perhaps there weren't all that many of them, it just seemed like it as they slept in bunk beds that didn't leave enough space to open the doors of tiny bedrooms with paper-thin walls, the ceiling lamp shaking as they charged about cramped flats on boring, wet Saturday afternoons. This was how Pablo lived, and how his neighbour no doubt lived, moving between weariness and disappointment, between monotonous resignation and the temptation to snatch a little pleasure, a glimmer of happiness anywhere, at any price. Sara knew about this kind of life; Socorro told her about it often.

'I've put him on a diet,' she'd say with regard to her husband, and Sara felt sorry for her brother-in-law, Marcelino, who'd have to get ten thousand pesetas from his mother's pension on the first day of every month if he ever wanted to have sex with his wife again. 'Don't be silly, Socorro,' Sara said to her, 'you can't do that to him!' 'Oh, can't I?' she'd reply. 'And why not? What else can I do? Can you tell me? It's what women have always done, it's the only thing that works, the only thing I've got . . .' 'What about you?' asked Sara. 'I mind less than he does,' her sister said, 'and anyway, I just put up with it.' That was the beginning of the end, putting up with it, until good intentions disappeared, and anger was more sustaining than supper when a very young, very tired man got home late in the evening to find two cold fried eggs covered with a plate and a wife, also very young and very tired, who wouldn't open her legs for him. 'Your loss,' the men would mutter, and Sara sympathised, but she sympathised with the women too, they worked as hard as their husbands and still they had to put up with them shouting because they'd drunk three beers in a row and the fourth wasn't already chilling in the fridge; women who'd got married before they were twenty because they were sick of doing it standing up in a bathroom, or lying on the ground in a dark corner of their local park, and who'd got pregnant two, three, four times before they were thirty, watching their husbands broaden, fill out, and stay young, growing more attractive, while they themselves went from splendour to collapse, stretch marks, sagging flesh, the same shape as the bread rolls they ate in the street, women who had only one weapon and used it so much the rope finally snapped. Sometimes they were lucky enough to get a meek one, like poor Marcelino, who ended up doing everything Socorro told him, and was passably happy, and made her passably happy, but sometimes they turned out bad-tempered, like Pablo, who summed up his philosophy of life in a single sentence, 'I'm going to do what I bloody well like and if you don't like it, there's the door.' And behind the door there was always another, younger woman, a girl, who was prepared to do all the things a lawful wife didn't have to do, who never said no to anything, who learnt fast, and caressed and flattered them, excited them, sucked them off, and let them suck anything they liked, for as long as they liked, until they realised that not only was it cheaper than going to a prostitute, but that if the girl was so devoted, it must be because she was crazy about them, because she really loved them. So then it started all over again, from the beginning, but with an extra person, an odd one out − the lonely, wrecked wife who didn't read books or newspapers, who didn't have a TV, or any idea that in the other half of the world there were women like her claiming as their right the duties her husband had demanded of her in vain for years, a woman who never could have guessed what young female students in Salamanca called liberation, a woman like her sister-in-law, Pili, who went to her mother-in-law's to cry, and cried until she was empty. Sara felt that, however much she had come to hate her, however many books and newspapers she herself had read and would go on reading, Pili's tears were heartbreaking, but no more so than the words of her brother, when he looked her in the eye and spoke to her straight. 'I'm thirty-three years old,' he'd say, 'and all I've done all my fucking life is get up at six thirty in the morning and work like a slave, so what do you want me to do now, eh? What do you want me to do?' So when Vicente González de Sandoval, with his slender fingers and carefully clipped nails, said that his story was sordid and ugly, Sara smiled and felt like adding, 'You have no idea. You'll never really know what a sordid, ugly, sickening story really is, Vicente.'

Everything else was easy. When Vicente came to pick her up to take her to the restaurant where his friend was celebrating his last night as a bachelor, he arrived on time, and she saw that he was wearing very different clothes – jeans, a checked shirt and a suede jacket – from the suit and tie she was used to seeing him in at the office. She was pleased by this, and even more by the fact that he couldn't take his eyes off her legs as she got into the car. 'You look great, Sara!' he told her. The bride and groom were saying farewell to their single status with a joint dinner, as befitted a modern couple who would be getting married in church the following morning in an almost clandestine ceremony (with only their closest family present, no confetti, white dress, veil or bouquet) as a way of keeping their respective families happy. The couple welcomed Vicente and Sara without surprise because, as she later found out, they hardly knew

Vicente's wife, and they were used to seeing him alone, or with a different girl each time. The comfortable combination of indifference and friendliness that Sara sensed in them, and in most of the guests at the dinner, helped to put her at her ease, to rise above the inevitable, occasional little smiles from a few back-biters. Vicente couldn't keep his eyes off her even when he was eating, enveloping her in an exclusive, tyrannical attention that Sara would have hated in another man, making sure she never ran out of wine, or cigarettes, or anything else, during the entire meal. That evening, he embodied the man that Sara had been yearning for ever since her fateful sixteenth birthday party.

This more than made up for any gaps, any hesitations or uncertainties. 'I've always wanted a boyfriend like him,' she thought as Vicente kissed her on the mouth in front of everyone, with a longing that tensed his delicate fingers as he held her; 'I've always wanted a boyfriend like him,' as he whisked her out of the restaurant, kissing and embracing her so that they swayed and staggered; 'I've always wanted a boyfriend like him,' as he pounced on her in the car and his hands explored her body; 'I've always wanted a boyfriend like him,' when he suddenly stopped and looked into her eyes, and said he was dying to have sex with her, but that he couldn't take her anywhere more comfortable, or discreet, or pleasant than a hotel. 'I've always wanted a boyfriend like him, always.' It was a profound truth, the most brutal and humiliating and purest truth she possessed. So that night, and many other nights, she behaved like a vulgar tart from the suburbs and said yes to everything, to be what he wanted her to be, whenever, wherever, however he wanted, repeating over and over to herself that he was the boyfriend she'd always wanted. And for a long time, that was enough.

But it wasn't enough, because Vicente González de Sandoval was a weak man, though it would take her years to find out.

At first, he seemed quite the opposite, a wise man, a prince, someone with the power to control reality and subject it to his wishes.

'Why didn't you bring me here the other day?'

The apartment was small but had magnificent views, on the top floor of a building in the Calle Bailén, almost at the Plaza de España.

'Because I didn't know it was empty,' he said, taking off his jacket and dropping it on the sofa. 'It belongs to my grandmother. She owns the whole building, but no one lives here at the moment. I went to see her and asked if any of the flats were empty. I said I wanted to use it as an office, that I couldn't work at home because of the children.' He took off his tie, unbuttoned the top two buttons of his shirt, and smiled. 'We agreed I'd return it to her whenever she needed it, but I don't think she ever will. She's loaded.'

This wasn't true. His grandmother was very rich indeed, but neither that apartment nor any other apartment in the building belonged to her, or any other member of his family. This was another classic ingredient of this classic story. He'd looked in the papers, called an estate agent, gone to see the apartment, liked it, paid a deposit, and for years, without Sara knowing, continued paying the rent by direct debit from a bank account his wife knew nothing about. He'd never felt the need to do anything like this for any of the other women he'd had affairs with since marrying María Belén, and this part of his story was true, although he'd looked only at furnished flats so as not to spend more than he had to, just in case things went sour, in case he suddenly went off Sara the way he'd gone off all the others.

'And the furniture?'

'It was already here.'

'It's hideous.'

'Yes,' he said, putting his arms around her, holding her tightly and kissing her on the mouth. As he gazed down at her, Sara had a feeling that she was going to fall hopelessly in love with him. 'I'll make sure I tell my grandmother off.'

The sheets on the bed were new. They felt stiff and rough, though not unpleasant, because they had never been washed, and the creases from being in their packaging were still visible. Sara noticed this, because she nearly always noticed everything. He undressed her like a greedy child at his own birthday party, not yet resenting the poverty of her responses, her inability to return what she was receiving, her need to remain in control at all times. The others Sara had been with had not minded, Manuel had not minded, but Vicente would come to find it painful.

'Did you buy them?' she asked, lifting a corner of the sheet, when Vicente collapsed beside her, convincing her that everything had gone well because he seemed so happy. She had enjoyed his weight upon her, his smell, and felt the same need to possess him and to give herself to him, that she had experienced many years earlier one August in a borrowed bed. It wasn't exactly pleasure, but it was the most intense thing she'd ever felt for a man, with a man.

'Yes,' he murmured.

'Did you come here specially to make the bed?'

'Of course,' he said, and she laughed and clung to him as she'd failed to do earlier, when he was moving inside her.

Perhaps it was this, her interest in such a trivial detail, the disproportionate reaction to his answer that enlightened Vicente in that instant. Perhaps, in such a brief space of time, he managed to link Sara's excessive delight now with her urge to take the little bottles of shampoo from the hotel bathroom that first night. And then there were all the strange questions he couldn't make sense of: 'Where did you live with your parents before you got married?' That was the first. 'In the Calle Montesquinza,' he'd answered. 'Which school did you go to?' 'To El Pilar.' 'Ah!' she'd sighed, inexplicably relieved, and on she went, her questions becoming more and more mysterious: 'Where did you hang out when you were at the university?' 'I don't know, around Moncloa, I suppose, like everyone else.' 'You didn't happen to meet a civil engineer from Vitoria whose name was Juan Mari García de Ibargüengoitia, did you?' 'No.' 'Or a very pretty girl called María Pilar Gutiérrez Rios whom everyone called Maruchi?' 'No.' 'Did your wife go to the Sagrado Corazón?' 'No.' 'Does the surname Villamarín sound at all familiar? Or Ochoa?' 'No, why should they sound familiar? Why are you asking me such bizarre questions?' 'Oh, I don't know, just because.'

'You've never told me why you're my equal and my opposite, Sara,' he said looking into her eyes, their noses still almost touching. 'Why you're my reflection in a mirror.'

Sara moved away from him and leant against the headboard. She took a deep breath and, staring at the ceiling, told him everything. It was the first time she'd told anyone her story, and it would be the last. She'd thought she wouldn't know where to start but she started at the beginning, with a frightened little girl called Sebastiana the day she started work at a big apartment in the Calle Velázquez, just after her twelfth birthday. After that, her words seemed to flow of their own accord, to issue from lips that felt numb, her tone neutral as she tried to defend herself from her memories. He let her speak, without interrupting or moving closer to her. Sara could hear his breathing when she paused, when she forced herself to pause, but talking soon became painful, making her throat feel tight and her mouth dry. 'I need a drink,' she thought, but she desperately wanted to get to the end of this story and didn't dare interrupt it now. Then she began to talk about herself, the extra piece that never fitted into any jigsaw puzzle, her confusion, her bitterness, her anger. She'd never wanted anyone to feel sorry for her, and she certainly didn't want him to, so she chose indirect routes, apparently trivial details, ordinary words. She talked of the white child-sized furniture, the silk dress, the washing line, the collection of coloured hairbands, the bunch of old photos, faded, yellowing images, torn and dog-eared. But even then, her tactic didn't work, and she wept silently throughout.

When she was finished, she turned to look at Vicente and thought she saw a trace of compassion in his eyes. He sat up, cleared his throat, and turned to pick up the phone on the bedside table.

'Hello, it's me, is my wife at home?' he said, in his confident, efficient tone. 'No, don't disturb her, just tell her I won't be coming home this evening because I'm still in Segovia. The meeting went on longer than expected, so I'm staying overnight. Yes, yes, I'll explain it to her tomorrow. Thank you, goodbye.'

He replaced the phone on the bedside table, sank back into the bed and put his arms around her, his embrace both protective and vulnerable, its strength contradicted by the childlike impulse to place his cheek against hers and press hard, so that she could feel his cheekbones.

'Sara, Sara,' he murmured. He seemed deeply moved, even guilty somehow, and made no attempt to hide it. 'My God, Sara.'

By now, she believed he could be her salvation, and she was convinced he would be as long as they both played the same game. From that night on, until the weariness of repetition changed the rules, Vicente González de Sandoval spent a lot of money pleasing Sara Gómez Morales, buying her beautiful, useless presents, always choosing the most expensive things, taking her by the hand to visit all the most luxurious places, from the most vulgar and ostentatious to the most refined and exclusive. He managed to surround every peseta he spent in a clean, transparent veil, a simple token of his love, and he never used his generosity to bargain, never asked for anything in return. He liked to look at her, to watch her enjoy the things she couldn't afford, gradually discovering her inexhaustible skills, the proficiency of her fingers, her eyes, her palate, the assurance with which she distinguished real silk from synthetic, genuine Armagnac from cheap Spanish brandy, and he enjoyed provoking her, tempting her, taking control of her will, her memory, her emotions, whenever he caught a gleam in her eye as they passed a shop window.

'Do you like it?'

It could be something small, insignificant even – a pen, a handkerchief, a diary – or something very expensive – a piece of jewellery, a crocodile handbag, an evening dress – but he always enquired with the same interest, the same adorable, mischievous look on his face, and she always answered in the same way, shaking her head, with the same silly, childish, carefree laugh, her hands sunk into her coat pockets as if she were trying to pierce the fabric with her knuckles.

'Do you like it?'

Vicente ran his tongue over his teeth, stood behind Sara and put his arms around her. He looked closely at her face reflected in the window while his fingers slid inside her blouse or skirt, going further, further every time until, eventually, she leant against him and closed her eyes, tilting her head and offering him her neck. He kissed it, or licked it slowly until he reached her ear, and asked for the third time: 'Do you like it? I'll buy it for you.'

Sometimes, by this time, the people inside the shop had noticed them. Some watched them, amused, whilst others were shocked. And if they were in a luxurious place, with thick carpets and plush sofas, and she detected the slightest suspicion in the shop assistant's eyes, she trembled at the thought of the things Vicente would say as he wrote out the cheque.

'It's amazing,' he'd mutter, clicking his tongue, as if he

were talking to himself, 'how horny spending money makes you, my dear.'

And she loved the disarming little postscript he added a second later. 'Your father never warned me about this. Had I known, I would never have married you.'

They left the shop almost choking with laughter, and Sara gave herself up to the happiness coursing through her body, the salty, sharp tingle under her skin, the sudden sparkle in her eyes, and the crackle of the expensive wrapping paper that seemed to hold out the promise of a new, easier life. The inebriation of all these pleasant sensations was unaffected by the flashes of common sense that occasionally struck Sara out of the blue. Vicente lived in El Viso, a smart residential area away from the bustle of the centre of town, so that protected them, made them invisible, another anonymous couple amongst thousands of others. But sometimes he would let go of her arm and make her hurry past certain restaurants, certain shops or entrances to apartment blocks. He gave no explanation, and she never asked why, because this was just the first chapter, the first stage in their story. Vicente always used that word on the few occasions when she'd dared speak about what was happening to them: 'It's just a stage,' he'd say, 'this is a stage.' And she believed him, because deep down it didn't yet matter to her, because what he gave her, what he allowed her, was enough. This was why she coped easily with being alone at weekends, in her single woman's bedroom now suddenly full of pretty, often expensive, objects that were hers and yet still seemed to belong to someone else. But when her jewellery box, and her wardrobe, and the bathroom shelves spoke up, asking her what she was doing, what she was really playing at, not realising the true price of things, she thought of Vicente and smiled, and it all made sense because he made it make sense.

'It isn't a waste,' he said one summer afternoon, as the sun lazily caressed the tops of the skyscrapers in the Plaza de

España and filtered between the slats of the blinds, painting her body with stripes. For once, she had spoken to him of her doubts. 'It's a calculated investment. I'm investing in you, your pleasure, in your happiness. I love you, Sara, and it's much better if you're happy with me, because I need you to love me back.'

Maybe, if nothing had changed, if external reality had not invaded the narrow confines of the capsule in which she spent her time with him, Sara would have recovered her ability to calculate, the essential detachment she'd gradually relinquished, almost without noticing it, as Vicente taught her at last to take off her clothes with joy. But the dictator's death foreshadowed the first signs of weariness in a love story that still seemed full of colour and nuance. In the spring of 1976, when Vicente applied to join the Socialist Workers Party, Sara felt reality give her a push. And while the whole country entered a state of turmoil that felt like an extension of her own private passion, she came to believe that there was only one way forward. She wanted Vicente at the very centre of the rest of her life. She had laid to rest her dream of a rifle and, with a faith, a hope that belied what she said aloud, she observed the fervour with which Vicente embarked on the various stages of his political career. The wind was now blowing in her favour, in favour of this young generation who were invisible until only a few months before, but who now – suddenly – had immense power and could stir the stagnant waters, explode the stale air, with their words and their actions. Things were changing so fast that nobody, not even they, understood the full extent of their success. It all seemed so genuine, so moving, so necessary, that she didn't pause to consider the elegant, discreet words that Vicente chose when he introduced her into his new world. Instead of keeping her hidden, he placed her right in the foreground, suiting both him and his ambitions. Sara also thought herself favoured, because of her story, the tragedy of her family, and she liked to hear her lover repeat the dates and names, the anecdotes and reminiscences that Arcadio Gómez Gómez had retrieved for him around the table at the flat in Concepción Jerónima, stories she'd heard a thousand times by the time she agreed to introduce Vicente to her parents, but that took on a new shine when she heard them uttered with the smiling, authoritative gravity of Vicente's voice. So she became accustomed to being the companion of a married man who, apparently, was not known to be married by anyone in the party, and she spent more time with him than his own wife, accompanying him on trips, sometimes long, sometimes short, on which she encountered people who became friends and who assumed they were putting off having children until Vicente was a member of parliament.

Then one day Sara couldn't conceal her nausea in front of a simple cup of coffee. They were in the restaurant of a five-star hotel in Athens, and by then Vicente was an MP. She was unaware that something else had changed too.

'I think I'm going to be sick.'

'You don't think you might be pregnant, do you?'

'Of course not. That's ridiculous.'

It was the spring of 1982, and by then the surveyor who had surprised her by inviting her out of the blue to a bachelor's dinner had been married for over seven years. Sara was thirty-five.

'I've told her about us,' Vicente said a couple of months after the 1977 elections, which was when she'd chosen to talk to him about their situation. She didn't dare cross the line between asking for something and demanding something, she issued no ultimatums, and didn't put any pressure on him, because she had calculated that there was no need. And yet, despite all her calculations, she saw him go white, look suddenly small and fragile, shrink visibly inside his shirt collar, when he revealed he'd already told his wife, but then said nothing more.

'And?' Sara said after a pause.

'Well, she knows.'

'And?' said Sara again, her voice fearful, thin as a thread.

'She says it's not important.'

For the first time in her life, Sara thought about this woman, tried to put herself in her place, and only then did she begin to understand Vicente's point of view. In the long pauses in the conversation, she became aware of the exact magnitude of an astonishing chain of errors, and of the true price of things, all those pretty, often expensive, sometimes very expensive things, that had no importance, not just because they were part of an honest, transparent game – 'You like it, so I buy it for you. You're happy, so am I. I love you, you love me, and money is for spending' – but also, above all, because they had never compromised him. The money in itself had never been significant to him, because it had never committed him to anything, just as all the half-promises and understandings had never committed him to anything; the ambiguous nature of a relationship that was public but also secret, an engagement that was also adultery, a confused love that had grown and become more complicated, thriving on its contradictions, adopting the sophisticated lifestyle of the educated bourgeoisie, providing the best seats for Arcadio Gómez Gómez and Sebastiana Morales Pereira at bullfights where they wept when the loudspeakers played the rousing opening of the *Internationale*. But none of this was important, because neither Vicente nor his wife found any valid reason to consider it important.

'At first she was beside herself. She hit me and shouted at me, then she started smashing things,' he said, his voice sounding strange, almost unrecognisable, as he covered his face with his hands. 'Then she flung herself on the floor, grabbed my legs and started crying. She said she was going to kill herself, that she wanted to die. You can imagine. And then she said it wasn't important. That she was prepared to wait for as long as it took me to get over it, she wouldn't cause trouble, she'd let me live my life. But I mustn't leave her, whatever I did, because I'm the only man she's ever loved, and she'd go mad if I left her, she'd kill herself.' He suddenly took his hands away from his face, and leapt up after Sara, grabbing her by the arm. 'Where are you going?'

'I don't know. I'm going home, I suppose,' she said. Standing in the living room that she had made her own by filling it with books, plants, and some of her own belongings, Sara had gathered up her coat and bag like a guest who'd just realised she'd outstayed her welcome. She shook her head so as not to meet his eye, but at a certain point she had to. 'I don't want to end up crying too. Not today. I think you've had quite enough people crying on you today.'

'Listen, Sara,' he said, holding her by the wrists. He pushed her gently until she was leaning against the wall and didn't let go. 'I'm crazy about you, you know that. The fact that I haven't been able to . . . sort this out, doesn't change a thing. I'm crazy about you,' he said again. 'You know that.'

And the worst part was that she knew this was true – she knew he was crazy about her. And she knew that Vicente González de Sandoval was much more than a weak man. He was also a conscientious lover, a generous man, an amusing travel companion, a good friend, admirable in many ways and adorable in many others, the boyfriend she had always wanted. Because of this, although she tried, she could never leave him. Because each time she saw him again, paler than ever, even more shrunken inside his shirt than the last time she'd told him she couldn't go on, her heart told her that she wouldn't be able to control herself, to rid herself of the need to go to him. It was love, and it was glorious, and damaging, and glorious all over again, all at the same time. Then, sooner or later, two plane tickets would appear, and everything would start all over again. First it was New York, then Cairo, Berlin, Buenos Aires, Istanbul, Havana, and finally Athens, where, one morning, Sara Gómez Morales couldn't get through her breakfast.

She was pregnant. She couldn't believe it, but it was what the pieces of paper said. They had turned almost grey because she had folded and unfolded them so many times. They gave the results of her two tests: the first one, which was going to be negative, but was positive, and the second, which was going to be negative too because the first one just had to be wrong, but was also obstinately positive. Between the two tests Sara, unable to accept that forgetting to take a little yellow pill could cause such a catastrophe, found that she was paralysed. She didn't want to think, and she didn't want to talk to anyone about it, and when she made all the arrangements for an abortion – on her own – she wasn't even aware of taking a decision.

And indeed, she hadn't made the decision. Without thinking or discussing it, without analysing her situation, she was simply playing a part, taking one more step in the banal, dog-eared script of a life that seemed so familiar it must be hers, the truest life, the only real one. This point was the convergence of Doña Sara's pearl necklaces, Arcadio Gómez Gómez's cape turned inside out, the apron with which Sebastiana vainly tried to shield herself from the ugliness of the world, Señora González de Sandoval's undignified resistance, and her husband's weakness of character. They all held up before Sara's eyes the image of an exploited, betrayed woman, abandoned to her humiliation with the unbearable burden of an innocent child who had no future. Better the fate of Señorita Sevilla of the Robles School of Typing. Sara could almost hear their voices, their thick, sour pity, the good advice they whispered in her ear – better the fate of Señorita Sevilla, condemned always to be Señorita and never Señora, with her plastic hairbands and six pairs of polished shoes, her average fate as an average single woman, averagely capable, averagely content, averagely happy.

Later, Sara would never be able to pinpoint exactly the moment when she woke up, but she knew it wasn't because of a kiss from a handsome prince. Simply, at a certain moment, she looked up and in the mirror saw the typing teacher, and didn't recognise herself in that face. So she looked in another direction, and saw the poor wretch that inhabited the popular songs her mother used to sing when she did the cleaning, and found this image as gloomy and useless as the other. She concluded then that she was not, could not be, the grey woman weeping at night as she rocks the humble cradle of her sins, nor the single woman with a modest wardrobe who uncomplainingly rubs the feet of another woman's husband a few days a month. This wasn't her, it couldn't be. She'd never faced up to such a simple, obvious truth. This wasn't her. It could never be her. She imagined the screenplay of her life ripped to shreds at the bottom of a wastepaper basket, and heard herself say aloud, 'It's over, Sara, it's over.'

It was so unfair. She knew it was unfair, but nobody had ever bothered to be fair to her. She knew from bitter experience that children don't always adapt, that they couldn't endure everything, but she decided that her body would be the home to which her child could always return, whether empty-handed or loaded with gold. She knew she could be making a mistake, but it was her own risk, a risk that wasn't in the script and would crush with a single blow the average future that awaited her. She knew no one would understand, and of course no one did understand, neither her parents, nor her brothers and sisters, nor her godmother, to whom Sebastiana appealed in a final desperate attempt, giving Doña Sara the opportunity to hang up the phone violently, terminally. At work they didn't understand why she was leaving so suddenly. The last call she made from her

337

office was to lie to Vicente. 'I've had an abortion,' she told him, 'but I shouldn't have done it, it was a mistake. I feel terrible and I never want to see you again.' As overwhelmed as any man would be, even a strong one, at the mere mention of the word pregnancy, he could find nothing to say, so she said goodbye, just goodbye, and hung up.

By that morning, she had it all planned. For weeks, she'd been doing sums, covering whole pages in columns of figures that all tallied, meek, cheerful accomplices on the bottom line. She had saved a lot of money because she hadn't spent a penny on herself for years. There was also her new flat, in the district of La Vaguada, which she'd been furnishing over the past two years out of a vague prudent instinct while she waited for her parents to make up their minds to move. They didn't want to live so far out of town, but they had no choice, because their daughter was now the head of the family. When she explained things to them, with a smile that did nothing to hide her determination to impose her own will, they did not even try to object. In fact they were more worried about other aspects of their daughter's decision.

'But at least tell him,' pleaded Sebastiana, screwing up her face and tugging at her bun. 'He's the father, and he's got money. You should let him know and he'd help you.'

Sara smiled, shook her head, and kept going, hanging pictures, positioning lamps, unrolling rugs, seeing Arcadio out of the corner of her eye shaking his head even more emphatically at this new development that was completely beyond him. She was more affectionate than ever towards him, and to her mother, and every day she assured them that it would all work out. It was easy, all she had to do was wait, this was what all the others had done – her mother, her sisters, her sisters-in-law, the wives of the men in her life, simply wait, furnish a nursery, buy a cradle, and shawls, and a pram, it was so easy. She was more worried about other things, vaccinations, colic, chickenpox, how far her savings

338

would stretch, getting a good job again afterwards; or the first bad mark in maths, a bloodied knee, a cruel, painful question. Perhaps, by then, she might be able to answer, she might know where the father was, perhaps not, but anything was better than having two mothers. It was easy, all she had to do was wait; wait and look after herself.

But she wasn't like other women, she never had been. One afternoon, after lunch, she felt a terrible, searing pain in her middle as she carried the plates to the kitchen. They slipped from her hands while her body screamed. She sat down and tried to calm herself, gripping the arms of the chair so hard her knuckles were white. She ordered the pain to stop, because she was only five months gone and she hadn't waited long enough. It would stop, it had to, but it didn't. She'd had an ectopic pregnancy, the young man – he looked so young – in the white coat told her in the murky dawn beneath the hospital lights. The foetus wasn't where it should be, in the uterus, but in a Fallopian tube, which was what had caused her to go into labour prematurely. Sara stared at him unseeing; she heard him but she didn't listen. She was inside a body that didn't feel like hers, her own treacherous, enemy flesh. A betrayal. But the young man went on talking: 'You're still fertile,' he said, 'the left ovary won't function any longer, but the right one hasn't been harmed and one is enough, you can have more children.' 'No,' said Sara, and he looked at her strangely. 'I won't be having any more children,' she added, but didn't say why. Children have no price, she thought to herself, that's why Vicente can't buy them for me.

She didn't say this to Vicente when he came to her house one afternoon, a couple of days later. By then she feared that nothing would ever change, that life would always be an armchair, a tartan blanket, sitting utterly and irrevocably still.

'What are you doing here?' she asked without getting up.

Arcadio and Sebastiana were standing at the door. They

quickly slipped from the room, as if Sara's curt greeting had chased them away.

'I've come to see you,' he said. And it was still him, with his old assurance, the calm confidence of a master of the universe.

'Who called you?' asked Sara, jerking her chin in the direction in which her parents had disappeared. 'Him or her?'

'Neither,' answered Vicente, taking a low stool on which Sebastiana used to rest her feet, and placing it in front of Sara's armchair. He sat down, his head on a level with her knees. 'It was me who called. I called straight away. I wanted to speak to you but your father answered the phone and I found out you hadn't had an abortion. I thought it would be better to wait a while, until the child was born, or until you were willing to talk to me again. Since then, I've called every week. That's how I found out about this.'

'Right,' she said, with a sarcastic laugh. 'My father's like that. He always gives in to people who give orders.'

Vicente didn't respond to this barbed comment, and instead searched for her hands beneath the blanket, but he didn't find them, so he rested his head on her knees and went on speaking without looking at her.

'I've been feeling awful without you, Sara, these last few months. I've been wretched without you.' He paused but still she said nothing, so he went on, hoping that Sara, who had broken out into a sweat despite herself, would realise that he was telling the truth. 'I've got it wrong so many times, I know. I've behaved like a fool. I've made mistakes, so many mistakes, but I can change.'

He shifted position, sitting up and looking at her. She returned his gaze, and saw that he was smiling. She realised that he thought his power over her was still intact, and that he was hoping she would smile back, but she couldn't force herself to smile, and when she saw his lips, she shuddered at

340

the memory of the love she'd felt for him, a reckless, endless love that was still trying to survive, even if only in the warm recesses of her memory. She realised she would have liked to please him, to smile at him, but she couldn't.

'It's amazing!' she heard herself say. 'What strength of character! If only I'd known, I'd have got pregnant deliberately, and sooner, when there was still time.'

He moved away from her as if he had a sudden bad cramp. Now when he looked at her, his face was different. She'd never seen him look like that before, so scared, fearful, eyes moist. She wondered what had happened, why she wasn't the one on the verge of tears, as usual, why it suddenly seemed as if he were the one with everything at stake.

'Get out, Vicente,' she said, her voice steady. 'Get out. Leave me alone. Please.'

But she couldn't watch him leave. She put her face in her hands, elbows resting firmly on the arms of the chair, and waited until she heard the front door shut. Immediately afterwards, her eyes still closed, she heard her mother's voice.

'What's wrong with you?' demanded Sebastiana, crossing the living room and shaking her until Sara looked her in the face. 'Have you lost your mind? Go after him right now, and throw yourself at his feet, you fool. You're such a fool!'

'Were you listening behind the door, Mama?'

'Well, of course I was, what do you think? I don't know what's wrong with you lately, but somebody's got to take care of you.'

'Leave me alone, Mama.' The voice – someone else's – that had taken up residence in her throat, was so harsh that it easily silenced her mother. 'Leave me alone, all of you. Please, just leave me alone.'

Andrés never liked Bill. He knew the others – Tamara, Alfonso and his mother – didn't like him either, but they didn't have to put up with him ruffling their hair. Because of this, and because each time Bill did it, it seemed like a mocking, even threatening, gesture, Andrés disliked him more than anyone else did. This was why he was the most pleased of all when Sara decreed, without a hint of regret or sadness in her voice, that the intruder was being dispatched.

He wasn't too sure what exactly it was that now seemed safe and sound, free at last of the American's worrying presence. He wouldn't have known how to describe the safe new place that formed the backdrop to his life – a new world, a new family, a new landscape. He knew, however, with complete certainty, that he liked it, whatever it was. And he knew that Sara liked it too. She was the only one who seemed to realise what was going on. Andrés may not have been able to find the words to express what he was feeling, but he often thought of the Olmedos, of Sara and his mother, as people stranded together in an alien land, people who were lost but who, when they met, had been saved, because they found they could understand one another, speak the same language, laugh at the same jokes. They'd found a place to stay where they no longer felt lost, even though it wasn't the place they had originally come from.

Perhaps he was more sensitive to movement than anyone else, because he had always stayed in the same place, the same small town where he was born and had grown up, a comfortable, narrow horizon that had now surprisingly unfolded like a huge sheet that could cover the sea and whose edges were out of sight if he looked straight ahead. But he wasn't looking straight ahead, only glancing out of the corner of his eye, when he discovered something even more worrying than Sara's involvement with the American, something that would confirm his suspicions.

'Do you know something, children?' Sara said at the end of Maribel's birthday lunch, after the songs and presents, when they were still sitting at the table but no one could eat any more cake.

'In the paper yesterday,' she went on, with the mischievous look she used when she had good news tucked up her sleeve, 'I noticed that they're showing that film about gladiators in Chipiona, the one we didn't get to see last summer because we couldn't get tickets, do you remember? Do you want to go?'

Then there was shouting, please, please, could they go, they'd do their homework tomorrow. Maribel was sitting at the end of the table with Sara at the opposite end; Juan was next to her and beside him was Alfonso with the children both sitting opposite them. Waiting to see what his mother would say, Andrés noticed Juan and Maribel glance at each other first, rather than looking at him and Tamara as they pleaded to be allowed to go. The glance lasted only a split second, but Andrés noticed it, and he noticed that they both smiled an identical smile. After another infinitely brief moment, they looked at the children. Their expressions were identical, and it was obvious they would let them go to the cinema.

'All right,' said Maribel. 'If you promise you'll behave and won't drive Sara mad.'

'OK,' said Juan, and then added: 'But Alfonso's not going.'

Alfonso hadn't paid any attention to the conversation until then. He appeared to be dozing, legs stretched out, hands lying limply in his lap, but he sat bolt upright when he heard his name.

'I am going, yes, I am, I am,' he said, eyes still blurry with sleep, but nodding vigorously to emphasise his words.

'No, I'm sorry,' said Juan, shaking his head, 'you can't go, Alfonso.'

'Why can't I?' he asked. 'I want to go. I can go, can't I?' He looked pleadingly at each of them in turn. 'I am going, I am going.'

'But you don't even know where!' said Juan, smiling. 'So where is it that you want to go then?'

'We're going to the cinema, Alfonso,' cut in Tamara, seeing how confused Alfonso was. 'To the cinema in Chipiona. Sara's taking us.'

'She's taking me too,' said Alfonso, looking very pleased. 'Aren't you, Sara? You're taking me too.'

'Of course I am,' said Sara. Andrés saw that she was smiling and realised that, although she was the cleverest of all of them, she hadn't noticed the look exchanged by Juan and Maribel. 'And I'll buy you a carton of popcorn this big. If Juan lets you come with us, of course.'

'No, Sara, really,' said Juan, shaking his head, but without much conviction this time. 'You've got enough with these two. You can't take Alfonso as well, with all the trouble he creates.'

'What are you talking about?' she said. 'He's always on his best behaviour at the cinema. He loves going, don't you, Alfonso?'

'Yes, yes, I'm going, I'm going, I'm going to the cinema. I'll be good, and I'll eat my popcorn quietly.'

'You really don't mind?' asked Juan.

'I really don't,' said Sara, smiling, and then gesturing towards him and Maribel. 'Why don't you both come too?'

Andrés thought she should have noticed then that something odd was going on, because both his mother and Tamara's uncle immediately looked away in opposite directions. He was certain he was right, that when they exchanged glances earlier, they'd agreed something, and it was something they didn't want anyone else to know about.

'Well, I've arranged to meet up with some friends,' said Maribel quickly. 'With it being my birthday and everything.'

'I'll go with you to the cinema, if you like,' said Juan half-heartedly. 'But I had planned on going home for a siesta.'

Sara burst out laughing and assured them they weren't

needed. It was true, they never needed anyone else to have a good time, the four of them had a lot of fun together. But as Andrés kissed his mother goodbye, he almost decided not to go to the cinema.

'You're going home, aren't you?' Maribel asked Juan, and he nodded. 'Would you mind dropping me off at mine first?'

'Of course not.'

'It means you taking a detour.'

'No problem,' Juan said, smiling. 'I'm not in a hurry.'

Then Sara called, 'Come on, Andrés,' and he turned and saw that Alfonso and Tamara were already sitting in the back of the car, with the passenger door open, waiting for him. He really wanted to see the film – he'd been the one who'd been most keen to see it last summer – but he was on the verge of saying he wouldn't go and slipping quickly into the other car, telling his mother he'd rather go out with her and her friends, though he was pretty sure she hadn't arranged to meet up with any friends. He was about to, but Dr Olmedo was quicker than him and started up the engine while he was still deciding what to do. Meanwhile Sara was hooting, 'Andrés, come on, hurry up, we don't want to find we can't get tickets again.'

He really enjoyed the film, even though he was only half paying attention to it. His mind was still on Dr Olmedo's red car as it drove off. In every actress on screen he saw his mother, her face in every face, her body in every body, and an imagined, imaginary, eagerness in the angle of open arms, parted lips, the open violence of hands and kisses. He was only twelve years old, but he thought he knew about that sort of thing, a few vague words, the hint of a murky mystery. Sitting stiffly in his seat, not responding to any of the comments Tamara whispered in his ear from time to time, he thought of his mother, and this made him think of his grandmother and the things she said to him, the revolting way she had of clicking her tongue and venting her mean, coarse rage.

'What does she care what I do, where I go, who I go out with?' his mother would say when she found him particularly quiet and withdrawn, and guessed that her mother had been criticising her again. 'The world's changed, your grandmother doesn't have a clue, she belongs to the past. Just ignore her.' This was what she said to him and then he didn't know what to think, other than that things were as they were, and even if he didn't like it, it might not be anyone's fault. 'A mother is a mother,' thought Andrés, this at least he was sure of, and that his own was a good mother, because she loved him and he knew it, he could feel it. He closed his eyes and felt safe against her body, in her arms, her warmth. But his grandmother never took any notice of his opinion when she started wondering aloud what her daughter Maribel was doing at night in those bars, in the lives of those men – always other women's – who treated her as if she were an old rag. When Andrés heard his grandmother, he didn't feel strong enough to stick up for his mother and give his own version of things. All he could think of was getting out of there, running away before his face became red with shame, and hiding somewhere where no one would see him.

A mother is a mother, and his own mother, who would be thirty-one the following day, was waiting for him at home, the table laid with a special dinner for the two of them.

'Prawns!' he exclaimed when he saw the dish in the kitchen, not noticing that she was wearing slippers and no make-up. 'Yum!'

'You haven't had a hamburger and ruined your appetite, have you?' she asked. He gave her a kiss and shook his head. 'Good. I won't be a minute. I'm going to have a shower and change into my house clothes. I'll be quick.'

It was nine o'clock on a Saturday night.

'Aren't you going out?' he asked, surprised.

'No,' she shouted from the bathroom, as if it were the most natural thing in the world.

Andrés didn't yet know the word 'paradox', but he didn't need to, as he welcomed the strange effect of that spring on his mother's usual lifestyle. Maribel still occasionally went out for a drink with friends in the evening, but as she left, she always told him where she was going, and with whom, and she almost always came home sober and steady on her feet, early enough to find him still awake and to tell him off for not turning off the TV at half past ten like she'd told him. Then Andrés remembered other nights when her voice had been thick and slurry, trying to reassure him when she staggered in at dawn, the light already filtering through the blinds. He remembered her slow, difficult sentences, her disjointed words: 'It's only me, sweetheart, I bumped into the chest of drawers. Go to sleep, dear, it's only me,' and he remembered her coming into his room carrying her shoes – 'Ouch, my feet are killing me' – lying down beside him – 'Let me give you a kiss' – falling asleep next to him fully dressed, and in the morning shielding her eyes from the light, her foundation dried and cracked like mud, eyeliner and lipstick smudged, hair in a mess, and the insatiable thirst that came with hangovers.

'You're very selfish, Andrés,' Sara had said to him the only time he had dared tell her about it, a few months earlier, during the Christmas holidays.

'No,' he said, very serious. 'Mama's the selfish one.'

'I don't see why.'

'Well, because she's my mother, isn't she? And I didn't ask to be born, did I? She brought me into the world because she wanted to, so she should take care of me.'

'Of course she should. So what's the matter, doesn't she take care of you?' asked Sara, raising her voice, as if she were angry with him. 'Doesn't she feed you and buy you clothes, and send you to a good school? Doesn't she look after you and make sure you have everything you need?'

'No, not when she goes out and spends all night out somewhere,' he said, getting cross now too.

'Ah, well, now we've got to where we were going. Considering the fact you're only twelve, you sound like an old lady, you know.'

'What if I had an attack of something and died while she was out?'

'What if you get run over by a car outside your school, what then? Is your grandmother going to come and give you the kiss of life?'

He didn't know what to say to this. Sara took advantage of his hesitation to put an arm round his shoulders. Then she went on, listing the kind of truths she liked, the kind he would have liked too if life hadn't sometimes turned them into a pack of lies.

'Your mother's much more than just your mother, Andrés. She's herself too, can't you see? She's very young and very lively and she has a right to enjoy herself. She'll have plenty of time to slow down in the future. You know how she lives, how hard she works, and she looks after you all on her own, making sure you turn out all right. That's a huge responsibility, and she hasn't got anyone to share it with. It's not a bad thing that she tries to have fun. Quite the opposite. I'm sure that if she was bored and bitter and sad, she'd be a much worse mother.'

'Yes, yes,' he said, nodding sadly. 'I know all that, you always say the same thing. But things aren't like that here.'

'No, Andrés,' Sara said. They were sitting on the seesaw, swinging slowly up and down. 'Things are the same everywhere. There are people everywhere who think one way, and people who think another way, and that's what matters, don't you see? What people think, what people feel. You've got to try and think about what you know, what you feel, not what other people tell you.'

'But you can't think bad things about people who love you,' he objected.

'Of course you can,' she disagreed gently. 'Because affection is no guarantee of anything. Your grandmother, for instance, might really love you but she could be wrong and she could be hurting you, even if she doesn't mean to.'

He understood – he always understood what Sara said. He understood the meaning of the words she poured over him gently, cautiously, like drops of balm stinging an open wound that never quite healed. But he'd never managed to stop being selfish, never managed to stop feeling sorry for himself, to face his grandmother with his head held high, to understand or forgive his mother's absences.

Nor had he ever found out exactly what she did, what she was looking for and never finding on those nights out. Yet now, when he was more than convinced, almost certain, that she must be performing scenes like the one in that film with Tamara's uncle, it turned out that at last he had a mother like other people's, a mother who no longer bothered to wear make-up all the time, or wear the tight dresses he hated when she went for a walk; a mother who sat on the sofa with him to watch TV every evening, who didn't bump into furniture or thickly curse her fate all the time, a mother who walked straight down the street and looked past the men who dared to wolf-whistle, a mother who saved up to buy a flat, a mother who had found something he didn't know anything about, and which he wasn't sure he'd like, but which meant he could at last feel calm and even strangely proud of her.

That spring was warm and peaceful, and in its light the nature of things began to change. Andrés quickly got used to this new feeling of security, and as he shed the responsibility of taking care of his mother, he felt a new lightness. He'd always liked Dr Olmedo, always thought he was very nice, and had even envied Tamara that she was in the care of someone like him, a man who knew how to do things and do them easily. After the first moments of confusion, of sudden, violent jealousy, like the one that had stopped him in his tracks outside the restaurant, he started working out the advantages of his new situation. Quite apart from the new state of domestic calm, he began to see this unexpected conquest of his mother's as a personal triumph.

One afternoon, as Andrés was cycling to the stationer's to get a pad of graph paper and an extra-long ruler, he saw his father in the distance, leaning on a car, beer in hand, outside his friend's bar. Andrés realised he wasn't hunching, stooping as he used to do each time he saw him, or feeling regret, or dread, or sadness, or shame. This sudden, unexpected robustness meant that his heart didn't start thumping, his legs didn't feel weak, and he didn't look down. He only checked to see if the man whose surname he bore had recognised him. Then, not giving his father the chance to rush off as he usually did, he turned down a side street to avoid him. And he never flushed at all.

Andrés's father was very handsome. The most handsome man she'd ever seen. This was what Tamara thought when she first met him. But also that Andrés had been unlucky.

Their art teacher was becoming impossible. The art materials he told them to bring to class were increasingly sophisticated, and harder to find at the shops in the centre of town, shops that sold all sorts of things – stationery, books, newspapers, magazines, gifts, toys, sweets, cigarettes – but never had very much of anything. Tamara was just thinking she'd have to get Juan to drive her to Jerez or El Puerto, when Andrés said he knew where they could get the extra-long steel rulers and A3-size graph paper they needed. The only technical stationer's in the area was in a part of town she didn't know, an area of red-brick blocks of flats, the streets lined with young trees only about a metre high. She and Andrés cycled there after school, pedalling slowly side by side along the Paseo Maritimo. As they reached the red apartment blocks, Andrés sped up and shot off down a side street as if he were trying to win a race. It meant he didn't see the man waving to him from outside a bar. At least Tamara thought he hadn't seen the man, or heard him calling out. She sped after Andrés and caught up with him at the traffic lights.

'Wait, Andrés! Somebody was calling to you back there.'

He shook his head, but she couldn't tell what he meant by that. He stared fixedly at the traffic lights and gripped the handlebars as if he were revving up a motorbike, and didn't say a word. Surprised at his attitude, Tamara looked round and saw the man again. He was heading towards them, apparently confident that he could catch up with them before the traffic lights changed.

'Well, what was all that about?' he said loudly, coming round Andrés's bike and grabbing hold of the handlebars. 'Why are you in such a hurry? Whenever I see you, you always shoot off.'

His hair was an unusual colour, dark gold, with paler yellow highlights that glinted as he moved his head. It was weird, so perfect it looked fake, and his face was the same. Tamara thought his eyes – large, hazel, almond-shaped, with the longest, blackest, thickest eyelashes she'd ever seen – could have been a woman's; and so too could his small, perfect nose, and his fleshy lips. But despite these delicate features, he had a man's face, large, with a square jaw. His skin was smooth and dark, without a single spot, line or blemish, and it looked soft. He wasn't tall, but he wasn't short either, and he looked as good in his jeans as a TV model. He was wearing a white shirt with half the buttons undone, showing a gold medallion with an image of the Virgin of El Rocio on a tanned chest, as deep a gold as his hair, and pointy snakeskin boots. Tamara thought he was the most handsome man she'd ever seen, and she couldn't think of anyone to compare him to.

'What do you want?' Andrés said without looking at him, still revving up that imaginary motorbike. Tamara wondered who the man was for Andrés to be so rude to him.

'Well, I don't know, what d'you think I want?' he answered. He had a very strong Andalusian accent, and his voice was very deep, better suited to a taller man. 'Just to say hello, see how you are, how you're getting on. I am your father, you know.'

Andrés screwed up his face but said nothing.

'At least introduce me to your friend,' the man insisted, turning his brilliant smile on Tamara.

'Her name's Tamara, she goes to my school,' said Andrés, and then, to Tamara: 'This is my father. He's got the same name as me.'

Andrés's father came over and kissed her on both cheeks.

'Isn't it you who's got the same name as me?' he said and burst out laughing. 'Come on, I'll buy you both a drink.'

'The thing is, we're on our way to the stationer's . . .' Andrés began.

'You can do that later, can't you? It's still early.'

The man turned round and headed for the bar, apparently assuming they would follow, as indeed they did. But just before they set off after him, Tamara glanced over at Andrés and saw a look on his face unlike any he'd ever given her before – an appeal for help, but also a look of anger and misgiving, indignation, uncertainty, and an ancient, icy resignation. Tamara didn't fully understand the message his look conveyed, perhaps even Andrés didn't fully understand it himself, but she felt a stab of fear – as if a red light were flashing, an alarm sounding – and she realised her friend was having a bad time. This much she could tell, and she didn't like it. So she followed him without a word, leant her bike against the same street lamp where he had left his, and put her hand on his shoulder as they made their way to the table where the handsome man, Andrés's father, was waiting for them, smiling. There was a fat woman beside him, with hair dyed a bluish black, wearing heavy make-up and a short, tight, cheap velvet dress. Her big fat legs were encased in fishnet tights that strained over the bulging flesh.

As she sat down, Tamara saw that Andrés was very pale. His father tapped him on the leg and then gave him a little shake, as if demonstrating that he wasn't about to give up despite Andrés's lack of enthusiasm.

'So, what would you like to drink?'

The big fat woman collapsed on top of him, grabbing him with both hands. 'Get off!' he said, pushing her away, not looking at her. She straightened up and crossed her hands over the tiny expanse of her skirt, all the time staring at Andrés.

'What's the matter?' his father said a moment later. 'Cat got your tongue?'

'I'll have a Coke,' said Tamara quickly.

'Me too,' said Andrés reluctantly.

But his father ordered chips as well, and when they arrived, he couldn't resist the temptation of grabbing a few from the plate himself.

'The bike's going well, isn't it?' the man said. He turned to look at Tamara: 'It used to be mine. I gave it to him as a present.'

'You were going to chuck it out,' said Andrés slowly, staring at the chips.

'So what? It was still mine. I was going to chuck it out but I gave it to you instead.'

'You didn't want it,' said Andrés, still not looking up, his face now suddenly bright red. 'So that's not really a present.'

His father glared at him, but just when Tamara thought he was going to start shouting, he burst out laughing, a sharp, high-pitched laugh like a madman's.

'You're just as stroppy as your mother, kid. Just the same, a right little prickly pear.' He gave a strange rat-like smile. 'How is she, by the way? Your mother – haven't seen her for ages, or rather, she hasn't seen me for ages. At least, she pretends she can't see me.' Andrés went a little redder, but didn't say anything or look up. 'Seems like she's a bit full of herself lately, and it's starting to piss me off, I can tell you.' ('She isn't your wife any more,' Tamara thought. 'It's none of your business.' But of course she didn't dare say it aloud.) 'Seems like she's been going round looking at flats, with that old bitch in the BMW.' He paused, leant forward suddenly and grabbed his son's chin, forcing him to look up. 'Speak to me, for fuck's sake!'

'What?' Andrés shouted back. Pleased to have got a reaction at last, his father leant back in his chair.

'Is it true she's going around looking at flats?'

'Yes!' Andrés spat out, his face scarlet. 'She's looking, so what? We're going to buy a flat.'

'Oooh!' his father said, raising his eyebrows with a look of mock amazement. Tamara began to feel scared of him. 'And with whose money, might I ask? Because I don't think she'll have enough with what they got from that land at La Ballena. I mean, taking money from your own mother. I couldn't believe it when your grandmother told me. How much did she get in the end – two million pesetas? Three?'

Andrés didn't answer.

'I'm speaking to you!'

'She's going to buy a flat with her own money,' Andrés said after a moment, 'with what she earns from her work.'

'Right. She's going to get a mortgage, is she? Well, I'm happy for her,' he said, looking at the woman beside him and nudging her with his elbow. 'She must be working *really* hard now. Day and night. Especially at night, because we don't see her in the bars around the port any more, and you know how keen she used to be on bars . . .'

'She's at home with me at night, OK?' Andrés stood up suddenly, knocking over his chair, sniffed loudly and pulled at the hem of his T-shirt. 'She's with me. At home. With me.'

Then he turned and ran out of the bar. Tamara jumped up and followed him.

'Leaving so soon?' they heard the man call after them. They didn't answer.

But the handsome man was fast and by the time they'd got on their bikes, he was standing in front of them once more with his indestructible smile, waving a finger, now not even bothering to raise his voice.

'You tell your mother to say hello to me when she sees me in the street, OK?'

His words, sounding more like a threat than a recommendation, floated after them as they cycled to the stationery shop, and they were still hanging in the air on the way back, when Andrés, without a word of warning, shot out in front of Tamara and guided her through the maze of identical streets. She thought they seemed to be going a very long way round and realised Andrés must be looking for a safe route, a way to get back to the Paseo Maritimo without passing the bar. She didn't complain; in fact, she wished they'd taken this route on the way there. Andrés took a right turn as they reached an area of beaten earth surrounded by an asphalt track, which was the sports ground for the school next door. The baskets and goals at either end were deserted. It was quite late by now, so there weren't any kids in the sand pit or on the swings. Tamara couldn't understand where Andrés was going, but followed him once around the track, until she grew tired. She stopped, propped her bike against one of the basketball posts and sat on the ground beneath it. From there, she watched him pedal around the track, once, twice, three times, going faster and faster, until he too started to grow tired and slowed down.

As she watched him, Tamara found herself suddenly thinking about her own father. She didn't do this often, perhaps because she didn't have to concentrate to remember him, perhaps because his image wandered in and out of her memory in the same way he'd wandered in and out of her life, always making it better, happier, more fun. She adored him, not in the way she loved her mother, yet in some ways more, because she'd always felt a different kind of love for him, a shiny, noisy, explosive kind, like a bunch of balloons, or a present wrapped up and tied with ribbon, like the pleasure of waking up early and knowing you could go back to sleep again because it was a holiday. When her mother died, Tamara missed her with an intensity so absolute, so radical, so closely linked to each and every one of her daily actions, that she surprised herself thinking that in some ways she'd always lived alone with her mother. It was her mother who put her to bed at night and got her up in the morning, made her breakfast and put out her clothes, took her to school and collected her, gave her a bath and sat next to her at the kitchen table while she had supper. And her mother arranged things so that she seemed to be there even when she wasn't, because there were times when she went out a lot in the afternoons, or the evenings, but she'd taught the maids how to do things exactly as she did. With her father it was different. Like a fairy godmother, or the genie in the lamp, he was rarely there, but he might appear at the door to her room at any time, for no reason, without warning, making it seem like the sun was shining even if it was night.

Papa worked a lot, this was what Mama told her and it was what he told her too. This was why he was almost always away from home, having meals at restaurants and so on, even at the weekends. But when he got home, he always had something for her – big, expensive presents, small ones – and he sat on her bed and told her jokes that would go down well when she told them at school, or taught her how to imitate the sound of a banjo with your mouth, or how to make a little figure out of toothpicks. Papa was like a big kid, a protective, generous friend, the solution to all her problems. 'If the princess doesn't want to eat her vegetables, then she doesn't have to. If she doesn't want to go to school, let her stay at home. If she doesn't want to get dressed, why should she?' Tamara smiled as she remembered this. 'Bring it here, I'll fix it for you.' And he did. Straight away. And then he lifted her up in the air and gave her a quick kiss before he left.

He was her father, and he was the best. Until everything went sour.

Perhaps this was why she didn't think about him often, why her memory greedily kept him for itself, refusing to share him with her conscious mind. Because one day everything did go sour. She almost stopped loving him then, because he started to behave strangely, doing things that were sometimes horrible and unfair, things that made him seem ugly both inside and out, like a different man from the one he'd always been. She almost stopped loving him, but one night, when neither of them knew how little time they had left, Papa came into her room at midnight and, finding her awake, lay down beside her and kissed her and said sorry. He didn't explain, he didn't say why he was sorry, and she didn't ask. She just kissed him back, curled up in his arms and fell asleep, and then he had rewarded her forgiveness with a secret.

Andrés was still cycling round the track, more and more slowly now. In the fading light of the afternoon the outlines of buildings began to blur, and Tamara felt an icy shiver down her spine, as if frozen needles were slowly piercing each vertebra. But it wasn't the falling night that made her shiver – it was the familiar icy touch of the secret. So she stood up, vigorously brushed the dust from her trousers, grabbed her bike and waited for Andrés to come level with her, then cycled one last time round the track with him.

'I'm going home,' she said.

'Can you get back on your own?'

She nodded, and waved as she cycled off. On the way home, she decided not to tell Juan she'd met Andrés's father, because she didn't feel like having him look at her with those eyes that sometimes saw right inside her, because she didn't want him to try to explain the world to her with words that seemed to be about someone else's father, but ended up judging her own father harshly. She knew it was best not to talk about Papa in front of Juan, not even to mention him. She didn't know why, she just knew. Juan had never discussed it with her, but he thought that, at the end, when everything went sour, her father had shown himself as he really was, not the other way round. She'd never heard Juan say this, but she knew he thought it, and that he was wrong.

Juan was a good person and she loved him. She'd always loved him, but with a different kind of love to the one she'd felt for her mother, and without the passion she'd felt for her father, and always much less than he seemed to love her. She knew this too, and the certainty cheered her up, bolstered her when she thought of all that she'd lost, because Juan was all she had left. So she'd decided not to say anything to him, but he was waiting for her at the entrance to the development, worried because she was so late − it was a quarter to nine − and when he asked her where she'd been, it didn't occur to her not to tell him the truth.

'We bumped into Andrés's father, and he bought us a Coke, and it got late.'

He didn't say anything at first, just walked beside her, not looking at her, simply staring up at the sky.

'Had you met him before?' he asked. 'Andrés's father?'

'No, I'd never seen him before.'

'What's he like?'

'Very, very handsome,' she answered, and Juan laughed.

'Seriously, he's unbelievably handsome. Andrés really looks like him. But an uglier version. I mean, at first I didn't notice, but then looking at them together, I don't know, they kind of look alike. It's a pity, isn't it? Because Maribel's pretty too, but Andrés . . .'

For reasons Tamara didn't really understand, Juan always stood up for Andrés even when nobody was criticising him. They'd reached the house and Juan went into the kitchen to start dinner.

'Andrés isn't ugly.'

'Yes, he is,' she said. 'I mean, he isn't hideous or anything, he's just thin – his legs look like sticks – and his hair stands up even though he combs it down with cologne, and his face looks like a bird. I don't know, I don't think he'll look like his father when he grows up.'

'You never know,' said Juan, facing away from her, keeping an eye on the potatoes. 'People can change a lot over the years.'

He passed by the baby unit to get the results of the newborn's check-up and then went straight in to see Charo. She was looking scrubbed and calm, smiling, her hair tidy. Her white nightdress – all frills and pale pink ribbons, chosen after she'd found out the baby was a girl – suited her. As he admired this perfect vision of new motherhood, he smiled too, realising it was the first time he'd ever seen her in bed with clothes on.

'Have you been to see her?' she asked.

'Yes. She's doing brilliantly. Very healthy, and very cute.'

'What about Damián?'

'He's gone to fetch Mama. He won't be long.'

Just then a nurse wheeled in a transparent plastic crib. Inside, a tiny, dark-haired baby lay asleep, all bundled up. Their attention immediately switched to her.

'Isn't she lovely?' said Charo after a moment, once the nurse had left.

'Yes,' said Juan. 'But I can't understand why you and Damián have given her such an awful name.'

'It isn't awful!' said Charo, sitting up abruptly, but the movement hurt, so she lay back against the pillow carefully. 'It's – exotic.'

'Whatever you say.'

'Well, of course it is! What would you have called her then?'

'I don't know,' said Juan, and he thought a moment. 'María, probably. Or Inés. Or Teresa. Or Almudena.'

'Like the patron saint of Madrid?'

'Yes.'

'Aren't we posh all of a sudden!' she said and Juan laughed. 'You'd never know you came from Villaverde Alto. Anyway, you should have told me before, you know. I mean, there's plenty of reason to take your opinion into account.'

'Don't worry. I'll be a good godfather even if I haven't chosen her name.'

'No,' said Charo, eyes wide, her smile fading a little now. 'In the end, we decided that Nicanor's going to be her godfather.'

'But Damián said—'

'Yes, Damián wanted you to be the godfather, but I made him change his mind. It would be too much, wouldn't it, if you were her godfather?' she said, looking away, focusing intently on the edge of the sheet. She tugged at the fabric several times before looking at him again, her expression serious, wary. 'It's enough that you're her father.'

Juan Olmedo's initial reaction was not to believe what he'd just heard. Then, he experienced the same amazed, guilty, foolish feeling he'd had one afternoon, many years ago, when he was so bored he took out his old chemistry set and didn't read the instructions properly. He'd absent-mindedly mixed two acids with the contents of a white bottle without checking to see what it was and the test tube had exploded. Shards of glass had flown at his face while a greenish stain with burning edges spread across the wall. His father had gone mad and made him repaint the wall, but nothing could get rid of the tiny scar beneath his right eye that reminded him every morning of the day he nearly blinded himself.

'It can't be true,' he said to himself, 'it can't be.' But it was – it was true. Somehow, he knew straight away that it was true. He suddenly felt cold, hollow, the rush of his cowardly blood emptying his veins. When he was able to speak again, his mouth felt dry.

'I don't know whether to laugh or tell you to go to hell,' he said, but Charo was the only one of the two to laugh.

'You can do what you like, nothing you do will change things,' she said, pointing at the crib. 'She's yours, Juanito.'

'You can't do this to me. You have no right to do this to me,' he said, his eyes as hard as he could make them. She looked calmer now, as if her confession had eased her mind. 'No right.'

'That's true,' she said. 'I had no right. But it isn't true that I couldn't do it. I could, and I did. I'm absolutely sure the baby is yours. There's no way that she isn't. If you like, I can fill in on the details.'

'No, thanks, I'll pass on that.'

'As you wish.'

Juan looked around the room, before standing up and walking to the door.

'Where are you going?'

'None of your business,' he said. He made an effort to speak calmly, and slowly, pronouncing each word carefully. 'I can't accept this, Charo. I don't have to accept it and I don't intend to. I don't want to hear any more about it. Not now, not ever.'

'Look at me, Juan,' she said. Her voice was both firm and despairing, and he had to obey. 'Look at me, and look at her, and think a little. Go on. You're not only the best one of the three, you're also the most intelligent – look at your daughter. She doesn't deserve to have a mother like me and a father like Damián, no one deserves that. Don't you read the papers? Everything is inherited from the parents, everything. Your height and the colour of your eyes, how fat or thin you are, whether you have a talent for painting or music, your voice, your will power, your brains, everything. It's all genetic – your personality, your tastes, even how good or bad you are.'

'That's a load of nonsense, Charo. You haven't got a clue.'

'Yes, I have,' she said, sitting up again, this time not giving in to the pain. 'It's all true. I've read about it, I've discussed it with people who know about these things. I found out about it.'

'You're crazy,' Juan muttered. 'That's what this is, a psychotic episode. I can't think of any other explanation. You must be stark raving mad.'

'No!' she shouted. 'I know what I'm doing. I even talked to a geneticist. I was scared of Damián, to tell you the truth. I don't know why, because he hasn't got a clue, but I thought it might occur to him . . . But the geneticist told me that for the time being you can't tell who the father of a child is if the two men being tested are brothers. The genes are too similar, or something like that. If Damián gets suspicious, which he won't, but anyway if he does, the test would be positive, the same result you'd get if you were tested. That's what the geneticist told me. So there.' She lay back now and went on: 'In ten years' time they'll probably be able to tell. So remind me and we can have a test done, just so that you can be sure.'

'You're a fool.'

Under other circumstances, he would have been surprised at his choice of insult, and at the contempt with which he uttered it, but he'd spoken without thinking, without weighing his words. He walked back to the bed with steps so weary they seemed to sap his remaining strength. He sat in the armchair beside it, looked at his sister-in-law, and felt pleased when he saw terror in her eyes. He'd spent his life being afraid of her and this was the first time Charo had ever been afraid of him.

'You're a fool,' he said again, and this time he was aware of every syllable. 'I'll never rest easy. Never again. But in ten years' time, this child will have a father, and that father will be my brother. I'll be her uncle, a nice man who comes to lunch every so often and gives her birthday presents. And that's it. That's what'll happen. It's what's right, and it's for the best. Don't you forget it, because no geneticist in the world can change it.'

'Yes,' said Charo, and she smiled again, with a gentle, enigmatically content expression he didn't even try to comprehend. 'That's true, but the child is still yours.'

'That doesn't mean a thing.'

'No. But she's yours, Juanito.'

'So what?'

'Nothing. Just that she's yours.'

'What I don't understand is . . .' He tailed off. He didn't feel like talking, but he had to go on. 'What I don't understand is why you told me. If all you wanted was for the child to be mine, you could have achieved that without saying a word to me. It would have been less risky, wouldn't it? Better for you.'

'Juanito!' said Charo, laughing.

'What?'

'I know exactly who you are, what you are. I know what you're capable of, and what you're not capable of. You'd never blackmail me, you'd never do anything that would be detrimental to me or the child. That's why I wanted you to know. I was going to tell you before the birth, but as this morning you got so . . . well . . .'

'But why did you tell me? That's what I don't understand. Why?'

'Just in case.'

'Just in case what?'

'Just in case.'

At that moment Damián, with a radiant smile and a huge bunch of flowers, appeared in the doorway. Juan looked away, because he realised it hurt to look at him.

'Oh, just look at her!' cried his mother, going straight to

the crib and picking the baby up without asking for permission. 'She's adorable, absolutely adorable. Look at her, Dami, isn't she gorgeous? Look at her eyes, and her mouth, isn't she lovely? You know who she looks like? Come here, Juanito.' He didn't move, so his mother took the baby over to him. 'She looks just like you did when you were born. Can you believe it? Absolutely identical. I could be looking at you, thirty years ago.'

'Don't be ridiculous, Mama,' he said. 'She looks just like her mother.'

'Yes, yes, that's true. But she also reminds me of you when you were born. Come on, hold her for a bit.'

'No.'

'What's the matter with you?' asked his mother, surprised. 'Don't tell me you're scared of holding a baby – you're a doctor. Take her, I want to put the flowers in water.'

'Let her father take her.'

'Come on, you take her, darling, don't be silly. Just for a second.'

'Yes, Juanito, hold her,' said Charo, her hand in her husband's, staring at Juan with a foolish smile. 'You're the only one who hasn't held her yet.'

He shouldn't have held her, he shouldn't have let his mother, with the foolish nonchalance of the ignorant, put her in his arms. He would never have felt how light she was, how incredibly tiny, he would never have known the powerful call of her smell, the extraordinary perfection of her features. He shouldn't have held her, at least not so soon, but he found himself holding her and he turned away from the others to look at her. Standing at the window, in the white, artificial light of the street lamps, they were alone together, he and the beautiful baby. She had black hair, darker than her mother's, just like his, grey eyes, perfectly drawn lips, tiny hands, and she had been in the world for barely two hours. 'She's my niece,' he thought, 'my niece,

my niece.' But he wasn't sure that this silent, private incanta-
tion would work. He stroked her face with the tip of his
index finger and she screwed up her face. He shouldn't have
held her. He turned, still holding the baby, to face the others
again. Charo had just applied lipstick – pale pink like the
ribbons on her nightdress – and she blew him a silent kiss.

'Well,' he said, not looking at anyone in particular, and
clearing his throat in an attempt to make his tone sound
distant, professional, 'this baby's got to go back into her crib
right now. Newborn babies can't control their body temperature properly until they're about twelve hours old.' He
put his daughter in the crib and covered her, tucking in the
blankets carefully. 'You mustn't keep picking her up or she'll
end up getting hypothermia.'

Five minutes later, when he was back outside, he knew
what was going to happen. He'd known it five minutes ago,
as he quickly took his leave of his mother and brother, and
kissed Charo on the forehead, just to annoy her. He'd
known it the second he heard the revelation that was still
causing turmoil in a part of his mind he'd been unaware of
until then. But he had an even greater need to tear himself
from the sweet, evil loop of happy endings, the trap into
which he'd allowed himself to be lured by his sister-in-law's
revelations. This was what his life was reduced to – an
unbearable succession of tugs that tensed the string of his
will without ever actually snapping it.

It hadn't been like this at first. At first, Charo had erupted
into his life like an explosion of fireworks, a furious flurry of
coloured streamers, a calendar where every day was a holiday. She made up for everything, absorbed everything,
justified everything. Elena had burst into tears when he told
her he was leaving her because he was in love with another
woman. She had burst into tears in a huge, brightly lit,
crowded bar, but he didn't care. He made himself look
apologetic, maintained a focused, temporary silence, paid

for their drinks before leaving and walked home from the Circulo de Bellas Artes, because he felt relieved. He was no less sensitive, no worse a person than before, it was just that nothing mattered. As he reached Callao, he went into a cake shop, bought himself a cake, and ate it as he walked along the street. Nothing mattered, nothing except the messages on his answering machine, the doorbell ringing, Charo.

He should have known; he should have been afraid of her. He knew her almost as well as he knew his brother, and he should have remembered the taste of anger, the logic of betrayal, the persistent poison of the telephone, but he didn't. She'd understood that he was the best and that was enough. She'd agreed, and he allowed himself to believe that he was responsible for what was happening. And when Charo curled up beside him, anchored him to the bed by laying an arm and a leg across his body, and when he was alone afterwards, in a room where every object retained the precise memory of her skin, her voice, her laugh, he reflected that her situation was more difficult than his, and that he had to be reasonable, flexible, patient. He took pleasure in his own quiet superiority. He was the most intelligent of the three, he always had been. So, with an emotional faculty not entirely devoid of reason, he perceived Charo's weakness, the fragile root of her vanity, but he could never have imagined the direction it would take.

'This needn't change anything.'

He felt as if a mirror had shattered and each and every shard had pierced him. He could find nothing to say.

'It was an accident,' said Charo, looking at him as if she couldn't understand why he was so upset by the news. 'I wasn't trying to get pregnant, it just happened. In a few months' time the baby will be born, and we can carry on as before. There's no reason why it should make any difference to us. It's completely separate from our relationship.'

'But I thought we weren't typical lovers.' Juan formed the

sentence in his head and blushed furiously at the thought of saying it aloud. 'I thought we had a serious, stable relationship. I thought your marriage was just a problem to which we'd eventually find a solution. I thought we'd end up living together, I want us to live together, I want to marry you, I love you.' He completed the speech in his head, like the fool he was and always would be.

'Tell me what you're thinking,' she said.

'Nothing.'

He'd just remembered – too late – that he couldn't trust her. This was the main conclusion he reached the first time he slept with Charo, after cheerfully acknowledging that he was exhausted. He couldn't trust her, he reflected, he couldn't believe anything she said, but there was nothing he wanted more, needed more, than to believe her. He couldn't trust her because she was never straight, because she took back half of what she gave, because she managed her secrets and her silences with cold calculation. She came and went from his home, his life, leaving behind invisible particles of a confused spirit that thrived on vague resentment and on the unbearable arrogance of the victim. Because, although she had no argument to justify her constant demands of the world, nothing of what Charo had, of what was happening to her, ever measured up to what she believed she deserved.

Juan had given a lot of thought to the elaborate dissatisfaction Charo wrapped around herself like a cloak, a second skin that isolated her from the ordinary lives of ordinary people. Being the local princess could make for an unhappy future, he concluded, and he shifted the blame onto Damián for his wife's chronic disappointment. He pictured scenes with Charo in her modest room, one of many siblings, looking at herself in the mirror she had to share, admiring herself, awarding herself a future as dazzling as her eyes, and the almost painful perfection of her body. Hooking Damián would have seemed like a triumph, a glistening road to glory.

Instead it turned out to be a narrow, rough, bumpy lane. Juan pictured Charo now too, trapped in a comfortable routine made up of identical, average days, the modest destiny of the trophy wife of the Bread King of Northern Madrid, a marginal, small-time magnate who would never appear in the Society section of a newspaper or magazine. He was very rich, that was for sure, and getting richer by the day, but he was a dull, mediocre man, with a mediocre future and mediocre ambitions. This was where Juan located the origins of Charo's endless, universal complaint; a princess cheated of her future.

'Of course, I wasn't able to go to university . . .'

The first time she said this, Juan reacted as if she were joking: 'What do you mean, you weren't able to? You weren't interested. You didn't even try.'

'Well, I'm not so sure about that.'

Juan realised she was serious, and he wasn't sure how to interpret her picturesque version of the past.

'I wasn't very happy as a child. My parents didn't love me. They didn't pay much attention to me.'

'How can you say that? I don't think it was like that. I never noticed it, nobody else did.'

'You don't have a clue, but it's true. They never forgave me for being prettier than my sisters.'

'Charo,' he began, becoming impatient with her self-deception, which seemed to distort her, rather than her past.

'Don't look at me like that. Do you think I'm a fool? I know exactly what I'm saying, and I'm right, even though you all always contradict me.'

He tried to argue back, to make her see reason, but she always found the pea under the mattress, the stone in the shoe, a new argument with which to sustain her role as victim.

'Actually, it was your fault I married Damián,' she said one day. 'You didn't fight for me.'

'Don't say that, Charo.'

'It's true. You didn't. You didn't try to win me back, you just disappeared.'

'I left so I wouldn't have to see you. I couldn't bear to see you without being able to kiss you. And I couldn't bear you not taking any notice of me. That's why I left.'

'Right. Very convenient, isn't it?'

This was the price he had to pay for his partial, inadequate possession of her; his part-time ownership of a woman who felt arbitrarily and endlessly wronged and who would never accept responsibility for anything that happened to her. He tried to understand her – fervently, unconditionally, desperately, the way he loved her. He tried to find any thread to guide him along the secret paths of her labyrinth, to find a solution to her unhappiness, or at least a reason for it. Charo's happiness was important to him because he loved her. He still loved her, still felt he'd do anything for her, always. He felt dizzy, with a black, amorphous panic when he thought he might end up despising her one day.

That day came, after many traps, and silences, and lies. But before this, Juan Olmedo learnt new things about himself, although they weren't things that he particularly liked. When Charo told him she was pregnant, he said that he couldn't go on like this, he realised it had all been a mistake, right from the beginning, and that this new development not only changed everything, but made him see that they should never have even begun. He pronounced every word with the calm, clear voice of someone who believed everything he said. But she was unfazed.

'You can't leave me, Juan, you can't. We're in this together. You might not think so, but we're locked together. You can't leave me. You'll never be able to.' She paused and smiled. 'I bet you won't.'

She stood, calmly picked up her bag, and went to the

door, closing it quietly behind her, leaving him alone, to learn what it was to be truly alone.

He knew the nature of this solitude wouldn't make up for the brutal destruction of all his dreams but, for a time, the certainty that he'd done the right thing brought some harmony to his life. Over the past two years, in all his plans and projects, he'd managed to view the figure of Damián from the most convenient angle: from a distance. Juan, who had thought of everything, hadn't thought of his brother. Charo's husband was a hindrance, a loose end, an annoying but residual inconvenience, a cretin who didn't deserve her. This man, whom he had once loved and who had been such a big part of him, had gradually disappeared like a snowman in springtime. It had seemed fair. Juan had seen her first, he'd loved her first, he'd suffered more, and one of them had to lose out. It should have been Damián, but it would be him, Juan, again. Always him. Juan Olmedo now knew he would never be reconciled with his brother. He didn't want to be, but stepping aside from his future with Charo and their accidental daughter who had united them once more – at least in the mind of her mother's lover – restored some harmony to his life. For a time. Too short a time.

She knew it. Charo knew that he was drowning, that he couldn't walk down the street without seeking out women who looked like her, couldn't say anything without feeling that his words were for her, couldn't sleep without seeing her in his dreams. That he dreamed of her even when he was awake, and that nothing mattered to him any more, not her husband, or her future, or her pregnancy, he didn't care about any of it. It had been more than three months since he'd last been alone with her, only seeing her in the company of others – a hundred days and nights of slow, exasperating despair – when one morning, Charo rang at his door as he was emptying the contents of his pockets onto the sitting-room table. It was a quarter to nine and he'd just got home after his night shift.

'Hello,' she said, as if she were turning up for an appointment and assumed he'd been expecting her. 'You can buy me a coffee.'

She was wearing a rather short, low-cut orange dress, gathered beneath the bust. Her legs were very tanned, and her pregnancy hardly showed. She was just entering her fifth month and hadn't put on much weight. She didn't throughout the pregnancy, following the diet her obstetrician had prescribed to the letter because she was too vain to do otherwise, although she liked to say she was doing it for the baby. She looked very beautiful, with the firm, fleshy roundness, glowing skin and soft features that characterised pregnancy. She was wearing an orangey-red lipstick, quite unlike the deep murderous crimson of seduction, or the pale pink of motherhood.

'To be honest, I feel terrible,' she announced, reclining on the sofa, her dress spread out over her golden thighs like the corolla of a tropical flower. She controlled her body and her posture with the same wisdom, the same marvellous cunning as before, not succumbing to the shapelessness that pregnancy so often induced in women. 'I've stopped smoking, of course, so I'm very irritable. Happy, but tetchy. That's normal, isn't it? Well, your brother can't understand it. He says he's scared of coming near me and that my belly gives him the creeps. Normally I wouldn't care, really, you know that, but the thing is I'm all on edge, so that's why I thought, "Come on, Charito, what do you bet, your stomach won't bother Juan."'

Even though he was stunned, Juan still felt like shouting 'Olé!', 'Bravo!', pulling out his handkerchief and waving it about in her honour, like at a bullfight, the theatre or a football match. He would have called for an encore, she deserved it, for being so clever, so daring, so irrepressible. He

372

would have liked to show her in some way how much he admired her performance, but he couldn't, because his feet carried him towards her and he simply did what he had to. Like a good boy. And that morning, as he discovered that he liked Charo just as much with a thicker waist, Juan Olmedo learnt that he had never known what it was to feel truly scared.

It wasn't a question of what he was doing, but of what he was capable of doing. He, who had so often and so cheerfully claimed he'd be prepared to do anything, sometimes realised it wasn't a question of mere words. Kneeling on the bed, he pulled his sister-in-law towards him and entered her slowly, his eyes fixed on her bulging belly, which suddenly seemed as soft as a grass-covered hillock, and then he stopped hearing the voice of Elena, the girlfriend he'd left for Charo, and heard his own voice instead: 'What the hell are you doing, Juan? Think about what you're doing. Have you gone crazy or something?' And he felt fear, and pleasure, and more fear, and more pleasure.

'Have you ever had sex with a pregnant woman before?' she asked, because she liked to talk in the early stages of sex.

'No, you're the first.'

'Well you're doing it very well. You're very gentle.'

'I'm always gentle with you.'

He loved her. Dishonest, confused and contemptible as she was, he loved her, and he wanted her for himself. His love consoled and sustained him; it absolved him of his mistakes and released him from his anxiety. But it did scare him. It terrified him to think of time, and limits. He'd gone back to her halfway through her pregnancy and they hadn't even discussed it, it hadn't occurred to him to ask her for an explanation, she hadn't given him any, because there was no need. She'd only had to knock at his front door to create the right situation for him to take all the responsibility, all the blame for what was happening. Her return, her essential display of boldness, loaded the gun, but it was he who had pulled the trigger. Charo simply appeared, sat down in front of him, and looked into his eyes, risking rejection but knowing it would never happen. And when she departed, she left him alone with his misery, the profound indignity of being a mere puppet, the weakness of his intentions, and the humiliating destruction of a desire that is love, but is not good.

He was terrified by his sudden inability to control himself. He couldn't understand what had happened to him, how he'd got where he was, and yet he also knew that it had only just begun, and that the end was a long way off. The morning before the birth of the baby who was to be his niece, Charo behaved strangely, after surrendering to him with the same eagerness, the same determination with which she used to annihilate him in the days when her waist was narrow and her body docile. Her pregnancy was very advanced, she was in the thirty-ninth week, and he thought it would be better to stop having sex with her at that stage. 'Honestly, it's fine,' she'd laughed, 'you should know that better than anyone. Sex is good for you right up to the end because it strengthens the muscles and it can induce labour – that's what they said at those classes you sent me to.' It was true. Charo hadn't wanted to do anything to prepare for the birth but he had insisted, and he'd been such a pain about it that she'd finally given in. That morning he didn't manage to be quite so persuasive because his sister-in-law attacked him with the kind of arguments that he usually used to disarm her, and he couldn't find a response quickly enough. So he let himself be disarmed by her, and when at the end he saw her lean over her now huge, low belly and look strangely at the fingers of her right hand, and sniff them, and look at them again with the same terrifying curiosity, he realised that of everything that could happen, the worst had already taken place.

She refused to go straight to the hospital. She was quite calm, and so sure of what she knew that she insisted he take her home first to collect her suitcase. 'We've got plenty of time,' she said, 'two hours, I learnt that at the classes too.' Juan felt so guilty that he didn't stand up to her, but as he drove, detached from what he was doing, pressing the pedals and stopping at traffic lights, mostly in their favour at ten in the morning, he could see a single staring eye everywhere he looked – in the sky, on the road, on the windscreen – an eye that was staring at him. He knew of course that foetuses couldn't see, didn't know, lacked any awareness or capacity to interpret what was going on around them, but he could still see it, a tiny eye staring at him, accusing him through the hole that had now opened up in its peaceful little world of watery echoes; an elemental world in which she'd swum like a drowsy happy fish until an enemy burst in and destroyed it.

He knew it was nonsense, of course, but he couldn't help himself.

'Hi, Damián, it's me.'

Her suitcase was ready and waiting in the hall. Juan picked it up and turned round, about to head back to the car, but saw that Charo was going towards the sitting room.

'Right, well, it's started. My waters have broken. My waters. So I'm going to the hospital. No, I haven't gone into labour yet, I haven't got any contractions, Juan says when I get to the hospital they'll give me something to get them started. What? No, Juan's here, with me. When I saw fluid coming out, I got a bit scared – I didn't know what it was, so I called him, and he rushed over. Well, he can drive me to the hospital, I'm sure he won't mind. OK, I'll see you there. Yes, silly, love you too, see you in a bit.'

On the way to the hospital, Juan Olmedo started to cry.

'Honestly! What's the matter with you?' Charo snorted impatiently when she noticed. 'Are you an idiot or what?'

Juan Olmedo was crying because it was all so ugly, so

sordid, so unfair that an awareness of his love for her could only make it worse. For at this most difficult time, she had gone back to being the person he didn't understand. He'd never wanted to live like this, in a state of continual anxiety, where all his wishes and actions had come to nothing. He loved her, he wanted to be happy, but everything he had now suddenly fitted inside this car and this monstrous, shameful situation. This was where so much love, such lofty ambitions, had got him: to the saddest form of madness.

'Please stop it, Juan. Please don't cry.' It was the first time he'd ever cried in her presence, and when he looked at her, it was the first time he'd ever seen her cry. 'Pull yourself together, please. Shit, don't do this to me now. Not now.'

They still hadn't quite recovered by the time they got to the hospital, but the receptionist in A & E didn't seem to notice.

'Don't leave me,' Charo said, holding the admissions form. 'Please don't leave me on my own.'

So he went to the room with her and stayed while she changed and unpacked her things. Damián arrived, and he too asked Juan to stay. Juan went into the delivery room with them, and he was the only one to stay with her throughout the labour because he made Damián go outside when he was about to faint. The hospital routine, the familiar smell of disinfectant, warmed him and restored a little of his confidence, the comforting company of a landscape he knew so well. But when he left the building through the main entrance, on the threshold of a night that seemed quite different, his mood had changed for other, more profound reasons. Because, even if he'd known from the beginning that this was what was going to happen, and that it wasn't advisable to be taken in – even a little – by the sweet, deadly loop of happy endings, Juan Olmedo already knew that the child was his, and he felt, even without wanting to know, that the eye was calling, not accusing him. He was terrified of limits, but also of time, and Juan Olmedo grew tired of denying with his head what he knew with his heart, and succumbed to a surge of pure, foolish joy because, that afternoon, Charo had given him a reason to hope.

For months, carefully, meticulously, literally, he went over everything Charo had said in her hospital bed: 'You're not just the most intelligent of the three, you're also the best. Nobody deserves to have a father like your brother, I wanted you to know just in case.' Sentences like images that fade slowly in a stack of photographs lying forgotten in a drawer, like an endless prayer repeated until it becomes meaningless. Tamara was growing, losing the blurry, undifferentiated features that make all babies look alike, turning into a dark-haired, unique little girl at the same rate as her mother was going back to being herself, wearing the same clothes, the same blood-red lipstick, and nothing happened, no path opened up to link the closed, parallel compartments in which his split existence unfolded.

Juan Olmedo could not understand that his sister-in-law had chosen him as the father of her child simply because at the time she got pregnant, she liked him better than her husband. This was too brutal, too cruel even for a professional victim, a deluded despot who had never paid the price for placing herself above everything and everyone. He couldn't accept that hers had been an irrational, arbitrary choice because, apart from anything else, Charo adored her daughter and in her own characteristic, and characteristically egocentric way, she lived for her. Juan had reckoned it would be so, not just because it was natural that Charo would feel this way, but because she'd always been like a surrogate mother to her brother-in-law, Alfonso, and her young nephews and nieces, the sick and the weak. Damián made fun of her, mocking her generosity, her often excessive self-denial when she thought someone really needed her. But this was the light that Charo radiated. Juan Olmedo clung to this thought for a long time, and as he watched Charo play with the child, change her nappies or hold her in her arms, singing her quietly to sleep. Yet all that happened was that time continued to pass.

'She looks adorable.'

Tamara was playing in the sunny garden, piling earth onto plastic plates and feeding it to her doll with a little yellow spade. He and Charo were sitting on the back porch watching her and waiting for Alfonso to wake up from his afternoon nap. Alfonso had moved in with Charo and Damián after their mother's death and it gave Juan the perfect excuse to call in often after work.

'Yes,' said Charo after a pause. 'She really is very cute. Even though she looks like you.'

'That's not true,' said Juan smiling, quickly recovering from the shock of his sister-in-law's words – she never mentioned the subject of her child's father any more. 'She looks like you. Exactly like you.'

He was scared of talking about it and he was just as guilty as she was of avoiding the subject. He was scared of what he might say, but also, above all, of what he might hear if he pushed Charo to the limit. In short, he was scared of the word 'no'. He absolved himself of blame, reflecting that he had nothing more to say and she knew it, knew that he was there, waiting for her, always, for as long as she liked. He had told her so many times he'd lost count, and he'd lost count of the times she had refused to answer, wrapping herself in an ambiguous silence that meant nothing because it hinted at too many things. But that afternoon it was the beginning of spring, the sun felt good and new, like a surprise gift. Tamara opened her own mouth every time she held the little spade to her doll's mouth, instinctively imitating what her mother did when feeding her. Juan had left a junior doctor asleep in his bed. He'd slept with her three times in ten

378

days, even allowing himself the luxury of calling Charo to cancel a meeting without any explanation.

His relationship with all the other women in the world had changed some time ago, although it hadn't reached its final form. At first, he was scrupulously faithful to Charo. It seemed ridiculous, but he felt incapable of desiring any other woman. The women around him, the ones he worked with, the ones he saw in the street, seemed like flat, lifeless images, more or less pleasing to the eye, but quite devoid of reality. He still looked at them, but he no longer wanted them even in his imagination. He didn't need them. When Charo announced she was pregnant, betraying him for a second time, the process became more acute until he was completely stripped of his capacity to desire. If he couldn't have his sister-in-law, he wouldn't have anyone. But one evening, when Tamara was eight months old, the friend of the girlfriend of a friend backed him up against the wall of a bar and asked him what the hell was he up to, and he said he wasn't up to anything, so they slept together, and they had a good time. From then on, and though she called him many times and he wouldn't see her again, Juan Olmedo recovered a certain neutrality. He didn't go in search of women, but if ever he liked one he let her find him. There came a time when he no longer recognised himself, a time during which he slept with and then rejected many women; a frenzied, feverish time when he went from one name to another, one mouth to another, one body to another, in an impossible search for an antidote, a poison that would cure him or destroy him completely. And yet, on that sunny, peaceful afternoon in April, he couldn't see the colour of his future. Before him was a scene so sweet, so right that it didn't even yield to the memory of that junior doctor he found so attractive, and who was so good in bed, but wasn't part of his true life. That afternoon, Juan Olmedo reflected that all of his life was there in that garden, on that porch, in the characters of a scene that belonged to him, a part of his life that had been hijacked by another. The certainty dispelled his fear and loosened his tongue.

'I think about the child a lot, you know. I wonder what's going to happen to her.'

'Well, nothing,' said Charo, looking at him with interest, and he realised she was gauging the meaning of his words. 'What could happen?'

Juan didn't want to reply to this question, and he fixed his gaze on his daughter before going on: 'I don't know. She's two now.'

'Almost two and a half,' said Charo, and from her look, Juan realised she already knew what he was going to say.

'I mean, when all's said and done, I am her father.'

'No, you're not,' said Charo, smiling without a trace of bitterness or malice. 'You're her uncle, remember? You were very clear about that. Nothing's going to happen, this is the only sensible way forward. That's what you said and that's how it is.'

'I know, but I was wrong,' he said. Deep down, he didn't care about the child, not yet; at the time all he cared about was her mother, and what Tamara, as their child, represented. But he wasn't lying. 'I can't help it, every time I see her, all I can think about is that I'm her father.'

'I'm glad,' said Charo, still smiling, comically unmoved by what she was hearing. 'That's best for all of us.'

'What about Damián?'

'Well, nothing, what about him? He's my husband, and he's Tamara's father. We're a happy family. Doesn't it show?'

'Yes,' said Juan. He stood up and collected his things, not looking at her. 'You look good in photos.'

This time she didn't ask where he was going. He couldn't bring himself to make an excuse so he just left. He wasn't sure what he was feeling, because a sudden, powerful weariness prevented his rage, pain and contempt from rising to the surface. When he got home, he collapsed on the sofa and switched on the TV. He didn't change the channel, which was showing a quiz show with big money prizes and hostesses in pink bikinis and a loud, bald presenter. A contestant from Teruel won half a million pesetas. A woman from Huelva wasn't so lucky, winning only a hundred thousand. The roulette wheel was turning again when the doorbell rang.

Charo threw herself at him without giving him a chance to say anything. She put her arms round his neck, her legs around his waist, and covered his mouth with hers. Only later, when they were in bed, naked and sated with each other, did she explain why she'd come.

'It wouldn't work, Juanito,' she said, moving close to him so that their noses were almost touching, their breath mingling in the tiny but constant gap between them. 'It would be a disaster.'

She looked at him as if she needed to hear him say something, but he remained silent. She closed her eyes and went on: 'I know what's going on. You're sleeping with other women. That's it, isn't it? I know you so well, Juan. I realised from the start.'

'But you don't mind.'

'Look, this is what we have, and it's the best we can have. You're very important to me, very important, because you're the only one who loves me, apart from my daughter and Alfonso who's like another child. You're the only one. And I don't know why you do, frankly, because I'm a shit.' She paused, but still he said nothing. 'I know I am, and I don't understand how you can be in love with me, but I don't want you to stop. If we lived together, you'd stop loving me, Juan, you wouldn't be able to stand me, I'm sure of it. I've often thought about it. It's better this way. Believe me, it's much better like this.'

'No.'

'Yes,' she said, smiling in her own special way, the same sad look with which, years earlier, she'd refused a second slice of chocolate cake. 'Yes. I know you better than you know me. You have no idea what I can do, what I can be. I love you, Juan, I can't love anyone more than I love you. I don't know why. But I know it's not enough, that for you it wouldn't be enough.'

These words would haunt Juan Olmedo for the rest of his life. He would never be able to overcome them, not even when he became strong and cynical, an expert at handling his misfortune. He realised that her words were no more than a partial, inadequate explanation; another trap, another stage in the endless deception. That night, he shared with Charo more than they had ever had together – his pain, his helplessness, his anguish on discovering with selfish but joyful amazement that she too was capable of suffering and that she too was in pain. He couldn't remember then how moved he had been by her faded, smudged lipstick, her lost look in the bustle of the Gran Vía, that Sunday afternoon when they had gone to the cinema and she had confessed without words that she was unhappy. But having lost all hope of ever being happy himself, her unhappiness comforted him and bound him to her with a different tie, a terrible solidarity in common defeat.

Juan Olmedo tried to get used to a different dream, a close horizon of small, immediate benefits, and known, calculated risks. But that didn't last long either. That sleepless night was the apex of a roller-coaster ride, the summit, the point of a needle on which he would have preferred to remain impaled, because the fall was brutal, and there was no safety net. Charo forgot what she'd said. All the mirrors shattered, and Juan went on cutting his hands and feet on the shards. His life became an endless, intermittent break-up, the chronicle of a failure repeated a thousand times, because she still won all their bets even though, every time, she had to give him more in exchange.

At a certain point, without realising how it happened, Juan started to see something hysterical, pitiful, almost comical in his sister-in-law's melodramatic reappearances. At a certain point, he began to be flippant with her, smiling sympathetically, using the diminutive of her name, not getting up when she left. He didn't think about it much, because he wanted to think less and less, but he sensed that the key to the process lay, not in Charo, but in himself. Sometimes he felt as if his arteries were drying out, as if all moisture were leaving his shell of a body, fossilised by the endless waiting and the inconceivable concessions he'd had to make. By the implacable, temporary nature of his life and the utter destruction of his pride. But still he couldn't leave her, couldn't resist her – her body, her smell, her voice – or the tyrannical, incomprehensible decrees of her will.

He couldn't even do so that night, near the end. By then he'd started to judge the passing of time by his daughter's age, not by her mother's promises. He'd agreed to meet Charo at the same restaurant where she'd stood him up two nights earlier, and once again he was the first to arrive and sit at their table. She'd stood him up so many times it had almost become a habit, a ritual that exerted a mysterious influence over him. This was why he had chosen the same restaurant, where the waiters looked as sorry for him as they had forty-eight hours earlier, offering him a silent sympathy that had bothered him at first. Not any more. Now he felt a wretched satisfaction at displaying his wounds in public, as if it were pleasant having everyone know he was a fool. He didn't really understand what was going on, and he didn't like it, but he was used to beating himself up more tenaciously than she ever did. He no longer recognised himself and perhaps he was becoming someone else – someone who was harder, unhappier, a worse person but better suited to the way things were.

That evening, however, Charo did turn up. Three-quarters of an hour late, by which time he'd already had more than half a bottle of red wine, and eaten all the bread and butter and olives. She turned up, and all the waiters glanced at him, impressed, suddenly knowing. Juan could almost feel the pats on his back. He watched her as she made her way to the table and sat down opposite him. She looked beautiful, if a little unwell. Maybe this was why she looked so attractive, because of the slight dark rings under her eyes and her sharp, almost gaunt cheeks. She seemed to have aged, though. That evening, Juan realised that Charo was starting to look older than she was, that she was ageing fast.

'Sorry,' she said when it became clear he wasn't going to say anything. 'I was running late.'

'Yes, two days late.'

She laughed.

'OK, well, I'm even more sorry, then. I'm mortified. Is that enough?'

'I hope it was worth it, at least.'

'Well . . .' She looked at him with that odious smile that said 'I know that you know that I know you sleep with other women, and you know that I know that you know that I sleep with other men. Isn't it great? Aren't we marvellous, and wicked, and grown-up? Aren't we having a wonderful time?' Juan felt a sudden, brutal urge to punch her in the face. 'Actually, it wasn't. I would have had a much better time with you. You're the one I most enjoy being with, as you know.'

She tried to take his hand but he moved it from the table.

'You're jealous, aren't you?'

He didn't want to answer, but the waiter's arrival disguised his silence, which became heavier, more noticeable once the waiter had departed.

384

'For God's sake, Juan,' said Charo after a while. 'I can't believe that after eight years you still don't know the score. You're sulking like a little kid. I don't know what's the matter with you, you've been very strange lately.'

Juan filled their glasses with wine but still said nothing, not just because he didn't feel like talking, but because he realised that Charo was finding his silence hard to take, and was getting nervous, maybe about to make a mistake.

'I suppose, all in all, it's logical you're jealous,' she went on, trying to sound casual. 'Really, it's as if you were my husband – it's been so long since I slept with Damián anyway.'

'Go to hell, Charito.'

He'd said it quietly – really he'd been talking to himself – but she heard him clearly.

'What?' Charo said, eyes wide with fury. 'What did you say?'

Juan Olmedo stood up slowly, took a ten-thousand-peseta note from his wallet, and calmly, carefully placed it on the table before saying, more loudly this time:

'I told you to go to hell.' She flushed. The people at nearby tables were staring. The waiter had brought another bottle of wine and was about to show it to them, but stopped. Juan added: 'Charito.'

As he left the restaurant he glanced at his watch. Twenty minutes later, his doorbell started ringing continuously. Charo stood there, weeping, her hair a mess, looking worse than Juan had ever seen her look. She tried to stuff a ten-thousand-peseta note into his mouth before flinging herself at him and starting to pummel him with her fists, screaming like a wild, frightened animal.

'You'll leave me when I tell you to! Is that clear?' Her mascara had run with her tears, forming thick black streaks down her face. Her nose was running and she was spitting out the words so furiously it seemed as if her teeth might fly out after them. 'You'll leave me when I say so! Idiot! Bastard! What do you bet, you'll only leave me when I say so!'

He failed to restrain her, to force her to stop and think about what she was doing, to recover the last remnants of the lovely, special girl with lips of caramel whom he'd kissed at traffic lights in the Calle Francos Rodríguez after a shift in his father's shop. And he also failed to hold on to himself, to resist the desire growing with every attack, every scratch, bite, punch she inflicted on him. He had desired her so much when she was at her best, but he now desired her even more when she was at her worst. He held her tight, and then slapped her hard. Instead of slapping him back, she laughed, and he kissed her, and put his arms around her, and caressed her, and possessed her from a place he'd never been before, feeling as if the floor were giving way beneath his feet. He accepted that he wanted to fall, to boil in the thick magma of the inferno into which Charo was dragging him, teaching him to despise her, and truly to despise himself.

Yet he still loved her. He loved her and despised her. But he felt so tired, wrecked, worn out; unable to take one more step, to hold out his hand to her once again. So it was Charo who started to make the first move, to humiliate herself, doing all the running, showing him that she wanted to keep him. Juan couldn't understand her, and he watched her circling, pretending that there was nothing wrong, that everything was fine, that they had something good. He didn't even try to see her as he used to, with the innocent eyes of the simpleton. His were now predatory eyes that anticipated, with a shrewd malice born of resentment, every one of Charo's moves – Charo, who made him feel utterly alone when she spoke, when she touched him, when she lay beside him.

The end came quietly, discreetly, without fuss or warning. They were in bed, about to go to sleep; she stayed at his place often now, lavishing upon his indifference the gift of sleep that she used to be so cunningly sparing with. She talked about her other lovers, perhaps to goad him into jealousy.

'Damián doesn't know a thing,' she said. He wasn't looking at her – perhaps that was why she chose this time to tell him. 'He only knows about you.'

'What?' Juan sat up and, turning towards her, grabbed her arm. 'What do you mean he knows about me?'

'Well, not that we're still lovers, but he knows that we once had something together.'

'How did he find out?'

'He was driving me crazy one day, so I told him. He's always done it himself, right from the start, he was always sleeping with one woman or another. He never made the slightest attempt to hide it.'

That night, Juan Olmedo couldn't sleep. He realised that he had never, ever, not even when Charo closed the door behind him for the first time, known what it was to be truly alone.

'I can't take any more, Charo,' he said at breakfast, looking straight at her, without hesitating, or hiding. 'I can't. I mean it this time. Don't think of coming back. Don't call me. Don't bother to make yet another scene, because I've had enough. I can't go on with this. I just can't.'

Charo realised that he meant it this time. She didn't cry, or scream. She didn't take off her clothes, or fling herself at him, or try to drag him to bed.

'You'll regret this, Juan,' she said eventually, eyes dry, lips firm. 'You'll regret doing this to me. I know you'll be sorry. What do you bet?'

It was the last time she ever wagered with him, but she won the bet easily, just as she had won all the others. Juan Olmedo was never alone with her again until he saw her lying by the side of the old Galapagar road, her lifeless body covered by a thick, grey blanket, and then he realised what it was to be truly sorry.

★

In mid-May, an optimistic east wind, moderate and brave, brought summer with it, spreading a salty joy of bare arms and cheeks tanned by the sun that felt like a victory over the persistent uncertainty of winter. In the south, the arrival of hot weather is a certainty, a guarantee of stability, a spontaneous scientific proof. The changeable weather that drives everyone mad ceases abruptly with the first blast of true heat. From then on, there is nothing but heat, the only variation a benevolent, refreshing foreign wind, or another drier wind, redolent of the desert.

Juan Olmedo's body welcomed the arrival of summer before his brain even had time to recognise it. At least this was what he thought when he at last managed to identify the insistent tingling that triggered nervous ripples just below the skin at the back of his neck, his arms and his legs. It was a Thursday afternoon, he was driving home from work on a road that shone like a mirror in the sun, and he was feeling uncomfortably hot. He took off his jacket, switched on the air conditioning, and this improved things slightly, but not enough. He spent the rest of the afternoon trying to tire himself out. He watered the plants, tidied his desk, reorganised the junk room, hung all the tools that had gradually been dispersed throughout the house over the past few months back on their board, emptied all the wastepaper baskets, carried a couple of rubbish bags out to the bin and, once he'd done all this, decided not to go for an evening walk on the beach, but headed instead to the telephone.

The woman he used as a babysitter was very happy to hear from him. He'd needed her only three or four times in the last few weeks, when he'd had to go out to dinner with colleagues, bonding sessions he'd gradually grown used to and even enjoyed, although he still felt a little reluctant to go, just as he always had back in Madrid. But these outings on Fridays or Saturdays were not the only way in which his life was becoming more settled, a process he found so disconcerting that he couldn't enjoy it fully. When he was alone, a sudden mistrust, a poisoned gift from another time, another man's memory, made him doubt everything that was happening, made him doubt what his senses were telling him. It was a need to regain control, regain faith in his senses, that prompted him to go to Sanlúcar that evening, to head down the path of beaten earth that seemed strangely unfamiliar considering it was only a couple of months since he'd last been there. The neon sign above the bar greeted him like an old friend, however.

'How lovely to see you!' exclaimed Elia, playing the hurt, forsaken sweetheart as he came towards her. 'I thought the earth had swallowed you up.'

'I'll go away again if you like,' he said very calmly, as he reached her side.

'No, stay.'

In an instant she went from sulking to being outrageously affectionate, and Juan couldn't help comparing her silliness, her superficial skill, her profitable, practised moves, with Maribel's greedy surrender. It made her rise in his estimation, even compared to a woman who was younger and more attractive. While Elia purred and coiled herself around him, he glanced around the bar which was unusually full for a Thursday night. 'Must be the wind,' he thought to himself, and then, because he was still thinking of Maribel when their drinks arrived, he took the opportunity to rid himself of the girl's embrace. Leaning both elbows on the bar, he asked casually: 'Do you happen to know someone from my town called Andrés? He used to deliver bread. I think they called him "Tasty Bread" or something.'

She smiled with only one side of her mouth and half closed her eyes.

'Yes, of course I do,' she replied. 'But they don't call him that because he delivered bread. It's because he's so tasty.'

'Right, well, doesn't make any difference.' Juan smiled, and she smiled back. 'He's not here now, by any chance?'

'He's always here. He comes nearly every night. Only for a drink, though. He's usually broke. He hasn't got a regular job, but he gets work from time to time and then he has a real party. He's the one over there, leaning against the pillar. See him? The one in the pink shirt.'

Juan Olmedo looked, not realising that the man had been watching him for some time. He now returned Juan's gaze unflinchingly. He must have been about thirty, of average build, with dark blond hair and the kind of doll-like face – clearly drawn eyebrows, large round eyes, small nose, fleshy lips – that usually graced male models. 'He's too old to pull off that teenage-heartbreaker look successfully,' Juan thought. He also thought he looked shorter than Maribel, which meant he wouldn't reach above Juan's shoulders. Just tall enough to impress an eleven-year-old girl. He smiled, so that the man would look away.

'You're fucking his wife, aren't you?'

Her comment made him start, and she noticed. He took a long sip of his drink, and thought a moment before answering. 'First, she's no longer his wife. Secondly, he doesn't give a shit who she's fucking. And thirdly . . .' 'Yes, I am fucking her. So what?' he thought, but didn't say it out loud, because he remembered how careful Maribel was about this, the strict, universal cautiousness that he found so disconcerting, especially since it was like the shame she might have expected him to feel, but which he didn't.

'Don't call me "usted", Maribel, it's too polite. Call me "tu",' he remembered to say at last, the third time they slept together.

'Why not?' She held him tighter under the sheets as a way of showing her gratitude for his request, although she didn't intend to act on it. 'Does it bother you?'

'No, it's not that. It doesn't bother me, it just seems silly.

390

It's ridiculous that you use a formal way of addressing me when . . .' He tailed off and shrugged, smiling, hoping to convey the rest of the sentence that he didn't want to say out loud – it's ridiculous that you address me as 'usted' with the same mouth you also use to suck my cock.

'Maybe.' She stopped to think, to find the right words. 'If I start using "tu" at this stage, I'll get used to it, because, well, that always happens, and then sooner or later it'll slip out when I'm telling Andrés about something we've discussed, or when I'm mentioning you to someone. And if Andrés hears, he'll realise what's going on, and then he'll get used to it, and if my mother finds out . . .'

'What?'

She didn't answer, only looked at him, and he guessed the rest of the explanation. 'This isn't an easy business,' her eyes told him, 'it can't be because, away from this bed, you and I are not equal, and if my mother finds out I address you as "tu", she'll immediately get suspicious, and I'll end up letting it slip and then everyone will know, and that won't be good for anyone, because no one will accept that in this difficult business we're both winners, they won't understand what goes on in this bed, and I'll get an even worse reputation, and you'll start to get a bad one too, and you won't care because you can afford not to give a fuck what people think of you in this town, but I can't, because times may have changed, but not in that way. Not for women like me, and for the children of women like me. That's why this affair, that's so easy when we're here in bed, is so difficult outside, because here you and I are equal, but outside we're not, and you are "usted", but I'm still me, and I'm not much.'

'The fact is, if you don't mind,' she said after a while, 'I'd rather go on using "usted".'

Then he kissed her on the mouth for a long time, passionately, with a sudden need to merge with her, to absorb her into himself and keep her there inside him, safe. He didn't bring the subject up again although it was always on his mind, so much so that he managed to lie to Elia so fluently and eloquently that he was sure she believed him.

'And thirdly, I'm not fucking Maribel. The fact is, I wouldn't mind, but I haven't even had a chance to try. I never see her.'

'But she works at your house!' Her look was shrewd rather than suspicious, which revealed the discreet reach of her intelligence.

'Yes, but only between one and five in the afternoon, and I'm at work then. Twenty-five miles away. At the hospital in Jerez, as you know.'

'Ah!' said the girl, showing her ugly teeth as she bit her lower lip, as if punishing herself for having made a mistake. 'I just thought, as you never come to see me any more, that must be it. And then Andrés said that maybe . . .'

'I've been very busy lately.'

He didn't feel he owed her more of an explanation, and she didn't dare ask. Instead, she twined herself around him again, like a trained, hungry snake, before pulling him down the corridor at the back of the bar.

Juan Olmedo, who had come very late to this seemingly complicated and problematic world only to discover that it was an easy place, assumed that Elia would take great pains this time. And he was right. His body was grateful to her for all her efforts, and yet, beneath the basic but costly gratitude, the dose of pleasure that she gave him didn't satisfy him, or make him feel any calmer. The following day when he woke up, he felt anxious and stayed anxious until, at two thirty, absolving himself in advance for all his past and future mistakes, he knocked on the door of his head of department's office. The sky was a vivid blue, the sun was hot outside the window, and the demon of the east wind was tirelessly practising new ways of insinuating itself into the landscape, and its inhabitants. Juan could feel it slipping inside his body, keeping him on edge, unable to concentrate properly on anything.

'Listen, Miguel,' Juan said. Sitting at a desk covered with piles of graphs, his friend looked back at him over his reading glasses. 'I was thinking, the department's pretty quiet, there's no one in surgery, no one due to come in, and I don't have any patients this afternoon. So, I was wondering if I could take a couple of hours off to deal with a personal matter.'

Miguel Barroso took off his glasses, leant back in his chair and smiled mischievously as he gestured for Juan to sit down.

'What for?' he asked, wrinkling his nose as if he hadn't heard what Juan had just said.

'A personal matter.' Juan Olmedo couldn't help laughing when he saw his friend's expression. 'It's in my contract. I have the right to take time off if necessary.'

'At this time of day?'

'Well, yes. It's a perfect time of day to sort out business.'

'Right, so you're going to the notary, are you?'

'Exactly.'

'So what's her name?'

'The notary?'

'No, the personal matter you've gone and got yourself.'

'Well,' said Juan. He knew his boss didn't believe a word he'd said, and he laughed, realising he'd have to tell him what it was all about. 'The truth is, I wasn't looking for anything. It just happened.'

'Right,' his friend said again, raising his eyes to heaven. 'So who is she?'

'Well . . .' He tried to think of a way of not telling him, but couldn't find one. 'The thing is, I'd really rather not go into it. It's complicated. And anyway, it wouldn't mean anything to you because you don't know her, and you never will.'

'You're kidding!' Miguel, who knew all about Juan's

passion for his sister-in-law, adopted a look of mock alarm. 'Not another one you have to keep secret?'

Juan shrugged, thought for a moment, then laughed. 'Well, yes. Let's say that technically it's incest.'

'That's right, make me green with envy, you bastard,' said the head of the department, waving a hand at the door.

Half an hour later, Maribel, who was standing on a chair polishing the mirror in the entrance, wearing the old, worn espadrilles Juan hadn't seen her in for months, almost fell off the chair when she saw him come in.

'Jesus!' she exclaimed. But she looked pleased rather than surprised. 'What are you doing here?'

He didn't answer. He held out his hand to help her down from the chair, put his arms around her and kissed her on the lips, leaning down a little as she was quite a bit shorter without her heels.

'Well, I haven't got anything for you to eat,' she said with a huge grin.

'Yes, you have.'

They climbed the stairs, not looking where they were going, but still managing to keep their balance and reach the floor above without stumbling, their eyes half closed, lips pressed together, hands under each other's clothes. The bed was made, the blinds pulled down, the tiles cool and freshly washed. Juan Olmedo noticed all this, and took it as a sign that things were on his side, that his possessions were welcoming him, greeting him happily. Forcing himself to move slowly despite his urgent desire, he undressed Maribel, keeping his eyes open so that he could see her old, mismatched underwear, a bra that must once have been white but was now an odd shade of pink, and flesh-coloured knickers with loose elastic which he recognised as the ones she was wearing the first time. This time though they didn't make him feel sorry for her, or guilty, but inspired in him a strange and deep tenderness. Maribel was obviously embarrassed at having been caught wearing her tatty under-wear. While he let her finish undressing quickly, he thought that it had been silly to give her a shawl for her birthday, and he felt moved when he thought how much care she must take of the two brand-new sets of underwear – one black, one white – that she wore, strictly alternating them, when-ever she came up to his room in the morning after he'd worked a night shift.

This encounter was taking place on what should, in theory, have been a working day, but this wasn't the only reason it was special.

'Now, let's see.'

Maribel didn't usually talk during sex, as if she couldn't concentrate on anything other than what she was giving and what she was receiving. Juan liked her instinct to forget everything else because it meant he didn't have to be on the alert. In this she was so different from Charo who, with her complicated moods, could surprise him at any time with a revelation without it affecting the quality of her surrender, at least it didn't seem to. And yet, that afternoon, at a point when neither of them seemed up to talking, Maribel allowed herself to speak for a moment and asked him a question:

'Didn't we have a deal?'

Juan raised himself up on one elbow and looked at her.

'Yes, we did.'

'And don't we have it any more?'

'Well, no, it doesn't look like it.'

'Good.' Maribel smiled and took him back into her mouth. A moment later, pronouncing the word with diffi-culty, she said again: 'Good.'

In a vague, indefinable way, Juan registered the satisfaction with which she had greeted his remark. He had made it without giving it too much thought, or attaching much importance to it, when perhaps it was quite important after all. This wasn't the first time Maribel had surprised him with an intelligence about their relationship that went far beyond her general understanding of things. In such cases, Maribel always realised before he did what was going on. Perhaps that afternoon was no exception and yet, after the final tremor, it was Juan who surprised her. It was five to four and he was starving.

'Did you get any bread?' he asked. She nodded. 'Have you had lunch?'

'No,' she laughed, 'you didn't let me.'

'OK, well let's put that right. I'm going down to the kitchen to make myself a ham sandwich. Do you want one?'

'No, no, let me do it.'

'You don't get it, Maribel,' he said, hugging her a little tighter and holding both her wrists with one hand. 'I'll say it again: I, yes, I, so not you, am going down to the kitchen to make a ham sandwich.'

'But I can do it.'

'I know, but I didn't say it so you'd offer to make it. I asked if you wanted one too.'

'OK.' And she relaxed, falling back on the bed. 'I'll have one.'

'Ham or something else?'

'Ham.'

'And what would you like to drink?'

'A beer.'

The tiles on the kitchen floor felt hot beneath his bare feet. The sun was streaming in, creating a puddle of light that he stepped in with pleasure. As he cut the ham carefully – he'd seen too many thumbs sliced open by a knife – he felt the heat through the soles of his feet, the fingers of sun lapping at his insteps, making their way up his legs to his knees, and he welcomed this caress like an unexpected piece of luck. Standing naked in the kitchen of his house, Juan Olmedo experienced a quiet, humble kind of peace, and in this vague harmony of sensations, he realised that he felt all right. He really did. This vague, general well-being felt so unusual that he just stood there, allowing the sun to climb up his back, spread across his shoulders, take over his face, his neck, his hands, closing a perfect circle, a capsule with invisible walls that kept him warm, safe from fear and doubt. He felt all right and he didn't really know why, didn't even feel the need to understand why, so he let his arms hang by his sides and closed his eyes, recognising a self that he thought he had lost for ever. Then he wondered if this feeling of warmth wasn't enough after all. He told himself it probably wasn't, but hoped he was wrong.

He knew his affair with Maribel was difficult – more than difficult. So much so that it would never have started had chance not placed them at either end of a taut, uneven rope that drew all its strength from its unevenness. Their difference, at first ensuring that nothing would ever happen between them, had become the essence of the bond that united them. Juan would never have gone up to Maribel in a bar, or tried to flirt with her in the street or at work, and when he was out and she was at the house, washing his clothes, tidying his wardrobe, making his bed, he became aware of the deeply perverse nature of their intimacy more clearly than when they were together, a wonder that had all the advantages of a clandestine relationship and none of the drawbacks. Whenever Maribel came to the house to collect Andrés in the late afternoon, on days when the children had a day off from school but the adults had to work, or if they bumped into each other at Sara's house over the weekend, almost always with the children as an excuse, they were both nervous, both looking out for any opportunity, however small, to suddenly remember something and have to leave. Sara would assure Juan she really wasn't bothered about the blind, she never opened it fully anyway, while Juan insisted it would only take him a minute to pop home and get a screwdriver. Maribel would remember that there was a loaf of bread in his freezer that she could use for supper that night, as long as Juan didn't need it, of course. Juan never needed it, because the loaf didn't even exist, and he and Maribel would cross the road with calm, unhurried steps, as if they were saving up their haste only to release it as soon as the door was closed behind them.

Juan Olmedo had taken much greater risks over the years, but he'd never had sex so fast, or suspected that eight, ten, twelve minutes could stretch for so long. Nor had he ever known a woman who always smiled just after she came. And he liked seeing Maribel's smile hovering over her face like a veil – stable, transparent – when they got back to Sara's, both of them quiet, keeping their distance, and walking even more slowly than before. All of this was important, and yet Juan Olmedo knew that their ill-advised affair, which was developing, against all logic, over the weeks, depended on its very precariousness, on the days between his night shifts when they didn't see each other, on the barriers that separated them apart from the few mornings, like lush desert islands, when they were together, the few hours when they made the most of every minute, each knowing absolutely nothing of the other's world. This was the strength of their relationship, and its danger.

Juan knew all of this only too well but, that afternoon, he felt all right and couldn't understand why. So he added a bar of almond chocolate – his favourite – to the tray with the sandwiches, and surrendered for the first time in many years to the comfortable relativity of the truths he preferred.

They ate in bed, propped up against the pillows, and though Maribel wanted to remake the bed, he simply shook the sheet a couple of times to get rid of the crumbs.

'I'm warning you, I haven't finished cleaning downstairs,' she said, making no move to get out of bed.

'It doesn't matter,' he said, hugging her. 'I forgive you.'

They fell asleep without realising it. Maribel woke up

before he did and, glancing at the clock, let out a shriek. By the time Juan managed to open his eyes, she was already half dressed.

'It's a quarter past five! It's a miracle your niece hasn't caught us.'

Tamara must have got home from school by now, but Juan was seized with a kind of lazy regret that prevented him from getting up, so he watched Maribel from the bed. Once she'd finished dressing, she went quickly to the bathroom, emerging a moment later with her hair tidy. She headed for the door, but stopped halfway there and walked back to the bed. She sat down, kissed him on the lips and left again.

'Maribel.' She was already by the door when his voice stopped her. 'I need to tell you something because, well, you're going to find out anyway.'

She gripped the door handle and didn't say anything. She looked scared, as if she was sure she was about to hear bad news. He realised he'd unintentionally made it sound alarming, so he didn't want to keep her waiting. He decided to be brief, to see if the special intelligence he thought he'd detected in her on other occasions was present now.

'I went to Sanlúcar last night.'

Her expression changed instantly. All fear gone, she closed her eyes, and a smile spread gradually across her features.

'You're a bastard, you know that, don't you?'

It was the first time she'd ever addressed him as 'tu', the first time he'd ever heard her do so aloud, so maybe this was why he spoke without thinking, without attaching much importance to his words, an importance which they perhaps merited.

'I really like you, Maribel.'

She closed her eyes again, and kept them closed this time. It didn't even occur to him that she might already know.

III

✦

*The Wind from
the East*

The water was freezing, but Sara Gómez fought the biting cold by paddling her arms and legs madly like a little kid. She was sure that when she got out, her body would be bright pink. She plunged underwater one last time, emerging a moment later looking like a plucked chicken, with goose pimples all over and a vague feeling of happiness reaching down to her fingertips. She had stood indecisively at the water's edge for rather a long time, successively attracted and repelled by the idea of her first swim of the year, but now the young May sun had warmed her towel, and it spread itself generously over her back, a guarantee of warmth that might, in a little while, encourage her to repeat the experience. While her body temperature returned to normal, Sara sat down and looked at the beach. The steady movement of the sea broke the silence – free of the noise of radios and conversation – with its perfect, rhythmic roar, producing foam that dissolved an instant later in a dance that seemed absurd, and was therefore always fascinating to a child of arid lands.

She went home at lunchtime, tired and happy, though on the last hill she had to force her feet forward as they seemed to have forgotten the way. She was hungry, but more importantly she needed to rest. Having negotiated the treacherous obstacle of the stairs, she pulled down the blinds, lay down on the bed and closed her eyes. In the cool darkness of the bedroom, she realised that the first swim of the season would become her own private ritual, something she would do every year. The repetition of such a simple act seemed like a guarantee of stability in a life that was no longer new, but felt more like it was her own than it had done a year earlier. It was a good time to take stock, and Sara felt that all in all, her time in the town had been satisfactory. Afterwards she fell asleep. She finally had her lunch in the late afternoon, and as she ate, she decided she would go back to the beach the following morning, taking a chair, a sunshade and a book. She wanted to try out all her beach paraphernalia in preparation for the season, a time of small pleasures, heat and constant movement.

The start of the school holidays intensified this feeling of freedom, as if her friendship with the children gave her the right to feel as if she too were on holiday. Tamara's end-of-year results would have seemed very good, had not Andrés's been even better, but she celebrated them with the same enthusiasm. The children had more than three months of holiday ahead of them, and during the first few days they seemed so bewildered, so incapable of handling all this free time that they even occasionally complained that they were bored. Sara, who took them with her to the beach every morning, teased them when she found them hanging listlessly around the development in the afternoons. She knew that sooner or later they would find things to do on their own, and she was right, but the children didn't stop including her in their plans. She didn't see as much of them as she had the previous summer, and yet her relationship with them improved, because apart from coming to her when they needed her help, they now also invited her out when they didn't need her, establishing a dynamic that ended up including Juan as well, and even Maribel, in a pleasant whirl of visits to the outdoor cinema, games of volleyball on the beach, and improvised theatrical performances in the garden.

June was good, and July was much better than Sara had

dared hope – indeed it was better than most months she could recall. At the centre of this oddball family who had adopted each other purely out of a desire to spend time together, Sara became the weight that balanced the scales, the judge who settled conflicts of interest, the organiser of outings and projects. And whether they were at the beach, the swimming pool, the cinema, standing by the barbecue, or at the games arcade where Andrés and Tamara met their deaths over and over again in their perpetual struggle against aliens, or sitting chatting with Juan after dinner, a drink in her hand, Sara Gómez thoroughly enjoyed herself. Life seemed easy, and was easy, in that pliant timetable of spontaneous arrangements and unexpected plans, in the gestures of affection and happy conversations. Sometimes Sara thought she sensed something more – a hidden, cohesive force, a shadow spreading and floating above their heads, marking them out with the sign of a common past; almost as if this were a shared convalescence in which the generosity they all radiated towards one other sprang from a fierce determination to escape their own loneliness and help heal each other's wounds. When Sara caught herself thinking like this, she told herself she must be wrong, that she had no reason to attribute to her neighbours the conclusions prompted by her own past. But then, in the first week of August, something happened that chilled her to the marrow.

The town had become impossibly crowded, and there were endless queues in all the bars and shops and petrol stations, but it didn't manage to spoil her mood. Nor did the east wind, which hadn't yet unleashed its full potential, but announced its arrival with a few, stifling blasts of hot air. This was why she greeted Ramón Martínez, the estate agent with whom she'd struck up a strange friendship one year previously, with a sincere smile, even though he'd picked the siesta, the worst time he could have chosen, to pay her a visit on such a hot day.

'Hello, Ramón!' she exclaimed as she opened the door. 'You've chosen a good day to come for a beer.'

'Yes,' he said. He looked hunched and nervous, and didn't return Sara's smile. 'I'd better stick to coffee.'

'Of course,' said Sara. She realised straight away that his visit was neither spontaneous nor informal. 'You're in luck, I've just made some. Come in, sit down.'

While she prepared a tray in the kitchen, Sara wondered why Ramón had dropped by and why he looked so serious. Whenever they bumped into each other, less frequently than one might have imagined given that his office was only a hundred metres from the entrance to the development, they both insisted that they must see each other more often, go for a drink and have a chat. But he couldn't have been more than thirty-five, he had an exhausting work schedule and a wife and two small children who hardly ever saw him, so he was always in a hurry, always trying to make his next sale. Well aware of this, Sara never pressed him. That afternoon, however, as she put the tray on the table and sat down opposite him, he looked at her as if he had nothing more important to do than talk to her.

'What's up, Ramón?'

'Well,' he began, shifting in his seat, sitting forward, leaning back, looking for somewhere to put his hands. 'The thing is, something's happened and I'm not sure if it's important or not. It's to do with your neighbour opposite, the doctor. Olmedo's his name, isn't it? But as I hardly know him . . . You're quite good friends with him, aren't you?'

'Yes, we've become good friends.'

'That's why I thought I'd tell you. He seems nice – he's polite, and seems like a good person, but I don't know. Anyway, I trust you, and if this turns out to be something important, well . . . it's better if you decide whether or not to tell him.' He stopped as if he expected Sara to start asking questions, but she didn't say anything. 'OK, I'll try to get this in the right order. Last Friday, I think it was . . . yes, the last Friday in July, wasn't it?' Sara nodded. 'Right, well I had a visit from Jesús, the security guard we've just employed. I'm sure you've seen him around.' Sara nodded again. 'So you'll have noticed that he's fairly young. It's his first job, and he's still a bit green, which is probably a good thing in view of what happened later. He was worried because he had noticed a man hanging around the entrance to the development, and when Jesús went to see what he wanted, he started asking some pretty strange questions about someone called Olmedo. The boy didn't even know who he was talking about, so he came to get me. The guy must have been about forty-five, tall, a bit on the fat side and bald. He was wearing sunglasses and he looked like all you lot from Madrid look when you first come here. You too. No offence.'

'You mean,' said Sara smiling, 'he was dressed in white.'

'Well, yes. In a pair of those crumpled drawstring trousers, a maroon T-shirt, and a jacket as crumpled as the trousers. He was even wearing white espadrilles. But he was acting tough, cocky. Well, all you *Madrileños* sound a bit like that, but . . .'

'Right, I know what you mean.'

'Well, he asked me if Dr Olmedo lived here and I said yes, but because I didn't much like the look of him, I asked why he was looking for him. He said he was a friend of his – I think he said a friend of the family, to be precise – and that he was spending a week's holiday in Chipiona, so he thought he'd drop by. I gave him the number of Dr Olmedo's house and explained how the entry phone works. I said Dr Olmedo was probably at work, but that he usually got home early, around six. I suggested he could maybe go and get something to eat while he waited for him. That's when he started acting strangely, because he asked me if there was somewhere private we could go to talk. I took him to my office, and he told me he was a policeman. A friend of the family, but also a policeman. And suddenly, without me asking, he took out his identity card and badge and waved it at me, like this.' He made the gesture a couple of times. 'Like the police on TV. His name is really weird. Like Nicholas . . . Nicomedes, Nico something. Shit! I've forgotten. Can you believe it?'

While Ramón Martínez searched his memory, Sara herself came up with the answer. 'Nicanor.'

'That's right! Nicanor. How did you know?'

'Because Tamara and Alfonso have mentioned him.' She spoke slowly, instinctively cautious. 'It's true, he is a policeman, and he is a friend of the family. He was a close friend of Juan's brother – Tamara's father.'

'Well, you wouldn't think so. That he's a friend, I mean. Quite the opposite. He looked very shifty and kept bombarding me with questions. The thing is, I didn't have a clue about half the things he wanted to know. He mainly asked me about the one who's a bit dim – Alfonso, his name is, isn't it? Did he go to a daycare centre, and where, and did his brother take him or did he go by bus, was it state-run or private, did he come home at weekends, did someone look after him here. Well, I don't know, I told him, because I don't. I told him he goes somewhere, to a school or something, because I've seen him waiting for the bus, but as for the rest, I don't know a thing. He kept noting everything down in a little notebook, and when he finished, I looked at him and thought to myself, this one's a nasty piece of work. Well, it's as if he could read my mind, because then he gave me this whole speech, saying he couldn't tell me anything specific, but our conversation might become part of an official investigation. He said I shouldn't worry, but he wanted to remind me that "it was my civic duty to co-operate", and so on, banging on about responsibilities and duties and obligations and police procedure, and Christ knows what else. Anyway, he told me not to tell anyone he'd been here or that I'd spoken to him, but he said it all as if he was being really friendly and that's what annoyed me the most. The thing is, he really put the wind up me at first, but then I thought about it for a few days and . . .'

'You came to tell me.'

'Well, yes. Because, I don't know . . . It's not as if I'm the suspicious type, you know that, but it was all very odd. I wasn't even sure he really was a policeman. I mean, it could have been a story, couldn't it? A trick, so that he could get in and burgle the doctor's house or something. And even if it was true, it doesn't mean anything, him being a policeman, because there are good ones and bad ones. The fact is, I didn't like that Nicanor bloke one bit. And it pisses me off that someone like him can go around sticking his nose in people's business just because he's a policeman. If something's up, he should say what it is. That's what I think, anyway.'

The coffee had gone cold in their cups, but they drank it anyway, in silence. Sara Gómez Morales felt a new, oppressive weight on her shoulders.

'He didn't do anything else?' she asked, assuming a responsibility she hadn't sought. 'He didn't go into the house, or leave a note for Juan? He didn't ask about Tamara, or look for her?'

'No. I think he just came here to track down Dr Olmedo, or rather his brother, but he didn't want them to know he'd found them. I don't know why. That's why I said I wasn't sure whether this might be something important or not. He might never come back, who knows. Maybe all he wanted was the address, to write them a letter or tell them about a fine or something. I mean, what else would the police want with poor Alfonso? Could be an inheritance, or something, I suppose. And if Nicanor's always that

cocky, maybe he just doesn't know how to deal with
people any other way. I wouldn't be surprised, because
they're all a bit like that in the police. Now, what I don't
understand is, if he really does know them, why doesn't he
just go and see them, and tell them in person whatever it is
he has to tell them? I don't know, I've gone over it a lot in
my mind and I still can't make any sense of it. Anyway,
when he left, I saw him out. He'd parked his car on this
side of the street, a little way down, and he drove past me
to get out onto the main road. There was a woman in the
car, young, with dyed blonde hair, in one of those faded
sundresses. Her face was all pink from the sun, so I think it
is true that they were on holiday near by. I don't know Dr
Olmedo well enough to tell him something like this, but I
thought it'd be a good idea to warn him, even if it turns
out to be nothing. Maybe he already knows that someone's
after him. Anyway, that's why I thought it'd be best to tell
you, because you know him better than I do, and you'll
know what to do.'

This last phrase echoed in Sara's ears like a prophecy, and
it was accurate. She was so stunned by the impact of what
he'd just told her that when Ramón stood up, she had
trouble reacting. Perhaps this was why she didn't realise that
he still looked uneasy, as if he'd found his own words a
little forced, even suspect. She only understood this when
Ramón, already at the door, turned back as if he were
reluctant to leave.

'I was born here, in this town, you know, but my mother
was born in Benalup, the same as the rest of her family.
Benalup de Sidonia. Does it ring a bell?' Sara shook her head,
wondering where all this was going. 'It used to be called
Casas Viejas. That's probably more familiar, isn't it?'

'Yes.' And then she began to understand. 'Of course I
know that name.'

'They changed the name of the village, because they were

so ashamed of what happened there, but they couldn't change my family's name, even though they'd left only the women alive. It isn't that I'm traumatised or that I've made some sort of vow. I don't dream of revenge or anything like that, but there's no bloody way I'm going to collaborate with all these law and order types. I just don't want to. I might be wrong, but there's no way I'm co-operating with them.'

Sara Gómez Morales looked at Ramón Martínez. She smiled, took both his hands, and squeezed them gratefully. When he had gone, she half filled a glass with the best brandy she had in the house, and sat back down in her armchair. In the following hour and a half, she got up only once, to refill her glass. When she went out, she realised it was still too hot to go for a walk along the beach, but she needed to move, so she went back inside to get her car keys. She'd had quite a bit to drink, but she didn't feel in the least bit drunk. Doubts, and a sudden anxiety, very like fear, kept her alert and focused. She drove to El Puerto, turned round and then drove to Sanlúcar, but could find no way forward however many miles she covered.

She would have to tell Juan everything, in as neutral a way as possible, and at the first opportunity. It was the logical thing to do; the most sensible and probably the best option. In theory, there was no reason why this man's visit should represent a threat to anyone. Sara went over Ramón Martínez's chain of reasoning again and again, but she was absolutely certain that there was more to the visit of this sinister policeman than a simple question of an inheritance or an unpaid fine. She was sure of it, but had nothing to back up her certainty, just a few scattered clues that didn't even amount to suspicions, held together by the insubstantial mortar of her imagination. She knew that Damián Olmedo had died after falling down a flight of stairs. She knew that his brother Alfonso succumbed instantly to sheer panic at the sight of any bald, fat policeman in a uniform. She knew that Tamara had learnt that certain compassionate lies were better for everyone than the truth. And Sara also knew that she had been terribly bored during the endless afternoons of a long, damp autumn, the season of brandy and idle speculation.

But things had changed a great deal since then. They'd changed so much that she was no longer even tempted to solve the puzzle, to give it form and weight. Sara Gómez Morales found herself thinking that she wasn't interested in any episodes from the Olmedos' past, in anything that had happened before fate had caused them to become part of her own life. After all, she too was an expert in moving from place to place, she'd spent her life going from one home to another, constantly changing her goals, always looking for somewhere she could finally call home. And the Olmedos were as much a part of this stable future as she was herself. If they moved, Sara didn't feel she would be able to stay, although she would always be on the other side of the line she had drawn for herself in the sand. This was the worry at the root of her fear and the reason she felt a strong urge to say nothing to Juan, to forget Ramón Martínez's warnings, to pretend that no stranger had come to disturb the profound, sunny peace of that summer.

But there, at the centre of it all, was Alfonso. Clumsy, defenceless, and always alone in his poor, small, empty world. Alfonso, who would never harm a soul, who was barely capable of harming himself, but who suffered just like everyone else, and when he cried he told them, 'Look at me, look how my tears are falling, it's because I'm crying, look, look at me.' Sara didn't know this man called Nicanor, but the thought of him coming face to face with Alfonso scared her. She couldn't forget the terror that had paralysed him in that hamburger bar in El Puerto. And she couldn't imagine what the police could want with a child like Alfonso, a thirty-three-year-old child who couldn't even wash his own shirts. The image of Alfonso alone, in a strange place as a stranger bombarded him with questions, Alfonso furiously tugging at his own hair until he pulled it out, as he did when he felt lost in certain situations, when he sensed he should understand what was going on but couldn't, filled Sara's eyes with tears. They make me do tests, he'd told her, I hate tests, I hate them. This was the most worrying aspect of Ramón Martínez's account, and the key to the quandary Sara now found herself in. Juan Olmedo was protected by life, by his knowledge, his position, his experience, his ability to take decisions, but his brother Alfonso was condemned to wander the world defenceless and alone, lost in the vast desert of a loneliness so absolute it stretched like a thick, impenetrable jungle around him, a loneliness like a moonless night on a bleak plateau, a loneliness like hunger, like pain, like the gaze of a torturer. Alfonso was always alone, even when they were all around him, listening to him, spoiling him. Alone, and in the company of sounds that only he could hear, shadows that only he could see, unable to understand the keys to a world that was real, yet terrifyingly alien.

When at last Sara Gómez Morales returned home that evening, it was almost dark, but a permanent illusion swam before her eyes – the image of a bare, white room in which Alfonso Olmedo sat huddled and whimpering like an orphaned puppy, cowering at the furious threats of a faceless man who punched the walls with his fists. Sara knew she'd have to tell Juan everything. Everything, in as neutral a way as possible, and at the first opportunity. But when she reached her front door, just above the hole the children had made in the frame by inserting one drawing pin after another, she found a handwritten note, in Tamara's clear, round hand. We're at home, playing Monopoly. Come over if you want.

Sara smiled to herself as she crossed the street. The door of the Olmedos' house was open. In the sitting room, half a dozen children were staring at the board, looking after their houses and hotels and piles of cash. Alfonso was sitting on the sofa, watching the game with a look of concentration intended to convey that he understood what was going on, when really it was beyond him. Sara sat down beside him and asked where Juan was.

'He's gone to have grilled sardines at the bar,' Tamara explained. 'We didn't feel like going – we're fed up with sardines, but he loves them. Maribel's gone with him, because she said what she's fed up with is pizza.'

'I'm not surprised,' Sara said sympathetically.

'Well, we've ordered some,' said Tamara laughing. 'It's just about to arrive.'

'I'll play with you.' Alfonso was looking at Sara, nodding.

'But I'm not playing.'

'Yes, you are,' he insisted. 'We'll play together, you and me. Let's have the horse.'

By the time Juan and Maribel got back, Sara and Alfonso had fleeced all the other players at the table. Mortgaged to the hilt, Tamara had given up. Andrés and another girl who lived on the development called Laura were still making a last stand, selling them streets and houses at a ridiculous price. All Alfonso understood was that his team was going to win, so he was clapping and shouting delightedly. He seemed so happy that Sara thought she'd never forgive herself if she ruined everything for what appeared to be so little, a distant shadow, a strange visit from another world to which nothing could force them to return.

Over the following weeks, the feeling of impunity, the certainty that her neighbours were at least as safe as she was in her new life, alternated with moments of sudden, alarming lucidity in which Sara forced herself to think about the fact that the police wouldn't waste their time or pursue any matter unless there was a definite reason. She was sure that her neighbours weren't in any real danger, but if they were under suspicion, some day things might change, in which case her warning might prove to be important. Nobody who knew him would ever dare think that Juan Olmedo was capable of committing a crime, much less his brother Alfonso. No one except Sara, because she had her own reasons for keeping quiet. This was the third factor that she considered during the final weeks of that summer – she didn't want the police anywhere near her. Although there was no connection between her own past and that of the Olmedos, although she'd never met them before moving here, although she had her own guarantees, and however much she'd carefully rehearsed all her answers, she didn't want anyone snooping around her asking questions.

Sometimes she felt as if her initial anxiety had been foolish. The days passed, August was stiflingly hot and as crowded as ever, the tourists arrived and left, filling pavements, café terraces and restaurants like a predictable tide, and nothing happened. Letters were delivered, the phone continued to work, Ramón sat in the same office, and nothing changed. Or so it seemed until reality came to contradict Sara Gómez Morales in a way she didn't foresee.

She had noticed a poster stuck to a lamp post at the entrance to the supermarket. She'd been to street markets in El Puerto a couple of times but this one was going to take place in Sanlúcar. Sara liked to browse these small, over-priced markets, and she always bought some trifle – an ashtray, a picture frame, a vase – paying more for it than she would have in a shop, but she never minded because it was all part of the fun. The children had accompanied her once but they'd been terribly bored, so, on the last Tuesday in August, she went to Sanlúcar on her own. She brought plenty of money with her and was in a good mood, but found nothing she liked. By the time she'd finished examining all the stalls, it was already half past nine in the evening.

Before she'd left, Tamara had invited Sara over to have pizza with her and Andrés, but Sara was also fed up with having pizza for dinner.

She drove to Bajo de Guía, found a parking space straight away in a car park full of cars with foreign number plates, and joined the river of people moving slowly between the beach and the crowded restaurant terraces, parallel to the mouth of the Guadalquivir. She was sure she wouldn't get a table, but she didn't mind eating at the bar. She didn't pay too much attention to the people she passed, but when she got to Joselito Huerta, the last restaurant on the seafront and purveyor of the best sea bass in town, she caught sight of Juan Olmedo. Her neighbour, who must have taken the precaution of booking, was sitting at one of the best tables by the beach. Sara was just congratulating herself on this happy coincidence, when she saw him burst out laughing and realised he wasn't alone. Sitting opposite him, a young woman with long hair and wearing a red dress was poking her tongue out at him. As he responded by throwing a ball of bread down her cleavage, Sara recognised Maribel. She instantly backed away and, hidden behind an ice cream stand, she watched them from a distance. Though apparently innocuous and childish, their relationship seemed very close and self-sufficient, but she didn't detect any other signs of intimacy until a waiter placed a tray of king prawns on their table. Maribel took one, peeled it and put it in Juan's mouth. Before he began chewing, he kept her fingers in his mouth and sucked them. Maribel parted her lips and started to breathe through her mouth. Sara was watching this scene with amazement rather than disbelief, when the stallholder asked her if she wanted an ice cream. No, she said, and walked slowly back to her car, turning round once or twice until she could no longer see their heads in the distance.

As she drove home, Sara felt clumsy and incapable, but

416

not cheated or let down by this discovery. It explained so many things, including the recent harmony that had reigned in their lives. She felt ambivalent, alternating between a painful understanding of the impulse that had pushed Juan down the slope of a secret relationship with someone from a very different social class, and a no less sympathetic fear of the future that awaited Maribel beyond the kind of affair that never ended well. Nevertheless, inspired by a silly vestige of romanticism that she never would have believed herself capable of, Sara also knew that whatever it was and however long it lasted, it was a good thing, and if it was good for Juan and Maribel, then it was good for all of them. Too good to spoil with bad news. So she decided to shut the news away in a corner of her memory where other secrets languished.

Some trains move very slowly, creating the illusion that they are at rest, inoffensive, peaceful. But they are still moving, and sooner or later they catch up with the naive hare that thought it could outrun them, running the creature over quietly, cleanly, quickly, economically, with no crushed bones, screams of pain, or the messy inconvenience of bloodstains. These trains then go on their way, tooting their whistles happily to passers-by; healthy, pretty, well-dressed children and young girls, who wave at them cheerfully as they travel onwards, soon forgetting the hare that stands up on its broken legs and struggles on, in a vain and desperate attempt to proclaim that it isn't hurt. Such is their character, their nature. The condition of trains. The condition of the hare.

As Sara Gómez Morales slid down to the bottom of the slope, the tragedy of her unborn child came to join her memories, bitterness, anger, rifles and love in a reality that was absolutely flat, grey, featureless, with no emotion and no surprises. Of all the lives she'd coveted in the warm dreams of her future, this was the only one she'd never wanted. But she hadn't shied away from it; Sara Gómez Morales kept going, always kept going, no turning aside, no looking back, without stopping to rest because resting can sometimes be worse than keeping going. She kept going, in her love of brandy and in the oblivion of that love. She didn't know what else to do, and she was now too old to learn.

The loss of the child that she had not sought, had not planned, hadn't even wanted until she gave in to the unforgivable weakness of making it a refuge, hurt her more deeply than she would ever have thought possible, because this selfish project had involved much more than the accidental promise of motherhood. It had been her chance to break the siege, the vicious circle of her life, and yet it had gone wrong all by itself, as if her cards had been marked since birth. The script of her life had never been so succinct, so obvious, so accurate. Sara Gómez Morales – borrowed life, superfluous daughter, mother of no one. She was nothing at all, and would never be anything; she'd be nothing for the rest of her life.

She missed Vicente. Very much. His arms and his words, the trips abroad, breaking up and getting back together. She'd always had so few things that she'd never learnt to let any of them go. She'd even come to miss the taste of disappointment, the company of her own tears, the intermittent shudder of all those truncated dreams. Behind the patient, inscrutable smiles with which she'd tried to calm her father's bewilderment, her mother's anxiety over the fate of the child, the mistake who had refused to keep growing till the end, there was less pride and more hope than it seemed. Sara hadn't been counting on Vicente, but she was still in love with him at the time, and the child was his, and with those three simple elements, the variations in the equation were endless. And yet, when Vicente came for her, she couldn't go with him because this defeat had devastated her inside. It had stolen her faith and changed her for ever. She missed Vicente terribly. She regretted having thrown him out of her life, but she knew it was the only way forward, the only thing she could do. She didn't have the strength to get hooked on disappointment again as a way of life. She knew by now that nothing would rise from the sterile ashes of hope, nothing except more ashes.

When her savings began to run out, Sara convinced herself that she'd recovered enough to start looking for a job. She didn't find much. She was thirty-five, had a pile of humble diplomas gained on obsolete correspondence courses and no higher qualifications, all of which made her prospects surprisingly worse than the last time she'd looked for a new job. It was as if universities had exploded like popcorn makers in the nine years since then, filling the streets and houses, businesses and factories, with graduates. Sara settled for the best job she could find, even though it was the most inconvenient – an accountant in the offices of a large supermarket where she had no lunch break, changed shifts every week, and was constantly forced to undergo training, sacrificing one Saturday after another to an endless succession of computer courses. This was the only noteworthy novelty in her life until the health of her father – a man who had always seemed relatively healthy despite his chronic lung disease – deteriorated definitively.

Arcadio Gómez Gómez died on the first dawn of 1984. Sara thought that death had chosen a good date for him, because he was conscious almost until the end and was able to say goodbye to his children and almost all of his grandchildren, a privilege he would not have enjoyed had his final hours not arrived during the Christmas holidays. Sebastiana was so bereft, however, that she wouldn't even let her family comfort her. She shut herself up in her room and told them all, one by one, that she wouldn't see another New Year's Eve.

She was wrong, but only just. She outlived her husband by sixteen months. Sara found her dead in her bed one morning in April, the sheets lying tidily over her body and a placid expression on her face, eyes closed, lips parted, as if she were snoring at death. In the middle of the night, her heart had stopped beating without waking her. Although this was a clean and pleasant end, compassionate, in fact the best end that Sara could have wished for her mother, it seemed cruel at first, and somehow more harsh than the long, dry agony that had slowly, mercilessly crumbled away the final weeks of her father's life. Before the peaceful corpse of the woman who had felt she was not cut out to be a widow, and had had her own way, Sara began to tremble, her fingers shaking, her knees weak. She felt suddenly hot, then cold, and realised that she was about to faint. She sat down quickly on the edge of the bed, on the side her father had left empty when he died. The dizziness threw her senses into disarray, making her feel nauseated for what seemed like an eternity. Later, much later, she was able to cry. By then she'd called work, called her brothers and sisters, and the undertakers were on their way, but she was still alone in the flat. Then she went to the kitchen, sat on a chair, leant her elbows on the table, covered her face with her hands, and wept; for her mother and her father, for herself, for the suffering that had parted them and the suffering that had brought them back together again, for the stories they'd never managed to tell her and for those she'd heard from other lips, for the stations in the metro every Sunday, and for the green and black lines of an apron, for the traps and tunnels of a duplicitous, lying memory, for the arcades of the Plaza Mayor in black and white, for the pavements of the Calle Velázquez in resplendent colour, Sara wept. For her parents' fate, which had been so dark, so unfair, and for her own, Sara Gómez Morales wept for a long time.

In the bewildering frenzy of the first few days, the constant visitors and sleepless nights, she asked herself many times why this second death had affected her so deeply, so much more profoundly than the first. She'd always been more like her father. She had the same personality, the same useless, obstinate pride, the same anger fermenting deep inside her. She'd inherited Arcadio's words and silences, his will, his determination, his way of suffering and telling no one. Things would have gone better for her had she been more like her mother, she thought sometimes, more flexible and yielding. Sebastiana adjusted better to the blows of fortune, as well as the caresses. In her, hatred was a requirement of love. In her husband, love had always been a manifestation of hatred. But they had loved each other equally, and had loved each other until the end. Sara, who had only ever loved another woman's husband, was amazed when she compared her own history of borrowed beds and guilty secrets with the astounding simplicity of her parents' love. In their whole lives they had fought only one war, and it was a war they had lost. But they'd survived defeat together, unaware that this was a way of beating history at its own game. She loved them both, each in their own way, but perhaps she had always loved her father, the one who was like her, a little more. She'd often felt guilty for this slight preference, although she never betrayed it in either words or gestures. Nevertheless she had mourned Arcadio more briefly, more fleetingly; her grief for him had been ample, private, acute and wide, but it had never paralysed her as her mother's death did.

Later, when all the visitors had left and sleep returned, Sara Gómez Morales realised she was alone. She was thirty-eight years old, and she was more alone than ever before. Her hands were empty and she had no home to return to. But then, as if she'd read Sara's thoughts from afar, the woman chose that moment to come back into her life.

The doorbell rang at exactly five o'clock one afternoon in June, the week after her birthday. Sara almost didn't open the door, because she wasn't expecting anyone. 'It'll be some awful travelling salesman,' she thought, but the doorbell continued to ring so insistently that in the end she gave in out of curiosity, and found the last person she was ever expecting to see standing in her doorway.

'Hello, darling,' said her godmother, with a smile that belonged to another time, as if the life they had shared had never come to its abrupt end. 'Won't you ask me in?'

Stunned and unable to move, Sara eventually stepped aside to let her in.

'Of course. I wasn't expecting you.'

Doña Sara Villamarín Ruiz slowly entered the tiny hall-way of her god-daughter's flat. Before, Sara had always been able to guess which direction she was walking in from the sound of her heels clicking energetically, almost furiously, across the floor, but now she realised that her godmother was shuffling her feet. It had been over ten years since she'd last seen her.

'Aren't you going to give me a kiss?'

'Of course,' she repeated, as if she were unable to say anything else. She leant towards her godmother, who'd grown smaller since the last time she'd kissed her. 'Of course.'

Doña Sara walked on into the flat, slowly and laboriously, without asking where the living room was. She didn't need to – the flat was so small it would be impossible to get lost. Sara, who had been dozing on the sofa in the darkened room when the doorbell rang, went ahead to open the blinds.

'Wait. It's just that it was so hot. There you are. Sit here, in this armchair, it's very comfortable. Would you like something to drink?'

'A coffee? But only if there's some already made.'

'It's all right, I can make some. It won't take a minute.'

Sara escaped to the kitchen and focused on the simple, methodical task of brewing the coffee as a way of calming herself, but she only half succeeded. By the time the steel lid of the coffee pot began to tremble, she still hadn't been able to guess what might have prompted her godmother's visit that afternoon. Many years had passed since their regular contact – first weekly, then fortnightly, then monthly visits that maintained the sham of a relationship between them – had disintegrated into an irregular routine of phone calls, always from her godmother to her, and ending with a promise to visit that Sara had never kept. Their final phone conversation had ended abruptly, and Sara believed it would be their last. In the autumn of 1982, her godmother had offered to speak to Vicente on her behalf, to force him to acknowledge paternity of the child Sara was expecting, hinting that this exchange between social equals would be more successful than any Sara herself might undertake. Sara had told her to go to hell, then hung up. End of story. Yet here she was, almost three years later, sitting in Sara's living room.

'What lovely coffee, darling,' said Doña Sara after her first sip, with her accustomed, fixed smile, so imperturbable it might have been painted on.

'All coffee's good nowadays,' thought Sara. But she said nothing, because her godmother's anachronistic comment, endlessly repeated by an older generation who were used to coffee made with chicory, reminded her that she had before her not the great lady of the past, but a bewildered old woman, overcome by age like any other. Her godmother had always had a rather bird-like face, her nose curved like a beak, with a pointed chin and bulging eyes, but she was no longer the majestic eagle with a predatory stare and back-combed hair who used to receive her in silence, pointing to her watch with her right index finger, but an old owl, the skin on her face wrinkled, soft and trembling, like a curtain flapping in the wind. She was seventy years old, had sunken eyes, and even her willing smile could not mask her weariness.

'I came to see you last week but you weren't in. Your neighbour said you were probably at work. I thought of leaving a note with the concierge, but as you don't have . . .' She paused, but Sara didn't fill the silence. 'I was very sorry to hear about your mother, Sara. I was very fond of her, as you know. You should have called me. In the end I found out from the mother of one of the girls who works for me who knew her. Anyway, there's nothing to be done now. My husband died too, did you know that? Eighteen months ago.'

'I'm sorry.'

'Yes. But he was in a very bad way. He was in a lot of pain and the left side of his body was completely paralysed. He'd been bedridden for years, and he couldn't speak any more, he could only grunt. Sometimes we understood him straight away, sometimes we didn't, and then the poor man would become exasperated. Because he was all there, you know. That was the worst part – he was aware of everything. I think he wanted to die. He'd been wanting to for years. He just wished it was all over, but it wasn't, he didn't die, and nobody could do anything for him.'

'I'm very sorry, Mami,' said Sara. Unexpectedly moved by the suffering of the bitter, disagreeable old man, she'd unconsciously called her by the name she had used when she was a little girl who hardly ever saw her mother but who, without ever quite knowing why, never called her god-mother 'Mama'. 'It must have been very difficult for you.'

'It's always been very difficult for me.' And for a moment her eyes filled with tears. 'You don't know how difficult.' She recovered quickly and started searching for something in her handbag. 'Well, let's not dwell on such unhappy matters. We've had quite enough of that lately, the two of us, haven't we? Look, I've brought you a birthday present. It isn't new,

424

but I hope you'll like it. I would have liked to buy you something, but I'm rather reluctant to go out these days. I often feel dizzy when I go to the department stores. And I've spent so many years at home, not going anywhere, always at Antonio's beck and call, that I wouldn't know which shops to go to. I've grown old. But what can you do?'

As she spoke, she rummaged in her bag, removing things one by one, piling them in her lap. Sara counted two glasses cases, a packet of pills, a purse, a wallet, two keyrings, a headscarf, a handkerchief, a pair of leather gloves – ridiculous in summer – a bottle of aspirin, and a handful of loose, crumpled papers; a chaotic collection of items that seemed to tumble from her grasp. She held them strangely, as if she couldn't quite grip them or straighten her fingers.

'Here it is!' she announced at last, holding up in her claw-like hands a small, square box covered in navy-blue silk that had lost its sheen with age. 'I may be wrong, because my memory isn't too good these days, but I seem to remember you used to love these.'

Sara got up to take her gift, looking closely at the hand holding it out to her.

'Yes,' said Doña Sara in answer to Sara's unspoken question. 'I have arthritis. My bones, my joints all ache, my fingers, my knees. I've spent my life looking after an invalid, fifty years to be precise. Fifty years of thinking about all the things I'd do, all the places I'd go, how happy I'd be once the poor man finally died, and now it turns out I'm an old crock too, and that's the truth.'

Sara looked into her eyes before opening the box. Inside she found a pair of long, antique gold chandelier earrings. They were inset with tiny pearls and finished off with two large pearls in the shape of teardrops. Doña Sara had remembered correctly – Sara had always loved them. And as she looked into the old woman's eyes, she understood – 'You've been a good daughter to your parents,' her godmother's eyes said, small and moist like those of a frightened animal, 'you took care of them till the end.' She no longer had the energy to pretend. 'I need you now. Take care of me and we'll both benefit from it.' This was what Sara Gómez Morales saw in her godmother's eyes. 'These earrings are nothing compared to what I could give you.' This was the key to the mystery of the unexpected visit; Sara had guessed it. She suddenly felt very hot again, and then very cold, but her wonderful capacity for calculation intervened, forcing her to wait, to stay calm, not to say anything until Doña Sara had said all the words she had intended to say.

'They're lovely, Mami. You were right. I've always loved them.' She went over and kissed her on the cheek. 'Thank you.'

'I'm glad you like them, darling. I . . . I often think about you. I know that many years have passed and a great deal has happened. Life is complicated, and yours hasn't been easy, but then nor has mine. But although we've grown apart and haven't even seen each other for a long time, the fact is you're all I've got, Sarita. That's why, when I found out that your mother had died, I started to think. You don't need me, that's quite obvious. You have a flat, a job, a salary coming in every month. But I'm alone now in that huge apartment with nothing to do all day, no one to talk to, or go for a walk with, or to the theatre. I love the theatre, as you know, but I never go nowadays because I don't dare go alone, so I thought . . . If you'd like to come back to live with me, Sara, I'd be much happier, I'd feel safer, with someone I love, someone I can trust, not like all those horrible nurses who looked after Antonio and forgot about half the things they were supposed to do. And it would mean you could stop working. I wouldn't bother you much. We could go out for a while in the morning . . .'

'But I can't leave my job, Mami.' Somehow realising the significance that this conversation would have for her future,

Sara interrupted her in time, at the point that seemed most advisable for her own interests, and leaving aside any other kind of emotion. 'I'm poor, as you know.'

She knew Doña Sara would blush at this, so she wasn't surprised when she saw her cheeks turn red. She also knew that her godmother would now struggle to get out the words she had prepared, but she did nothing to make it any easier for her.

'Well . . . I . . . I could compensate you in some way, of course. We could come to some arrangement.'

'So,' said Sara, leaning back in her armchair, lighting a cigarette and looking straight into Doña Sara's eyes, 'you're offering me a job.'

'No, no, darling, no.' Her godmother closed her eyes and rubbed them. She looked even more lost, helpless. 'I . . . Well, yes, it depends on how you look at it.'

'I can only look at it one way, Mami. I have to earn my living.'

Doña Sara said nothing. With her clumsy, bent fingers she collected all the things in her lap and put them back into her bag. Once she'd finished she looked at Sara. The uneasiness of her speech contradicted the wide, conventional smile:

'Speaking of money is always so unpleasant, isn't it?' Her god-daughter smiled on hearing this outrageous maxim again, after all these years. Not perceiving the irony in her expression, Doña Sara went on, encouraged: 'I simply can't. I've never been able to. But I understand, really I do. Look, I'm going to the seaside the day after tomorrow. To a sanatorium that's like an old-fashioned spa. A wonderful place, on the Costa del Sol. It's the best thing I can do for my joints – plenty of rest, lots of massages, thermal baths, exercise, but with a physiotherapist making me do all the exercises, not those dreadful balls all the doctors here seem so keen on. I never go to Cercedilla now. I can't – that huge house, and the nights are so cold, even in summer. Whatever they say about mountain air, being by the sea suits me much better. I'll give you my phone number at the hotel. You could come to visit me, spend a few days there. I'm sure you'd like the place, although if you have something else planned we could talk after the summer. I . . . well, I'll have a word with the man who manages my finances. I'll give him instructions to agree something with you. Whatever you want, darling. As far as that's concerned, there is no problem, you can rest assured.'

'All right. I'll think about it, and I'll let you know at the beginning of September.'

'Please do agree, darling.' And for the first time in her life, Sara saw need in her godmother's eyes. 'Please.'

Then she stood with some difficulty and went to leave, shuffling her feet, taking short, quiet steps in which nobody would have recognised the woman she once was.

'Would you like me to drive you home?'

'No, there's no need. The chauffeur is waiting for me at the door.'

'I'll come downstairs with you anyway. I'll see you out.'

Once she was back upstairs, Sara sat down in the same armchair as before and prepared to examine the situation with a cool head. But she felt too agitated to sit still, so she got up and, taking a pen and paper, she sat at the dining table that occupied the other half of the room. She placed two sheets side by side, intending to make a list of the pros and cons of this new move, this return to a lost world, a journey in the opposite direction to the one that had begun twenty-two years earlier when she saw the true face of a treacherous reality. But she didn't write a single word. As she filled the pages with increasingly complex geometrical patterns that tangled around each other, creating an erratic, chaotic maze, her powerful, arithmetical mind weighed up all the arguments.

Nobody had ever hurt her as much as the defenceless,

decrepit, lonely old woman who had just shattered the unwanted peace of her life. But she was fed up with working, fed up with getting up at a quarter past seven in the morning and not having lunch until four in the afternoon, fed up with clocking in at three in the afternoon and not having supper till eleven at night, fed up with traffic jams in the mornings and traffic jams in the evenings, fed up with doing courses at the weekend, fed up with her paltry salary, fed up with cooking on a Sunday so she could fill the freezer with meals in plastic containers, fed up with having to get a loan every time she needed to replace an electrical appliance or her car broke down, fed up with always being tired, fed up with having to choose between eating and sleeping, between sleeping and having fun; in short, fed up with being fed up. Wrapping herself in the immaculately soft skin of the prodigal daughter and returning to the house in the Calle Velázquez wasn't like signing a declaration of peace – it was giving in, handing over her weapons, bowing down, kissing definitive humiliation on the lips. But she was no longer leaving behind great dreams or battles, tiny seeds that would one day sprout like a touching miracle before her castaway's cabin. She'd be leaving behind a tiny flat, a tiresome and not very well-paid job, a grey life, a flat, monotonous horizon; pride that didn't put food on the table, the damp gunpowder of a toy arsenal, and a balcony full of spider plants, geraniums and money plants that were part of an endless chain of gifts that had no price, small gestures of courtesy in a world that was only just decent. Her life was better than her parents', than her brothers' and sisters' lives had ever been, but she was still in the same half of the world as them; in the land of small, hard-won pleasures, the uglier side of reality.

'I still have time,' she told herself, 'I still have time.' But every morning she had more and more trouble getting out of bed, and every Saturday sacrificed to yet another spreadsheet pierced her like a thorn. She no longer had the comfort of the fierce intransigence she had at sixteen, the fervour that had sustained her during the hardest times, the absolute determination that helped her to keep her head held high and her hands busy. She no longer believed in miracles, only in the modest life she'd been able to scratch out for herself as she slid back down to the bottom, falling over the same cliff time and time again. Because she had tried. Tenaciously, tirelessly, desperately. She'd tried but she could count her victories on the fingers of one hand. A diploma in English. A collection of framed certificates. A small treasury of pretty things, often expensive, sometimes very expensive, always wrapped in the precise, unbearably intense memory of the cold mornings, the rainy evenings, and the caresses that had brought them to her. A spectacular collection of photos taken in some of the most beautiful places on the planet – Brooklyn Bridge with Manhattan in the background, the pyramids at Giza, three columns of the Temple of Poseidon at sunset at Cape Sounion, the brightly painted tin facades of shanties against the murky immensity of the Río de la Plata, the Kaiser's old palaces on Unter den Linden, the Malecón in Havana. It was her booty and it was all as useless as spoilt milk.

She didn't retain any love for her godmother, but after all these years she no longer hated her. She still knew her very well though, and she knew the rules and regulations that governed her life, her house, and the way she looked at the world. Sara had seen fear in her godmother's eyes and she was sure that, if she accepted the offer, that fear would give Sara the kind of power that perhaps no one had ever had over her godmother before, a power that Sara herself had never experienced. She knew it would suffice simply to be there, not to leave, to take her to the doctor, to the theatre once a week, in order to reconquer time and space, an acceptable level of freedom, and all the leisure and comfort in the world.

This may have been the factor that tipped the scales, because during the August holidays she didn't leave Madrid as she usually did, and she felt that every minute of this precarious, finite period of rest compelled her towards another, longer one with seemingly limitless boundaries. Perhaps it was this, but she didn't think she'd made a definite decision yet, when, one morning, she came across a strange photograph on one of the back pages of the newspaper. A young woman, probably under thirty, was posing for the photographer holding a bunch of white feathers in her hand. She was wearing a rather flamboyant but elegant white dress – short at the front, long at the back – and her hair was done in a high knot adorned with long, stylish feathers. Had Sara seen her in a magazine or Sunday supplement she would have taken her for a model and moved straight on, but she was in the newspaper, standing between the President and Vicente González de Sandoval, who in turn was standing beside the Minister of Finance. Sara read the caption and grimaced.

'Well!' she said aloud. 'Their children will certainly have very long surnames!'

Then she went straight to get a bottle of brandy, half filled a glass, drank it in one go and told herself she didn't care. 'What difference does it make to me?' she thought as she refilled her glass. 'Absolutely none at all.' She looked at the photo again and read the caption carefully. The woman was very beautiful and above all had a spectacular figure, with long, perfect legs like exclamation marks. She was twenty-eight, and there was a double 's' in the first half of her surname. You never get a double 's' in Spanish. It doesn't exist. When Sara found herself with an empty glass in her hand, she refilled it. Vicente hadn't wanted to accept her rejection of him. He'd looked for her, called her, chased after her for months. He wanted to live with her, so he said, but Sara hadn't believed him. In the beginning, the only thing she'd asked of him was not to lie to her, and she had believed she'd never ask him for anything more. He said he'd be honest with her, but he'd done nothing but lie. He'd told too many lies. She was sure he'd never leave his wife, and now it turned out he'd married someone else. And not any old person, but a cover model with a double 's' in the first half of her first surname. Sara Gómez Morales had short, simple, common surnames, with not a double 's' in sight, because in Spanish surnames usually end in a 'z' and only contain single 's's. There is no double 's' in Spanish, or at least there hasn't been for centuries. When she finished the brandy, Sara moved on to whisky. But there wasn't much of it, so she had to resort to the anisette with which she used to drink a toast with her mother at Christmas.

She was drunk for two days, and spent two nights throwing up. Afterwards she slept for so long that, when she opened her eyes again, she didn't know what day or time it was. When she checked, she found that she had only three days of her holiday left. But then she told herself no, she had many more – in fact, she had years. Her godmother's eyes filled with tears when Sara phoned her at her spa by the sea to tell her that she would accept her offer and live with her once more. And on 15 September 1985, Sara Gómez Morales returned to the grand house in the Calle Velázquez where she'd lived for the first sixteen years of her life, bringing much less luggage than she'd left with. From the very beginning, she realised she'd made the right decision.

After all those years, but for very different reasons than had prompted her when Sara was a child, Doña Sara Villamarín Ruiz was once again prepared to pay any price to make her god-daughter happy and keep her by her side. Sara thought she'd be back in her old room, but her godmother gave up her own bedroom – a very large, light room, with a bay window that looked out onto the trees in the street, and a dressing room and bathroom en suite. Beside the door to the bathroom, there was another door that led to a square room that served as both a study and a living room, which her godmother had always called the 'little room'. In order to give her god-daughter this suite of rooms which was almost independent of the rest of the apartment, Doña Sara had moved into Don Antonio's old room which had been their conjugal bedroom until his illness made it impossible for them to share a bed. Sara interpreted this gesture as a hint that the subject of her wages, so distasteful to the mistress of the house, would remain hidden behind the guise of a relationship that was familial in public. And so it was. Doña Sara introduced her to the servants as her god-daughter and, at that moment, she became Señorita Sara once more.

They both knew that things were not exactly as they appeared, but they took equal care to ensure that the status quo was maintained, avoiding any unpleasant clarifications. Sara realised immediately that she'd underestimated her godmother when she'd thought of her simply as another old lady, alone and disorientated like so many others. The uncertainty and moral ambiguity that had accumulated over time – in the long, lonely years spent living with an invalid, whom she must have wanted to suffocate with his own pillow on more than one occasion, although she would never have acknowledged this – had warped her character, leaving her diminished, cowed, devoid of the pride that had moulded her for so much of her life. Now everything frightened her, and the slightest mishap in the house would worry her so much that she couldn't sleep. The television breaking down, a medical check-up, notification that the gas company was going to check all the appliances in the building, a circular from the tenants' association or simply seeing yellow barriers on the pavement outside the house, made her whimper and complain as if such events were catastrophes. Her arthritis, which was increasingly painful and untreatable, was not only a source of suffering, but also of shame – at the odious scrawls to which her handwriting had been reduced, the deformity that would eventually force her to give up the showy rings she'd worn in a desperate, futile attempt to disguise her gnarled and twisted fingers. She'd had bad luck, very bad luck, worse luck than Arcadio or Sebastiana, hardly better than that of the man with whom she'd shared her life. Sara realised all this, yet she couldn't feel any compassion for her, although she did try to help her as much as she could, to make her life easier. She'd always been an excellent worker, honest, conscientious and responsible, and she tackled her new duties with the same spirit that had helped her move ahead in much worse circumstances. This was her new job, and it wasn't too demanding.

Very soon her life returned to being as peaceful and regulated as it had been when she was a child. She got up late, though never later than ten, and had breakfast in the dining room with her godmother. Then every day at around eleven, the morning physiotherapy session would begin. Every Monday, a trained therapist would join them at the house, supervising her patient's slow progress. Little by little, Sara learnt how to help Doña Sara with her exercises, although her godmother hated them and was reluctant to give up the ones she had already mastered in favour of new, more painful ones. Yet when Sara forced her to do these exercises regularly, she began to get much better, and when she realised that even her hands had improved, she stopped complaining. After the exercise session, they usually went out for a short walk – towards the Retiro when the weather was good, or to look at the shops when it was too cold or too hot. Rainy mornings were greeted as if they were some kind of punishment by the old lady, who could conceive of nothing worse than being shut up within the four walls of her house, but Sara improved the situation with the simple purchase of a video recorder. Her godmother had vaguely heard of such devices, another of the many mysterious items she felt were beyond someone her age, but she became hooked on the new toy so quickly that Sara soon became a regular customer of all the video shops in the area. Doña Sara didn't enjoy watching films as much as going for a walk, but they provided a new subject of conversation during their aperitif before lunch. This immutable ritual had survived all the misfortunes of the occupants of the house, and continued to be celebrated every day at two o'clock on the dot. Doña Sara drank a glass of port as she had every lunchtime for the past fifty-five years of her life, and her god-daughter, who preferred vermouth, would keep her company for precisely a quarter of an hour, before they went into the dining room. After dessert, the mistress of the house, with a loyalty as unshakeable as her devotion to her glass of port, retired to her room for a siesta. At six thirty, Sara joined her again to have coffee and a light snack before beginning another exercise session, which was shorter and less taxing than the morning one. This last session was often cancelled if it conflicted with an outing to the theatre or the cinema, or if any of the old friends Doña Sara still kept in touch with happened to visit. If they had no plans for the evening, they went for another walk or stayed at home and watched a film. At this point, they went their separate ways. Doña Sara ate very little in the evening and went to bed straight afterwards as she was always tired. The medication that relieved the pain in her joints contained a derivative of morphine that made her drowsy and slightly dopey, something that was obvious to everyone but her. This meant that Sara had at least half her afternoons and the latter part of her evenings free.

For over a year, she relished the blessing of time, limiting her daily activities to a few, essential tasks. She read a great deal, slept, spent whole hours doing nothing, lying on her bed or wandering about the house, searching through wardrobes, opening drawers, recognising every one of the old, familiar items that called to her once more, after so many years. Her social life, which had never been particularly busy, except in the good old days of her relationship with Vicente, was now reduced to a minimum. Apart from her god-mother's lifelong friends, Doña Loreto, Doña Paloma and Doña Margarita, who immediately made room for her at their card games – now increasingly rare because of the ailments of one player or another – Sara saw no one other than the servants and Amparito, Doña Sara's other god-daughter, who came to lunch every Wednesday and with whom she'd always got on as badly as her godmother did. The truth was she didn't have much to do, so, to fill her spare time with something useful, she gradually took on extra responsibilities. Doña Sara had never managed her own assets – the only task befitting the head of the family that her husband had carried out till the end – and she was deeply grateful to Sara for taking steps that gradually freed her from the distasteful duty of looking after her own money.

The first stage in this process took place one afternoon in January 1987. Seeing the look of desolation that darkened her godmother's face on receiving an envelope that the concierge had just brought up, Sara offered to check the balance and the service charges of the building for her. That very evening, Doña Sara asked her, as if it were a very special favour, to do the same for the other buildings in which she owned properties. Sara agreed. It was no effort for her – she'd always loved figures and was used to this kind of work. When she'd finished and was delivering a simple summary of the statement of accounts for each building, the old lady raised her hand as if calling for a break.

'You have such a wonderful head for figures, darling!'

'It's obligatory, Mami,' Sara said, smiling. 'I've been working as an accountant for over twenty years.'

'Well, I could certainly do with some of your skill – it makes me feel ill just thinking about spending a whole afternoon with all this mess. And what's the point anyway? Everyone just starts arguing over a few pesetas and they end up insulting each other as if they'd all gone mad. Take the man downstairs, for instance, the general. He looks like such a gentleman, doesn't he? Well, you should see him at the tenants' meetings. He starts shouting over the slightest thing – a thousand pesetas – it's incredible. The number of afternoons that wretched man has ruined for me! Antonio used to deal with everything, as you know, but when he couldn't move about any longer, I had to take his place. It was dreadful! If only you knew the behaviour I've seen in this building. And all over money. It's always the same. That's why I thought, well . . .' And in that instant she lowered her voice and seemed to collapse in on herself, to shrink, so that she resembled a frightened little girl, as she always did lately whenever she had to ask her god-daughter a favour. 'If you could go . . . I know it's a bore, I know, the meetings are terribly tiresome, but I get so befuddled and—'

'All right,' Sara interrupted her before she turned red. 'I can go, if you like. I really don't mind. It's all quite straightforward and I'm used to dealing with figures. I'm sure it's possible for you to nominate someone to attend in your place. Let's have a look. Yes, here we are. We just have to fill in this form, you sign it, and I can represent you. Honestly, I really don't mind.'

Doña Sara had already opened her mouth to continue speaking, but now she closed it again without a word. The beginnings of a pleased smile that had lit up her face for a moment disappeared, and she fidgeted in her armchair as if she were suddenly uncomfortable. Sara realised immediately what the matter was. She went over to her, took her hand and shook it gently, until she looked up at her.

'Would you like me to sign it for you?'

'Would you?'

'Of course,' said Sara, nodding, suddenly moved by her

godmother's distress and embarrassment. 'Give me your identity card or your passport – anything with your signature on it. I won't be able to imitate it exactly, but it's only a tenants' meeting, not an official form. There won't be a notary involved, so it doesn't matter.'

But notaries did become involved. The annual increase in service charges prompted Sara to look into the situation of the companies, together with the rest of the assets, that Doña Sara had put into the hands of her friend Loreto's son-in-law following her husband's death. This man had just committed the unforgivable sin of leaving his wife for one of his company's secretaries. Sara had never liked him. When they met to sign her work contract – because from the first she'd insisted on having a document drawn up that guaranteed her Social Security payments, the right to fourteen payments a year, and a specified yearly review – he had looked down his nose at her and told her that, in his view, she was going too far.

'Isn't that enough already, sweetheart? Two hundred and thirty thousand pesetas a month? Too much for you to start setting conditions as well.'

Sara took her time before replying. She knew that she was going too far, because in deciding on her salary she'd doubled the amount she was paid by the supermarket. But she also knew that this shitty little fascist, who used hair gel and fastened his tie with a gold tiepin featuring the colours of the national flag, was just another employee like herself, and she wasn't prepared to allow him to speak to her in that manner.

'I couldn't care less what you think, Santi. You're not paid to give your opinion, so from now on, when it comes to my affairs, do me a favour and keep your views to yourself. It's not your money, as far as I can see.'

They didn't get on, but Sara came to feel sorry for him as she listened to his former mother-in-law tear him apart mercilessly, airing all his dirty linen in public, from his sexual inadequacy to his mediocre professional skills. When it came to this last point, however, Sara agreed. Before the circumstances of his separation from his wife led her to maintain a compassionate silence about her findings, Sara had remarked on occasion to Doña Sara that her financial manager seemed incapable of retaining a general idea of the state of all her assets and that, perhaps because of this, her books weren't being kept up to date. Doña Sara wasn't too worried about it, but Sara got into the habit of phoning Santi to remind him of important dates in her godmother's financial year and, from time to time, she'd discuss certain points with him when she didn't agree. By June, when she was completing her own tax return and not paying too much attention to the old ladies' conversation as they sat having coffee in the same room, she hadn't brought up the subject in months. She had been working on the form in her study until her godmother sent for her – 'Loreto and Margarita are here, dear. Why don't you come in here with us? You can sit at the writing desk over there' – and her industriousness hadn't gone unnoticed by the mother with a grudge.

'I tell you something, Sara,' exclaimed Doña Loreto, pointing at her friend's god-daughter. 'With such a treasure here, why are you still paying my layabout son-in-law, when all he'll do is spend the money on that tart of his!'

'Oh!' Doña Sara's jaw dropped. 'I never really thought about it.'

'Well, it's time you did, my dear. It really is.'

After that, Doña Margarita started talking about her impending cataract operation and they moved on to the subject of surgery, something they all found fascinating. Nobody mentioned Santi again, but at breakfast the following morning, Doña Sara raised the issue.

'I'd like to know your opinion, dear. About what Loreto said yesterday, I mean. What do you think?'

'I don't know, Mami. I'm not too keen on Santi myself, as you know. He's unpleasant and he's conceited. And I can understand Doña Loreto and her daughter, because it must be awful, but I also feel slightly sorry for him too. It's as if he's gone from being an angel to a devil overnight.'

'But he can't be trusted any longer. You must agree with that. A grown man who abandons his family and runs off with some twenty-four-year-old slut is not someone you can trust.'

Sara looked at her godmother and realised that nothing she could say would change her mind. Such were the rules of her world, the weapon of women of her class, a tried-and-tested, time-honoured tactic, like the sexual abstinence her sister Socorro had imposed on her husband in order to get what she wanted. They were all in agreement on paying one another and keeping their wealth amongst themselves so that not a single peseta would leave the reduced circle of their acquaintances, but there were requirements and rules for remaining within this charmed circle. In this case, the money belonged to Señora Villamarín, and her friend Loreto's son-in-law had committed a terrible breach of their code.

'Maybe.' Sara paused, reflecting that, in the end, Santi was still a bloody fascist. 'No, he's not to be trusted. You're right.'

'Would you be able to . . . I mean, would you be able to manage it all on your own? The taxes, and the properties, and Antonio's company shares . . . well, all of it?'

'Of course I would,' said Sara, smiling. 'With my eyes closed, Mami. It's really not that difficult. I mean, we'd have to hire someone to deal with all the paperwork, because if I did it I wouldn't have time for anything else. But I could take care of it all – taking the decisions, thinking up a strategy so that you'd pay as little tax as possible, managing your investments and the income from your properties, dealing with the banks, dealing directly with your stockbroker. I could definitely do everything that Santi does. That's what my job has always involved.'

'And you could pay yourself whatever you thought appropriate, you know that.'

'No, no, no.' And for the first time since she'd lived with her godmother again, it was Sara who blushed when money was mentioned. 'I already earn enough. Really, Mami, you're paying me quite enough. I have plenty of spare time and I enjoy this kind of work. Don't worry about a thing.'

Doña Sara took her hand, squeezed it and kissed her.

'I'll never be able to thank you enough for what you're doing for me, darling. Never.'

But it didn't stop her trying. From that day on, Sara became her head and her eyes, her hands, her voice and her memory. By mid-September Sara's signature was authorised for all her accounts, and she had a power of attorney so wide that the notary, after demonstrating his objectivity by congratulating her on a series of decisions he'd thought extremely wise, read it aloud twice to make sure that the old lady understood how fully she was placing herself in her goddaughter's hands once she'd added her shaky, distorted signature to the papers. From then on, Doña Sara rewarded her with expensive, extravagant gifts, and began to talk aloud of Sara's inheritance.

When she was a child, Sara had been sure that the apartment would one day be hers. Doña Sara was old, her husband was even older, and there was no other child on the scene. Children ended up inheriting the house they'd grown up in, it had always been so, it was the logical, reasonable and natural thing. Amparito and her brothers, who lived in Oviedo, would sometimes come to stay for a few days at Christmas, or at Easter, but her godmother always treated them as visitors, outsiders, strangers passing through Madrid. But then afterwards, when it all ended, Sara realised that the López Ruiz children, those 'cousins' of hers, would be the only happy heirs of their aunt's fortune. Reality, ugly and harsh, lurking on street corners around the Puerta del Sol, sank its teeth into her once more. Sara never, not even after she went back to live at the Calle Velázquez and saw how much her godmother still despised the fatuous, conceited Amparito, had any doubt as to the future heirs of the Villamarín fortune, the immense wealth whose control now lay in her modest but capable hands. Her godmother's promises, far from dispelling this conviction, only secured it more firmly.

'I think it's best if we don't mention any of this to Amparito, don't you agree?' she said to Sara one day when they sat down together, at Sara's instigation, to deal with financial matters. 'I mean, she's so stingy, and she's always thinking about her wretched inheritance. If she finds out, we'll never be rid of her. Anyway, now that you're living with me again . . .' Doña Sara looked into her eyes with warmth, and a combination of gratitude and trust born of long-standing affection. 'I'll do what I have to do, dear. You won't end up in the street, far from it, you can be sure of that.'

Sara blushed and could think of nothing to say. At the time, towards the end of 1987, she had no idea of the course her life would take soon afterwards. She'd always been an excellent worker, honest, conscientious and responsible, and her commitment to managing her godmother's assets had not had the slightest detrimental effect on the conditions of her job. Certainly it now took up more of her time, but she preferred her new role to the monotonous routine of lady's companion, in which she had begun to feel she was wasting her talents. She'd never be able to leave Doña Sara. She'd go on supervising her exercises until the end, even though they were now producing increasingly insignificant results. When Doña Sara felt like going out, Sara still took her to the cinema and the theatre, and had tea with her and her friends in the afternoon. But when Sara had a more urgent meeting, she'd send her godmother out for her walk with one of the maids, and she often stayed in her study doing paperwork in the afternoon while Doña Sara watched television. Her godmother never complained, because she never felt neglected – quite the contrary. Just as Sara's relationship with her parents had changed, so Doña Sara's relationship with her god-daughter gently and easily became the exact opposite of what it had once been. Sara accepted full responsibility for the old lady's fate, and realised that this new situation was better for her.

She was forty by then, but still too young to be living like an old lady herself. This was the main advantage of the change – it freed her from the feeling of lethargy, of becoming fossilised, that had overcome her sometimes in her spare moments as her life slowed down, her own pace slackening to keep time with an elderly and infirm woman. The new demands of the job made her feel young again, interrupted the stultifying routine, and gave her life momentum, restoring a familiar sense of satisfaction as she accomplished each task brilliantly. Her days gradually filled with small appointments, duties that varied depending on the time of year and the day of the week: visits to the banks, drawing up quarterly statements, meetings with the managers who ran Doña Sara's country properties – farms in the province of Salamanca, a large estate in Toledo, two in Ciudad Real – working lunches with the solicitor, the agent, the stockbroker. These were occasions when she could do herself up, buy clothes, go to the hairdresser, put on make-up, even flirt with men who often ended up staring at her with a captivated smile before expressing their admiration for her ability, and who occasionally went a little further, risking a proposition that, more than occasionally, Sara decided to accept. None of these mild flirtations turned into anything serious, but she had to admit they were entertaining.

The only person who was unhappy with this new turn of events was Amparito. Although she hadn't been informed of the legal arrangements that had turned Sara into her main rival, she sensed that there had been a change that was detrimental to her interests, and she responded by increasing the frequency and length of her visits to her godmother. Doña Sara complained constantly of how tiresome Amparito had become and the visits bothered Sara too, until she found a solution in a dry, withering reply that guaranteed a lasting, if tense, truce between the two of them.

'Look, Amparito, to me this is a job like any other,' she told her the umpteenth time that Doña Sara's niece wondered aloud what Sara might be taking from the house. 'Move in here if you want, and take care of your aunt yourself. You only have to say the word and I'll pack my bags right now and go back to my flat. You decide – whatever suits you better. But as long as I'm living here, there'll be no more of your stupid allegations.'

And she meant it. She was an excellent worker, honest, conscientious, responsible, with hands as clean as her conscience. But none of what occurred subsequently could have happened had Sara Gómez Morales – self-sacrificing, disinherited, poor but admirably capable of taking care of herself and anyone else – not completed the final stages of a metamorphosis that returned her to all she'd been taught before she left that house, together with everything she had learnt outside its privileged walls. Difficult lives produce difficult adults, and Sara knew the price of things only too well. Sara Gómez Morales had been nothing, but now she was prepared to be everything all at once. All she needed was an opportunity. And life came to meet her after the last frost of 1988.

When a maid rushed in and told her to hurry to the living room in the faltering, urgent tone of true emergencies, she feared that her godmother had had a fall, hurt herself, or had a serious accident. Instead she found her sitting on the sofa, holding the phone, weeping, shaking her head and saying repeatedly, 'What are we going to do, dear God, what are we going to do?' Sara gently took the receiver from her and heard on the other end of the line the voice of Victoriano, the gardener at the house in Cercedilla, who'd been taking care of everything since the housekeepers died, a few months apart, in the same year as their master. This was how Sara found out that the roof of the house, a country mansion that the grandfather of Doña Sara's godmother had built in the first half of the nineteenth century to use as a hunting lodge, had collapsed spectacularly, taking with it the attics and the floor of a good part of the second storey.

'Don't worry, Mami,' said Sara, sitting beside her god-mother and trying to comfort her once she'd hung up. 'I'll go and take a look at it this afternoon. I've agreed to meet Victoriano there at five. I'm sure something can be done.'

Sara had happy, luminous memories of the huge house surrounded by ancient pinewoods as far as the eye could see, its large gardens, swimming pool and tennis court; she'd spent the best summers of her life there. But she hardly recognised the wondrous paradise of her childhood memories in the abandoned ruin, standing there humiliated and forgotten. It had been over fifteen years since anyone last lived there, over fifteen years since anyone had turned on a tap, switched on the lights or the boiler or the cooker. Victoriano, who was very old and stooped, had done little more than occasionally prune the hedges closest to the main building, and had ignored the rest of the garden. The paths had disappeared, the rose bushes had died and weeds thrived between the dirty, sparse remains of the gravel.

'I don't know what to say, Mami,' she confessed to her godmother when she arrived back in Madrid, just in time for dinner. 'It's a complete ruin. It's not just the roof that needs repairing. The staircase is so rotten it's dangerous, the plumbing doesn't work, and as for the electrics . . . it's still the old wiring that's covered with cloth, and that has split in so many places it will mean one short-circuit after another. Everything needs attention, even the garden. It will cost you a fortune, but I don't think you have any choice.'

Doña Sara closed her eyes despondently before opting for the easiest solution:

'What if I sell it?'

'As it is now?' asked Sara. Doña Sara nodded. 'You wouldn't just be selling at a loss: you'd be giving it away. I thought about it on the way home – you know I find it easy to think while I'm driving.' She paused and tried to sound more gentle, because she could see her godmother was upset and she knew that what she was about to say would upset her even more. 'Look, first of all, I don't think anyone is going to pay you what that house is really worth. People don't tend to have such incredibly large houses any more. Particularly in a place like Cercedilla. But if you are going to sell it – which is what I think you should do, because you know what the weather's like in the mountains and if you don't live in it once you've done it up, you'll be back in the same position in ten years' time – you've got to sell it as a grand old mansion, not a ruin. With this sort of project, you'll always get the money you spend on building work back, no matter how long it takes, and however much it all costs. If you do the house up, it gives you the chance to find some impulsive millionaire who'll pay you a reasonable sum for it. If you sell it as it is, it'll be the millionaire who gets a bargain, because after paying you a pittance, he'll have the work done himself and end up with an incredible house that's worth double what he paid for it.'

She was an excellent worker, honest, conscientious, responsible. She proved it yet again by hiring a builder, supervising the work, redesigning the bathrooms, choosing colours for the walls, thoroughly checking the quality of the finished work, dealing with an estate agent who failed to find a buyer after several months, changing to another agent but with no greater success, taking over the task of advertising the sale and showing people round herself in the winter of 1989. She had better luck than the agents. At the beginning of May, a predictably mismatched couple – he a white-haired, pomaded old man wearing a cashmere scarf, she a bimbo in her twenties who looked more like his grand-daughter, let alone his daughter – fell in love with the house before even seeing the inside. The woman announced that her name was Letizia, spelt with a 'z', talked nineteen to the dozen, and was crazy about nature, the environment and all that, as she told Sara several times. He had to hold his knees as he climbed the stairs but seemed prepared to sacrifice his remaining strength exclusively to the future glory of his young squeeze, and was constantly touching her breasts and smiling as he admitted that he could never say no to her. They tried to beat Sara down on the price, but she remained firm, and eventually they agreed an acceptable sum of ninety million pesetas, with all expenses to be paid by the purchaser. Her godmother, who'd just persuaded her doctor to increase her medication, was very pleased because it meant she'd be able to go to the seaside on the date planned, but she didn't seem particularly interested in the actual deal. 'With things the way they are,' she pronounced, 'selling the house just means one less problem to think about.' Sara could understand her point of view.

But the sale was delayed. For one reason or another, clinging to legal technicalities and the slowness of the banks, the buyers drew the whole thing out for over a month. Sara was convinced they were going to pull out of the deal, when Letizia with a 'z' rang her to give her the name of their notary and the date on which the sale was to be completed. At the end of the conversation, in a different, slightly embarrassed voice, she added: 'Bring a couple of bags, or a travel bag, something like that, because, well, I don't think we've mentioned this before but if you don't mind, we'd like to register the sale at seventy-eight million and pay the rest in cash.'

'In cash?' repeated Sara, smiling at her embarrassment.

'Yes. Maybe I should have mentioned this before, but talking about money is always so unpleasant.'

'Of course.' Sara smiled again, working out that this amount of undeclared money was acceptable because she'd easily be able to hide it from the taxman. 'All right, we can register it at seventy-eight. Whatever suits you.'

She was an excellent worker. Honest. Conscientious. Responsible. And she was used to counting money. The twelve million pesetas in bank notes that changed hands in the notary's office when he stepped out for a moment – deliberately – slid from her hands into the two small bags she'd brought for the purpose. But she hadn't foreseen what would happen next. The weight of the notes. Their value. Their significance.

Back out on the Calle Núñez de Balboa, the palms of her hands felt strangely hot and tears pricked her eyes. She was losing her head, but it didn't matter. She was more keenly aware of a shudder, an impure pleasure made up of anger and a desire for revenge that suddenly filled her mind, sharpening it to a point as deadly as a poisonous arrow, and making her heart beat faster. She was carrying twelve million pesetas that didn't exist, twelve million that nobody had seen, that nobody would ever claim to have handed over, twelve million that the former owners would claim never to have had. Twelve million pesetas that existed only in the weight she could feel in each hand. In each of her two hands, the hands of a lost little girl who'd never had a home to return to.

Her godmother's house was near by, but on reaching the corner of the Calle Ayala, Sara turned left instead of right, going up the hill instead of down. She got to the Calle Principe de Vergara and went on, holding on tightly to the two bags, a gentle flame in her heart, 'money's always so unpleasant', but it kept her rooted to the ground, and made her feel more alert, kept her warm. Money could be so pleasant, it just had to mean more than the money itself. Sara Gómez Morales walked along, striding purposefully, an unfamiliar energy propelling her, going round the block once, twice, three times. Her mind was going crazy with a wild sequence of calculations: twelve million pesetas, how long would an accountant at the supermarket in El Pinar take to assemble that much money, twelve million pesetas, how many years would it take Doña Sara Villamarín to die for her god-daughter to have been able to save that much, twelve million pesetas, how many nice things, often expensive, sometimes very expensive things could a person buy with that much money?

Sara felt a shudder, a pressure across her chest like a full cartridge belt, a savage brightness, the certainty that the justice of rifles could be achieved beyond the humiliated land of her dreams.

Sara couldn't stop thinking about the visit from the policeman from Madrid, not even when she found out Juan Olmedo's other secret. So when she saw the development's security guard at her front door, she felt sure the man must have come back. The guard had knocked so frantically and rung the bell so insistently that, as she went to open the door, she'd thought it must be the children, come to drag her off on one of their expeditions – after all, they had only ten days of holiday left. But it was Jesús, the security guard, and something was wrong, very wrong, because he was panting like a cornered animal and sweat was pouring down his face even though it was a cool afternoon and the west wind was blowing.

'Come with me, please!' His eyes were open very wide, and his lips were trembling as if he were about to cry. 'Please, hurry, come with me!'

Sara was so alarmed that she didn't even stop to lock the door. As she left the house, the security guard started running and she hurried after him as quickly as she could, but it obviously wasn't fast enough for him.

'Run!' he shouted, turning his head as he ran. 'Please! Run!'

She started running, feeling a little ridiculous because she was so unfit, but she kept going. As she reached the entrance of the development, her smoker's lungs started to scream and the muscles in her legs protested loudly. She was coughing and spluttering, but she kept on going. Then she saw that the guard had stopped a few yards from the gate beside a red shape that was lying on the pavement. She stopped to catch her breath a moment, before realising what that colour meant. When she did, she started running again, but this time all her tiredness had disappeared. She felt terribly cold, panicky, but above all very scared.

Maribel was lying on the ground, on her side, curled up in a foetal position. She was wearing the same dress she'd had on when Sara spotted her with Juan in Sanlúcar. The blood rushing from her side formed a red puddle with wavy edges, like a monstrous carnation.

Sara screamed Maribel's name and, crouching down, placed her hand on her forehead. She kissed her face, then took her hand and met her bloodless, exhausted gaze, unable to comprehend what she was seeing, what was happening, unable to take a decision or even wonder what she could do, how she could help, while the security guard shifted his weight from one leg to the other, as if he too were at a loss as to what to do. He managed to string a few words together.

'A woman at the bus stop came to tell me . . . She must have come out from behind that hut over there. The woman saw her, and came running to get me. When I got here, I found her lying on the pavement. She must have crossed the road – God knows how – you can see the trail of blood.'

At this point, Maribel closed her eyes. Sara looked up and saw the hut, a simple construction of corrugated iron with a bloody handprint on one corner, and a trail of red drops, some more like puddles, leading across the road. Then she heard Maribel's frightened voice, a whisper as thin and sharp as a needle.

'Juan,' she said, and she squeezed Sara's hand. 'Call him. Please call Juan.'

'Of course! I'm such an idiot.' Sara turned to the security guard who was standing beside her, frozen, resigned, as if he could no longer even think. Sara waved her hand at him vigorously to make him react and get him moving. 'Run to number thirty-seven, straight away. Ask for Juan Olmedo and tell him everything. He's a doctor, he'll know what to do. Hurry, please!'

The wound had made a dark stain on Maribel's bright red dress. When Sara dared look at her, the precarious calm she'd obtained from telling the guard to go and get Juan evaporated instantly and her feelings of powerlessness and terror returned. Maribel spoke again, and tears slid slowly down her cheeks.

'He knew,' she whispered, looking at Sara, and she squeezed her hand again. 'I don't know how, but he knew. He knew that I was signing the contract for the flat on Monday, and it was his last chance. He's been pestering me for money for months – he wanted us to set up a business, he said I'd be rich. But that's not what he told me today. He said they were going to kill him and that it was all my fault. He said he needed at least half the money – two million pesetas, and that I had to give it to him, or he'd kill me himself . . . He said that he loved me, that he was the father of my child, I was his wife, and he'd always loved me. I told him to fuck off and leave me alone . . . "I'm going to kill you" – that's what he said. "I'm warning you, you're a worthless whore, and I'm going to kill you" . . .'

A car pulled up beside them, and a moment later Juan Olmedo appeared. His face was white and there was a mechanical abruptness to his movements that belied his apparent calm. Without a word, he gently pushed Sara out of the way and knelt down beside Maribel, making a strange sound with his tongue, the kind of rhythmic clucking mothers use to soothe their babies. He was frowning in concentration, and there was a look of brisk efficiency in his eyes as he swung into action, doing a thousand things at once before examining the wound. While he extracted a packet of sterile gloves from his trouser pocket, he looked closely at the pool of blood. Still staring at the ground, he put on the left glove, and as he pulled on the other glove, he estimated the distance between the hut and the body lying on the ground. Before he'd even examined Maribel, he already had answers to a number of questions.

'Try to speak as little as possible and answer only yes or no, OK? Do you feel cold?'

'Yes.'

'How cold?'

'Getting colder.'

'But you're not shivering.'

'No.'

'Do you feel as if you might start shivering at any moment?'

'No, I don't think so, but . . .'

'Don't speak more than you have to, Maribel. What's your blood group?'

'A-positive.'

Only then did he lift the dress to examine her. He parted the edges of the wound, then pressed them together again and, keeping his hand firmly positioned against the gash in her belly, he leant down towards her.

'What did he do it with?' he asked quietly. Sara, who had begun to cry without even realising it, now understood why Juan hadn't dared look at her at first and why his voice was little more than a whisper. 'A kitchen knife, hunting knife, a flick knife . . . ?'

'A flick knife.'

'With a blade about twenty centimetres long.' Then he looked at the wound again and, with chilling calmness, inserted his index finger into it. 'Or a little less?'

'I don't know.'

'He moved it around, the bastard.'

'I don't know,' she repeated.

'No.' Juan cleared his throat and when he spoke again he sounded more like his usual self. 'It wasn't a question. OK, Maribel. It looks dramatic but it isn't serious. We're going to go to the hospital straight away so that they can stitch you up, and then you'll be fine. I'm going to put a towel in the wound to plug it.' He looked round at Sara and she saw that the colour had returned to his face. There was something else too – a look of fury in his eyes. 'In the car there's a white towel wrapped in a pink towel. Could you bring it to me? But don't touch it directly, only touch the pink one.'

On the passenger seat of Juan's car there was a small case, a blanket and two white towels wrapped in pink towels. When Sara handed them to him, Juan unwrapped one of the white towels and rolled it up. Suddenly Maribel grabbed his wrist.

'Am I going to die?'

★

When they got to the hospital, the first thing Sara noticed as she entered the Accident and Emergency department was a clock. It was eight minutes past six in the evening. Then she remembered that when she'd heard the doorbell she'd glanced at the clock on the video and seen that it was five twenty-nine. The hospital clock must be wrong, but her wristwatch seemed to be in agreement. A porter confirmed that it was indeed only eight minutes past six on a day that now seemed endless – long, thick and slow as if each second were a drop of lead – and this sudden cruelty on the part of time scared her more than thinking of the suicidal speed at which Juan must have driven there. He had acted quickly, so she accepted that perhaps no more than seven or eight minutes had passed from his arrival to the time they left for the hospital, but she'd always recall the scene as if every word, every gesture, every movement had happened in slow motion. Until Maribel asked if she was going to die. Then time came to an absolute halt.

'No, you're not going to die,' Juan had answered, and looked away. Holding the rolled-up towel by one end he had inserted it neatly and precisely into Maribel's wound. 'Not you. You're not going to die. Could you give me a hand, Jesús?'

The security guard rushed forward, but Maribel wouldn't let go of Juan's hand.

'If I die, we've never talked about . . .'

'You're not going to die.' Juan slipped his right hand under Maribel's neck and lifted her head, resting it on his thigh. He leant over her and stroked her hair with his thumb as if she were a little girl. 'I won't let you die, do you hear me? You're not going to die.'

Since arriving at the scene, Juan had been a blur of movement, doing several things at once, but now he stopped and looked deep into Maribel's eyes. He leant over and kissed her on the lips just once, then once again.

'You're not going to die,' he repeated quietly. 'Now keep still, don't speak and only do as I say.'

As if he'd become aware of the almost obscene intimacy that had just filled the air, he rested Maribel's head on the ground once more and stretched out her body on the pavement before getting up and issuing instructions.

'Open the back door of the car, Sara. You sit in the back with her. I'll explain what to do in a minute. Could you come here, Jesús? Stand by her knees, there. We're going to crouch down, slip our hands under her and when I count to three, we're going to lift her and put her in the car. OK? I'll hold her by the shoulders and you take her legs. Understood? OK, here we go. One, two, three, now!'

A moment later, Maribel was lifted, leaving on the pavement a red stain with wavy edges that no longer resembled a carnation. Sara suddenly felt her grip on reality slacken. But then Juan grabbed her by the arm and led her a few metres away from the car.

'Now, Sara,' he said, rubbing his face with his hands, and revealing just how anxious he really was. 'It's a miracle she's alive. But I mean it when I say she's not going to die. At least, I don't think she is, I'm almost sure. But I think the wound might have reached her liver. It's a deep, long wound and she has major internal bleeding. Whoever did it moved the knife about to do even more damage, and she's lost a lot of blood. Too much. She can't afford to lose any more. That's the major risk, if she goes on losing blood. And that's why I haven't called an ambulance – we can get to the hospital by car in half the time it would take an ambulance to get here and back. So I want you to sit in the back with her. You've got to lay her legs over yours and press on the towel the whole time. I'm going to give you a pair of gloves. Put them on and make sure you don't touch anything, because if the wound gets infected, she's finished. Do you understand? And if you notice that it's stopped working, that the towel isn't absorbing the blood, or that blood's starting to gush out, you have to tell me. I've brought plenty of equipment, and if things get ugly I can stitch her up myself temporarily.' At this point, Sara realised that she must have looked so terrified that Juan felt he had to reassure her: 'That's not going to happen, Sara. I'm almost sure. But if it does and we don't do something quickly, she could die en route. But it's not going to happen, OK?'

Sara nodded, and Juan took her by the shoulders and squeezed them quickly. Before he went back to the car, he said:

'One more thing. It was her husband, wasn't it?'

Sara nodded.

'Why did he do it?' His face was suddenly white again. 'Do you know?'

'Yes,' she heard herself say when she'd thought she'd never be able to utter a single word again. 'It was because of two million pesetas.'

'Fuck!' Juan Olmedo punched his fist violently against his palm. 'I can't believe it! That son of a bitch! Fucking unbelievable!'

For a moment Sara Gómez Morales allowed herself to think that Juan would have accepted a crime of passion more readily than this cold, futile stabbing, this desperate last resort. She thought he would even have understood it, and just for a moment she was scared. Later she felt that these thoughts had more to do with her own guilt, but at the time everything was happening too fast to analyse it. A moment later, she was sitting in the back of the car, struggling to put on a pair of surgical gloves. Meanwhile, Juan, who seemed to have calmed down, had the presence of mind to ask Jesús to find the children and tell them to go home and wait there until he phoned.

'Tell them to stay at the house. But don't tell them what's happened. Just say that Maribel suddenly felt ill and I've taken her to the hospital, but they mustn't worry, it's nothing serious.' Then he added, 'Oh, and don't mention Sara. You don't know where she is or what time she left – nothing.'

As he finished saying this, he switched on the ignition. A moment later, as he drove along, he dialled a number and started talking on the hands-free phone Tamara had bought him for his birthday, although they'd gone to buy it together and he'd paid for it.

'Hello, this is Dr Olmedo from Orthopaedics. Could you put me through to Accident and Emergency immediately.'

Sara followed all his instructions. She could feel Maribel's hand squeezing her own gloved hand as she pressed down on the wound beneath the blanket Juan had covered her with, as if she too found the sound of his words comforting although she probably didn't understand what he was saying.

'Accident and Emergency? Hello, this is Dr Olmedo from Orthopaedics. I need you to prepare an operating theatre and a supply of A-positive blood. This is an emergency. I have a seriously injured patient in the car – a woman, aged thirty-one, in good health, with a knife wound to the right hypochondrium, very probably involving the liver, in a state of hypovolaemic shock. I'll be there in about fifteen minutes. Please have an operating theatre ready, and get Dr Barroso – I need to speak to him. And if Dr Iglesias is around, could you get her too? Thank you.'

Before reaching the main road, taking a short cut that forced him to drive the wrong way down a one-way street, Juan passed a group of houses under construction – half a dozen square apartment blocks with three floors. The only one that was completed had salmon-pink walls and white balcony railings. The flat on the ground floor had a sitting room with French windows looking out onto a tiny, private garden. The flat on the second floor had an extra bedroom, but the top-floor flat had a large, oblong balcony that Andrés had liked so much his mother had decided to buy it. Sara had gone with her to look at the show flat, and thought it perfect. The following day they all went back to see it together. It had a large L-shaped living room, a practical, well-designed kitchen, one bathroom and an extra cloakroom leading onto an area for hanging washing, where there was also room to put a larder. It cost a million pesetas more than the ten million that Maribel had set as her maximum price, but Juan had encouraged her too: 'You can always sell it if you have to, before you've paid off the mortgage,' he said, repeating almost exactly what Sara had said twenty-four hours earlier. Maribel was so keen on the flat that she listened to their advice. Keeping her hand pressed down firmly on the towel that was plugging the wound, Sara thought about the flat. She listened to Maribel gasping for breath and, in the background, Juan's voice was gradually blocked out by voices from her past: 'This is how things are, Sari, there's nothing you can do about it,' her mother had said to her once, 'this is how things are and it's nobody's fault.' Andrés was twelve years old and he knew this already. 'This is how things are done, Sara, this is how they've always been done.' The older, more powerful Vicente knew this well. 'This is how things are, Sara, Sari, Sarita. What can you do? This is how things are.'

'If I hadn't put the idea of buying a flat into Maribel's head,' thought Sara, 'she would have taken Andrés off to Disneyland and that bastard of an ex-husband would have coaxed his way back in, slept with her, even moved back in with her if necessary, until he'd got all the money off her and left her without a penny. That's the way things are, and there's nothing you can do about it. But Maribel would be all right – no more humiliated or hurt than she has been before, nor worse off than she will be when Juan Olmedo leaves her, because Juan will leave her, he'll have to leave her sooner or later. She wouldn't have this gash in her side, and for a time she would have served some purpose, she would

458

have been deceived and robbed, and she'd have obediently performed every scene of the corny screenplay that had been her lot since the day she met the handsome boyfriend who bought her a pair of coral earrings and gave her a ride on his horse. Things are the way they are, and nobody's to blame. And maybe, if Mr Tasty Bread had been on the scene, she wouldn't have given in to temptation and fallen in love with the wrong man, at the wrong time, in the wrong place. Instead, she's almost died, because her life is only worth two million pesetas, and because I talked her into buying a flat, because I gave her the stupid idea of trying to raise herself up.'

'How's it looking, Sara?'

'Good.' She lifted the blanket to take a look, and saw that there was no blood around the edges of the towel and almost none on her hand. 'Very good.'

Juan was still talking. Maribel squeezed her hand, opened her eyes and looked at her, then closed them again.

'What about the flat?' she whispered in a feeble, cracked voice. 'What's going to happen to the flat? What if I lose it, after all the trouble I had finding it?'

'Don't speak, Maribel.' Juan had heard her whispering. 'Please don't speak and don't move.'

'Nothing's going to happen to the flat, don't worry.' Sara felt an overwhelming urge to hug her, but she remembered that she mustn't move her, so she tried to convey the warmth of an embrace with words: 'I'll go to the bank first thing on Monday morning and have a word with them. If they can't wait, I'll grab them by the ears and drag them to the hospital, with a notary and everything, and you can sign the contract there. I promise, Maribel. But whatever you do, please don't worry about the flat now.'

Sara turned to look out of the window, and saw Jerez in the distance, at the top of a hill. 'She's going to pull through,' she told herself, eyes closed, 'she's going to pull through, she's going to be OK, we're all going to be OK.' Then Sara felt something hard and heavy in her stomach, as if she'd swallowed a large stone without realising it, but the tension eased as she looked out of the window and saw Jerez again, much closer now. Maribel was going to be OK. Sara could count the buildings, distinguish one from another, read the names painted in big letters on the white fences of the wine cellars. She heard the car horn – Juan was blowing the horn constantly – and felt something damp and warm against her hand.

'Juan,' she began. She didn't know how to continue, but he understood.

'Is it gushing out or is it just that the towel's soaked?'

'No, I don't think it's much.' Sara lifted the blanket again and peered at the wound, trying to interpret what she was seeing correctly. 'No.'

'Doesn't matter. We're here now.'

They were driving up the ramp to the hospital. The last part of the journey was almost comforting, like waking up from a nightmare. At the entrance about a dozen people were waiting for them, a small crowd of white coats and green scrubs standing around a trolley, faces alert, legs tense, like athletes waiting for the starting pistol. Juan put on the handbrake and all four doors were immediately opened from the outside.

A hospital porter held out his hand to Sara and pulled her out of the car. She stood a little to one side, took some deep breaths and removed the surgical gloves. By the time she turned round, the car had disappeared and Maribel was on the trolley, with a drip in one arm and a bag of blood serum above her head, and another drip, as yet unconnected, in her other arm. Juan was beside her with two or three other people. Then they took her inside. The wheels of the trolley screeched as they rolled across the cement surface and Sara couldn't remember ever having heard a more welcome sound. She was tired and very dirty, with sweaty hair and bloodstained clothes, and two trails of dried blood ran up her arms. But she felt happy – more than that, as euphoric as a general who has just won a battle he thought he had lost. After standing there a few minutes without knowing what to do, Sara also went inside. She saw the clock in the entrance hall and couldn't believe her eyes. She glanced at her own watch and didn't believe that either. She asked a porter what time it was and he replied that it was almost ten past six. She sat on a bench and, not long afterwards, a nurse – small and friendly looking – came towards her.

'Hello, you must be Sara,' she said, without waiting for an answer. 'My name's Pilar, I work in Orthopaedics with Dr Olmedo. Would you like to come with me? I can lend you some clean clothes – only hospital scrubs, but at least they'll be clean. You can even have a shower if you want to. You look as if you need it.'

The hot water and soap cleaned her on the outside but also washed away her feeling of euphoria, which hadn't survived a quick review of the situation.

'How long will it take?' she asked the nurse.

The nurse was at a desk, filling out forms, and she smiled when she saw Sara dressed in scrubs, her wet hair dripping down her back. She didn't answer immediately.

'Depends what they find. I think it'll be at least two hours, but it might be three.'

'Was the liver damaged?'

'Yes, it was quite a gash.'

'Where's Juan? In there?' The nurse nodded. 'Is he operating on her?'

'Oh no!' The nurse smiled as if this were a ridiculous idea, so Sara realised it must be. 'He's a good doctor, but this isn't his field. There are two surgeons working on her, and they're both very good. And she has the best anaesthetist in the hospital. Dr Barroso's taken care of everything. She's lucky because sometimes, however much we try . . . Anyway, all the doctors here are good, but don't worry, she has the best. She's in very good hands. By the way, Dr Olmedo said if you want to go home you can take his car. I have the keys here. But if you'd like to wait, there's a room over there. It'll be less worrying.'

'Can I make a phone call?'

'Of course. Just dial zero.'

Sara spoke to Tamara first, then to Andrés, telling them both the same story – Maribel had been mugged, she'd been wounded by a knife, they had no idea who could have done it, she was in surgery, but in absolutely no danger. Sara would wait for Juan to come out of the operating theatre and tell her how it had all gone, and then she'd call them again. She'd get back there as soon as possible, but they mustn't worry, they must take care of Alfonso and keep themselves occupied. Tamara was calm for most of the conversation but then, at the end, she burst into hysterical sobs. Andrés, on the other hand, didn't make a sound.

'Andrés, are you still there?' Sara had exhausted her supply of half-truths and now felt increasingly anxious. 'Andrés, say something, please. If you don't answer, I'm heading back there right now. Do you want me to do that? Do you want me to be there with you? I can ask them to tell Juan to phone us at home, and I'll be there in no time.'

'No,' Andrés said at last. 'Stay there. I'll pass you back to Tam.'

But it was Jesús, the security guard, who came on the line. His shift had ended but he was happy to stay with the children for as long as he was needed. Sara asked him to keep an eye on Andrés, and gave him the number of the hospital and the extension she was calling from. After she hung up, she remained very still, feeling increasingly anxious, convinced she'd got it wrong and managed the conversation badly. By the time she saw Juan again at around nine, Tamara had already rung twice and she hadn't known what to say to her.

'It all went very well,' Juan said. He looked exhausted, but then he smiled and the frown, the tension around his mouth, disappeared. 'She's in Recovery now. As long as nothing goes wrong during post-op, fingers crossed,' and he held up his crossed fingers, 'she'll be home within a week. I'm going to stay. I want to be here when she wakes up. Have you spoken to the children?'

'Yes, but I think I put my foot in it.'

She told him quickly about her phone conversation but he didn't look too concerned. He had spent the last two hours in an operating theatre, after all.

'I think you did the right thing, Sara. You had to tell them something. The problem will be when Andrés finds out it was his father. But it's not your fault.' He stopped and thought about what he'd just said, as if it had only just occurred to him. 'That's going to be really hard, isn't it? Poor kid. Anyway, we'll see. Go home and try to get some rest. Tam knows where I keep the babysitter's phone number. Get Tamara to call her and she can look after everything. I'm going to call the kids now.' He went to the phone and then suddenly remembered something: 'Oh, yes, Sara, make sure Andrés stays at my house tonight. The last thing Maribel said to me before she went into surgery was that she didn't want to see her mother. And thanks.' He put the phone down, walked back to her and gave her a hug. 'For everything.'

He'd just started dialling when, as if he didn't know what he was doing, who he was calling or why, he hung up and stopped Sara just as she was about to leave.

'One more thing, Sara,' but he didn't complete his sentence until she had turned to look at him. 'This afternoon, the wind . . .'

'It was the west wind,' she said and wondered why he was mentioning it. 'I'm sure of it.'

'That's right, the west wind.' He turned away and dialled, striking the keypad much harder than necessary. Sara was again amazed at the violence hiding inside such a placid man. She heard him mutter under his breath a threat she didn't understand. 'The west wind. We're going to fucking get him.'

The day Maribel was stabbed, Juan Olmedo hadn't been due to go to the hospital because he'd just worked a night shift. In accordance with the restriction that the school holidays had imposed on the unconditional freedom the adults had enjoyed during term time, they had had lunch early, all of them together, and then Juan had tried to persuade the children to go to the beach because it was one of their few remaining afternoons before term started. At last, accepting he wasn't going to convince them, he ended up settling for second best and allowed them to go to the pool.

Alfonso had just fallen asleep on the sofa, and Juan wasn't prepared to waste any more time. He took off his shoes and tiptoed out of the sitting room, bumping into Maribel in the hall, who was coming out of the kitchen also barefoot, smiling and removing her apron. Maribel had a great range of smiles, and this particular one conveyed desire and an almost wild enthusiasm. The kind that engulfed her face later, as she stifled her moans against the pillow so as not to wake Alfonso, was blissful and self-absorbed, but also expressed the gratitude that she sometimes liked to describe aloud.

'If you knew how much I like it, if you could imagine how good it feels,' she'd said once. 'You can't imagine how grateful I am, really, you can't imagine.'

Barely an hour later, Maribel was very cold and had lost almost a litre of blood. As he drove to Jerez at suicidal speed, Juan couldn't get her words out of his head. 'You can't imagine how grateful I am, really, you can't imagine.' Wrapped in her pleasure was her death, and he felt more responsible for the latter. His head felt as if it were full of ice, about to crack like a glass wall, and Dr Olmedo struggled to resist the urge to collapse on top of the steering wheel. He'd told Sara it was a miracle that Maribel was alive, and this was true. He didn't know how to define the mercy of a fate that had directed the knife blade straight to the liver without severing a major artery on the way. The blade must have stroked the mesenteric artery without even scratching it. The mesenteric artery. The femoral artery. A hidden curse. When he saw Maribel lying on the pavement, his heart had stopped. 'I'm a dangerous man,' he thought, 'a dangerous lover.' He'd performed many tasks at once, fast, but his heart, the muscle that pumped blood with the mechanical regularity of a well-oiled machine, had not started up again until he had inserted a finger in the wound and confirmed that merciful fate had decided to allow both of them to live.

'What do you need?' Miguel Barroso hadn't bothered with greetings or unnecessary questions. 'Let's see: an operating theatre, A-positive blood – well, that's lucky, at least – a surgeon . . .'

'Or two.'

'Two?'

'Yes. And make sure they're good ones, both of them.'

'Two good surgeons.' Miguel's voice, even on the phone, betrayed a surprise that Juan had expected. 'And an anaesthetist.'

'No,' Juan interrupted again. 'Not just any old anaesthetist. A great anaesthetist. I mean it.'

'Fine, I'll get you the best, don't worry. Who is she, Juan?'

'She's my cleaner.'

Juan Olmedo had heard many nurses – tens, hundreds, thousands of nurses – say the same thing, with the same regulation smile: 'They're all good', to reassure a mother, a husband, a wife, a son. 'They're all good' – the standard phrase accompanied by a bright smile, while a fragile body on a trolley was wheeled down a corridor and through double doors that closed behind it with the disconcerting smoothness of silk. The relatives remained on this side, tortured by their imagination, abandoning themselves to fate, to their faith in God, science or progress. 'They're all good.' Maybe it was true, maybe all doctors were good, but some were better than others, and some were good, but not good enough. Juan knew this. He took a deep breath.

'Miguel?'

'Yes?'

'It's her. And it was her ex-husband. You understand, don't you?'

Miguel Barroso took a moment to answer, as if he didn't know what to say.

'Do you want me to send an ambulance?' he asked at last.

'No, I don't think so. I think I'll get there quicker by car. If it gets bad, I'll ring for one myself.'

'OK, I'll tell them to stand by, just in case. And don't worry. I'll take care of everything here.'

Juan had kissed her on the mouth to stop her talking, not knowing what she was about to say, just in case she tried to tell him that she loved him. In a way, she'd already told him, with oblique, reassuringly ambiguous words, and with that surprising instinct that is often mistaken for intelligence in cunning spiders that slowly, steadily weave their webs.

'What are we going to do when the school holidays start?'

They were lying in bed, naked, one lunchtime. It was very hot and they were both sweating. The blinds were down, the ceiling fans were on, but barely making an impression on the stifling air of a prematurely, tropically hot June day.

'We can send the kids to the beach,' he said. He was leaning on one elbow, caressing her with his other hand. 'It's good for them, gives them an appetite.'

But it hadn't been so easy. Alfonso, at least, was out of the way for a time. In return for a promise from Juan that he wouldn't have to go back to the daycare centre until Tamara's term started in the autumn, he continued attending the centre until the twentieth of July. But Andrés and Tamara seemed to be coming and going all day long. And they had friends. Lots and lots of friends. Andrés would get to the Olmedos' house around nine, which was the time Maribel was due at Sara's, and about an hour later, he and Tamara would peer around Juan's bedroom door to say they'd be back at lunchtime. But ten minutes later Tamara would appear at the back door – 'Hello, it's me, I've come to get the ball.' Andrés would follow about three minutes later – 'Hello, it's me. Tam, are you getting the ball or what?' Five minutes later, their friend Pablo, or Fernando, or Laura, or Alvaro, or Teresa, or Lucia, or Curro, or Rocio would ring the bell – 'Hello, can Andrés and Tamara come out to play?' And a quarter of an hour later, the dance of the fridge door would begin – 'Hello, it's me, I've come for a glass of water, have you seen Andrés? I can't find Tam, is she here?' – and the bell would ring again and a lost child would politely say – 'I've come for Andrés, I've come for Tamara, could I have a glass of water? There's no one home at my place.' Juan couldn't understand why their friends had such trouble finding them because they were in and out of the house all day. But he was much more tolerant of the interruptions to his mornings after a night shift than those after lunch, because they ruined the only two hours he had to accommodate the lust he'd been patiently nurturing all week. 'Maribel, have you seen my goggles? Mama, can we have a snack, please, we're going to the beach. Maribel, I don't like paté, can I have ham instead? I can give this one to Alvarito, he's always hungry. Mama, I wanted paté, why did you give me ham? Hello, it's me, I forgot to take the lilo. Hello, is Andrés there? Hello, it's me, I've come to get sun cream for Rocio, she's forgotten hers and she's going to get burned. Hello, it's us, we've come back because the wind was blowing really hard and we couldn't stand all the sand. Switch on the TV, let's see what's on. Why don't we go to the pool? OK, let's go and find the gang, we can do something with them. Are you coming with me? No, I'll wait for you here.'

'Why didn't you open the door to Marina this morning?' Tamara asked, aggrieved, one lunchtime in July. 'We'd agreed to meet up, and when she couldn't find us, she had to go shopping with her mother.'

'Because I was bloody sleeping!' yelled Juan, getting up and lunging at the little girl like an ogre in a fairy story. 'Because I've been working all bloody night and I was asleep! Because I'm fed up with you not letting me get any sleep!'

Maribel leant across the table, put a hand on his arm and squeezed it.

'I'm sorry,' said Juan. 'I'm sorry. But it's true. You never let me sleep.'

That afternoon, the children left together right after lunch and didn't come back till half past six. If they saw Maribel's bag and shoes in the downstairs cloakroom, neither of them remarked upon it, or asked why she hadn't left yet. They just took the sandwiches that were ready on the counter in the kitchen and rushed out again. The following morning, Andrés made a sign with a white card and coloured pens: 'Please don't ring the bell, Juan is asleep.' A week later, the sign was lost and the bell began to ring incessantly once more. On top of that, Alfonso's daycare centre had closed for the holidays. These were all banal, predictable setbacks. The fact that in the Bay of Cadiz the sky had clouded over at three in the afternoon on the last Thursday in July was unusual, but not extraordinary. But when it turned a dark, dirty grey more reminiscent of a November afternoon, Juan Olmedo took it to be a sign of pure spite on the part of the elements.

'I don't fucking believe it!' he muttered to no one in particular.

'It's going to rain!' yelled Tamara. 'It's incredible!'

'I don't fucking believe it!' said Juan again, and Maribel laughed.

'It's already raining,' yelled Andrés, getting up from the table and running out into the garden.

Tamara and Alfonso joined him there, and they all started shouting like a pack of happy savages, running about in the rain. Maribel stopped watching for a moment and leant towards Juan.

'If I were you, I'd go and get some sleep,' she said, smiling. 'This doesn't look good.'

'I know what we can do!' said Andrés, standing in the middle of the garden, his hair, T-shirt and swimsuit all dripping wet. 'Let's go and ask Fernando for his Scalextric! We can connect it to mine and Alvaro's and set it up on the porch. What d'you think?'

'Yes!' cried Alfonso, waving his arms about enthusiastically.

'And we can ask Juan for his too!' said Tamara. Then, delighted with her brilliant idea, she ran to the sitting-room window and shouted much more loudly than she needed to: 'You'll lend us your Scalextric, won't you, Juan?'

'Of course I will,' he said, laughing resignedly. 'That's just what I fancy, playing with the Scalextric all afternoon.'

'Great!' shouted Andrés.

'Go and get some sleep,' insisted Maribel. 'I mean it.'

Then Juan, not thinking what he was doing, turned towards her and discreetly brushed her fingers under a napkin.

'Have dinner with me tonight, Maribel.' He whispered it, but he knew very well what he was saying. 'I'll pay. We can go wherever you like.'

He'd thought about it before, many times. He'd even

picked up the phone on a couple of occasions, just before leaving work. In those instants, it suddenly seemed so easy, so obvious – Maribel was at his house and in his head, she was ironing his clothes, tidying his wardrobe, making his bed, and she was touching him, caressing him, placing a hand on his face, stroking it with timid, hesitant fingers, as if she could hardly believe he was still there, hadn't melted away, disappeared like a warm, welcome ghost down the passageways of a pleasure fulfilled. But he was still there, he continued to exist outside the house on days when he went to work, in the routine of his daily commute to Jerez and the smell of disinfectant in silent corridors. He had a phone on his desk and he knew the number by heart, and she'd answer at the other end – it was easy. He'd taken a long time to admit it, but he wished he had more night shifts. While he was wandering about the development at weekends, bumping into Sara on purpose to ask her if she had any plans, suggesting to Tamara at breakfast that she ask Andrés to stay for lunch, listening out for the doorbell and the phone, the process of plotting kept him busy, although sometimes he didn't even get to see her and went to bed on Sunday nights feeling the same disappointment that used to ruin his evening when he was a kid and Atletico were playing at home and lost. At weekends he had no control over Maribel's life, no control over where she went and when. But the rest of the time he did, so he began to see her occasionally, always at one, two or three in the afternoon, and these sporadic, fleeting encounters became more regular as spring progressed. While he spoke to patients, read their case histories and examined them, he pictured her cleaning, moving about the house, cooking, eating, opening windows and closing them; he could see her, and he could count the pores, glistening with sweat, on her face like a freshly washed apple, and even her ribs when she arched her back like a majestic wild beast. He could hear her voice, her peculiar way of asking him something, 'Please'. And over her voice, another one urging him on: 'There's a phone on your desk, you know your home number, call her, she'll say yes.' He knew she'd say yes, to everything, anything, whatever he liked. He'd thought it over many times. Too many. He'd even picked up the phone on a couple of occasions, as he was about to leave work. But he'd always put it back down again, without dialling.

He wasn't trying to behave like a gentleman. His attitude was cold, thoughtful, calculating. It wasn't in his interest to rush things, to extend this rather surprising relationship – a surprise that he was enjoying – into other areas beyond those where it had originally blossomed. He didn't want to be Maribel's boyfriend – he wanted more. He wanted to continue fucking her in secret, with the windows closed and the blinds down, in a place with rules but no name, the private refuge of his bedroom. But it wasn't enough, he wanted more. He knew he couldn't have it all, that it was impossible, and that is why he was hooked. Without realising it, he'd become obsessed with this mysteriously common woman – the more common, the more mysterious she was – who, when she took off her clothes, shed a skin, her name, her memory, everything that she knew and everything she would rather not have known. He'd become addicted to a Maribel who didn't really exist. She needed him so that she could emerge, new and radiant, from the lustreless armour that kept her hidden from the eyes of others and kept her intact for him, because she was simply a part of him, the best part. She couldn't save him, but she could occasionally make him forget what he knew. Because he was hooked, he was convinced the best thing to do was endure, so that's precisely what he did. He forced himself to imagine the kind of conversation he might have with Maribel at a hypothetical dinner, where he might take her afterwards, the kind of horrendous bars she'd like, how many metres she'd stay away from him while she checked the tables for anyone she knew who might tell her mother, the look of terror on her face on hearing the word 'hotel' (one of those places where you had to give your name, address and identity card number before they'd give you a room), the sad, ugly way they'd part without having found each other, him returning home irritated and with his nerves jangling. Juan made himself imagine all this, and put the phone down again. He put it down, even though he didn't want to, even though the persistent voice of the obvious whispered a different story in his ear, an account of the evening that awaited him – helping Tamara with her homework, dealing with Alfonso, cooking supper, eating supper, watching TV, going to bed early. Even though that same voice asked whether he wouldn't rather see Maribel, drive her somewhere far away, stop the car in the middle of the countryside, throw himself on top of her, he hung up. He hung up, and went home feeling irritated, his nerves jangling, still wrestling with his indecision.

But the first time he invited Maribel out to dinner, he forced himself not to think about anything, either what would happen or how she would interpret it, the consequences of his invitation. Nothing. He didn't even try. It was the last Thursday in July, it was raining, and he couldn't stand it any longer.

'Have dinner with me tonight, Maribel.' She was still smiling, quietly enjoying his anxiety. 'Please.'

'OK,' she said at last. 'But what can I do with Andrés?'

That afternoon, Juan Olmedo had only a very short siesta. Afterwards, he drank two cups of coffee and spent almost three hours designing and assembling the largest Scalextric track the children had ever seen. At nine o'clock, when he came downstairs, showered and dressed to go out, the children were still organising their first serious competition.

Juan had a couple of test runs and when he'd finished, he looked at his watch, then at Andrés.

'I'm going out for dinner,' he said in a tone that progressed from casual to conspiratorial. 'Your mother asked me to drop you off home on the way, but I'm thinking that would be a bit of a bore for you, wouldn't it?'

'A big bore.'

'Well, why don't you stay here tonight? Give her a ring.' Andrés's eyes lit up as if a hundred-watt light bulb had been switched on behind them, and Tamara rushed up to give Juan a big hug. He kissed her back and tried to look serious. 'The babysitter will arrive soon. Maribel made a potato omelette before she left, it's in the kitchen. Be good and don't go to bed too late. You can carry on playing tomorrow, OK?'

A quarter of an hour later he picked up Maribel at a petrol station about three blocks from her house.

'Where are we going?' he asked.

'To El Puerto, to eat crayfish.'

But instead of pressing the accelerator, he turned to look at her in the fading light of the summer evening, the afternoon's rain now a distant memory. He was used to seeing her dressed up, but when they'd gone out for a meal before, they'd always had the children with them, and Sara had often come too. That evening, Maribel looked much more extreme, more vampish. She was wearing a dress he'd never seen before – tight and black, with a long, split skirt and a neckline that was dangerous rather than daring, a deep V that showed off her admirable cleavage. She was wearing dark red lipstick that seemed familiar to Juan, even though it was nothing like the shade Charo used to wear, and thick black eyeliner.

'What's the matter?' she asked after a moment. 'Why are you looking at me like that?' She knew why. 'We agreed that I could choose where to go, didn't we?'

'Of course.'

El Puerto de Santa Maria was packed full of cars, people, children yelling and chasing each other, carousels with their music at full volume, street mimes, clowns and stalls offering all sorts of items from the mundane to the extraordinary. Maribel walked slowly, looking at everything with a radiant smile, her eyes shining like those of a little girl. But Juan observed from the start how she was also keeping a scrupulous tally of the men looking at her as they passed, although she pretended not to notice. He enjoyed this little performance, although he wouldn't have been able to explain why. He also liked to watch her eat, closing her eyes for a moment before her first bite, as if she sincerely wanted to be reconciled with the crayfish she was about to devour, sighing with satisfaction as she ate, discreetly sucking the heads although it wasn't a very elegant thing to do.

'You can say what you like about grilled sardines,' she insisted after she'd finished the last crayfish, 'but there's no comparison.'

'I'm a man of simple tastes, Maribel.'

'Yeah, right,' she said, looking mischievous, knowing.

Juan could find no answer to this, and simply laughed.

'So what are we going to do now?' she asked, rummaging around in her bag.

'Well, I don't know. Go and have a drink somewhere?' He didn't dare go any further.

Maribel opened a small, golden compact and, holding it in one hand, she reapplied lipstick with the other.

'Would you like to come back to my place?' she said, not looking at him, her eyes focused on the reflection of her lips in the tiny mirror.

'Of course,' Juan heard himself say in a tiny, stifled voice. 'Of course I would,' he said again, more firmly. 'Your place or wherever. Wherever you'd like to take me.'

But she wouldn't let him drive right up to her house. She

made him pull up a few metres from the petrol station where he'd picked her up earlier.

'Park here,' she said and started to get out. Juan stared at her, confused. 'Wait ten minutes and then walk there. You know the way, don't you?'

'Maribel.' He caught her arm and she turned. 'Are you serious? There's no one around.'

'That's the deal,' she said, suddenly very serious. 'I always keep my side of the bargain, now you've got to keep yours.'

'OK,' said Juan, letting go of her arm. 'Would you like me to cover my face with my shirt before I ring the bell?'

'No,' she said, and laughed. 'There's no need for that.'

She left, and Juan Olmedo sat wondering whether Maribel's concerns were justified – all the meticulous pre-cautions, the permanent state of alarm about what her neigh-bours, her in-laws, her mother, her ex-husband might think. It was a subject she didn't like to talk about, and she refused to see sense even when Juan tried to reason with her. 'No, they can't do anything to me,' she'd say quickly, 'I know they can't, but they can talk about me, and I'd rather they didn't, that's all. I know it's no big deal but I'd prefer it if they didn't go around saying, "Poor little Maribel, silly little Maribel." It's not much to ask, is it?' 'No,' Juan would always agree, 'it isn't, but . . .' He could never finish the sentence because he realised that nothing he could say – 'You're over thirty, you're independent, you're separated from your husband, you can do what you like, it's none of their business who you sleep with' – would make her feel better, or stop her hearing their remarks in her head – 'Poor little Maribel, she's gone and got herself involved again, silly little Maribel, she's found another one to take advantage of her.' He understood, but he persisted, pointing out her insistence on calling him 'usted', the way she always hung back and walked beside Alfonso when they went anywhere in town, sitting in the back if there was ever anyone else with

476

them in the car, the ridiculous need for so much secrecy. He found it all touching, but above all hugely exciting, and as he sat in his car, glancing at his watch and discovering how exasperatingly slowly ten minutes could pass, it occurred to Juan Olmedo that perhaps Maribel was deliberately exaggerating her fears in order to keep him dangling at the end of a rope she'd learnt to manipulate so wisely. As Juan jumped out of the car, he didn't realise that this was the first time he'd ever suspected any hint of a planned strategy in Maribel's actions. Before the night was over, he would find it incredible that he'd ever doubted it. The fuck he'd been looking forward to for over ten hours was memorable, but what Juan Olmedo would never forget was what happened afterwards.

'I've been thinking . . .'

Maribel had got out of bed naked and gone to the kitchen – 'Let's have a drink, shall we?' – leaving Juan alone in her tiny bedroom with rough, white walls in which the showy Empire-style bedroom suite barely fitted. A disparate army of soft toys that Andrés had won for his mother at funfairs over the years filled every available surface, although the place of honour was reserved for a doll in a First Communion dress. Maribel came back with a glass in each hand and a well-prepared speech.

'Don't take this the wrong way,' she said, handing him a drink and getting back into bed, 'but for the last few days I've been thinking that, because of the holidays – which I really need, because I'm knackered – but as Andrés is at your house all day . . . . Well, it's no wonder, is it? I mean, compared to this place, you have the pool and the garden and everything, so it's not surprising he'd rather be there. He was over at your place all the time last summer. Of course I didn't take any time off last year because I'd only just started my new job. Well, anyway, I can't really take proper holidays. That's how it is when you're a single mother, you've still got to do the shopping, and washing, and cooking every day. So that's why I was thinking – please don't take this the wrong way – that I'm just as happy to cook at your place for all five of us as I am to cook here for just me and Andrés. Just as happy. And that way I wouldn't have to argue with him all the time, and you'd have one thing less to think about, and the kids would get proper meals. Anyway, that's what I've been thinking.'

She'd said all of this with her eyes fixed firmly on the bottom of her glass, but when she finished, she had no choice but to look up at Juan. Her cheeks were flushed and there was a childishly candid expression on her face. As he stared at her, Juan Olmedo felt like getting up and shouting 'Bravo!', producing a handkerchief to wave in her honour as they did at bullfights. But he just smiled and sat up, intending to convey his admiration for her little show.

'Why are you looking at me like that?' she asked, but this time she didn't know the answer.

'Because I really admire you, Maribel.'

'You admire me?' She looked disconcerted, almost scared. 'Why?'

'Because you're a good person. And because you're very good to me.'

'Yes, well, I thought . . .' She was blushing furiously now. 'I know you like going to the beach in the mornings – people from Madrid always do, I don't know why, I prefer the afternoons. We could take turns, with the kids, I mean.'

'I don't think I'll be spending much time at the beach this year, Maribel.'

She burst out laughing and then, as if she felt more confident now, she was more direct:

'The thing is, I don't think I could take a whole month without being alone with you.'

He took the glass from her hand, put it on the bedside table, and lay down, taking her with him.

'What are you going to tell your mother if she finds out?' he asked, putting his arms around her and kissing her.

'That you're paying me overtime.' She laughed. 'I have it all worked out.'

'So I see.'

This was how the pleasantly chaotic summer holiday began for Juan Olmedo, ending with his lover almost bleeding to death on a pavement. For a whole month, they lived well, and together, an odd couple living an odd existence with odd hours, in the gloom of a house with its blinds down, where people had their siesta in the morning and lunch in the afternoon, and nights stretched on until everyone was on the verge of collapse, simply in order to take advantage of the time, when even Sara, an obstinate night owl, would have given in. Sometimes, by the time they were alone together on the porch, they were so tired, so sleepy, that Juan only just had the energy to get up, walk to the car and drive Maribel home. One of those times, at around three in the morning when even the garden hammock was looking attractive, he felt so torn between desire and laziness that he had a brilliant idea.

'Let's go to bed, Maribel.'

'What?' she said, as if she hadn't understood.

'Let's go to bed.'

'Now?' she said, eyes wide. 'Are you crazy?'

'The kids are fast asleep. Your son's sleeping in Alfonso's room at the end of the corridor, and Tamara doesn't even wake up when her alarm clock rings, so let's go to bed, come on.' She didn't dare move. Knowing what she was like, he arched his eyebrows and decided to force things. 'What, would you prefer the hammock?'

'No, please, not the hammock,' she said, laughing.

'Well, then. Let's take off our shoes and creep upstairs. We can lock the door and we'll set the alarm for ten, or nine if you like. No one here will wake before eleven at the earliest.

Alfonso's always the first one up, and he just heads straight for the TV without bothering anyone.'

Maribel seemed convinced by his arguments and the following morning, Juan's predictions came true so accurately that at ten thirty they both left the house, having had a shower and breakfast without anyone even knowing she'd slept there. Juan went to knock on Tamara's door and said he was off to the street market, he wanted to buy some new trousers. The little girl responded with a grunt and told him to let her sleep. Maribel needed a red zip and a small frying pan, and she asked if he'd mind taking her into town. Juan said of course he wouldn't.

'And you don't mind about last night, do you?' she asked as they got into the car.

'What do you mean?'

'Well . . . that I stayed in your house overnight and all that.'

Juan looked at her, but he couldn't see her face because it was turned towards the window.

'Does it matter to you?'

'Yes.'

He said nothing more until they got to town. He parked in the first space he found that was reasonably close to the market and suggested they walk the rest of the way. He already knew what he was going to say.

'My father was a baker, you know.'

'Oh! So was mine.' She sounded surprised but Juan couldn't tell if it was because of what he'd said or the way he'd come out with it so suddenly. 'Well, only for a short time,' she added.

'Mine was a baker all his life. He died outside his bakery. His aorta burst just as he was unlocking the shop, and he fell down dead. He wasn't very old, only in his late fifties.'

'I'm sorry.'

Juan Olmedo stopped a moment, looked at her and

480

smiled. He felt like putting his arm round her, but remembered in time that they were in public, so put his hands in his pockets instead.

'You don't have to be sorry, Maribel, it was a long time ago. I just told you about it so you'd realise there are many things about me you don't know. That my father was a baker, for instance. Or why I'm alone, why I've never married, why I came to live in this town.'

'So, why did you?' she said, looking at him as if this were a guessing game. He sighed before answering.

'Oh, because I felt it was all over for me, I suppose – it's a long story. But I'm still alive, I'm walking along here with you now. Nothing really matters to me any more. But that has one advantage: now I only do what I want to do. If I don't want to do something, I won't do it. Do you understand?'

'Sort of. But it's enough.'

'Now I don't understand.'

'I mean it's enough for me.'

'You're happy with so little, Maribel,' thought Juan Olmedo, and he felt the meanness, the hypocritical selfishness of his words. 'I wasn't always like this,' he would have liked to say to her, 'I wasn't, I swear,' but he didn't add anything more, because he didn't want to risk telling her the truth, that he'd asked her to stay the night because it was three in the morning, because he didn't fancy taking his clothes off outside, and he felt even less like getting the car out of the garage and driving her home. He'd liked having her there in his bed in the morning, but it didn't change a thing.

But the knife that had gone straight to Maribel's liver, without severing a major artery on the way, was about to change things for ever. After he had spoken to Miguel Barroso and knew that the only thing he had to do was carry on driving towards Jerez like a madman, Juan Olmedo began thinking and feeling without wanting to, and seeing, superimposed upon the narrow band of road ahead of him, bodies and names, faces and expressions, images of past and other more recent sins. Deep down, he'd never believed Maribel, he'd never taken her seriously, he'd managed to convince himself that her fear and caution, the anxiety so similar to a shame she might have expected him to feel, but that he did not feel, was simply a happy game, a clever move in a match she'd initiated and controlled from the start. And he'd admired her for it, since it benefited them both. He'd admired her as much as he'd despised her ex-husband, that little man with a big head who surely couldn't be all that frightening because he looked so comical, with his doll's face and wannabe gangster mannerisms, the ridiculous way he challenged Juan with his eyes as he raised his shirt collar. He was pathetic. Juan Olmedo knew he was the better man, and the most intelligent of the three, so he'd met the man's gaze with a proud smile and thought how small and weak he was, without stopping to wonder what lay behind that weakness, the same factors behind the reality now lying on the back seat of his car. He hadn't taken Maribel's fears seriously, he hadn't wanted to see a motive in her ex-husband's eyes, he'd refused to. Juan was the better man, the most intelligent of the three, that had been enough, and it wasn't the first time he'd been in this position.

'When you stab someone, you have to turn the handle with the blade inside the body, like this, see? As if it's a screwdriver, so it does more damage.' As he drove like a madman towards Jerez de la Frontera, Juan Olmedo remembered the gruesome tales of fights he'd overheard as a receptive child living in a tough district, in a tough town, in a tough time. 'You can blind someone using two fingers, like this, see?' Without wanting to, Juan was thinking, and remembering his passivity, his indifference, his guilty superiority as he went to the small-town brothel to do exactly what all the others did. He should have done something, said something to the man, threatened him while there was still time. But what for? When you punched someone it was a good idea to have a battery in your fist or, even better, a sugar cube soaked in brandy then left to dry, so that it crystallised, with the edge protruding between the middle and ring fingers of your good hand. He knew all these things, and a few more besides. He pressed the accelerator, honked his horn, drove on the hard shoulder, rushing to get to the hospital, remembering and regretting. He should have punched the man's lights out, smashed a bottle over his head, because you could have seen this coming, it was obvious from the start. He should have grabbed him by the lapels, got right up close to him and said: 'Don't mess with me, you little bastard.' He should at least have said this. But what would have been the point? The man was only interested in Maribel, in her money, and he knew exactly how to turn the knife so as to cause the most damage. He would probably even have guessed that Juan was capable of kissing his ex-wife on the mouth simply to stop her talking.

He was the third, the best of the three, the most intelligent, but still the third. Sometimes the most defenceless, sometimes the most powerful, sometimes insensitive and egotistical – that was him. But now it was Maribel who was on the losing side. This was why Juan Olmedo couldn't make sense of it all, still wondering why pain and guilt, error and blood, had to repeat themselves in his life, the life of a man who had only ever wanted to be a good boy. 'I should have killed him,' he told himself, and it didn't frighten him, so he repeated it: 'I should have killed him.'

He had time to think and he wanted to think. But when they brought Maribel up from Recovery, conscious, with all her vital signs under control, one thought was at the forefront of Juan's mind, coexisting with alarm and relief, fear and guilt, good memories and bad, and even with the first hint of a feeling of possession that had been born with the stabbing of a knife, a feeling that had never flourished while there was only one woman in the world, and that woman wasn't his. Seeing him, nobody would have guessed any of this, neither the porter who took Maribel up to her floor, nor the nurse standing by the door of one of the quietest rooms, where a hand-drawn cross on one of the two identification labels revealed that the other bed inside was to be kept empty. 'I'll take care of everything,' Miguel Barroso had said and Juan smiled when he saw how completely he'd kept his word. Once Maribel was comfortably installed, Juan's eyes met hers. He took a step forward, stroked her face, and asked her how she felt. She responded by resting her face against his hand. At this point, the porter and the nurse both left the room quietly. Nobody watching the scene would have guessed, but then, and later, Juan Olmedo was thinking only one thing: 'Don't cross me, Mr Tasty Bread, do not cross me.'

By the time Damián Olmedo crossed his brother Juan for the last time, Tamara was ten years old. 'Well, if it isn't Mother Teresa of Calcutta herself! What's the matter? Look, Juanito, one of these days I'm going to punch you so hard you won't know what's hit you, is that clear? I'm a grown-up. I'm thirty-seven years old and I can do what the hell I like, get it? I don't have to justify myself to anyone, least of all you, so get out. Now!' El Canario's real name was Amador, but he liked to say that there was no one in the whole of Villaverde with the balls to call him that. Tamara hadn't liked the doll's house. It was very big, very pretty, and, above all, very expensive – a crazy, ridiculous present for a little kid who wouldn't know how to appreciate it – but it was what she wanted. Damián had told him so two days earlier on the phone: 'She wants a doll's house,' so Juan had bought her one. 'I don't know what the hell you think you're doing in my house at this time of night, waiting to tell me off. What are you, my wife or something? Who do you think you are, you wanker?' El Canario had never known his father, and would probably have preferred never to have known his mother. Everyone knew her, her name was Benigna, she worked in a bar and she drank – anis, wine, vermouth, beer, whatever was left in the customers' glasses. Of course she wanted a doll's house! Tamara was crying, in her new dress with tiny bunches of grapes embroidered on the collar, a green ribbon in her hair. 'I wanted my daddy to give me the doll's house, not you, my daddy.' 'Why don't you just fuck off, Juanito? I didn't get home earlier because I couldn't. So what? If Tamara's in a mood, she can just shake herself out of it. What's the problem? You were here, weren't you? You're the saint, after all, everyone's grandmother.' El Canario wasn't from the Canary Islands, he was born at the Doce de Octubre Hospital, like everyone else in the area, and his mother was from Valdepeñas de Jaen, but they called him that because he went to a gym to do Canaries wrestling. It was one of Benigna's lodgers who introduced him to it, a sales rep from Teruel known only by his surname, Parra, who was fond of the boy. Because of this, and because he'd met a boxing coach by chance, and because he watched lots of films on TV, and because El Canario was always bunking off school and hanging around on the streets, smoking joints and kicking empty bottles about, he took him to the gym. The boxing coach could see immediately that El Canario would be no good at boxing – he wasn't agile or flexible enough – but he suggested that with such a great big body, the boy should maybe try Canaries or Graeco-Roman wrestling. Damián hadn't appeared all afternoon. By the time Juan arrived at around six, his sisters were there with their children, and some of Tamara's school friends. Others arrived over the next quarter of an hour. After that, no one else arrived until the children's parents came to collect them at around eight thirty. The birthday cake was still sitting, untouched, in the middle of the dining-room table, with two red candles in the shape of a one and a nought. Tamara refused to blow out the candles and cut the cake until her father arrived, but her father didn't arrive, and some of the children kept asking if there wasn't going to be a birthday cake at this party. To play for time, Trini brought out the *piñata*, and then, at eight o'clock, Paquita ran to the nearest shop, bought the first cake she saw, ran home with it and gave each child a slice, except her niece who had a terrible tantrum and locked herself in the bathroom, crying because her father wasn't there. The second cake was as big as the first, but when Juan offered to pay his sister for it, she said there was no need. It hadn't cost her a penny because the nearest cake shop was, of course, Damián's. 'Come on, let's have the cake now.' 'Are you sure?' 'Yes. I'll grab Tamara, we can sing Happy Birthday to her and have the bloody cake, even if it is three in the morning and her birthday was yesterday, I don't care.' 'You know what, Juanito? Do you remember Papa? Well, I'm starting to feel like him – I've had it up to here with your superior little tone, up to here!' El Canario respected Parra because he didn't sleep with Benigna, and for a time he took going to the gym quite seriously, although he refused to give up smoking or drinking beer, and he stopped running when he'd had enough rather than doing the extra five or six kilometres he was supposed to. But somehow he won his first fight. Then he lost three, won another two, lost three fights in a row and gave it up, but his record was more than enough for a legend to grow. 'You'd better watch out, that guy's a champion wrestler!' El Orejas, a skinny boy with glasses who was always keen to play the role of right-hand man, would warn whenever El Canario lost his temper. And whoever heard him would be out of there like a shot, but not before hearing the phrase that El Canario, the hardest gang member in

Villaverde Alto, made famous in all the districts this side of the river: 'Don't cross me, boy, don't cross me.' Tamara was refusing to come out of the bathroom. Meanwhile her friends were getting their coats and their goody bags, leaving without asking any questions, but looking at their parents with an expression that spoke volumes. Juan had lost count of how many drinks he'd had. He got himself another one and then sat down in the corridor outside the bathroom, attempting to talk to Tamara. Before this, he'd said goodbye to his sister Trini, who rushed off saying she had to give the kids their baths and supper. As he watched them leave, he reflected that he really ought to do the same. He had a dinner date and nothing was forcing him to stay there in Damián's house, trying in vain to reason with a distraught child, when he was pretty sure it would do no good. Tamara had become unbearable recently – capricious, tyrannical, irritable – an expert at emotional blackmail, although she didn't yet know that it worked because her victims were aware that she was alone, and that her mother's death had brought the sudden, spectacular abandonment by her father in its wake. Juan should have left, he should have decided to ignore Tamara's tantrum, but he stayed, and spoke for a long time outside the locked door. He talked about traffic jams and unforeseen events, of the pressing business that adults engaged in and the way things became complicated, of what it meant to love someone. At a quarter to ten, Paquita said she had to leave, but Tamara refused to say goodbye to her. Juan poured himself another drink, drank it, ate a tuna sandwich and a handful of crisps, and had time to refill his glass again before Tamara finally emerged from the bathroom with a red, tear-stained face. Juan should have left, he should have turned his back on it all, but he stayed, because that was his nature, his character. As she came out of the bathroom, his niece told him that what she'd said earlier wasn't true, that she had liked the doll's house, a lot, and Juan Olmedo reflected that the world would be a better place if his brother Damián weren't living in it. 'So what if Tamara's unhinged? What d'you think I am? Every time I see her, I see her bitch of a mother. I can't help it, I just can't. It's not my fault, Juan, I didn't want to have any children, you know that. When Charo got pregnant, I didn't want children. But that's the least of it. Marrying that woman was the worst thing that ever happened to me, it was the worst fucking decision I ever made. So leave me alone and stop pissing me off, will you?' El Canario's enemies said he liked to be hit, that he looked for it, and that's why he only fought with opponents who were stronger and more dangerous, more violent than him. It was true that he often took a beating and was out of circulation for a few days afterwards, reappearing with split eyebrows, reeking of disinfectant. But Juan Olmedo preferred the other version, the one his friends, his loyal followers put about – the official myth of the local hero who never picked on the weak, never mistreated anyone he had an advantage over, but just dealt with insults from any fool who dared challenge him. The most he'd do would be to lift someone by the lapels and then drop him, giving him a couple of slaps and the same warning as always: 'Don't cross me, boy, make sure you don't cross me again.' Juan really admired him for it, and felt a strange sympathy towards him. The others – El Rubio, El Chino, El Choto, El Toledano, the leaders of the other gangs – scared him, and he crossed the road when he saw them, but not if El Canario was around. Like every other kid in Villaverde Alto, Juan knew that no one would dare make fun of him. Damián, on the other hand, didn't like El Canario at all. He thought he was weird, vicious, that he had an insane glint in his eye, as if his mind were always elsewhere. Juan didn't find El Canario odd, only sad sometimes, a strange, intense melancholy that he recognised only many years later, and which could be summed up in a single word: tormented. Juan had had too much to drink. He knew he'd had too much, but he went on drinking, and eating methodically between drinks so as to diminish the effects. The alcohol plunged him into a blank, elastic state in which he was selectively lucid. A couple of weeks earlier, the maid who worked at Damián's had phoned Juan at eight thirty on a Sunday morning. The master of the house had got home an hour before to find Alfonso still up, masturbating in front of the TV, watching an Open University programme in which a young, pretty teacher was explaining the correct use of the preposition 'off'. Damián had flown into such a rage that he'd gone to the kitchen for scissors and threatened Alfonso with them. Alfonso's screams had woken Tamara, who'd seen her father brandishing the scissors, and had started screaming even more loudly than her poor uncle. The maid didn't know what to do. By the time Juan got there, smiling, now he'd got over the shock, at his younger brother's grammatical perversion, Damián had gone to bed, Alfonso was still crying on the sofa, and Tamara was attempting to comfort him, as if he were some monstrously large doll. Juan took them out and spent all morning telling them stories about Damián, when he was still called Dami and was the quickest, the most cunning, his best friend. They arrived home for lunch in a much better mood. As they were having pudding, Damián appeared in his pyjamas, with a big smile, wanting to put everything right. But he didn't apologise. In this, he resembled Charo – she never apologised either. 'Don't bring up the business with Alfonso now, for fuck's sake. You didn't really think I was going to cut off his prick, did you? Though frankly, for all he uses it . . . I just wanted to give him a fright, that's all, a bit of a shock, it's the only way he's going to learn. If he lives in my house he's got to follow my rules. I pay for his upkeep, for everyone's upkeep around here, and I don't want him sitting around wanking all day. It drives me crazy, seeing him go at it like that, with that stupid look on his face. And don't say you'll take him to live with you, because you're not taking him, and you're not putting him in any kind of home either. He's going to carry on living here and I'm going to make him stop doing it, because if he doesn't, I'll have him operated on and that'll fix him. One less problem for him and for me. I've already made enquiries – it's not difficult, or dangerous. And don't give me your opinion because I don't need it. Some doctors believe in . . . What's the matter? Why are you staring at me like that? Don't you dare look at me like that again, d'you hear me? I'll fucking punch you, Juanito.' The only thing Damián admired about El Canario were the girls he hung about with. Juan had noticed them too, it was impossible not to, like not noticing a shiny red Ferrari stopped at traffic lights. Sometimes they were blondes, sometimes they were brunettes, once there was even a redhead, with tiny freckles on her cleavage – it made you dizzy just looking at them, let alone imagining what she was like lower down. They were spectacular, amazing girls, but none of them lasted very long with El Canario. You'd just got used to seeing one when he'd appear with another, and by the following weekend he'd already found a new one, drop-dead gorgeous like all the others. It was as if, instead of a diary, he had one of those salacious girlie calendars, but with real women, just for him, and he tore off a new page whenever he felt like it. The truth was that afterwards, those girls didn't seem all that great. Juan realised it one afternoon when he saw the redhead in the street. She was on her own, in jeans and a navy T-shirt, hair tied back, wearing no make-up – an ordinary girl, like so many others, in white plimsolls, carrying a bag of shopping in each hand. But it was her, the same girl who'd set the pavement on fire two or three weeks earlier, in the days of her ephemeral reign, when El Canario had his arm around her, stopping to feel her up every so often, because he liked that, pawing his girlfriends, kissing them, displaying them in public for all to see. And the girls reflected the light of the local hero, it shone through their bodies, enveloped them like a benign spell, making it impossible not to look at them and desire them, so pretty, so made-up, in high heels and the tight clothes they wore for him, smiling – sluts, favourites, smug whores with a big smile on their faces because they were so pleased with themselves. Juan Olmedo knew that Damián didn't mean what he'd said about Alfonso. He wanted to believe that Damián didn't mean it. But Damián had indeed considered having Alfonso operated on, perhaps he'd even consulted someone about it. Standing at the top of the stairs, leaning one hand against the wall and gripping the banister with the other to block Damián's path, Juan remembered a piece of paper, and Nicanor stuttering as he tried to explain, eyes fixed on the carpet. He couldn't understand what Nicanor wanted, or how he knew this doctor whose surname was Miguel (at first Juan thought it must be his first name), or what his relationship was with him that he was asking Juan not only to sign a mysterious letter of support, but to pass it round his colleagues at the hospital as well. 'Give it here,' said Damián impatiently. 'Look, Juanito,' he said, 'I'll explain everything. It's all been a misunderstanding, a huge and terrible misunderstanding. The loonies adore him, they adore José Antonio. It's logical, they're alone, they've been abandoned by their families, most of them don't have anyone at all, so they pay for the residential home out of their pensions or their savings.' 'Who's José Antonio?' interrupted Juan. 'Miguel, José Antonio Miguel,' clarified Damián, and then Juan understood, the strange combination of names jogged something in his memory. Someone at work had mentioned the case and he'd heard something about it on the radio – a very profitable, and particularly repugnant racket dreamed up by one or more of the psychiatrists at a private clinic not far from Juan's hospital. They obtained legal guardianship of patients who had no relatives with the excuse that it was necessary to preserve the interests of the patient, but then they sold their property and pocketed the proceeds. On the surface, it appeared clear-cut, easy, legal. 'He's their heir, d'you see, Juan? José Antonio's their heir because they've left it all to him. Poor things, they're alone, they don't have anyone, and the loonies adore him so they leave everything to him. He looks after them, takes care of them. It's all been a huge misunderstanding.' 'Nicanor's getting a cut,' Juan realised then, 'I bet he gets a cut. They get him to check things out, and in return, he gets some of the proceeds.' 'He's a friend of ours and he's a good man, he'd do anything for them,' Damián went on. 'He might end up in prison through no fault of his own, so that's why his colleagues at the clinic have written this letter to express their support, and we'd like you to sign it and pass it around your friends. We need all the signatures we can get.' In the end, the case was dismissed through lack of evidence, as often happens when the only witnesses – who in this case were also the victims – are mentally ill, their testimony dis-counted as a matter of course. The letter never became public. Juan wasn't surprised. No doctor with any con-science would ever sign such a document. So in three or four years' time Dr Miguel would still be working in a clinic, maybe even the same one. He might be one of the doctors that Damián had mentioned who was in favour of operating on poor Alfonso. Juan knew that Damián had meant it. The world would be a much better place if his brother and his friends weren't living in it. 'Let me past, Juanito, for fuck's sake. Let's have a nice birthday party for Tamara. I've come back to have a shower and change my clothes, and then I'm going out again. Nicanor's waiting for me with some girls. You've had your say, so let me past, Juan. Just get out of my way! Do you really want me to punch you? Shit! If you weren't such a poof, I'd tell you to come with us, see if we could wipe that holier-than-thou look off your face.' When they were kids, they never fought. Later, when they were teenagers, they started fighting a lot, too much. In those days the younger Olmedo was no threat, but the older wasn't capable of holding back for long. Dami was quicker and more experienced, but Juan, to everyone's – including his own – surprise, could be much more violent than his brother. So they were more or less equal, though Damián would never admit it. El Canario didn't know this either. One Saturday, Juan had caused a row between them, although he didn't feel responsible. He'd put on one of Damián's shirts that he really liked because he and his friends were going to a cinema in Madrid, as they called the centre of town, as if they lived in a different city. The girls were coming too, but Damián wasn't. He was grounded, because he'd had some bad marks at school, so it made no difference to him if Juan wore the shirt – it was just lying in a drawer. Juan had asked if he could borrow it and Damián had said no. Their mother had intervened, suggesting then ordering Damián to lend it to him. In the end, Juan had just grabbed it. He had already left the house when Damián appeared on the street, snorting like an angry bull, and Juan didn't know what to do, because the others were waiting for him at the corner. His brother took advantage of his indecision. He headbutted him, knocking him to the ground, flung himself on top and raised his fist, but then suddenly disappeared. Juan, who had closed his eyes, opened them to see El Canario releasing Damián's shirt collar, having dragged him off. 'If you want to be a hard man, pick on people who are stronger than you are, idiot,' El Canario said to Damián. 'Leave me alone, Canario,' Damián answered, 'keep your nose out of my business.' El Canario laughed, made as if to punch him, and laughed again. 'Don't cross me, boy,' he added, smiling, 'just don't cross me.' Then he turned to leave, but Juan jumped up, unbuttoned the shirt as quickly as he could and called after him: 'Hey, Canario!' Naked from the waist up. Juan ran up to Damián, flung the filthy shirt at him and continued after El Canario. 'I'm stronger than he is, Canario,' he said, 'I'm stronger.' El Canario looked at him and smiled, but said nothing. In those days, Damián was taller than Juan. Everybody thought it would always be like that, but Juan grew more later on, until he was taller than Damián. The evening of Tamara's birthday, as Juan stood at the top of the stairs, Damián seemed shorter than ever. He'd lost a lot of weight very quickly, but he still had a paunch, like a pregnant woman's belly. He looked old, he was almost always drunk these days, and he was hard — so hard that sometimes Juan thought he could have stuck a pin in his arm and Damián wouldn't have felt a thing. Damián ate cream cakes, drank malt whisky, and snorted over a gram of cocaine every day. Juan liked cocaine, but he didn't like his brother. Damián didn't like himself much either, although he didn't realise it. There were many things he didn't know about himself, above all that he'd always been a weak man, with a personality as soft and fragile as the cakes he devoured without savouring them. Whenever he saw Damián stuffing a cake into his mouth, it always struck Juan Olmedo that this was what Damián's life had become — swallowing without chewing, missing out on the taste of things, the contrasts. Perhaps this intrinsic weakness was why Damián hadn't been able to handle Charo — bittersweet and salty, bitter and acid, and sweeter afterwards if need be — while she was still alive, or to get over the supreme insult of her death. Juan had never managed to understand her, but in loving her and banging his head again and again against the arbitrary walls of her maze, he'd learnt to anticipate her movements, and he'd never understood how Damián and Charo had ever managed to live together in the same house for so many years. That night, seven months after his sister-in-law's death, he was left with two theories. The first, and best, was that Damián, deep down, didn't care much about his wife's fate. The second theory was that they were both so alike that nothing, except death, could ever separate them. The second theory was the correct one. Juan feared this when his brother picked the only argument that he, Juan, did not want to hear. 'Please don't give me a sermon, Juanito, for God's sake. I don't care about my health, I've already told you. So I'm not well? I know I'm not, of course I know that. I told her clearly, from the beginning, "If you ever cheat on me, I'll kill you." Well, she cheated on me but I didn't kill her. In the end she killed herself, she killed herself while she was cheating on me, the bitch. How can I get over something like that? You don't know what you're talking about. I could have accepted anything between us, anything but that, shit, everything but that. She was a hell of a woman, Charito, she was unique. And she killed herself cheating on me. And I hate her for it, I hate her. I forgave her lots of times, you know, and she forgave me even more, but I just can't forgive her for this. I'd kill her right now, kill her even though she's already dead, that would be enough. How on earth could I be all right, Juanito, how?' After that Saturday afternoon, which ended up with no cinema, no girls, no shirt – the shirt Juan liked best perhaps only because it wasn't his, because it was Damián's – El Canario began to acknowledge him when they passed in the street. Juan would greet him back with a brief, sober wave of the hand, the way men are supposed to, and he was very conscious of how this almost incidental deference conferred a prestige upon him that he'd never enjoyed before. In the sixth year of the *bachillerato*, Juan Olmedo picked up a girl for the first time, and for one wonderful, magical term, he went out with one girl after another while El Orejas, El Rubio, El Chino, El Choto, El Toledano all learnt his name and called out to him with a friendly grin from across the street. The older Olmedo, so serious, always so polite, such a nice boy, started pulling up a chair to El Canario's table without being asked and having a beer with him, and this was where he learnt about turning the handle of a knife when the blade's already inside a body, and that it was good to hit someone with a battery in your hand, if you were stupid enough not to have with you a sugar cube that had been soaked in brandy and left to dry. 'So that it crystallises, of course,' said Juan the first time he heard this advice, understanding the trick and its advantages. El Canario had laughed. 'So that it what?' He'd never heard the word 'crystallise' before, he seemed almost proud of it, and patted Juan on the back. 'You'll go far, Juanito! Shit! You'll go far!' El Canario might not have known the word 'crystallise' but he knew lots of other things. Juan never got him to pass on a girlfriend, or get her phone number for him, or to give him advice on winning a girl over. El Canario did this for his other mates, but to Juan he always said the same thing: 'Who, that one? No fucking way, she's a slut, she'd be no good for you. Trust me, I know what I'm talking about. She's OK for El Orejas, he couldn't get anything better, but you, you'll go far, Juan.' But then, one afternoon, he asked Juan if he'd like to go for a walk as far as the barracks. Juan thought he must want to buy some hash, and said yes, he'd go with him. They walked for quite a while, just the two of them, chatting about all sorts of stuff, official fights and street fights, referees and scores, champions, broken noses and broken dreams. Until they reached a fence, just a fence like any other. 'Let's sit down for a while?' El Canario suggested. Juan agreed, and thought they must be waiting for a dealer. He couldn't understand why they'd come all this way to find one, maybe it wasn't hash El Canario had come to get – this is what Juan was thinking when El Canario put a hand on his shoulder, pressed himself against him, and then started to stroke his back as he brushed Juan's nose with his own. 'Wouldn't you like to come to the gym with me one day?' he said, his hand moving down Juan's back, his lips brushing Juan's face. 'You've got such a good body.' 'Don't speak to me like this, Damián,' Juan thought, 'don't tell me all this, don't make me feel sorry for you, you bastard.' He needed all his pity for himself by then; he had none left over for his brother. Damián had never spoken of love before, neither when Charo was alive nor later, when he'd collapsed with a single word on his lips, 'whore', as if he'd sworn never to call her by her name again. Juan had made the most of Damián's weakness, his bitterness, the brutal magnitude of his stupidity, which confirmed Juan, once again, as the best, the most intelligent of the three. He couldn't accept any other version, any other reality – it would be unbearable. Jealousy gnawed at his insides like a dog maddened by hunger, a dry, burning sensation that warped everything around him, just like before, when he'd asked God to do whatever he liked, as long as he gave Charo back to him. The time for jealousy and anger was past, but Damián's hoarse lament had reminded Juan that he was still the third, now, still, always. The best, but always the third. 'I was the one who had a unique relationship with her, you son of a bitch. It was me who forgave her anything, even the grotesque mockery of her death and her shattered body.' When his memory began to play tricks on him, Juan Olmedo finally moved aside to let Damián past. He moved down two steps and they were level. They could have passed each other for the last time that night if Juan had done what he should have done, if he'd left quickly, and gone home. But he was thirsty. He'd had a lot to drink but he was still thirsty. Maybe nothing had ever been true. Maybe Charo had told Damián everything she did with Juan, what she said to him and what he said to her, what she asked for, what he promised. Maybe they had laughed, the two of them, together in bed, after Charo had made Damián forgive her for her umpteenth marital infidelity in the only way she knew how. 'So what, Juanito?' he asked himself. 'What does any of this matter now?' But it mattered because it bothered him. He should have left, but he didn't, because he could be much more violent than his brother. To everyone's surprise, including his own, Juan was still the more violent of the two, and this violence had become part of his personality, his nature. Juan poured himself another drink, telling himself it would be his last, and slowly went back upstairs. When he got to the top, he heard the shower and told himself again that the world would have been a much better place if his brother hadn't been in it. 'Are you still here? Shit, you've really got it in for me tonight! Or are you just dead drunk and you can't leave because you can't see straight? Don't worry, I can take you home. You really shouldn't drink, Juanito, you can't take it. And I'll tell you something else, you've been drinking too much lately. Ha! What do you think of that? I know how to lecture too, it's easy. You shouldn't drink because you're the good one. That's your thing: being good. That's why you spend your whole life pissing me off. Don't look at me like that, Juanito, I've already told you. How about a line? It might clear your head.' El Canario was still stroking his back very slowly, as if he were in no hurry, as if he could wait all day for Juan to answer him. Juan was looking at him with his eyes wide open. He didn't know what to say, how to refuse without offending him, how to reject him without losing him for ever. He wasn't scared of him. The last thing he wanted to do was go to a gym with him, but he wasn't repelled or embarrassed – he admired him too much for that. He was stunned and totally confused, but he'd begun to understand a few things. El Canario smiled at him with parted lips, show-ing the tips of his teeth, not yet knowing, or perhaps guessing how Juan felt, and at that moment Juan would have given anything to turn back time, wind back the last half-hour of his life. 'No, I don't think I will,' Juan said at last, stumbling over his words. 'Go to the gym. No, better not.' 'OK, mate, that's fine.' El Canario took his hand from Juan's back after caressing it one last time, regretfully, like an abandoned lover. Then he smiled a strained, false smile. 'Don't try to be nice, Canario, shit,' Juan thought but didn't say it. He said nothing as they walked back, more quickly than before, taking all the short cuts back towards the buildings and lights, to the street where the fighter's friends and current girlfriend – a brunette with large breasts who drew a beauty spot just above her top lip – were waiting. Neither of them spoke, but El Canario was humming a rumba about birds and stray dogs, accompanying himself by clapping from time to time. 'Do me a favour,' he said to Juan quietly when the bar's neon sign came into view in the distance, 'don't tell anyone about what happened this evening, OK?' 'No, of course not,' said Juan, 'I swear I won't, Canario.' Two minutes later, El Canario looked and sounded quite different. 'No luck!' he announced, slapping his thigh, and the others, who had no idea what he'd gone looking for, laughed as he sat down, grabbed his girlfriend by the shoulder and squeezed her, 'Shit, Canario, you're hurting me', and he kissed her on the mouth. 'Have a beer, Juanito,' only after this display did he look at Juan again, 'it's on me.' Juan wanted to leave, he didn't feel like staying there, but he stayed and had not one beer but two, because he'd sworn he'd never tell anyone what had happened and that was exactly what he was going to do. Afterwards, he got up and headed home like any other evening. He passed his house and kept on walking. Walking slowed down his heart but it brought tears to his eyes and he let them slide gently down his cheeks. He knew he wasn't crying from sadness, but he didn't really know why he was crying, perhaps because of the beating El Canario would go looking for the next day, or because the world was upside down, or because he was suddenly angry at everything. For once, Juan Olmedo thought his brother was right. It was true that he'd been drinking a lot lately, too much, but he couldn't reconcile himself to his memories. He missed her – so much, so intensely, so desperately, that every night when he went to bed he heard her last question, the one he'd thought would be rhetorical: 'What do you bet you'll regret it?' He drank to rid himself of the obligation of replying, of admitting that he'd never forgive himself for having abandoned her. When he was sober, it was much worse, because then he could clearly distinguish truth from lies, the real lies from the merciful ones, Charo's lies from his own. She would have killed herself even if he hadn't left her a few months earlier. Things would have been just the same if he'd let her come back, let her ring the bell, drop her handbag on the floor, throw herself at him, bind him with the ties of her own pleasure, her own anxiety, her own miserable and irrevocable ruin. He'd always known that Charo was ruinous, but he had never been able to choose any other direction. There was no way out, and there never had been, either at the beginning or the end, and when he was sober it was worse. This was why he had been drinking so much lately, and the reason he fell into bed every night whimpering like a fool, with a futile belief in his own qualities, his nobility, his moral superiority. 'I loved you, I would have done anything for you, because I loved you more than you knew, more than you deserved, I loved you.' What a fool. And yet, anything was better than accepting the truth, that Charo, in her cruel, incomprehensible way, had always been loyal to Damián, that he, Juan, had merely been one of her lovers – the most transgressive, secret and enduring – but just one more, and that she had tired of him, and had allowed him to believe that he was leaving her. But he wasn't sure of this either. He wasn't sure of anything, except that he was thirsty. He recognised his thirst and he drank. 'Well, yes, I'm going to do a line here, so what? This is my house, and I'll do what I want, wherever I want, whenever I want. Look, Juan, just leave me alone for two minutes, that's all I ask. Well, because I can't fucking be bothered to go to the bathroom to do it there! OK, OK, I'll stop shouting. I know this isn't just about the line. I bet you didn't give Charito such a hard time over it. She couldn't get enough of it, the bitch. Well, do you want one or what? No, of course you don't, not today. Today you're in Mother Teresa mode, I could tell as soon as you walked in, I could see it in your face. Bet you didn't look like that when you went crying to my wife, did you? When you snivelled down the phone to see if you could soften her up and make her feel sorry for you, because that's the only way you'd get to screw her again.' Juan never told anyone, not even when what was bound to happen sooner or later did happen. Twenty years later, when Juan saw him again in the Plaza de la Princesa, he was still faithful to the promise that had created a strange and exclusive bond between them. Since that evening neither of them had ever mentioned the gym again, but they had spent a lot of time together, alone, in silence, going for walks or sitting where no one they knew would see them – on a fence, a bench, in a bar in any district but Villaverde. El Canario often had a bruised face and an absent look. He'd throw stones into the distance but didn't laugh when he hit a billboard or wall or dustbin. 'Do you know what I'd like to do, Juanito?' he'd say sometimes. 'Set off a bomb – a fucking huge bomb – set it off, cover my ears and run away, and blow the whole fucking place up.' Juan nodded and waited for him to get over it. Then his friend gave him a tap on the back and said, 'Come on,' and was his normal self again. He looked the same but older, more smartly dressed and with short hair, when Dr Olmedo saw him coming out of a cinema with a very young boy, tall, dark, shy-looking but with something fierce in his eyes. Juan had insisted on taking Charo to the Vips café before driving her home, because that evening she'd seemed particularly eager, and he liked to keep her in that state. All his attention was directed at Charo, her movements, her hunger, but he still recognised El Canario when their eyes met by chance in the crowd that spring evening. 'Canario!' El Canario looked at Juan in surprise as if he wasn't sure whether to answer to the name any more, but then his face lit up and he strode over, arms open. 'Olmedo!' They hugged, patting each other on the back and laughing without knowing why. 'Shit, Juanito, you're all grown up!' 'How's it going? What are you up to these days, Canario? It's been ages.' 'Yes, ages.' ' "Canario?" ' asked the boy, beside them now, looking at them curiously. He seemed annoyed when they ignored him so he tried again: 'What did you call him?' 'No one calls me that any more,' said El Canario quickly, 'everyone calls me Amador now.' 'So you don't need to have balls now?' said Juan, and El Canario laughed. He put his arm around Juan and walked off, taking no notice of his companion, or Juan's. 'You always had balls, Juanito. Not much else, but you had balls.' They went into the nearest bar for a drink, ignoring the reluctant looks of their companions, and filled each other in on their lives, while the boy yawned, and Charo alternated between utter boredom and sudden fits of passion, pressing against Juan and whispering in his ear that she wanted to leave. But the two friends ignored them. They had another drink, and another, and Juan found out that El Canario had done his military service with the paratroopers, then re-enlisted and ended up as a mechanic. He now ran a garage in Villaverde, very near to where the Olmedos used to live. 'I never see you round there.' 'No, we moved to Estrecho just before you left, don't you remember?' 'Right! And now you're a doctor, a real doctor. Shit, Juanito, I knew you'd go far!' And he jerked his chin in Charo's direction, as she headed to the ladies for the third or fourth time. 'She's not my wife,' confessed Juan, and he smiled before leaning in to confide: 'Actually, she's my brother Damián's wife.' 'Fucking hell!' El Canario laughed. 'I always said you were something else! It's so great to see you, Juanito, really great.' And Juan was pleased to see him, to see him looking and doing so well, and he told him so. El Canario was a few years older than Juan, so he must have been about forty, but he looked great, his skin was firm and his eyes bright, with no sign of the tension and sadness they used to contain. They exchanged phone numbers before parting, although they both knew they'd probably never call. 'Look after yourself, Juan,' said El Canario and kissed him on both cheeks. Juan kissed him back, and they hugged: 'Be seeing you.' 'He looks like you, you know,' said Charo as they headed back to her house at last. 'Who? El Canario?' asked Juan surprised. 'No, not him, the other one. He looks a lot like you did when I first met you.' 'Really?' She nodded, and he smiled. 'You're very fond of him, aren't you?' Juan nodded – it was true, he was. 'You've never mentioned him.' Hearing a hint of suspicion in her voice, he looked at her, realised what she was getting at, and laughed. 'I've never slept with him, if that's what you're thinking.' 'Well, in that case, I can't think why you'd be friends with that fag.' 'He's not a fag, he's a good man. He always was and he always will be. That's why I'm fond of him.' 'A good man but he's still a fag,' she insisted. 'Leave it, will you, Charo?' said Juan. 'Or I'll get a taxi and you can go home right now.' She realised he was angry and didn't mention it again until he'd calmed down. 'Won't you tell me about him?' 'About who? El Canario?' Juan was caressing her. 'No, I'm not telling you.' 'Why not?' 'Because you wouldn't understand.' And he went on caressing her, wondering how he could be so much in love with a woman and not be able to share the story with her. His memory played tricks on him, deceived him, and together with the elastic blankness caused by alcohol, created a false, selective awareness. As Damián leant over the little table on the landing, Juan Olmedo said to himself that it wasn't just the line. The problem was Damián's weakness, his habit of talking endlessly, of challenging Juan, of being superfluous in a world that would have been much better without him. The problem was Damián, it had always been Damián, as he spoke of a woman Juan didn't recognise but who must be the real, the true Charo, Damián's Charo, not Juan's. Since the last night they'd spent together, Juan Olmedo, who'd always stopped himself thinking about his brother when he slept with his wife, had wondered many times what Damián would have felt if he'd heard Charo's confession, what he would have thought and how it would have affected him. Yet Juan was sure that such a scene had never taken place, that Charo had never told her husband anything, that she had lied to him. Damián had never shown any sign of knowing what was going on between Charo and Juan, neither while Charo was alive nor after the dreadful morning of her death – until tonight, when he mentioned the subject almost casually. Juan Olmedo had had a lot to drink, too much, and Damián's words – 'you snivelled down the phone to see if you could make her feel sorry for you, because that's the only way you'd get to screw her again' – bored right into Juan's brain, fermenting there and making him even more drunk. When Damián straightened up, still sniffing, Juan began to shake. He wasn't cold, he didn't feel sick, he had no other physical symptoms to explain it, but he was shaking. Charo was his life, had always been his life. The world would be a better place without Damián. Juan Olmedo had had too much to drink, far too much. He'd never felt such fury as he did then, and he felt the black, anguished silence inside himself, the profound sense of failure at his core, the terror at being betrayed by his memories. He had never before seen the true face of anger, but at that moment he could touch it, feel it burning in his eyes. But he didn't push his brother. His lips, his hands, his voice shook. But he didn't push his brother. 'What? Did you think I didn't know? I've always known. She told me about all the times you went crying to her, and what a pain in the arse you were, and how you took advantage of the time when she told you I was having an affair with one of my shop assistants. You talked her into it. You're a son of bitch, you know that, a real son of a bitch.

You didn't stop until you'd screwed her, that's what she told me, and you were always getting her to compare yourself to me, wanting to know how I did it to her, always wanting her to tell you that you were the best, that you had the biggest prick. You're a bloody fool! I even felt sorry for you. That's the truth, Juanito, you're pitiful. You're even worse than Alfonso. I mean, he's got no choice, but you – all that studying, and for what? For nothing! That's why I never said anything to you about it, and that's why I don't hold it against you, because you're fucking pitiful. So, now you know. I've always known, always.' When what was bound to happen finally did happen, the Olmedos had already moved to Estrecho. Juan was the only member of the family who still went to Villaverde, because of his classes, but he had never told anyone about El Canario. Then, one Saturday, Damián's friend Pirri called and was on the phone for almost half an hour. He told him the story in minute detail. When Damián hung up, he went straight to find Juan. 'Hey, El Canario's been caught with someone's prick in his mouth!' Juan closed his eyes and said nothing, but Damián told him the whole story anyway. 'It was on some waste ground,' he said, 'near the barracks. The other guy was really young, underage, almost a kid, it was kind of a rape.' None of this was true, only that El Canario had had a prick in his mouth. But the story was so shocking that on the Monday at school, no one talked about anything else, although everyone knew by then that his lover had been older than him, and was married. Juan didn't see El Canario that day or the next or the day after that, but on the Thursday, as he was on his way to the bus stop, he heard a loud scream and laughter. 'Canaria!' Juan saw El Canario hurrying away, head down, hands in his pockets. A group of kids was following him, taunting him. 'Hey! Canario, wait!' He must have recognised Juan's voice because he stopped. 'What's going on?' Juan rushed across the street, put a hand on El Canario's shoulder:

'Where are you going?' But El Canario didn't answer, only looked at him with his left eye – he couldn't open his right. His face was bruised, he had stitches in one eyebrow, and his lip was split. Juan wondered what he'd had to do this time to get beaten up so badly. He must have crossed the river, picked a fight in the centre of Madrid, where they didn't know him and hadn't heard the news. The group chanting taunts was getting closer, so El Canario walked on and Juan followed. 'You shouldn't be seen with me, Juanito,' El Canario said after a while. 'Why not?' asked Juan. 'Because of those idiots? I couldn't give a shit.' And then he told him what he'd wanted to say: 'Listen to me, Canario.' He made him stop, looked him straight in the eye, framed his bruised and swollen face with his hands. 'You're my brother, OK? Whatever happens, whatever you need, you're my brother, and that'll never change. Remember that. We'll always be brothers.' The group taunting El Canario was getting bored, but didn't go away. El Canario wiped a tear from his face and looked at Juan with his good eye. Then Juan, without thinking about what he was doing, leant towards his friend and kissed him on the lips. 'Well, you're right, Juan,' said El Canario at last, and his voice sounded clear and steady in the absolute silence around them. 'You are stronger than Damián, you are going to turn out to be the strongest of the lot.' Juan Olmedo didn't push his brother. He was absolutely sure he didn't push him; he didn't even touch him. Damián fell on his own, as he turned to look at Juan. Juan was leaning against the wall after moving out of his way, Damián went down a step, turned round and asked him if he thought he didn't know about him and Charo. And as he was telling him he'd always known, confident that he was going to place his foot on the second step, he lost his footing and fell down the stairs, never gaining much speed, bumping against every step, against twenty-seven of the twenty-eight steps of a long, straight staircase, the ideal staircase on which to kill yourself.

'I didn't push him.' Juan watched him fall, heard his body breaking against the steps, but all he could think was: 'I didn't push him.' He hadn't pushed him but as Damián's body reached the bottom, his head coming to rest on the last step, curled up like a sleeping child, Juan heard the sound of bone breaking. Before rushing downstairs, Juan had two thoughts. The world would be a much better place without Damián. And if his brother had hit the back of his head after such a fall, Juan would bet anything they now had a tetra-plegic in the family. His drunkenness disappeared instantly. Juan felt sober, focused and alert, as he joined Damián at the bottom of the stairs. This was something he would never be able to deny later, although he was sure he hadn't pushed him. But he would never be able to explain the sudden frenetic activity of his memory, the swift, powerful process that filled his mind with images as he rushed down the stairs. Dami sitting on the kerb, outside the house in Villaverde Alto, looking up from the gadget he was fixing and smiling at him like the best brother in the world. Charo dancing in front of the cracked mirror, in shoes that were too big for her despite the thick socks she was wearing on the hottest day of the summer. His father about to slap him, while Damián stood there, pretending to hold a microphone, doing his Rafael impersonation. Juan throwing his biology exam into the umbrella stand in the hall of his parents' flat. The taste of strawberries turning bitter as Charo told him she was leaving him because he was too good for her. The black body stocking worn by the locksmith's wife at Conchi's bar so she could earn some extra money. Damián laughing at him and asking if he'd fucked Charo yet, when she was begging for it. Charo and Damián sitting together at Mingo's Bar, he fondling her breast, she smiling as he did so. Charo tied to a chair in the school basement, sweating, exhausted, looking up at Juan, trying to show with her eyes that she understood. Damián striding around the dining-room table holding a newspaper and bellowing about creating wealth, new jobs, economic prosperity. Charo sitting at that same table, in the same dining room, and him staring into his plate of soup and saying silently, 'I love you, I love you, I love you,' not daring to look up at his brother's girlfriend. The Bay of Cadiz, the light, the comforting immensity of the ocean, and the impossible ghost that controlled his days and his nights. His mother weeping, Paca's voice, his father's death, seeing Charo in every tree, every cloud, every house, every corner of the carriage as the train took him back to Madrid, and he didn't know whether he wanted to go back or not, but he knew he still loved her. A lipstick that was a strange colour, dark and dangerous, almost brown. Elena, who was a paediatrician, and had red hair and the best backside in the hospital, and spoke German, and played the cello, and who wanted to marry him and have kids, one with red hair, the other with black hair like his father. The smell of Charo's hair, the happiness in the air around her. The princess of Estrecho, with sadness in her eyes, on the verge of tears in the Gran Vía. The urge to press on the accelerator, to leave Madrid and drive, two hundred, three hundred kilometres, until they found a hotel; the split second that urge had lasted. Charo's head on the pillow, as she told him it was his fault she'd married Damián. An orange dress, her pregnant belly, and Charo winning her most difficult bet. A newborn baby girl, dark-haired and fragile, her tiny round head peeping out from the sheet swaddling her, lying in a transparent hospital crib. The mother of this child, who was his, not Damián's, comforting him with the naked, bitter truth, because she loved him more than anyone but didn't love him enough. A different Charo, who lied and was always late, but was even more desirable, more spectacular, saying she was sorry before humiliating him, humiliating herself, trying to make him believe she no longer slept with her husband. The violence and cynicism and utter degradation, breaking up with her, insulting, hitting her, and the fear of having unintentionally become something he had never wanted to be. His love surviving, for ever. A body covered in a thick grey blanket on the hard shoulder of the old Galapagar road, the gap where her legs used to be, the absence of her caramel-coloured thighs. Damián's version of the story, that hateful but feasible version he'd mentioned so casually. And El Canario. As he reached the bottom of the stairs, Juan Olmedo thought of El Canario, who was the only brother he would have wanted, and he pictured the tear rolling down his face as he told him that he was right, he was stronger than Damián, Juan was the stronger of the two. He knelt down beside his brother's body and observed him, not touching him. The world would be a much better place if Damián were dead. He, Juan, was the stronger of the two, and Charo knew it, she'd always known it. Damián was unconscious. 'He's probably dead,' thought Juan, and Damián's version of the story, his indifference, his lack of emotion, his contempt would all die with him. It was difficult to survive such a fall. Dr Olmedo put out a hand towards the victim's head, grabbed it by the hair, lifting and tilting it towards him, and what he saw confirmed his suspicions. He'd heard right: there had been a crack as Damián's head struck the bottom step. But the impact hadn't affected the back of the neck – it was the base of the skull which was now inflamed, with blood pouring from it. A deadly blow, especially if there was internal bleeding as well. And Damián's version of the story would die with him, so that Charo would live again in Juan's memory just as he had loved her, bittersweet and salty, bitter and sour, sweeter still if she needed to be. It would be difficult to survive such a fall. Difficult, though not impossible. Almost nothing was impossible. Reviving the dead, maybe, finding a way of turning back time. Juan held his brother's head, and told himself that Damián was dead, dead, dead. He could have taken his pulse, but he was dead.

He could have tried to revive him, but he was dead. He could have checked to see if he was dead, but he was dead, and Charo would live again after having died twice, once when her lover's Audi crashed into a granite cliff on a cold, sunny April dawn, and again in the words Damián had spat at him that dreadful night. Then, Dr Olmedo laid his brother's head back on the step and in that instant his mind, or his memory, threw back at him the things Damián had said that evening: 'I'd kill her right now, kill her even though she's already dead, that would do, that would be enough.' Juan Olmedo had thought he would do it gently, but instead he dashed Damián's head hard against the step that had killed him, killing him again. He could have checked to see if he was still alive, but he didn't. It was impossible to survive such a fall. There had been a loud, unmistakable crack. Blood flowed obediently from the wound, down the corpse's neck, staining his shirt. The world would be a much better place. Damián was dead and his version of the story had died with him. Then it started to rain. It seemed impossible, but it was raining, a fine rain that landed on Damián's clean blood and on his brother's dirty hands, a downpour of tiny, dry particles, covering everything. As he struggled to understand where it was coming from, Juan Olmedo looked up. His brother Alfonso, eyes very wide, pyjama top buttoned up wrong, had grabbed Perico, the teddy bear he'd had since he was four, and couldn't sleep without, and was banging the toy's head against the handrail on the first floor. Sawdust was flying out of the bear's body, but Alfonso, oblivious, went on bashing it against the rail, again and again.

'Damián's fallen down the stairs,' said Juan, looking at Alfonso, and he was amazed at how firm, how steady his voice sounded. 'I'm trying to revive him.'

'Revive him,' repeated Alfonso, 'revive him.'

And he went on bashing the teddy bear against the handrail until there was nothing left.

Maribel's recovery was going well but then, two days after her operation, her mother burst into the hospital, wailing and weeping so uncontrollably that a nurse stopped her and made her sit down when she emerged from the lift. The nurse sent a colleague to fetch Dr Olmedo because she didn't dare leave the woman alone. When Juan arrived, he saw a woman who was much younger than he'd expected – she must have been about Sara's age – with an attractive face, her hair dyed black, wearing high-heeled sandals and a tight dress in a large flowery print that her daughter would have liked. He held out a hand and introduced himself. She grabbed his hand and kissed it quickly, repeatedly, until it was covered in lipstick smudges. Maribel often kissed his palms once her lipstick had worn off, and Juan was relieved to note this difference. He withdrew his hand as soon as he could and, suppressing the urge to speak harshly, he attempted to sound neutral, and professional.

'I'm sorry, but your daughter doesn't want to see you,' he said.

'Why not?' She leant over and took her head in her hands, tensing her fingers as if she were about to tear her hair out. 'I didn't know anything about it, I swear! I've only just found out. If I see that bastard, I'll tear his eyes out. Please, Doctor, please, I just want to see her, just for a moment. I'm her mother!'

The people in the waiting room had been staring with interest through the glass partition for some time, and some had even come to the door. A patient in a wheelchair pretended to be looking at the prices on the vending machine, and a couple of nurses stopped in their tracks, as if awaiting the rest of the scene.

'Wait here a moment,' said Juan, gently guiding her to a chair. 'Please calm down. I can't let you in to see her in this state.'

Maribel was awake, sitting up in bed with the television on, reading a magazine. She smiled when she saw him.

'Your mother's out there. She's been kicking up a terrible fuss. I'm surprised you didn't hear her from here. Look what she did to my hand.'

Maribel raised her eyes to heaven, then closed them for a moment, and tutted. Then she wearily took Juan's hand and wiped it on the sheet until all the lipstick had disappeared.

'I knew it. I knew she wouldn't want to miss this,' she said. 'She loves this kind of thing – hospitals, operations, patients . . .'

'I'll do whatever you want,' he said. Seeing that her mother's arrival was affecting Maribel less than he'd expected, he dared give her his opinion: 'But I think it would be best if you let her in to see you.'

Maribel nodded, resigned.

'All right, let her in, but would you mind staying too? I'd rather have someone else with me.'

As he left the room, Juan realised Maribel had addressed him as 'tu' again. Since she'd been in hospital, since she'd dug her nails into his arm while a nurse stuck a drip into her, she'd stopped using 'usted'. 'You do the stitches, Juan,' she'd said, 'please, you do it.' 'No, I can't do it, and I wouldn't be allowed to either,' he'd answered. 'This isn't my field, and anyway doctors never treat patients they have a personal relationship with.' At the time, he was still so agitated that he hadn't noticed the change in the way she addressed him. But now, as he walked down the corridor to fetch Maribel's mother, he wondered what it all meant, and instinctively felt that the ex-husband's knife had changed everything in some vague and as yet indefinable way. The brief, tense meeting between Maribel and her mother confirmed this impression. Maribel remained calm, while her mother, seeing that her display of grief was having no effect, switched to remorse. Maribel, who was gradually growing stronger in her hospital bed, had broken down only once, when her son came to see her for the first time.

As Juan expected, Sara had ignored his advice and, instead of ringing a babysitter and going home to rest, had stayed with the children herself. They had even ended up, all three of them, sleeping in Juan's bed. As she opened the door to Maribel's hospital room, Sara glanced at Juan, her eyebrows raised in warning, and he realised why immediately. Andrés was even paler than his mother had been when she was stabbed. He stood, frozen, motionless, at the door. Maribel, who still felt weak and couldn't move without severe pain, reacted immediately when she saw his small figure, his face as blank as a robot's. She opened her arms and called to him, but he didn't move and even, for a moment, looked away, staring at the corner of the room. Maribel burst into tears and then Andrés ran to her and huddled against her. She turned her head to one side, a grief-stricken look on her face, and made room for the child beside her on the bed. When Juan left the room with Sara and Tamara, Andrés was crying even more copiously than his mother. Half an hour later, he had calmed down but still clung to Maribel, while she looked anxious, scared by his reaction.

Her mother's visit, on the other hand, hardly affected her. Juan was pleased to see how detached, how firm Maribel was with her, and how casually, even affectionately she spoke when she said she thought she ought to leave with Juan when a nurse came to fetch him. As he walked the woman to the lift, he realised the relationship between mother and daughter would never be the same, because one of them had almost died, and the other had once sided with the man who had tried to kill her. The shedding of blood had shifted the balance of power for ever. Juan wondered whether something similar wasn't about to happen in his own relationship with Maribel. He had been pleased that she'd suddenly started addressing him as 'tu', but it also worried him more than he would dare admit. While part of him welcomed this sign of normality, another part feared it. And there were other aspects of his life, and Maribel's, that had changed.

It was inevitable. He knew he had to do it but he still waited till the last minute, the day before Maribel was due to leave hospital, after Sara had told him how Maribel's replacement (one of her cousins, a girl called Remedios, whom Juan had only seen once) was getting on.

'You see, Sara,' he began, not knowing how he would continue, as he walked her to the door. 'There's something you should know, because, well, I'm sure you've already guessed, Maribel and I . . .'

'I know,' said Sara, smiling. 'I've known for some time. I saw you one evening at a restaurant in Bajo de Guia, doing rude things with prawns.'

Juan burst out laughing.

'And you didn't say anything?' he murmured, sounding amazed, as if he couldn't believe how discreet she'd been.

'No. I thought it was none of my business. It's up to you, you're both grown-ups. But,' she said, taking Juan's arm and squeezing it briefly, 'there's something else I haven't told you, and I think you ought to know. It might be nothing but, at the end of July, a policeman from Madrid called Nicanor turned up at the development, asking questions about you. Ramón Martínez, the man from the estate agents, talked to him.' Juan nodded, trying not to show any emotion. 'Anyway, Ramón found it a bit odd because the man kept badgering him with questions, but didn't explain why. It was as if he was just checking where you were, you and Alfonso, but didn't want you to know he'd been there. Ramón didn't like the look of him at all, but he didn't mention it to you because he doesn't know you very well. Which is why he told me. I've given it a lot of thought, but it never seemed the right time to tell you. I don't know if it's important or not, but with this happening to Maribel, and the police being involved, well, I thought I ought to tell you.'

'Right,' said Juan, pacing up and down and searching his pockets for cigarettes, as if he'd forgotten he was in a hospital and wearing scrubs.

Sara took a pack of cigarettes from her bag and offered him one. They went outside and he lit up.

'It's an old story,' he said at last. 'Nicanor thinks I owe him something, but he's wrong.' He looked at Sara, put a hand on her shoulder and smiled. 'Don't worry, it's nothing serious. But thanks anyway, for being so discreet – well, for everything. And thank Ramón from me.'

Sara walked back to her car and Juan finished his cigarette. There had been two autopsies: the initial one had been requested by Nicanor through police channels after the doctor who examined Damián's body discounted an investigation into the cause of death, and then another one, of which Juan, as closest relative of the deceased, was only informed when he received the reports in the post. The opinion of both pathologists had been the same, and was conclusive. And judges would never accept the testimony of a mentally disabled man. Nicanor knew this as well as Juan did, he knew there was no case to be brought, which was why he hadn't taken any official steps, only visits and muttered warnings. Juan Olmedo knew better than Nicanor – an orthopaedic surgeon with clinical experience knows more about falls and their consequences than anyone – but when he went back to the hospital he looked dazed and there was an unbearable tightness in his chest. There had been two autopsies, two pathologists' reports, one accident and one mentally disabled man. He repeated this over and over to himself like a mantra, but it didn't help. Nicanor's perseverance, his stubbornness, worried Juan because he could find no rationale behind it. A long time had passed since Damián's death, over a year, almost two, and it seemed incredible that while his own life had changed so radically, Nicanor's continued to be anchored to the tragedy on the stairs. It seemed impossible that, in this time, nothing had happened to interest or inspire him more than the dead end of suspicions he would never be able to prove. As he drove home from the hospital that afternoon, Juan remembered finding Nicanor, more distraught than anyone, in Damián's kitchen only a few hours after the accident. He had to admit that there was something noble, even admirable, in the loyalty of this grim, silent man who always followed one step behind his brother like a shadow. He seemed to have no life of his own, neither a wife, nor children, nor a family, nor interests, no goal or purpose in life other than his work and his endless devotion to Damián Olmedo. Despite being surrounded by all sorts of people – colleagues, neighbours, friends from his youth, girlfriends – Nicanor hadn't found anyone new to protect and admire, no one to depend on the way he had depended on Damián for over twenty years. Perhaps the righteous fantasy of vengeance and the excitement of the hunt had filled the immense hole that Damián's death had left in his life. Perhaps Nicanor Martos thought of Juan Olmedo every night before falling asleep, as faithfully as a spurned lover. Perhaps he would never tire, because hating Juan, threatening him, stalking him, scaring him, was his only remaining link to Damián.

That night, Juan Olmedo couldn't sleep, but in the early hours of the morning, he managed to convince himself that Nicanor's visit wasn't a new development – it was simply another stage in the vicious circle in which Damián's friend had become trapped ever since Juan had made his one and only mistake, a simple slip. His brother was dead and buried, they couldn't exhume the body without his knowledge, and it would be of no use, because another autopsy would only give the same results as the first two. Nobody, maybe not even a pathologist, knows as much about accidental deaths as an orthopaedic surgeon. Alfonso was now living with Juan, who was his legal guardian, and any meeting or interview, whether official or otherwise, could only take place with his prior, written permission. This hadn't happened, and would never happen, because there was no point, so Nicanor's recent visit had to be just another of his veiled threats. 'I'm after you,' he'd said to Juan the penultimate time he saw him. 'Oh, really? You don't say!' Juan had replied, in a cocky tone like the one El Canario would have used. Nicanor had done nothing, because he knew there was no case to be made, all he could do was harass Juan, threaten him, first in Madrid and now perhaps here too. Juan hadn't gone into hiding, he'd travelled over six hundred kilometres and found himself in the same place he'd always been. It was mid-September. If Nicanor had managed the impossible and found evidence where there was none, Juan would have known about it by now. The police didn't take the month of August off.

Juan got up with a headache and a feeling he knew well: not exactly fear, more a state of active alert, a particular way of keeping his eyes wide open. As he walked to the car, turned on the engine and set out on the familiar route to Jerez, he berated himself for not having been more open with Sara the previous afternoon. But then he realised that the impassive front he'd adopted, out of sheer surprise, would have been more convincing than a lengthy explanation full of half-truths. Anyway, Sara could be trusted. Juan Olmedo wouldn't have been able to say why, but he was absolutely certain she could be trusted. Perhaps this was why he felt so intensely weary of silence – he would have liked to talk – but he never brought the subject up again.

This was easy, because he didn't see Sara until that evening and by then many other things had happened. After her last check-up, Maribel was allowed to leave hospital in the late morning. Beforehand, she'd announced two things: that she didn't want to have lunch at the hospital, and she didn't want to leave before him. By the time Juan managed to get away it was already four o'clock and she'd been waiting for several hours in her room. He would never know how much the news that Nicanor was still dogging his steps influenced what he felt when he saw Maribel, in a T-shirt and skirt that looked too big for her, collapsed rather than sitting in an armchair, one hand placed over her wound as if trying to protect it. Her feet were swollen and she was resting them on top of her sandals, waiting until the last moment to put them on. She had dressings on both arms, and her hair was tied back. She'd been in hospital for nine days and had lost a great deal of weight, enough to make her face seem more angular, her cheekbones and jaw more prominent than before. Dressed and ready to leave, it was much more noticeable how pale Maribel's cheeks had become, how dull her eyes, but when she saw Juan she gave him a brilliant smile that seemed to contain all the other smiles she had ever given him – the mother, the horny girl, the grateful lover, the cunning spider, the cautious libertine, the confused child, the wise old woman, the generous cook, the conspirator, the nocturnal seductress, the conscientious worker, the wounded wife, the dying lover; all the women that Maribel had been for him and through him. Juan Olmedo recognised all these women in the woman now smiling up at him, and he recognised himself in the man who went to meet her. He felt a sudden, unfamiliar urge, somewhere between the desire to possess her and the need to take care of her, and it was only then, seeing her so fragile, so helpless now that she was out of bed, that he stopped thinking about Nicanor. He told himself that without Maribel, without the opportunity to feel useful, good, generous, essential, everything would have been worse.

'Take me out to lunch,' she said after hugging him tightly, kissing him on the lips. 'I want something fried and greasy, and very salty. Please.'

'No,' he said, teasing her as if she were a child, but he couldn't help smiling. 'It's bad for you.'

'No, it's not.' She laughed. 'It's extremely good for me. I've been dying for a plate of fried squid and a beer for days. Seriously, last night I couldn't sleep for thinking about it!'

Without Maribel, everything would have been so much worse, and definitely less interesting. This thought occurred to Juan again as he watched her tuck into the plate of fried squid, hungrily devouring the first few mouthfuls, then slowing down and stopping. To her own amazement, she had to admit that she couldn't eat any more, even though the plate was still almost full.

'Maybe my stomach's shrunk,' she said, smiling as if delighted at the prospect. 'No need to diet ever again.'

'I don't think that's likely.'

'What a shame. Now that I'm never going to be able to wear a bikini again, it would at least be nice if I could stay this slim.'

'Why aren't you going to be able to wear a bikini?'

'Because of the scar.'

'Don't be ridiculous, Maribel!' said Juan, pleased to be able to reassure her, to take care of her internally as well as externally. 'The navel's a scar too, and you weren't ashamed of people seeing that, were you? This one will gradually fade and seem less obvious, even to you. Once you've got used to it, you'll stop noticing it.'

'What about other people?'

'They'll be looking at you,' he smiled, and so did she, 'not at your scar.'

Internal scars are more problematic, he might have added, but he didn't because he was looking after Maribel and it made him feel good, needed, the best once more, the most intelligent, far removed from Nicanor and his whispered threats, remote from his own mistakes. Yet it was she, keeping to the script of ambiguity that had always governed their relationship, who freed him of the responsibility of looking after her by confirming that nothing would change between them.

'Christ!' she exclaimed as she got home, looking around the tiny living room that was spotlessly clean. 'My mother must really be in a state if she came and cleaned the house.'

'It wasn't your mother,' said Juan, taking her suitcase to the bedroom. She followed, frowning in confusion. 'It was your cousin, Remedios.'

'Remedios?' Maribel sat on the bed, shaking her head as if she couldn't understand. 'Why?'

'Because I told her to. I've asked her to come over every two days, until you're better.'

'Oh yes? And who's going to pay her?'

'Me.' When he saw the expression on Maribel's face – a mixture of shock and irritation – he explained, 'It's a present.'

'Well, I'm not happy about it, OK? Not happy at all.' Juan stood in the middle of the room, looking so baffled that Maribel relented slightly: 'I'm a cleaner, don't you get it, Juan? I don't need a cleaner. It's the stupidest thing I've ever heard.'

'But you're convalescing at the moment.' As Maribel calmed down, Juan began to feel a little angry. 'Your only job is to rest, and move as little as possible until the scar has healed. That's all I wanted. If you start moving around the house, carrying things, bending down, filling buckets of water, the stitches could burst and you'd be back to square one. You can't do any cleaning, not even your own home. Not for the time being. You need someone to help you, and that's all I was trying to do – help you.'

'Right, well it was a bad idea. Things aren't like that . . .'

Still shaking her head, Maribel lay down on the bed and gestured for him to lie down beside her. She put her arms around him and put her face close to his.

'I'm sorry, it's just that . . . it's a bad idea,' she said again. 'Things aren't like that. You don't have to worry, I'll sort myself out on my own. I can call my friends, my sisters-in-law, even my mother if I have to. I don't need anyone to come and clean for me. What would it look like if you were paying Remedios to clean my place – I mean on top of everything else, she's my cousin. It's not that I'm not grateful, I am, but there are some things that just aren't OK, and this is one of them.' She paused, frowned, closed her eyes, and seemed to struggle with what she was about to say next. 'I did a lot of thinking while I was in hospital. Well, I didn't have much else to do, did I? And it's all the same now with everything that's happened, but I think you were right, at the beginning, when you said it was stupid for us to get involved. Stupid.' Juan Olmedo, who could never quite get used to the way Maribel was constantly surprising him, burst out laughing even though he didn't really understand. She laughed too, but continued, 'Very stupid. But we went ahead, and here we are. It's complicated. Very complicated. That's why I think we ought to leave things the way they are, because if they change, they'll only change for the worse. I can't really explain it, it's just I'm sure that if things do change, they'll change for the worse. I ought to go back to calling you "usted", but I don't think I'll be able to, because when I was lying there on the pavement and I saw you arrive, I suddenly knew I wasn't going to die. So I can't call you Dr Olmedo any more, I can't say "usted" to you, that's just how it is. But one word doesn't make a big difference, does it? Or does it?'

He looked deep into her eyes, understood more than she had said, and wondered how far he would be capable of going, at what point the clean, transparent pact – that Maribel had apparently willed into existence and with which she was now again offering to relieve him of any responsibility – would become unbearable, stiflingly comfortable, too narrow even for his guilty conscience. He wondered what would happen afterwards, what price he would pay to give her up or to keep her.

'But you don't have to spend your life working for me, Maribel.' The words didn't surprise him as he said them. 'You could do something else, find another job. Then everything would be easier.'

'Yes, I've thought about that,' she said with a sweet, melancholy smile. 'I could try, if you like, I could look for another job. But the thing is, I don't know how to do anything else. I have a son and lots of other expenses, and the only thing I know how to do is clean houses. I realise there are other jobs for people like me, but they pay less. A supermarket cashier might not have to get dirty or ruin her hands, but she earns less than I do. And it's not just the money. Sara and you, especially you, and your brother, and Tamara, of course, well, you're like family now. I'm very fond of you. I'm most fond of you, but I'm also fond of Sara, and I don't mind doing her favours because I like being with her. Sometimes, when I get to her house in the morning, and we have coffee together in the kitchen and chat, I almost forget why I'm there. I like working for you both and things have never been as good as they are now. But I understand what you're saying, and I know why you're saying it. So if you want, I could look for another job.'

'No, no, Maribel, that's not what I mean.' Juan shook his head and bit his lip, searching for the right words. 'I want things to be good for you. I don't know, I can't explain it either.'

'It's not your fault, Juan,' said Maribel. She took his head in her hands, stroked his face, and showed that she was the more intelligent of the two, whenever she needed to be. 'You feel bad about the way things are sometimes – I know, I can sense it – but it's not your fault, it can't be. It's my fault. I was the one who didn't apply myself at school, I'm the one who left school at an early age and got involved with that bastard, got pregnant at eighteen, and didn't know how to deal with my mother – I've done everything wrong. But that's just the way things are. I can't do anything about it, only cry over spilt milk. But I don't want to cry any more. It's not your fault, Juan, really it isn't. I feel happier with you than I've felt with anyone, but you were right, it is stupid.'

From then on, Juan Olmedo learnt to live with a paradox – he accepted the role of immoral, opportunist boss that the ex-husband's knife had assigned to him when it put an end to what could previously have been considered as simply good fun. But he did it so that Maribel would feel happy with him, and he never again put money in her hand. When she came back to work, it was a few days later than she had intended. Juan had insisted partly because he didn't want her to take any risks with her scar, and partly because he liked visiting her in the afternoons, under the pretext of examining the wound, and climbing into her warm bed. 'I'll be very careful,' he promised the first time. 'You're always very careful with me,' she answered. He asked for her bank account number and said, casually, that he'd thought it would be more convenient if he paid her wages by direct debit. She smiled and said that was fine.

So, after a warm summery September, autumn arrived, and Juan Olmedo's life reverted to its usual routine of work and pleasure. Once more, Maribel drew down the blinds on the mornings following his night shifts, a ritual that retained its symbolism even when their planned encounters began to alternate with furtive meetings on Saturdays and Sundays. And while he sometimes thought that Maribel's attitude – her insistence on never pressing him, her docility, and their private language that let him speak of love in ways that would always remain oblique and comfortably ambiguous – was simply part of her plan, things returned to how they had been before. Or at least they seemed to.

During the days that Maribel spent in hospital, and later, while she was convalescing, Sara moved Alfonso and the children into her own home. She did so as if it were the most natural thing in the world, without explaining why it was necessary – either to Juan and Maribel, or to herself. 'It seems like a good idea,' was all that Juan had said when he found out. He didn't exactly thank her, just as Sara had not exactly asked his permission when she told him what she was intending to do. But it was no longer a question of standing on ceremony or favours between them, and perhaps this was why the children didn't ask any questions either. They'd always had fun together, but this was different. Andrés and Tamara were model guests. They ate everything that was put in front of them, carried their plates to the kitchen when they'd finished, accepted her suggestion that they have their bath or brush their teeth as if it were an order, and when Sara suggested they all go out – for a walk on the beach, or a meal, or to the cinema – they never argued, although Alfonso's comical attempts to imitate them made them burst out laughing. Sara smiled as she bent down to pick up the broken plates that resulted from his clowning, but in truth she never truly felt worried about the children.

It wasn't true that children would adapt to anything, endure anything, and Sara knew this. Tamara was still very scared. She was frightened of any shadow, any noise and of strangers. A gust of wind making the awning creak, the telephone ringing late at night, the wheels of a car screeching or someone suddenly turning to ask her the time, made her tremble and turned her voice into that of a pathetic little sparrow as she asked: 'What was that? Did you hear that?' The second night of Tamara's stay, Sara couldn't sleep and she heard her coming. It was twenty to four in the morning, over five hours since she'd put her to bed, but when she heard the door handle being turned slowly by a fearful little hand, Sara knew it could only be Tamara. The little girl tiptoed across the room, slipped quietly under the covers, moved her foot carefully until it was touching Sara's leg, and instantly fell asleep.

'I had a horrible dream,' she explained the following morning. 'I dreamed that I was in my old house in Madrid. I was in the bathroom, and my mother was alive, and she was brushing my hair. She kept telling me to be still, but I knew it couldn't be real, because she was dead, and I didn't dare tell her. And she just went on brushing my hair, talking to me and kissing me as if she was still alive. And she had to be still alive because I was the same age I am now, and I was wearing the dress I had on yesterday. But then I woke up, and I realised it wasn't true, of course, because Mama's dead, but I'd believed it, so it was suddenly like she'd died all over again. When she had the accident, I used to have this dream a lot. Now I only have it sometimes, but it goes away if I get into Juan's bed. That's why I came to sleep with you last night. I hope you didn't mind.'

'No, of course not.' Sara smiled. 'If you like, you can sleep with me every night, until you dream about something else.'

'Great!' Looking very relieved, Tamara gave her a kiss. 'But don't tell Andrés, OK? If he finds out he'll say I'm a baby. You know what he's like.'

But Sara didn't know what Andrés was like. At night, she would sometimes chat to Tamara for hours. The girl would ask her questions – what was her room like when she was a little girl, her school, her friends? What marks did she get and what was her favourite toy – and then she'd answer the same questions herself, attributing as much value to Sara's curiosity as to her own. Finally she'd close her eyes and fall asleep, plunging into sleep as if into a swimming pool, while Sara remained awake, thinking about her former closeness to Andrés. This special child, the first person who'd become important to her when she moved into her new home, was gradually filling up with all the screams, tears, anger and words that he hadn't allowed himself to express. Like a dam ready to burst, Andrés hadn't grieved properly over his mother's injury yet. At least not outwardly. Sara didn't know where he went when he disappeared mid-afternoon, without telling her or giving any hint of his destination. 'I'm going out,' he'd announce in neutral tones at the door, and not even Tamara dared say she'd go with him. She and Sara assumed he wanted to go out alone on his new bike – the ultra-light silver mountain bike he'd been presented with at the start of the summer – so they stayed at home with Alfonso, watching TV or baking a cake, waiting for him to come back. When he did return, he seemed as placid and calm as before, and was always ready to taste the cake, lay the table or play a game. But his willingness to join in did not conceal his complete indifference to the world around him, including them. Sara felt like shaking the boy, slapping him, forcing him to spit out the slow anger, the shame and grief that was poisoning him, turning him into nothing more than a robot. She tried to talk to him, but ended up chatting to herself when she came up against the brick wall of his silence. She would have given anything to wake him up and convince him that whatever happened, she'd always be there for him, she'd always be on his side. Yet she never felt truly worried about him, because it wasn't true that children would simply put up with everything, and she knew that sooner or later, Maribel's son would have to find his own path back to screaming and crying and feeling again. Sara was sure he'd manage it eventually. But still, Andrés's absence, his blank stares, his forced, empty smiles, the sudden awkwardness of his arms and legs, took her back to her anxiety in Juan's car, when Maribel had almost died and she'd felt it was all her fault.

At the beginning, there had been Andrés, so helpless, so lost in his hand-me-downs, the ridiculous flowery swimming trunks that were too big for him, and the green T-shirt that was so tight Sara could see his ribs through it when he appeared at the kitchen door, always holding one of those little toys you get inside chocolate eggs. This was how she explained her tenderness, the instant affection she felt for the child, a little boy so greedy for images, for names and sounds, for distant cities that were much more than mere points on a map, for mythic animals and real monsters, for emotion, for vivid colours, for depth. As she spoke to him and told him about her travels, as she asked him about the winds, she had fed his curiosity and turned it into faith, had given shape and solid ambition to it, before inspiring a different ambition in his mother. She never thought she was succumbing to Doña Sara's weakness in doing this. And she hadn't wanted to adopt the equivocal mantle of a benefactor when she decided to introduce a little arithmetic and common sense into Maribel's hare-brained schemes. And yet, especially at the beginning when Maribel was still so weak, Sara sometimes felt tempted to consider another version of reality. Sara Gómez Morales, with plenty of money and time on her hands, tied to the memory of the few things that had belonged to her and whose only ambition for the future was to accept her ageing, had slipped almost without realising it into Maribel's life, but hadn't recognised herself in the poor, unlucky girl, with family burdens but no home of her own, whom she'd pushed just as she'd always pushed herself.

When fate wearies of being stubborn, it is cruel, and Sara had more than enough reason to distrust patrons, philanthropists, and do-gooders. Sara knew the price of privilege, the cost that lurked on the flipside of every reward, every smile, every gift, the casual, lazy way anything good could be snatched away as abruptly and arbitrarily as it had previously been bestowed. But time doesn't progress in a straight line. Sara thought of herself, of Maribel, of things that were as they were and couldn't be changed. If Maribel had died, Sara would never have been able to forgive herself for convincing her that her life was so poor, so unfair and so thankless that Maribel would have swapped it, with no regrets, for a dream of a new, different life that had resulted in nothing but her death. But Maribel was still alive and she had survived – not Sara's good intentions, nor Juan's best intentions, but her ex-husband's knife. Time would go on passing, and some day it would start to work in her favour, to fade all the pain and fear. When this occurred, they – Sara and Maribel, Andrés and the Olmedos – might still be together in the same place, or they might be far apart, but they would always remember the events that had united them that summer. Sara was sure of this. In her mind, all the images and fragments of the story began to merge into an extravagant fictional plot that was suddenly made flesh one morning, when a loud clicking of high heels came to a stop outside Maribel's room, announcing a visitor that no one was expecting.

The woman was very young, twenty-five at most. She wore a lot of make-up and huge hoop earrings, and her hair was dyed red. Her body was rather bulky, and her uniform too tight. She unconsciously drew attention to it by tugging at the edges of her clothing all the time, never managing to smooth out the waist or stop the skirt riding up at the front. As she observed this battle, Sara got the impression that the woman's size put her in a bad mood, something that might have made her seem more agreeable had she not soon demonstrated that she was, indeed, in a bad mood. She was chewing gum, and appeared to be in a hurry, glancing at her watch as soon as she came in. She went straight over to Maribel's bed without paying attention to anyone else in the room.

'Hello. My name's Aguirre, I'm from the police.'

Sara was in an armchair beside the bed. She looked up and saw Alfonso, who was sitting on the unoccupied bed, suddenly look confused and cover his face with his hands. In the other armchair, Andrés also hid his face, bending right over and hugging his legs, resting his forehead on his knees. Tamara was standing beside him, looking bewildered and unsure what to do. Meanwhile, the woman opened a file, unfolded a sheet of paper and began reading, pointing to each paragraph with her pen, as if Maribel couldn't read.

'I'm sorry,' said Sara, standing up. She moved closer to the bed but decided it wasn't worth introducing herself. 'I don't think the children should be here for this.'

Aguirre turned round, looked at her a moment without asking who she was, and nodded.

'Yes, I've just realised that. Would you mind taking them out? And it would be better if you waited outside as well.'

'No way,' Sara thought to herself, 'no way.' She went out into the corridor with the children, and suggested they go to the cafeteria. 'I'll give you money for a milkshake, or a Coke, and chips, anything you like,' she said, 'you'll only get bored if you hang around here.' Tamara and Alfonso agreed, silently, but Andrés refused.

'No, no,' he said, and then as if two 'nos' weren't enough, he shook his head before going on: 'I don't want anything to eat or drink, and I don't feel like talking. You go if you want. I'm staying here.'

Had this been any other day, Tamara would have stamped her foot and complained: 'Oh, Andrés, you always ruin everything!' And Alfonso would have repeated her last words like a parrot: 'Ruin everything!' But that morning, they said nothing and simply sat down on the bench in the corridor. Sara was surprised by their sudden unanimity, but couldn't detect anything new or different between them. Aguirre, on the other hand, reminded her of the midwife who had attended her many years earlier, in another hospital, when she'd had her ectopic pregnancy and all her plans came crashing down around her ears. Sara had also been in a bad mood, fed up, tired and desperate to go home. 'I feel terrible, absolutely dreadful,' she'd said at last, tired of the midwife's resentful looks and her impatience, 'don't you understand?' The midwife looked down her nose at her and replied, 'Well, if only you knew how I'm feeling,' and at that moment Sara hated her more than she'd ever hated anyone before. Later, lying numb and alone, with the rest of her life ahead of her, she was amazed by how violently she had reacted, how viciously she had inwardly wished the woman dead. 'Die, you bitch!' she repeated to herself like a litany, a spell to escape the long tunnel she felt she was in. 'Die, you bitch!' The midwife had simply been in a hurry, wanting to finish things off and go home. Perhaps she had problems as serious, as bad as Sara's, but still Sara had wished her dead, and she wasn't about to leave Maribel on her own, wishing the policewoman dead. When she went back inside the room, closing the door behind her, the woman didn't even glance at her. She'd stopped listing the resources that the State made available to victims of domestic abuse and was addressing Maribel in a different, more direct tone.

'There's nothing to think about, seriously, take my advice.' She glanced at her watch, took out a pile of forms, and went on: 'If you don't report the assault, you risk not only a second attack, but also becoming your attacker's accomplice.'

'I know, I know, it's just that . . .' Maribel was looking at her, shaking her head, then turned her gaze towards the window. 'I don't want to think about it right now, not yet. I need to get this right and I have to discuss it with my son first. It is his father.'

'No, at this point, he isn't his father.'

'Of course he is!' Maribel sat up and looked at her, wide-eyed with amazement. 'He'll always be his father, and there's nothing I can do about it.'

'No,' the woman said again, wearily, giving a speech she must have repeated a thousand times. 'Now he's your attacker, and that's all. Do you understand? That's the only thing that matters. And, as I told you, he's on the run. He's not at his place of residence. This is very serious. I'm not sure you realise quite how serious it is.'

She was absolutely right, but listening to the way she spoke and her offhand tone, Sara felt that it would almost make you want to side with the enemy. Sara could detect the first signs of weakening in Maribel. Having been so strong during the worst times, she was now on the point of cracking, about to give in faced with the impatience of a woman who seemed entirely without compassion. Sara wondered if Aguirre was always so insensitive, whether she was still so hard-faced when she was out of her too-tight uniform. The woman didn't know how to combine the essential in-gredients for her job in the right amounts: her authority suggested simply hostility, her inexperience was disguised as superiority, and her inability to judge the right tone made her sound contemptuous and made the victim feel like a criminal. Just then, Juan Olmedo came into the room and he glanced questioningly at Sara. Maribel had been unlucky, very unlucky, once again. Andrés was still so young, and he was so lost, so confused, so determined not to cry, that Sara couldn't help picturing his small, dark, fleeting form as she listened to Maribel.

'You're right, you're absolutely right, I know, but I'd like to think about it, and talk to my son. It may not seem important to you but . . .'

'But he almost killed you!' Aguirre raised her voice, showing that she still had a little more patience to lose. 'Two days ago he tried to kill you and now you're telling me this? How could I possibly understand? I'm sorry about your son, but he'll have to face up to what's happened sooner or later. Really, I don't understand you – you, or all the other women like you. I just don't understand.'

'But all I'm asking for is a little time. I'm not intending to forgive him – I'd never do that, I swear.'

'Sometimes I think you all deserve what happens to you.'

This was too much. Sara wondered if she'd heard correctly, and from Juan's shocked face she realised she had. She couldn't decide if it was worse that the woman had expressed her opinion aloud or that she had resorted to using such tactics. If this was part of some cunning police strategy, it definitely yielded results, because Maribel burst into tears. Aguirre was busy writing notes, so Maribel had to tug on her sleeve to get her to look up.

'Why aren't you listening to me?' Maribel said, but the woman didn't answer. 'Why don't you want to listen to me?'

'Look,' the policewoman said, looking at Maribel at last. 'I haven't got all day.'

This really was the final straw. Sara was no longer in any doubt about what she'd heard, and she tried to think of a way of intervening to end the ordeal. She would have liked to give Aguirre a piece of her mind, but Juan intervened first. He moved so fast that before Sara knew it, he'd grabbed Aguirre by the shoulders and pushed her against the wall.

'Listen, I couldn't give a fuck how busy you are, d'you hear me?' The veins in his neck stood out as he shouted, but he didn't look as if he was about to lose control. 'Don't you dare speak to her like that! Don't you ever speak to her like that again!' He was calming down now, but kept the woman pinned to the wall. He went on, his voice back to its normal volume. 'You may have forgotten, but this is a hospital. And in this room, the absolute priority – the single, absolute priority – is the recovery of the patient. This woman has already suffered quite enough without you coming in here and making her cry. I will not allow you to stay here one moment longer. So, please leave, now.'

Sara smiled inwardly – visible satisfaction would have been unseemly. And it wasn't simply a question of the delight of the spectator witnessing a desired outcome, the ending she'd hoped for, for each character. There was something else, a mysterious feeling of solidarity that Sara couldn't yet define, a sense that she was sharing something more than this small victory with the wounded woman who had now closed her eyes, as if mortified at being the cause of such a scene, and with the man with a grim face, still magnificent in his fading anger, silently watching the intruder who was bending to gather up her papers that had fallen to the floor. The whispering that had been going on for some time behind the door now stopped, and the door opened timorously as the children peered in. Tamara's eyes were huge, startled, and Andrés's were also wide open and tense, like the fists of one condemned always to expect the worst. In the eyes of these clean, well-fed, well-dressed children, Sara could recognise the identical gaze of other children – dirty, ragged and undernourished – but who were just as alone, and just as frightened.

'What's happened?' asked Tamara in a tiny voice, pronouncing every syllable carefully.

'Nothing.'

Sara smiled and opened the door wide, but she didn't let them in. Instead, she went out into the corridor with them, and suddenly all the images, all the fragments of different stories, joined together in her imagination in an extravagant fictional plot – the adventures of a group of humans lost in space, abandoned together on a strange planet with a hostile but breathable atmosphere. This was how she had felt, how

Alfonso probably always felt, how the children were probably feeling now, and Maribel, and Juan, about the arrival of a stranger whose surname was Aguirre and whose first name they would never know, but who, by the simple fact of existing and being as she was, had awakened in them an absolute, violent need to get rid of her. She was the key that made Sara Gómez Morales, who had never been anything completely and never had a home to return to, understand that she belonged to them, to Juan and Maribel, to Alfonso, and to the children, and they all belonged to her, because something more crucial than love, than fear, more than pleasure or the need to live together, had united them at that moment, in that place, making them strong as long as they were together.

'Nothing's happened, don't worry,' Sara repeated, sitting down on the bench. Alfonso was crying very quietly, as he always did when he heard shouting, and she took his hand. 'Maribel's very tired and that's to be expected, isn't it? She doesn't want to talk, and nobody should force her to. She needs to rest, but that policewoman kept firing questions at her.' Andrés and Tamara now sat down, as if accepting Sara's explanation even if they didn't entirely believe her. 'That's why Juan got cross. But he's calmed down now – you know what he's like.'

Then the door to Maribel's room opened, freeing Sara from the need to lie.

'I'm terribly sorry,' the policewoman was saying to Juan, as he saw her out. 'I may have gone too far, you're right. But compassion doesn't help in this job, that's what my boss is always saying. Anyway, I've not been having a good day.'

'I'm sorry too,' said Juan. Now that his anger had subsided, he looked as sorry as she did. 'But you really shouldn't have spoken to her like that. It's been very difficult and we're all very tired.'

This exchange of apologies appeared to be the end of it,

but in fact it was a beginning, for Sara as well as for Maribel. The following morning, Maribel asked to have a moment alone with Andrés, and after a long talk in which she still didn't quite manage to get through to her firmly closed-off son, she denounced her ex-husband in the afternoon, giving her statement to two policemen whom Juan described as much more sympathetic, and therefore more efficient, than the ill-tempered Aguirre.

By the time Andrés Niño González, alias Mr Tasty Bread, was arrested in a small town in the province of Seville in October, having been on the wanted lists for over a month, Sara was able to identify her feelings more clearly. She couldn't forget that simple chance had brought them all together, apparently selecting them at random to be the crew of this unexceptional, earthbound spaceship – two neighbouring houses by the sea. They were all survivors – they had survived a mortal wound caused by a knife, a death, a loss, a threat, the implacable misfortune of their own birth. They all had a secret, and each private secret fed their common bond, the source of the force that united them.

Sara was able to sleep again, but every morning, when she went out into the garden, she looked up at the sky. Often, she found it clean, calm, at peace with the winds. At other times, it had clouded over, or was misty. Still, it was always familiar. She never found anything worrying or strange in the blue expanse. Meanwhile, with the return of autumn, the children went back to their respective homes, and to school, Alfonso to his daycare centre, Maribel to work, and Sara to her leisurely routine of identical days in which she no longer felt alone. But still, every day when she got up, she looked at the sky, checked the direction of the wind, its nature, called it by its name, without knowing why, and waited.

The only original feature left in the apartment building was its facade. Everything else had been completely restored or renovated, including the lift, which had a mirror. As she went up to the third floor, where she'd agreed to meet the estate agent, Sara looked at herself and saw not one, but two faces, both of them alike. She was forty-two, and her hair was short, and she was also sixteen, with long chestnut hair, the ends made golden by the sun of many afternoons spent walking around Madrid. Then, as now, it was the end of summer. Then, as now, Sara Gómez Morales was herself, and another person.

'I think apartments on the upper floors of a building are much more pleasant,' the estate agent said, as she raised the blinds. Light flooded the spacious living room that had mouldings on the ceiling and a brand new wooden floor.

It was smaller than the apartment Sara had just sold, but much more expensive. The Calle Hermosilla was in that other half of the world, the exact opposite of her old district, in a different reality that would now be hers.

'This is the master bedroom. It has built-in wardrobes and an en-suite bathroom. If you're thinking of renting it out, I'm sure you'll have no trouble finding tenants. It's ideal for a young couple with a child.'

'Is the flat above the same?'

'Yes, exactly the same. Would you like to look round it?'

'Well . . .' Sara glanced at her watch. She didn't want to get home late, but she still had time. 'If you wouldn't mind.'

By the time she stood outside hailing a taxi, she'd decided to buy both of them, in order to use up every last peseta of her booty. Perhaps this was why she saw her again in the taxi window, in the streets, at the traffic lights, halfway between a memory and a character in a play, the girl with her name and longer hair, a lighter body but a heavier heart, legs that were twenty-six years younger as she rushed down the stairs of the kind of building she had never imagined she would live in again. Sara knew why the girl was running, and that she would only feel safe once she was back out in the street, breathing in the warm still air. She knew that she felt lost, ill, filled with shame and self-loathing, but she also had the strength to run like a hare, ready to do battle with whatever train crossed her path, with nothing to help her but her almost childishly agile figure. She could still feel the pain in her side, hear the miserable words with which she sought encouragement rather than solace: 'I'll get used to it.' This was all she'd managed to tell herself back then, and now she knew how true those words had been: 'I'll get used to it.' The image made her smile, and her eyes filled with tears. She'd been so young then, so good and naive, so gullible, so gauche and intransigent. She could still feel the pain in her side, and there was a taste in her mouth that was more bitter, more salty than tears. She'd kept on going, always moving forward, because she didn't know how to go in any other direction, and she'd been prepared to do anything – courses at secretarial college, at the Arce Academy, the Open University – to pay any price for a future that would never fully compensate her for all her efforts. Sara knew this and it was why, that afternoon, as she headed back by taxi to the Calle Velázquez, she would have given anything to find her, that brave, defenceless girl, to hug her and kiss her, to look her in the eyes and tell her: 'Look at me, you're like me now, one day you'll be what I am, don't forget it. When the streets shrink and the sky falls in on you, and every day seems dull and cloudy and all your love has expired, when your child refuses to be born and your parents die, and you sit and cry in the kitchen without knowing why, think of me and wait for me, because I've learnt to outrun the trains, I've found a way to take you home.'

'How did it go?' asked her godmother. She was in the sitting room watching a film, but she paused it when Sara arrived. 'Did you find anything?'

'No,' Sara said quickly, pretending to be fed up. She collapsed on the sofa and crossed her legs. 'Well, I saw a couple of things I liked, but they weren't right for a wedding. It's difficult, isn't it, a wedding at the end of October? If I get a suit, I might be too hot. If I get a dress, I might freeze. So I can't make my mind up.'

'I told you,' her godmother said, delighted to have been right. She started the film again. 'This time of year is terrible for buying clothes.'

Sara didn't set the date for the wedding she'd invented until she knew the date on which the contracts were to be signed. When she was given a morning appointment at the notary's office, she told her godmother that the wedding was going to take place in a registry office, and she even bought herself a new suit for the occasion. It was very elegant – a white jacket with black edging, and a black lace skirt – too elegant for going to the notary's and then to the bank where she'd opened a new account, into which she'd be paying the income from the flats, but nobody remarked upon it. Nor did the estate agent comment as he counted twelve million pesetas paid over in cash. Afterwards, as it was only two in the afternoon, she went – alone – to a restaurant she'd been to many times with Vicente. She told herself she chose it simply because it was near by, and because a woman her age, alone and in such a smart outfit, wouldn't attract attention there. Many of the waiters had changed, but the maître d' recognised her and the cloakroom attendant came to say hello.

'How are you, Señora? How lovely to see you! How many years has it been? We do still see your husband in here, but only very occasionally. He said you were well, but I must say you look better than well, and so elegant.'

'Thank you so much.' Sara smiled, playing for time. She told herself it was foolish, but still she continued: 'Actually, I was supposed to be meeting him here, but I just called and he said he didn't think he could make it, he's been held up. He's always so busy.'

'Yes, we see his picture in the paper sometimes.'

'Not on his wedding day,' thought Sara. Yet she was in such a good mood that she kissed the attendant on both cheeks again before going to her table and left a thousand-peseta tip in the cloakroom tray, even though she didn't have a coat. The girl was simply making conversation no doubt, but the thought that Vicente might have remarked to her, even once, that Sara was well, that he'd be bringing her for dinner one of these days, caused such violent, sudden emotion that Sara spent the next week fantasising about calling him.

She did eventually call him many months later, but for very different reasons, when her accumulation of wealth had acquired such a frenzied pace that simple arithmetic came before any emotional considerations. And yet, she hadn't pushed her godmother down that road. Sara hadn't even allowed herself to wonder if the episode of the money that came looking for her – that fell into her lap, making her sixteen-year-old self rush downstairs and look into her eyes – might somehow be repeated. When she got back to Doña Sara's the morning she'd been handed twelve million pesetas, and found the table laid for one, the only thing she knew was that she was not going to feel guilty about taking the money. That was the only thing she'd decided.

Her godmother had already gone to stay by the sea. A little over a week earlier, she'd become fed up with waiting for the buyers of the Cercedilla house to sign the contract. She seemed so desperate to leave Madrid that Sara had encouraged her to change her travel arrangements. She'd been trying to convince her godmother to make the journey by car, as she did every year, but Doña Sara had flatly refused, as she also did every year. Doña Sara liked trains. So, reluctantly taking a maid with her instead of her god-daughter, she had left by train – a day after her chauffeur, with all the suitcases, made the same journey by road, arriving in plenty of time to collect her at Malaga station, drive her to Marbella, and help her to settle in. Usually the chauffeur would return to Madrid the following day by train, but this year Doña Sara didn't want him to leave until Sara had arrived, because the maid who was with her couldn't drive, and she didn't like relying on taxis. It was a ridiculous arrangement that was repeated in reverse in September, but Doña Sara had become a capricious old lady who did not allow anything to thwart her wishes, and who never spared any expense – or the efforts of others – on making her life more pleasant. 'I mean, I won't be around for much longer,' she'd say when her god-daughter tried to make her see reason. That afternoon, Sara had her own reasons for opposing Doña Sara's plans. She should have been leaving to join her godmother by the sea, but instead, Sara phoned her and told her that some errors had been found in the Land Registry entry for the house they'd just sold. She said they had to be corrected, and promised that the process of doing so would only delay her departure by twenty-four hours.

Sara kept her word, but only after dealing with the promises she had made to herself. Although it was very hot, she didn't have a siesta and after lunch she shut herself in the only room in the apartment that she hadn't set foot in since returning to live there, almost four years before. Occasionally, when she went down the corridor, she'd found the door open, so she knew that the furniture was still there. However she hadn't expected it to look so old, so worn, the once-white lacquer now dirty and yellow, as if it had grown weary of the passing of time. When she lay down on the bed, she had to curl up her legs, but soon found a comfortable position. She had to close her eyes in order to see. Her godmother would sit on a tiny little chair to tell her a bedtime story. She never chose Sara's favourites – stories about princes and princesses who ran away from wicked stepmothers and ended up kissing each other by the bedsides of their children. Instead, at her own bedside, there was a woodcutter and his wife; poor, hungry wretches who conspired in their kitchen, and rose at dawn the next day to take their children into the forest. Sara didn't like these stories, but her godmother ignored her complaints. 'Wait and see,' she'd say, 'it will all end well.' The end was a goose that laid golden eggs, a cauldron full of diamonds and gold coins, treasure hidden inside a chocolate house, the pathway home. 'Wait and see.' Sara didn't like these stories, but her whole life could be summed up in them. She would never be a princess, no handsome prince would ever kiss her on the lips to wake her from the dream she'd always preferred to real life. But now she was like Jack, who swapped his cow for a handful of beans, or even Gretel, so prissy, so blonde, as odious as her brother, who tricked the old witch and so made their fortune. 'Wait and see,' her godmother would say, and fate had forced Sara to follow this advice: 'Wait and see.' She had waited, this was the ending, and it was a happy one. For once, Sara agreed with her godmother. As she emerged back out into the street in the mid-afternoon, her body felt more agile, flexible, younger. Yet she carried inside her all the women she had been before, and the burden of a loyalty that could not be destroyed – she owed these women more than she owed anyone else.

The young man in the estate agent's nearest to her old address spoke easily of money, never complaining how unpleasant it was. He didn't think Sara would have much problem finding a buyer for her old apartment – he had a few clients looking for a flat in that area himself – but he didn't believe they would find someone willing to pay cash. 'People here only have what they earn, you know,' he said, and Sara nodded: 'Of course.' As she was leaving, she said the place where she'd be spending the summer had no phone, so she'd ring him once a week instead. By the third time she called him, the property had been sold.

She did nothing apart from the obvious, made no plans other than deciding the best area of Madrid to buy in, the size and features of the one large or two small apartments on which she would spend the contents of the two bags that had spent the last few weeks at the bottom of her wardrobe. For the time being, this would be all. She was satisfied, her life continued to be comfortable and pleasant, her work just as well paid. She earned much more than she spent, slept at least nine hours a night, and wasn't prepared to take any risks. But the sale of the Cercedilla house hadn't only been profitable for her. Doña Sara didn't spend a single second of her holiday discussing the matter, but Doña Loreto, who liked to think she was very sharp and could sort out other people's lives, brought up the subject at their first get-together after the summer holiday.

'I'm delighted for you, my dear. It's wonderful. Such a piece of luck,' she said to Doña Sara before even tasting her coffee. Then she turned to Sara: 'How much clear profit was made from the sale?'

'Well,' said Sara, frowning as if she was working it out, and assuming that Doña Loreto was no expert in tax law, 'after expenses, capital gains tax, and all that sort of thing, almost eighty million.'

'Goodness!' Doña Loreto looked at her friend, smiling from ear to ear. 'Over seventy million more in the bank, and one less headache in Cercedilla! How I envy you, Sara. If only I had property, instead of a half-share in a company that my sons-in-law keep interfering in. If I were you, I'd sell the lot, all of it, really I would. Money in the bank at a good rate of interest, and that's the end of your worries. Wonderful! I mean, you don't have any children to leave it to, so what's the point in saving? You can't take it with you.'

'That's true.' Doña Sara nodded in agreement, while Sara felt the blood rushing through her veins. 'You can't take it with you, I mean.'

Doña Sara felt the same distaste for country properties as she did for unfaithful husbands, and for the same reason. Doña Loreto knew this, and so did Sara, because she'd heard Doña Sara say it so many times – 'I hate the countryside.' It seemed a trenchant declaration when delivered to a child, but many years later Sara finally understood that it was the product of a bad experience. When he was first married, still strong and vigorous, Don Antonio Ochoa often used to leave home without warning. At first he would only be away for one night, and would return with flowers, chocolates and an amusing story that laid all the blame on one of his friends, and was usually incredible enough to be believable. Later on, his absences became lengthier – almost always two or three days, even a week occasionally – and he would offer no explanation when he returned. There was no need. His wife never knew who he was with, but she always knew where he was. Don Antonio only stopped being unfaithful to her when his body chose, not fidelity, but impotence. Yet he still took pride in being a landowner, and he genuinely liked the countryside more than anything. At the apartment in Calle Velázquez, lost amongst the drawers, were photos of a handsome man – the body that Sara had only ever seen lying down, or slumped in a chair – upright in hunting boots, with his shirt open, a hat and a happy smile, standing on some crag overlooking a huge plain planted with crops, beside a vineyard, or with a flock of sheep, a sheepdog at his heels. This was why he stayed away so long. He liked to take his conquests to his estate near Toledo, but he also took care of the estate and looked after the other properties – the land in Salamanca that his wife had inherited from her mother, and the estates in Ciudad Real that were part of her family fortune and were the most valuable. This was why Doña Sara hated the countryside.

'The thing is, I like spending time with you,' she told Sara at dinner that evening, 'and I think maybe Loreto's right about all those properties being a headache, even though you manage them. The less you have to do, the more time you'll be able to spend with me. And it's true, I don't have any children to take care of the estates once I'm gone. What will my nieces and nephews do with them? Sell them, of course. And if I leave you the estates, what will you do? Well, probably sell them too. Anyway, I don't care about that land, I haven't visited any of it in years, not even the Toledo estate, which is closest. You know I hate the countryside. I think Loreto's right.'

The first course was Swiss chard, which neither of them liked, but which was still served once a week because it had always been served, and because it was good for you. As she listened to her godmother, Sara swallowed a mouthful with difficulty and wondered why she didn't feel nervous. She ought to, yet she felt calm, alert. She could almost hear the cogs and gears, the humming of the machine in her head, above the old lady's weak voice.

'I don't know, Mami,' she answered after a while, once she'd decided which persona to adopt, which would be most appropriate. 'Selling everything like that, all at once. It's a bit frightening, isn't it? Why don't you think about it some more? Property is a secure investment, because it never goes bust.'

'No, but roofs cave in, and sometimes there's hail in April, or it's hot in January.'

Sara smiled. Her godmother, who had a poor memory, had managed to list the three disasters that had occurred over the past two years. Sara could not, however, agree with her so easily. Faithful to the role she had chosen, and therefore sensible and conservative, she remained firm.

'We can think about it anyway – see what we have, check out the market. We need to take things slowly, don't you think? We should consider the consequences before doing anything.'

Sara hadn't planned this. After all, she'd been a good, honest, conscientious worker all her life.

'What consequences could there be?' asked her god-mother, intrigued. 'Fewer problems and more money in the bank, as Loreto says.'

Sara closed her eyes briefly, put her napkin on the table, sat back and crossed her arms before replying. It wasn't easy for her to continue because she'd just realised that she needed to measure every word, to tug carefully at the gold thread she had just found by chance.

'Well, it's not as simple as that. Your financial situation would change overnight. Doña Loreto knows nothing about tax – why should she? – but land isn't taxed in the same way as capital, Mami. Owners of farms get subsidies, advantageous credit terms with low interest rates, they can defer tax if the harvest has been poor or worse than expected, and of course they can claim a large part of their expenses against tax – wages, costs of machinery, repairs, things like that. You know all this already, or it should sound familiar, because I've told you about it several times. Money in the bank, on the other hand, has no tax breaks. Quite the opposite, in fact.'

At this she stopped, though she was no longer playing for time. She knew exactly what she was going to say next, but she wanted to check the old lady's reaction first. It was entirely as she expected.

'So what could we do?'

'Well, we'd have to do something else with the money, find other investments, choose funds with tax advantages, and we'd need to keep changing our strategy as your capital increases. If you decide to sell all of it, and sell it quickly, we'd have to take more risks. Otherwise, the Revenue could claim over half of the profit.'

'Oh, no!' exclaimed the old lady. Sara had won the first round. Now furious, as befitted a wealthy Spanish lady who hadn't paid a penny in tax during the forty years of the dictatorship, Doña Sara clenched her fists, banged them on the table and leant forward. 'Absolutely not! Do whatever you think is best.'

'Well. Let's not be hasty,' Sara said, as she tried to calm the storm she'd just unleashed. 'First, we need to consider what we're going to do, and how we're going to do it. But if you do decide to sell, I think it would be a good idea to look for another stockbroker, someone who's less conservative than Don Ricardo.'

Sara couldn't possibly use Don Antonio's stockbroker, but she didn't know who else to go to, or more precisely, she knew that the only person who could help her was the one person she didn't want to ask for a favour. That night, as she went to bed, she discounted the idea. She continued to discount it every night and every morning that autumn, while she had meetings with managers and tenants, agricultural experts and town clerks, so as to divide up her godmother's country estates into lots to be sold, the best ones quickly – such as the land with good water, very valuable in a province as dry as Ciudad Real – the others more slowly. She discounted the idea all winter as well, when the owner of the neighbouring land decided to buy the plots she was selling in Salamanca, thus creating the largest livestock farm in the region. And in March, when Doña Margarita's son made an offer, low but irresistible, for the house where Doña Sara's husband had conducted many of his adulterous escapades, Sara pushed aside the idea yet again. Every night as she went to bed, and every morning as she got up, she thought about it again, decided to go ahead, then forbade herself to do so; yet right from the start she knew there was no one else she could turn to. Her social life, which had never been very active, except in the good times she wanted to forget, had dwindled to nothing. Finding a business partner through one of the intermediaries she'd met as her godmother's financial representative would not only mean she ran the risk of being reported to the police, but also, in the least bad scenario, of being blackmailed for the rest of her life. She couldn't see another way, couldn't make up her mind. Meanwhile, time was passing,

By the spring of 1990, the banknotes were piling up in the bottom of her wardrobe at such a rate that, on occasion, she opted to forego some of the undeclared money that she had so far reserved for herself. The money was no longer the problem. While she struggled with the idea of calling Vicente, Sara Gómez Morales, without the crutch of her past, began to wonder what she really wanted to be. Before her stretched two different paths. One led to being a wealthy and fairly honourable woman, a sort of luxury version of Señorita Sevilla. The other would turn her into a seriously wealthy fraudster. For the past few months she had been viewing apartments again in her spare time, although she was now looking for something different – a very large, old apartment, cheap enough that she could buy it using the rent from her other two apartments, and so dilapidated that the refurbishment would absorb all the money accumulating at the bottom of her wardrobe. The plan was to add value to her investment, and then eventually sell it off and start all over again. This was the safest, least nerve-racking path, and the one that most involved Vicente. But without completely abandoning this scheme, she chose the other path.

When at last she sold the house in Toledo, Doña Sara divided the money up between her nephews and nieces, and paid the gift tax out of her own funds. 'I never liked that house,' was all she said. She bought Sara a new, very expensive car – her first BMW – but she didn't give her any money. Sara had been expecting this. However fond Doña Sara was of her, however much she needed her and preferred her to Amparo and her brothers, Sara would never inherit the shawl, only the fringes. Children of servants are only fostered, never adopted, because blood is thicker than water, and rules are rules. She wasn't going to cry over it at this stage but, beyond her own feelings, the situation of her godmother's current accounts was becoming unsustainable. Sara would have liked to let another summer go by, to give herself longer to reflect, rein in her ambition or prepare herself better inwardly, but she didn't have the time. She'd wasted almost a year. If she waited until September and the transaction was delayed for some reason, the tax year might end with no income declared. And now there was much more at stake than her prestige in managing Doña Sara's finances efficiently.

He wasn't in the phone book, of course. As she dialled the party headquarters, Sara's hands felt clammy, her legs were shaking, and when she spoke her voice suddenly sounded halting and childlike. The first person she asked for, however, was at his desk, and he remembered her. 'I don't think I can get hold of him right now,' he told her, 'but I'll be seeing him in a couple of hours – we're having lunch together – so leave me a number he can contact you on. That'll be the best thing.' He was lying, but ten minutes later the phone rang, and it was Vicente González de Sandoval, not his secretary.

They agreed to meet the following day, at two thirty, in a restaurant that was new to her, a big place that must once have been the cellars, or coach houses or even the stables of a palace. The walls were exposed brick, the windows small and high up, and ceiling fans cooled the air, lending the place the air of a grotto in an eighteenth-century garden. The teak furniture was in a vaguely colonial style that lightened the classical look of the rugs, and there were plenty of large lustrous plants cleverly placed for maximum effect. The glasses were Portuguese blue glass, the plates white, and there was no cutlery to be seen. The place suited Vicente's taste for pared-down luxury, one more station on the journey that Sara had enjoyed with him for a while. She was sure he'd been thinking about the place the day before as she tried to explain, hesitantly, a little incoherently, that she'd like to meet up with him to discuss something too important to talk about on the phone. The asphalt outside was so hot it seemed about to melt beneath the merciless June sun, but as she entered the restaurant, Sara was shocked by more than just the change in temperature. The echo of another time, another place stopped her dead in her tracks for a moment by the bar. Then she saw him. He was sitting at a table at the back, looking over some papers, and wearing small reading glasses – something he'd never needed when they were together. He was fifty now, with grey hair and a weary look – the only man she'd ever loved. For a moment, she felt as gauche and naive as a sixteen-year-old, but just as she was about to run from the restaurant, he looked up, saw her, removed his glasses and stood up. She smiled involuntarily as she walked over to him.

'How are you?' he asked.

'I'm fine,' she said. He kissed her on both cheeks – real kisses, his lips touching her face as he put an arm around her waist and held her against him a second longer than necessary, so that she became very aware of his embrace. 'I'm well. And you?'

'Hm.' He frowned and shrugged, then he laughed. 'I suppose I'm well too. Sit down. I'm so pleased you called me, I really wanted to see you.'

The courtesies continued with a conversation on the possibilities of the menu, which led to a quick summary of their respective lives. Vicente's children were well – the eldest was already at university whilst the youngest was about to start. Sara's parents were both dead, and she was living with her godmother again. Vicente raised his eyebrows when she told him this.

'I saw your wedding photo in the paper,' she couldn't help saying, and even added: 'Your wife's stunning.'

He smiled wryly.

'She certainly is stunning. But she's no longer my wife. We divorced a couple of years ago. But, of course, the photographers weren't interested in that.'

'Oh,' said Sara, trying to keep any hint of bitterness from her voice, to remain detached and light-heartedly ironic. 'There I was thinking you'd never leave María Belén, and it turns out you've left several women on the trot.'

'Well, yes, that's how it goes,' he said. 'You can get used to anything – getting divorced, getting married, getting divorced again.'

'So, any day now you might be getting married again?'

'I don't think so.' He paused, looked at her, and laughed. 'Marriage has always ended up being rather expensive for me. Although my girlfriend's rather keen on having a wedding, that's for sure.'

'I suppose she's very young.'

'Not that young. She's thirty-six, although she doesn't seem it. Because of the way she acts, I mean.'

'And she's stunning?'

'Well, fully dressed she's fairly normal, but without her clothes she's impressive.' Sara laughed and he looked at her. 'What about you?'

'Oh, I can't think about that sort of thing nowadays. I have other plans, which is why I called you.'

'I was crazy about you, Sara.'

He said it firmly, quietly, with the same voice he would have used to order a bottle of wine – a much graver tone than the urgent, anxious voice he'd used when he said, 'I'm crazy about you, Sara,' after every row, after every parting and every inevitable reconciliation. 'I'm crazy about you, Sara, and you know it.' Sara tried to smile, to appear composed, and wondered why everything had to be so difficult.

Again she felt tempted to rush out, but that would have seemed ridiculous, so after folding her napkin yet again and taking a few sips of wine, she managed to collect her thoughts, and reminded herself of the reason she was there.

'I . . . I need to ask you a favour, Vicente. A very big favour.' He abandoned the nostalgic pose of the rejected lover and sat up straight in his chair. 'Before I begin, I have to warn you, it's quite a delicate matter – definitely risky for me, but possibly dangerous for you, because of your position and your political career. If you can't help me, you must tell me – I'll understand.'

'I'm getting excited,' he said. Sara couldn't help laughing at this and it released all the tension that her words had created. 'What's up?'

'I need a stockbroker or a financial adviser for a rather special piece of business. The person would need to be very capable, very discreet, absolutely trustworthy and above all, not in the least bit curious. They mustn't ask questions, or pass on any gossip. And they must be prepared to run certain risks, possibly even to operate on the fringes of illegality.'

She said it all in one burst, not daring to look up from her plate. When she did, she found him looking very surprised. But he was also grinning and his eyes shone like those of a little boy who'd got to pick the hand containing the present.

'I'm getting more and more excited,' he said, drumming his fingers on the table. 'Are you bankrolling a guerrilla army or dealing with the Mafia or something?'

'No, no, nothing as exciting as that. I told you I'm back living with my godmother again. You remember that whole story, don't you?' He nodded, and she went on: 'Well, she's quite elderly now and she doesn't have any family, apart from three nieces and nephews who only visit occasionally, but they will inherit her fortune when she dies. However, I'm looking after all her business interests – everything, including managing her assets, because I'm her legal representative. She's very wealthy. Extraordinarily wealthy. So, let's just say that I have an opportunity to inherit some of her money.'

This revelation wiped the smile off Vicente's face. He pushed his plate to one side, sat back and looked at her with an expression she found hard to interpret – a slight, sad tension around his lips, as if the past, his story and Sara's, all the years during which they'd never managed to live together, and all the intervening years, had suddenly landed on the table.

'What's the matter?' Sara asked, unable to stand his gaze.

'Nothing.' He shook his head, quickly recovering his composure. 'You know that I've always thought you were clever and strong, capable of anything. But I wasn't expecting something like this. Not from you.'

'Have I shocked you?' He shook his head again, but she insisted. 'Are you disappointed? Do I seem despicable?'

'No.' He took Sara's hand and squeezed it. 'In fact, it's good to see you like this. In a way, I find it reassuring.'

She removed her hand, but didn't stop to reflect on his words.

'Are you going to help me?'

'Of course I am. I know someone who might do. Is that all you need?'

'Yes, that's everything.' She smiled and she would have liked to force him to smile too, to convince him that everything was over between them. 'Thank you, Vicente. You don't know how grateful I am.'

'No, but I'd like to.'

This was bound to happen. Sara looked into his eyes and everything around her began to grow dim, everything merged into the background, the plants, the furniture, the music, leaving her on her own in a sudden void, a blank space filled only with the two dark eyes looking at her from across the table.

'I was crazy about you, Sara,' he said, and his voice sounded as it used to.

She wasn't sure how she avoided the trap, where she found the strength to stop her hand from advancing across the tablecloth towards his, but then she glanced at her watch, gave a small cry of alarm, and said it was late and she had to leave. He did nothing to hold her back, but cupped her face in his hands and kissed her on the mouth. 'I can't, Vicente, really I can't.' And it was true. At that moment, she didn't want anything – neither money, nor power, nor revenge – as much as she wanted him, but she knew the price she'd have to pay, the terms and mechanisms of her poverty. Ten years ago she would have returned home in tears. That afternoon she couldn't cry, but it was even worse. She felt so sad, so shrivelled up inside, that she told her godmother she wasn't feeling well, and spent the afternoon in bed, her fists clenched and her eyes open, empty of any sign of life apart from a single obsessive thought – the unbearably clear memory of his body on top of hers.

The following morning she felt no better. She was just sitting down to lunch when a maid came to tell her she had a phone call. From the voice, it sounded like a very young man. She didn't recognise the name – Rafael Espinosa – when he introduced himself. But he said he'd been given her name by Vicente González de Sandoval, and he wanted to make an appointment to meet her, whenever it was convenient. Moved by the speed with which Vicente had kept his promise, Sara took down the address and agreed to meet the young man in a couple of days' time. When she saw him standing in the reception of a firm of investment managers that occupied an entire floor of a skyscraper in the Azca district, it took her only a moment to recognise him.

'Do you remember me?'

The last time she'd seen him he was a teenager, a scruffy boy with long hair and a permanent grudge against the world, who slouched and swore with every other sentence. Now his hair was short, he wore highly polished shoes, a deliberately showy tie, a suede jacket and very clean, pressed jeans – a small concession to rebellion.

'Wow, Rafa! You've really changed!'

'Well, you look just the same.'

He was the youngest son of Vicente's elder sister, and his favourite nephew, maybe because he played the same role in the next generation as Vicente had played in his own. He was also the only member of Vicente's family that Sara had ever managed to meet. In those days he was a far-left activist and his views were much more radical than his uncle's, with whom he was always arguing, after ordering twelve-year-old malt whisky or the most expensive dish on the menu: 'You can fucking afford it!' Vicente would find it all highly amusing. Sara liked him too; she enjoyed listening to him, because he held up a mirror in which she could see a young economics student, more passionate and naive than the man she'd fallen in love with, and because she herself was sometimes the subject of the reproaches the boy hissed at his uncle – 'What about you? Look at you, for fuck's sake – you've got a hot girlfriend like this, but you still stay married to that posh bitch. Some example you set for the working classes!' Once the boy had left, Vicente would tell her that Rafa had a huge crush on her, but she'd never believed him. Maybe this was why she was so pleased to see him again, and felt much more confident than she'd expected as she followed him down the corridor. He closed the door to his office carefully after offering her a seat.

'Right, let's see.' He sat down at his desk, immediately adopting a serious, professional manner in keeping with the framed certificates from universities at home and abroad that were displayed on the walls. It was clear that he'd also been radical when it came to reinventing himself. 'Vicente didn't say much. I gather it's a question of opening two lines of investment, is that right? One investing a specific amount of capital, the other investing the income generated by the first.'

'Well, yes, that's basically it.' Sara nodded.

'OK. And the capital would be in your name. I mean you would be the person with the legal capacity to authorise the investments.' Again Sara nodded. 'And I assume that we don't want the original capital to be at any risk – I mean that in principle the investments we pick should be sufficiently safe and reasonable to justify the fact of choosing them.'

'Exactly.' Sara smiled, grateful that he'd said 'we'.

'And we can be more daring, more . . . unorthodox, let's say, with the second account – I mean, the capital generated by the income from the original sum.' He raised his eyebrows, and she nodded.

Then he opened a drawer, took out a sheet of paper and slid it across the desk to her together with a pen.

'How much money are we talking about?'

Sara wrote down a figure with eight zeroes and returned the piece of paper to him. He looked at it, looked at her in amazement, looked at the figure again, then whistled, loosened his tie, tore up the paper and threw it into the bin.

'It's very hot today, isn't it? Shall we go for a drink? I'm parched.'

Neither of them spoke again until they were sitting at a secluded table on the Paseo de la Castellana. Then Rafa asked her what she wanted to drink. Once the waiter had taken their order, he looked at her.

'So you're going to fleece the old woman, eh?' He laughed, amused by his assessment of the situation.

'Thank goodness I asked your uncle for someone discreet!' complained Sara. Although his remark had shocked her, it also confirmed that Rafa was clearly up to the task.

'But that's precisely what I am – super-discreet. And that's why I brought you here, so no one would hear what we're discussing.'

They never met at his office again, and she only called him there a couple of times. If she wanted to talk to him, she'd leave a message on his answering machine at home, though mostly he called her, always after eleven at night, when no one apart from Sara was likely to answer the phone. Their conversations were short, usually just long enough to arrange their next meeting. They almost always met in the evening too, for dinner or a drink, when Doña Sara had gone to bed and her god-daughter could leave the house without having to provide an explanation. This was why, in all the years they lived together until her death, the old lady was perfectly happy. Tortured by her arthritis, Doña Sara no longer wanted to go out and it was increasingly difficult for her to move, but she almost always had her god-daughter close by, ready to help her, to read her the paper, to sit with her and watch television.

'See how well things have turned out?' she'd say to Sara occasionally. 'I knew it was a good idea to sell all that land. Before, you were always rushing around – to the bank, to the property manager. It was nothing but trouble. But now look how nice and cosy we are, spending all day together.'

Doña Sara never asked about the state of her accounts, but to begin with Sara always insisted on giving her details. Indeed, while Rafa was making her rich, he was also adding to her godmother's wealth. She soon stopped obsessing about the security of every transaction when she saw how capable Vicente's nephew was. He was such a skilful, shrewd investor, so accustomed to seducing Lady Luck, that no impartial observer would have been able to condemn his client for condoning his daring. Despite the fact that Rafa cultivated a taste for risk that Sara found excessive at first, the truth was that the Villamarín fortune had never been so well managed. Rafa was very good at what he did, with a confidence surprising in one so young, but Sara never discovered anything suspect in his way of working, not even when his first transactions produced profits so spectacular that she decided to watch him more closely. During the autumn of 1990, they constantly kept in touch by phone, and became used to seeing each other about once a week. Later, when Sara simply accepted his brilliance, his skill at predicting the future, and the speed with which he made money, it was he who insisted on meeting occasionally even though he had nothing new to tell her. She always agreed, because she'd honed her role as the model daughter at the same rate as her ambition grew, and therefore she had few occasions to escape, to have fun and do herself up for an evening out. She and Rafa got on very well, as well as they had done when she was still with Vicente. Rafa liked to show off, revelling in her admiration when share values went up or down in line with his predictions, and Sara had no trouble flattering him, enjoying the figures as much as he did, and listening hungrily to all the tales he told to amuse her.

'I don't know what I would have done without you, Rafa. I really mean it,' she said to him one evening, towards the end of a meal she insisted on paying for to celebrate an especially brilliant deal.

'Well, imagine what you could do with me.'

He said nothing more and Sara didn't attach much importance to his words. Rafa was thirty, single, fairly handsome and a huge flirt; less seductive than Vicente had been when she first met him, but much more fun. Sara noticed that he smiled at waitresses, cashiers and girls in the street, so she assumed that he extended the same treatment to his female clients. For the first time in years she felt good, she felt young, and she was aware of the effect she had on certain men, who'd turn to look at her in the street or when she entered a restaurant. She'd always been elegant, but until now she'd never had the money to prove this to the world.

She also still had a good figure, and wanted to make the most of it. Sometimes she realised that the men looking at her, who were always about twenty years older than her financial adviser, took Rafa to be her lover and this clearly made them even more interested. Yet when she went out with him, she felt like a maiden aunt being taken out by her thoughtful nephew. Until one evening, when she was forty-four, the ambiguous words and double entendres sprinkled throughout Rafa's conversation made her think otherwise.

'Tell me something, Rafa. You wouldn't be flirting with me, would you?'

'Well, of course I am! I've been flirting with you for months. It's about time you noticed.'

He was smiling and looked completely at ease, ready to seduce her. She burst out laughing. 'But that's ridiculous!'

'Why?' He suddenly sat forward, leaning his elbows on the table, preparing to do battle. 'I find you very attractive, Sara.'

'No.'

'Yes.'

'But I'm old enough to be your mother.'

'I don't think so. Unless you had me when you were fourteen.'

'Seriously, Rafa,' she said, already seeing him in a different light, 'I'm much older than you. Just leave it. You wouldn't want to.'

'Of course I would,' he said, prepared to press the issue. 'I'd love to. We fund managers have a weakness for millionaires, don't you know – it's our ideal sexual fantasy.'

Sara couldn't help laughing. Nor could she ignore the tingling she was feeling inside.

'But you've known me for years.'

'Yes, but it's not the same now. You may not have realised it, but you've become a different woman.' He stopped, and when he went on his voice was deeper, more husky. He tapped his index finger on his chest. 'I've turned you into a different woman.' Sara smiled despite herself, overwhelmed by the confidence that had turned the boy she had known into a man. 'A year ago, when I first saw you again, you hadn't changed at all. I told you so when I saw you, and I meant it. You were like . . . like a primary school teacher.'

'Oh, come on, Rafa!' She too was now leaning forward and was no longer laughing.

'Seriously, that's what you looked like – a self-sacrificing teacher or an office girl. I liked you then – I've always liked you – but now: it's not just that having money suits you, it suits everyone, but you've turned into something wild and ferocious. You're a dangerous woman, Sara, you could swallow us all whole. You're frightening.'

'And that's what you like about me, that I'm frightening?'

'Yes, I always go out with women who are more powerful than I am.'

'That's not it, Rafa.' Sara was smiling. She'd given in, accepting the sudden gifts that fate had bestowed on her once more, driven by her own appetite, her desire to devour him, to possess Vicente again through him. Perhaps this was why she suddenly understood Rafa. 'That's not why you want to sleep with me. What you want is to sleep with your uncle's girlfriend. He was your idol. It's a teenage fantasy, not a professional one.'

'Maybe.' He laughed. 'What difference does it make?'

She could never claim, however, that he was a lover with no personality. Nor that their desire was constrained by the fact that their affair had arisen from another, more difficult, love. Rafa wasn't seeking love with Sara, nor was he offering it, but she found in him a simple pleasure for which the price was never too high. They both came out on the winning side, although Sara got more out of their affair than he did, and she knew it. Rafa was a luxury on whom she never dared depend, a miracle that occurred anew each week. It wasn't just the basic physical pleasure of touching another body beneath the sheets, the body of a young man – fit, cheerful and eager. It was also what that body stood for, a certain sort of peace, an unlikely point of equilibrium. Rafa never troubled her, never created a void within her; he never took over her mind, her will or her imagination. He never possessed her, yet he was there, and it was good being with him. He spoilt her and made her laugh, and he never tired of fucking, never gave up before she had raised the white flag. Sara had never had such an easy, basic relationship with a man. In the apartment where they met, there were signs of other women – packets of cigarettes, lipsticks, jackets and shawls, books, sometimes university textbooks. He would pile them all up on a bench, like a display, by the front door. When she arrived, she often noticed that the contents of the display had changed, and she tried to spot which exhibits had disappeared, and which ones were new. However, the certainty that she had competition and the youth of her rivals reassured her and put her in a good mood, never the reverse. 'When you get bored, just tell me. I don't want any drama or silly games,' she'd say to him, and he'd laugh. 'Are you in a hurry? No? Well then!' Sara sometimes thought Rafa would have liked something else, total passion, total addiction, a middle-aged woman losing her head over a younger man, but she was sure that the balance they had struck was best for both of them.

They didn't have to discuss what they wanted, or check the terms of an alliance that moved from the bars and restaurants where they used to meet, to a bed. They could still talk about anything – amounts and percentages, interest and investment strategies – but they never spoke of the shadow that was always with them. While Rafa's desire strengthened her, and the amount in her bank accounts soared, Sara knew that, despite the fact they had never mentioned him since their affair began, Vicente was still there between them. It was his hand she felt when his nephew caressed her, and his skin she kissed when she returned his caresses. It was Vicente who was the possessor, the possessed, when another man collapsed on top of her. Sometimes, when she was bored during her godmother's physiotherapy sessions or as she sat watching the old films Doña Sara liked and whose dialogue Sara knew by heart, she thought of Rafa, recalled his face, his body, the tone of his voice when he became excited, the way he moved, the way he moved her with him on the bed, and gradually another face, another body, another man took control and she was back in his arms. Vicente was still the source of everything that was best in her life – this time, her affair with Rafa. But this tacit trio ceased being secret in a most unexpected way.

'Next week, probably Wednesday – I'll let you know when exactly – you'll have to come to the office. I need you to sign an authorisation.'

She didn't move or speak. They were lying in bed, he on his back, she on her side, with her head on his shoulder, and an arm and a leg around him, as if she feared he might get away.

'We have an opportunity to do a deal that's completely out of the ordinary. Fucking incredible, in fact. It's very clean, very safe, but if we want to buy, then first we have to sell.'

Sara propped herself up on one elbow and looked at him. He'd never spoken to her like this, and he'd never needed her signature to do a deal. Also, his expression contradicted the apparent euphoria of his words. He looked uneasy and afraid, like a little boy confessing to a misdemeanour. Sara was suddenly reminded of how young he really was. She'd noticed that he'd been a little quiet that evening, and that he'd made love to her without any of his usual banter. Rafa clearly hadn't been in the mood for games, but she hadn't guessed why he was suddenly so serious.

'How much?'

'Half.'

'No way,' said Sara. She sat up and started getting dressed. 'I've told you over and over again, Rafa, nothing dangerous. It's not worth it.'

'You don't understand,' he said, sitting up and leaning against the headboard. He'd never used this curt tone with her before. 'You have no idea. Honestly, you've never seen anything that was more worth your while than this. Listen to me, please. On Thursday morning, four people are going to buy a huge amount of land, hectares and hectares of it in three different provinces. You're going to be one of those four people. And next week, you're going to sell your share to the Ministry of Defence for much more than you paid. They're going to build an air base – it's already arranged. It's a dead cert, Sara, there's no risk involved. You'll make an absolute fortune overnight. You can't refuse.'

'I don't understand.' But later, when things became crystal clear, she'd have to admit to herself that in that instant, she had indeed begun to understand, because she already knew the answer to her next question: 'Are you another one of these four people?'

'No, no such luck.'

He was so clever, so shrewd, so used to seducing Lady Luck, that Sara felt the urge to give in to him at this point, to finish dressing, agree to everything, and insist she didn't want any more information about the deal. He would have been grateful for this, she knew, but she couldn't do it, couldn't prolong the heroic dream.

'So who then?'

'So who?' he echoed sarcastically, refusing to make things easy for her. Sara couldn't help the quaver in her voice as she said the name they had both been avoiding.

'Vicente?'

'Of course,' he said, lying down again and looking more relaxed. 'He's going to concede over half of his share to you.

He thinks we're taking things too slowly. Your godmother's really quite old, and she could die at any moment. And whatever she promises you now, in the end you probably won't get a thing. That's what he always says, and I think he's right. He and I both know what these people are like. After all, we're . . . well, you know. Anyway, he thinks we're moving too slowly.'

'He thinks? What does he know about our business? Why haven't you ever mentioned him before? I don't understand.'

'Oh, for God's sake, Sara!' It was Rafa who now seemed surprised. 'Don't tell me you didn't know, or at least have some idea? I can't believe that you're that naive. I'm good at what I do – very good – but I'm no miracle worker. I'd never have achieved so much without a little help.'

'Help?' She could barely even talk.

'Privileged information. A telephone call from time to time. "Buy this, sell that, do as I tell you." He knows, Sara. In his job, he knows about everything that's going on.'

'He's been behind you from the beginning.' Rafa nodded. 'He's known about everything, all along.' He nodded again. 'But why? Did he tell you?'

Rafa wouldn't answer. Sara finished dressing, put on her shoes and went to the kitchen to pour herself a drink. She drank it down in one, refilled the glass and lit a cigarette. Nothing had changed, everything was the same, right from the start. Every episode of her life had been written in advance, every decision taken for her. She should have been pleased, but she felt lost and defeated, manipulated by the only man she'd ever loved. The man for whom she'd have given up everything. Vicente had come back into her life by the back door, robbing her of her revenge. She should have felt protected by the all-powerful shadow of the only man who'd ever loved her, and who behaved as if he still loved her. She knew that he would see things this way, and that Vicente was probably convinced he was doing the right thing for her. She imagined him savouring his magnanimity, the aristocratic pride of someone who'd decided to become her benefactor without letting her know, just in case she ruined the meticulous plans he'd made for her. A person who would hold a fabulous birthday party for her, lend her a pearl necklace, have her new shoes covered in yellow silk, all for her. But Sara no longer wanted adoptive parents, or a different surname, or a bedroom kitted out with made-to-measure furniture. She had lived her story alone, and she alone had planned the happy ending. Had she known about Vicente's intervention earlier, she never would have agreed, because to her only the quality, not the quantity, of her revenge mattered. Her ambition couldn't be measured in numbers, but in hours, images, memories. This was what Vicente would never understand. But it was too late now – things were too far gone. Arcadio Gómez Gómez watched his youngest daughter from the bottom of her brandy glass, and he looked serene, as if nothing could surprise him. 'Bad luck,' he was saying, 'bad luck. In another country, another time, things might have been different.' As she drained the second glass, Sara felt a strong desire to hate Vicente, although he didn't deserve it. She knew she'd never be able to find the right words to describe her bitterness: it wasn't ingratitude, or folly, or arrogance. But she also knew she'd never be capable of hating him. All true stories were alike, they all ended up in the same place, with the same lie, and it didn't matter if the battles were real or fictional. When she went back to the bedroom, Rafa was still in bed. Sara sat down beside him.

'When it all started, Vicente imposed two conditions. The first was that I was not to use the information he gave me for any other client. In return, he'd give me a few tips on other deals for myself. The second condition was that I wasn't to tell you. Every Monday morning at nine, I send him a fax with a statement of your accounts. Based on that, he sometimes makes the decisions himself, and of course he's always right. He didn't want you to know, but I wasn't willing to do this particular deal without telling you. I couldn't have invented a source for a deal with such enormous profits. He understood.'

Sara stubbed out her cigarette, lay down on the bed, and looked at him. She suddenly wanted to embrace him, but differently, like an aged aunt would kiss her kind nephew on suddenly discovering he was an impostor.

'I think he's always been in love with you, Sara.'

'That's ridiculous.'

Then she started to cry, and wept for a long time, convulsively at first, as if she wanted to drown in her own tears. Bewildered by the explosion of a grief he would never understand, her lover put his arms around her and kissed her like an older brother, as if he knew they would never share the same bed again.

'Would you like me to buy your share and then sell it in your name?' he asked when she'd calmed down.

Sara shook her head. It no longer made any sense to try to escape, to keep on running. She was exhausted, and nothing mattered any more. Her father would forgive her. He'd always been very forgiving of those who knew, who gave orders, who'd had an education. On the appointed morning, Sara again put on the lace skirt and white jacket with black edging that she'd bought three years earlier.

Her heels clicked resolutely down the empty corridor. When she opened the door of the office where they were waiting for her, she found half a dozen men, all rather similar, smartly dressed, though not as smartly as her. She already knew some of them, although she had trouble recognising them. The rest she'd never seen before, but they all looked at her closely as they greeted her. Sara realised they were wondering whether she really was worth the price

Vicente was about to pay for her. He seemed to be in no doubt.

'You look wonderful, Sara,' he whispered as she sat down next to him. 'Whatever they say, younger lovers do a lot more for women than they do for men.'

'Perhaps.'

Just then, the notary entered the room. While he spoke, and passed round documents for everyone to sign, Vicente kept looking at her out of the corner of his eye. His head was bowed, and he kept drawing on a sheet of paper – a sign of nerves that was unusual in him, no doubt disconcerted at finding a different woman from the one he had expected.

'Are you going to consider my proposal?' he asked after signing the contract, then passing it to her together with a pen.

'Yes,' she replied, passing it on to the next buyer with a smile. Only then did she look at Vicente. 'Yes. Now, I can consider it.'

She would have preferred a different kind of defeat, for their reunion to be bitter or insipid this time. Instead it was a victory, and that was even worse. She wasn't like other women, so this aged lover rejuvenated her more than any other. That afternoon the pleasure she felt in Vicente's arms was identical to the pleasure she'd felt in the days when she still had hope. Only the pain afterwards changed, becoming wider, more muffled, like a constant dull ache rather than the sharp stabbing of an open wound. Sara would have preferred defeat, but since cutting him out of her life, eleven years earlier, she had never desired a man as much as she desired Vicente that afternoon, had never received or given as much, and yet it was no longer enough. She would have preferred to tell herself a different story – the tremulous epilogue to a romantic passion, a flame that can never be extinguished, a love more powerful than time, than money, than power.

Perhaps this would have been an opportunity to change their story, but she wasn't even going to try, and he knew it.

'How you despise me, eh, comrade?'

She stroked his face, kissed him on the lips and tried to smile.

'Less than I despise myself, Vicente,' she said. 'But I'll never have to go back to being an accountant. Whatever happens, I'll never have to do that. I owe that to you, and I'm grateful.'

It wasn't what he wanted to hear, so it took him a moment before he went on:

'This is how things are done. It's nothing new. It's ugly and unfair, I know, but it's nothing new and it's never going to change. You've always been on the side of the losers. It's time you changed sides.'

She held him close, clinging to him like a castaway to driftwood.

'You don't understand anything, Vicente,' she said. 'But it's not your fault.'

By the time Doña Sara Villamarín Ruíz, widow of Don Antonio Ochoa, died a few months before her eighty-fifth birthday, Vicente González de Sandoval had married for the third time and had a two-month-old son. His party had been in opposition for several years, but his previous lover hadn't rejected his marriage proposals because of that, and he knew it. Their relationship had simply died of weariness, unable to bear the weight of so many other relationships, so many endings that were all the same ending, so many stories that were all the same lie. Yet they still saw each other from time to time. He loved her. She loved him too. They remained loyal to each other until the end. So when her godmother's will was read and Sara found that she had been left a derisory sum compared to the amount she had been promised, she simply laughed. Sitting beside her, Amparo López Ruiz looked at her suspiciously, confused by Sara's reaction. Sara couldn't stop laughing. She was still laughing as she said goodbye to Amparo and her brothers at the door to a house that was no longer her home and that she would leave that very afternoon. She had told Vicente she was leaving Madrid, that she'd send him a card occasionally, and not to look for her. He promised he wouldn't, and never did.

Tamara knew that Andrés didn't love his father. They'd never talked about it, but she'd seen Andrés with him – the man who was so handsome when his son was so ugly, puffing himself up like a prize turkey; the boy shrinking gradually, as if every word he heard from his father oppressed him. 'You couldn't love a father like him,' thought Tamara, as Andrés pushed his heavy, old bicycle that still looked tatty despite several coats of inexpertly applied metallic paint. He never wanted to talk about his father to her, so Tamara assumed he didn't want to talk about him to anyone.

But Tamara also knew that Andrés loved his father. She'd known it right from the beginning, months before she'd even met his father. She'd guessed it from Andrés's silences, from his expressions, and from a few things he'd said, quick, jumbled confessions that seemed to have no meaning. But words always mean something, and Andrés's words conjured a dark, fleeting, mysterious figure. At school, if a classmate mentioned that his father had got a promotion or a new job, or bought a new car, and the rest of the class immediately began talking about their fathers, only he and Tamara remained silent. Tamara no longer had anything to tell, but Andrés always found an occasion to whisper in her ear later, when no one else was around, that his father knew a lot about engines, and could sail a boat, and used to have a horse. She accepted these confidences with unconditional trust, without asking what engines or horses had to do with the conversation they'd listened to earlier, and she pictured Andrés's father as a kind of modern bandit, a cunning smuggler or a pirate. So, although he was frightening, she wasn't impressed by his boasting or his threats. But she could tell that Andrés was ashamed of him, of his twisted vulgarity, his sinister posturing. Yet she was also certain that Andrés loved him, because you can't not love your father, whatever he's like.

Tamara knew a lot about love and shame. She noticed that Andrés was often rude to his mother, and told her off, as if she were the child and he the adult; that he berated her for silly things like getting home late, or drinking too much wine, or not dressing like a mother should. Tamara disapproved of this and she told him so. 'You don't know how lucky you are. If your mother died suddenly, like mine did, you'd be sorry.' Andrés became angry, but he soon got over it. She and Andrés did talk about Maribel. All of his complaints about her grew out of his love for her, his absolute dependence on his mother, which gave shape to his life. Tamara knew that you were lucky if you could depend like that on a father or a mother. She depended utterly on her uncle, and nearly always kept any reproaches or complaints to herself, although they were usually so trivial – what to watch on TV, what to eat for dinner, not wanting to wear wellington boots when she went out to play in the rain – that she soon forgot about them. But however much he loved her, however good he was to her, Juan wasn't her father. Tamara attached a lot of importance to this because she'd been unlucky, she'd had to learn at a very young age what love and shame were.

'Are you awake?'

She hadn't been able to sleep, but didn't reply. It was one of those nights when it felt as if the walls of the house were shaking. Nobody else seemed to notice, but she could see it so clearly that she had to close her eyes when the walls started to sway and bulge, and the air became thick with a premonition of the dust that would rise when the ceilings toppled in on them. Then the shouting would suddenly stop, and in the unhealthy silence that followed, Tamara opened her eyes and found that everything was the same as before – the walls, the ceiling, the furniture, the clothes she was wearing, and the thick fog inside her head.

'Are you asleep?' whispered her father again.

'No,' she said quietly. 'I'm awake.'

The fog never cleared. It was there when she got up in the morning and it was there when she went to bed at night, dominating her dreams. It was the fog that made her mother appear in the bathroom mirror and she'd brush Tamara's hair for a long time, kissing her and fooling around just like she used to. The fog killed her again every day at a quarter to eight, when the maid came into her room to wake her. Tamara couldn't see it, but she knew it was fog, and that it was damp and thick and dirty.

'I'm sorry, Tam,' said her father as he lay down beside her. He felt for her in the dark and hugged her tightly. 'I'm sorry.'

She loved him very much; as much as before, when he was always happy and full of fun. She couldn't stop loving him even though he was always cross now, in a permanent bad mood that seemed nothing like sadness. Yet she knew he was sad, consumed with grief, and that it made him shout and lose his temper over the slightest thing. It made him behave horribly towards her in a way he never used to, to hit Alfonso, and fire the maids, and hardly eat, and drink too much, and forget everything, and have parties with loud music and lights switched on in the house at four or five in the morning, parties that woke her and Alfonso up. But they didn't go downstairs. They'd done it once, at the beginning, and found lots of strange people lying on the sofas, a woman dancing naked, another rushing from the sitting room covering her mouth with her hand, a row of white stripes on the glass coffee table, and her father laughing, looking quite unlike himself, as if he was wearing a mask. She had been so scared and ashamed to see him like this that she'd tried to get away before he saw her, but she couldn't get Alfonso to move. He'd stood there, rooted to the spot, holding her hand, staring at the naked woman. Then her father noticed them, told them to come in, and began introducing them to everyone, until Nicanor came over and said that was enough, he ought to let them get back to bed. After that night, whenever they heard music downstairs, Alfonso would always rush to his room and they'd both hide under the covers and pretend to be asleep. But they couldn't sleep, because her father didn't know how to be sad any other way, because he couldn't control his pain, and turned it into the thick dirty fog that now filled his daughter's head, replacing all that she had lost.

'I don't know what's wrong with me. I feel bad, really bad. But I love you, Tam. I'm so sorry I've got like this.'

One evening, it was the soup. The maid, who was new, had found an open packet of soup with pasta letters in the cupboard that was almost past its expiry date, so she'd decided to use it. But the master of the house didn't like soup with pasta letters, he liked ordinary noodle soup: 'I loathe this kind of soup, I really can't stand it.' He could have left it at that; instead he tipped the contents of his bowl onto the floor and then threw the bowl down for good measure. 'But it's all just pasta,' said the maid in a terrified voice, 'letters or noodles – what difference does it make?' This made the master of the house so furious that he flung a full bowl of soup at the wall and started shouting, which made Alfonso burst into tears. Tamara had simply closed her eyes and waited for the house to come crashing down on top of her. She didn't know exactly when they'd started living on shifting sands, because she didn't know if the things that were happening were real. She didn't know how to get rid of the fog in her head that made her life seem cold and dirty. When her mother died, Tamara felt as if she'd lost everything, but she didn't realise she was losing even more than she thought.

'I'm sorry,' her father kept saying. 'I'm sorry.'

She loved him very much, but she was terrified of him. She put out her hand and stroked his face, put an arm around his neck and kissed him. Everything was so difficult now. She used to sit on his lap, ruffle his hair and tickle him. Now, every morning when she got up, she'd tiptoe to the top of the stairs, and if she heard him walking about or talking on the phone, she'd go back to bed for a little while, and didn't go down for breakfast until she heard the front door slam. That summer they hadn't left Madrid. Her father had said he didn't feel like going away, and she hadn't complained because at the house by the beach – which was small and only had one floor and a tiny garden with hardly any trees and stuck-up foreign neighbours – there was nowhere to hide. At the beach they'd always be together – Papa, Mama and Tamara – sunbathing, splashing around, swimming to the red buoy, walking to the bar, having a siesta in the same bed. That was why it was best they stayed in Madrid all summer, in the big house with three floors, where she could get away quickly, quietly, always upstairs if he was downstairs, always downstairs if he was upstairs. Her father didn't seem to notice that she was avoiding him. She knew she was avoiding him, and she knew she was scared of him, but she couldn't control her fear. All she could do was wait for the thick dirty fog and her father's terrifying sadness to disappear.

'Mama didn't love us, you know,' he'd said and started crying just like Alfonso did when he was being told off. 'She was going to leave us. When she killed herself, she was going to leave us. She went off with other men. She didn't love us.'

'That's not true.'

'Yes, it is. Mama was bad, Tam, she was very bad. And she didn't love us.'

'She loved me, Papa,' she said firmly, and he didn't say anything. 'She did love me.'

You can't not love your father. Tamara knew this. Even if he was horrible, and did horrible things, and said horrible things that slipped like an icy draught into your ears, you couldn't stop loving him. Even if one day he fell down the stairs and disappeared, and a thick dirty fog filled your head, flowed down your throat into your stomach and down your arms and legs until you became a stone, a frozen hollow statue of yourself. Even if the pain of this loss carried within it a seed of relief – instant, odious relief – the promise of a life without shouting or fear. You can't not love your father, you can't stop yourself loving him, you can't stop suffering for him, Tamara knew this.

Andrés knew it too, she was certain of it. Andrés had to know, because the fog that had gradually left Tamara, without her realising it, over the past year, was now inside him too – she could sense it in Andrés's head, in his anxious face, the fog of love and shame. But at a certain point, her own experience stopped being enough, stopped helping her to understand what was happening. Andrés had been less lucky, and yet much more lucky, than her. His father had gone beyond shouting and anger, silence and fear, and done something truly horrible, but his mother was OK, she was still alive and would soon be ready to return to a normal life, something Tamara had lost for ever.

They had all suffered with Maribel, including Tamara. The reappearance of violence, blood, uncertainty and all the words – accident, injury, prognosis, emergency – that she'd never wanted to hear again, had plunged her back into her deepest fears, where all sounds became screams, all shadows appeared to be threatening, all strangers were murderers. Before all this happened, Tamara had grown very fond of Maribel. She'd always liked her because she behaved like a mother – she talked and worried and smiled and kissed like a mother, and she was there, with a meal on the table, a fridge full of food and plenty of plasters at the ready. She could solve almost any problem around the house in ways that Sara and Juan couldn't, and when they were all together, which was almost always, she didn't differentiate between her and Andrés. This was why Tamara had been the only one who wasn't amazed or bothered by the fact that her uncle sometimes went out with his cleaner. She'd never understood why Andrés always complained that Maribel wasn't like other mothers. And she couldn't understand why he wasn't happy now that the worst hadn't happened and Maribel was still alive. It was true that his father had run away, that the police had searched for him and caught him and that he was now in prison, awaiting trial. But it was also true that Andrés had never lived with his father, and that he'd always avoided him if he saw him in town, pedalling away on his bike like a maniac. Tamara pondered all of this but couldn't understand, however much she tried.

They didn't see each other so often now, and things felt different. In the first few weeks of September, while Maribel was recovering at home, Andrés had refused to go to school. 'I'm staying at home to help my mother,' he'd said to Tamara. She had thought it slightly odd, but all the adults – Juan, Sara, the teachers at school – said he was right, and that he had to recover too, give himself time to get back to normal. But when he came back to school, he was a different Andrés. He didn't say or do anything that the other kids didn't do, but he always seemed separate, alone inside himself, as if he didn't care about anything. He ate, spoke and moved about mechanically as if he were following instructions he didn't understand. It was the thick dirty fog. Tamara recognised it and hated it, but she didn't know how to make it go away. This was important, however, because, sensing the fog in Andrés, Tamara had looked inside herself and realised that it was no longer there. She'd overcome it, somehow managed to get rid of it without even noticing. She was very absent-minded; she often left her espadrilles behind at the beach, her books on her desk at school, bags of sunflower seeds on the counter where she'd put them down while searching in her purse for the right change. But now, she didn't have to retrace her steps to remember where she'd left the burden of her worst times – it was there, in Andrés's eyes.

The first week of October, Andrés came to school every day. He sat at his desk next to Tamara and did as she did, but when he opened his books he didn't read, when he picked up his pen he didn't write, although he heard the teacher he didn't listen. The second week, he missed two days of school. The third week, he was only there on the Monday. This was when Tamara mentioned it to Sara, but Sara told her not to worry.

'He's upset, it's to be expected. He probably wants to wait until everyone at school has forgotten what's happened, and make sure they're not going to bother him about it.'

'But nobody's bothered him.'

'It makes no difference.' Sara smiled. She didn't seem at all worried. 'Anyway, Andrés is very bright. He can easily make up the classes he's missed later on.'

'But he tells Maribel he's going to school and then he doesn't turn up.'

'Stop worrying about it, Tam, seriously. He must know why he's doing it.'

Tamara had often thought that adults were stupid, but she'd never been so sure as she was now. So, when Andrés didn't show up at school the following Monday, she waited until late morning and then went and told the teacher she wasn't feeling well – she thought she was going to be sick and her head really hurt. As she'd expected, the teacher said she could go home. Then she picked up her bike and went to look for Andrés, but she didn't find him at the sports track he'd taken her to the afternoon they'd bumped into his father, or the old road that was so good for racing because cars didn't use it any more, or in the pine woods between the beach and her house, or at the port, or in any of the places they went together. She cycled around town not knowing where else to look, and was riding around aimlessly – she couldn't go home yet as Maribel would be there and school wasn't out yet – when she saw him, sitting on a bench with his rucksack beside him, in a new part of town near the industrial estate. The place was deserted.

'What are you doing here?' he asked as she sat down next to him. 'You should be at school.'

'So should you.'

'Have you come to get me?' She nodded and he got up. 'You're an idiot.'

He put his rucksack on his back and walked off. Tamara watched him cross the square and wondered where he'd left his bike. It was too far for him to have walked, especially as he now had a brand-new, lightweight, silver mountain bike. He'd got it back in July and it was exactly what he'd always wanted. 'What d'you think?' he'd asked as she admired it and gave it a test ride. 'Wow!' she'd said as she got off. 'It's really cool! Did your mother buy it for you?' 'No, my grandmother,' he'd answered, 'she's owed it to me since my birthday. It was in January, and she said that was a very bad time of year for spending money.' Since then, Andrés had taken his bike everywhere. He'd cleaned and oiled it, and spent most of his pocket money on it. He'd bought a tiny ultra-modern pump, a wing mirror, and a new, more powerful headlight. But here he was, walking back into town without his bike. Tamara went after him.

'Where's your bike?' she asked as she caught up with him and dismounted, wheeling her bike alongside him.

'I haven't got it.'

'Did you take it to be repaired?'

'No,' he said, looking straight ahead. 'I've thrown it away. I didn't like it.'

Tamara didn't believe him – he must be completely stupid if he thought she was going to believe that. She said goodbye and set off home. At the first set of traffic lights she looked back at him. He was still walking. She cycled on and suddenly caught sight of his bike in a dead-end street lined with low houses. A little boy who was too small for it was trying to ride it, watched by a smiling woman holding a baby. She was sure it was his, so it must have been stolen. That was the only possible explanation and Andrés was probably just too embarrassed to tell her. Tamara waited until the woman took the baby inside and then went up to confront the thief.

'Hey!' she said, trying to sound as threatening as she could. 'Where did you get that bike?'

The little boy didn't look scared. He stared at her, smiled, and proudly rang the bell a couple of times.

'My dad gave it to me,' he said.

'Oh, yeah?' Tamara was disconcerted, but unwilling to give up so easily. 'Well, it belongs to a friend of mine.'

Now the little boy looked scared.

'Mama!' he shouted.

The woman came out and explained that the boy's father had found the bike in a skip, and if she didn't believe her she could just look at the paintwork – it was all scratched.

Tamara cycled home, suddenly feeling very weary. By the time she got there, her eyes were stinging. Juan was in the sitting room looking at the paper, with Alfonso beside him watching the TV. She turned the volume down.

'You've got to do something, Juan,' she said, looking at the floor. 'Andrés is bunking off school. He tells Maribel he's going, but then he doesn't turn up. He spends all morning just sitting on a bench near the industrial estate, and don't tell me that's normal because it isn't normal. It's weird.'

Tamara looked up, and in her uncle's eyes she saw a reflection of her own alarm. So she told him everything. It was very important. The fog was thick and dirty, it filled you up and it blocked out the sun.

Sometimes the mass was dense and black, sometimes it was grey and more diffuse, splitting unexpectedly, dividing into a million black dots against the sky, then coming together again and returning to its original form – a dense black cloud that appeared alive, elastic, suspended in the air by some mysterious law.

'What is that?' Juan asked.

He had returned from the bar carrying a glass in one hand and a bottle of Coca-Cola in the other, and now stood by the table staring at the strange phenomenon.

'Mosquitoes,' Andrés said confidently, not looking at Juan. 'They're angry because they're going to die. They know winter's coming, and the east wind's made them all go mad. They're attacking a wasp.'

'A wasp?'

'Yes. It'll manage to kill quite a few of them, but the rest of them will finish it off.'

Juan Olmedo sat down at the table and pushed the Coca-Cola towards him, waiting for Andrés to lose interest in the mosquito cloud, which was still expanding and contracting outside the window. Then suddenly it vanished, along with its invisible trophy.

'That's it,' the boy said. The mosquitoes had disappeared, leaving the windy beach behind. 'They've killed the wasp.'

'What's going on, Andrés?'

The boy turned back to the window, as angry with himself, with Juan, with everything, as the mosquitoes and the dying wasp and the east wind. He didn't really understand what was happening to him. When he thought back over the past few months, he remembered odd details, fragments of conversations, isolated images, but he didn't dare put them into a logical, coherent sequence. Yet in his heart of hearts, he knew what they meant, the way the elements all belonged to the same story and linked together to acquire meaning, even though he was unwilling to link them. He'd also known he couldn't avoid it, and that even if he didn't tell his mother or Tamara the truth, he'd eventually have to tell Juan. He sat up straighter in his chair. Juan was watching him expectantly, little suspecting that whenever Andrés saw him, or heard him, or whenever somebody mentioned Juan's name, he remembered the words that had somehow issued unbidden from his lips: 'I suppose you'll be getting her to scrub floors on her knees again, won't you?' This was all he'd said, and then he'd blushed as he'd never blushed before, the redness thickening around him like a dark clot, gagging him and making it difficult to breathe. He still felt this way as they sat in the little bar at Punta Candor, the town's furthermost beach. When the doorbell rang and he went to answer, he was at home on his own. 'Mama's not here,' he'd said, about to close the door in Juan's face. 'She's gone out to do some shopping.' But Juan quickly stepped in. 'I haven't come to see her,' he said, 'I've come to see you.' Andrés didn't want to go with Juan. He didn't feel like a walk or a Coke, and he certainly didn't feel like talking. He knew what would happen, he knew it, yet he offered only a feeble excuse: 'I'm watching TV,' he said stupidly. 'You can watch it later,' Juan replied, 'we won't be long.' So Andrés fetched his jacket, telling himself it made no difference, if it wasn't Juan, it would be someone else – his mother, Sara, his teacher, the headmaster – and he'd had enough, he was tired of wandering around all day, his mind held hostage by a few words, a few images, a few details that he didn't want to put in their proper order. His mother's lover was still looking at him, calmly, expectantly. 'I suppose you'll be getting her to scrub floors on her knees again, won't you?' Andrés decided to tell him everything. When he spoke, his voice sounded strange, as if it belonged to someone else.

'It was me,' he said, and stopped. Juan Olmedo nodded slowly, his face quite expressionless, as if he were determined not to be surprised or shocked by anything Andrés said. 'It was me who told my father everything.'

'I'm your dad, aren't I? And you're my son. Nothing can change that.' The first time, Andrés didn't dare tell him. The first time, he didn't even know that his father had come from Chipiona to see him. It was his grandmother who phoned: 'Why don't you come over for tea?' she'd said. 'I have a surprise for you.' Andrés thought it must be the bike – she'd promised him one so many times since his birthday in January that his mother grew cross every time he mentioned it. 'Why on earth do you want a new bike? You already have one that works perfectly well. When it breaks, I'll buy you a new one. You don't need to go asking other people for one.' These days, all his mother ever thought about was saving her money, and there were some things she'd never understand. Andrés had been taken aback when he'd found his father at his grandmother's house. They were both in the living room, all smiles, as if they thought he'd be delighted. 'What about the bike?' he'd asked. 'What are you going on about a bike for?' his grandmother said, getting up to give him a kiss. 'Your father's here! Aren't you pleased to see him? Surely you love him more than a bike!' 'Well, no,' thought Andrés, 'I don't.' But he didn't say so. He sat down beside his father and agreed to have a chocolate milkshake, because he knew he had no choice. He'd last seen his father over two months ago, the afternoon he and Tamara had gone to the stationery shop, and he was pretty sure that was about the longest he'd ever spent with him, the longest conversation they'd ever had, and even then, his father had said just enough to make Andrés feel deeply ashamed. He'd always loved his father from a distance, loved a version of him that was secret, hidden, and which the man himself had destroyed, publicly, in one fell swoop.

'He . . . I . . . He said he missed me, that everything was going to be different.'

When his grandmother had finally stopped going on about how well he was doing at school, his father took out his wallet and started searching through it. Andrés thought he must be looking for money, and he was surprised because his father had never given him a penny, but what he showed him was even more of a revelation. It was a photograph. Not a very good one – maybe the flash hadn't gone off, or it simply hadn't illuminated the corner where his father was posing, a white bundle in his arms. 'Bet you've never seen this before, have you?' Andrés shook his head. He'd never seen it and didn't even recognise the place where it had been taken, the furniture, his father's wide smile, the clothes his mother was wearing as she stood beside her husband, looking happy, fat and very young. 'That's you,' said his father pointing at the white bundle, 'you were a week old. What do you think of that?' Andrés held the photo and took it to the window as if he wanted to see it more clearly. 'I've always been very proud of you, you know,' his father went on. 'And I didn't even know how well you were doing at school. Your mother never calls, she never tells me anything. I have more of these,' he added as Andrés handed the photo back to him without a word. 'If you like, I can bring them another day, so you can take a look. In one of them, you and me are on the beach, playing football. You must have been about two. And in another one, I'm taking you on my horse around the fair. That's my favourite. Would you like to see them?' Andrés nodded, without really knowing why. Maybe he was just being polite, or maybe he really did want to see them, to see if what his mother had told him was true – that at first, when he still lived in town, his father used to take him out, buy him presents and play with him. Andrés couldn't remember any of it, all he could remember was absence, eyes that looked past him without recognising him. He still felt very uncomfortable with his father; he needed to see the photos to know more about him. 'I've got to go,' he said after a while, 'my friends are waiting.' 'OK,' said his father, 'but let's arrange to meet another day? And I think you deserve a present for getting such good marks at school.'

'He gave me a new bike, a really brilliant one. He'd never given me anything new before. He talked a lot about when he and my mother were going out, and about when I was small, when we all lived together. Mama's never talked about that, and it was nice to hear about it.' Andrés glanced up. Juan Olmedo was still looking at him as calmly as ever. 'He was my father, wasn't he? He is my father.'

It was such a lovely bike, really light, and it shone in the sun as if it was made of silver. 'Do you like it?' his father asked, and laughed when he saw how emphatically his son nodded. 'Actually, it's my bike too. My girlfriend bought it for my birthday last week, and I've hardly used it. I really wanted a motorbike, but she said she didn't trust me, I'd kill myself on a motorbike and anyway, they're much more expensive. But I'm glad she gave it to me, because now I can swap it for your old one, OK?' It was such a lovely bike, really light, and fast too. Andrés was so happy that he leant the bike against a tree and hugged his father. 'Thanks, Papa,' he'd said. His mother had told him that 'Papa' was the first word he had ever said, but Andrés didn't think of this as he hugged his father, and he didn't realise it was the first time he'd called him that since he'd been old enough to remember. The bike was so beautiful and light and fast and silver that Andrés couldn't think of anything else. They took turns riding it around a square in town that was deserted during the siesta, and timed themselves against the clock. Andrés had fun in a way he never had with his mother – not exactly more fun, just different, the type of fun only fathers and sons share. But just before they parted, his father said something else: 'I wish I could have bought you a new bike myself,' he'd said. 'I wish we'd gone to a shop to choose it together and all that, but I'm skint. I've done everything wrong, and I'm sorry. I've ruined everything – my family, my wife, my son – and now I've got nothing. Anyway, that's life, I suppose.' He looked at Andrés, smiled, gave him a kiss and rode away on his heavy old bike. His words echoed in Andrés's ears as he watched him leave.

'He said he was sorry about everything, about having left us and not taking an interest in me. He said he'd tried to put things right once, but my mother had made it too difficult. I believed him, I thought he was telling the truth. After all, he's my father, isn't he? I'd never had a father, and it was nice to have one. It was fun to go out with him and joke around and play football.'

'Do you have a football?' his father had asked one afternoon. Andrés fetched his ball and they'd practised taking penalties at the sports ground Andrés had cycled round with Tamara only three months earlier, when he didn't know his father and would never have imagined they could get to know each other so quickly. It was the beginning of July and his father had said how lucky it was that the holidays had come and Andrés could go out whenever he pleased without having to tell his mother where he was off to. 'When you go back to school, we won't be able to see each other so often,' his father said, slipping a little anxiety into his son's mind. He never spent very long with Andrés – maybe only an hour or two – but as the summer wore on, he saw him more frequently. It suited them both, Andrés's absences were short enough that no one, except Tamara, really noticed, and when she asked where he'd been, he always said he'd been out on his new bike, and Tamara seemed satisfied with his answer. His father often told him that he couldn't stay long 'because of that bitch', meaning his girlfriend. 'She's a pain in the arse. I work all day long but she still doesn't stop nagging me. She doesn't even pay me, because she says the bar belongs to both of us, and that if I want to live there, I have to work there too, but then she goes and keeps my tips. Only gives me a thousand pesetas from time to time, as if I was a little kid. I can't stand her, you know, I really can't stand her.' 'Why don't you leave her?' Andrés asked. 'Where would I go?' his father replied helplessly, suddenly looking very small. 'I've got nothing, no qualifications, no training, and the way things are nowadays, what work would I get?' He sounded so forlorn that it didn't occur to the boy to think that his father was only thirty-three, he was young and healthy, and that other people's fathers took whatever work they could find without complaining about it. 'If only your mother would listen to me,' he said at last, 'it would be different. I could come back to live with you, take my time looking for a job, or start a business with all that money she got. How much is it, by the way? Where does she keep it – at home? Oh, in the bank, right. Well, well.'

'Then he kept on saying he wanted to come back, he'd really like to live with us again, so we could be together as a family. He was always talking about the money Mama got from her grandfather's land. He said it didn't sound like much, but it would be enough for him to start a business. He could get a loan for the rest, or find a partner or something.'

'What would you like best – one of those shops where they develop photos, or a stall selling roast chicken? They'd both be pretty cheap to set up, especially the roast chicken stall, because all you have to get is the roasting machine, and you could just hire that, you wouldn't even have to buy one. If we did the photo place, I could go halves with my brother-in-law – he knows all about it because he worked in one of those shops for years. He's always saying that if he had the money he'd set one up.' Andrés listened, enthralled, the way he used to listen to fairy stories when he was younger, knowing that ogres didn't exist but still believing in them a little, knowing that magical princesses weren't real either, but dreaming of the most delicate maiden with golden hair. 'Of course, the roast chickens would be a good business in summer, with all the tourists who don't feel like cooking, but in winter, well, I don't know. Another thing I thought we could do is set up a little shop, one that's part of a chain. The problem is, all the cheap ones sell clothes or sweets, or perfume, and you'd be less interested in that, wouldn't you?' Andrés nodded. 'I've given it a lot of thought, and it's important you like whatever we choose, because it's obvious – if your parents own a shop, you'll end up running it when you grow up.' They spent a long time like this – the father talking, the son listening – viewing their magnificent castle in the air, opening all the doors and windows, exploring all the nooks and crannies, looking out from the balconies and seeing a different world: a house, a family. 'I'm your dad, aren't I? And you're my son. That'll never change.' The fantasy acquired colour and depth, and seemed so real that Andrés felt as if he could climb inside and live there for ever. And then his father asked for his help: 'Could you do me a favour and tell Mama about our plans? We can't do any of it without her.'

'I even tried to convince my mother that he was right, I don't know if she told you.' Juan shook his head. Andrés went·on, his cheeks burning: 'It all sounded so great – we'd live together, they'd have the shop, and everyone would be happy. First of all, I said to Mama that she could set up a business with the money from her inheritance instead of buying a flat. She said I was crazy and asked what kind of business I thought you could set up with four million pesetas. I told her that some people thought you could, and she said maybe, but they must be the sort with plenty of money who could afford to take a risk. "What if I set up a business and it didn't do well?" she asked, so then I told her I'd seen my dad and he had lots of ideas, and he said he was sorry about us. Well, she went straight to the phone and started yelling.'

Andrés could hear her from the kitchen. 'Haven't you done enough to me already, you bastard? And now you go filling your son's head with nonsense. There's no way I'm going to agree to meet you, I'm not interested in anything you have to say. I don't believe a word, do you hear me? I never want to see you again, and I want you to stay away from Andrés. Just go to hell!' And she hung up and went in search of Andrés. She found him in a corner, crouched by the fridge. 'What's the matter with you?' she demanded, still furious but with tears in her eyes. 'Have you forgotten what your father's like? He's never taken the slightest interest in you, never given us a penny, never even called you on your birthday! I don't understand you, Andrés, I really don't understand, sweetheart. How could you believe all his lies? Don't you realise the only thing he cares about is the money? He's trying to find a way of taking it from us.' But Andrés withstood the torrent without flinching. He was prepared for every word she spat out, every tear that slid down her cheek. His father had predicted the scene; he'd given his son both the poison and the antidote. 'She won't want to listen at first,' he'd told him, 'because she's got a thing for that bloke, the doctor. They're seeing each other, aren't they? I knew it. She's a fool, I bet she's getting her hopes up. As if he'd marry her! Stupid woman, she's crazy – even her mother says so and she loves her more than anyone, because who's going to love her more than her own mother? He's taking advantage of her. He'll mess around with her until he's bored and then he'll be off. He's a pig, I'm telling you, sleeping with a poor woman who's only working there to earn her living. I bet he gets her to go down on her knees to scrub the floors, doesn't he?' He stopped and looked at Andrés, whose face was burning. 'I'm your dad, Andrés,' he went on, putting an arm around him and hugging him, 'I'm your dad and you're my son and that'll never change.'

'I told him I was sorry, I hadn't been able to do anything, and he said I wasn't to worry, we had plenty of time. I just had to keep talking to Mama and telling her that I wanted him to come back. He said that sooner or later she'd give in, she'd always been crazy about him, everybody said so. He thought she was still looking at apartments and hadn't decided which one to buy, so I . . .' Andrés stopped. He wasn't sure if Juan was looking as calm as before because everything seemed blurred. 'I told him. I told him everything.'

His father had suddenly become very jumpy, very on edge. He'd called the waiter, paid for their drinks, patted Andrés on the shoulder and left without even waiting for his son. 'No, no, it's OK, don't worry,' he said when Andrés finally caught up with him, 'I just suddenly realised I had to go. I forgot I had to be back in Chipiona by now. See you the day after tomorrow, OK? Come to the bus stop with me, I haven't got the bike today.' His father's tone was back to normal and he was smiling again. 'Well, this apartment makes things a bit more difficult, doesn't it? Because of course when Mama signs the contract . . . I suppose she could sell it later on, but . . . It's a shame. I think I should go and have a word with her myself. What do you think?' Suddenly Andrés's whole world seemed to have collapsed around him. Everything seemed vague, unreal, a sham. He'd been living in a dream for over a year now, enjoying the benefits of a life that would never be his. He hadn't understood this until his father appeared, and began talking about concrete things – a photo lab, a machine for roasting chickens, a little shop, a business, real things that were within his reach; a life without pools or gardens, without the posh accent of the capital. His father stood on solid ground, he knew the texture of the earth and the stones, not like Andrés – he was treading on sand, walking along a fickle beach that gave way beneath his feet. He'd been as stupid and naive as his mother. He could no longer believe in Sara, or in Tamara. It bothered him when they took an interest in him, asking him things – what film to watch or what pudding to have. 'What do you care?' he thought to himself as he chose the film or said he'd rather have ice cream than cake. 'What do you think you're going to get from me?' Juan Olmedo, who was so polite, such a good person, got his mother to scrub the floor on her knees, and his father knew it – he'd said so. Suddenly everything was turned upside down. How could he have been so stupid? Why did he believe that the arrival of Sara and the Olmedos really had changed his life? How had he let himself be deceived by their easy friendship and affection? He wasn't like them, he never would be, and one day they'd grow bored of him, Tamara would start going out with one of the idiots in their class, and Sara would find another little boy to keep her amused. 'When did you say your mother's signing the contract? What time does she finish work? Where does she normally leave the development – it has a few entrances, doesn't it? Does she normally walk home along the road?' 'No,' Andrés answered, 'she usually goes past the fish farm, round the back of that bar – the one that's been closed for years.'

'He said he was my father, and I was his son, and nothing could ever change that, and I believed him. He said he wanted to wait for her after she finished work, to talk to her and make her change her mind. That's what he said.' Juan Olmedo was looking at him with the same expression as before but Andrés could no longer see him, trapped in the repetition of that single thought, the treacherous truth that had completely annihilated him: 'It's all my fault. But he's my father and I'm his son, and he kept on saying that nothing could ever change that.'

'But it's not true, Andrés,' said Juan, speaking for the first time in a long while. 'It's not your fault, it can't be. You're only twelve years old and he tricked you, that's all. You didn't know any better. Your mother is the only father you've ever had.'

'That's not good enough.'

'Of course it is.' Juan spoke softly, slowly. 'It's the only thing that matters.'

Andrés couldn't reply. He collapsed over the table, clutched his head in his hands and burst into tears. It was a long time since he'd cried like this, until he was exhausted. Not even on that September afternoon, when he was busy keeping his eye on the time as he swam at the pool, thinking he ought to leave if he didn't want to be late for his father, and the security guard had arrived, looking white as a sheet, and told him his mother had been taken ill and Juan had driven her to hospital. He'd fallen apart when he'd seen her lying there in her hospital bed, pale, with all those tubes stuck into her, so small and alone. He remembered how she'd smiled and opened her arms to him. But even then, he hadn't been able to shed all his tears. All his feelings of guilt and betrayal had remained locked inside, haunting his days as he rode off on his bike, trying to find his father, and all his nights. And then there was that terrible morning when they finally caught him, when he was arrested and put in prison, and Andrés had thrown his bike into the skip. He wouldn't have known what to say even if he had found his father. And he didn't know what to say when he saw his grandmother, looking thinner and more hunched than before, as she hugged him in the middle of the street. He didn't know what to do, or where to go in all the hours he spent wandering about town, longing for the intensity of pain rather than this deadening numbness. Sometimes, he would even kick a bench or punch a rubbish bin, just to feel something. He needed to be alone because he was not the person he used to be. When he was with his mother, he performed the actions and rituals of a distant normality that now seemed like someone else's life. She pretended that she didn't notice, watching him as he ate listlessly, or sat in front of the television and stared at the ceiling, or smiled at the wrong time. But she never said a word. Time expanded and contracted around him, like the cloud of doomed mosquitoes. Had he been four or five years older, he would have left, gone as far away as possible. But he couldn't do that, so he'd succumbed to paralysis. Until Juan Olmedo rang the doorbell that afternoon, and drove him to the beach, and bought him a Coca-Cola in a bar, and gave him an opportunity to talk.

Andrés had cried until he could cry no more, but he didn't know whether telling Juan everything had made him feel better or worse. His eyes were swollen and his cheeks felt numb. Outside, it was almost dark, and the dim, yellowish light inside the bar seemed to submerge them both in a miniature sea.

'He's my father,' he said for the last time, his voice now meek and weary. 'And I'm his son. It's true, whatever you say. But we – you, Sara, me and my mother – I don't know what we are.' He stopped and looked at Juan. 'That's the problem – I don't know what we are.'

'It doesn't matter what we are.' Juan sounded so sure he might have spent all his life preparing this answer. 'What matters is *how* we are. And we're fine. And we're going to go on being fine. That's all that matters.'

Neither of them spoke on the journey back. Juan stopped the car and Andrés got out without saying a word, but as he closed the door, he said goodbye and thank you. He felt exhausted. Somehow he got the key into the lock and turned it. Inside it was warm, and smelled of cooking, and as he came in, his mother called out to him in the absent, sing-song tone she used when she was busy. Andrés went into the kitchen and found her making ratatouille. He put his arms around her, pressed his face against her apron and told her everything.

Perico the teddy bear died, disembowelled by his best friend, at four thirty in the morning. Having committed the crime, Alfonso Olmedo threw the remains to the floor and ran off. His brother Juan was too scared, too confused and too drunk to be able to think, so he sat motionless by Damián's corpse for some time, unable to decide what to do next. He'd always worried about Alfonso. He couldn't remember a time when his concern for him had ever disappeared entirely, and yet, as happens to parents of young children, his anxiety eventually became a habit, a duty he no longer paid much attention to. This is why children drown in swimming pools while their families are sunbathing, why they get lost in shopping centres, their mothers not noticing that they've let go of their hand for a moment; this is why they become addicted to alcohol or heroin while their parents boast to their colleagues about how well they're doing at school.

Juan Olmedo dialled the number for the police, but he hung up before anyone answered. His whole body started to shake more violently than before and he broke into a sweat. Then an absolute awareness of his situation emerged from some remote part of his brain. He hadn't pushed his brother.

Damián had fallen down the stairs all on his own, cracking his skull on the bottom step. Juan hadn't pushed him, but no one knew this, and there was no one else around because it was late, and they had both been very drunk. He thought things over again, slowly this time. Even if Juan hadn't intervened, even if he hadn't touched him, Damián would still have died. And Juan would have been calling for an ambulance so that another doctor could certify that Damián was dead and take charge of the corpse, so that he could feel he'd done everything he could after the accident. The accident. He took several deep breaths, then picked up the phone again. Instead of dialling the emergency number, he called the hospital where he worked. He wanted to be on familiar ground, to feel protected and understood, comforted by his colleagues. He felt a sudden, terrible thirst, an over-whelming desire to drink in order to regain control of his body and focus his mind. He knew that one more drink would, for a time, mitigate the effects of all the others he'd drunk earlier, so he swallowed it down fast, without search-ing for a clean glass or getting ice from the freezer. Only then did he go looking for Alfonso.

He couldn't remember a time when his concern for his younger brother had ever disappeared entirely. Later, he could not even remember having forgotten about Alfonso. But as he carefully stepped around Damián's body, getting blood on his shoes so that he left bloody footprints on the stairs, Juan Olmedo realised that he'd have to explain the sawdust as well. Alfonso had reacted very badly to Charo's death. He'd stopped eating and sleeping, become listless and lost all his hair. There was no knowing now he would react this time. Juan had spent his life watching him, observing him, trying to guess what he was thinking or feeling, what he wanted or feared, but he'd never managed to establish any systematic pattern to his behaviour. The specialists treating

Alfonso had warned Juan that he never would. Alfonso's reactions could only be predicted in basic, rudimentary processes of stimulus and reward, but when he found himself in a situation outside these parameters, when he was facing something new and unfamiliar and didn't know whether he would receive a punishment or a reward, he gave in to the most random impulses, and these were rarely logical. The hospital was near by, so the ambulance wouldn't take long to arrive. When Juan entered Alfonso's room, he was already composing his version of events, the one he knew he must memorise so that he could repeat it later, word for word. But despite his apparent calm, the instinctive, mechanical efficiency that felt as if it belonged to someone else, he couldn't help feeling deeply moved, and sorry, when he found Alfonso lying motionless, face down on his bed. His brother didn't look up but as Juan approached he huddled against the wall, cringing as if he were about to receive a blow.

Juan didn't merely want to reassure him and comfort him. Earlier, as he emptied his glass in one gulp and cursed himself for having smashed Damián's skull against the step when he was sure that fate had already done the dirty work for him, he realised that the only real risk he faced was the deliberate, simultaneous murder of Perico the teddy bear. This was why he had come in search of Alfonso. He wanted to make him doubt what he had seen, confuse him, convince him that all he'd been doing was examining the wound, and that this was why he'd lifted Damián's head and held it before laying it gently back down on the step. It shouldn't be too difficult. Alfonso was docile and obedient – he believed whatever he was told by the people he loved. That evening, however, when he finally turned round and held out his arms, it was Juan who started to cry, and Alfonso who stroked his back and wiped away his tears, while Juan stammered that it was horrible, Damián had fallen down the stairs and he thought he was dead. Then the doorbell rang and the eldest Olmedo brother went to answer, appearing so distraught and incoherent that the doctor, who knew him, wondered for a moment whether he shouldn't deal with Juan first before seeing to the wounded man.

For Juan Olmedo, that moment – the arrival of the ambulance team, the sound of their equipment as they set it out on the floor, the whispering that was soon replaced by sympathetic looks and words of condolence – remained imprinted on his mind like a milestone, a line, the end of the day. This was how he would always remember it. And he would always remember the following day, the horrendous hangover that felt as if he was wearing a helmet that was far too small for him, the cocktail of analgesics he took in an attempt to get rid of it, and his equanimity, his ability to grasp what was going on around him, what had happened, and what might happen in the future. By then, Dami was with him. He couldn't see him, but he knew he was there, sitting on the kerb outside their old house in Villaverde, wearing shorts and a striped T-shirt, his wavy chestnut hair looking almost golden in the sun. He was holding something, a broken gadget he'd found in the street and was fixing, and he looked up at Juan and smiled, showing his dazzlingly white teeth. Dami was there inside him, somehow slipping through a crack in time and sitting down beside him, lodging his smile in the absolute blank of Juan's mind.

His mind had been empty, disconnected from the world for several hours. For the rest of his life, Juan would always remember how the cold white dawn of that day had seemed to stretch endlessly until, in the afternoon, he woke up sweating, with a merciless headache, not knowing where he was. He had fallen asleep on a sofa in the sitting room at Damián's and someone had covered him with a blanket. Dami was looking at him, smiling, forcing Juan to remember. But he never remembered everything. He could recall the doctor offering his condolences, a paramedic holding out a form, and he remembered signing it, nodding as someone told him that in a case like this – obviously a domestic accident – an autopsy would not be necessary. He remembered that he'd carried on drinking. They must have removed Damián's body before the rest of the household woke up, but he wasn't sure. He was aware of having spoken to the maids, telling them what had happened, and asking them to clean the stairs before Tamara got up. He could remember – as if in a dream – the deathly pallor, the horrified expression of one of the maids. She was South American and she broke into panicked sobs at the idea of cleaning up the blood. The other maid, who was calmer, must have cleaned it up, or maybe it was one of his sisters, because he remembered seeing his sisters. He must have called them, although he was unaware of having done so. They later confirmed that he had been the one to phone, waking them at around seven in the morning, such an odd hour to ring on a Sunday morning that they had feared the worst before he even spoke. When they arrived at Damián's, they found Juan asleep in a chair. Paca got him onto the sofa, covered him with a blanket, then shut the sitting-room door and told the maids to let him sleep. 'There was nothing else you could do,' she said to him later. He'd apparently told them the whole story when they arrived and was so distraught, so incoherent, that they were worried about him. 'Please get some rest, Juanito, or you'll fall to pieces, and that's all we need.' Tamara's voice was what woke him. He wanted to see her and give her a kiss before she left. This was his first mistake. The little girl was surprised to find her two aunts there when she came down to breakfast, and she immediately asked where her father was. Trini said Damián had called them because he had to go on an urgent trip, and he worried Tamara might get bored being alone all day with Alfonso, so he'd asked them to pick her up and take her to spend the day with her cousins. Usually, Tamara would have been delighted at the idea, but this time she was reluctant to accept, and kept asking questions. Her father didn't usually go away, all his business was in Madrid, and her aunts were acting very strangely, smiling a lot but with reddened eyes as if they'd been crying. Anyway, she always stayed at home with Alfonso and the maids when her father went out, which was happening more and more lately, and he'd never seemed concerned about her before. But she got ready to spend the day with her cousins because she had no other choice. She was almost at the door when Juan appeared, as pale as a ghost, and she realised they'd been lying to her. Going to see Tamara was Juan's first mistake, but he wasn't aware of it at the time.

His second mistake was less a matter of chance, and more a clumsy miscalculation on his part. The only decision that Juan Olmedo would later recall having taken during those hours when he was absent, when he never managed to fall fully asleep nor to be fully awake, concerned Alfonso. His sisters had agreed that Trini would take Tamara back to her house, and Paca would take Alfonso, but Juan had asked her not to: 'No, he already knows what's happened,' he explained, 'he woke up with all the noise and saw Damián on the floor. I've spoken to him and I'd rather have him here with me. We don't know how he'll react when he wakes up.' This was true, he wanted Alfonso there so he could talk to him before he had a chance to talk to anyone else, to tell him what he should say. He was sure that Alfonso would be asleep for a long while yet, because he'd given him a sleeping pill. He wasn't sure when he'd given it to him, but he knew what he'd given him, and sleeping pills always had a strong effect on his brother's nervous system. Juan calculated that he would probably not be able to sleep properly himself, and would therefore wake up before Alfonso, but he was wrong. Alfonso had already had several hours' sleep when Damián fell down the stairs, and the next day he woke up around one in the afternoon, still terrified, and very hungry. A couple of hours later, emerging from the bathroom after washing his face and combing his hair, Juan heard Alfonso talking in the kitchen, and recognised the voice of the person he was talking to. An icy shiver ran down his spine.

Alfonso was sitting at the kitchen table, playing with a spoon and the pot from the crème caramel he'd just eaten. He smiled when he saw Juan. He was looking quite cheerful, as if he didn't really understand what had happened. Nicanor, on the other hand, looked devastated. He and Juan had never got on, but that morning they hugged each other tightly.

'Why didn't you call me?' asked Damián's best friend. His eyes were red and swollen, his hands were shaking, and his voice was weak. 'I was with your brother last night. He said he wanted to have a shower and get changed, and I waited for him for ages. I couldn't think what had happened. I only found out from the maid, when I phoned a little while ago.'

'I'm sorry, Nicanor,' Juan said sincerely, almost affectionately. 'I'm so sorry. I just didn't think of phoning you – it's all been such a shock. I know I called my sisters, but I can't even remember doing it. But I should have called you too, you're right, I just didn't think.'

Nicanor hugged him again, to show that he accepted Juan's apology, then he sat down. Meanwhile, one of the maids offered Juan some coffee.

'I was scared something like this might happen,' said the policeman. 'Really scared. I kept telling him he was going to kill himself, crash his car or something. He was really overdoing it. I don't know how his body could take it. I mean, he was still going to work. I thought he was going to fall ill, and in the end . . .'

He couldn't finish his sentence. For a few minutes, all that could be heard was Nicanor sobbing violently despite his efforts to stop. Juan felt sorry for him. Nobody, except possibly Tamara, would ever grieve as deeply for Damián as this abrupt, severe man who was quite unused to weeping.

'I loved him like a brother, more than a brother. I loved him more than I loved anyone, you know that.'

Juan nodded – he did know. When the family moved to Estrecho, Nicanor's district, he and Damián still shared a room and lived at the same pace, but they had already cut the invisible thread that had bound them in childhood. Then Juan had fallen in love with Charo, and Damián had become friends with Nicanor. 'Little Martos', as he was called in the neighbourhood, was well known because his father was a policeman who liked to do his job outside office hours as well, although he only ever intervened to calm situations down, restoring order and breaking up arguments before they became fights. He had a reputation as a good man because he never went too far, and had never beaten anyone up, not even when he arrested someone on his own initiative and hauled him off to the police station in handcuffs. Nicanor was his only son and he liked to boast about his father, his uniform, his gun, the status these things brought him, but when he met Damián – who was not only more of a show-off than him, but also more used to being a leader – he stepped back and gave him the limelight, becoming his faithful shadow.

In all this time, over twenty years, Juan had never had much to do with Nicanor. Unless they bumped into each other in the street, they'd never met without Damián being there, and even then they hadn't got on well. Juan didn't like Nicanor. He didn't like his job, or his manner, or his way of walking, of looking, of intimidating people. Now with his own uniform and gun, Nicanor had become as much of a show-off as Damián, but he was never as clever, amusing or seductive. He was a hard, insensitive, dull man, grim and silent. And he was jealous of Juan, of his position as Damián's brother, of the influence he sometimes had over him, and their past closeness. Juan and Nicanor had never got on, but on the day of Damián's death, as he watched Nicanor struggle to regain his composure, Juan Olmedo realised this was the worst thing that had ever happened to Nicanor and he pitied him.

'How did it happen?' asked Nicanor.

'I saw it, I saw it, I saw it,' shouted Alfonso, still playing with the spoon and the glass pot. 'Damián fell down, right to the bottom, boom! I saw it, and then Juanito revived him. Boom! Boom! Boom!'

As Alfonso slammed his fist on the table again and again in time to his words, Juan felt a cold sweat running down his back.

'Go for a little walk, Alfonso, go on,' said Juan, but Alfonso went on banging the table as if he wanted the others to join in. Nicanor, head bowed, was paying no attention to him.

'But I saw it, I saw it.'

'Why don't you go to Damián's room, Alfonso? You can lie down on the bed and watch TV there for a while.'

'He gets cross. He gets cross if I do that. He comes and shouts at me,' said Alfonso.

'He won't get cross with you today, Alfonso.' Juan looked at him, and saw out of the corner of his eye that Nicanor was looking too. 'Not today.'

'Where is he?' asked Alfonso, looking first at Juan, then at Nicanor. 'Where's Damián?'

Neither of them answered. After a moment, Alfonso got up, asked Juan if he was sure Damián wouldn't be cross, and then left the room. Nicanor stretched in his chair and Juan told him everything – almost everything – in the exact order in which it had occurred, including his own drunkenness,

Tamara's tantrum, his anger at Damián for missing her birthday party, then his worry about him when he didn't call and nobody knew where he was. He told Nicanor how, when Damián got home at last, he'd looked terrible and was barely able to walk in a straight line. He'd seemed furious with himself, and then was angry with Juan when he'd told him to start taking care of himself, saying he didn't have to take lectures from anyone. He'd gone to his room to have a shower and change, and then he'd sniffed another line of cocaine. He'd started down the stairs and Juan was about to follow him. He'd gone down the first step, then turned round as if he wanted to say something else to Juan, but then he lost his footing.

'At first he fell sideways, then head first. He somersaulted over and landed face up. At some point during the fall his head struck one of the steps. When I got to the bottom of the stairs I examined the wound. He'd hit the base of his skull. I lifted his head carefully and blood just poured out. I called an ambulance straight away, but I knew there was nothing anyone could do.'

Nicanor didn't say a word. He sat very still, staring at the ceiling and looked as if he were about to cry again.

'What are you going to do now?' he asked after a moment.

'I don't know,' said Juan. 'I'll take Alfonso back to my place for a couple of days. Tam's with Trini and I think it's best if she stays there, at least until after the funeral. That way her cousins can keep her company. After that, I don't know. I have no idea.'

'Call me,' said Nicanor, putting a hand on his arm and squeezing briefly, 'and if there's anything I can do . . .'

At that moment, they should have parted and their lives would have continued on their separate paths, until they'd lost sight of each other completely. But Alfonso, usually so meek, so obedient, was not upstairs when Juan saw Nicanor out.

'I saw it.'

He was kneeling in the same position as Juan when he'd examined Damián's body, and was thumping something that looked like a dirty old rag against the bottom step.

'I saw it, I saw it,' said Alfonso, laughing. 'Damián fell down the stairs – boom! And Juan took his head and revived him. Boom! Boom! Boom!'

Nicanor went over to Alfonso and took the old rag from his hands – it was the remains of a teddy bear. He handed it back to him, turned around very slowly, and looked into Juan's eyes. The blood froze in Juan's veins.

'Why is he doing that?' Nicanor asked.

'I don't know.'

'I saw it, I saw it.' Alfonso laid Perico the teddy bear's corpse in his lap, grabbed him by the snout, turned him as if he wanted to place his fingers behind his head, and then smashed him against the step. 'Revive him – boom! Revive him – boom, boom!'

Juan moved a little to his right, seeking the support of the handrail to stop himself from falling, trying to make his move look casual.

'Why is he saying that?'

'I don't know that either.'

Juan was sure all the colour had drained from his face, but somehow he managed to keep his voice steady. It had sounded natural, firm, but he didn't think he'd be able to keep it up for long, so he thought it better to remain silent and appear surprised by what Alfonso was saying – his poor brother with a defective brain, a witness no court would ever accept. But Nicanor was looking at him strangely, and Alfonso realised it.

'Where's Damián?' he asked, but no one answered, and he started to get cross, crying and tugging at his hair. 'Where is he, Juanito? Where is he?'

When he understood that neither of the two men was going to answer, he let go of his teddy bear and flung his arms around Juan's neck.

'I assume there'll be an autopsy,' said Nicanor.

'No. The doctor who certified the death thought it wouldn't be necessary,' Juan replied, not looking at him, grateful for the distraction Alfonso was providing as he cried on Juan's shoulder.

'Really?'

'Yes, that's quite normal if a body shows no signs of a violent death. Saves the taxpayers' money.'

'Right. And where was that doctor from?'

'From Puerta de Hierro.'

'Well, well!' Nicanor raised an eyebrow. 'That's the hospital where you work, isn't it?'

'Yes,' said Juan calmly, as if the policeman's hard tone had dispelled his own fear. 'It's the closest. That's where the ambulance came from.'

'Well, there is going to be an autopsy,' said Nicanor, looking him straight in the eye. 'There is going to be an autopsy, because I'm going to request one. I'll see you when we get the results.'

Nicanor closed the door behind him and Juan didn't move. Leaning on the handrail, he held Alfonso, stroking his face and hugging him until he'd calmed down. There was no longer any point in saying anything to him – Nicanor now knew his version of events. If Alfonso went around saying that his older brother had tried to make him change his story, to get him to lie, it would only make things worse. If Alfonso was going to talk – and at some stage he undoubtedly would – it would be better if he also said that Juanito had comforted him, hugged him, taken care of him as he always did. As he felt his body return to normal and the blood begin to flow again, Juan Olmedo tried to think on his feet. There would now be an autopsy, but he knew what the results would be. He hadn't pushed his brother. Damián had had enough toxic substances in his system to make even a much larger man lose his balance. This was why he had fallen down the stairs, all on his own, and his body would preserve a memory of the accident, bruises and cuts that would enable the forensic pathologist to reconstruct precisely the trajectory, the speed, the phases of Damián's fall, and the moment when he cracked his skull against the step. It would be difficult to survive such a fall. Juan, like any good orthopaedic surgeon, knew that it was impossible to calculate the force that would be needed to break a bone when the body of a heavy adult male fell down a long straight staircase. Juan had done a great deal of studying in his life. So he was sure that he'd exerted exactly the right amount of force, striking hard enough to break a bone that was already cracked without producing any secondary fractures, any shattering that might enable a forensic pathologist to find signs on Damián's skull of a violent, excessive, intentional assault.

The autopsy report echoed all of this so exactly that Juan might have dictated it. The report was definite, conclusive: accidental death, with nothing discordant, nothing suspicious, no margin of doubt. As he read it, Dr Olmedo reflected that the text was almost identical to the passages he'd studied in textbooks. He didn't know the forensic pathologist who'd signed it, but the name of the pathologist who had carried out the second autopsy, whose report was stapled to the first, sounded familiar. The second report consisted of only two points, with an introductory paragraph in which the author agreed with all her colleague's conclusions, underlining the levels of alcohol and other substances detected in the victim's body. She emphatically discounted the possibility that Damián might have been pushed down the stairs, specifying that, had this been the case, the fall and the injuries would have been different. She also stated with equal vehemence that the skull fracture showed no signs of having been produced by a deliberate blow to the head, and therefore confirmed that the death had been an accident.

Dr Olmedo could have approached the pathologists at any time – they were colleagues of his, after all, even if they worked in a very different speciality – to comment on the case and ask who had requested the second autopsy. But he didn't do so. The day of the funeral, Nicanor kissed Paca and Trini on the cheeks, and dragged Alfonso, who was so bewildered and frightened he was using Juan as a shield, out from behind his brother to give him a hug. He didn't even acknowledge Juan, but nobody seemed to notice. That day, Tamara went back to her parents' house and Juan moved in to live with her and Alfonso, while he decided what to do next. At that stage, the idea of leaving Madrid hadn't even occurred to him, but he did know he wanted Tamara to live with him – he'd always wanted this – and Alfonso had no one else. His two sisters were too busy with their jobs and their children to be able to take care of Alfonso, with all the complex requirements and duties that entailed, although Trini was so enamoured of Damián's house that she would have taken on any amount of responsibility if it meant living there. But Juan rejected Trini's offer and convinced Paca that, for the time being, it was best if he lived in the house with Tamara and Alfonso, although this was, by no means, a permanent move. He didn't want to live in Damián's house. Had his own place been larger, had he had an extra bedroom, he'd have taken Alfonso and Tamara there, and closed up his brother's house for ever. So he'd decided to sell his flat and buy a larger one, in Estrecho or somewhere near by, so that Alfonso could continue at his daycare centre and Tamara could stay on at her school. But he didn't have time to put it up for sale, because escape, leaving Madrid for ever, soon became a necessity that could not be delayed.

If he'd had to make a list of all the things that were worrying him, he wouldn't have known where to .start. Perhaps it would have been Tamara, who had withdrawn into herself, sunk into a deep, private pit from which she never emerged, only pretending to be happy and have fun. Juan tried to keep her entertained, doing things with her in his spare time, taking her to the cinema, the theatre, the funfair, her favourite places to eat, and she applauded, rode the roller coaster, pondered her choice of pudding and then thanked Juan afterwards, like a polite little girl. But she never shed her new skin, or the rigid, empty smile that could not hide the sadness in her eyes. The world was not a better place without Damián in it. He would appear, a child of the same age, the same size as Tamara, and with him a fierce, yellow sun beating down on a poor district of Madrid in the seventies, the merciless glare making the child squint as he looked up and waved slowly at Juan, as if he were tracing a question in the air, a cheeky, innocent question typical of a child of ten: how do you expect her to smile at you when you killed her father? He hadn't pushed his brother. Damián had fallen down the stairs, all on his own, first sideways, then head first, somersaulting over before landing on his back, and that was how he'd cracked his skull on a step. Juan had heard it, he knew the sound bones make as they break, the base of the skull was swollen, blood was streaming from the wound. Juan had studied hard, and he was very intelligent, the most intelligent one in the family, and he'd carefully calculated the force he exerted as he struck the blow, and he'd made such a good job of it that both pathologists had discounted the possibility of foul play. He'd simply finished off what had already been started, the skull fracture that had caused his brother's death. The world wasn't a better place without Damián. Dami went everywhere with him, looked at him with the bewilderment of Alfonso's eyes, the indifference of Tamara's eyes, the disgust, fear and defeat in his own eyes.

Then there were Charo's eyes, as large and dark as her daughter's, but more lively, more mischievous – Charo laughing, Charo lying to him, Charo calling him in tears, all the different women that she had ever been, her words surviving her death and refusing to fade. Juan hadn't killed his brother – he never would have done that. He'd simply given in to a ridiculous, stupid, almost childish impulse when Damián was already dead. He must have been dead, but Juan hadn't checked to see if he was still alive. It would have been easy, as easy as putting out his hand and feeling his wrist, but he hadn't done it. He'd never know if Damián was still alive when he slammed his head against the step. He knew only that it was difficult to survive such a blow. And if he really had killed him, there had been no point to it – because the world was not a better place.

Juan had never despised himself as much as he did the day he finally decided to go down to the first basement and follow the purple line painted on the floor. Yet he still followed the purple line, round the corner where it diverged from the red, the blue and the yellow. He followed it to the end, telling himself for the umpteenth time that he had no choice, no other way of scratching at a corner of the truth. But he felt as if he were going crazy, as if he wouldn't be able to hold himself together in one piece for much longer. He could accept anything, but not in this state of chaos – Juan needed order, a principle, but all he had was this purple line to help him find a reason to go on defending to himself his version of his life. It had to be like this – a private matter, one more secret between him and Charo, a silent, posthumous conversation. He opened the door, walked up to the reception desk and spoke to the nurse, yet the only thing that mattered to him just then was finding out if Charo had told the truth, because if she'd lied about this, she must have lied about everything else. And if she'd been truthful, then maybe she had been on other occasions too. This was all he wanted to know – he had no other way of either continuing to love Charo's memory, or accepting that he'd wasted his whole life.

He was looking for a woman, an acquaintance of a colleague in Orthopaedics, but she wasn't at work that day so he was seen by a male doctor. The man was quite a bit older than Juan, with white hair and glasses but not at all paternal, rather unfriendly in fact. But Juan was for ever grateful to him for keeping his composure while Juan told him why he wanted the test, using the stock phrase that made most doctors raise an eyebrow and not believe a word of what they were hearing: a friend of mine. A friend of mine has been on holiday to the Philippines and thinks he might have caught syphilis. A friend of mine who's HIV positive wants to change his drugs. A friend of mine has a girlfriend who wants to have an abortion. A friend of mine wants to get a paternity test. The doctor explained the procedure, the tests he'd have to order, the form he'd have to fill in, and he wrote down the name of the nurse he'd have to see. 'There may be a factor that could skew the results,' added Juan at the end, and this time the man did raise an eyebrow. 'There are two possible candidates, and they're brothers, so their genes may be very similar. Also, one of them is dead.' 'It makes no difference,' said the doctor with a wave of his hand. 'Ten years ago, we wouldn't have been able to distinguish between the two, but things have progressed since then and the margin of error is statistically negligible.' The man seemed so sure that there was nothing more for Juan to do but stand up and shake his hand.

When he got back to Damián's, he spent all evening with Tamara. He helped her with her homework, let her choose what to have for supper, ate with her in the kitchen, and then stayed and watched television with her until she fell asleep. He sat and looked at her for some time. He was sure she wasn't his child, but he'd always loved her, and would go on loving her just the same. He was responsible for her being alone, sad and bewildered. He had abandoned her mother and finished off her father, having loved them both. Now, this little girl, who no longer cried or made a fuss, had no one but him. The test results couldn't and wouldn't affect her. Juan Olmedo reminded himself of this once more as he wondered what his life would be like once a letter on hospital notepaper – like the one containing the verdict on Alfonso, years ago, and the one that had saved Juan a few months earlier – had confirmed that he had never been the protagonist of the central story of his life, merely an extra, a badly paid supporting actor in a humourless comedy. At least he would have the solace of a murky, withered peace, finally driving Charo's image from the dominions she had reigned over with tyrannical ferocity for more than twenty years. Juan Olmedo stroked his niece's face, gave her a kiss, and wondered what life would be like without her mother, the moment when he would at last be free of Charo.

He'd told Tamara that he wanted to take her to the hospital so that she could have some tests done to check how she was and, the following day, when he reminded her about it at breakfast, she'd simply nodded. The nurse at the desk asked where he wanted the results sent and he said he'd collect them. A few days later, as he took the envelope, he was so sure he knew what the results would be that he didn't even feel anxious. But this time, he was wrong: the results said that his niece was his daughter.

Against all his convictions, against the theory that he'd used like a club on her mother's arguments the day of Tamara's birth, Juan Olmedo found himself looking at the child differently. He'd always loved her like a daughter. Now he loved her because she was his daughter. But he couldn't linger too long over this feeling – so new and surprising that it hardly interfered with his final, definitive reconciliation with Charo, who would now remain in his memory as the very young, slightly melancholy girl who had stood on the pavement along the Gran Vía, asking him in a whisper to risk his life for her. This was the woman he wanted to remember – a soft, warm mystery, without thorns or hard edges, only warmth and sadness and confusion. He was left with her once more, with her fears that he didn't understand, with the words she didn't say, with the lies he believed, and with the best of her – her laughter, her eyes, her thighs the colour of caramel, and the love she'd inspired in him, a love that had changed him, a love that had raised him up and dragged him down, to the highest and lowest points of his life. He'd touched the sky, and he'd toyed with madness. Now, on the even ground that lay ahead of him, Charo would never change. She would always be the same, always the best.

Then, one cold, wet afternoon in March, the maid who'd gone to meet Alfonso at the bus stop said he hadn't appeared. The teacher on the bus had told her that a friend of the family had collected him from the daycare centre by car and would drop him off at home. Five minutes later the door-bell rang and Alfonso arrived, dripping wet, holding an enormous half-eaten bun.

'Nicanor brought me,' he told Juan. 'He bought me a bun.'

'Did he?' said Juan, drying his hair with a towel. 'How come?'

'He bought me a bun,' repeated Alfonso.

'Yes, but why did he go to collect you? Why did he want to see you?'

'Ah!' said Alfonso after a long pause. 'He asked me about Damián. He's told his friends I saw it – boom! Boom! Remember?'

'Yes, of course I remember.'

The following day, Juan phoned the director of Alfonso's daycare centre. His first instinct had been to shout at him and tell him he should never allow anyone, not even the police, to take his brother without his knowledge or express authorisation. But that night, as he tossed and turned in bed unable to sleep, he realised it would be much more sensible to deal with the matter calmly, so he had simply asked the director why his brother had not come home by bus the previous day. He added that the man who had collected Alfonso had indeed been a policeman and a friend of the family, but still, with someone as vulnerable as Alfonso, it was unwise to take any risks. The director apologised, and assured Juan that he'd look into it and make sure it never happened again. But then, a fortnight later, Juan had arrived home from work and found that Alfonso wasn't there. The maid said that Mr Damián's friend had called that morning to say he'd bring Alfonso home by car. Juan immediately called the centre and was told that Alfonso had never arrived. Someone had phoned first thing to say that he had a cold. The man hadn't given his name so they had assumed it was Juan. When Juan phoned the police station where Nicanor was based, he was told he couldn't speak to him because he was in a meeting. Juan asked who he had to speak to in order to make a complaint and the policeman on the other end of the line said Nicanor was just heading out of the door. A short while later, Alfonso arrived home on his own, crying and terrified.

'He took me to a really big place, with lots of rooms,' he said between sobs. He confirmed that Nicanor had been waiting for him at the entrance to the centre that morning. He'd asked him if he'd like to go on a nice outing. 'I talked to people, and they did tests. I don't like tests. You know I don't like tests, Juanito. They're scary, and I hate them. Nicanor got cross with me. He got very cross with me. He took me like this.' Alfonso grabbed Juan by the lapels. 'He says you killed Damián. I said no, not Juanito. Revive him, revive him. He's very cross with me.'

It was almost four months since Damián's death, and three

since Juan had received the two autopsy reports. He couldn't understand what had happened, but he wasn't going to wait to find out. Nicanor wasn't at home when Juan called, so after a supper during which he hardly touched his food, he went out to look for him. If he wasn't on duty, he'd be at one of the three bars where he used to hang out with Damián, places he'd gone to almost every evening for over twenty years. He wasn't at the first place Juan tried. But as he entered the second, he saw him standing alone at the bar.

'You've gone too far this time, Nicanor,' he said as he reached him, tapping him on the shoulder before Nicanor had seen him. 'Just like your father used to. What you did this afternoon was illegal. Unlawful detention, I think it's called.'

'Alfonso came to the station of his own free will,' Nicanor answered calmly.

'In the eyes of the law, Alfonso has no will. His consent has no legal value, and you know it.'

'The thing is, Juan,' said Nicanor with a twisted smile, 'I've been having trouble sleeping. I've been tossing and turning, going over Damián's accident in my mind – the stairs, his fractured skull, and what Alfonso says about you trying to revive him by bashing his head against the step. It's all very strange, don't you think? I couldn't understand it until I started thinking like one of those detectives on TV. You had the opportunity, Juanito, and you certainly had a motive, because you've always been in love with Damián's wife. And you were having a row with him – you told me so yourself. So I mentioned it to some of my colleagues. I had trouble convincing them, but in the end they saw it my way. They all knew and liked your brother. And now they know that you killed him. I might be able to prove it, or I might not. You never know. But I'm going after you, Juanito.'

'Oh, yes?' said Juan, and realised that he too was smiling, although he didn't know why. To throw Nicanor off balance, Juan called the waiter and ordered a whisky. Neither of them spoke while his drink was being served.

'I'm going to tell you something, Nicanor: I didn't kill my brother. And if Tamara finds out, if she hears one word, even if it's only a rumour, if you ever think of telling her that I killed her father, I'll kill you.' Then he drank half his whisky in one gulp, feeling the excessive, innate violence that had always surprised everyone, including himself, rise to the surface. 'Remember what I said, because I mean it. If Tamara hears any of this, I will kill you, Nicanor. Remember, because I swear I've never been so serious about anything in my life.'

He'd finished his drink, put some money on the counter and left. When he was outside, he found he was shaking, and suddenly felt uncontrollably nauseous. He hardly had time to reach the corner and grab the first lamp post before he vomited. He wasn't deceiving himself – he was afraid. While he was inside the bar his fear had fortified him, sustained him, given him the grave, metallic hardness that had stunned Nicanor. But now fear was making his entire body slack so that he was reduced to a puppet. Still, he was pleased, although he suspected that his display would not be enough to scare off Nicanor.

It wasn't, but Damián's friend took over a month to reappear. He chose a bright Saturday in April, the day one of Tamara's classmates was having a birthday party. Around five, Juan drove her to the party, which was some distance away from Damián's house, on the Avenida del Mediterraneo. It took him almost an hour and a half to get there, find a parking space, take Tamara to the door, ask what time he should come back for her, stop off at his flat to check on things and collect his post, and then get back to Damián's. He was thinking of setting out again at around eight, taking Alfonso with him, so that all three of them could go to the cinema afterwards. As he entered the house, he called out to

Alfonso, but he wasn't downstairs. Then he heard his brother screaming. Juan rushed upstairs and Nicanor moved away from the door when he saw him. Alfonso had crawled under the bed and wouldn't come out.

'Just paying a visit,' said Nicanor, opening his jacket. 'As a civilian – no gun. I wanted to see how you all are.'

Juan said nothing; he didn't even look at him. He went straight to Damián's room and picked up the phone.

'Who are you calling?' Nicanor had followed him.

'The police.'

Nicanor disappeared, leaving so quickly that the front door had slammed even before Juan had reached the stairs. Alfonso told him that Nicanor had got very cross with him – as cross as the last time, if not more so – and Juan had assured him that he'd never have to see him again, that Nicanor would never shout at him or hit him again, and that the three of them were going to go away, far away to a place he knew and that Alfonso would like because it wasn't cold there in winter, and summer lasted almost all year round. It was by the sea, and it was called Cadiz.

The east wind blew until the middle of November, making the autumn warm and gentle, as if it had decided to take pity on them and keep the west wind out until the end of Maribel's convalescence. In one way or another, they had all taken part in it, yet no one could help her in the final stage of her recovery. Not even Juan Olmedo, who on speaking to her son realised that Maribel must have had a premonition, even before she was stabbed, that Andrés's new closeness to his father would inevitably lead to her encounter behind the builders' hut, where he'd tried to convince her he loved her with a knife in his hand. Juan was sure that Maribel would suffer more from the effects of this last wound than the first, and he was impressed by the fortitude with which she'd assumed the burden of Andrés's pain in addition to her own, continuing to be both a mother and a father to him, never repaying his betrayal with a betrayal, never saying a word to anyone. Only later did he come to understand other things – Maribel's reluctance to report her ex-husband to the police before speaking to her son, the look of powerlessness on her face after the interview with the policewoman, the indifference with which she greeted the news that the police had caught her ex-husband in a village near Seville. She was neither upset nor pleased by his arrest, and it definitely hadn't dissolved the nameless tension, the anxiety that Maribel claimed not to feel but which Juan could detect even when she assured him, with a bright smile, that she was fine. The arrest had, on the other hand, enabled Juan to unravel a personal mystery, which he had never mentioned to anyone. His indignation at the policewoman's brusque treatment of Maribel had not entirely supplanted a strange, impure feeling that had sprung from the suspicion that Maribel did, after all, want to protect her ex-husband, and this feeling wasn't dispelled even when he saw her sign her statement. When he realised that he was wrong, that the victim didn't shed a single tear for her attacker, he had to accept that the uneasiness gnawing away at him might be impure, but it wasn't unfamiliar. He knew its name. He'd lived with it for most of his life. It was jealousy, although he only recognised it once it had gone.

'Do you love her?'

Miguel Barroso had asked him this question out of the blue a couple of weeks after Maribel had left hospital. They were in the bar where they sometimes had a drink after work, on an evening that was no different from any other. Miguel, as usual, did most of the talking while Juan listened, responding occasionally to one of his friend's remarks, a mixture of professional gossip and depressing tales about his private life. Miguel was terminally bored with his wife of many years. Paula, the anaesthetist with whom he'd had an affair the previous autumn, had left him in the spring. Miguel sometimes felt he missed her, but sometimes he was relieved to be rid of her. He told Juan that she'd said she wanted to rebuild their 'relationship': 'Those were the words she used, can you believe it?' He'd just confessed that he'd started looking at the older girls at his kids' school, when he suddenly asked about Maribel. 'She's fine,' said Juan. Then Miguel asked him if he loved her and Juan burst out laughing.

'Don't be so sentimental.'

'I'm not.' Juan saw that Miguel wasn't laughing. 'Do you love her?'

Juan lit a cigarette, took a couple of drags and started playing around with his glass, centring it exactly on the beer mat. He took a sip of his drink, and as he swirled the ice cubes around in the glass, the image of Charo, alone in the courtyard, dancing before a cracked mirror, appeared unbidden before his eyes. 'No,' he was about to answer, 'I don't love her.' But he did want to sleep with her, and he thought about it a lot every day. He still wanted more. He wanted to go on fucking her in the gloom of a deserted house, with the windows closed and the blinds pulled down. He admired her, and he liked watching her as she spun her web slowly and steadily, playing with her, falling into her traps, observing her reactions. She was uneducated, had no conversation, no passionate experiences to recount, no mysteries to solve, but she was the cleverer of the two when she needed to be, and he enjoyed being with her.

'I don't know,' he answered eventually.

'What do you mean you don't know!' Miguel laughed. 'Of course you know.' He waited but Juan still said nothing, so he added: 'She's very sexy, that's for sure.'

This trivial exchange, a fragment of the ongoing conversation that formed the basis of his friendship with Miguel Barroso, in which women were a recurring theme, acquired an importance that Juan Olmedo wasn't expecting as he sat in the little bar in Punta Candor, listening to Andrés unravelling the tangle of his faith in his father and his own guilt. The skinny little boy, who was so quiet and serious, didn't know what his mother had asked Juan one afternoon in March, nor what he had offered her in return. Juan recalled her words: 'When it's over, it's over.' Andrés knew nothing about this, and had anyone told him, he wouldn't have understood, yet Juan felt that the boy had, without knowing it, been part of their relationship. When Maribel took all those precautions so that nobody would find out about them, when she arranged to meet him at the petrol station three blocks away from her house, or let one of the children sit in the front seat of the car, or walked beside Alfonso when they were in town, Juan had thought she was concerned about her own reputation. It had never occurred to him that she might be trying to preserve Andrés's admiration for him and protect him from her ex-husband's spite. He'd always been convinced that neither of them could care less about his reputation, but the knowledge that Andrés now despised him – that his father had taught him to despise him – hurt him more than he would ever have expected. 'You and I are on the same side, Andrés,' he thought as the boy told him his story, 'we're both good boys, we study hard, we're vulnerable, and people can deceive us. You're more like me than like your father.' He would have liked to say something like this, but he didn't dare. 'When it's over, it's over.' Maribel hadn't realised the full meaning of her words when she'd said them, but six months later, when she came out of hospital, she was fully aware of what she was saying when she admitted that he'd been right when he said that what they had started was foolish. But now, this bright little boy had found a way of forcing Juan to define the relationship he was prepared to have with him, and with his mother. 'I don't know what we are,' he'd said, and Juan, as

618

he watched him cry, had had time both to wonder whether the most sensible thing would be to leave Maribel, and to be overwhelmed by a sudden, uncontrollable urge to sleep with her. In the end, he'd told Andrés that what mattered was that they were fine. 'And we'll go on being fine,' he'd added, realising, as he did so, that he'd just made more of a commitment to this child than he ever had to his mother.

The next day, when he got back from work, he found her sitting on the kerb by his parking space.

'What are you doing here?' He was still so moved, so overwhelmed by her son's confession, and so pleased to see her, that he put his arms around her and kissed her on the lips, even though they were outside and anyone could see them.

'I've been waiting for you,' she said, not pushing him away or telling him off. 'I wanted to thank you for yesterday. Andrés told me everything when he got home. I thought he was never going to tell me.'

Juan glanced at his watch. Tamara would be home by now, Alfonso too.

'Shall we go for a drink in the hotel bar?'

Two days earlier, they'd met in town and he'd told her what Tamara had said about Andrés skipping school, wandering about the industrial estate all day, and then throwing his beloved bike in a skip. She'd nodded slowly, looking as if she wasn't hearing anything she didn't already know. 'He never tells me anything,' she'd said when he finished. Juan offered to talk to Andrés before he was summoned before the headmaster and, after considering the idea for a moment, Maribel accepted with another nod of her head. 'It might be a good idea, if you don't mind doing it. Maybe he'll talk to you.' But she didn't tell him what she already suspected, out of loyalty to her son. Forty-eight hours later, however, she was able to admit that Andrés had been acting very strangely all summer, that she knew his father had been brainwashing him, and as she'd watched him wander about the house, silent and pale as a ghost, she'd realised he was ashamed and was able to guess why. 'But I couldn't convince him that what had happened wasn't his fault,' she added.

'Last night, we cried together, and I sat hugging him for a long time. But then this morning he had breakfast and went to school without a word.' She glanced at her watch, indicating that she had to leave. 'He's having a terrible time, much worse than his father. That's what makes me angry.'

Then, unusually, she took a note from her purse, picked up the bill from the table and paid for the drinks. Juan allowed her to pay without saying anything, and followed her out. As they got back to the development, he offered to give her a lift home.

'It's OK, I can walk,' she said, but then, as if she was worried she might have offended him, she quickly added: 'But if you don't mind dropping me off, that would be great.'

Juan Olmedo realised that Maribel had changed. It was as if the suffering she'd endured in the last few months had made her view her life in a new light, more objectively. What she'd said to him when she came out of hospital was true: she'd done a lot of thinking while she was there, and the result was plain in her face, her actions, and in encounters such as this one – over an hour and a half during which she hadn't smiled once, hadn't made any suggestive hints, hadn't shown the least sign of desiring him. Surviving is never easy, he knew this. And suddenly, he was scared. Before realising that it was ridiculous, before remembering that he'd once thought he didn't find her attractive, and that it was she who had changed his mind, he was scared that it would be Maribel who would decide that the most sensible thing to do was to leave him. As he drew up outside her building, he looked up and saw that the lights were on in her apartment.

'Andrés is home, isn't he?'

'Yes,' she said, glancing up at her windows and giving him one of those smiles that made him feel entirely naked. 'I'm sorry too.'

He fell on her, kissing her neck, feeling her breathing grow ragged. He pressed his face against her throat, her shoulder, her neck, and smelled the faint hint of her morning cologne beneath the stronger scent that her body exuded after a day's work. Unsurprisingly, he discovered that his desire had rewarded – or punished – him with a ferocious erection.

'Right now,' he said, straightening up and trying to appear composed, 'I'd give anything to fuck you, Maribel.'

'Oh, yes?' She laughed and, turning in her seat, she reached for the bulge in his trousers. 'And what's anything? A month's wages?'

He laughed at the prosaic nature of her calculations, and decided to be generous.

'A year's wages.'

'Wow!' She increased the pressure of her hand and he thanked her with a grunt. 'That's a good deal.'

Then, while Juan gently removed her hand, regretting that neither his age nor the circumstances enabled him to surrender to her, Maribel leant in and kissed him. Though they were outside her house, although all the street lamps were on, although anyone might see them, she kissed him just as she would have had they been alone.

'Why did you tell me that?' she asked as she got out of the car.

'Well, just so you'd know.'

Some forty hours later, when she slipped into his bed quietly, waking him up after his night shift, she behaved as if she would never forget it. This was exactly what he'd hoped for, and welcomed, as she moved over his body. He didn't understand that Maribel had realised before him, as usual, that his earlier show of sincerity was the mirror image of the smiles she used to seduce him, the first deliberate public act of seduction in which Juan had taken the lead. Before, he'd expressed his desire many times, but it had always been Maribel who made things happen, who had created the right mood, who'd pushed him with her words, with a movement of her eyebrows, with the curve of her lips.

The second gesture Juan Olmedo made in that direction was much more conscious, and was an even greater surprise, although Juan wasn't quite sure what had prompted him to do it. Maybe it was because the care Maribel took to appear unaware, to hide from him her new confidence as a coveted object, excited him just as much as her caution at the beginning. Or because none of what he'd said or done until then had come anywhere near the commitment he'd made to Andrés with her in mind. Or because at a certain point, he realised that he, Sara and Tamara were all so worried about the boy that Maribel seemed to have lost her privileges as the victim. Or because he still felt terribly uncomfortable in his role as the immoral, opportunist boss, and couldn't resist the temptation to be the fairy godmother for once. Or because he felt like testing her, seeing what would happen if he took away her pink housecoat and mop, and made her sit beside him in the car, driving across an open landscape, without locked doors or lowered blinds. Perhaps it was simply that he didn't feel like leaving her behind in this small town, going back to Madrid with Tamara and Alfonso but without her, and sleeping alone in a hotel bed.

'Have you ever been to Madrid, Maribel?'

They were in bed, listening to the wind whistling through the blinds. It was an unpleasantly cold day towards the end of November. It was way past lunchtime, but neither of them seemed prepared to confess they were hungry as they huddled beneath the covers.

'No, of course I haven't,' she replied. 'We were going to

go there on our honeymoon, but a week before the wedding my ex disappeared and didn't come back for three days. When he did, he said all his money had been stolen, so we didn't go anywhere.'

Juan stroked her face before continuing. His sister Trini was about to get married for the second time. This was the reason that she'd never come to visit, despite telling him on several occasions that she would. Paca, who'd spent a week with them in August, before the knife had turned everything upside down, told Juan that Trini had found a new boyfriend, someone she'd met at work. He was separated from his wife, had no children, and let Trini boss him about. 'She says she's thinking of getting married again,' Paca had said in a tone that made it clear she didn't believe the wedding would ever happen. Juan had also assumed that his younger sister's boyfriend would escape while he still could, but then at the end of October, Trini called to announce that she would indeed be getting married on the second Saturday in December. 'We set the date with you in mind,' she said, 'it's during the bank holiday so you have no excuse. I'm dying to see you all.' It was over a year since they'd last seen each other. When he left Madrid, Juan had promised to come back for Christmas, but he knew it wouldn't be possible. After three months of a special schedule with no night shifts, he knew he wouldn't be able to take any extra days off. At Easter he had just started seeing Maribel so he didn't even consider going up to Madrid, and in the summer Tamara had refused to go and visit their relatives in the city. 'But it's so nice here in summer,' she'd said. 'Let them come to us – that's why we live beside the beach, isn't it?' On the other hand, she seemed delighted when he told her about the wedding. Andrés was at their house, studying for a test the following day. 'You're so lucky, going to Madrid,' he said, staring at his feet. The rest followed naturally. Juan still felt indebted towards him, he knew the boy wanted to go to

Madrid even more than he wanted a new bike. Juan was always answering his questions about the place and one more passenger wouldn't make any difference. He was planning to go by car and stay in a hotel, because Trini would be too busy to put them up and there wasn't room at Paca's. It certainly wasn't worth opening up Damián's house just for four nights. Juan glanced at Tamara before asking him. 'Would you like to come with us, Andrés?' He hadn't seen such a lively expression on the boy's face in a long time. He was hoping for a similar reaction from Maribel, but things didn't turn out as he'd expected.

'Would you like to come with me to Madrid?'

'Me?' She moved away from him quickly, sat up in bed and looked at him in disbelief. 'To your sister's wedding?' He nodded, and she shook her head. 'No way. Have you gone crazy? I can't go.'

'Don't you want to?' He looked astonished.

'No, I . . . Of course I'd like to,' she said and lay down again. She let him put his arms around her to warm her up. 'I'd love to go to Madrid with you, but I can't.'

'Why not?'

'Well, because I can't, because I . . .' She was going to say something, then changed her mind in mid-sentence. 'What would your sister say?'

'Well, "Nice to meet you", I expect.'

'No, I mean your other sister.'

'She already knows.' Maribel closed her eyes. Juan smiled. 'She knows all about us. She always asks after you when we talk on the phone.'

It was true. When he'd introduced them, Juan had simply said that Maribel was Andrés's mother, but Paca, his favourite sister and the only sibling with whom he still got on as an adult, realised immediately that there was something between them, so he told her the truth – that Maribel was both his cleaner and his lover. Paca had put a hand on his shoulder and raised her eyes to heaven, shaking her head. 'What the hell's wrong with you, Juanito? Why can't you get together with a normal girl? There are thousands of them out there.' Juan took a moment to answer. 'Maribel is a normal girl,' he said, smiling calmly. His sister said nothing more. He'd asked her not to tell anyone, not even her husband, and she'd said, 'Who do you take me for?' He realised she'd crack and tell someone sooner or later, because it was far too juicy a secret to keep to herself for long. But he realised he didn't care.

'Right,' said Maribel nervously. 'But she'll have told everyone.'

'No, she won't.'

'Yes, she will.'

'No, I'm sure she won't have told anyone.'

'Anyway, if the kids were smaller, we'd have an excuse. You could say I was there to look after them. But they're too old for that, nobody would believe it.'

'Maribel.'

But she wasn't looking at him. She'd moved out of his embrace again and was lying on her back, staring at the ceiling. She was strangely sad all of a sudden.

'Maribel,' he said again, shaking her gently so that she'd look at him. 'In Madrid, nobody knows you. Nobody knows you're my cleaner.'

She turned towards him and took his face in her hands.

'But I know it, Juan,' she said. 'I know.'

At that moment, Juan Olmedo guessed what would happen sooner or later. As she kissed him, and climbed on top of him, and tried to console him, he guessed that they didn't have much time left, that sooner or later he'd have to choose – ask her to find another house to clean, or to move into his and find herself another job. And when his prick reacted for him, his stomach tensed, he gripped her hips and entered her body, finding it as soft and warm as he remembered all those times during the day when he found himself thinking about sleeping with her, and went over it in his imagination, trying to find a trace of what love had once been for him. 'I'm not in love with you,' he thought, but her body was soft and warm, and it could speak, sing without words, lull him with an inner music, a humble, luminous harmony, and not even the most stupid of men would give up a woman who possessed such strange powers. 'I'm not in love with you,' he thought again, as he kissed her, made her roll over and do things his way, but not even then did Charo come to his aid, he couldn't picture her dancing in front of the mirror, or putting on lipstick, or asking him to come closer, to risk his life for her. When he opened his eyes, all he saw was Maribel.

She enjoyed it more than he did, and the intensity of her pleasure was enough to make him feel miserable. But it didn't change his view of things. He couldn't prolong this situation indefinitely, he'd known that right from the beginning. He didn't want to leave Maribel, he couldn't think of anything more stupid, but he knew that the woman who woke up beside him every morning and started getting dressed, pulling any old underwear out of the drawer, would be different. He'd never lived with a woman but he was too old to ask for another pack of cards. He was forty-one years old and he knew the alternatives, the white coats with whom he'd never had much luck, the road to Sanlúcar which he could no longer be bothered with. He didn't have much time left, and whatever happened in the end, it would all be his fault. He held Maribel in his arms and closed his eyes. He knew that sooner or later he'd have to choose between two mistakes, and he didn't know which of the two would be worse. Maribel chose that moment to speak.

'I've been thinking, well, the thing is, I'd go anywhere

with you. So if you still want to take me, I'd like to go to Madrid with you.'

Juan Olmedo said nothing. Not even that he admired her a little bit more every day. He had little time left, but he was prepared to make the most of it.

An Ending

❧

Sara Gómez saw him standing by the garden gate, when she went out after lunch to check that she hadn't left anything outside that might get wet in the rain. The weather forecast on TV had announced a moderate east wind over the bank holiday, but instead a cold, damp west wind had been blowing all morning, and Sara didn't need an expert to tell her that it was going to rain that afternoon. So she went out to the garden and that's when she saw him – a middle-aged man, medium height, rather fat and rather bald, wearing a red anorak and sunglasses despite the fact that it was a dull day. She was sure she'd never seen him around before. So few of the houses were occupied in winter that everybody knew their neighbours' cleaners, friends and relatives by sight, and this man was not one of them. 'If he's having a look round because he's thinking of renting or buying a house, he hasn't chosen a very good day,' thought Sara, as she checked the awnings and piled the cushions from the garden furniture in a corner of the porch. Then, she glanced at her watch and saw that it was four o'clock – a film she wanted to watch was about to start, so she went inside and forgot all about the stranger.

Alfonso Olmedo was sitting on the sofa in front of the television, covered with a blanket. He was recovering from flu and still looked poorly. Sara sat down beside him, and wiped the sweat from his forehead. He hadn't had a temperature since yesterday, but she was still following the instructions Juan had left stuck to the fridge to the letter.

'I think it's going to rain.'

'Will it be raining in Madrid?'

'No, I don't think so. When Juan phoned earlier he said it was cold, but bright.' She picked up the remote and handed it to him — she knew he loved changing channels. 'Put it on channel five.'

Alfonso smiled and flicked through the channels until he stopped at the image of a ship in full sail.

'Is it about war?' he asked.

'I think it's about pirates.'

'Good!'

He took Sara's hand and smiled.

'In a while we can make popcorn, if you like.'

He squeezed her hand and smiled again. He didn't seem upset to have been left behind while the others went to Madrid, and Sara was glad Juan hadn't cancelled the trip, because Alfonso had been no trouble. When she'd seen him in bed four days earlier, she hadn't thought he'd recover so quickly. Tamara and Andrés had come to tell her: 'Alfonso's ill, he's got flu, Juan says we can't go to Madrid, what do you think about that?' 'It's a bloody shame,' she thought. But she didn't say so because they looked so disappointed. Alfonso's temperature had been so high that even by looking at him, Sara could tell he was burning up. He was no better the following morning but by the afternoon his temperature had gone down slightly. The children, who were in the sitting room waiting for news, for any sign of improvement, told her as soon as she arrived, but Juan said quickly: 'There's no way we can go. I'm really sorry but you'll just have to accept that. Alfonso's not at all well, and even if his temperature is back to normal by the time we're meant to be leaving, he'll still be very weak. We could leave a day later, but that would be too much of a rush.' 'Why don't you leave him with me?' After a moment of absolute silence, the children started yelling and clapping, ignoring Juan who was shaking his head. 'Absolutely not, Sara. Alfonso's a terrible patient, he's tiresome and he has tantrums.' But Sara assured him it would be no problem, reminding him that Alfonso had stayed at her house for ten days when Maribel was in hospital and had behaved impeccably. She had plenty of room, and time, and she was used to looking after invalids. 'It's up to you,' she added, 'but I think it would be ridiculous to cancel your trip. Alfonso will be fine, and if he isn't, I can always call that nurse you use as a babysitter.' The following day, Alfonso had only a very slight temperature and he was even able to get out of bed in the afternoon. The day after that, at eight in the morning, Juan dropped him off at Sara's and set out for Madrid. At three that afternoon, he called to say they'd arrived and were having lunch. He called again at six to tell her they'd ended up in the Calle Concepción Jerónima and were thinking of her. At nine Sara forbade him to ring again until the following morning, when she was even more firm: 'Alfonso doesn't have a temperature any more, we're both fine and we don't like the telephone ringing all the time! I have your mobile number, and if anything happens I'll call you, otherwise don't even think of calling me until Sunday morning to tell me what time you think you'll be back.'

She would have liked to speak to Maribel, but she knew she wouldn't have wanted to say anything in front of the others. Maribel had offered to stay behind with Alfonso before Sara did – and she was the only one who hadn't been grateful when Sara stepped in – but Juan wouldn't hear of it. 'Either we all go or none of us goes,' he'd said, and Maribel didn't dare object. While pirate ships chased each other across the screen, were fired at and sank, and Alfonso asked incessantly what was happening, Sara thought about Maribel, her doubts, her fears, her sense of imminent disaster. They'd spent two afternoons together at Sara's, Sara taking clothes out of her wardrobe while Maribel tried them on, looking at herself in the mirror as if she were a condemned woman.

Sara sympathised, but didn't believe Maribel had any reason to worry. 'Who am I going to talk to? And what have I got to say? Nothing!' she moaned, searching amongst the clothes. 'Just stay close to Juan, don't say a word and you'll see, everyone will think you're lovely.' 'What if they ask about my job?' 'Well, tell them you're unemployed, or that you work in a shop, anything.' 'What if they look at my hands?' Sara could find no answer, but found her a pair of black gloves in a drawer. 'There you go. It's fairly cold in Madrid in winter,' she said. 'They're too small,' said Maribel. 'Well, buy yourself a pair that fits.' 'But I'll have to take them off to eat lunch.' Then Sara brought out the black lace skirt and white jacket with black edging that no longer fitted her, but had looked so devastating twelve years before. 'Look, this is what you're going to wear.' Maribel had to have the skirt altered as it was a little big for her, and the jacket needed to be let out, and she had to buy a pair of high-heeled court shoes that cost her a small fortune, but when she went back to Sara's to try it all on, it suited her perfectly. But she'd still looked anxious, and was delighted when Alfonso fell ill and Juan said they'd have to cancel the trip.

Sara sympathised, but didn't believe Maribel needed to worry. She understood her fear, her embarrassment, the pride that sometimes drove her to the back of her cage, the only space she could control and feel safe in. Sara thought her fears were ridiculous, but they did give her a sense of the logical structure that had sustained Maribel in a relationship that had no future. Sara was fifty-four years old, she'd learnt that those who have so little that they don't know how to let anything go, also have nothing to lose. She'd witnessed many curious things during her life. The metamorphosis of Maribel – whose Andalusian accent now seemed less marked, and whose laugh was much less explosive, who observed what was going on around her more attentively, and kept her conclusions to herself – was by no means the strangest. This was why, the last time they were alone together before the trip to Madrid, Sara dared to speak openly to Maribel, even though the whole thing was ridiculous and she didn't believe Juan and Maribel's relationship had a future: 'Look, Maribel,' she said, 'I was in a similar situation once. I felt like you do, I did what you're about to do, and I put my foot in it. So go to Madrid, be yourself, forget about everything, and just have a good time.' 'Especially in bed, if you know what's good for you.' But she didn't add this, because she suspected Maribel already recognised it better than she ever had.

'Shall we make popcorn now?' Alfonso asked when the film was over.

'Yes, come on,' Sara said, but as they were heading to the kitchen, the doorbell rang.

'Who's that at the door?' Alfonso asked in the mischievous, sing-song voice he always used when someone rang the bell.

'I don't know.'

When she went to open the door, she found the man in the red anorak she'd seen earlier.

'Good afternoon,' he said, but didn't add anything.

'Hello,' said Sara, and realised that Alfonso had gone back to the sitting room and had switched the television on at full blast.

'My name's Nicanor Martos, and I'm with the police.' He showed her his badge. 'I was a close friend of Damián Olmedo. I know his brother Alfonso's here – I just saw him – and I'd like to have a quick word with him. Can I come in?'

'I'm not sure,' said Sara, looking at him closely, feeling her arms and legs go tense. 'We're here on our own. Alfonso's been ill, and I think he's still feeling very weak. I'd rather you came back when his brother Juan was here.'

'Look, lady,' Sara realised that the polite preliminaries were over, 'I've been following Juan Olmedo for a long time. I caught a plane from Madrid this morning to come

633

and see his brother, precisely because I found out that Juan Olmedo wouldn't be here. At the moment it's simply a personal visit, but at some stage it might form part of an official investigation. I assume you wouldn't want to be accused of obstructing justice, would you?'

'Maybe I would,' thought Sara, seeing his oily smile. 'Maybe I would.' But his words had had their desired effect: she stood aside and let him in. He looked round at the hallway, the doors leading off it, the furniture, as if he wanted to fix them all in his memory. Sara remarked to herself how quickly he'd gone from politeness to cocky impatience. He seemed like a thug, and she noticed his nails were very long. She could understand why Alfonso Olmedo was terrified of him.

As she followed him to the sitting room, she was prepared for the worst, assuming Alfonso would start to shout and scream, or else lapse into a blank, trembling silence. But Alfonso's reaction was quite unexpected.

'You don't live here,' he said when he saw him, and continued channel hopping. 'You live in Madrid, not here. You can't do anything to me here. You don't live here.'

He seemed quite calm, but he was looking straight ahead, as if he were talking to himself.

'No, I don't live here,' said the man. 'I live in Madrid. But I've come to see you.'

'You can't,' said Alfonso, still flicking channels. 'You can't come here. You live in Madrid, not here. You can't do anything to me here.'

For a few seconds, nobody said anything. Then, very slowly, the man went and stood in front of the television, blocking Alfonso's view.

'Get out of the way,' he said, still avoiding the man's eyes. 'I can't see. I know how to change channel. I can do it on my own.' He was pressing the button on the remote frantically. 'See? See? Get out of the way, Nica, get out of the way!'

'I've brought you some sweets,' said the policeman. 'A whole packet just for you.'

He took a red packet with gold lettering from his anorak pocket. He shook it and at last Alfonso looked at him.

'Are they for me?' Alfonso asked. The man nodded. 'All of them? But you can't come here, Nica, you can't. You live in Madrid, not here.'

Looking utterly confused, he put down the remote and turned towards Sara. But she couldn't answer his mute appeal, couldn't tell him why the man had come to see him – she had no idea. Nicanor switched off the television and sat down on the coffee table in front of the sofa, his knees almost touching those of Alfonso, who was looking at him as if he were a ghost. But when Nicanor waved the packet of sweets in front of him again, he grabbed it and opened it immediately.

'He loves these,' Nicanor Martos said, turning towards Sara. 'He's always loved them, ever since he was a kid.'

Alfonso put three sweets in his mouth at once.

'How are you, Alfonso?' asked Nicanor.

'I'm very well. I live here now. You can't do anything to me.'

The policeman smiled sympathetically, but Sara realised this was only for her benefit.

'Of course I'm not going to do anything to you. I've never hurt you.'

'Yes,' said Alfonso, nodding emphatically. 'Tests. The men do tests on me. I hate them, I hate them.'

'But those men live in Madrid.'

'Yes.'

'They haven't come with me. They're not here. See?'

'You get cross,' said Alfonso, looking at Sara again. She felt scared now. 'You get very cross with me. I saw it and I tell you, but you get cross. Revive him, revive him.'

The policeman sat up and started searching his pockets

until he found a pack of cigarettes, then asked Sara with a smile:

'Do you mind if I smoke?'

'You know I don't,' she said, making no attempt to disguise her hostility. 'There's an ashtray full of cigarette butts right next to you, so it's obvious I smoke myself. So it follows that I don't mind.'

He lit a cigarette and waited. Alfonso, who had been very still, his arm frozen as he took another sweet from the packet, now put it in his mouth and started chewing it slowly.

'Would you mind if I had a few minutes alone with Alfonso?' Sara had been expecting this for some time. 'It won't take long. I want to ask him something, and he's not going to tell me if you're here.'

'I don't get the impression he'd be too happy if I left him on his own with you.'

'It's . . . an important matter. Very important. I assure you you'll understand when you find out what this is about. I need your help here. It'll only take ten minutes, fifteen at the most.'

Sara looked at her watch, then at Alfonso. His eyes were open very wide, but she felt she couldn't refuse, couldn't prevent this man from doing what he had come to do.

'Alfonso, I'm going to the kitchen for a moment to make popcorn,' she said, immediately regretting this excuse because he gave a happy smile. 'Is that OK?' He stopped smiling, but said nothing. She turned to the policeman: 'Ten minutes. Not a moment longer.'

As she left the sitting room Nicanor closed the door behind her. She, on the other hand, left the kitchen door open and didn't go near the cupboard where she kept the popcorn. The microwave was noisy, and she wanted to listen to what was going on in the sitting room. She had a feeling the conversation taking place in there was going to have an impact on her life, even though she had no idea exactly how.

Anything that affected the Olmedos affected her as well, just as the knife in Maribel's side had done, and her son's stubborn, silent grief. They all lived here now, even Alfonso knew this – he'd said so to the policeman, as if it made him feel safe. They all lived here, in a mysterious equilibrium that made them strong as long as they were together. 'You can't do anything to me,' Alfonso had said. 'I live here now.' And Sara realised that the policeman did not understand how true this was. It was her only advantage in the face of the authority he'd managed to exert over her, almost effortlessly. Nicanor Martos would never imagine that everything that was important to Alfonso was also important to her, that they all knew that the past of each individual could become the enemy of them all – it had happened once, and it wasn't going to happen again.

Only eight minutes had passed when the man raised his voice enough that she could hear him from where she stood. Then Alfonso screamed. Sara rushed from the kitchen and opened the sitting-room door, hearing as she did so the violence in the stranger's voice. She couldn't see Alfonso but guessed he must be huddling at one end of the sofa, hidden by Nicanor, who was leaning forward, almost kneeling on the cushions. As she moved closer, she saw something else: a glass on the table that had been on the drinks trolley earlier, together with a bottle. She smelled the familiar, sweet aroma still hanging in the air. In that instant, Alfonso saw her and called her name.

'What's this?' she asked, picking up the glass and sniffing it, a boundless fury growing inside her.

'Wait a minute,' said the man. He got up, took her by the arm and moved her to one side. She could see Alfonso now, hunched and pale at the end of the sofa.

'What's going on?' she asked, still holding the glass. Then she saw that Alfonso was clutching something that looked like a teddy bear.

'Do it now, Alfonso,' said Nicanor, leaning forward to shake the soft toy. 'Show Sara how you revive Perico.'

'This isn't Perico,' said Alfonso. 'This isn't Perico.'

'It doesn't matter, Alfonso. Just show her, show her what Juan did.'

But now Sara was shouting, forcing the man to pay attention to her:

'This is brandy.'

'Yes,' he admitted, again leaning over Alfonso, who was hiding his face with the teddy bear.

'Did you give him some brandy?' He didn't answer. She tugged at his arm. 'Have you made him drink brandy? What kind of animal are you?' She glared at him. 'How could you do such a thing?'

'Look,' Nicanor said, shaking free of her grasp, 'Juan Olmedo murdered his brother Damián, and Alfonso saw everything, I'm sure of it. But Juan's tricked everyone into believing his story and a court would never admit the testimony of this idiot. So I want you to see . . .'

'Get out!' Sara shouted and gave him a shove. As she moved nearer to the sofa, Alfonso put his arms around her legs and pressed his face against her hip.

'Have you gone crazy?' said Nicanor, eyes wide with astonishment.

'Get out of my house!' Sara shouted. She sat on the arm of the sofa and stroked Alfonso's head. 'Get out now!'

Nicanor's expression changed, as if he realised he'd underestimated the woman. He did up his anorak and put his hands in his pockets, trying to recover his authority and his composure. When he spoke his voice was calm, but there was a hint of desperation:

'I'm telling you the truth, I swear. Juan Olmedo is a murderer.'

Sara felt Alfonso squeezing her more tightly. She too was

calmer now. But she knew exactly what she had to do and what she had to say.

'Please leave,' she said firmly. 'Right now. I'm not going to say it again. Leave or I'm calling the police.'

'I am the police,' he said.

'Not here,' Sara said. 'Not in this town. Not in my house.'

The children had wanted to spend the rest of the morning at the Rastro market, but at breakfast Juan had announced, in a tone that would brook no argument, that they would be leaving immediately and having lunch en route, so that they could arrive home in the afternoon. They didn't dare object. They had all gone to bed very late the night before, and it was past eleven when Maribel had gone to their room to wake them. While she was doing that, Juan phoned Sara and asked her, even before enquiring about Alfonso, whether she'd had an unexpected visit. 'Yes,' she said. 'Nicanor,' he said. 'Yes,' she said again. For a few seconds neither of them spoke. 'But he's gone,' Sara went on, 'and I don't think he'll be back.'

When she joined them in the hotel dining room, Maribel noticed that something was up. 'It's nothing,' he said, and he tried to smile. 'Just a slight hangover – I overdid it last night.' And it was true, he had had a lot to drink the night before. At one point Trini had sat down beside him and while she eyed Maribel, she'd remarked upon Nicanor's absence: 'I'm surprised he didn't come,' she said. 'He seemed very keen to see you when I phoned to invite him. He asked if you'd be coming. I spoke to him a couple of times after that, and I mentioned that Alfonso had flu. Then he phoned to ask about presents and I said that in the end it would only be you and Tamara coming and . . . well, some friends of yours, and that Alfonso would have to stay behind with a neighbour. He definitely said he'd be here, but there you are.' That's when Juan had started to drink, one glass after another, making sure he ate between drinks to diminish the effects of the alcohol. Nobody noticed how much he was drinking because everybody always drank a lot at weddings and because Maribel, despite being a great hit that evening, was having a terrible time and had started drinking even before he had. 'Don't leave me on my own, please don't leave me on my own,' she'd whispered as they entered the function room where the reception was being held. He took her hand and didn't let go until they sat down for dinner. 'Everyone's staring at me,' she said, so quietly she seemed to be talking to herself, as she unfolded her napkin and placed it on her lap. 'Of course they are,' he said, 'it's because you look so lovely this evening, and they don't know you − it's the first time they've ever seen you.' But she was so nervous she didn't even smile or acknowledge his compliment. He, on the other hand, was amused by the situation and by Maribel's panic, her vain attempts not to stand out, not to attract attention, hiding behind the children whenever anyone approached her. Juan Olmedo knew that Maribel was wrong about why people were staring at her. He knew that she looked spectacular that evening, that she deserved all the admiring stares, and he liked it.

Later on he was the one who caused people to stare, but by then he'd had a lot to drink and didn't want to be alone, didn't want to think, not yet, not in front of his sisters, or his brothers-in-law, not in front of friends and acquaintances he'd known all his life. He was scared, but he didn't want to be − surely he was safe by now. There had been two autopsies, both of which had uncovered nothing surprising, nothing suspicious. But Nicanor was back making threats again, and Juan didn't want to be alone. When he started kissing Maribel and caressing her through her clothes, pushing her up against a column beside the dance floor, she was alarmed at first. But she'd had a lot to drink too, and Juan's sudden display of affection dispelled her nervousness, as if his desire returned her to a place where she felt safe, a dark, shuttered house where no one could see them. Then she dragged him to the dance floor and they began to dance. They'd never danced together before. Despite the amount of alcohol they'd consumed, they somehow managed to synchronise their movements fairly well, and continued dancing and drinking until the music stopped and they found Tamara fast asleep on a chair. The following morning, Juan held Maribel in his arms, his eyes serious, mutely pleading with her not to leave him on his own.

He hardly spoke during the journey back, although he made an effort, responding to the children's excited chatter with the occasional word or smile. When they stopped for lunch, Maribel let the children run on ahead and looked at him questioningly. He smiled and made an inconsequential remark about how easy the journey to Madrid was now that there was a motorway. She agreed and continued looking at him, trying to convey that she understood his anxiety, although she was unaware of what had caused it. As the kilometres passed, and light drained from a dirty December sky, Juan Olmedo felt increasingly cold. Fear made his stomach churn, throwing his thoughts into disarray.

They reached the development at around six. It was dark, but as they got out of the car, they were greeted by a warm, dry breath of air, a promise of spring on the threshold of winter. The east wind was blowing in from the Straits, driving out the cold and damp, cleaning the air as if to welcome them, to prove that it was pleased to have them back. Juan locked the car and followed Maribel and the children, letting them reach Sara's house first. They rang the bell and all began talking at once. But when he stood in front of Sara, even before they exchanged a word, he understood that he was safe, he was out of danger.

'Did you have a good time?' she asked, looking into Juan's eyes, while Alfonso flung himself at him and hugged him.

'Really good,' said Tamara. 'And the hotel was cool.'

'Did you like Madrid, Andrés?'

'Yes, it was brilliant. I've brought you a present.'

'So have I,' said Maribel. 'But it's in the suitcase.'

'Oh, good!' Sara smiled, still looking at Juan. 'You should go away every week!'

'Maribel,' said Juan, 'would you mind taking Alfonso and the kids back to the house and making sure they have their tea and their baths? I need to have a word with Sara. We can all go out for dinner later, if you like, and tell her all about the trip.'

Maribel knew something was up, so she ushered the children away without asking any questions. Sara and Juan watched them cross the road, open the gate to house number thirty-seven and go in.

'How did Maribel get on?' Sara asked as they entered her house. 'Did you all have a good time?'

Juan nodded. She gestured for him to go into the sitting room.

'Let's sit in here. Would you like a drink?'

He nodded again, and sat on the sofa while Sara went to the kitchen for ice. When she got back, she looked very calm and she smiled before sitting down beside him.

'The thing is, Sara,' he began, putting ice cubes in his glass before pouring himself some whisky, 'Nicanor believes I killed my brother Damián, Tamara's father. Well, he wasn't really her father, he was her uncle, because Tam is my daughter. But I didn't kill my brother. It's a very long story.'

'I'm sure it is,' she said, and smiled again, as if nothing, not even the news that he was Tamara's father, could surprise her. 'I could tell you quite a tale too. One of these days, I'll probably tell you the whole story, but we've plenty of time and right now it doesn't really matter.'

Juan Olmedo looked into her eyes, that were sometimes grey, sometimes green, but always the colour of storms, and in them he read that the only way forward was to keep going, always keep going, to follow the tracks until you found the place where poppies flowered, to imagine a place that trains never reached, and to stand facing the ocean, learning that if it blows from the right, it's a west wind, if it blows from the left, it's an east wind, and if it comes from straight ahead it's a south wind, but they all erase the pathway back. There was a great deal of life in those eyes, a long story. And the future.

'Anyway,' she went on, putting her glass down and taking his hand. 'I'm pleased you stayed behind, because I wanted to suggest something. The other day, at the supermarket, I had an idea. It was only the first of December but they'd already put out their Christmas displays. Well, as you know, I'm not very keen on Christmas – to tell you the truth, it always puts me in a terrible mood. When I was little, I never knew where I'd be having Christmas lunch. If I went to my parents' house, it made them terribly sad, and if I stayed at my godmother's, I'd be upset. So, anyway, I've always hated the whole business and never gone in for celebrating it. I've spent nearly all my life living in other people's houses – first my godmother's, then my parents', then back to my god-mother's – until I came here. This is the first time I've ever really had a home of my own. Anyway, at the supermarket I was looking at the turkeys. They were all neatly laid out and wrapped up with red ribbons, as if they were presents. I'd never seen them done up like that – I think it must be an American thing, so it must be because of the airbase. So then I thought, I love cooking and I've never done a Christmas lunch, why don't I do one this year? I'd like to invite you all – you and Tamara and Alfonso, and Maribel and Andrés. I'll cook one of those turkeys and we can all eat it here together. I know it might sound silly, but I'd love to do it. What d'you think?'

Juan squeezed Sara's hand now, deeply moved.

'Are you saving my life?' he asked, and she laughed.

'Well, at the moment I'm just inviting you to lunch.'

Juan closed his eyes and nodded. When he opened them again, he smiled, and Sara was smiling too.

'All right then,' he said. They stood up and hugged. 'I'll bring the wine.'

'Great,' she replied. 'That's just what I expect men to do.'

She told him to go on ahead – Maribel would be worried and the children would be wondering where he'd got to – but she wanted to tidy herself up a little first, before they went out to dinner. However, once she was alone, she opened all the sitting-room windows and went out into the garden. The east wind rushed into the house with the energy of an impatient lover, making the curtains dance.

Outside on the porch, Sara gripped the rail with both hands, closed her eyes and gave herself up to the wind, which swept through houses, dried sheets and cleaned the air, cleansing the blood and the murky sadness of the shortest days. The east wind lashed her face, danced inside her head, and filled her lungs with the regular rhythm of an aerial tide that sharpened the meaning of the verb to breathe. The weight of lead, the chemistry of rust, the velvety poison of moss all fled before the formidable force of the wind, like the powerful breath of a classical god, and, this evening, Sara Gómez Morales felt that it was blowing through the other half of her life as well.

She wasn't outside for long, maybe only five minutes, but when she went back inside, she found a house that felt different, new, clean; a house that retained the spirit of the wind. She thought of what the townspeople said, and smiled. Because the east wind blows it all away.

Reading Group Guide

❦

The Wind from the East
Almudena Grandes

In brief:

Two strangers arrive in a small seaside suburb: Juan
Olmedo, accompanied by his mentally disabled brother
and his young niece, and Sara Gómez, an enigmatic
woman in her fifties. Both have their reasons for fleeing
the city. Sara grew up in an environment that was never
truly her own: adopted by a wealthy benefactor but
returned to her family aged sixteen she has always been
caught between her love of the good life and her
feelings of duty towards a family and a poverty that
repelled her. Juan also has his reasons for starting a new
life. A doctor in the local ER unit, he is haunted by a
tragedy in his family's past and by a secret sexual
obsession that threatens the fragile equilibrium he has
found in his new home. Like the coastline on which
they live, dominated by capricious winds that bring
chaos or clemency in their wake, the lives of the two
protagonists are pitched from fortune to adversity by
forces beyond their command.

In detail:

Dr Juan Olmedo, his mentally disabled brother Alfonso and young niece Tamara arrive at their new home by the sea, hoping for a new beginning. Their lives have been fraught with tragedy: Juan has lost the woman he loves in a horrific car accident, and his loss is compounded by the fact that the car was driven by his lover's lover. Tamara has recently lost both her parents and Alfonso the security of his family unit.

They are watched by their neighbour Sara, who is also a new resident and, like the Olmedos, is seeking a new life away from Madrid and an escape from her history. When Sara's father returned from the Spanish Civil War a broken man, her mother Sebastiana fell pregnant with Sara. Already struggling to make ends meet they accepted Sebastiana's childless employers' proposal, allowing them to raise Sara with just a visit to her natural home for a few hours every Sunday. The feelings of duplicity, confusion and displacement this instils in a young Sara stay with her throughout her adult life, and the betrayal of being returned to her natural parents at sixteen sets her on a path of revenge and survival at all costs.

Sara and the Olmedos are drawn to each other, and together with their cleaner Mirabella and her son Andrés they become an unlikely but close-knit family unit. As each of them grows and learns about themselves they begin to heal, supporting each other as their lives move forward, buffeted and comforted in turn by the local winds.

The Wind from the East takes place over the space of a year, and as the characters tell their stories we explore the nature of class, sibling rivalry, obsessive love, infidelity, duty, poverty and duplicity. Almudena Grandes has constructed an epic Spanish saga in which the dramas unfold like the coastal winds, sometimes charging in without warning, stirring everything up and leaving the characters raw, at others sweeping gently through the landscape and clearing the air.

About the author:
Almudena Grandes is one of Spain's top-selling authors. Her first novel, *The Ages of Lulu*, sold over a million copies worldwide and was translated into 21 languages. She has won a number of awards, including the Crisol Readers Prize, which is voted for by the public. Two of her novels have been made into films.

For discussion:

* *The Wind from the East* was originally written in Spanish. How well do you feel this translation works?

* The Spanish Civil War plays a central part in the lives of many of the characters – how successfully does the novel convey this period of history?

* Juan's first meeting with Charo occurs the day he receives his exam results, the best day of his life:

'Delighted, stunned, drunk with joy and pride, his faith in himself finally confirmed. He could never have imagined that life would feel as good as it felt when he held this little piece of white paper with his name on it [. . .] On the journey home, Juan Olmedo felt a new serenity, a new command over himself and others, an utterly new feeling of control over his present and his future.'

How significant to their relationship is the fact that the two events occur on the same day?

* Social inequality appears in each of the generations. How and to what extent do the characters transcend these boundaries?

* Should Tamara ever be told that Juan is her father?

* Sara's parents chose what they thought was best for Sara when they accepted Doña Sara's proposal; given the circumstance, did they make the right decision?

* Was Juan's act of ensuring his brother was dead murder? Given the evidence in the book could you see him behaving in the same way again? Is he a criminal? Is he a violent man?

* We never hear Charo's voice, her story is only told through Juan. Is their any evidence to support an alternative version of events?

* Was what Sara did to her godmother wrong or was it justified? If you knew someone who was doing the same, would you report them to the police?

Suggested further reading
The Shadow of the Wind, Carlos Ruiz Zafón
My Lover's Lover, Maggie O'Farrell
Disgrace, J. M. Coetzee
The Weight of Water, Anita Shreve
Lovesong, Nikki Gemmell